John Macker
windowless
Little Lies, is a published by Corgi Books.

www.rbooks.co.uk

Also by John Macken

DIRTY LITTLE LIES

and published by Corgi Books

TRIAL BY BLOOD

John Macken

TRANSWORLD PUBLISHERS
61–63 Uxbridge Road, London W5 5SA
A Random House Group Company
www.rbooks.co.uk

TRIAL BY BLOOD
A CORGI BOOK: 9780552154628

First published in Great Britain
in 2008 by Bantam Press
a division of Transworld Publishers
Corgi edition published 2008

A CIP catalogue record for this book
is available from the British Library.

Addresses for Random House Group Ltd companies outside the UK
can be found at: www.randomhouse.co.uk
The Random House Group Ltd Reg. No. 954009

The Random House Group Limited supports The Forest Stewardship Council (FSC), the leading international forest-certification organisation. All our titles that are printed on Greenpeace-approved FSC-certified paper carry the FSC logo. Our paper procurement policy can be found at www.rbooks.co.uk/environment

Typeset in 11½/13pt Garamond by
Kestrel Data, Exeter, Devon.
Printed in the UK by
CPI Cox & Wyman, Reading, RG1 8EX.

2 4 6 8 10 9 7 5 3 1

For Alison, Joshua and Fraser

TRIAL BY BLOOD

ONE

1

Detective Inspector Tamasine Ashcroft leaves the office block, her excitement swirling through the double doors after her. This is the once-in-a-career moment of breakthrough, the link that unites several separate pieces of evidence. After two years, she knows that all three children have been killed by the same man. More importantly, she knows exactly who the man is and where he lives.

Tamasine skips off the pavement and across the road, fresh and excited, despite the fact that it is almost two a.m. Tamasine has been working almost without pause for eight days. When it is as important as this, her reserves of energy are almost boundless. And then, as she knows all too well, she will crash, struggling to get out of bed, a cold coming on.

There is the sound of footsteps behind her. She looks back and sees the figure of a man in the half light. He is moving rapidly, a squeak of trainers on damp paving stones. She is suddenly awake and alert. The alleyway is high-sided, a gap between office blocks and shops, and easily two hundred metres long. Joggers don't take short-cuts to taxi ranks, she recognizes.

DI Ashcroft quickens her pace and risks another glance back. This is no runner. Something in the way he is leaning forward, heading towards her, smacks of hunger. Tamasine hesitates. It is probably nothing, but she should be on her guard. She curses that she has no weapon, no stab jacket, no police radio. He is gaining, and quick. She considers how to tackle him if need be. Think like a copper, she tells herself, not like a frightened panicking female. Stay low, aim a kick to the crotch, that ought to do it.

She stops and turns round, pulling out her warrant card. He is twenty metres away, fifteen, ten.

'I'm a police officer,' DI Ashcroft says, cool and slow, just like she has been taught.

The man stops. Tamasine sees him clearly for the first time, a small light illuminating his features. He is big, wide, bony and unhinged. Dense black hair, thick eyebrows, burning eyes. Teeth bared, a real-life psycho. From his jacket pocket he pulls out a six-inch hunting knife and a clear plastic bag.

'I am a police officer,' she repeats. 'Put the knife down.'

The man stares at her. Tamasine stares back. Her heartbeat is frantic, everything else shut out.

Classes on disarming assailants flash through her brain. He smiles at her. Tamasine slides her warrant card away. She knows that if she fails to disarm him, she is utterly alone and at his mercy. The plastic bag scares her. He has done this before. For an instant, she pictures the man she is going to arrest in the morning. Is this just coincidence? she asks herself. And then, an instant decision, an automatic response: she turns and runs.

Halfway down, the alley dog-legs to the left. After that, the main road will be in full view. Tamasine sprints with all her might. Panic is good, she tells herself. Nothing else matters. Forget the child-killing creep. Forget the urgent need for sleep. Just get the hell out of this alley and on to the road. Now.

For as long as she can bear, she doesn't look back. There is a noise behind her, and she glances over her shoulder. He is flat out, twenty metres away, but gaining. There is something in his eyes, and she knows she has to escape. Tamasine puts her head down, the lights of the main road just eighty metres ahead.

Forty metres. She flails, knuckles scraping the bricks. A couple of taxis pass the end of the alley in quick succession. She can hear traffic. He is too far back. When she reaches the main road she will be safe. A night bus pulls up and stops opposite the mouth of the alley. There are people on board, witnesses, her protection. Tamasine risks a final look back in her last few paces. He is ten metres behind, and no longer gaining.

And then she stops dead. The buildings are looming over her. A strange feeling of reverse vertigo dizzies her mind. A flashing whiteness crashes behind her eyes. A bleeding numbness in her mouth. She is unable to move. It takes a second to register. Her brain tries to right itself. She is on the floor.

She tries to get up but can't. Something is weighing her down. The man who was chasing her comes to a halt. He keeps his distance, glancing down at his knife, and then slowly back up again. Tamasine attempts to right herself, but she is wedged firm. The reason floods into her, the last few seconds finally making sense. Something has smashed her clean in the mouth. And that something is now pinning her to the floor.

She cranes her neck round as far as she can. Another man. He is large and firm, an unshakeable bulk. Tamasine looks back at the psycho with the knife. He is bristling, the blade gripped so hard she can see his knuckles in the half light. His full attention has switched from her to the man holding her down. There is nothing but the sound of the psycho's breathing for a few long seconds. Tamasine watches his face gradually alter beneath his brush of black hair. He is boiling over, on edge, almost quivering with intent. But she can also see that he is conflicted. And what she detects in his eyes as she focuses more intently into them scares her more than anything so far.

He is afraid.

And then, pace by pace, he gradually backs away, swallowed by the shadows, never averting his eyes from the man above her.

Tamasine starts to thrash on the floor. A gloved hand reaches down and clamps itself over her mouth. She smells the rubber, her nose desperately sucking air in and out, the oxygen debt needing to be repaid. Another hand fixes itself across her windpipe. She sees the bus pull away from the stop, passengers oblivious, just metres away. Detective Inspector Tamasine Ashcroft tries to scream but the air is blocked. As she fights and kicks for dear life, two burning questions fill her head.

What did the psycho see? And what was it that scared him?

2

Wide-open pupils stared hard into the fluorescent light, fixed and unblinking. Dr Reuben Maitland dragged a cottonwool earbud across the cold surface of one eyeball, feeling it judder, dry friction jerking its progress, shivering along with it. Up close, fibres of cotton stuck to the surface, while others grabbed at corneal cells and tore them off. He flipped the earbud round and drew it slowly across the other eyeball. Its frozen pupil continued to suck in the penetrating brightness. Surrounding it, burst capillaries oozed into the white, leaking a congealing redness.

Reuben frowned at the man standing over him. Kieran Hobbs half smiled, fascinated and appalled in equal measure. He straightened, scratching at his blond hair.

'Nice line of work,' he said.

'Yeah,' Reuben grunted, dipping each end of the stick into a different tube of blue fluid.

'What's next?'

'You enjoying this?'

'I'm just asking.'

'I've got cheek, hair, blood and eyeballs.'

'Sounds like you're starting a collection.'

'Belt and braces, Kieran.'

'And fucking cummerbund, by the looks of things. I mean, is there any bit of him you don't want?'

Reuben stared sadly down at the corpse on the floor. Or at least what was left of it. It had an amorphous quality, beaten literally to a pulp. The light shirt and trousers were seeping into redness. Reuben imagined for a second that the clothes were all that was holding it together, skin and bones mashed into an oozing paste that was straining to be free.

He lowered his voice. 'Look, if your boy had been a little less sadistic—'

'*Efficient*.'

'Then it might have been a bit easier. But as it is, the body will be contaminated with his fists, his boots and his iron bar.'

'Like I said, efficient.'

Reuben stared into the dead man's face. Efficient indeed. The nose was spread, the forehead collapsed, the mouth a gaping hole, the chin split open. His long black hair was tangled and matted, a burgundy sheen to it. Reuben tried and failed to imagine what he would have looked like before he made the mistake of trying to assassinate Kieran Hobbs. During his time running the élite GeneCrime unit of the Forensic Science Service, Reuben had seen a larger share of corpses than seemed fair. But rarely had he encountered one which had been so systematically ruined.

'I'll give him his due, though.' Kieran dabbed at a small stain on his tailored shirt. 'He didn't speak a word.'

Reuben glanced towards the rear of the disused factory. Leaning against a table was Valdek Kosonovski, one of Kieran's two full-time minders; on the tabletop lay a dark iron bar. Valdek was brooding and still, wearing a grey flannel sweatshirt flecked in red. His torso sustained an ugly musculature which yelled steroid abuse. He stared straight back at Reuben, his eyes lifeless, his face shiny with sweat. Suddenly nauseous, Reuben returned his attention to the ruined corpse on the floor.

'I mean, fair's fair. He came here to kill me. What does he expect?' Kieran asked. 'A cuff around the ear, and on your way, sonny? So my boys get a bit carried away from time to time. Well, tempers tend to fray when someone comes along trying to put a bullet in you.'

Reuben looked momentarily into the eyes of Kieran Hobbs. Thick knitted eyelashes blocked the light, pale blue irises prowling behind, lurking in the shadows. This was the law according to men like Kieran. Someone comes to get you, you get them first and you finish them off. The more brutal you are the better. Word gets around. Even psychopaths baulk at the idea of being beaten to death should it all go wrong.

Reuben glanced back at the mashed face beside Kieran's shoes. 'All the same . . .'

'Don't go soft on me now, Rube. You seen worse than this before.'

Reuben closed a small plastic box of tubes, and slipped it inside his case. 'Yes,' he said, 'I've seen worse than this. And I've also caught the people responsible.'

'What're you trying to say?'

'Keep your boys under control, Kieran. You can't afford to have them killing people like this.'

Kieran glanced over at Valdek, who was now busy cleaning up, a stringy mop soaking up small patches of red and diluting them in a bucket of water. Kieran scratched his chin, his skin so pink and clean it almost shone, his fingernails leaving thin white tracks.

'Yeah, well,' he said, appearing to consider Reuben's words.

'Otherwise . . .'

'Otherwise what?'

Reuben removed his blue plastic shoe covers. He had helped Kieran on and off for almost a year, and still didn't feel comfortable around him. But Kieran had proved increasingly useful over the last twelve months, in ways that Reuben could never have imagined. There had been a time, at the beginning of their relationship, when events had almost come to a head. Like a couple who had rowed and made up, however, it had only brought them closer. But there were days like today when the whole thing stank. Now he found himself fighting every urge in his body to call for back-up, to have Valdek arrested, to have the factory isolated and searched. But he checked himself. He was no longer in the police, and no longer had any back-up to come and rescue him. As he screwed up the shoe covers and squeezed them tight in his fist, he reminded himself that he was an outsider, a civilian, an exile.

'Just keep them out of trouble.'

'OK,' Kieran answered quietly. 'So, when will you let me know?'

Reuben pulled his bloody gloves off and sealed them inside a small plastic bag, which he zipped into his case.

'Soon.'

'How soon?'

'Flat out? Forty-eight hours.'

'Great.'

And then Reuben asked the question he'd been trying to avoid. 'What will you do with the body?'

Kieran flashed him a comforting smile. 'You let me worry about that, sunshine.'

He placed his thick fingers on Reuben's shoulder and gave it a playful squeeze, and for a second, Reuben tried his hardest to stop his muscles from recoiling.

3

Reuben picked his way across the weed-strewn car park of a derelict block of flats in Mile End. The tarmac was sprinkled with chunky cubes of shattered windows. The burned-out vehicles had long since been towed away, but the glass lived on, a sparkling reminder of past damage, slowly being ground into the floor. Crunching towards an unpromising doorway, Reuben passed a metal sign proclaiming 'Quebec Towers', its black enamel paint cracked and peeling, its shiny steel supports browned with rust. He glanced around and pulled the main door open. 'Out of decay . . .' he whispered to himself.

Inside, the cold footwell of the stairs clung on to a faint impression of piss. It was no longer intensely acrid, people now urinating elsewhere, but an acidic dampness had invaded the concrete and was reluctant to leave. Reuben ascended quickly, carrying his small leather case.

On the third floor, he entered a weed-infested

corridor and stopped outside a flat. The window and door had been sealed with anti-squatter steel plating, grey and unyielding, perforated by an army of small regular holes. As Reuben ran his fingers over the perforations of the door, he imagined the flat breathing and sighing in the chilly afternoon air, redundant and retired, marking the days until its consignment to rubble.

He moved his hand to the top of the surface and fumbled for a second, until a quiet click released a hidden catch. Reuben pulled the heavy door open and closed it behind him, stepping into a gleaming white room. He glanced around at the grey equipment which lined the benches, at the series of fridges and freezers buzzing away in the corner, at the industrial light fittings bolted to the ceiling. Reuben hoped to God his two companions were home.

'Anyone in?' he called.

Almost immediately, two people shuffled out of the back room.

'You're late,' Judith Meadows announced. She was petite and dark, and, for Reuben's money, enigmatic sometimes to the point of frustration.

Reuben blinked in the brightness for a second, lights glaring off the antiseptic surfaces, the pulped man in the warehouse refusing to leave him.

'Blame the Reaper,' he said. 'He's not always as punctual as you might imagine.'

'So, what have we got?' she asked, squeezing herself into a stiff lab coat. Through the shapeless layer of protective clothing Reuben sensed she was putting on a little weight, her small frame not quite so lost in the garment.

'Eyeballs. Earbuds. Don't ask.'

'Nice. So then we'll find out who the hell he was?'

Reuben handed his leather case to Judith. 'That's the general idea.'

'What do you want doing with the samples exactly?' Judith smiled briefly, a light going on and off in her face. 'I'm late for work.'

'I'll cut you a deal. If you get them dissolving, I'll finish up.'

'Done.'

Judith extracted the earbud from its bag, snipped it in two and manoeuvred each half into a separate tube. She pipetted some clear fluid and pulsed the tube in a small noisy centrifuge.

Over the metallic whine, Moray Carnock cleared his throat. 'What is it they say about the ends and the means?'

Reuben took in the compressed, shabby look of his business partner, glaringly out of place in the ordered laboratory. Even now, after everything, his sheer untidiness still made him smile.

'The less the better.'

'Look, I've got some more work for you.' Moray raised his Aberdonian burr a notch to be heard. 'A little bit borderline, if you catch my drift. But the money's good.'

The centrifuge slowed like a jet engine being turned off after landing. Glassware on a shelf vibrated, dull clinks as closely packed bottles rattled against one another. Judith extracted several more tubes from Reuben's case and slotted them into a hot-block.

Reuben drummed his fingers on a lab bench. 'Good enough for a new centrifuge?'

'Just about. And it's all fully legal and above board.'

'And morally?'

Moray licked his lips. 'Up to the usual high standards.'

Reuben hesitated for a second. 'If we don't do the bad things . . .'

'We can't do the good things.'

Reuben frowned at Moray. Judith raised her dark eyebrows in conspiracy. Regardless of what had happened before, this was Reuben's team, the two people he trusted more than any other. Rights and wrongs were complex beasts. To hunt the truth often meant engaging in deception. But with Judith and Moray, there was an almost osmotic sense of what was just and what was not.

Reuben's thoughts were interrupted by a noise at the door.

'Either of you expecting visitors?' he asked.

Moray and Judith shook their heads, almost in time with each other.

He glanced round as the door swung wide open. In the doorway stood a uniformed police officer. She was late thirties and strikingly beautiful, pale blue eyes offsetting her blonde hair, which was pinned so tight it looked painful.

'So . . .' she said, stepping inside.

'So indeed,' Reuben answered.

'The infamous Dr Reuben Maitland.'

'It's been a while.'

'I've been busy.'

'To what do we owe the pleasure, DCI Hirst?'

'Just being friendly.' Sarah Hirst flashed an icy smile around the flat. She flicked her eyes at the tubes Judith was holding. 'And this might be?'

'Probably not the sort of thing a detective chief inspector wants to know too much about.'

'Which goes for a lot of your activities, Dr Maitland.'

'Really though. What do you want?'

Sarah Hirst chewed her lower lip. 'Robert Abner requires a word with you.'

'*Requires*?'

'Big-boy Abner?' Moray asked. 'Is Dr Maitland in trouble?'

Sarah turned to face him. 'Ah, Moray Carnock. Long time no see. They say you should judge a man by the company he keeps.' Still staring at Moray, she said, 'Well, Dr Maitland, I'd say you were having problems.'

'Good one,' Moray answered dourly.

Behind them, Judith held a couple of tubes up in the air, pointed at them and said, 'Dissolving.' She wriggled out of her lab coat, picked up a pale blue motorcycle helmet, shouted goodbye, and left the flat in a rush.

'Seriously,' Reuben asked, 'what does he want?'

'No idea. Don't have anything to do with him these days. He just came into my office and asked how he could contact you.'

'Something going down at GeneCrime?'

'Just the usual. The odd murder. Maybe a serial rapist . . .'

'And?'

'And that's all I know.'

'If I say no?'

'I'll bring him round here.'

Reuben glanced at Moray, who grimaced a silent 'ouch'.

'What the hell,' Reuben said. 'Let's have a look at the mess you've made of my old department.'

Sarah Hirst's unmarked police Mondeo stuttered through the crowded streets and alleys of East London, heading towards Euston. A bitter easterly wind was getting up. It flapped at the coats and jackets of the people they passed, who walked quickly, their movements staccato and jerky, as if their whole bodies were shivering. At a set of traffic lights, and surrounded by waves of freezing shoppers, Sarah turned to face Reuben, both hands firmly on the wheel.

'So, how've you been keeping?' she asked, her voice softening.

'Fine.'

'Really?' Sarah glanced from the lights to Reuben and back again. 'You look like shit.'

Reuben smiled. 'It's all the fresh air and exercise. What have you been up to for the last few months?'

'This and that.'

'Anything I need to know about?'

'Certainly not.' Sarah risked another glance away from the lights. 'What's eating you up? You seem a little . . .'

'What?'

'Rough around the edges.'

'Thanks again.' Reuben rubbed his face. He was reluctant to talk. DCI Sarah Hirst wasn't the sort of person you opened yourself up to. But things were getting on top of him, and as long as he stuck to generalities, he couldn't see much harm in spilling his guts. 'Oh, I don't know, Sarah. Things are tough. I can't get access to my son, who always seems to be ill anyway. Lucy is using all her legal skills to keep me away. I spend my days in unsavoury company – no offence – and my evenings, well . . .'

The lights turned green, and Sarah pulled off briskly, tyres squealing in complaint.

'Where, exactly?'

'Sorry, Sarah, you know the rules.'

'Oh come on. Just because you scare the pants off half the Met doesn't mean you have to hide all your life.'

'It's not just the police. I mean, you appreciate that an ex-copper digging into the affairs of an occasionally corrupt police force won't necessarily be welcomed with open arms. But there are others out there. The private investigations—'

'Which I should have you arrested for.'

'Involve some nasty punters.' Reuben reached over and flicked the heating up a notch, already regretting opening his mouth. 'Identifying killers can be taken personally.'

'You play with fire.'

'You're going to get burned by Abner.'

Sarah indicated and pulled over in one seamless movement, braking hard. Reuben pitched forwards, his seatbelt biting.

'I'll drop you here.'

'Do you have to drive so much—'

'What?'

'Like a copper?'

'Just trying to enjoy myself.'

Sarah turned to face him. Reuben noted the concern in her face, a slightly pinched brow, her mouth tight. But Sarah had made a career out of hiding her motives deep below the surface of her expressions.

'Reuben?'

'Yes?'

'A piece of advice. Be nice to him. He's got a lot on his plate.'

Reuben winked at DCI Hirst and left the car. He crossed the road and walked towards a blank and unmarked building. Around the corner, and hidden from direct view from the street, was a security checkpoint manned by an officious-looking guard. As Reuben approached, the guard straightened and took a step forwards.

'Well, well. The long-departed Dr Maitland.'

'Hello, Amit,' Reuben answered, holding his hand out.

Amit gripped it and shook it vigorously. 'Good to see you,' he said, 'after what happened.'

'Likewise, my friend. How's things?'

'Quiet since you left.' Amit picked up a security clearance badge, and waved it under a scanner. 'So, what brings you back to GeneCrime, doc?'

Reuben shrugged. 'Your guess is as good as mine.'

Amit passed the security badge through his window. 'Who are you meeting?'

'Commander Abner.'

'The great man himself. You are indeed honoured.'

'We shall see.'

Reuben raised his eyebrows and opened the door marked 'Forensic Science Service, GeneCrime

Unit'. It had been a long time. The antiseptic hum of its corridors rushed to meet him. He paused, breathing deep, the inhalation sucking in a wave of unpleasant memories. Then he stepped forwards, and was slowly swallowed by the building.

4

Reuben took in the sheen of the furniture and the size of the ornaments. Things had changed. The carpet was thicker, his shoes silent across the floor. On the walls hung a number of wooden plaques embossed with obscure mottoes and interlocked pistols. The glass desk was large and round and seemed designed to concentrate attention on its occupant like a lens.

Commander Robert Abner, thick-set, angular and greying, looked up from his paperwork, brown eyes sparkling as he flashed a smile. He gestured for Reuben to sit down.

'Miss your old office?' he asked.

Reuben pushed his pupils around the room. 'You should see the one I have now.'

'What's it been? Nine months?'

'Ten.'

'Still angry?'

'I've moved on. But the personal stuff still gets to me.'

'Nature of the beast. You spend all day hunting the truth at work, there's a danger it'll follow you home.'

'Yeah, well. And now I'm paying for it.'

Reuben looked up from the desk and into Commander Abner's face. He appeared tired and haunted, and Reuben understood that this was an occupational hazard of running GeneCrime. Similar pressures had driven Reuben deep into amphetamine dependency.

'But you know what still bothers me, Robert, a year on?'

'What?'

'How easily it leaked into the public domain.'

'Once things were in the papers . . . It's no consolation, but letting someone as good as you go wasn't easy.'

'Because I heard a rumour recently. That someone here had been feeding information to a reporter.'

'I thought you'd moved on.' Commander Abner smiled.

'So did I. But when you suddenly realize that maybe your career didn't end the way you thought it did . . .'

'It's possible, I suppose. Leave it with me, Reuben, I'll keep my ears open. I owe you that much.' Commander Abner flicked at some small specks of white on the shoulder of his black uniform. 'So, what are you up to at the moment?' he asked.

'The only things I can do.'

'Which are?'

Reuben sighed. The questions had barely let up since Sarah had arrived at the lab. They would have made a good double act, if they had got on, and if Sarah had been capable of taking orders from anyone, including her boss. 'Identity. Paternity. Fidelity. Whatever comes along. Private cases, commercial cases, you name it.'

Commander Abner stood up and walked over to the partially blinded internal window that faced into Reuben's old laboratory. Through it, scientists were pipetting, chatting, assessing and comparing. He beckoned Reuben to join him. Reuben watched them; some he recognized, some he didn't. He was suddenly struck by the thought that they looked like lab rats, sniffing their way round as if searching for an exit. Among them Reuben saw Judith, who was flushed after her moped journey, her cheeks reddened by the biting wind.

'You know, Reuben, before I came over to Forensics, I never realized what a dirty science it was. Grubby, oily, filthy. Blood, semen, saliva . . . vaginal, anal, buccal . . . Mopping up other people's spills.' Commander Abner's tone was gentle and contemplative, an off-the-record frankness to it. 'And every day as we get smarter, the criminals get more careful. Sure, miscarriages of justice occur. Sometimes we get the wrong man. And as you know, on occasion this hasn't always been by accident. Which is why I'm here. To sort this mess of a division out. And it's also why I've asked you here.'

'Sir?'

'You know I appreciate what you did for us after you left. Helping bring a corrupt officer down . . . Believe me, Reuben, if it was within my power, I'd reinstate you today. But rules, as we're fond of reminding the public, are rules.' Commander Abner looked absently through the glass. 'Still, there are other ways.'

'What are you getting at?'

'That sometimes as a police force, we can't go where we want to go. Sometimes we can't do what we want to do. We're the good guys, Reuben. We have strict procedures and protocols to keep us on the straight and narrow. Outside GeneCrime as well as inside it.'

'So?'

'So maybe sometimes they're too strict.' He sighed, a low moan of career-long frustration. 'You take the sickos out there raping and murdering seemingly at will. And all the time we're being held back, slowed down. Forms to fill in, boxes to check, health and safety, ethics committees, civil liberties . . . I'd like to just get out there, do some covert testing, rattle a few cages.' Robert Abner rubbed his face wearily. 'Sarah Hirst is smart though. She keeps tabs on you. And not just for your advice. She can see what I can see. That one day we might need you, Reuben. Because you're the only person in the world with a predictive phenotyping system that actually works.'

'Which is why I don't come cheap.'

'I'm serious. One day, I'm going to come knocking. Everything will be *sotto voce*, and there will never be any traceable lines of communication. But the way events are unfolding . . . Well. I'm just saying.' Commander Abner smiled, almost apologetically. 'You know how things are.'

Reuben nodded. He'd felt exactly the same when he was running the forensics section of GeneCrime.

Lost in overlapping thoughts, they continued to watch the scientists ensconced in their antiseptic cage below. Reuben stared at Judith, who glanced up momentarily. But the window was a two-way mirror, and her eyes failed to track him down.

5

A tracksuited, athletic and well-presented man steps off a quiet tube train many metres beneath the crowded streets of West London. His hair is curly, dark, and shines as if wet. Just behind him, Reuben Maitland and Moray Carnock exit from a different door moments before it closes. The train slides out of the station, a piston within a cylinder, dragging warm, thin air behind it, which ruffles their clothes.

The man turns into a corridor, heading for another platform. The corridor is divided, those coming on the right, those going on the left. Reuben and Moray hug the wall and keep left. The glistening mosaic tiles on the wall catch Reuben's shirt and Moray's jacket. The man peers quickly back, as if aware that he is being followed, but the curve of the corridor protects Reuben and Moray from his straight line of vision. Reuben checks Moray's face. It is etched with concentration and intent.

The passageway continues to bend and twist

deep beneath the city. Moray glances behind, making sure the coast is clear. He nods to his partner. Reuben takes a small gun-like object from his pocket. It is warm in his palm. Still walking, he aims it at the neck of the tracksuited man. Ahead is an opening, the junction of several passageways and escalators. Moray has a final look around. There are no direct witnesses. He taps Reuben on the shoulder. Reuben hesitates a second, sighting down the barrel. There will be one shot, a single opportunity. He knows he must not miss. And if he hits, it has got to be silent and undetectable. Small round CCTV cameras are everywhere, bolted to the walls, taking everything in.

Moray steps in front, shielding Reuben from direct view. Reuben directs the implement over Moray's shoulder. Then, just as the man begins to exit right, Reuben pulls the trigger. The man turns into the corridor and disappears. Moray stops and bends down, examining the floor carefully, picking up a small plastic object the size and shape of a match head. Reuben keeps walking, tracking the target, making sure.

Around the corner, the tracksuited man steps on to an escalator. As he does so, he scratches his neck irritably, a delayed reaction, as if bitten by a mosquito. Reuben knows it doesn't hurt. The man looks around, but sees nothing untoward and continues on, Reuben edging along further behind and allowing Moray to gradually catch up.

* * *

Judith Meadows gripped the small plastic probe with a pair of disposable forceps. Her hands, usually steady, trembled slightly, and she struggled to hold the object. She was well aware that working for Reuben was the wrong thing to do. Judith knew she was a trusted and respected technician within GeneCrime, a safe job in a dangerous world, watching murderers and rapists appear as bands on gels and sequences on screens. Remote from the carnage, but watching it all the same. She dropped the probe into a bullet-shaped Eppendorf tube, and bathed it with several drops of a red liquid which smelled vaguely of antiseptic. Judith glanced over at Moray Carnock, who was lounging on a sofa in a grubby overcoat, examining the intricacies of the SkinPunch gun, which was capable of firing a tiny probe and snatching a microscopic sample of skin. But the real action, she thought with a frown as she slotted the tube into a hot-block, lay outside the FSS. It lay in the passions and obsessions of her former boss.

Judith looked at Reuben, who was pushing his arms into a lab coat. He was putting on a little weight, she noted, and she saw this as a good sign. Maybe he was taking things easier, lightening up. But even as she thought the words, she dismissed them. Reuben was always one step ahead, caught up in the next case, the next problem to be solved, just as he always had been when he ran the forensics section of GeneCrime.

'So, remind me again,' she said, to no one in particular.

'This is Mr Anthony McDower,' Moray replied without looking up.

'And his crime?'

'Possibly having an affair with the wife of a Mr Jeremy Accoutey.'

On the far side of the room, Reuben extracted a slide from an elongated cardboard box. He walked over and picked up Judith's tube, peering deep into it. As he did so, Reuben pictured the sinister beauty of the microscopic world of forensics. He saw the human skin cells rushing out of the probe and dispersing, bursting open like grenades, spraying their contents like organic shrapnel, double helices of DNA dancing in the solution, thrashing around one another like aquatic snakes, slowly and inexorably falling to the bottom of the tube.

'As in Jeremy Accoutey the Arsenal defender?' Judith asked.

'None other.'

'Jeremy Accoutey the ex-jailbird?'

Reuben slotted the warm tube into a small blue centrifuge on the lab bench. 'Reformed character, apparently,' he said.

'I don't know,' Judith smiled. 'If you'd seen the game the other night . . .'

Moray treated himself to an extravagant yawn.

When he had finished, he said, 'Yeah. The ref blew so much he looked like Louis fucking Armstrong.'

'Well, saint or sinner on the pitch, it's his wife's behaviour that concerns us now.'

'Aye, true enough,' Moray muttered, rummaging in the folds of his substantial coat. 'Here,' he said, passing Reuben a muddy brown envelope, 'this came for you.'

Reuben guided his gloved thumb under the flap and opened the envelope. Inside was a note, thin white paper, Times New Roman font. He read it silently and passed it to Judith.

'What is it?' she asked.

'Read it.'

'"Michael Jeremy Brawn, Prisoner #362847, Pentonville; False genetic identity; More deaths will follow; Find the truth."' Judith raised her full dark eyebrows. 'What's all that about?'

'Beats me. Moray?'

Moray sat partially up on the sofa, battling the considerable gravity of his abdomen. 'Just came via the PO box. Your guess is as good as mine.'

Reuben retrieved the note from Judith and pocketed it. 'Name rings one. Judith?'

Judith shrugged, adjusting the hot-block temperature. 'Maybe.' She took the tube from the centrifuge and placed it into the small metal heater. 'Maybe not. You got the suspension buffer sorted?'

'Must be out of practice. Give me a minute.'

Reuben weighed out a gram of white powder with a spatula. The electronic scales took a moment to settle, digital numbers flickering as the balance fought for calm. Reuben stared down at the powder and licked his dry lips. He then glanced up at the shelf in front of him. On it, among bottles and beakers and jars, was a small white vial marked 'Oblivion'. Reuben dragged his eyes away, forcing them instead to scan the labels of the cold, colourless solutions there, which read NaOH, EtOH, HCl, Tris, NaAcetate, EDTA and TBE. On the shelf above, a large dewar flask bore a peeling sticker which announced 'Liquid Nitrogen'. Reuben ground his teeth as his eyes once again hunted down the vial called Oblivion.

'That's the minute,' Judith said, bringing him round.

Reuben half smiled, tapping the fine white powder into a tube of water, and shaking it vigorously. He appealed for inner calm.

'Well, for now,' he muttered almost to himself, 'let's find out what stories Mr Anthony McDower's DNA can tell us.'

6

The streets close to GeneCrime were a tangle of human movement, people walking, riding, running, driving and fighting their way to their next destination. Roads battled to funnel the movement into ordered directions, white lines keeping the masses apart, yellow lines preventing them stopping, hatched boxes barring their entry. Overall, Sarah Hirst thought with a shrug as she left the war zone of the pavement and entered a glass-fronted café, this was life. Most people on the straight and narrow, some crossing the line, a minority doing just what the hell they wanted.

Inside, Reuben was sitting at a table so square it almost looked sharpened. He was reading a newspaper, its upside-down headline LEADING CID OFFICER RAPED AND MURDERED. Silently, she took in his fair hair, his green eyes, his lean frame with its wide shoulders, the cleft of his chin, the almost perpetual frown of concentration. A sharp mind, a genuine radical, an obsessive visionary with police hang-ups. Be careful, she told herself.

Sarah stepped forward and drummed her chewed fingertips on the cold surface of the table.

'Dr Maitland.'

Reuben took a second to look up, deep absorption clawing at him. 'Detective Chief Inspector Hirst,' he said, shaking himself round.

'May I?'

'What?'

Sarah nodded at a chair.

'You're late.'

'Things are crazy at GeneCrime.'

'More crazy than normal?'

Sarah sat down heavily. 'Multiple crime scenes, huge sets of forensic samples, the usual backlog grinding through the system.'

'Hell, it's a big unit, I'm sure you'll cope.'

Sarah reached forward and grabbed a couple of chips from Reuben's bowl. 'You mind? I'm starving.'

'Go ahead. Enjoy yourself.'

'Barely enough time to eat at the moment.' Sarah swallowed the deliciously greasy fries. 'So, what did the big man want?'

'Commander Abner? Something and nothing.'

'What was the something?'

'Said he might need my services one day.'

'And the nothing?'

'The usual. How he wished I hadn't taken matters

into my own hands and got myself sacked.'

'Any idea what he might need you for?'

'Who knows.'

'But something unauthorized?'

'Guess so. Can't imagine it appearing on any official audits anywhere.' Reuben slid the remnants of his lunch towards Sarah. 'Especially since I'm persona non grata with all of GeneCrime's senior staff.'

Sarah plucked another chip from the bowl. 'Not *all* of them,' she said.

Reuben folded his newspaper and leaned forward. 'Listen, Sarah, what do you know about someone called Michael Jeremy Brawn? Currently serving time in Pentonville.'

'Dunno. The name sounds familiar. You got any more info?'

Reuben hesitated a second. Then he pulled a piece of paper out of his jeans pocket and passed it across to her. 'This came through the post.'

Sarah scanned its contents. '"Find the truth."' She broke into a smile which made her eyes glisten.

'What?'

'Someone knows how to press your buttons.'

'So?'

'So ignore it. It's a note. Plain and simple.'

'But don't you think—'

'Look, Reuben, not everything has to be some sort of conspiracy. Chill out for once.'

Reuben slid his bowl back and out of Sarah's reach. 'If you're going to be like that.'

'So I'm working on a no-win-no-chip basis now?'

'You scratch my back . . .'

'I'm a trained firearms officer, Dr Maitland. It might pay you to be nice to me.'

'That's more like it. The old Sarah Hirst. Cold, calculating and heartless.'

There was a snap to Reuben's words, making them sound as if they'd been spat directly from his thoughts. He was regretting the outburst almost before it reached Sarah's ears. She stopped, the playfulness disappearing from her face.

'Bit low.'

'I just meant . . .'

'Things change, move on.'

She fell silent. One of her earrings caught the light, winking in the sun, flashing as she moved her head. Reuben marvelled at the vivid reds and deep blues hidden in the pale rays of spring, split and refracted, rescued by the diamond. It was an expensive item, the sort of thing someone else buys you. He wondered for a second who had given the earrings to Sarah, and when.

'Sorry. Crossed that line again,' he said with a sigh.

'I hope I don't need to spell it out.'

'I know. What happened before—'

'I take a calculated risk with you, Reuben, every

time I see you. As you say, persona non grata. Disgraced police civilian whose activities I shouldn't turn a blind eye to.'

'Oh come on, Sarah. You get as good as you give.'

'How so?'

'The advice, the technical input. How many times have I helped you?'

'And how many times have I ignored the fact that you have GeneCrime samples in your freezers, a member of GeneCrime doing your dirty work; that you're associating with gangsters like Kieran Hobbs . . .' Sarah made a show of checking her watch. 'Look, I'm late. I'd better run.'

Reuben unfolded his newspaper. 'Sure.'

'OK, take care of yourself, Reuben, because you're in a very precarious position.' Sarah stood up to leave. 'Seems to me that if you work for gangsters and investigate the police, you've got things all wrong.'

As she strode out, Reuben muttered to himself. Sarah Hirst, as hot and cold as ever, a fragile relationship built on mistrust. Each needing the other, each uneasy with their role. But Reuben was smart enough to know why he unnerved coppers, and what he had that they needed so much.

7

Reuben loitered on the doorstep of a smart suburban semi, dodging a freezing spring shower. He examined his watch, and ran a hand through his damp hair. He glanced around at the tended garden, the immaculate German car, the recently swept pathway. It irked him momentarily that his wife had swapped her quest for domestic perfection so easily from his house to someone else's. Orderliness almost seemed to emanate from her, symmetrizing everything in its wake. He took another deep breath, scanned his watch again, noticed that the hands had barely moved, and finally pushed the doorbell. There was a pause, then the sound of movement, the rumble of carpeted stairs taken in stockinged feet. Reuben stepped back a pace. Keys rattled, the lock fumbled, and then the door was pulled open by a smart-looking woman with a dark bob and piercing green eyes.

'You're early,' she said.

'Good to see you too.'

'Look, there's a problem.'

'What?'

'Josh isn't well.'

'Again?'

Lucy Maitland sighed, sweeping at her disciplined fringe. 'It's nursery. Breeding ground for germs. Anyway, I'm not sure I want him going out, especially in this weather.'

'But we agreed.'

'Before there were germs.'

Behind Lucy, Reuben noticed for the first time the shape of a man lurking deep in the hallway. He approached, the light gradually revealing his brown hair and tanned skin. Reuben raised his eyebrows briefly at him. 'Hello, Shaun,' he said flatly.

'Reuben,' Shaun replied.

'Look, Reuben, I'm sorry your journey has been wasted,' Lucy continued, 'but that's the way it is. Surely you don't want him getting worse?'

'Can't I even see him?'

Shaun paced forward so that he was standing shoulder to shoulder with Lucy. Together, they filled the doorway, a human barrier.

'You know, legally,' Lucy answered, 'you shouldn't even be within four hundred metres of him.'

'But I thought we'd agreed—'

'Or this house.'

'You said you would be flexible.'

Shaun took a step towards Reuben. 'The answer is no. Not when he's sick.'

Reuben held the stare, his eyes wide, his muscles tight, his jaw clamped. Large, fat drops of rain soaked the denim of his jacket. Then Shaun stepped back and slammed the door.

Reuben stood still for a few seconds, facing the door. In its shiny black paint he saw his helplessness staring back, distorted and rejected. Then he turned to walk down the drive and towards the street. But as he passed the front of the house, he glimpsed his eighteen-month-old son through the streaming bay window. Reuben stopped. He tapped his fingernails against the thick double-glazed glass. Joshua looked up from the plastic car he was crashing into the skirting board, and started to totter rapidly and eagerly towards him. 'That's my boy,' Reuben whispered to himself, his breath on the window. 'You still recognize your old dad.'

Then Joshua came to an unsteady halt, caught up in a coughing fit. Reuben watched as his son screwed up his eyes, his mouth wide, his chest silently spasming. He fought the impulse to kick open the front door and hold him. Instead, Lucy entered the room and picked Joshua up, turning him away from Reuben, shielding him with her arm, kissing the back of his neck. She stared coldly at Reuben. He touched the glass with his fingers. Between the double-glazed panes was a fine film of moisture. He saw layers of glass and air, distorting his vision, deadening noises, separating the warm from the cold.

Reuben turned and paced disconsolately back down the short spotless drive, through the lacquered gate and on to the smart South Kensington street that Lucy now called home. He swore under his breath, moist air defeated by the rain. She had only moved a mile and a half since they had separated, but this part of the city was as alien to him as Novosibirsk.

As he crossed the road and headed towards the shelter of an Underground station, Reuben's mobile rang, disrupting his gloominess.

'Dr Maitland?'

Reuben paused. 'Hello, Sarah,' he said.

'About that note.'

'Which note?'

'The one you showed me earlier.'

Reuben turned down a side street. 'The one I should ignore on account of being perpetually suspicious?'

'Right.'

'Well?'

'According to Metropolitan records, Michael Jeremy Brawn got four years for sexual misdemeanour. Pleaded guilty to assaulting a woman on a train. Must be ten or eleven months ago.'

'I'm touched. But why are you ringing me?'

Over the line came the sound of keyboard

tapping and coffee being slurped. 'Perpetual suspicion. What else do *you* know about Michael Brawn?'

'Nothing, except his name rings a bell, and the note alleged he has a false genetic identity. Why?'

'Because he's an interesting one. I've had an ask around. Touched a few nerves, especially with senior uniform.'

'Really?'

'Really.'

'Look, about earlier—'

'Forget it.'

'I just . . . considering what we've been through, sometimes I forget the rules.'

'Well, there's a simple way of remembering them. *Professional* and *personal.* Two different things.'

'I know.'

'I don't have a lot of time right now, bigger fish to fry. But I'll try and pull Brawn's record.'

'Very good of you.'

'You're going to be paying me back for this.'

'I was worried about that.'

Sarah took another swig of coffee. 'Be afraid, Dr Maitland,' she said, 'be very afraid.'

Reuben closed his phone and frowned. Mostly, he understood people. How they worked, what they wanted, what they needed. But not Sarah. A Ph.D. in biology and years of detective intuition and still Sarah remained a mystery to him. Unreadable, inconsistent, contrary. And very beautiful. Almost gratefully, Reuben allowed Gloucester Road tube station to beckon him into its dry subterranean world and swallow him up.

8

The Underground lifted Reuben up and nudged him out on to a slowly drying street. Tyres were cutting into the remaining moisture and spraying it into the air. On the pavement, the tread of shoes picked up droplets of water from saturated paving slabs and moved them to new locations. Reuben's jacket tried to rid itself of its invading wetness, an almost invisible steam coaxed out of it by the emerging sun. He shrugged his shoulders, shifting the clammy denim momentarily away from his skin.

He crossed the road, and tracked left and right through a succession of junctions, echoing through an underpass and emerging on to a wide straight road which contained a row of uninspiring shops. After a furniture store, Reuben paused in front of a tall, fortified metal gate. He heard the buzzing click of acceptance and pushed through. A long narrow alleyway took a kink to the right and ended in front of a steel door. Reuben pressed the buzzer twice, waited a second, and then walked through.

Inside, the factory floor was concrete and empty. Strip lights hung down at regular intervals from the low ceiling. There were no windows. At the far end, a lorry-wide shutter was bolted shut. Several industrial tables occupied one corner. They were stainless steel and countersunk, with gleaming taps at each end. Kieran once told him the area had originally been used for gutting fish, and the rest of the factory for packaging, before the business went bust. Reuben scanned the room for the ruined corpse, beaten and pulped, bleeding into the porous ground, almost expecting it still to be there. He sighed to himself, repeating his mantra under his breath. The ends and the means. The ends and the means.

He spotted Valdek towards the rear of the building, leaning against the same table that had held a bloody iron bar a couple of days earlier. Reuben walked towards a dark green door halfway along the opposite wall. As he did so, Valdek straightened and began lumbering towards him, aiming to cut him off. Reuben slowed his pace, allowing him to catch up. He glanced around. There was no sign of blood on the ground now, the floor scrubbed meticulously clean. An area of darkness was the only sign, still wet where it had been scoured. Reuben wondered whether Valdek had disposed of the dead man himself, dumping him in a river or feeding him to pigs, or some other such underworld treat. What Reuben had found out about the deceased man had lessened his sympathy. Still, nobody deserved to be slowly battered to death in a dingy warehouse by a psycho like Valdek Kosonovski. Reuben tried not to let his disgust show as Valdek reached him.

'What do you want?' Valdek asked.

Reuben said, 'Is your boss in?'

Valdek frowned, his jaw locking. 'He's busy.'

Reuben had met Valdek a handful of times and had failed to warm to him. He had an Eastern European look which verged on the Slavic, his nose blunt, his face square, his hair receding and lank, longer on the sides and back than was truly fashionable, as if compensating for its retreat. His neck was thick and firmly set, his ears, under his hair, big and bold. Reuben saw the iron bar, clenched fists and leather boots. He pictured muscles swelling and contracting. He imagined flesh bruising, blood leaking, bones cracking.

'How long for?'

'You got an appointment?'

Valdek's English was perfect, despite his roots. He spoke in a low rumbling monotone, verging on the hoarse at times, a canine growl you instinctively didn't want to get on the wrong side of. Reuben wondered whether the steroids he undoubtedly took were fucking with his voice box.

'Yeah,' Reuben answered, stepping over to lean against the bare brick wall.

Valdek followed him. 'Well, while you're not doing anything . . .'

'What?'

'I want to know about it. Forensics.'

'In what way?'

'How long do DNA samples last?'

Reuben squinted at him. 'Depends. Minutes, hours, days, years.'

'Where are people's DNA samples kept?'

'What do you want to know for?'

'And what information do the police keep?'

'Anything else?'

'How do you know if you've been DNA tested? I want to hear all of it.' He glanced around the empty warehouse. 'Here. Now. You and me. Man to man.'

'Why?'

'Because I'm asking you and you're standing here.'

Reuben shrugged. 'Not a good enough answer,' he said.

Valdek appeared to swell. Maybe he just changed his posture, pushed his chest out or lifted his shoulders. But beneath his World Gym sweatshirt there was a standing to attention of muscles, an urgent readiness for action that Reuben knew he was supposed to notice. The guy was on a very short fuse.

'What kind of fucking answer do you want?' Valdek asked, stepping closer.

The air had changed. Menace. Straining at the leash. A finger trembling on a hair trigger. Valdek glared down at him. Reuben met his eyes head on. Blazing, full beam, wide pupils.

'Something better than that,' he answered.

Valdek stood toe to toe with Reuben. 'You arrogant cunt,' he spat, drops of moisture spattering Reuben's face. 'What's your problem?'

Reuben refused to be intimidated. 'My problem is that I don't want to talk to you about forensics.'

'You got an issue with me?'

'I've got an issue with your attitude.'

A door opened ten metres away. Out of the corner of his eye, Reuben recognized Kieran's other minder Nathan strolling over.

'What's going on?' Nathan asked.

'We'll come back to this,' Valdek whispered, scowling, his teeth bared.

Nathan approached and Reuben knew that Valdek had had his moment. Valdek stepped away, keeping his distance, brooding, the low ceiling holding the intensity tight.

'Hey, doc,' Nathan said, 'how're you doing?'

Reuben glanced back at Valdek, who avoided his eye. He made a mental note not to antagonize him again. Witnessing the aftermath of a Kosonovski beating had been shocking, but seeing Valdek up close and on edge had surprised him. How quickly things could escalate from nothing, how little provocation was needed. Reuben suspected that Valdek wouldn't have hurt him. Kieran had him on a tight leash. And it had been too tempting not to push him, to see what it took to get him angry. Reuben sensed that one day in the near future, when Kieran had no use for him any more, Sarah Hirst might be getting an anonymous tip-off about Valdek Kosonovski.

'Fine, thanks,' Reuben said.

Nathan was mid-thirties, a serious weight-lifter like Valdek, just as wide but slightly taller. He was the friendly face of Kieran's ever-present minders. Nathan seemed to grin almost permanently, as if he was practising the look for a bodybuilder competition.

'What were you talking about?' Nathan asked. 'I bet it was what you do, wasn't it? Forensics and all that?'

Reuben nodded.

'My missus loves all those shows. With those shiny labs and the way they outsmart the bad guys. Can't get enough of it.' Nathan had the kind of chirpy cockney accent that almost seemed to have died out in the capital. 'That how it is in real life?'

Reuben glanced around himself, at the factory interior, the two minders, the scrubbed floor, the grubby stench of crime. 'Just like it,' he answered.

'Great. Well, he should be ready for you now,' Nathan said. 'Go on up.'

Reuben pushed through the green door. He thumped up the stairs and paced along a plushly carpeted corridor. At the end, Kieran's office door was open. Reuben found Kieran sitting upright in his leather chair, leaning slightly forward, his blond eyelashes flickering in the bright sunlight like butterfly wings.

Reuben sat down opposite him and said, 'You should keep your boys under control.'

Kieran grinned, a flash of teeth to go with the glint of Rolex and the bling of jewellery. 'They're OK, aren't they? So one of them's a bit, what? *Excitable.* Nothing wrong with that in my business. Sends out the right message to the right people.'

'And everyone else?'

'You get a bit of rough treatment?'

'Something like that.'

Kieran leaned forward and opened a drawer. 'I'm sorry, Reuben. I'll have words. Here, maybe this will help.' He pulled out a thick wad of pristine twenty-pound notes, and slid them across the empty desk.

Reuben hesitated, rubbing his face and sighing.

'What's up?' Kieran asked.

'I'm not proud of what I do for you.'

Kieran puffed his cheeks. 'I'm hurt.'

'Let me tell you a story, Kieran.' Reuben frowned at the bundle of notes, as if they were in some way repellent. 'When I started out in forensics, you were exactly the kind of villain I was after. In fact, I actually spent time on a case involving one of your many syndicates.'

'And then?'

'And then I came to see that what's good and what's bad isn't necessarily so clear cut. I saw coppers beating people up, innocent people. I saw criminals helping others in times of need. And then I started to see something worse.'

'What?'

Reuben moved his eyes away from the money and stared out of the window, looking at the flat, soiled roofs of two-storey shops. 'Around the time I left GeneCrime, a copper began using forensics to put people away. He reasoned that forensics is the one thing juries don't question, the one infallible truth among the chaos of evidence. And it was easy. As long as you had access to the databases and the specimens, you could do what you wanted. Identities could be traded, samples could be inserted or deleted, matches could be found. Science is just people. And people are a mixed lot.'

'There's always been bent coppers,' Kieran shrugged. 'Here, I'll write you a fucking list.'

'But now they're smarter. A new breed using new tools to get what they want.'

'Forensics, you mean?'

'Sometimes. And as a result, innocent punters languish in jail to further careers, or to substantiate hunches, or to punish suspects in unsolvable crimes.'

'Can't be *that* widespread though.'

'Not necessarily. But it's out there. And I'm worried it might be happening again. Single coppers rarely act alone.'

Kieran Hobbs caressed the smooth skin of his cheeks, feeling for the meaning of Reuben's words. 'So, basically, if I've got this right – and tell me if I haven't – you waste your time running round trying to solve crimes that have already been solved?'

Reuben made a sound halfway between a grunt and a laugh. 'Something like that. Because no one else does. No one else seems to care about the fact that science can be used and abused. No one else seems to care about the truth any more. Just arresting punters and putting them away.'

'So things change, move on. It's life. This place for example.' Kieran waved his arm around the office. 'Nowadays, most of the capital's fish comes already gutted and prepared, a lot of it even flown in from all over the world. Friend of mine runs an import business. It's how I found this place. Nice and quiet and out of the way. And it don't even smell too bad!' Kieran chortled to himself, his smile fading over three or four seconds. 'So new circumstances get exploited by new men. Why you though? What do you care?'

Reuben sighed, blinking away the sunlight. 'Because occasionally things happen that change the way you think. You either ignore it, or you do something about it.'

'Oh fuck. An ex-copper with principles.'

'The rest is only a sideline to finance the big stuff. Paternity suits, industrial espionage' – Reuben took a piece of paper out of his jacket – 'tracking the identities of assassins . . . I mean, no offence, Kieran, but it's small potatoes.'

'It ain't small potatoes when someone comes to kill you.'

'Thought that was just an occupational hazard.'

'So who was he then?'

Reuben squinted, recalling the warehouse below and rubbing his cottonwool bud slowly over the open eyes of the pulped man lying on the floor. 'Ethan de Groot. Dutch in origin, but lived here for some time. There's his last known address and phone number. Thirty-two, single, one previous conviction for possession of cocaine, two for ABH and another for intent. Nice guy.'

'I've seen worse.' Kieran casually scanned the piece of paper, before slotting it into his shirt pocket. 'What I don't get is who sent this Dutch cunt after me. Who is it wants me finished that badly?'

Reuben stared balefully out of the window. 'I'll write you a fucking list,' he whispered to himself.

9

Sarah Hirst loitered in the doorway of the flat, a metal cylinder marked 'Cryo-Store' in her hands. From it, a heavy white vapour leaked slowly down towards her stockinged legs and over her leather shoes. Reuben watched her for a second as she walked past him and into the room, vaporized nitrogen swirling behind her like a cloak. There was a fluid loveliness in the way she moved, as if she'd been poured out of a bottle, viscous and honeyed, which the gas exaggerated, like the vapour trails of a banking aircraft. 'Professional and personal,' he whispered to himself. 'Professional and personal.' He locked the metal door and turned to face her.

'What you got?' he asked, pointing with his eyes at the cylinder she was holding.

'I thought you might be asleep.'

'So why did you come?'

Her eyes widened. 'Because what I've got here is good enough to wake you up.'

Sarah paced over to the lab bench. She placed the

Cryo-Store carefully down and opened it. Reuben took a pair of elongated forceps from a shelf and retrieved a frozen and preserved Eppendorf tube from the volatile liquid.

'And this is?'

'A DNA sample from none other than Mr Michael Brawn, Pentonville's finest felon.'

'How the hell did you sanction that?'

'Sanction? You don't sanction the removal of a classified forensic sample into the wider community.' Sarah propped herself against a stool, half leaning, half sitting. 'Thought you might have a dabble with your wonder technique of predictive phenotyping. You never know what it might find.'

Reuben ran his eyes quickly around the lab, over its busy shelves, its blank surfaces, its humming freezers, its anonymous equipment. 'Sure. It's that or get a good night's sleep.'

'Anyway, I've got to shoot. We've just had reports of a potential victim, dredged fresh out of the Thames.'

'Like Tamasine Ashcroft?'

'Got to go and oversee the prelims.' Sarah glanced directly at Reuben. 'But, yes, could be another.'

'What have you got so far?'

'Not a fat lot. Except there may be more than one man involved.'

'How so?'

Sarah straightened, the stool complaining as

it scuffed the vinyl floor. 'Sorry, Dr M. Need to know basis.' She tugged at the sleeves of her black jacket and smoothed her dark skirt. 'Gotta dash, otherwise the FSS will have already started bitching about GeneCrime taking over. Good luck with the predictive phenotyping.'

'If I decide to do it.'

'Oh, you will.'

Sarah unlocked the door and left the lab with a sad smile which seemed to linger in the room after her. Reuben paused a few seconds, thinking, wondering, trying to decide what made Sarah tick, and what she truly wanted from him. As he slowly inserted himself into the stiff restraint of his lab coat, he whispered, 'I know I should trust her, but . . .' And then he grunted, taking in the empty space around himself. Whispering to yourself. That was one step closer to lunacy than talking to yourself.

The idea behind predictive phenotyping was a simple and brilliant one which had done much to ruin Reuben's career and personal life. The science was good, unexpectedly robust and unerringly accurate. What hurt with predictive phenotyping was the potential for misuse. The ability to determine what a stranger looked like from a microscopic sample of their blood, or hair, or saliva even, brought with it a number of temptations Reuben had been unable to resist. For when your wife is having an affair with an unknown person who leaves hairs behind in your bed . . . Reuben shuddered for a second, revisiting the events of the previous year which had precipitated his sacking from GeneCrime. Sarah's words tracked him down a final time. When the personal and professional get mixed up in a sticky tangle, that's when you know you're in trouble.

As Reuben popped open the tube and extracted a small sample of its contents with a pipette, he felt the spark of the technique's possibility ignite once more. He knew he wouldn't sleep, and that he would work through the night. It wasn't that Michael Brawn interested him per se – a single piece of paper with a few words on it was only a minor red rag – but that the excuse to delve, to probe, to use the technology that only he had access to, bit into him like a snare. Besides, the purity of doing something for the sake of its methodology appealed to him after the grubby, filthy commercial cases he was pursuing. As he flicked a sequencer on, he once again recalled Commander Abner's words, his assertion that predictive phenotyping could be the answer to his problems.

The hours began to get soaked up in an enveloping series of activities and actions: tapping information into a laptop; lying horizontal on a sofa reading a book; taking down the vial marked 'Oblivion' from a shelf; flicking tubes with his index finger; using the same finger to rub amphetamine into his gums; slotting the tubes into a machine; chewing his teeth; reading data off a screen; pipetting coloured fluid on to a DNA chip; staring into screens of numbers; mapping facial coordinates . . .

Reuben pulled his head back from the glow of his laptop. A clock in the corner of the screen read 13:27. He'd worked solidly into the next day. He hesitated, savouring the pause, and then pressed the return key. Slowly, on the screen, a 3D face began to come to life.

Reuben watched, fascinated. Textures and colours, contours and coordinates, depth and tone, pushing and receding, narrowing and widening, lightening and darkening, shaping and defining. He stretched, amphetamine muscles relishing the chance to extend and unfurl. The computer stood still, its result illuminated on the screen. The face was that of an Afro-Caribbean male, mid-forties, mildly obese. In a text box in the corner was printed 'Psycho-Fit of Michael Jeremy Brawn: moderate intellect; schizophrenia negative; likely benign'. Reuben squinted at the 3D image, rotating it with his mouse so that it seemed to be shaking its head.

'So, Mr Brawn,' he frowned, 'nice to meet you at last.'

10

Twelve faces glanced up at Prison Guard Tony Paulers with a dozen expressions ranging from expectation to hatred. Among the negligible middle ground were irritation, apathy, disdain and guilt. Tony Paulers had become adept in his twenty-one years of prison service at simultaneously noting and ignoring what he saw staring back at him from the inmates of Pentonville. Those who beamed were generally up to something, those who growled and snarled either weren't or didn't care who knew it. Either way, he had been spat at and sworn at and kicked so many times in the last two decades that it had become a matter of survival simply to avoid confronting what he saw in the eyes of his inmates.

The TV room was half full, prisoners slumped on plastic chairs, absorbing the daytime trivialities of a world they were locked away from. Tony would be happy if they watched television all day. The lulling, soporific immersion in home improvement and cookery programmes seemed to dampen their spirits. Tony had never been assaulted in the TV room.

He allowed himself a moment to examine the assembled ranks in front of him, naming them in his head, being quietly vigilant, seeing who was where. Hardened cons, care-in-the-community cases, lads who were only months too old for borstal. Tony appreciated that status in here was not a winning smile, or a professional job, or a beautiful wife, or a platinum credit card, or anything else you might strive for on the outside. No, status here was simple and brutal. It was in the twinkling of a bicep, the girth of a chest, the length of a charge sheet. And as he focused on the prisoner he had come to fetch, he realized that this one was different. This one was outside the normal rules of categorization. This one was the exception that proved the rule.

Tony cleared his throat, most prisoners having already switched their attention back to the screen. 'Michael Brawn,' he announced, 'you've got a phone call.'

Tony watched Michael Brawn stand up. He was slow in his movements, almost compellingly so. He recalled the first time he had seen him, nearly a year ago. Tony had been mesmerized from the start, unable to keep his eyes off him. They were drawn to Michael Brawn, fascinated, incapable of moving away. Moths to flames, rabbits to headlights. Tall, lean and intense. A bony hardness about his face. Calm, ordered, in control, and extremely psychopathic. The kind of man who unnerved prison warders, whom they tried to stay on the right side of.

Michael Brawn looked Tony in the eye, standing still in front of him. Tony nodded at the waxen face, pale and gaunt, almost stripped of expression, something unbreakable in the boniness of the cheeks and forehead. He saw the impression of power, almost inviting Tony to try him, and that was what unsettled him. His silent confidence. Tony knew that Brawn rarely spoke, seldom even acknowledged those who talked to him. He just watched them with fixed eyes, and a slight twitch of the eyebrows. As Brawn stepped forward, Tony appreciated that there was intellect there as well. You knew that this man saw into people, understood their motives, read their body language, sized them up before they were even aware of the scrutiny. And that this man had been in situations. He had been beaten, kicked and threatened. He knew what pain and suffering were, and what effect they had on other people.

Michael Brawn passed close, the air from his tall, lean body breezing across Tony's face. Tony turned and followed him, a couple of yards back. Brawn walked briskly along light green corridors and through sets of prison doors. Tony watched from behind, taking in the expressions of prisoners as Brawn passed them. He was no body language expert but had spent enough of his career observing the interactions of criminals to know that Michael Brawn didn't just worry the guards.

They entered a wider corridor housing a series of wall-mounted phones, each with its own graffitied metal hood. Tony watched Brawn snatch the receiver, glance up and down the walkway, and listen intently. He sauntered past, stopping to pass the time of day with a fellow officer. Swivelling slightly, he continued to monitor Brawn. He was hunched over, his head pressed hard into the metal hood, extracting all the privacy he could from it. And then he began to speak, slowly and deliberately, his accent dry and Mancunian. Tony strained to hear over the bland nothingness his colleague was spouting.

'Yeah?' Michael Brawn whispered. 'December. The seventh. Third Sunday. Second Monday. The fourth. Tuesday. August seventeenth. May twelfth . . .'

The other guard continued his spiel, and Tony turned back to him momentarily. 'But the governor wants an anti-smoking initiative, apparently. Some national scheme. And him on, what, sixty a day? Easy. Like to see him come down on to the shop floor reeking of fags and booze and try and implement that one.'

But Tony wasn't really listening. Once again, Michael Brawn was dragging him away, his very presence captivating. This time, it wasn't simply his indefinable difference from the other prisoners. Tony had just learned something new: Brawn was passing code out of the prison.

He watched him hang up and walk nonchalantly back the way he had come. Tony Paulers ended his half conversation with a noncommittal smile, and headed off to his office. He had a phone call of his own to make.

11

He was breathing quickly, but this was good. He liked to feel his lungs expand in his chest, cold with the ache of stretching slightly too hard. The second one had been easy. She had made it possible, had put herself in the right position, given him her vulnerability on a plate. The only problem had been the mugger, the scumbag who had wanted her purse, or whatever he was after. He spat out a wet, sour-tasting ball of phlegm. Wankers like that made him mad. And when he was mad, there was no one who could harm him. When he was angry, truly angry, he was on fire. Untouchable.

The mugger had seen it, and had turned and fled. Half of him had wanted to chase him, hunt him down, punish him for scaring the woman half to death. But then again, the mugger had presented him with an opportunity he couldn't overlook. He had almost made the decision for him. Sometimes all it took was a small nudge, and suddenly you were standing on the other side of the line that most people won't cross. And with the first and second decisions, a series of events was now inevitable.

He watched and waited. The thing was timing, not availability. Lots of women were available. It was not being seen. In a city of eight million pairs of eyes, there were eight million chances to get caught. You had to be selective. Many nights he would go home having accomplished nothing. Having taught no one any lessons at all. But remaining at liberty, free to try again another night.

He knew things would change. At the moment, it was straightforward. No one was hysterical yet. But give it two or three more, the police would finally link them, they would begin to understand what they were up against. Then different rules would have to apply.

Lights bounced off the Thames, dulled by their association with the browny grey mass of water. He watched it silently flowing by, cold and uncaring, keeping a chill wind tightly wrapped around it like a scarf. On the opposite side were new blocks of flats, supposedly interesting in shape – wedged or curved – designed to seduce the eye rather than assault it. Not like the blocks where he had grown up. Big, straight, towering monstrosities, most of which had now folded in on themselves, dynamited to make way for the smoother shapes of designer living. But at least the old blocks had character. You knew who you lived next to. No need for video phones or remote entry. Just flats full of people getting on with their lives while the Thames quietly went about its business.

He heard a horn . . . then he shook himself round, glancing at his watch in the gloom. Not quite a black-out. Just a few seconds of tuning out, being elsewhere. Small wedges of time which seemed to go missing occasionally. Where they went he didn't know. He didn't physically move anywhere or do anything, his mind just wandered. A side-effect, the doctor had called it. She had said a lot of things about side-effects. But he had kept his cool. The medical profession didn't understand much about living, about being truly and utterly alive. They were more concerned with lessening symptoms, patching you up, making you feel that you were better. Not with actually making you better. There was a difference, a large difference, which seemed to be lost on the GP. Being good and feeling good, being healthy and feeling healthy, being alive and feeling alive.

And she had spoken names. Big, ugly, strung-together medical names. Words like car crashes, smashed into long pile-ups. Hypothalamo-gonadal-pituitary axis. Follicle-stimulating hormone. Hypogonadotrophic-hypogonadism. A leaflet spelling it all out. He had looked the terms up, Googled them on his computer, learned how to say them, and what they meant. He repeated them rapidly under his breath, waiting and watching. Follicle-stimulating hormone . . .

He shook his head, his hair damp, cold against his face as it moved. Back again. More lost seconds somewhere. The burning itch that needed to be scratched brought him round. He checked his watch. One thirty-four. Very few people around now. Just the odd one or two shuffling home, or looking for cabs, or drawn to the Thames. He stamped his feet. Keep moving, stay ready, be alert. His breathing was still quick. He was excited and on edge.

He closed his eyes and listened. Noises across the water, drifting, swirling in the air, being blown from who knew where. He blinked. Among them the hypnotic tick-tock of high heels. He clenched his teeth, rolled his neck, opened his eyes wide and stepped back into the shadows, ready.

12

'Mock fucking Tudor,' Moray groused, his voice as rough as the gravel drive which stretched before them.

'Who'd have guessed?' said Reuben, his footsteps crunching in unity with Moray's, echoing their arrival.

'You coming in?'

'I'll lie low. Let you earn your money.'

'Great,' Moray replied. He examined the house in more detail. 'Footballers. Was there ever a group of people less deserving of over-payment?'

'Lawyers?'

'Ach,' Moray said with a grin, 'the familiar sound of Dr Maitland's axe being ground.'

Reuben smiled back. 'I'll wait here.'

'Cheers.'

Moray pulled an envelope out of his coat and tramped towards the front of the house. As he did so, he swore under his breath. An eight-bedroom mock-Tudor Barratt home. No class, no character, no soul. He stopped by the door, which had a dark glass panel at head height. Moray quickly glanced away from the reflection of his untidy form. Below was a spotless doormat, inviting him to clean his shoes before he entered. Moray inspected his tatty footwear for a second, sighed, and rang the oversized doorbell. After a couple of moments it was pulled open by a man in smart jeans, a tight jumper and pristine shoes. Moray took in the square jaw and the highlighted hair, the post-ironic mullet and the previously broken nose.

'And?' the man asked, holding a large black remote control in his hand like a weapon.

'I've got your results.' Moray nodded towards the envelope, which he was swinging between his forefinger and thumb. 'Can I come in, Mr Accoutey?'

Inside the lounge, an enormous flatscreen TV was illuminated green. Figures in red and yellow tussled across its shallow glassy surface. Jeremy Accoutey pointed his remote at the screen, freezing the image. Moray glanced from the TV to Jeremy and back. On the screen, Jeremy Accoutey was in the process of taking a penalty kick in front of a packed crowd. The ball remained frozen, stopped midway on its trajectory towards the goalmouth, oval and distorted in its movement.

'You like to watch yourself play?' he asked.

Jeremy grunted. 'Depends on the result. Do you want a drink?'

Moray shook his head.

'You sure? I've just opened a bottle.'

'No thank you, Mr Accoutey.'

Jeremy hesitated, then picked a bottle of Courvoisier off a coffee table and poured some into his glass.

'So,' he said, swirling his drink, 'you've got my answer.'

'Yeah.'

'And?'

Moray pushed the envelope towards him. 'Inside you'll find screen-shots of all our analyses. Everything should be self-explanatory.'

'So what does it say?'

'It's best you read the full report. But any questions, contact us via the usual PO box.' Moray let go of the envelope, allowing Jeremy to take it. 'And we'll need the remaining three and a half thousand.'

Jeremy Accoutey snatched the envelope, his fingers immediately moving to tear it open. Then he stopped, his jaw twitching, appearing to change his mind. He walked over to a dark office desk which sat brooding in the corner, surrounded by lighter Scandinavian furniture. Moray pictured the desk lurking in an antiques shop somewhere, solid and defiant, happily gathering dust. Jeremy unlocked a drawer and pulled out a bundle of notes.

'Should be all there,' he said, passing it to Moray. 'Three and a half.' Jeremy then reached into his jeans, and with a practised movement pulled out a couple of additional twenties. 'And here, this is for you and your partner. Get yourselves a drink or something.'

Moray didn't look up from leafing through the wad of notes and silently counting them. 'We don't do this for the tips,' he said.

'So what do you do it for?'

'It's a long story, Mr Accoutey. And just as we respect your privacy, we expect the same in return.' Moray finished counting, and glanced at Jeremy, who was still holding the purple and blue notes, unsure what to do with them, unused to having his money refused. 'A two-way street,' Moray added with a smile.

'Right.'

'And remember, if you have any questions, you know how to get hold of us.'

Moray made his way to the door, past the screen image of Jeremy Accoutey – his penalty kick in mid-flight, an instant of expectation pixilated and frozen – and walked out, crunching back up the sandstone drive.

Behind him, and with the door still open, Jeremy stared hard at the envelope. He closed his eyes for a second and crossed himself. He took a heavy swig of his drink, baring his teeth as it burned its way down. He took a deep breath which stretched the ribbing of his jumper. And then he tore at the envelope with trembling fingers.

13

DCI Sarah Hirst hesitated for a second, her arm stopping mid-motion. Rules and regulations, a voice whispered.

'I shouldn't really,' she said.

Reuben stared through the windscreen. A thin rain was falling, mist-like, layering the glass with a film of almost imperceptible droplets. He counted four seconds between sweeps of the intermittent wipers.

'Do you want my help or not?'

Sarah allowed her arm to complete its journey, handing the photograph over to Reuben. 'OK, but prepare yourself. Some of these aren't nice.'

'Compared with what I've seen recently . . .' Reuben began, but then he stopped. The colour photo showed a naked female corpse with strangulation bruising and a sick pallor which spoke of a breathless death.

'We've tried extracting from all six of the blue regions here.' Sarah pointed with slender unpainted fingers. 'But no joy. We're absolutely stumped.'

Reuben focused into the picture, examining the blue spots of negative DNA testing. She was lying on her back on a cold white table, lifeless and inert. Sometimes all it took was a photograph, and he was there. In it, seeing it, feeling it. The arteries gorging, the muscles clenching, the airways fighting, the heart spasming. Alive and thrashing, the single most animated instant of life always in the seconds before death.

'The body was discovered in water?'

'The Thames, no less.'

'And for how long?'

'We think she's been dead for three or four weeks. This is just a hunch, but she could be linked to the DI a few days back.'

'Tamasine Ashcroft?'

'That's the second time you've mentioned her by name. Did you know her?'

'Not really. Think I might have met her once or twice on an investigation a few years back.' Reuben cleared his throat. 'Up-and-coming DI taken out in her prime. Any connection between her profession and her death?'

'How do you mean?'

'Could she have been working on something . . .'

'Nothing that checks out. Some paedophile stuff, but it doesn't look to be linked. Even coppers end up in the wrong place at the wrong time.'

'Yeah, well.'

Sarah reached for the picture, holding her hand out, palm upturned. 'Could I?'

Reuben passed it back, frowning. 'You're saying it might have been the first?'

'I'm not saying anything. But you're aware what happens with first-time murders.'

'Like first-time lovers. Don't really know what they're doing till they've done it and it's over.'

'So this could be important.'

'If it's linked.' Reuben rewound to the case that still haunted him. No mistakes then with the first one. Just slow, methodical torture and death as Reuben's career fell apart and his marriage disintegrated. 'But it doesn't always work like that. You remember?'

Sarah half turned in her seat. The bad memory was still raw. 'Sorry . . .'

The wipers dragged again across the windscreen, shuddering and screeching in protest. It had stopped raining. Reuben blinked a couple of slow blinks. It was amazing. You could stare through a windscreen for long sluggish minutes and not notice that the wipers were still flicking back and forth, the wetness having dispersed, the glass no longer needing clearing. The brain and its ability to miss the obvious and lose itself in memories you hoped you'd buried.

'Sometimes,' Reuben said after only a brief pause, 'if they've been in the water a while, particularly where there are boats, you get this weirdly impenetrable mix of oil and algae.'

'Oil?'

'From outboard motors. This is good because it preserves the DNA, but bad because it makes it almost impossible to get at.'

'So what do we do?'

'Ask the lab to try again using a dilute ethanol solution. Then precipitate with sodium acetate and re-sequence. Might need five per cent glycerol in the PCR mix as well.'

'You think it will work?'

'It's the only thing that stands a chance.'

Sarah frowned. 'We'll give it a shot. Thanks. Now, I've got something for you.' She pulled another colour photo out of the pocket of her charcoal jacket. 'Have a look at this one. Recognize him?'

Reuben squinted at the mugshot of a dark-haired Caucasian prisoner taken at the time of arrest. 'Possibly . . .'

'You *did* carry out your predictive phenotyping on those samples last night?'

'You're joking. This is Michael Brawn?'

'None other.'

Reuben patted the pockets of his denim jacket, then slid out his pheno-fit of Michael Brawn. He searched the digitized features: the shallow nose, the rounded pudgy cheeks, the distended earlobes, the anterior curve of the chin, the slight overbite.

But mostly Reuben stared into the blackness of the face, with its dark pigmentation, pure-line Afro-Caribbean, unmistakable in its ethnicity. He placed the picture next to Sarah's mugshot, shoulder to shoulder, head to head.

'White Michael Brawn, meet black Michael Brawn.'

The wiper juddered across the dry screen again, and Sarah finally turned it off.

'There's something else, something more important than this,' she said.

'What?'

She bit into her lower lip. 'He's one of ours.'

'Shit. I thought the name—'

'This changes things, Dr Maitland.'

'Fuck, yeah.'

'I used Charlie Baker's access to check back through GeneCrime records.'

'Charlie Baker?' Reuben sucked in a breath that held a faint tinge of Sarah's perfume. 'Are you sure that's wise?'

'As I say, I am trying to catch what looks like a serial rapist at the moment. You'll forgive me if I take short-cuts.'

Reuben surveyed DCI Hirst's flushed cheeks and flared nostrils. 'Sorry,' he said.

'GeneCrime performed the forensics on him, the forensics which sent him down.'

'And if they're bent . . .'

Sarah whistled, a low note somewhere between

a sigh and a hum. 'I need to have another ask around, see what people know. Pull his file and have a proper look.'

'It doesn't make sense,' Reuben said, partly to himself. 'We profiled him, and his phenotype and genotype are entirely opposite.'

'Just as the note suggested.'

She flicked at her hair in the mirror. Reuben continued to focus on his pheno-fit, a million unsettling notions blurring his vision. Michael Brawn. A false genetic identity. DNA used and abused. It was still going on. Sarah's mobile rang, and she answered with a quick series of yeses and nos. Reuben scratched his forehead hard, trying to dismiss the notion. Sarah ended her call.

'No rest for those who hunt the wicked,' she said. 'Drop you somewhere?'

Reuben shook his head slowly. 'Here's fine.'

He climbed out of the car, slotted the pheno-fit away, and allowed himself to be swallowed by the sea of bodies flooding the pavement, immersing himself in other people's rights and wrongs, in their truths and inconsistencies.

14

Reuben lined up four colour photographs on the white lab bench. The first was a picture of Lucy, of her shoulders and her head. He recalled taking the photo, Lucy reluctant, self-conscious from the attention. They were on holiday somewhere, Portugal he guessed, and she had a reddening tan from too many hours in the sun. Her sunglasses were in her hair, which was slightly lighter than normal. Reuben estimated that it was near the end of the holiday, and they had been about to return to England, to their pre-Joshua lives, which seemed to revolve almost entirely around work. Lucy's eyes were smiling, despite the reluctance. The light which bounced off them projected carefree happiness, a future together, marriage and children, endless possibilities. Reuben scrutinized her face, absorbing every detail of the moment, a shutter's blink of everything that used to matter.

Joshua's photo, in comparison to his mother's, was slightly blurred. There was almost a halo around him, the haze of movement of his pale body lending an ethereal aura to his skin. Reuben estimated he was around fifteen months. When he saw photographs of his son, he half wished he could fast-forward them to an age when his features would start to really crystallize – five or six maybe. Even now, when he looked at him, he couldn't be sure. The darkness could just as well be from Shaun Graves as from Lucy. The nose was still a snubbed mound of tissue waiting to bud. The mouth and ears, the chin, the line of the eyebrows, the cheeks . . . all were beginning to talk to him, but would always remain supporting evidence. The eyes held the real clue. They were a light blue, with, from some angles, a hint of grey-green, and Reuben never tired of staring into them. But eye colour, he was well aware, could change up to the age of two. After that he would have a good idea. Reuben's irises were green, as were Lucy's, and Shaun's were hazel. He had done the maths, performed the permutations for the two locus trait with its three alleles. A complex inheritance with some guesswork involved. But a lot hinged on whether Joshua's eyes remained blue or began to turn more green.

He put Joshua down and picked Shaun Graves up. He was in a dark suit and light shirt, caught unawares, frowning slightly, his face almost square on to the camera. A Moray special, snapped covertly from some distance, one of a series of shots he had taken for Reuben in the days when the exclusion order had been rigidly enforced, and his only contact with Joshua was holding illicit photographs of him. Shaun had, Reuben was forced to concede, charismatically good looks. His chin was long, with the hint of a dimple in it. His ears were relatively small and symmetrical, and his cheekbones high and prominent for a male. Shaun's light eyes offset his golden skin. His hair was dark brown, but not quite as dark as Lucy's. Reuben focused on the face which had taken everything away from him, forcing himself to be cold and scientific, to map the details of his features rather than glare at them with lasting bitterness.

Closing his eyes and imprinting Shaun's characteristics, Reuben dropped his photo and picked up the final one. It was a perfunctory picture of his own face, expressionless and deadpan, taken from his old GeneCrime ID card. A terrible photograph, but ideal for the purpose at hand. There was no dishonesty of a forced smile or any other expression developed for the camera, just his nose, mouth, eyes, chin, ears, hair and cheeks. It was almost like an autopsy picture, so lifeless and drained of colour by a bright camera flash.

As he examined it, he recalled the period when it was taken. GeneCrime had just updated its already heavy security and had required new photo-ID cards for all personnel. It was three months before his dismissal. Reuben sensed the wildness in his own eyes, tried to immerse himself for a second in the suspicions, the pressures, the abrasive atmosphere of the division, at a time when everything was starting to go wrong. The root cause of where he was today. The seeds of protracted suspicion, the need for results starting to push one or two of his colleagues over the line that should never be crossed by CID.

And then Reuben paying the ultimate price. He saw Commander Robert Abner, red in the face, shaking his head sadly at Reuben, while DCIs Phil Kemp and Sarah Hirst stared at him in quiet silence. Sarah Hirst, cold and elegant, undisguised resentment on her face. Phil Kemp, dark-haired and squat, an unhealthy pallor to his skin. Clearing his throat, raising his eyebrows at Reuben and reading the charges against him. Then, minutes later, when all the talking was done, leaving the room, barrelling down corridors, DI Charlie Baker standing in his way, making him scrape past, giving Reuben a slow handclap out of the building.

Reuben blinked rapidly, returning to the now. He arranged and rearranged the four photographs on the bench, constructing family trees. Reuben and Lucy, with Joshua beneath; then Shaun and Lucy, with Joshua beneath. He superimposed features, measured distances with a pair of callipers, squinted and scribbled notes into a lab book. And then he turned Lucy's photo over and moved

Joshua's picture next to his own face, and then next to Shaun's, running his eyes rapidly back and forth between the images.

Reuben stood up. He slid a clear bottle labelled '100% Ethanol' from a lab shelf and poured a slosh into a Pyrex beaker, measuring out roughly a hundred millilitres. A quick calculation told him that this approximated to half a bottle of 40 per cent spirits. He pulled down the small glass vial marked 'Oblivion' from a rack of chemicals, and shook its powder back and forth. Its fine off-white grains arranged themselves into hills and valleys, ups and downs. Reuben flicked the tube with his middle finger, deciding.

He knew he could never bring himself to perform a paternity test. To sully Joshua, to drag his DNA into his lab, through his equipment, into his tubes . . . It was the purest form of hypocrisy, but Reuben had fought the impulse a thousand times. And at least this way there was still hope. To test his son and come up with a cold statistical number, the answer 'no' spelled out in a long stream of digits, truly that would finish him. He uncapped the vial, wet a fingertip and dabbed it inside. Then he rubbed the bitter powder into his gums, a small quantity which would keep him alert and awake.

Swigging from the beaker, he slotted the photos of Joshua, Lucy, Shaun and himself away, and sighed. He sat upright in the chair and pulled out two other pictures. And as he sipped the drink and felt the first tingles of the slow onset of amphetamine, he began to inspect and re-inspect Michael Brawn's contrasting photos in minute and utter detail.

15

Sarah Hirst supported the weight of her head with the fingers of both hands. A cold, gnawing headache was burrowing deep into her sinuses. On the desk in front of her lay a multitude of papers and photographs, covering almost the entire surface. The photos showed crime scenes, bodies and fragments of bodies. She felt a sense of overwhelming atrocity in the redness of the colour close-ups and the coldness of the black and white mortuary shots. Sarah pushed her fingertips into the thin skin of her forehead, lowered her chin and shifted the pressure from the top of her nasal passages. Like a ball of pain which moved position as she altered the angle of her brain, the headache seemed to relocate to her frontal lobes.

Three unsolved murders in little over a month, and now this. A body dredged from the Thames. Maybe linked to one or more of them, maybe not. There was no Missing Persons report, no search. Just a bloated corpse spotted by a woman walking her dog. Pathology had refused to commit themselves to a time of death. Three to four weeks was the best they had come up with. Sarah sighed. To disappear and to die, to have no one miss you, and to wash up naked on the brown cloying banks of the Thames . . . She rubbed her aching head, and again felt the pain move as she did so. This was loneliness on a scale even London found shocking.

Sarah had run Reuben's suggestions past Dr Mina Ali, the senior forensic technician of GeneCrime. Since Reuben's departure, the unit had promoted from within. The publicity and the sudden openness of the division had had that effect. CID, Forensics, Pathology – everyone looked inwards, as if trying to rediscover the privacy they had lost when everything spiralled out of control.

The press had swarmed all over the covert unit. In the subsequent nine months, wounds had closed and scars had formed, but actual healing was still a way off. GeneCrime's greatest strength was also its greatest weakness. A unit of élite CID and brilliant scientists, supported by gifted programmers, pathologists and criminologists, had pushed crime detection to world-leading levels. Cases previously beyond the scope of straightforward resolution had been brought to fruition through new methodologies and cross-discipline cooperation. But it had come at a price. The disparity in personality, outlook and approach between GeneCrime's police and scientist factions had sometimes threatened to overwhelm the unit. Mistakes had been made, lines had been crossed, egos had taken hold. And then DCI Phil Kemp, Sarah's opposite number, and the man who initially took over from Reuben, had begun to change the rules.

Sarah reached for her coffee, which was cold. The thought of Phil Kemp distracted her from her grinding headache. It was possible that caffeine was to blame for it, but she drank the bitter liquid anyway. Sarah knew she had to keep going; had to run through the evidence, get Forensics to cross-match samples found around each body; had to chase Mina to see if she was willing to use Reuben's method of extraction. The unit had fucked up once before, and Sarah was damned if it was going to happen again.

A knock at the door made her look up from the slim comfort of her cold coffee. Detective Inspector Charlie Baker was standing in the doorway, dark-haired, swarthy, a model IC2 if ever there was one. Sarah wondered just how hairy he was beneath his white shirt and black trousers. The short beard that covered much of his face and neck seemed almost ready to overwhelm him.

Charlie passed Sarah a heavy brown CID file, holding on to it a moment longer than was necessary. 'Here,' he said. 'This was in your pigeon hole.'

'Thanks.'

Charlie paused for a second, and Sarah knew that something was up.

'This the file Reuben Maitland's interested in?'

'What makes you think that?'

'See this here?' Charlie pointed to the title on his security badge. '*Detective Inspector* Charlie Baker.'

'So?'

'So, I *detect* and I *inspect*.'

'Well, do you think you could detect the door and inspect your way back out again?'

Charlie scratched his beard and grinned. Sarah noted the way his teeth fitted tightly together, worn upper incisors meeting equally worn lower ones.

'Touché,' he said, before spinning round on his black heels and leaving the office.

Sarah returned her attention to the carnage in front of her, seemingly a hundred corpses lying at subtly different angles with multiple patterns of wounding. But all sharing the same horrible truth. Lives ended in unimaginable pain and violence.

She picked up a picture of the bruised corpse of DI Tamasine Ashcroft. Married with one child. Her eyes fixed open, horror in her expression. Knowing about men who did this, and finally meeting one face to face. And then the most recent discovery. Slightly bloated, pulled out of the river after a few weeks. And, as she looked more closely at the Pathology report, similar patterns of injury to DI Ashcroft. 'Killing them first and then raping them. Asphyxiation, death, and then, and only then, penetration.

Sarah picked up her drink and forced another sour mouthful down.

'So what are you so scared of?' she asked.

16

Lesley Accoutey poured another drink, her hand shaking, the bottle clinking against the rim of the glass. Her slender fingers gripped the gin and tonic and carried it across the room, ice cubes rattling and slices of lemon slowly sinking. She sat down on the cold laminate flooring. They had chosen it together. Natural oak. And it looked good, virtually indistinguishable from the real thing. As she ran her eyes over the surface, Lesley noted the simulated imperfections which had been imprinted into its pattern, meticulously designed, a sad parody of the random beauty of real wood. She pressed her palm hard into the façade. It felt cold to the touch and didn't seem to give anything back. Not like real wood.

She glanced up at her husband Jeremy, perched silently on a large cream sofa, staring intently at her. Anthony's name came to her, and his face. She blinked him away. This was more important than anything, even Anthony. This was her marriage. And yet . . . Lesley began to cry again.

'No more lies, Lesley,' Jeremy said, after a few moments.

Lesley continued to sob, unable to look her husband in the eye.

Jeremy took a heavy slug from his glass. 'His DNA matched samples found in your underwear.' He picked an A4 manila envelope off the sofa and held it up for emphasis. 'They said the odds were ten million to one. You know me. I like a flutter now and then. And I know those odds are pretty tight. So no more lies.'

Lesley raised her tear-stained face, blonde hair tumbling into her eyes. Again, an image of Anthony hunted her down, tracksuited and smiling, stroking his trained hands over her slender body, making her laugh and exciting her all at the same time. She glanced around the room. Could she give all of this up? she silently asked herself. A footballer's salary for a physio's? She ran her fingers over the unyielding laminate flooring.

'We keep this quiet, and no more lies,' Jeremy repeated.

Lesley looked up at him and whispered the word 'sorry'. She tried to picture Jeremy taking her used panties from the laundry box. Choosing a likely pair, one of her favourites, expensive and sheer. Or maybe he had given them several sets to choose from. She was filled with a sudden disgust. Having her dirty knickers opened, revealed, examined by people she didn't know. Violated. All looking for stains, for Anthony's essence which had leaked out of her and into her underwear. Lesley felt a sudden flare of anger.

'You had no right going through my things,' she said. 'Giving them to sordid men who delve about in other people's private—' She stopped herself, trying to choose a different word, on the verge of saying 'affairs'. 'Business.'

'Yeah, well, sometimes you've got to do these things.'

'Do you?' she asked angrily.

'When you get whispers, sniggers. When suspicions won't go away, month after month. And when you hear there's a way of telling you one hundred per cent yes or no.'

'Oh God.' Lesley swallowed her gin, the ice cubes clattering against her teeth. Such a mess. Such an ugly fucking mess.

'They got DNA from him, and DNA from inside you . . .' Jeremy battled the anger and the humiliation. 'Look, if we're going to survive, we have to face this thing together. Openly and honestly. OK?'

Lesley stared at him, and shook her head slightly. She mouthed the word 'sorry' again and pushed her long manicured nails hard into the imitation wooden floor.

17

The secret, Reuben conceded, was always to stay one step ahead. And as he was driven east along concrete carriageways and brightly lit thoroughfares, he appreciated that sometimes this meant isolating yourself from cold, hard logic and following the random vagaries of your heart. But ahead of what? His old division was stitching itself back together. It was only with the benefit of time and distance that he was finally understanding all that had happened, and all that was still happening.

No one was sure how many miscarriages of justice there had been. Or, more worryingly, whether new ones were being perpetrated. Reuben knew it, Sarah knew it, Abner had even alluded to it. Phil Kemp couldn't have been acting alone. He simply didn't have the insight or the ability to trade genetic identities without being detected for so long. That required access to samples, to databases and to methodologies that a CID officer would struggle with. Reuben could see now that in neutralizing Phil Kemp, he had created a more subtle problem. You feel the bulging tumour under the skin, you cut it out, and you assume you've solved everything that's bad. But what about the ones you can't see? The small, thriving metastases hiding in the bones? Sometimes, Reuben frowned, the obvious symptom blinds you to the more serious diagnosis.

As the taxi turned off the dual carriageway, Commander Robert Abner's words hunted him down and found him. *Sarah Hirst is smart. She keeps tabs on you.* Reuben had never been sure about Sarah. Not in the way that you're sure that you are single, and happy half the time, and miss your son like crazy. Not in the way that in knowing your own strengths and weaknesses you also know those of others. Sarah had always been closed. Cold, distant, almost deliberately unknowable. With certain exceptions. There had been a time, several months ago, when Sarah had lowered her defences briefly, when Reuben had witnessed emotion and feeling and empathy. When they had nearly crossed the line. Nearly. But now the circumstances were different, and Reuben appreciated that he was, as Commander Abner had pointed out, being kept close. Not that close to Sarah Hirst was a bad place to be.

Reuben patted his jacket pocket for the envelope Moray had given him earlier. He examined it closely for a couple of seconds, turning it over and inspecting both sides. The PO box address was typed and printed, screaming anonymity a little too loudly. He ripped it open and retrieved a note from within. It was a slim strip of good-quality paper which may at one point have been part of a larger sheet. He read the printed words out loud to himself.

'The truth to your sacking from GeneCrime lies in Michael Brawn's identity.'

Reuben glanced again at the nondescript envelope, re-read the words of the note and put both in his pocket. When you mess with forensic scientists, he thought, it's best to do it cleanly and unidentifiably.

The taxi slowed and stopped, and Reuben looked up. They had arrived. The Lamb and Flag was buried deep in East Ham, the kind of establishment that had proudly watched the changing faces of a million men and women walking through its doors over hundreds of years. Reuben pushed through the front door as his taxi pulled away to find another occupant to transport around the capital. The bar was rough, vainly aspiring towards spit and sawdust, its drinkers raw and edgy, and overwhelmingly male. The air was sour with drink. Almost immediately, a figure who had been leaning against the wall interrupted Reuben's path. He was late twenties, medium height and very tattooed.

'You Stevo?' Reuben asked.

'Only if you're Reuben,' the man replied.

Reuben stepped further into the pub and offered his hand. It was taken by Stevo's, which was so tattooed that it shone blue in contrast with Reuben's white offering.

'Thanks for meeting me.'

'Any friend of Kieran Hobbs is a friend of mine.'

Reuben grimaced, and hoped it didn't show too badly. 'Not a friend, exactly. I sometimes do some work for him.'

'Either way. He told me to look after you.'

'How do you know Kieran?' Reuben asked.

'Done some stuff for him. Mainly through Nathan, who's an old mate.'

'What kind of stuff?'

Stevo smiled. 'Friends of Kieran shouldn't ask that sort of question.'

'So where's it happening?'

'Follow me.'

Reuben followed Stevo through the pub and out into the rear yard. It was concreted, and two powerful floodlights hung in opposing corners. Thirty or forty people were milling around, a jittery excitement in the air, their voices clipped, their movements quick and twitchy. Reuben and Stevo pushed their way through until they could see what was going on. At the centre was a crude square marked out on the floor.

'You watch. The old pros, the ones who usually win, will be sober as judges. It's the young lads, they've had a few – call it a bit of Dutch or whatever – and they're vulnerable. Bravado higher, reflexes slower – walking targets to a geezer who knows what he's up to.'

Two men appeared from opposite sides of the crowd. Both were dressed in jeans and T-shirts. They walked over and shook hands, eyes not meeting, scanning the people surrounding them, sensing the intensity. The crowd fell silent.

'What are the rules?'

'No rules,' Stevo answered, 'except when one of you's had enough the other has to stop.'

Each man took three paces back, facing the other. A whistle blew. They rushed forward, and within seconds were kicking, tearing and punching each other with a ferocity that took Reuben aback.

'Smaller guy will win,' Stevo said.

'How do you know?'

'Wants it more. Plus, you've got to have balls to be a small guy and get into this ring.'

Both men were soon bleeding, the fluid black under the artificial lighting. Sickening blows continued to be traded. The crowd shouted and cheered. The larger man suddenly doubled up, bent over, spitting blood and teeth.

'Jesus,' Reuben whispered.

'You never see the punch coming. Even with practice. Believe me.'

'No?'

'No. What you do see is the body shape. You see the cunt shaping up to put one on you. You get to know when he's about to swing. And that's when you have an instant to make that decision.'

'Which decision?'

'Do I get out of the way, or do I get to him first? And this geezer just made the wrong call.'

The smaller man paced around his fallen opponent and kicked him smartly in the head, snapping his neck up. The larger man keeled over on to his side, and the smaller man walked up and kicked him in the head again. The man on the floor raised a bloody hand before he lost any more teeth. A whistle blew from deep within the crowd. The smaller man stopped, then turned round and bowed to the crowd. A low cheer went up, echoing around the enclosed yard.

'You seen enough?' Stevo asked. 'Plenty more where that came from.'

'I think I get the idea.'

'Right then. Maybe you're ready.'

Reuben managed a half smile. He had the sudden need for a drink.

Staying one step ahead. That had been his rationale for this. Sensing that things could turn nasty at any moment, and suspecting that learning how to fight might be a useful skill. He was increasingly putting himself on the line, and no longer able to call for automatic police back-up. A sixth sense had recently started gnawing away at him, telling him to be prepared for anything. And that was exactly what he now planned to do.

18

'Ah, DI Baker, I've been meaning to speak with you.'

'Sir?'

Commander Robert Abner closed the door to the Gents behind him and paced over to the urinal. Charlie Baker half turned, unsure how to react.

'I guess this place is as good as any,' Commander Abner commented as he unzipped his flies, noisy and exaggerated in his movements.

As he did so, he turned his avian eyes on the man standing next to him, appraising him one final time. DI Charlie Baker was bearded and sharp, with small dark eyes and a paleness which spoke of too many hours under the strip lights of GeneCrime. Commander Abner knew he worked hard, and was reasonably unpopular, with no obvious allegiances in GeneCrime. People didn't trust him, or want to share their space with him. The closest thing to a loner that the interreliant police unit held. But Commander Abner considered this to be a good thing. A man with ostensibly few friends was unlikely to have fostered strong alliances. For this reason, Robert Abner considered him low risk. Not that that was any guarantee, but what could you do? he asked himself. You had to start somewhere. He had pulled his file, cross-checked with a couple of old colleagues, watched him closely. There was no substitute for the copper's instinct. Especially when you were policing the police.

'What I'm about to say is in confidence, and I expect it to stay that way. You understand?'

Charlie Baker nodded, acutely uncomfortable. He had barely needed the toilet, but had decided to stretch his legs nonetheless. Now here he was, standing shoulder to shoulder with six foot four of area commander, his bladder suddenly closed off, and not knowing where to look or what to say for the best. 'I understand,' he answered quietly, looking down at the dry porcelain, empty except for a couple of blue toilet cubes.

'Good.' Robert Abner began to piss, a powerful hissing jet which filled the silences. 'Look, Baker, we need to sort this division out. We're doing OK, the situation is better than it was, but still I hear things.'

Charlie stared mournfully into his section of the elongated urinal as Abner's yellow stream flowed past him on its way to the drain. 'What kind of things?'

'Rumours, inside and out. Impropriety. Surely I don't need to say it, man?'

Charlie grunted noncommittally.

'I want you to keep an ear to the ground. No one must know. Someone in this unit isn't playing fair. Trouble is, I can't have an open audit. It's all too vague, too easy to walk away from. Unless, that is, we catch them at it.'

'And, specifically, what is "it", sir?'

'That's my business. But I recently had an idea, a way to sort things out. Someone who could help us.'

Charlie remained distinctly unnerved, barely listening to the unit commander. He had spoken to him maybe two or three times since he had taken over the jurisdiction of GeneCrime. He wasn't a boss who interacted with his staff unless he really had to. Charlie had always imagined his inaccessibility was a strategy for maintaining discipline, the unapproachable head who unsettled his staff and kept them firmly on their toes. And now this. Standing next to him, scared to death, unable to piss. The warning hanging in the sharp damp air of the toilets. Someone not playing fair. Catch them at it.

'Who have you asked to help?' he asked.

'Maybe I'm not making myself clear.' Commander Abner glared down at him. 'Your job is not to question what I'm doing. Your job is merely to report anything out of the ordinary, anything new that happens which doesn't sound right. I don't want you ploughing through past cases. We're too busy, and that's something that, as I say, I'm trying to take care of.'

'Right.'

The flow from Charlie's left was easing, trickling down to virtually nothing. And still Charlie couldn't go. He heard the commander shaking out the last drops. Amid his misery, Charlie felt a shot of apprehension. Abner poking about in the division could only be bad news. He wondered what he was really after, what had brought him to this course of action. This was a long way from standard operating procedures.

'So I expect you to keep me up to speed. Anything unusual, or unorthodox, or doing the rounds – scandals, hints and insinuations – I want to hear about it. From now on, you are my ears on the inside of GeneCrime.'

With that, Commander Robert Abner hoisted his zip up as energetically as it had come down, turned and walked out of the toilets.

As Charlie stood at the urinal, partially humiliated, embarrassed and impotent, he pondered Abner's words, and worked through the implications. Why was Abner sharing this with him? Was he being set up? What was the commander trying to achieve? And what had got him so spooked? But as he thought, he quickly saw that this could become a position of trust, reporting directly to the big man, a situation of safety, of protection, of immunity. As he relaxed, he began to piss. He whistled, steam rising from the porcelain. From now on, he would be burrowing his way into the centre of GeneCrime, listening, watching, and biding his time, his every move sanctioned by Abner.

19

The footwell of Moray's ageing Saab was littered with piles of fingernails, which looked to Reuben like the bones of a tiny mammal. Some were long and femur-thick, others shorter and curved like ribs. It was clear that Moray chewed his nails as he drove, then flicked them towards the generally empty passenger side. As Reuben peered closer, he saw that the fibres of carpeting were entwined with the fragments, as if subsuming the bones into the nylon earth.

'You don't have many passengers, then?' Reuben asked.

Moray continued to chew into the tip of his middle finger for a few seconds. 'Not so many.'

'Or manicurists?'

'Mani-what-now?'

As they crossed Southwark Bridge, the Thames appeared choppy, and military grey in colour. Reuben shivered for a second, imagining being dredged from its muddy depths, the clay sediments in his hair, a mix of oil and algae coating his skin. And he wondered whether GeneCrime had successfully isolated DNA from what might be the first victim linked to DI Tamasine Ashcroft.

'Did you explain the possible outcomes to him?' he asked.

'I did.' Moray finally detached the remaining piece of nail. He plucked it from his mouth, glanced at Reuben, and flicked it out the window. 'There,' he groused. 'Happy?'

'Ecstatic.'

'But you know at this rate we're going to have to set up a fucking counselling service.'

'Fancy it?'

'Yeah, right. "Mr Accoutey, I'm afraid your wife is fucking the Arsenal team physio behind your back. Now, can I have the cash please?" Or, "Mr Bloggs, your actual father is the man you've been calling Uncle Pete all your life. Twenties will do, or fifties if you're pushed." Reckon you could do better?'

Reuben bit into his own nail, feeling the slight flexing, the reluctance of the hard, translucent substance to yield. 'Paternity suits aren't exactly my thing.'

Moray took a quick look sideways. 'Could save you a lot of grief in the long run.'

'I can't do it. You know that, Moray. I just can't. Call me a hypocrite. It's just when it's your own flesh and blood . . .'

'Aye. Sorry.'

'And this way, at least there's still hope.'

'It's not the despair that kills you . . .'

'I know. It's the hope.'

Reuben rubbed his face, a slow, heavy movement of his hand dragging his features down. The other side of the Thames was equally as frantic as the one they had just left. For a second, Reuben saw the myriad of bridges which criss-crossed the river as slender and elongated escapes from the mayhem, calming moments over water, before it all began again. They stuttered and barged their way through the streets of cars, buses, taxis and cyclists. Reuben made a silent promise to himself that he would retire to the countryside. Somewhere static and silent where clocks seemed to run slow, the only sound the sighing of cows and the music of birds.

He held on to this image for several quiet minutes, until they pulled up outside a café bar. It was metallic, Italian, and looked expensive, its designer modernity clashing with Reuben's daydreamed fields. Moray eyed the entrance intently.

'You sure about this?' he asked.

'How do you mean?'

'That you trust her one hundred per cent?'

'One hundred's a big number,' Reuben said, loosening his seatbelt. 'But I don't see what she would have to gain from stringing me along.'

'Yeah, well. Just be on your guard.'

Inside, DCI Sarah Hirst was sitting bolt upright at a polished aluminium table, in a polished aluminium chair, both of which struck Reuben as being wildly uncomfortable. As he walked up and pulled out a chair, he wondered if the furniture was simply too painful for slouching.

'Hello,' he said.

'Thanks for meeting on my territory.'

Sarah looked tired, but her eyes were wide and busy, taking in everything around her. Reuben glanced at her large black coffee, a legal amphetamine, with little of the pleasure but all of the heart thumping.

'So . . .' he began.

'So indeed.'

'How's things?'

'Absolutely snowed under.'

'You said on the phone you were trying to tie it to the latest killing.'

'Ninety-five per cent. Sex post-death. It has to be.'

'Any joy with the DNA?'

'Mina Ali's on it. But no luck as yet.'

'There was one other thing. Tell her to try a pre-amplification step with random primers and low magnesium. That's about all I can think of. And if that fails—'

'I'll pass it on. If we can get it sorted, you never know.'

'What is it that you couldn't say over the phone?'

Sarah drank deeply from her coffee. Reuben sensed that she was making him wait, preparing him for bad news. She used both her hands to replace the mug, which rattled against its saucer.

'Well?' he asked.

'You might want to look closely at this.'

Sarah pulled a thick brown file out of her slim leather case and slid it across the table. Reuben picked up Sarah's coffee, took a swig and grimaced. The front of the file read 'Michael Jeremy Brawn; GeneCrime CID'. Reuben opened it and began to leaf through its thin white and yellow pages. There were more photos of Brawn, distinguishing marks, witness statements and dates of arrest.

'Who else knows about this?'

'No one.'

'You sure?'

Sarah sighed. She turned her coffee round to drink from a different side to Reuben. 'As you're aware, you can't be sure of anything in GeneCrime. You put that much ego under that much pressure and grant that many exceptional powers, you don't expect things to be straightforward.'

Reuben paused, suddenly lost in something. He stared at the Final Evidence form, scanning left and right, up and down. An inventory of samples collected from Michael Brawn and results obtained. The last piece of paper before a laboratory investigation officially became a CID one. Figures and statistics and outcomes. And there, at the bottom, his own signature. Fuck. He looked again, blinking rapidly. His brow furrowed.

'Is that what you mean?' he asked, holding the document up.

'Why don't you show me?'

Reuben pulled out a pen and scrawled two words on another piece of paper from the file. Then he turned them both round and pushed them across the table towards Sarah.

'You really do sign a shit autograph,' she said, frowning and leaning her head forward, her light hair cascading towards the papers. 'But my point was, either one of them was signed through a major hangover . . .'

'Or?'

'Or by someone else. It just struck me when I flicked through the file. That signature is different from others of yours.'

'But who the fuck could have done that?'

Reuben stared at the two signatures. The more he thought about it the surer he was becoming. Dots were joining, actions linking themselves together. His sacking. The shift from the private to the public. A commander with deep-rooted suspicions about the very officers supposed to be solving crimes. A metastasis inside GeneCrime. Michael Brawn sitting in Pentonville with a false genetic identity. Someone faking Reuben's signature on an evidence document to get Brawn put there.

He looked up and frowned at Sarah. 'You want to know something?'

Sarah drained what remained of her drink. 'Why don't you spell it out, Dr Maitland?'

'Michael Brawn has just become personal,' he said.

Other decisions now needed to be made, other courses of action followed. Something deep in his coffee-sour gut told Reuben that things were going to get nasty. He took out his mobile and dialled Stevo.

20

Immediately, there was something in his nose which spoke of school PE lessons. A rough comp in West London, which had nevertheless splashed out on a state-of-the-art gymnasium, almost as if it had decided to swap physical education for mental. Although it had been built several years before Reuben began attending the school, the pinch of sweat, the sweetness of leather and the freshness of wood had hung permanently in its air. Now, as with all nasal matters, the smell seemed to travel up through his sinuses, diffusing through the sphenoid bone directly into his brain. Dusty memories were slowly coming alive, as if they had been lying there for twenty-five years waiting only for that one unique odour to wake them from their coma. Reuben saw sadistic PE teachers, shivering boys running the full gamut of pubertal development, games treated more like punishments than pastimes.

He scanned the gymnasium. All around, wooden

bars lined the walls. Several well-pounded punch bags were supported from the ceiling, and battered medicine balls loitered in heavy static lines. Reuben looked back at Stevo, who was standing in front of him wearing a head-guard, his tattooed hands out front.

'We ain't talking about boxing here,' Stevo continued. 'This is different. This is *fighting*. You saw what went on the other night.'

'Unfortunately,' Reuben answered, adjusting his tracksuit top. He had wanted to witness the way men fight, knuckle to knuckle. Sooner or later, Reuben suspected, the knowledge would come in useful. Now he had decided to take the next step.

'You get punched in the ring, fine, it hurts, but you're OK.'

Stevo reached forward and jabbed Reuben in the shoulder. Reuben peered through Stevo's padded head-guard and into his eyes, trying to gauge what to expect.

'You know what I mean? You take one from a fist – no gloves now – or an elbow, or a knee . . .'

Stevo jabbed him again, harder this time.

'Right,' Reuben grunted, his shoulder complaining. Stevo was enjoying this, his eyes ablaze, and for a second the apparition of a PE teacher returned to Reuben.

'One of those and you're going down.'

Stevo stood still, in control, his hands by his side. Reuben felt his shoulder, which jarred slightly as he moved it. Then Stevo punched him sharply and suddenly in the guts.

'Doesn't matter who you are.'

Reuben bent over, caught out, winded, unable to breathe. He had barely had time to react. He fought for air, angry, his brain struggling to keep up. The rules were changing by the second. Stevo was going to hurt him.

'And forget the films. No one's coming back at you after two or three good punches.'

Reuben straightened, hands on hips, finally inflating his diaphragm. He monitored Stevo intently. He was examining his knuckles, rubbing his thumb over the point which had connected with Reuben's chest bone. Stevo looked up. There was meanness in his face. He smiled, blue eyes and yellow teeth. This was for real. Reuben lifted his hands, ready to protect himself. Stevo continued to wait, revelling in the moment, and Reuben wondered what he had actually let himself in for. People like Kieran had very nasty contacts. Men who did what you asked them to do, with no question or hesitation. Men like Valdek Kosonovski, iron bar at the ready. If these were the sorts of friends Stevo had, then Reuben should be on his guard. This wasn't a game. This was fighting. But Reuben had made the rash decision when he saw his counterfeit signature staring back at him the previous day. It was time to toughen himself up. He had a bad feeling about what lay ahead.

Stevo lowered his hands. He was grinning under his head-guard. And then he launched a punch. Reuben tried to duck, but it struck him on the side of the head. His ear rang; it was on fire. Then something changed. PE teachers, playground fights, Phil Kemp . . . Stevo aimed a kick at Reuben's gut, but Reuben reacted and grabbed Stevo's leg. He jerked it round and pushed it hard, sending Stevo reeling back, slamming on to the mat.

Stevo picked himself up, taking his time, slow and deliberate, breathing hard. 'Not bad,' he remarked with a laugh. 'Not bad.' He took off his mask and wiped his forehead with the back of a hand. 'Nathan told me you were a bit of a pussy. In fact, Kieran said so as well. But maybe not.'

'Thanks.' Reuben grimaced, dismissing the notion that he had been about to launch himself into Stevo, fists blazing, kicking and punching, on the verge of losing control.

'I guess we just have to get you angry.'

21

Kimberly Horwitz pushes through the last physical barrier clawing at her to remain at work. The revolving doors hesitate, resisting her efforts for a second, before gaining a reluctant momentum and then propelling her forcefully on to the street. Increasingly of late, Kimberly feels as if the seventeen-storey building is swallowing her in the morning and spitting her out at night.

As she walks, she swings a slim case, trying not to count the days. Three months in London had sounded ideal. A chance to get away and start again. But that was the very problem. She was alone in a foreign city, perpetually out of time-zone synch with family and friends back home in Boston. If she was entirely honest, the reason she accepted the bank's invitation to aid its acquisitions team had been more about not saying no than actually wanting to say yes.

Corporate banks seem to sway over her. Only a few persistent lights are on in the buildings which stare blackly down at her. When she looks up, she feels dwarfed by the towering office blocks which back on to the Thames. Kimberly checks her watch. Nearly two a.m. Sixteen-hour days, just like at home.

She walks around a corner, and heads towards the main road. She pictures her bed in the apartment the bank has rented for her. Her stomach growls loudly, and she is glad for the moment that she is on her own. The result of a client's attempt at an ice-breaker, a buffet of Traditional London Fare. Or Fayre. Some bizarre Limey post-war food known as tripe, a selection of severed eels in a ridiculous type of gelatin, a paper cup full of gritty shells called cockles. She smiles to herself, her digestive system complaining again. What were they trying to do, poison them, for Christ's sake?

Kimberly cocks her ear to one side. Amid the clacking of her high heels, a softer noise. She spins round but sees nothing. An echo, maybe, sharp spikes from her footwear bouncing back from the office blocks, muffled and restrained. She listens acutely. The rhythm stays fixed, the hard and the soft answering each other. But then they start to lose synch. The duller noise becomes quicker than her own pace.

Understanding is soon upon her. Kimberly glances left and right. A parallel street to the right, an intersection straight ahead. Someone who had been matching her pace for pace is speeding up.

There is no one around. She suddenly feels a long way from Boston, homesickness mingling with fear, making it feel colder and more desperate.

The taxi rank is just one block away. Kimberly tells herself not to panic. She has come to London to do a job, then get the hell back again. Besides, the streets of England are safe. Downtown Boston, no way she's going to be walking the streets at this hour. Central London, however, is fine. She hurries towards the intersection, scanning the cold commercial frontages of office blocks and the dull black windows of insurance agencies.

And then, from nowhere, with no sound, a figure. Coming towards her, fast and intent. She starts to scream, but doesn't get the chance. The air is out of her before she hits the pavement.

22

The tube train surfaced in a hurry, as if it were coming up for air. Reuben blinked in the light, staring through the opposite window. The platform was bathed in a pale spring yellowness, one of the stations where the Underground poked its head out to see what was going on. He stretched, aware that he was stiffening up, leaking blood vessels forming deep bruises where Stevo's fists had rammed home. He again pictured the ruined body of Ethan de Groot, destroyed by an iron bar, a mess of internal haemorrhaging, ruptured organs and broken bones. Being beaten to death was truly horrific, and Reuben shuddered for a second with the memory of having to take DNA swabs from the corpse. But this, he acknowledged sadly, was what his life was becoming.

He scratched his chin. It hadn't always been like this. From being a junior CID officer, the return to education, a Ph.D. in molecular biology, the switch to forensics. Academic publications, pioneering research, high-profile breakthroughs. Head-hunted for GeneCrime, an élite national forensic detection unit being assembled in Euston. Rising to the position of lead forensics officer. Becoming a media spokesperson on crime. Building a loyal team who looked up to him and helped him push the science of what was possible. And then everything going wrong, with Lucy, with Shaun Graves, with GeneCrime. The very newspapers Reuben had written for demanding his dismissal for abuse of position.

The train began to move, accelerating in small electric jolts, disappearing down into the ground once again. Reuben's options had narrowed. He had lost his wife, child, job and home, in a matter of weeks. But he knew that GeneCrime needed monitoring. Rumours from his old team abounded. And so he had set up a covert lab, had begun testing GeneCrime evidence smuggled out by Judith, while pursuing private cases to finance the investigations. Holding hands with the devil in order to do what was right.

Reuben shook his head. Ten months, and he was starting to sleep properly again. But things were still messy. A new lab, new private clients, helping the gangster Kieran Hobbs figure out who was trying to kill him. The police taking a sporadic interest in the form of Sarah Hirst, keeping him under observation, tolerating his activities in exchange for his insight. None of it sat well. He was caught between just about everything: between the police and the underworld, between his wife and his son, between what was right and what was wrong. But all the time knowing that if he didn't police the activities of GeneCrime, no one else was going to, and wondering how many other Michael Brawns were out there, the scent of false genetic evidence leaking from their skin.

At the next station Reuben stood up and left the train, climbing two sets of escalators to emerge into the tainted air of the city. No house, no car, no bank accounts, no nothing. That had been the idea. Invisible and untouchable, free to go where he wanted, beneath the radar of the people he investigated and the clients he served. As a disgraced police civilian, Reuben was well aware that his only protection was anonymity. That and fight training. He made his way to a bus stop and stood in line. Once famous, respected and feared, now just a scientist in a bus queue.

Moray had beaten him to the laboratory. He was sitting on the sofa fingering a padded envelope, looking apprehensive.

'Post,' he said quietly.

Reuben inspected the package. 'Funny, the print . . .'

'It's the same as the other ones.'

Reuben pulled on a pair of gloves and ripped it open, pouring its contents on to the bench.

Several very tightly wrapped wads of used fifty-pound notes dropped out, along with a piece of paper. Reuben scanned the note and slid it along to Moray.

'The truth to GeneCrime lies in the genes of Michael Jeremy Brawn,' he muttered. 'Find out who he is. PO box 36745.' Moray whistled a long, low note and picked up two bundles, weighing them in his palms as if he could guess their value.

'What do you reckon?' Reuben asked.

'Twenty to twenty-five.'

'I mean, about the note.'

'Someone has an axe to grind about GeneCrime and is prepared to pay.'

'But who? And what are they really after?'

'They need you to get involved in whatever's going on.'

'But what *is* going on? All we know is that GeneCrime seem to have put someone away based on false DNA. And someone else wants to know the truth.'

'Who do you figure?'

Reuben picked the note up again. The same font as before, used by just about every computer in the world, probably cut from the same sheet of paper as the others. The envelope was self-sealing. He examined the adhesive flap up close, knowing that it could have trapped enough skin cells for forensic analysis. But Reuben's instinct told him that whoever sent the notes was being more careful than that.

'If I was a gambling man, I'd put my money on Abner.'

'Why?'

'Just a few things he said last week. Dropping hints like they were going out of fashion.'

'About what?'

'GeneCrime is a mess that Abner's trying to mop up. One bent officer doesn't spoil a division, but things take time to settle down. And while they do, everything has to be right. Abner needs to have independent knowledge of any potential impropriety.'

'But why not come to you directly?'

'He couldn't risk it. Anyone got wind of the fact that I was digging about in GeneCrime and he'd have all sorts of nightmares on his hands. Think about it. The press, his fellow officers, GeneCrime CID and Forensics . . . there'd be mutiny. And all this in the middle of a major investigation.'

'So what about Michael Brawn?'

'What's really weird is he pleaded guilty at his trial.'

'So?'

'A fake DNA sample should have got him off the charge. There would have been no forensic way of linking him to the crime. It's the wrong way round.'

'Maybe that's why Abner wants you to pursue it.'

'If it's him.'

'But what can you do anyway? The guy's in prison.'

Reuben shrugged. 'At least he isn't going anywhere for a while.'

'And where's a copper going to get twenty-five grand?'

'I hope you don't need me to answer that. Believe me, for paying off informants and oiling the wheels, there's always money available. Just look at the sums seized on drug raids. Twenty-five grand is child's play.'

Moray smiled. 'I always did wonder what happened to all the seizures of cash, and the sale of assets.'

'Another grey area in the universally grey area of crime detection. Whatever you've got to do to catch the bad guys.'

Moray stood up and made a show of checking his watch. 'Should be our motto. Listen, I've got to run. What do you think, though? Twenty-five grand could buy a lot of equipment, keep us going for a few months.'

Reuben was still holding the note, gazing at it, almost focusing through its neatly typed letters. 'How could I not be intrigued?' he asked.

'Right enough,' Moray answered, heading for the door. 'But a word of caution. When someone wants you to do a thing so bad, you've got to wonder why.'

'So you're saying I should do what exactly?'

Moray shrugged. 'Fucked if I know,' he said.

Reuben pulled his gloves off. 'Thanks a lot.'

Moray grinned, opened the heavy door and slammed it as he left. Reuben glanced up at a vial labelled 'Oblivion', and licked his dry lips. There had been no point asking Moray. He knew exactly what he was going to do.

23

DCI Sarah Hirst was beginning to regret the large Danish pastry she had just eaten. It wasn't that being around the dead made her nauseous any more, or that the smells and sights of the GeneCrime morgue still unsettled her constitution. It was simply that as she watched the pathologist's retractor open the deep scalpel wound just below the sternum of Kimberly Horwitz, she knew what was coming next. There was something about viewing the contents of a dead person's stomach that resonated deep in her guts, almost as if intestines could see and had empathy.

Sarah enjoyed watching the scientists the most. They were awkward, disjointed and withdrawn during the pathological investigation, impatiently waiting to take samples – a skin punch here, a swab there, a scrape wherever possible. By contrast, CID were stolid and unmoved, cracking gags to while away the time and camouflage their discomfort. Even after so many investigations, the professions kept themselves isolated. Sarah wondered whether the gulf in personality would ever be bridged. Reuben Maitland had come close – a scientist with the loyalty of CID and Forensics alike – but then his work and home lives had collided like light bulbs smashing, imploding and showering shards of debris far and wide.

The thought of Reuben ate away at Sarah like the sharpness of the formalin invading her sinuses. She took a lot of risks on his behalf, turned a blind eye to his investigations, maintained communication with him when most of her colleagues still bore grudges. But much as she kept him where she wanted, Sarah was aware that using someone whom you only partially trusted was a dangerous way to proceed.

Sarah focused on the examination in small bursts. The Path technician held open a clear plastic bag. Symbiosis wasn't quite the right word with Reuben. He was more like a commensal parasite. Digging his way into the soft underbelly of GeneCrime. The chief pathologist slit the bluey green stomach, which was distended and bloated. And while Sarah didn't doubt that GeneCrime investigations had gone awry, Reuben's motives almost seemed too self-absorbed. There was a thin leaking of gas, putrid and sick, which nearly made Sarah retch. She glanced away, hand over her nose. That, or she had underestimated Reuben. Sarah had made that mistake once before, and it had proved costly.

Still, his obsession with knowing the truth about his former unit bordered on the fanatical. The incision was widened, teased apart with two pairs of blunt forceps. A thick acrid liquid seeped out, running darkly over the surface of the gland, like a punctured animal bleeding.

Sarah watched Charlie Baker for a second. He was mesmerized by the dissection, taking it all in, eyes moist with fascination. Other members of the room were contrastingly circumspect. Working silently and efficiently, the pathologist used a sterile plastic spatula to spoon the lumpen stomach contents into the bag.

Sarah appreciated the risks Reuben was taking as well. An underground lab, associating with known criminals, the type of men he had hunted prior to his sacking – this wasn't easy. The bag slowly engorged, its corners inflating, its middle bulging. There was a slurry of orange paste, fragments of fibrous meat, a white-ish slime which Sarah took to be detached stomach lining. For a second she saw the intensity of Reuben's motivation, the willingness to sacrifice everything in order to hunt down the corrupt, the criminal and the fraudulent, those who falsified, altered and distorted, the users and abusers of forensic science, the police officers and scientists who undermined the whole of criminal detection through their deliberate actions. While Sarah knew that these people were the exception, she had seen it happen with her own eyes, but had failed to recognize it. Only Reuben had been sharp enough to spot what was going on.

The pathologist struggled for a second, digging his spatula deep into the recesses of the shrivelling organ. He gave up, instead pushing his gloved fingers inside and pulling out a series of pale stringy remnants. Sarah looked away again. And now, in a society where the underworld were wising up to the power of forensics, where police needed better and better methods of detection, where the pressure to identify and arrest those who murdered and raped had never been higher, the stakes were massive. This was what Reuben had seen from the outset. The power of forensics for good, and also for bad.

The pathologist muttered something through his mask, and Sarah's brain scrambled to process the words, trying them on for size. Then she understood. 'Tripe,' he had said. 'No idea people still ate it.' Sarah belatedly appreciated the reason for the slow progress: he hadn't been clear whether he was removing parts of a cow's stomach or the corpse's. She shook her head slightly at the thought of a stomach lying within a stomach. Sarah had seen more bizarre things come from the bellies of the dead, but still, she had yet to witness anything pleasant.

Mina Ali, senior forensic technician, stepped forward and passed the pathologist an extended cottonwool bud, which he delved deep into the open stomach before passing it back to her. She watched Mina carefully insert it into another plastic bag and seal it. Mina, petite, dark and bony, raised her eyebrows at Sarah on her way out of the morgue. For a second, Sarah longed to follow her, but she knew that she should be seen to be present.

Aside from the rare sight of partially digested tripe, nothing untoward had come out of the corpse's digestive tract yet. They had no DNA, no nothing. Just striation marks and signs of condom-protected rape. But last meals occasionally revealed things that no one alive could tell you.

24

The door crashed open, a dull thud echoing through the lab, metal plating slamming into the wall. Reuben looked up, pipette mid-stroke between two sets of coloured tubes. Moray was holding a bulging carrier bag in one hand, a folded newspaper in the other.

'What's up?' Reuben asked.

Moray paced quickly into the flat, locking the door behind him. 'Trouble. Big trouble.'

'Like what?'

Moray tipped the contents of the carrier bag on to the floor. A multitude of newspapers tumbled out.

'So you've got a paper-round?'

'This is serious,' Moray answered.

He stooped down and arranged the papers – the *Sun*, the *Mirror*, *The Times*, the *Mail* – so that their front pages could be seen. Reuben scanned the headlines, which screamed FOOTBALLER AND WIFE DEAD, SUICIDE RIDDLE OF ARSENAL

FULLBACK, ENGLAND DEFENDER IN DEATH PACT and ACCOUTEY'S FINAL SCORE.

'Fuck.' Reuben picked up the *Mirror* and focused intently on the text sheltering under the huge headline. 'Says here the police aren't looking for anyone else in their enquiries.'

'Right, but listen to a couple of these. They don't make good reading.' Moray rummaged through several editions, licking his thick stubby fingers for grip. '"Jeremy Accoutey, who was imprisoned in 2004 for his part in a brutal fight outside a nightclub, was yesterday described by team-mates as having a long-term fascination with firearms."'

'Why didn't we know this?'

Moray continued to read from the article. '"During his Arsenal career, Accoutey was capped twelve times for his country. It appears that, after taking his wife's life, he turned the shotgun on himself."'

'Oh God.' Reuben was scanning the inside pages of the *Sun*. '"Lesley Accoutey was described by a close friend as bubbly, vivacious and beautiful, with not a care in the world,"' he quoted. There was a colour picture, an amateur modelling shot taken, he presumed from the clothes, some time ago. Reuben had never met Lesley Accoutey. She was elegant and lovely, smiling out at the camera, unknowing. A few years later, a shotgun to the head, her cranium shattering, her face collapsing, her world ending.

'There's worse. Check out *The Times*.'

Reuben picked up the paper with a look of sad premonition. He read out loud, half whispering, his voice tight with misgiving. '"Commander Robert Abner, head of GeneCrime, a pioneering Metropolitan forensics unit, commented, 'The investigation is currently centring on the circumstances which led up to and precipitated the tragic and bloody events.'"'

'Like an envelope full of forensics,' Moray muttered, 'explaining how his wife was banging the team physio.'

'With our prints all over them.'

'Fuck, indeed. And look, even your old mate's getting involved in the action.'

Reuben took a copy of the *Daily Mail* from Moray, folded to reveal a half-page editorial. He mouthed the words to himself. '"DI Charlie Baker, leading the inquiry, said, 'It is only a matter of time before we make an arrest.'"'

Reuben pulled off his latex gloves, which were grey with newsprint, and threw them in the bin. He scratched the back of his neck, angling his head to the side, biting into his top lip. This was never supposed to happen. No one was supposed to get hurt. That was the code they had adopted. Forensic detection for independent corroboration. Final proof when all other avenues pointed to the same conclusion. But nobody had mentioned firearms.

Reuben slumped down on a plastic and metal lab

stool, designed more for leaning against than for comfort. As he scanned the room, he appreciated that laboratories rarely offered solace. The benches were sharp and unyielding, the machines cold and grey, the solutions stoppered and toxic.

Moray tidied the papers into a pile, equally silent and absorbed. After a few moments, he straightened and said, 'So, what now, big man?'

Reuben remained still. Two people had died as a consequence of his actions. He saw the next few weeks. CID sniffing around, finding the lab, closing him down. The balance shifting. Being compromised again. Making himself vulnerable. And all the while having to stop trawling through GeneCrime cases, letting doctored science slip through the net, allowing it all to happen again.

He made a quick, silent decision, brutal in its simplicity, dangerous in its implication. It had been gnawing at him for days, but he had kept it at bay. Now he saw that it was the only option.

'Gotta go,' he said to Moray. 'There's someone who can help.' He smiled a sad smile at his partner, and opened the door. 'I'll catch up with you later.'

Reuben took out his mobile as he walked, and dialled a number. 'There's only one person who can make it happen,' he whispered, waiting for the call to be answered.

25

Central London at rush hour. Barging, jarring, pushing, jostling, forcing. Reuben stared through Admiralty Arch and up the long straight drag of Pall Mall. At the end, and out of sight, Buckingham Palace sat in stony defiance, gazing over the vehicles grinding their way past like a huge impatient parade. The traffic was virtually static, four lanes fighting to get home, engines running, tyres heavy, fingers drumming on steering wheels.

Reuben glanced at his watch. A light changed somewhere, or a roundabout opened up; a momentary easing, vehicles moving forward, first gear to second, then quickly back again. He watched a battered maroon Fiat Punto take advantage of a gap and pull over in front of him. A rear passenger door opened and Reuben peered inside. Kieran Hobbs was grinning at him, all white hair and white teeth. Even at dusk, he was virtually a beacon. Reuben climbed in next to him and closed the door. In the front, Kieran's minder Nathan indicated and pulled back into the traffic.

'Hey, doc,' Nathan grinned in the rear-view mirror.

'Hi, Nathan,' Reuben replied. He took a moment to survey the interior of the car, and turned to Kieran. 'Hard times?' he asked.

'Invisibility.'

'How do you mean?'

'I drive my Range Rover,' Kieran explained with a sigh, 'half the journey your boys are in my rear-view. I travel about in this, nothing.'

Reuben ran his fingers over the cracked plastic interior of the door, which had lost its fascia, its skeletal workings open to the world. He examined the window winding mechanism for a couple of seconds, with its coil of wire and corroding levers, simple and functional, never meant to be seen by the world. 'But still . . .' he said.

'You're saying you drive something better?'

'I don't have a car, Kieran. Or a house. Or a bank account. Or anything.'

'After all the money I've put your way?'

'Invisibility.'

Kieran grinned. 'I hide from the good guys, you hide from the bad guys. Right?'

'Something like that.'

Reuben was unsettled and on edge. Images of Lesley Accoutey and her husband continued to eat into him. He knew that you couldn't legislate for the extremity of a person's actions, but still, his activities had resulted in two deaths. Even though he told himself that Jeremy Accoutey in all probability knew the identity of the man his wife was fucking, and just needed final proof, it still didn't sit comfortably. All of his career had been about taking the correct path, doing what was just and right. He looked over at Kieran. Even when that seemed to be wrong at the time. But sometimes, sometimes life isn't that simple.

'So, where are we going?' he asked.

'Thought we might eat while we talk.' Kieran leaned his chubby form forward. 'Nathan,' he instructed, 'the usual, please.'

Nathan glanced in the rear-view, his thick neck turning slightly. 'Sure, boss,' he answered. 'I'll cut down the back way.'

Reuben stared silently out of the window as they picked their way around Piccadilly Circus, exiting towards Oxford Circus, cutting down side streets. He didn't feel like talking to Kieran. Not yet, anyway. After a few stop-start minutes the ageing Fiat Punto pulled up outside a row of shops, and parked on a double yellow line. Reuben saw a traffic warden spot them and amble over, increasing his pace as he got closer, pulling out his ticket book as a visual warning.

'Don't even think about it, sonny,' the traffic warden began. 'You can't park on a double—' He stopped. He had noticed Kieran Hobbs climbing out of the back.

'Is there a problem?' Kieran smiled.

'Oh, sorry. I never realized . . .'

Kieran waved a dismissive hand and the warden nodded obsequiously, replaced his book and sauntered away.

Reuben followed Kieran out of the car. He walked a couple of paces behind, taking a few strides to catch him up. When food was in the offing, Kieran didn't hang about. Reuben noticed with interest that during their short journey along the pavement, four people nodded, smiled or otherwise acknowledged the presence of Kieran Hobbs. This was, he conceded, a genial and well-known gangster, old-fashioned, liked and respected by his community.

Kieran pushed open an unmarked door, which was sandwiched between a couple of shops. Reuben tracked him down a flight of stairs, which opened out into a dingy restaurant. Immediately, two waiters hurried over and escorted them to a table which appeared to be the best of a bad lot.

'Drinks, Mr Hobbs?' one of them asked. 'Before you order?'

'Leave us for a bit. We've got business.'

Both waiters scurried away again. This was power. Proper power. Not the sort the police wielded or governments manipulated. This, Reuben was aware, was direct and instant authority over people's actions. For a second it irked him that a man like Kieran Hobbs should have such sway over the lives of other individuals, while those seeking only to help, to enforce and to support had none. Even a copper of Commander Abner's seniority couldn't muster the influence Kieran had.

'So, this makes a change,' Kieran said, puffing his cheeks out. 'Dr Reuben Maitland, famous forensic scientist, ex of Scotland Yard, comes to me, asking a favour.'

'Believe me, I don't feel good about it either,' Reuben answered sadly. 'And I need it to be a free favour.'

'That's what I like about you, Reuben. You've got balls.'

'At the moment, anyway.'

'So, what can I do for you?'

Reuben glanced around the restaurant, making sure he couldn't be heard. This had to be done discreetly. No one must know, or else the whole thing could go dangerously wrong.

'It's really a case,' he said quietly, 'of what your friends might be able to do for me.'

26

Moray Carnock summed up the punters in the bar with the bitter word 'aspirational'. Moray hated bars. What was wrong with pubs, old-fashioned cosy retreats, warm beer, a warm fire, a place to wallow in what was good about the country? Not the country he still called home, of course, his accent refusing to lie down and surrender to pervasive English vowels and softly spoken consonants, but his naturalized home, here on the wrong side of the border. Fucking London and fucking bars, he sighed.

He picked up the drinks, trying to blend into the background, being careful not to catch the man's eye. Again, he cursed the fact that this was a bar and not a pub. Who was going to notice one more overweight slob in a public house? But in a smart Islington bar, Moray was well aware that he stuck out like a tramp at a temperance meeting. Cursing his luck, he placed the glasses down in front of Reuben.

'Fucking hate these places,' he grumbled.

'So you've said. About twenty times now.'

'I mean, why does the cunt have to choose a place like this?'

Reuben glanced around at the stylized fittings, which looked to have been ripped wholesale from a series of studio apartments. Not that he would admit it to Moray, but he did have a point.

'Could be worse. What's he done?'

Moray tapped the side of his nose. 'Need to know basis only.' He took a swig of his beer. 'But it's nasty. Could get himself in a lot of trouble from the law.' Moray glanced over in the direction of the man he was tagging. 'That's if the company decide to turn him over.'

Reuben ran his fingers across the CID file in front of him. It was slightly creased, and he felt the soft undulations in its cardboard surface. He had finally persuaded Sarah to lend it to him for a few hours.

'Let's get back to this,' he said.

'OK. But when he leaves, I'm leaving.'

Opening the file, Reuben said, 'So GeneCrime helped in the convictions of forty-two criminals that year. Now, a lot of those would be as outside help – where we took over cases the FSS was struggling with and got a result for them.'

'And the rest?'

'Would have been split fairly equally between my lab and Phil Kemp's old lab.'

'And the Michael Brawn case?'

'Not one of mine. Which is why I guess the name was only vaguely familiar to me. Just one of GeneCrime's forty-two cases in an average year.'

'So what we're saying is that Michael Brawn was convicted about the time you were genetically profiling your wife's lover and getting yourself sacked for gross misconduct.'

'Thanks for the memory. But the sacking has something to do with it all. OK, I crossed the line. And when Shaun Graves announced he was bringing a public prosecution against the Met for wrongful arrest, that's when it changed from being a reprimand to a dismissal. But Robert Abner is reasonably convinced Phil Kemp forced Graves to go public, which effectively ended my career.'

'What makes you so sure Phil leaked the details? Could have been anyone.'

'Like who?'

'Like Sarah Hirst. Or Charlie Baker. Or Mina Ali. Or anyone else in GeneCrime who had something to gain from your dismissal. Kemp's the obvious one, but he's only one of many.'

Reuben took a moment for a contemplative sweep of the bar. 'I guess so. But here's the thing, Moray. Have a look at this sheet.' He extracted a thin piece of paper from the file and handed it over to him.

'What?'

'You see the scrawl at the bottom? Supervising forensic officer on the conviction. Someone ripped off my signature. It's close to mine, but too shaky, like it was traced from something.'

Moray inspected the writing closely and frowned, a succession of deep parallel creases rippling the surface of his forehead. 'Now that changes things. Why would someone falsify your signature?'

'I had the authority to pass the evidence on to the next level.'

'But how come you didn't spot it at the time?'

'Things were messy. Must have happened right when I was getting myself sacked.' Reuben breathed in the fumes of his vodka as he swallowed the liquid; it was as if he was getting two hits for the price of one. He felt the anger return, the violation of having his signature used and abused. 'But what really matters is this. My authority was misused to get Michael Brawn put away on fake evidence. Meanwhile, Brawn is languishing in Pentonville making no waves about false imprisonment.'

'And the fucker who did all this?'

'Maybe still active inside GeneCrime. Now that's a scary thought with multiple other investigations going on every day.'

'And how.'

'I mean, they could be doing anything.'

Moray was only half listening, a wary eye trained on the man in the pinstripe suit talking earnestly on his mobile. He glanced back at his empty glass.

'I don't get it though. What would they gain from all this?'

'It's not necessarily about gaining anything.'

'No?'

'I reckon this is about hiding something.'

Moray stood up. The man in the suit had ended his call and was beginning to leave, his drink still half full. 'That's one for you to ponder, my friend,' he responded.

Reuben watched Moray instantly change mode, from lugubrious Scotsman to trained security expert. Moray took out a cigarette, lit it, and made for the bar. 'OK if I take this ashtray?' he asked the barmaid, picking it up anyway. While she moved off to serve someone, he gathered the man's discarded drink and carried it back to the table. 'Here,' he said, 'quick favour. Can you profile this? I think there are some sterile plastic bags in the car. The rim should be clean.'

'What are you now, a forensics expert?'

'Fortunately, no,' Moray answered, handing over his car keys. 'Catch you later.' He left the bar as swiftly as he could, heading after the man in the suit.

Reuben examined the glass for a second, noting the profusion of fingerprints on its surface. But as Moray had suggested, the rim would be where the DNA was hiding, buccal cells from the mouth caught up on the glass. He poured its contents into Moray's empty pint, and walked out of the bar with the glass in his hand.

In Moray's car, with its skeletons of discarded fingernails, Reuben carefully inserted the glass into a clear plastic bag. He tucked it away in the glove box, then drove back towards the lab, the afternoon traffic light and well behaved, large streams of hot exhaust gases churning in the wind.

He focused through the cars, buses and taxis around him, seeing back into the past, hunting down images of his previous life. He saw the other main laboratory of GeneCrime, gleaming and empty, save for Phil Kemp, leaning against a bench, short and stocky, his shirt tucked tight into his trousers, his collar un-ironed, his pallid skin haunted by a dark stubble which lurked deep in its pores. Phil Kemp chatting and smiling at Reuben, two friends who had become distanced by their career aspirations. Reuben blinked rapidly, retrieving the words that had passed between them, the deeds, the actions, moments that even now loomed large, hard-wired in, like all the millions of random events of a life, just needing a spark to light them up again.

Reuben pulled on to a long stretch of dual carriageway and accelerated hard, the big thirsty engine of Moray's Saab relishing the attention. He frowned, picking through the options. Phil Kemp could have authorized the Final Evidence document himself. There would have been no need to fake Reuben's signature, except to distance his own motives from it. The dial surged past eighty, and Reuben narrowed his eyes in concentration.

What he really needed to know now, though, was what was so fucking vital about Michael Brawn.

27

Judith Meadows pushed her head into her powder blue helmet, her matching scooter gleaming in the underground lighting of the GeneCrime car park. The helmet was tight, and as she forced it on, her ears filled with the scrape of the foam lining, and her chocolate-brown hair pulled taut against her scalp, falling over her face so that she had to stop and tuck it into place.

She was cold and tired. It had been another long shift, ten hours with only one break. Robert Abner had circulated an email asking for volunteers to work double shifts, and Judith had reluctantly offered to help the following day. The thought sapped her even further. She wanted to be home, curled up in front of the TV, avoiding the news, just relaxing like normal people did, ones who weren't caught in the aftermaths of carnage on a daily basis. And with a potential rapist at large, and the investigation gathering pace, she felt the need for escape even more acutely than ever.

Judith knew that most of the details had been kept out of the press, but it would be big news soon. Evidence was falling into place. Profiling and pattern matching were confirming what the GeneCrime scientists intuitively knew already. The word 'serial' – which needed utter proof, rather than supposition, before investigations were scaled up – had begun to infect conversations in corridors, in offices and in laboratories. But still there was no DNA. Despite all the double shifts, all the technologies, all the insight and experience, the advanced methodologies were floundering. At least two, and probably three, of the cases were linked; everyone believed it. But proving it forensically was hurting.

Judith pulled her strap tight, feeling it bite into the skin beneath her jaw, sensing the heaviness as she tilted her head. A headache was beginning to gnaw its way through her cerebral cortex, and the compression of the helmet seemed to be engaging it in a battle for supremacy, pain pushing in and pushing out at the same time. The unit was under pressure, and these were the times when it showed its limitations. When a serial killer was active and successful, when bodies were coming in at the rate they were, then GeneCrime started to reveal its cracks, as it always had. Admittedly, Judith told herself, pulling on a glove, things were better than they had been. Commander Abner was instilling a sense of unity, pacifying the eager CID, mollifying the gifted but fragile scientists. Bringing GeneCrime closer to its original remit – a cutting-edge unit able consistently to push crime detection beyond what was currently believed feasible.

A door opened behind her, and Judith glanced around. DI Charlie Baker stood in the doorway, his arms folded. Judith had never been sure about Charlie. He was ambitious to the point of disruption, a copper who rattled the cages of all around him. He had a knack, doubtless developed from countless interviews, of unsettling people through the mildest, barely perceptible insinuation or suggestion.

'Judith,' he said. 'Glad I caught you.'

Judith fiddled with her other glove, trying to pull it on. 'Sir?'

'You wouldn't happen to have a whereabouts for Reuben Maitland, would you?'

'No, sir.' When you lie, Judith told herself, be decisive. 'Why would I?'

'I heard a rumour that you two were friends.'

'Really?'

He watched her intently. 'That's what I heard.'

'Well that's the danger of rumours.'

DI Baker scowled, a sharp grimace partially hidden beneath his beard. 'What about a fat Scotsman by the name of Moray Carnock?'

'Like I said . . .' Judith pushed the start button of her Italian scooter. The small engine put-putted away, fast and erratic at first, quickly settling down.

She wanted to be the hell away from DI Baker and his remorseless stare as soon as she could.

'You sure?' he asked. His eyes narrowed and his mouth tightened. Something told Judith that getting on the wrong side of DI Baker was not an advisable course of action.

'Like I said,' she repeated.

DI Charlie Baker continued to monitor Judith for a couple of long seconds. 'Well, if you do, you know where to find me.' He furrowed his brow and turned round. Then, almost as if he'd practised it, he half turned back, seeming to remember something. 'Maybe the cold air will jog your memory,' he added, smiling coldly at her as the door shut on him.

Judith climbed on to her scooter, beginning to shiver slightly. She revved the machine up and squealed through the underground car park, out into the icy wind and on to the dark streets.

28

If he strained, Reuben realized he could actually see the snagged fibres from the cloth which had polished the front door since his last visit. This is what the gate to hell would look like, he thought. Black, lacquered, almost mocking. He closed his eyes and words from the three notes played across his retinas. *Michael Jeremy Brawn. False genetic identity. Your sacking from GeneCrime.*

Reuben blinked rapidly, returning to the present. He rapped the knocker hard, anticipating trouble. Moments later, the door was pulled open. His ex-wife looked flushed and pretty, in a hassled kind of way. For a second, he longed to grab her, to hold her, to pull her close to him.

'What do you want?' she demanded. 'I'm late for work already. I've got a big commercial suit pending.'

Reuben half smiled at the fact that his thoughts could be so far away from hers. This had not been an unusual occurrence, at least not towards the end of their marriage, when Lucy's were presumably preoccupied with another man.

'Let me drop him off at nursery,' Reuben said. 'I've got a couple of hours and thought—'

'You can't just turn up like this.'

'I'm offering to help, Luce. What possible harm could there be?'

'I'm serious. The answer is no. And he's coming down with something again.'

'Although he's well enough to go to nursery?'

Lucy made a show of sighing out loud. 'That's my decision. My final decision. And if you don't leave, I warn you, Reuben, I'll call the police.'

'Just this once.' Reuben tried not to plead. 'It's just that I might not be around—'

'If it was up to Shaun, we'd have called them a long time ago. I mean, what the hell do you expect? You DNA-profile him, have him arrested—'

'You're making it sound deliberate. His name just ended up on the wrong list. Things got out of hand.'

'Then you keep turning up demanding to see Joshua, violating your exclusion order. Come on. We're lawyers, for Christ's sake. And you, I'm afraid, are breaking the law.'

'Your law. Not mine.'

Lucy treated Reuben to the icy smile she reserved for the defining moments of arguments. He pictured her using it in court, and it scaring the shit out of the opposition. 'Read the statutes, Reuben,' she said. 'Disgraced coppers don't get to make the rules.' She stepped smartly back and slammed the door.

Reuben remained where he was, bitter and resentful. In the background he could hear his son, somewhere behind the foreboding surface of the door. He knew it was the product of desperation, but he couldn't suppress the notion that he had heard the word 'Daddy'.

Reuben stepped away, walking quickly and angrily up the drive. He took out his mobile phone and dialled a number.

29

Sarah Hirst examined two depressing pieces of paper, both still warm from her printer. She could have read the information direct from her screen, but even in the twenty-first century, police departments ran on print-outs rather than pixels. The sheets quickly lost their heat as she held them up and read them again, and as they did so she sensed another trail go cold.

Everything pointed to the same man being responsible for at least three deaths. DI Tamasine Ashcroft. The unidentified female found after four weeks. And now Kimberly Horwitz. Everything except what really mattered. The MOs were identical: bodies discovered in the Thames or within half a mile of it, raped post-suffocation. But no DNA. And if GeneCrime couldn't find DNA, there wasn't any to discover.

Sarah pictured this for a second. Rape with no DNA. A condom – that was the easy part. But putting surgical gloves on first, without contaminating them, and then putting the condom on, seconds after killing, the body slowly cooling, becoming aroused but still being calm and careful enough to think clearly, not leaving hairs anywhere on the victim, no pubic hairs, no head hairs . . . This wasn't just difficult. This bordered on the obsessional.

Both sheets of paper yielded negative results. On the first, no semen sample, no DNA found at any site on Tamasine Ashcroft's body, internal or external. On the second, the stomach contents of Kimberly Horwitz had come back similarly pointless. The tripe consumed at some sort of buffet, mild alcohol residue, partially digested vegetables. No deposits or silt from the river. She had been killed somewhere close to her final resting place, and dumped in the river after death.

Sarah leaned back in her chair, its springs groaning as she pushed her feet up on to the desk. Soon they were going to have to go public with everything they had. The capital's female population would be sent into panic. They would stay away from the river, avoid taking any risks at night, get chaperoned wherever they went, and the deaths would stop for a while. Sarah cursed. And then the killer would get even more careful, and would come back for more, and would be even more difficult to detect.

She shook herself, knowing that she had to stop thinking like this. People had died, and maybe others would as well. But still the detective urge made her see everything in terms of results instead of tragedy. Sarah was honest enough with herself to appreciate that this was a perennial failing. Being too hard-nosed. Breaking friendships in order to solve cases. Using people and spitting them out to achieve her ends. She thought guiltily of Reuben, of what had happened before, of what could happen in the future. The reason he would never truly trust her. Sarah frowned. One day she would kick back and relax, put friendships first, become well liked, open and honest. But until that day – when people stopped mutilating others, when women ceased being dragged out of cold rivers brutalized and battered, when police morgues were empty of the hacked and slashed – Sarah's means would continue to justify her ends.

The phone erupted into close-spaced double rings, indicating an external call. Sarah leaned slightly forward, still with her stockinged feet on the desk, and poked at the speakerphone button with the end of her pen.

'DCI Hirst,' she said.

'Sarah, it's Reuben,' came the reply.

'I was just thinking about you.'

'Should that worry me?'

'Only slightly.' Sarah squinted at the clutter in her office, telling herself again that catching bad guys was infinitely more important than treating people fairly. 'So, what's up?'

There was a crackly pause, Reuben's breathing mixing with the background noises of hurried London movement. 'Sarah, can you pull some strings for me?'

'What kind of strings?'

'Difficult ones. Illegal ones.' He paused again. 'Quiet ones.'

Sarah slid her feet off the desk and sat upright, her mouth closer to the phone. 'How quiet?'

'Silent. You, me and nobody else.'

'Why?'

'I've finally decided.'

'What?'

'There's a couple of things I need to do. And then . . .' His footsteps coming to a standstill. An audible breath. The stubble from his chin scraping against the mouthpiece.

'Reuben?'

'Pentonville.' A clearing of the throat. 'I'm going in.'

It was Sarah's turn to be quiet. She chewed the inside of her cheek. Eventually, she said, 'Why?'

'Look,' he said with a sigh, 'there's something in all this that concerns me. Something serious. Something we haven't talked about.'

'Go on.'

'Let's say you have a serial case. Let's say the murders you've told me about are linked.'

'They are. So?'

'We know something in GeneCrime isn't right.

Someone, maybe working alone, or maybe with others, has already doctored official forensic evidence.'

'But that was months ago. And it might have been Phil Kemp.'

'I don't think DCI Kemp did this. Or if he did, that he acted alone. Phil had the authority to pass Michael Brawn's forensic evidence through the system, no questions asked.'

'You're saying, then, Dr Maitland, that a rogue scientist or CID officer or both got Michael Brawn sent down, and is now just sitting pretty in the middle of this advanced forensics unit?' Sarah glanced over at the door, at its observation panel, the safety glass distorting the light from the corridor. 'And none of us has noticed anything? None of the senior detectives, none of the experienced scientists, none of the multitude of people who are paid solely and professionally to detect wrong-doing?'

'But not within. Not inside the division. You know how it is in the force. You're always looking *out*, at the criminals out there, the ones who are perpetrating all the evil.' He sighed down the line, in danger of losing momentum. 'I'm saying that when you're caught up in a manhunt, you don't have time to look inwardly. Think about it. A rogue element slap bang in the centre of a big investigation.'

'What could they have to gain though?'

'That's exactly the point. We don't know. Michael

Brawn willingly going to jail. A psycho murdering and raping women. And then person or persons unknown in the thick of it all. The question you need to ask yourself, DCI Hirst, is do you trust the way the manhunt is progressing? Why do you have no pattern matches at all? Why aren't you picking up any DNA? How is the attacker evading the country's most advanced forensics unit?'

Sarah let the words sink in. 'You're saying they could be deliberately fouling up a big investigation?'

Reuben inhaled a deep breath and took time over his words. 'I'm saying anything's possible. And the sooner we sort out who Michael Brawn is, and who put him away, the more faith we'll have in the rape investigation. One rotten apple—'

'Can do a lot of damage,' Sarah answered, almost to herself.

'Brawn was charged on false CID evidence. Someone wanted him in prison or out of the way. Whatever it is lies at the heart of what's happening in GeneCrime. Maybe at this very minute.'

'It's a sobering thought. And the answer is?'

'The only lead we have is Brawn. And that's where I'm going to start. I need you to make the call straight away.' Reuben's footsteps started up again, movement and determination coming through the line. 'I'll talk to you later,' he said. And before she could react, the connection was cut.

Sarah stared at the phone, which was making the

sound TVs used to at the end of the evening, in the days when schedules actually stopped for the night. She let it continue, thinking hard, wondering about Reuben's motives, deciding whether to help him, working through worst-case scenarios, reasoning whether she should inform anyone else, calculating what she would need to do to keep everything quiet, and all the time focusing on the negative pieces of evidence scattered across her desk.

After a full five minutes, during which the complaint of the phone grew inaudible to her, Sarah picked up the receiver and dropped it again, and the noise stopped. She hunted in a packed drawer for a directory of Metropolitan CID numbers, and began cross-referencing names against on-line lists of information. Soon, she was running her little finger across the screen, hostile static following its progress. Then she used her other hand to dial a number. And as she waited for her call to be answered, she convinced herself again that friendships were expendable in the midst of a murder investigation.

30

Reuben marvelled at how quickly city streets could turn from the exclusive to the downright execrable. Even in the most desirable areas of London, you were only ever three or four wrong turns from the types of people and housing that money helped keep out of sight. Reuben didn't know the address of the shop he was seeking, but he knew the kind of road which would take him there. Within minutes, the number of shoppers had eased, the proportion of boarded or shuttered properties had rioted, and the number of youths hanging around on corners had reached epidemic proportions. He knew he was heading in the right direction.

The shop, when he found it, was more welcoming than he had imagined, but he still felt nervous. Not because he was afraid, but because this was a moment of commitment, of not turning back, of utter permanency. His hand gripped the wooden handle of the door, which was flaky and dry. He examined the pictures in the window for the one that he wanted, but couldn't see it. Reuben loitered another second, before pushing the door open and stepping inside. A facially tattooed man looked up at him from his magazine and raised his pierced eyebrows.

Sitting in the padded chair, Reuben recalled the words of his father, who had always told him that no matter what anyone else said, it hurt like hell. Even after a few drinks, and a lot of bravado, the pain was still acute. And he had been right. Reuben focused on the buzzing source of discomfort, the minute needle shooting in and out, carrying with it a dark blueness, depositing it firmly under the epidermis and out of harm's way, and in his soreness he felt a rare and sudden empathy with his father. They were finally bonding, long after his death. He closed his eyes, the hum of the instrument loud in his right ear, encouraging his mind elsewhere. They both had sons, and they had both made a clear mess of parenting. They both had weaknesses – spirits for his father, stimulants for Reuben. And they had both sat in a chair like this, feeling this pain.

Reuben shook his head. That was about it. But then a memory of his childhood tracked him down, one he had long since forgotten, pricked by the tattooing. With Aaron in the front room of their fourth-floor flat. Eleven-year-old twins in the same dark blue Adidas shorts and shirts, white stripes on the sleeves. Looking at Aaron, fair and freckled, with long blond hair, unkempt and shoulder-length. Watching him run his fingers over his father's forearm. His father, tall and fair, with rougher and more blunted features than his sons'. On his arm a fresh tattoo of a dagger, firmly in the process of scabbing over, the pattern only just discernible. Aaron asking how much it hurt, and his dad smiling and saying even more when he had to pay for it. Reuben desperately waiting his turn, wanting to touch it and not wanting to, drawn and repulsed at the same time.

And then pushing his hand forward and Aaron withdrawing his. Reuben's fingertips brushing the raised surface of the tattoo, red and blue ridges budding through the damaged skin, a stubble of fine blond hairs mapping out the area, a large, angry scab forming and brooding. Almost seeing it forensically, the damage to the layers of skin, the irritated response from the body. The warmth of his father's arm beneath his fingers. Silently wondering why his father had had this done, what it meant outside the living room, outside the flat, on the streets and in the pubs he frequented. Seeing Aaron eyeing it almost enviously. His brother already knowing what it implied, and to whom, and wanting one himself. Reuben asking what would happen when the scab fell off, whether it would take the ink with it, and George Maitland laughing that fluid cackle of his, saying no, what will be left behind will be the real deal.

Reuben looked down at the needle. The real deal indeed. But this was going to be his calling card, his way in. The change in his identity that would get him what he wanted in Pentonville. The tattooist had changed needles, red shading with a finer point now filling in the gaps. Every line, every dot, every nuance would be there for life. Layers of skin would be shed, cells dying and falling away, scattering like dust. And always there, deep in the epidermis, the red and blue and black ink would shine through, getting duller and weaker with each tier of skin, but still lurking entrenched in the flesh like a memory that can't be shaken.

The tattoo artist was silent, concentrating hard, flicking his eyes back and forth between Reuben's arm and a picture in a book. Reuben was happy not to distract him. He looked away, the discomfort gnawing but not unbearable. He had experienced worse. A broken ankle, a dislocated shoulder, a spill of phenol on his hand. Physical and chemical damage. And that was neglecting the mental torture of watching a stranger play daddy with your son.

Reuben closed his eyes, wondering if Sarah was making the critical phone call on his behalf, and whether she had the authority to pull it off without alerting her superiors. Things were getting messy. When having a tattoo done seems like a step in the right direction, Reuben conceded, things were undoubtedly untidy.

31

Detective Inspector Charlie Baker brooded in the corner of the large open-plan living room. For his taste, the ceiling was on the low side, symptomatic of a new house masquerading as an old one. The furnishings were light and breezy, neutral to the point of banality, the walls cream, the flooring a patterned wood effect. It was, Charlie thought, chewing his teeth, a fucking vacuum.

He surveyed the forensics team in front of him bitterly. Above almost everything, Charlie resented forensics. It was middle-class detection, crime-solving for academics, criminality for people who didn't want to get their hands dirty. The fuckers even wore gloves all day, wrinkled white fingers inside, isolated from the truths they delved into, and the human mess they poked about in. And not just any gloves. Surgical gloves, like they were carrying out life-saving operations, with divine power over the outcome of an investigation. Charlie had never been afraid to get involved, to bang heads together, to do house to house, to work all day and all night questioning some shifty fuck who was holding out on him.

Of course, he could see that there was a place for forensics, that you needed two types of policing these days: those who got out there and rattled cages and chased bad guys, and those who skulked in laboratories looking down microscopes. The one helped the other, and this is where GeneCrime had derived a lot of its success. There was an important distinction between the different elements, however. A case could be solved without forensics, but it could never be sorted without standard, no-frills police work. Both disciplines needed each other, but it wasn't always a two-way street. He smiled thinly to himself. Let some of these overqualified nerds get out of their gloves and lab coats and chase a villain. Lock them in a cell with a wife-beating psycho. Get them to question a gang of paedos. Ask them to infiltrate a crack ring. Let's see them take an armed robber down.

Charlie snatched a wad of forms from Dr Mina Ali, senior forensic technician. She was thin and angular, dark and lopsided, and he imagined snapping her like a twig. He signed all the yellow copies and returned them silently, seeing it in her eyes, as it was in most of their eyes. The animosity, the lack of trust. Charlie thrived on it. He wanted them to dislike him, to not be sure of him.

'A couple more sample requisitions and an

evidence exclusion,' Mina said, producing a thin stack of blue forms.

'And I thought CID had all the fun,' Charlie answered curtly.

Mina stared at him a second longer than was absolutely necessary. She was sharp and outspoken, a force to be reckoned with, despite her diminutive height. Charlie stared back, deadpan. Now Commander Abner had put his trust in him, he was a man with power. No one knew that yet, but they soon would. And Dr Mina Ali had better watch her forensically protected step. He scrawled his biro over the pages and shunted them back, watching Mina shuffle away, nonchalant and unconcerned but, his copper's eye informed him, ever so slightly flushed and trying to hide it.

All around the elongated living room, technicians inched along on their hands and knees, teasing out samples with plastic forceps, opening drawers, filling tubes with minute volumes of liquid and cataloguing specimens with practised patience. Charlie's gut rumbled somewhere deep inside him, an uncomfortable readjustment of his bowels. He wondered whether the forensic technicians could somehow detect his contamination of the scene if he broke wind. Charlie had sat through enough meetings on the promise of new technology, on their incredible levels of detection, on their sublime specificity of action. And yet no one ever spoke any more about the instinct of a copper, of his ability to pick one miscreant out of a crowd, or to recognize the one key fact in a whole dossier of information; of the diligence which identified the single strand of evidence among the tangle of crossed wires. The sensitivity and specificity of a chemical reaction was, he believed, nothing compared with the precision of the detective mind.

Charlie watched a junior CID officer carry something towards Mina, his movement rapid against the measured progress of the rest of the team. He was instantly alert, pacing over to the far side of the room, arriving within a few seconds. Charlie saw that it was a fragment of paper, thicker than normal, photographic perhaps, and decorated with a series of slender, closely packed coloured lines. It looked like a bar code drawn with randomly assorted pens. Mina held it in her upturned palms, frowning. Charlie reached forward and snatched it from her.

'What is it?' he asked.

Three or four technicians who had shuffled over stood uncomfortably, not meeting his eye.

'What?' he barked.

'If you'd give it back,' Mina said.

Charlie ground his teeth, then pushed it towards her. Fucking forensics, a voice inside him screamed.

Mina ran her dark eyes over the piece of paper. 'An ABI 377 screen-shot,' she answered.

'In English?'

'Before you get the actual bases out of an ABI sequencer, it produces an image file. And this looks like one of those.'

'So this is sequence data?'

'Kind of,' Mina said quietly. 'Though not the sort you see every day.'

'And what the fuck would a footballer be doing with DNA sequence data?' Charlie asked.

Mina turned to him, black irises huge through her glasses. 'That, DI Baker,' she responded with a smile, handing the scrap back, 'would appear to be your problem now.'

Mina encouraged the team to return to work, and Charlie remained in the centre of the room, a name coming to him, a link where previously there had been just a dead footballer and his wife, an idea that grew and grew, a connection that made him happier the more he pulled it apart in his mind.

32

Reuben ran his hand through his short-cropped hair, getting used to the feeling. Grade 2 all over, a classic eighties crew-cut. It felt like the fur of a short-haired dog, or like stroking suede the wrong way. There was something good about the honesty of a skinhead, he felt. It wasn't styled or coloured or otherwise tainted. It was the truth, before it twisted and turned and became distorted. This was, he thought, what he should have done years ago. But until now there had been no need.

In front of him, Stevo glared back. Reuben still wasn't sure about him. He suspected that under different circumstances Stevo would have liked to hurt him for real. Stevo was helping him, but there was an undercurrent of malice in every practice punch that landed, and every kick that put Reuben on his back. Ex-coppers were rarely popular at the best of times, especially with borderline hoodlums like Stevo. The thought made Reuben shiver involuntarily. Things were going to get a lot worse where he was heading than Stevo's muzzled hostility.

Reuben glanced up as the door to the gym opened and closed. Kieran Hobbs paced towards him, flanked by his ever-present security. Nathan sauntered over to Stevo and exchanged a high-five and a hug, his large frame almost swallowing his friend between distended muscle groups. Valdek remained where he was, arms folded and eyes glaring.

'Thought we'd come and watch,' Kieran announced with a grin. 'Stevo tells me you're getting better.'

'Better than what?' Reuben asked. He was on edge, not wanting to fight in front of Kieran and his minders.

'Better than a lab monkey should be.'

Reuben once again felt the familiar unease of being around gangsters. Even Kieran, genial and good-natured, worried him. Not because of who he was, or what he did, but because every time he saw him Reuben pictured his own fall from grace. At GeneCrime, Reuben had spent a short period of time on a case involving one of Kieran's many syndicates. And now, immersed in the duality of his existence, Kieran, underworld enforcer, the type of man who had would-be assassins like Ethan de Groot tortured and pulped, was closer to being a friend than an adversary.

'Let's raise the stakes a bit,' Kieran said. 'Fifty

quid on Reuben. Nathan? Valdek? You want a piece on Stevo?'

Valdek slid a note out of his pocket and silently handed it over. Nathan left Stevo and similarly gave his boss a fifty. Reuben saw that the experienced cash of hardened enforcers, of virtual street fighters, had little confidence in his abilities.

Kieran clapped his hands, firing a sharp echo through the high-ceilinged room. 'Now we're talking,' he roared. 'Come on, Reuben, let's see what all this training has done for you.'

Reuben examined his hands. This time there were no pads or gloves. Bare feet, jeans, T-shirts. They were fighting for real.

Stevo said 'Ready?' and Reuben nodded. He breathed deeply, watching Stevo, letting him attack first, as he'd been taught. Subtleties of body shape, of posture, of readiness all taken in and assimilated. Stevo switched his weight from foot to foot, his torso shifting and adjusting. He held his arms out, bent at the elbows, fists yet to form. And then he launched forward, three quick punches, right, left, right. The first catching Reuben around the ear. Stepping back from the second two. His ear ringing hot. He shook his head. Stevo kicked at Reuben's midriff. He parried it and pushed him to the side. Stevo brought his right fist abruptly round. Teeth jarring together, his lip splitting, the taste of iron.

'Come on, Reuben,' Kieran shouted, 'sort the wiry fuck out!'

Reuben ignored the buzzing numbness in his mouth. Stevo came at him again, fists first. He ducked smartly and drove his knuckles up into Stevo's guts. Winded, Stevo grabbed Reuben round the neck, pulling him to the floor. Reuben's face was forced into the mat, bleeding into its shiny rubber surface. Reuben kicked and thrashed. Frantic. He broke free and spun Stevo on to his back. Reuben forced his weight down on him, straddling his chest, knees pinning Stevo's tattooed arms. Stevo was breathing hard, his ribcage heaving beneath Reuben. He looked up, eye to eye, and grinned. Bad teeth with ominous gaps stared back at Reuben.

'That's my boy,' Kieran said, walking closer. 'Now finish him.'

Reuben felt Stevo squirm. He was light and wiry, smaller than Reuben, but strong and quick. Reuben formed a fist and held it above Stevo's face. 'You want to quit?'

Stevo smiled again. 'Hell no. I'm just catching my breath.'

And then Reuben's head pitched forward, pain arriving in the back of his head in two almost simultaneous blasts. Off balance, he tumbled away. Stevo was instantly behind him. He pushed Reuben's arm straight into its socket. A paralysing agony tore through his once-dislocated shoulder.

Reuben fought to spin round, clawing at Stevo. He was mute with pain, helpless and desperate. He felt the bandage on his arm rip, and then the pressure ease. There was a moment of nothingness and silence. Then Stevo let go of him and stood up.

'Jesus,' he moaned.

Reuben pulled himself to his feet, his heart racing, the fire in his shoulder subsiding, the back of his head still smarting, his ear ringing. 'What?' he gasped. He looked down at his arm, the bandage hanging off, the tattoo exposed. The scab was partially detached, revealing pristine new skin below. He noted that Kieran and his minders were examining him closely. 'What?' he gasped again, but this time with less conviction.

'I dunno.' Kieran shook his head, half serious, half mocking. 'First you lose me a hundred quid, and then that.' He pointed with his eyes at the tattoo. 'I thought you had more taste.'

Reuben pulled the bandage back up, feeling naked for a second. And this coming from a borderline albino with a penchant for gold jewellery. He snorted to himself, in discomfort, feeling future bruises, wiping the redness from the corner of his mouth.

Stevo came over and wrapped an arm around his shoulder. Reuben took comfort from the fact that he was breathing hard. It hadn't been easy for him.

'Nice one,' he muttered.

33

Through the third-floor window Reuben spotted Sarah Hirst's barely camouflaged police Volvo pick its way across the rubbled car park. He watched her talking on her mobile, a short, terse call which made her frown. Even from this distance he could see the lines on her forehead and the irritated pinch of her brow. He wondered who she was talking to, and whether it was work or private. As far as he knew, she was still single. But there were a lot of things Sarah didn't talk about, a lot of territories their conversations were firmly steered away from. Reuben often asked himself what Sarah was protecting, why she felt the need to draw lines between people, who really mattered to her outside the job. Once he thought he had broken through, was close to seeing through the façade, but the shutters had come down again and he had been left with her three-word mantra of conduct – personal and professional.

As he waited for her to end the call and come

up to the lab, he rocked the small toy in the palm of his hands. It was a Kinder egg, oval and slightly elongated, the sort which pulled apart at its equator to reveal a few small fragments of plastic which inevitably required assembling into something or other of little interest to a child once it had been constructed. He spotted an envelope on the lab bench and wondered momentarily whether he should send the egg's contents to Joshua. The words 'choking hazard' were printed on the scrap of paper which had fallen out of the egg along with its plastic innards. He frowned briefly to himself.

Laid out on a clear perspex tray beneath his hands was an Eppendorf tube, half full of a pink liquid, a minute pair of disposable tweezers, several dabs of double-sided tape, a scalpel blade, a cottonwool bud and a nylon glove. Through the rear window he saw Sarah climbing out of her squad car. Reuben worked quickly, packing the items into the Kinder egg and forcing it closed again. It was a tight squeeze, but they just about fitted. He spent a few long seconds staring at the object and slowly shaking his head. Then he slid it into his pocket as a knock sounded at the door.

Sarah appeared hassled, in a pretty sort of way, almost as if vexation suited her features. Her light straight hair, not pinned back under its usual discipline, worried her eyes. She wore very little make-up, and her clothes hadn't seen an iron recently.

'Jesus, look at the state of you,' she said.

Reuben neglected to comment on her appearance. 'Thanks.'

'What happened?'

'Training and preparation,' he answered, running his tongue over his swollen lower lip.

'I won't ask. Probably a good thing to look like that where you're heading. You ready?'

Reuben had a last scan of the lab, its fridges and freezers, its anonymous machines, its industrial light fittings, its spotless benches. Containers housing solvents, buffers, powders and liquid nitrogen crowded its shelves. In the freezers he pictured thousands of small opaque tubes, each with a unique sample of DNA. He flicked off his computer and shut down the lights. 'Yes,' he answered, 'I'm ready.' Under the bandage, his right arm itched like crazy. A small pool of blood had leaked through, scabbing brown at the surface of the cotton. He checked his pockets, certain that he had everything he needed. And then, Sarah waiting impatiently by the open door, he locked up and left.

Reuben remained quiet as Sarah drove out of the ruined housing estate, with its skeletons of vehicles and carcasses of buildings. Inflated carrier bags were tangled in the branches of skinny trees. A cold easterly wind blew through the broken windows of empty tower blocks, a lifeless howl tearing at the thick glass of the Volvo. Sarah's police radio burst into life and died again, inaudible words crackling and fading.

'So this is it then,' Sarah muttered. 'Any last words?'

'It's only going to be a few days.'

'A long few days, though.'

'Maybe. But it will be worth it.'

'I guess so.'

Reuben surveyed the dismal concrete atrocity which surrounded them. He fell silent, listening to the engine as Sarah turned on to a main road and worked her way quickly through the gears.

'If there was a way of doing this through official channels . . .' he said after a while.

'There isn't. Not without him finding out.' She drove quickly, relying on motorists to spot the understated police markings. 'In which case you'll never find out who he is and get to the truth.'

'Yeah.'

Sarah turned to him as they waited at a traffic light. 'Well it won't be your worst assignment ever. Remember what happened last year?'

Reuben fingered the Kinder egg in his jacket pocket. It was warm, unyielding, and critical to the next few days. He recognized where they were, knew they were getting close.

'Jesus, yes.'

'Just don't compromise yourself in there.'

'Compromising, as you know, is not something I do well.'

The rest of the journey passed in silence, Reuben watching the outside blur by, thinking things through, knowing it was the right course of action but wishing there was another way.

'OK, we're here,' Sarah said eventually as she pulled the squad car into an underground car park, blinking in the momentary darkness, her tired eyes struggling to adjust. She parked rapidly and brusquely, and Reuben couldn't help but be impressed.

'I'm going to have to go on one of those driving courses one day,' he said, climbing out.

'Sorry, Dr M,' Sarah countered with a smile, 'for proper CID only.' She walked around the car and stopped in front of him. 'I think you're forgetting something.'

Reuben looked into her eyes, brilliant and clear despite the fatigue. 'What?' he asked, caught for a second in her beauty.

'Give me your hands,' she answered.

He paused, unsure. And then, almost disappointed, he understood. Reuben pushed his arms towards her. Sarah took them in her own, keeping eye contact, something playful in her face. Then she handcuffed his wrists.

'Come with me, Remand Boy,' she said, leading him towards a door and up a flight of concrete steps.

They walked along an off-white corridor which opened out into a larger hallway. At the end, they entered an office. It was small and modern, designed to be functional rather than comfortable. A duty sergeant was seated at a cramped desk. He was late twenties, thick-set and surly, clearly resenting being bound to his desk. He looked up at them with little enthusiasm.

'DCI Sarah Hirst, GeneCrime Forensics, Metropolitan CID,' Sarah announced, an abrupt and official intent to her voice. 'This is Reuben Maitland, on remand for attempted spousal murder. Hearing's been postponed for a week, and bail denied, while we repeat a series of DNA tests. He's now due to be transferred in the interim. Can I leave him with you?'

The duty sergeant sighed audibly. 'You got his forms?' Reuben noted that he had an untidy mouth, lower lip too big, teeth elongated and badly aligned.

Sarah passed him a sparse bundle of paperwork from her case. 'I'm afraid we're still waiting for his I-26 and his 2052 Self Harm.'

A practised look of doubt shaded the man's features. 'Without the 2052 there's no—'

'Look, sergeant,' Sarah interrupted, 'I've got another case due upstairs. Court three. I'll have one of my team fax the Self Harm through as soon as it comes.' Her tone hardened. 'Now, let me ask you again: can I leave this prisoner with you?'

'Fine, ma'am,' he replied, straightening in his seat but avoiding eye contact. 'You uncuff him, I'll take him through.'

Reuben marvelled at the power Sarah could generate just by raising her voice a notch. Sarah turned and unlocked his cuffs. She stared into his eyes again, a long second which excited and unnerved him. There was something there, but he struggled to decide what. Sarah then moved out of the way, pausing in the doorway as the broad and looming duty sergeant stood up and gripped his upper arm.

'From now on, he's all yours, sergeant,' she intoned.

Reuben felt the tightening grip and knew that this was a taste of what he was about to face. Constraint. Restrictions. Limitations. He was suddenly nervous.

An hour later, in a prison van with blacked-out windows, Reuben swayed on his feet as the vehicle emerged through the double security gates of the courthouse and swerved around the corner. Surrounding him, prisoners were standing, trying to peer through the obscured windows, banging on the walls with their fists, shouting and hollering. The van shifted direction again and the prisoners swayed, bouncing off one another. Reuben punched the metal lining of the van hard, his knuckles jarring, his teeth clenched hard.

He was about to take his own personal trip to hell.

TWO

1

Reuben paced the cell, restless, curious and on edge. He examined it from every conceivable angle, a habit he had developed in the many hotel rooms he had called home over the last year. There were two slender single beds, a metre and a half apart, tubular metal frames, dark green blankets and light green sheets. A partition just over a metre high abutted the pillow of Reuben's bed. Behind it sat a toilet, its plumbing open and exposed, and next to it a brown plastic bucket. There was a pair of boxed fluorescent lights, one on each wall, and the floor was sealed with a tightly glued vinyl. A white painted board attached to the wall ran the length of the bed, just above it, blank except for an infestation of drawing-pin holes. At the end of the room, a window, a metre wide, with integral white-painted bars. In between the bars resided a thick layer of perspex which felt warm to the touch.

Reuben stopped in front of a chest of drawers with inset blue handles. He examined a small sink in the corner which was full of socks soaking in the murky water. Two hot-water pipes ran through the cell, one of them feeding the sink. A few pairs of dark blue boxer shorts adorned both pipes, and were slowly drying. Over the other bed was a collage of posters: a wolf, close up and hungry; Homer Simpson, drunk and watching TV; an England flag, hand-drawn; a Liverpool FC banner; two composite pictures of lingerie-clad women in a variety of poses; a calendar with a picture of a castle; a BMW Auto Sport sticker; a grisly bear with an arching salmon in its mouth. Reuben tried and failed to picture the man who would be his cellmate from the images he chose to surround himself with.

Since arriving he had been interviewed twice, searched naked, then asked about his health but not examined. He had filled out questionnaires, had helped complete a Shared Cell Risk Assessment form, and had barely uttered a word of truth. The induction process, which had been rumoured to last two days, had been rushed through in hours. It had been brisk but friendly, prison personnel happy to push him through the procedural stages, into the next waiting room, and into the next, until they were satisfied he wasn't going to kill himself or anybody else. Reuben had often read reports on Pentonville when he worked at GeneCrime and consigned killers there. Prisoners in bleak, often dirty cells; inadequate first-night procedures despite occasional self-inflicted deaths; night staff unaware of the location of new prisoners; lack of training in basic emergency procedures; prisoners locked up for twenty-two hours on some wings; vulnerable prisoners routinely moved into stained cells alive with cockroaches. He had known what to expect. And not just from what he had read.

Reuben recalled that feeling, alone, cut off, scared, incarcerated for the first time, surrounded by men you would pay to avoid on the outside. The intense concentration of murderers, rapists and the mentally unstable. Not knowing who was who, the people to stay clear of, the inmates to not even look at. Appreciating the cold statistics of bullying, self-harm, sexual assault. Hearing the stories about men cutting themselves just to spend a night in the safety of the hospital wing, of punishment beatings, of sugarings, of buggerings. Seeing prisoners sitting in their cells smoking crack all day, indifferent warders ignoring everything except what they wanted to see. The insomnia, the helplessness, the hidden hierarchies, the all-pervasive fear.

Reuben knew, because he had been there before. A different institution, a long time ago, almost in a previous life. Three months for possession of Class A narcotics with intent to supply. Aaron's narcotics. Protecting his brother from breaching his parole and going down for five years. Identities traded, Aaron promising to stay clean and make it up to him. It had been a poor decision, one that still rankled with Reuben. But the knowledge of prison life, which he repressed and had always been ashamed of, now gave him strength. He knew what to expect, and how he would react. Reuben was no virgin. He was an ex-con.

He walked over to the metal door, which again was painted white, with an enlarged letter-box aperture, a metal flap which folded out into the corridor and couldn't be opened from the inside. There was no door handle. He ran his fingers over its cold surface wondering who was going to walk through.

Reuben turned and examined himself in the wall mirror, which was metal, not glass. The barely reflective surface showed a man with a crew-cut, narrowed eyes and gritted teeth. A week could sometimes be a long time. Still, he would do what he had come to do, then get the hell out. Undetected and unnoticed. A viral particle that floated in on the wind and floated out again.

He glanced towards the door as its lock turned. The man who walked in was mid-thirties, scruffy and slightly shorter than Reuben. He tossed his folded newspaper down on the bed, the whole time maintaining eye contact, spending a few critical seconds weighing Reuben up. Reuben looked back at him. He wore loose tracksuit bottoms and a red hooded sweatshirt. Dense cropped hair, dark eyebrows, stocky through his clothes. He said the words, I'm Narc, and Reuben replied, I'm Reuben. The voice was north-western, Merseyside probably, but could have stretched into Cheshire.

'So, what're you in for, like?' Narc asked.

'On remand. Tried to kill my wife.'

Narc sat down heavily on his bed. 'Why?'

'She'd been cheating on me.'

'How did you know?'

Reuben had had time to invent his story, and knew it inside out. But verbalizing it suddenly felt empty and unconvincing.

'I caught her out,' he answered.

'How, like?'

'What are you in for?'

'How did you catch her?' Narc repeated.

'I don't want to talk about it.'

Every time he had rehearsed the words in his mind they had sounded plausible. On remand, awaiting trial on the grounds of attempted spousal murder. He had even smiled when Sarah had suggested it. Trying and failing to kill his unfaithful wife seemed to ring true, as if this was something he had thought about doing, Lucy in the arms of Shaun Graves finally pushing him to violence. But there was just something about saying it out loud which didn't sit right with him, confessing to a crime that hadn't happened.

Below dark, thick eyebrows, Narc screwed his eyes up and squinted at Reuben. He leaned forward on his bed, hands on his legs. 'You want to be nice to me,' he said curtly. 'I could save someone like you a lot of bother in the long run.'

'What do you mean, someone like me?'

'Someone who hasn't done time.'

Reuben sighed, unsure for a second what to say. It had been fifteen years ago, before the force, a short sentence. The image of his brother came to him again. But time moved on, and to someone like Narc, Reuben clearly didn't look the type any more. He wondered whether that was a good thing or a bad thing.

'That obvious, huh?' he said eventually.

'Only to the whole prison. And this ain't a nice prison. I've done Winson Green, Scrubs and Dartmoor, and this little shithole is the worst of them all.' Narc stood up and took a pace towards Reuben. 'And as for this wing, it's the shittest wing of the shittest prison. Suicide hot-spot of the whole penal system. Two people a week die in UK prisons. You know that? And some weeks both of them seem to come from this cesspit. You get me?'

Reuben nodded.

'You don't fuck about in here. When someone asks you a question, you fucking well answer it.'

Reuben avoided his eye, sensing a quick temper and a refusal to give ground. There was no point in facing his cellmate down. He had to get in and out with the minimum fuss, ruffling as few feathers as possible.

‘I came home early from work and found him in my house,’ he began quietly. ‘When he’d got the hell out I calmed down. And then I started hitting my wife and couldn’t stop.’

Narc relaxed his chest and shoulders, which had been on alert beneath his hooded top, prepared for trouble. ‘You see?’ He grinned. ‘You stick with me, you’ll go a long way.’

Reuben turned and sat on his bed, staring at the blank ceiling above him. His cellmate wasn’t ideal, but shouldn’t present a problem. Seven days and seven nights, by his best estimate. Lying low and doing what needed to be done. Redressing the balance, searching out what Michael Brawn had to hide, snooping into the affairs of GeneCrime. And all the time closing in on the truth about his sacking from the country’s leading forensics centre, burrowing into the heart of one institution to find his way into another.

2

Reuben felt acutely observed. He was in the lions' den, and knew it. Without doubt he would have put away some of the prisoners he was walking past. It was an unnerving thought. As he negotiated his way down steel stairways and along catwalks, he tried to blend in, dressed in grey tracksuit bottoms and a baggy T-shirt, his tattoo obvious, his crew-cut unremarkable.

From the inside, Pentonville was a Matrioshka doll of metal cages within metal cages, a web of suicide netting connecting everything. In between, corridors were freshly painted in pastel colours. Several of the passageways had suspended ceilings with neon strip lighting. Reuben could see where towering Victorian corridors had had their wings clipped, the arches above doors squared off. The largest prison in the country, captive in the twenty-first century, being bent and twisted into shape as it served its time.

The dining room had retained its high ceiling.

Reuben received his evening meal – a cube of lasagne, a portion of carrots and a scoop of chips – and looked round for somewhere to sit. Inside, an almost insistent voice repeated the words *blend in*, *blend in*. Most of the plastic seats were taken. He headed towards a virtually empty table in the corner, and lowered his tray. A large, tattooed prisoner glanced up, his forehead wrinkling into a bulldog frown.

'Fuck off,' he said.

Reuben lifted his tray and changed direction, spying another empty space on a different table, this time opposite a shaven-headed inmate.

'Not there, darlin',' the man growled without looking up.

Reuben paused, about to sit down regardless. *Blend in*, the inner voice urged. He took his tray and walked away, glancing around, aware of the scrutiny. The dining room was packed, the conversation loud, inmates seated in what looked like established groups. Reuben tried for a third time, a free chair at the end of a long table. He dropped his tray down gradually, making eye contact, attempting to appear firm but not too firm. The answer came back instantly.

'No one sits there, fuck-face.'

Reuben hesitated, weighing the prisoner up. He was bearded and intense, but not too large. Reuben pulled the chair out and sat down, staring at the man, refusing to be messed about again.

'Did you fucking hear me?' the prisoner asked, his voice rising, his eyes wild.

'Yes,' Reuben replied, 'I heard you.'

He picked up his fork and stabbed it into the lasagne, slicing down and dissecting it. The man slowly rose to his feet.

'You are a dead man,' he said.

Two other inmates at the table stood up. Reuben squinted at them. They were larger than their companion. Reuben watched them check for guards before walking round the table to him. The first, a snub-nosed man with thick black stubble, reached down and yanked the fork out of Reuben's hand. The second, balding and sturdy, with a thin mouth and piercing blue eyes, lifted Reuben's tray off the table.

'You don't sit there, new boy.'

'No one fucking sits there.'

The two men walked over to the table Reuben was first turned away from, and dropped his fork and tray in an empty place. The tattooed prisoner moved to say something, but was dissuaded by the stares of the two men. Behind them, Reuben reluctantly stood up and headed over to his tray.

'You sit there and eat your dinner,' the prisoner with the black stubble instructed.

'Then we'll come and find you, explain a few things to you,' his partner added, cuffing Reuben's cheek with the palm of his hand, a mock slap used to emphasize the point.

They sauntered back the way they had come, their eyes fixed on Reuben, not letting up until they reached their food. Even then, for a few long seconds, they monitored him between mouthfuls, muttering to each other. Please, Reuben said to himself, don't let them have recognized me. The newspaper interviews, the late-night current affairs programmes, the odd appearance in court. It was more than possible. The mission would be finished before it started.

Reuben slouched over his tray, opposite the tattooed prisoner, who stared at him with open contempt. So much for blending in. He had been in Pentonville just seven hours. It would only take one attentive soul, one bright spark, one prisoner he had come across before, and he would have to get the fuck out and quick. Forget Michael Brawn, it would become a matter of survival. He had heard the stories – everybody had. Ex-coppers in prison brought the psychos out of the woodwork. He made a stab at eating his food, which was suddenly cold and unappetizing.

3

Reuben entered the toilet block, his head down, the need acute. There was a urinal which ran along the length of the far wall. At right angles to that stood four sinks, small metal mirrors above each, and opposite the sinks was a row of flimsy formica cubicles, with walls and doors which stopped half a metre above the red-tiled floor. Reuben appreciated that privacy was not encouraged in the toilets of Pentonville.

He pushed his way into an empty cubicle and sat down, his stomach suddenly fluid, his colon spasming. Reuben had pictured this moment numerous times since leaving his laboratory in the morning, and none of them had cheered him. There was no other way to do what he needed to other than accept that it was going to be unpleasant and messy. He closed his eyes and pushed, hovering slightly off the seat, his hand in position. It hurt like hell, hard and unyielding, a sensation he wasn't eager to prolong. He gritted his teeth and made it happen, his eyes watering, blood on the toilet paper, an acute stinging pain making him smart.

When he had finished, Reuben flushed and left the toilet. He checked that he was alone before running the hot tap and squirting some soap into the water. Then he dropped the Kinder egg in, wedging it so that it blocked the plug hole. He squirted out more soap, washed the egg and scrubbed his hands. The door opened and an Asian inmate with two pierced earlobes wandered in. Reuben picked the egg out, sure that it was clean, and took it to the towel. The prisoner watched him. Reuben kept his back to him, dried the Kinder egg and towelled his hands. He left the toilets, the egg in his pocket, one vital part of his mission accomplished.

Reuben headed for the TV lounge. Finding the prisoner he needed to track down was going to take time. It was a big place. One needle inmate in a haystack of twelve hundred miscreants. Reuben knew what he looked like, and the wing he had been assigned, but that was it. He hadn't been in the dining room, or in any of the other areas Reuben had been able to gain access to. Now, after dinner, he was free to roam until nine p.m. That gave him almost three hours. And if there was one thing prisoners liked to do after their evening meal, he knew from experience, it was watch TV.

It was difficult to define the space as a room. Without walls, it felt more like a cage than a lounge, a metal enclosure with a concrete floor, and barred walls and ceiling. Twenty inmates were slouched on chairs, watching a TV which was mounted high in the corner. Around it, nothing but space, extending high into the atrium, suicide netting and steel walkways the only things visible for fifteen vertical metres.

Reuben skirted around the outside, careful this time to choose a seat that wouldn't raise anyone's interest. He was about to sit down on an orange plastic chair when the two men from the dining room entered and walked straight over to him.

'Oh no you don't,' the taller man said. 'You get to come with us.'

They steered Reuben out and down a long corridor to a room with brick walls and a rough plastered ceiling, part of the old communal area. Two inmates were in the middle of a game of table tennis. The hypnotic ricochet of the ball, from bat to table to bat and back again, was as rhythmic as a clock, the noise echoing in Reuben's ears, his eyes darting to follow the motion. And then, in a feat of surprising speed and agility, the shorter man with the thick stubble sprang forward and caught the ball in mid-flight. The noise stopped and Reuben's eyes came to a standstill on him.

'Match fucking point,' he said, stamping on the ball.

The two players glanced at each other. Then they

dropped their bats and walked out. On his way to the door, the one closer to Reuben met his eye. Reuben recognized what his face was betraying. His expression said, I wouldn't swap places with you for the world.

Reuben clenched his fists behind his back. He watched the man who had caught the ball pick up the table tennis bat and turn it over in his hands, aware that his reactions were quick and his coordination extraordinary. His colleague closed the door, and said quietly, 'We know who you are.'

'Got word from the outside.'

Reuben tensed himself. He had been recognized already. The men paced closer to him.

'From now on, you do what we say.'

'And you stay the fuck where we can see you.'

'If you want to stay alive.'

They talked almost in unison, as if they had already rehearsed what they were going to say to him. He thought momentarily of the interview rooms at GeneCrime, where he had witnessed the same approach to countless cases, CID officers working as a team, insinuating and intimidating, a double act of interrogation.

'You play by our rules.'

'Or you don't play at all.'

A cold, leaking nervousness tightened Reuben's stomach. Fingernails dug deep into the palms of his hands, curled fists ready.

'But, see, Mr Hobbs wasn't very forthcoming.'
'So you tell us why you're here.'

Understanding finally came to Reuben. He let out a long breath and slowly moved his hands to his back pockets. 'I tried to kill my wife,' he muttered through a disguised breath of relief, the words again feeling false and lacking substance.

'And why should that interest Kieran Hobbs?'

'We're friends.'

'You don't look like one of his friends.'

'I've been helping him with a few things.'

'Like what?'

'Can't say.'

The two men, Kieran Hobbs' associates, glanced at each other, unsure.

'See, if we're going to look after you—'

'Someone tried to kill Kieran. I was able to find out who it was.'

The shorter of the two scratched his dark stubble, his eyes wide. 'So you're a snitch?'

'No,' Reuben answered. 'I just know people. Kieran paid me to find out who sent the assassin, a man called Ethan de Groot, and I did. And he owes me the odd favour. So when I knew I might be going down—'

'He agreed to have you minded.' The taller prisoner softened. 'Look, I'm Cormack. Cormack O'Connor. And that there's Damian Nightley.'

Damian managed a brief half smile before

saying, 'But look, see, if we're going to mind you, you're going to have to do a fuck of a lot better than you did at dinner. The last guy you sat down opposite, you want to stay well away from. If Boucher comes looking for you, we ain't going to be able to help.'

'Aiden Boucher?' Reuben asked.

'You know him?'

'I've heard of him.'

Reuben cut to a large wooden lecture theatre a few years earlier, packed with an attentive audience of police and CID. Slides flicked on to the screen, showing the face of Aiden Boucher from different angles, clean shaven and looking younger than he had in the dining room. DI Charlie Baker had been standing at the lectern, briefing CID on Boucher's possible involvement in the murders of four homeless men. What had stuck with Reuben about the talk was the way Charlie had directed his laser pointer, hovering on the pupils of the projected face, which made it look like there was a demonic fire in Aiden Boucher's eyes.

Cormack cleared his throat. 'So you keep yourself to yourself, and don't step on anybody's toes.'

'Especially not psychos like Boucher,' Damian added.

'And we'll look out for you.' Cormack stepped away from the table-tennis table and opened the door. 'We can't protect you from everyone, but you'll be OK if you stick close to us.'

Reuben walked out, following Damian and Cormack, suddenly feeling immune and protected among twelve hundred restless criminals, most of whom would see an ex-copper as fair game.

4

The green phone card had the letters HMP stamped deep in black across its middle, indented, almost branded. Reuben pushed it into the slot, a process that the mobile phone had made almost obsolete, outside prison at least. He dialled from memory, slouched over so that his head was almost covered by the scratched metal hood which guarded each of the telephones in the row. The hood reminded Reuben of the imitation of privacy which Pentonville sought to encourage. Like the flimsy cubicles in the Gents, the barely partitioned toilet in the cell and the walls made of bars rather than brick. Designed to make you feel there was seclusion when really that was the last thing the prison wanted.

The call was answered swiftly with the words, 'DCI Sarah Hirst, Metropolitan CID.'

'You OK to talk?' Reuben asked.

'Sure.' The sound of a door being slammed. 'Any signs of Michael Brawn yet?'

''Fraid not.'

'Has anyone twigged?'

'I thought they had, that I'd been recognized. But no, so far so quiet.'

Sarah was silent for a second. 'Good,' she said eventually. 'So, what's it like?'

Reuben glanced out of his hood. A short queue of tracksuited prisoners were chatting and fidgeting, waiting their turn. The other three phones were occupied by inmates, similarly slouched over, all trying to muster some privacy for their words to loved ones, or lawyers, or associates. 'Not great,' he said quietly, acutely aware of the need not to be overheard. 'Fair share of psychos here, one or two of whom we've put away. Aiden Boucher, for example. Almost ended up being his fifth victim.'

'Jeez. Nasty piece of work.'

Reuben cupped the end of the receiver with his palm and continued to talk as quietly as he could. 'It's going to be a long week, but I'll survive. Just got to find a way of taking a DNA sample from Brawn that is one hundred per cent dependable.'

'Any ideas how?'

'I'll have to wait and see. Not sure how close I can get to him yet.'

'Don't get how you're going to do it without him noticing.'

'Nor me. But the good news is Kieran Hobbs has two of his men keeping an eye on me. Cormack O'Connor and Damian Nightley.'

'I'll look them up,' Sarah answered, 'see what they're in for and whether you can trust them.'

Reuben heard the scratch of pen on paper, and heard Sarah whispering their names under her breath while she jotted them down.

'Thanks,' he said. 'I'll call you back later.'

'When you've nailed Brawn, go see the governor. I've spoken to him and he knows the score.'

'Who else is in on this?'

'That's about it. You, me and the governor makes three. And Moray and Judith of course. That quiet enough for you?'

'Any quieter and they'd need radar to detect us. Thanks.'

'Then the governor will get you transferred back to the same courthouse, and I'll pick you up from there. And, Reuben?'

'Yes?'

'Don't take any unnecessary risks.'

Reuben smiled. 'Don't worry, I won't.'

He scanned the corridor again quickly. And then he saw him. Coming his way. 'Shit,' he said.

'What?'

'Got to go.'

A tall, lean man was picking up the next phone along as the previous caller headed off. Reuben replaced his receiver. The man had his back to him. He was slightly taller than Reuben, his hair jet black and neat, his wide shoulders hunched, his sweatshirt pulled up to reveal his forearms. His face in a dozen different arrest photos. Obvious and unmistakable.

Michael Brawn, in the flesh.

Reuben picked the receiver back up and pretended to dial another number, frantically wondering what to do, all the time straining to hear what Brawn was saying. He faced him slightly, watching his jaw move, unable to see his features but catching fragments of his conversation: 'The last Friday. October. The third of the fourth. May.' Reuben pulled out a small address book and quickly started to scribble down the words. Brawn's accent was Mancunian with hard vowels and, almost hidden among them, rounded London consonants.

'Saturday the eighth,' he continued, 'the first of the first—'

'Oi! Virgin! One fucking call, man.'

Reuben half turned, continuing to record Michael Brawn's words while pretending to talk. A couple of prisoners were glaring at him.

'Hang the fuck up, or I'll do it for you,' the closest to him said.

'The penultimate Monday. Ash Wednesday . . .'

Reuben inscribed the last few words.

'Cunt-face! Put the fucking phone down now!'

Reuben paused, weighing up his options. The second prisoner was twitching, his teeth bared. He flashed back to Stevo's training, seeing the punches, the kicks, the actions of defence and attack. And then the mantra returned: *blend in*. Reuben replaced the phone.

Without looking back, he walked away, past Michael Brawn and past the scratched metal hoods of the phones, and loitered at the end of the corridor, where it gave way to a communal space dominated by a pool table. Two inmates were playing, lost in the shot one of them was taking. Reuben watched for a second, sensing the seriousness of the game, excited that he had encountered Michael Brawn on only his second day, wondering how the hell he was going to DNA-test him.

Moments later, Brawn strode past him, turned right down an adjacent hallway and disappeared. Reuben waited a second, fingering the address book in his pocket, full of days and months from Michael Brawn's mouth.

Then he turned the corner and followed him.

5

The TV room was packed with eager prisoners, forty or fifty of them, standing and sitting. On the screen, twenty-two football players were arranged around the circumference of the centre circle, their heads bowed, wearing black armbands, observing two long minutes of silence. The TV room was hushed as well – a rare moment of reverence. Reuben had now learned which block Michael Brawn was housed in, which floor and which corridor. The exact cell, though, had been difficult to narrow down. Reuben had lost him behind a closed set of doors, but he knew he was confined to one of twelve potentials. Although Reuben had loitered in the vicinity on three separate occasions during the day, Brawn had remained firmly ensconced in his room, blank metal doors hiding him from view.

Until now. At the very front, and towards the right, Michael Brawn was sitting bolt upright on a blue plastic chair. As the two minutes' silence ground on undisturbed, Reuben, standing to the side and slightly behind Michael Brawn, observed him for a few seconds. He was inanimate, statue-like, straight and erect. His skin shone white, blue veins bulging below the surface. He pulled deeply on a skinny roll-up every few seconds. And then, with no warning at all, he jumped to his feet and screamed 'Cockney wankers!' at the television. In Reuben's peripheral vision, he saw hardened lags glance at one another. Others stared at Brawn with obvious hatred. The organized silence continued to hang in the heavy smoke-laden air.

Then, near the back, another shout erupted from a thick-necked prisoner with a shaven head. 'Shut it, Brawn,' he said.

Michael Brawn swivelled to face him. 'John fucking Ruddock,' he said with a smirk. 'Why don't you come here and make me?'

John Ruddock stared. The smoky silence seemed to deepen. All attention had now switched from the screen, prisoners mesmerized by the two inmates. Brawn was taller than Ruddock, but less bulky. His was a lean frame, all bone and sinew. In contrast, Ruddock was thick-set, a weights-room physique, someone who had turned civilian flesh into prison muscle.

From the TV, a loud whistle cut into the room. An ironic cheer went up. Michael Brawn returned his gaze to the game and the commentator continued his interrupted football commentary: 'And it will be interesting to see how Jeremy Accoutey's unfortunate death last week affects Arsenal's performance tonight. Certainly Manchester United will be looking at that area of central defence and wondering—'

The TV voice was drowned out by a shout from Ruddock. 'Come on Arsenal!' Several other prisoners repeated the refrain. It was clear to Reuben that Pentonville was a prison which would favour anybody over Manchester United. And in North London, Arsenal was virtually the home team.

Reuben rolled up his right sleeve, slowly and deliberately. He took a packet of cigarettes that he had traded with Narc from his front pocket. With an almost practised casualness, he passed a cigarette forward to Damian. Damian glanced at Reuben's tattoo and shook his head. And then Michael Brawn noticed it, out of the corner of his eye. He turned and looked slowly up at Reuben. The look was cold and appraising, an expressionless reading of Reuben's face. Reuben was suddenly on edge. This was the man he had come for, the prisoner whose DNA evidence had been falsified, the inmate someone wanted investigated, the criminal who might hold the key to Reuben's sacking and GeneCrime impropriety. Brawn's wide-spaced eyes revelled for a second in Reuben's discomfort, and then returned to the game.

* * *

Reuben squinted at the digital counter in the corner of the elevated screen. The game was fast approaching half-time. All around him, prisoners continued to be nervy and excited. He guessed they didn't see many live games, especially not clashes between footballing enemies, the big grudge matches of the season. He continued to focus most of his attention on Michael Brawn. A short-haired prisoner was leaning over and speaking to Brawn, who was taking very little notice, absorbed in the game. Occasionally he blinked, but other than that, he was inanimate. On the screen, a Manchester United player surged into Arsenal's eighteen-yard box, and a mishit shot deflected into the net. Suddenly, Brawn was on his feet, arms in the air, shouting.

'Fucking get in there!'

No one else moved. Brawn turned around, arms still aloft, teeth clenched, eyes ablaze. Mostly, prisoners avoided his gaze. Reuben stared at him, taking everything in. For the first time, he appreciated that there was something unhinged about Brawn, something outside the normal rules, something that was best left alone. Reuben also sensed that the other inmates knew this already. While he tried to sum up what exactly it was that was different about the man, Brawn shifted his head slightly to look hard at him, and Reuben found himself caught in the headlights of his eyes.

In the background, the commentator was beside

himself with excitement. Reuben grinned slowly at Brawn, an expression designed to say, our team has scored. Brawn stared back, waxen and cold. Reuben scratched his tattoo, almost involuntarily. The other prisoners fidgeted quietly in their seats. Then Brawn left Reuben's face and ran his eyes around the room. The commentator was saying, 'And the unfortunate lad at the back, Jeremy Accoutey's replacement, seems to have deflected that past his keeper and into his own net.'

The peep of the referee's whistle sounded. Michael Brawn swivelled round and sat down again. Reuben waited a couple of moments before leaving, shouts once again erupting in the room, inmates screaming at the TV; twenty-two players running to the baying of the crowd, one of their number lying dead inside a morgue, gunshot wounds to his head, samples of his wife's DNA sitting in Reuben's freezer, a large sum of his money in the glove box of Moray Carnock's car.

6

Judith Meadows rotated the slim platinum band of her wedding ring with her thumb and index finger. It was a nervous habit, something she often caught herself doing when her mind was busy, or she was unsure, or she was impatient between long stages of laboratory protocols. She pictured her husband for a second, sitting at work, chair tightly pushed under his desk, maybe twirling his own wedding ring absently, wondering whether it was really working out or not. A fresh start, they had both agreed. A time to reappraise their relationship. What Judith needed, he had suggested, was a baby. And whereas Judith would have happily slapped him for such a brazen lack of insight into her desires and needs, the words had instead hit her a smarting blow, which still stung three months later. The insensitive bastard was right.

Judith followed one step behind Moray Carnock as they exited the lift and made their way down the long, plush corridor of the hotel. She let go of her wedding ring and continued to think. It was as if her finger had finally slipped off the mute button of her alarm clock. The suppressed buzzer had begun to sound and there was little she could do to stop it again. She was in her mid-thirties, soon it would be too late. And now, slightly nauseous and feeling tired, Judith realized that things might be about to change. The sick feeling in her stomach was compounded by guilt, and by the knowledge that her work would inevitably suffer. Days spent pulling double shifts in the hunt for a serial murderer would be numbered. And there would be other issues.

She knew she would give her heart and soul to Reuben's cause as long as she could. She believed in her former boss and what he did, knew that it excited her and kept her alive, understood that scientific impropriety within GeneCrime could blow holes in UK forensics which might never be repaired. Judith just hoped that if her tiredness and queasiness were anything more than fatigue and a rushed lunch, she still had enough time to make a difference.

Moray stopped outside a blank door and inserted a card in its slot. They pushed through and into the room, which housed several heavy pieces of gym equipment. A floor-to-ceiling window revealed a couple of miles of London rooftop. The carpet was thin and hard-working, and contrasted with the rest of the hotel's deep luxury. Judith reached for her wedding ring, and cursed, stopping herself just in time. Moray walked forward and extended his hand in Kieran Hobbs' direction.

'Mr Hobbs,' he said.

Kieran took his hand and shook it. Judith deliberately held her arms by her sides. It was not good practice for forensic technicians to shake hands with known criminals.

'Hey, Judith,' Kieran said with a wink. 'How're you doing?'

Judith smiled back, a cement mixer of emotions churning her stomach. Her husband wanting a baby, fighting to disagree and not really winning, beginning to feel strange, long shifts hunting killers spacing her out, meeting real-life gangsters in the flesh, her former boss undercover and in prison. None of it sat right when she put it all together, but individually, things seemed to make sense.

'Fine,' she said.

Kieran extended his pink fleshy hand, a twinkle of gold catching the light. Judith shook her head, quickly and demurely, her hair amplifying the refusal.

'From such a beautiful woman, that hurts,' Kieran grinned. 'But fair play. Still, you can't be telling me CID are interested in semi-legitimate businessmen like me.'

'Semi? That's pushing it,' Judith answered. 'But no, not so much. Bigger fish at the moment, I'm afraid.'

She turned her attention to Nathan and Valdek, who were pushing free-weights. Nathan was lying down on a bench, forcing a monumentally stacked bar upwards, with Valdek standing at the side, his arms hovering close, ready to help if necessary. All that muscle, Judith thought, and so few neurons. For a second, she allowed her eyes to enjoy the spectacle. The rippling, engorging flesh, sinews straining, veins enlarging, teeth clenching, eyes bulging . . . she took in Nathan's face, his locked jaw, his grimacing smile, his creased forehead. Nathan caught her eye momentarily, and seemed to flinch, almost embarrassed by his exertions. Judith glanced quickly at Valdek. He winked at her and flicked his tongue around his lips. Judith returned her attention to Kieran, suddenly feeling uncomfortable. He was taking a tightly wrapped bundle of notes out of an inside pocket and handing it to Moray.

'That's what I owe Reuben up to date.'

As Moray struggled with the cellophane binding, intent on counting the money, he asked, 'You found out who sent the Dutch guy to kill you?'

'Working on it.'

'And?'

'Slowly slowly catchy monkey. But I've got something here that might just help.'

Kieran pulled a small plastic bag out of his inside pocket and passed it to Moray, who examined it briefly and gave it to Judith.

'What is this?' she asked.

'A mugshot of yours truly. God knows where it came from. But we found it in the lining of the Dutchman's jacket just before we burned his clothes the other day.'

Judith peered through the plastic. A thin red residue coated its inner surface, the black and white image of Kieran's face tinted pink by the blood.

'So?' she asked.

'Someone must have given it him, right? And that someone might be who wants me gone.'

'Who's touched it?'

'Just me,' Kieran answered. 'And those two.' He nodded in the direction of his minders.

Judith frowned, thinking, wondering what Reuben would do. 'I might have to get DNA swabs from all of you for elimination,' she said. 'Then we'll test it, see if there's anything worth looking at. Might need a few days though.'

'Fine, darling,' Kieran answered. 'You're the boss. Whatever it takes to wrap this thing up.'

Moray peered uneasily in the direction of Valdek. Reuben had almost been shocked by what was left of Ethan de Groot.

'Nasty business,' he said.

'Yeah, well,' Kieran responded. 'The man tried to kill me. Purely self-defence. You think your lot would take a harsh view of someone defending themselves from a hitman?' he asked, turning to Judith.

'You leave me out of this,' Judith replied quietly. 'I'm hardly a spokesman for the police.'

Kieran scrutinized Judith for a second, running his pale blue eyes over her. 'No problem,' he said. 'No problem at all.'

In the lift back down to the lobby, Moray said, 'That's Hobbs' private gym. Not that he uses it too much himself, by the looks. Just a perk for his boys.'

'Why in the hotel though?' Judith asked.

'He's got financial stakes in a lot of property round here. The ultimate aim of the money launderer – to convert it into bricks and mortar, in legitimate businesses.'

'I don't like working for him.'

'You don't say. But it's fine for me and Reuben. Hobbs is one of a dying breed, an old-school gangster. You know where you are with him. He's big enough not to have to go looking for it, if you know what I mean. Stable and sorted, with no axe to grind.'

'Until someone comes along who wants to kill him.'

'Which is where we come in. And without his money, we wouldn't be able to do the important things.'

Judith was silent. She knew the arguments, had heard them over and over, and appreciated their stark truths. But they never reassured her. If she was photographed shaking hands with a man like Kieran Hobbs, or even within his vicinity, her career would be over. Covert surveillance was a matter of fact. It happened, on both sides of the law. Just like the picture of Kieran she had in her pocket.

'I know,' she muttered. 'We've just got to be careful not to get mixed up in the things he's mixed up in.'

'That,' Moray shrugged, 'is the tight-rope we walk.'

The lift pinged, its door slid open, and Moray and Judith walked out through the lobby, surrounded by tourists, staff and businessmen, multiple worlds converging in the bright foyer of a London hotel.

7

As he walked, a fine mist permeated the air and slickened Reuben's face. It was the kind of borderline rain which closes in, turning everything grey, making you squint. He wiped his eyes, still staring down at his trainers. The tarmac, usually lifeless, was glistening. Cormack O'Connor, pacing shoulder to shoulder with him, his head similarly bowed, continued where he left off.

'Officially, money laundering. Five years. But let's say there might have been a bit more to it.'

'How do you mean?'

Cormack smiled at his feet. 'You'll learn not to ask those sorts of questions.'

'So, what about you?' Reuben said, turning to his left.

Damian Nightley cleared his throat, a low rumble through his voice box. 'Gun smuggling, you know, firearms offences. We had half of London sewn up. You name it, we could get hold of it.'

There was nothing boastful in Damian's tone of voice, just a matter-of-fact statement of the truth. And Reuben knew it was the truth. He already understood exactly what Damian and Cormack were in for, and what they had done in the past. Sarah had recited their litany of criminal activity down the phone to him, and it had taken several minutes.

'Pretty straightforward,' she had said. 'Nothing unsolved or untoward. Just bad boys who got caught out and are doing their time, until they're released back into society and we lock them up again.'

'What makes you sure they'll re-offend?' Reuben had asked.

'Call it a DCI's intuition. Career criminals from Kieran Hobbs' organization. Take away the criminal part and they've got no careers.'

Reuben stole a surreptitious glance at the prisoners on each side of him. Human beings, people who had drifted into illegal actions, men who risked their liberty and lost. Until ten months ago, Reuben's contact with criminals had mainly involved the microscopic parts of themselves that they left behind at crime scenes. More recently, he had been dealing with them in the flesh, and what had shattered his preconceptions was their ordinariness. Criminals were normal people who had different moral outlooks. Forensics, as well as police detection in general, demonized men like

Damian and Cormack. Reuben had often stared at DNA sequences or profiles and seen not the human but the satanic, a molecular reductionism which shrank a criminal down to the one act they had perpetrated, the one evil they had given in to. But Reuben was increasingly coming to see that it wasn't quite like that. And while he would happily have hunted both men who were protecting him, and would have been eager to avoid their company outside Pentonville's walls, he couldn't escape the conclusion that Damian, Cormack and their ilk were not evil so much as misguided and morally askew. Just like his father.

Cormack lifted his damp face towards Reuben, then thumbed in the direction of Damian. 'Ask him how long he's got left of his ten-year stretch,' he said.

Reuben glanced at Damian. 'How long have—'

'No fucking remission,' Damian spat, his tone suddenly harder. 'I got two months left.'

'He's almost a free man. And do you think he's happy about it?' Cormack turned his face to Reuben again. 'Ask him if he's happy about it.'

Reuben did as he was told, wondering why Cormack felt the need for an interpreter. 'Are you—'

'Drop it, the both of yous.' Damian's cheeks flushed with anger, his eyes narrowing. An undeniable darkness surfaced on his brow. He bent his head down and kept walking, veering off the exercise path towards a door marked 'Block B'. Reuben watched him go, puzzled at how quickly he had changed.

'Miserable sod,' Cormack muttered. 'If it was me, I'd be counting the days.'

Seconds later, a whistle was blown somewhere, and the forty minutes of exercise came to a halt. Cormack told Reuben he'd meet him after lunch, once he'd made a couple of calls, and they agreed to track Damian down. Reuben headed straight for the canteen, his stomach rumbling.

Already, after only three days, he felt firmly on the road to being institutionalized, food the trigger that kept him regimented, synchronized and under control. It was like hospitals, or old people's homes. Ridiculously early lunches and dinners, which always left you on the verge of hunger, perpetually waiting for the next meal, in line and orderly, obedient and submissive. Reuben shrugged as he walked, an involuntary twitch, feelings rising to the surface. Sometimes, on important cases, he had worked for sixteen hours straight and had barely eaten a morsel. But that was the all-consuming nature of forensic detection – the cooling body, the scattered skin cells, the drying blood. And the amphetamine had helped, from time to time. Now, however, locked up with nowhere to go and little to occupy him, he was ravenous, as if eating were a substitute for living.

Reuben entered the high-ceilinged dining room,

with its flaky paint and warming odours. He stood at the back of the queue, waiting his turn to receive several ruined lumps of food on a plastic tray. Someone joined the queue behind him and Reuben turned slightly, monitoring him in his peripheral vision. He was well aware that this was a safer option than staring directly. The grainy, blurred edge of his sight sensed something important. He turned a little more, the man coming increasingly into focus. Reuben's heart began to pound, his stomach forgetting about lunch. Michael Brawn was standing next to him.

Reuben shuffled forward in silence, closer to the food. He weighed his options. An unambiguous sample of DNA wasn't something you could easily take at the best of times. And without someone knowing, it was virtually impossible. Michael Brawn was two or three inches taller than Reuben, expressionless, his wide eyes sucking everything in. Reuben's tattoo – the crest of Manchester United Football Club – was facing him, clearly visible on the forearm sliding an aluminium tray along the steel rails of the serving counter. From Reuben's angled view, he could see Brawn's similar but lower-quality depiction on his right arm. He silently thanked Sarah for providing his CID file, which detailed the distinguishing mark.

Reuben knew he had to get close to Brawn, to find out where he went and when, and which of the small cluster of cells was his. Only then could he plan how to snatch a pure sample of him without his knowledge.

'Good result last night,' he muttered.

Michael Brawn remained quiet, just staring. It was clear to Reuben, as it had been in the TV room, that Brawn was a man who controlled every situation he was in. His silence undermined, hanging in the air, making men talk when otherwise they would be mute. But Reuben needed a result.

'Now it's just Chelsea to try and catch,' he said.

Again, Brawn glared at him. Reuben remained half turned, trying not to look directly at him, feeling the discomfort of the scrutiny. They shuffled a couple of paces closer to lunch.

'But with our away form this season, who knows?'

Brawn cut into him with his eyes. Reuben held his tray firmly as a dollop of vegetable landed on it, a similar portion left clinging to the ladle. The clank of metal on metal. A background hum of chatter. A soft whoosh of steam from a water heater. Utter silence from Michael Brawn. Reuben's trainers squeaking as he stepped up to the next server.

'I heard we might get bought out again, though. Did you hear anything?'

Michael Brawn dropped his tray beside Reuben's. A similar dollop of greenness landed on it, the server avoiding his eye. And then the sound of a snort, barely audible, but unmissable to Reuben's ears. Michael Brawn blowing air through his nostrils. The suggestion of don't-make-me-laugh.

Reuben turned away, focusing on the next server in line. Hidden from Michael Brawn, he allowed himself the briefest flicker of a smile.

8

The low-ceilinged room thundered and cracked, gunfire ricocheting off its surfaces, funnelling the fury so that it pounded DI Charlie Baker's ears until they felt as if they should be bleeding. He ripped a pair of ear defenders off a rack and paced quickly along the row of shooters. As he fitted them over his ears, the noises dulled, their edges rounded off, though still forceful enough to rattle his skull.

There was room for six officers at a time, the stalls divided with rough planks of plywood, looking to Charlie as if they had been knocked up in someone's spare time. He walked along the dark green carpet. Above, the ceiling was strip-lit and suspended, like in a cheap shop. Even by Metropolitan standards, this was an untidy gun range. He peered at the damage as he passed each stall in turn, two female officers and four male. The targets were black bowling-pin shapes on a fawn background, successful hits appearing as specks of white where light poked through from behind. He reached the final marksman in line and waited, allowing him to discharge a volley of shots in quick succession. Then Charlie reached forward, his arm angling up to tap Commander Robert Abner on the back.

Commander Abner turned his head, then swivelled his upper torso round, a two-stage process which seemed to Charlie slightly robotic, as if one cog controlled another. He pulled his own ear protectors away. 'What is it?' he asked.

'Sorry to interrupt you, sir. Just thought you should see this ASAP.'

Charlie held up a clear plastic bag, which contained two fragments of a sheet of paper. He glanced past his superior officer at the target near the end of the room. Robert's shots were clustered in two regions, one in the rounded head area and the other in the approximate torso. Charlie noted with satisfaction that the torso holes were in a tight cardiac formation. He also observed with interest that the skull shots were in no way random, and appeared to concentrate around the area where the right eye would lie. The commander hadn't lost his touch. And while Charlie considered himself a good shot, and had been trained to roughly the same standard, he knew that he wouldn't fancy his chances against him in a twenty-five yard competition. The old man was still a star.

'What is it?' Commander Abner asked again.

'I retrieved them from the house of Jeremy Accoutey.'

Robert Abner laid his pistol flat on the deep wooden shelf in front of him, making sure its short, chopped nose was pointing away from Charlie. He took the evidence bag in both hands, savouring its silky plastic feel, layers rubbing and sliding over each other. The paper inside was thick and vaguely familiar to him.

'So . . .' he said.

'It's output data from a sequencer. The screen-shot patterns you get for quality control prior to sequence analysis.'

'I'm more than familiar with what gel files are, detective inspector.'

'Sorry, sir.'

Commander Abner shouted to be heard over another barrage of shots. 'But I don't recognize the format.'

'That's because it's probably from an ABI 377. Still in operation, but less fashionable these days. The dog's knackers a few years back, and not the sort of equipment generally used by amateurs.'

'Do we use them currently?'

'Decommissioned our last one about ten months ago, sir.'

'Ten?'

He peered down at Charlie, a stern uncle with a glint in his eye. Charlie did his best not to be unnerved by Commander Abner's reputation for detail, or his status as one of the country's leading detectives, or his decorations for smashing gun rackets and drug gangs, or his no-nonsense progress in the world of forensics. It was, Charlie was forced to concede, a lot to try not to be daunted by, and it left him with the worrying fear that Abner saw right through him and into his motives and actions. It was bad enough a criminal getting on the wrong side of Commander Robert Abner. But a policeman . . . Charlie moved his thoughts to safer ground.

'Give or take a couple of weeks, sir.'

'So, let me get this clear,' Robert Abner growled. 'A footballer kills his wife, then turns the gun on himself. Some time prior to this event, he has been given sophisticated forensic information which hasn't come from ourselves.'

'Exactly, sir.'

'Charlie?'

'Sir?'

'Drop the sirs. We're both on the same side here.' Commander Abner raised his eyebrows, a brief smile twitching on his lips. 'Besides, it unnerves me. Now, what kind of information do you think Mr Accoutey received?'

'Impossible to tell.'

'But if you had to guess?'

'The obvious, given the death of his wife, would be some sort of infidelity test.'

'And who do we know who is currently offering such a facility?'

Charlie felt as if he was being tested, a senior officer asking what he already knew. 'Well, commercial outfits – you know, private labs that advertise in the back of magazines and just cover paternity tests, that sort of thing. If it was something to do directly with Lesley Accoutey, and that's simply a guess, there's only a couple of names that spring to mind.'

'Which are?'

'There was a private lab out near Heathrow, set up by some ex-human genome staff from the Sanger Institute—' Another volley of rapid gunfire burst through Charlie's words and he waited for a period of quiet. 'You know, when the human genome was essentially mapped, a few punters branched off into more exotic stuff. Screening for inherited syndromes in potential partners, picking up viral infections at an early stage, HIV testing, deciding which partner had got the virus first, a few borderline activities for employers and insurance companies . . .'

'And they're still active?'

'Very much so. We've been keeping a quiet eye on them.'

'Good. Maybe it shouldn't be so quiet from now on. Go over and see them, have a nose into their business.'

'I will. Only . . .'

'What?'

'There is the other possibility.' From the outset, a name had come to him thick and fast. A bell ringing, a nerve firing. 'There are whispers about Reuben Maitland,' he said. 'That he's still sniffing around, and offering forensic services.'

Robert Abner's face hardened. 'I want you to leave Reuben Maitland out of this.'

'But, sir. Surely he's a potential suspect.'

'I have my reasons,' he said, picking up his gun again. 'And that's all you need to know for now.'

He emptied the chambers, and Charlie watched him slot six new rounds in their place. Commander Abner replaced his ear protection and turned back to the target, and Charlie appreciated that his audience with the big man was over.

He walked back the way he had come, once again running the gauntlet of multiple weapons being discharged, and seeing tiny bright holes appear in distant targets, almost as if light itself was forcing its way through the cardboard in spontaneous bursts. He wondered why Robert Abner was protecting Reuben Maitland, and whether there was a bond between the two he didn't know about. It was not a thought that cheered him. The chance to squeeze Maitland was one he would have relished. And if it was true that he was still poking his nose into prior GeneCrime business, then having him put out of harm's way would have been a massive bonus for Charlie. As it was, he decided to convince Abner that he wasn't interested in Reuben Maitland, while all the time getting closer to him.

I know this smacks of you, Charlie thought, examining the evidence bag one more time as he left the range, and now, Dr Maitland, I'm coming to get you.

9

Joshua Maitland lay serenely asleep on his back, a blanket half on and half off him, a stuffed dog which had seen better days just out of reach. As his right arm stretched, it pulled a thin clear tube with it, which entered a vein on his wrist. The cannula was disproportionately large, and held in place with a plaster decorated with cartoon robots. A small amount of dried blood surrounded one edge of the plaster, wrinkling its surface.

While Joshua slept, a nurse approached his bed and adjusted the flow-rate of a bag of saline hanging from a small metal frame. 'Just keeping an eye on his fluids,' she said with a smile. Lucy Maitland attempted to smile back, a terse flick of her lips revealing a glimmer of teeth. When the nurse had left, Lucy glanced anxiously at her watch, and then at the clock on her mobile phone. She sighed, and looked back at Joshua, peaceful and still, with all the untouched beauty a sleeping child possesses. She stared in wonder for a second, the way she always did when Joshua was asleep, his noisy exuberance gone, leaving behind only a delicate loveliness in its place.

Sometimes, from a certain angle, he reminded her of Reuben. She saw it more when he was still. But when Joshua was charging around the place, boisterous and rowdy, Lucy thought he looked more like Shaun. But still, at eighteen months of age, she was unable to tell definitively. And the more quiet he had been recently, the more withdrawn and the less likely to run about screaming Shaun's house down, the more he had seemed to resemble her estranged husband. Lucy smiled briefly to herself, that illness could change the way her son looked to her. In rude health he was Shaun's son; in ill health he was Reuben's.

Lucy stroked the warm softness of his skin. She desperately hoped that Joshua wasn't Reuben's son. It was impossible to be certain either way without a DNA test. But Reuben didn't seem keen on the idea, and, though she battled to suppress it, neither was she. At the moment they had a status quo, which, given the last ten months, was a hell of a lot more acceptable than further turmoil. What she did hope, however, was that the hospital tests on Joshua would be rapid, and as decisively negative as she knew they would be. These days, doctors seemed to test for anything they possibly could, desperate to avoid the career-threatening instance when they missed something big. As a practitioner of law, Lucy knew that medics were petrified of meeting her ilk in any context other than the doctor–patient relationship. She secretly believed that this was why Joshua was being singled out for such invasive testing, given two or three months of just being mildly under the weather.

Lucy checked her watch again. Where are all the bloody staff? she asked herself. Her mobile rang. Work would be hunting her down, wondering why she wasn't keeping any of her morning appointments.

'Hello, Lucy Maitland,' she answered, trying to sound upbeat.

On the other end, from a corridor in Pentonville, Reuben said, 'It's your ex-husband.'

Lucy gave a half laugh. 'Not till the paperwork comes through, sonny. Until then, estranged would be more accurate.'

'Anyway . . .' Reuben paused, his breathing scratching through the receiver. 'Look, I just wanted to know how Josh is. Last time I saw him he had a bad cough.'

'He's fine,' Lucy replied flatly. And then, 'Actually, he's not fine.'

'What do you mean?'

'He's in hospital having blood tests.'

'Hospital?'

'Don't panic. Just as an out-patient, referred by the GP. Useless bugger that he is.'

'But what are they testing for?'

'Christ knows. But I wish they'd get on with it. We've been here so long Joshua has fallen back to sleep. Tell the truth, I wouldn't mind joining him.'

'If you had to take a wild guess though?'

Lucy noted that Reuben sounded edgy. 'Like I said, probably nothing, simply a precaution. Bloody inconvenient – I've got an eleven o'clock. Actually, I don't suppose you could . . .'

In Pentonville, with his head pressed close to the metal hood, the phone jammed in the crook of his neck, and a phone card pushed in the slot, Reuben watched a succession of prisoners pass him by. 'I'd love to,' he said with genuine regret, 'but I can't. I'm a bit . . .' Aiden Boucher walked past. He glared intently at Reuben and gave him the universal throat-cut sign. 'A bit busy at the moment. For a few days at least.'

'Fine,' Lucy muttered.

'Look, when will you know?'

'When I've managed to see a bloody doctor, which in this place might not be any time soon.'

'I'll ring you,' Reuben said. Aiden Boucher was disappearing into the distance, swallowed up by other inmates. Reuben pictured his son in the hands of medics, wanting only to hold him himself. 'Good luck, Lucy. And will you give him a kiss for me?'

In the brightly lit hospital room, Lucy ended the call with a curt yes. She bent down to Joshua's face and gave him a very brief peck on the cheek. 'That's from Dr Maitland,' she whispered, not wanting to wake him. 'Which is about all he's ever given you.'

A medic entered the ward and she straightened again. She knew she could be fearsome if she put her mind to it. Colleagues at her law firm often joked about it. 'Being Lucied' was the phrase they had invented – on the wrong end of one of her tongue lashings. She stood up and straightened her skirt. Woe betide the doctor who came between Lucy Maitland and getting her son tested and out with a clean bill of health as fast as possible. In fact, woe betide anyone who came between Lucy and anything she wanted.

10

Moray Carnock ambled his considerable bulk along the pavement. A light rain that didn't seem to carry wetness with it, just freshness, was beginning to come down. His clothes stayed dry, barely touched. Yet the droplets continued to fall, whipped up by the wind. Fifty metres in front of him his quarry was making similarly unhurried progress, untouched by the moisture, talking on a mobile, stopping occasionally in front of shop windows, gesticulating with his free hand. Moray noticed that a good deal of his attention was focused on checking his own reflection. He seemed to focus particularly on his hair, with its permanent wet-look and irritatingly rakish sweep. Moray ignored what he saw in the windows he passed. It was, he told himself, what lay on the inside that mattered. His stomach began to rumble. Moray allowed himself a brief smile. A pasty and two sausage rolls were what lay on his insides, and they rarely helped matters at all.

Anthony McDower started walking again, and Moray continued his progress. From what he could gather through Judith, the police conclusion had been murder followed by suicide. Jeremy Accoutey possessed an illegal firearm, had been in trouble with the law before, and knew with one hundred per cent certainty, thanks to Reuben, who his wife was fucking. Stranger things had happened, however. And Mr Anthony McDower, the team physio, examining his profile in a series of high-street shop windows, certainly didn't look overly distraught. He had been questioned and released by the police. But at the very least, Moray and Reuben had concluded, he was worth keeping an eye on. So Moray had decided to devote his afternoon to seeing exactly what Mr McDower did during his time off.

Moray watched Anthony enter a sunglasses and watches shop, the kind of place you go when you want to buy something but can't really figure out what. He checked his own watch. Three thirty-six. That awkward period between lunch and tea. He rummaged in the folds of his coat, but his fingers discovered only empty wrappers, the plastic remains of saturated foodstuffs. McDower was taking his time. Moray imagined him trying on a series of similar sunglasses, relishing the chance for more self-examination, paying more attention to his face than to the potential purchases. Although Moray was 95 per cent sure he was innocent, obvious vanity only days after the death of his lover seemed inappropriate at best. He tried to imagine how he would have felt if his ex-wife had died when they were still together, and reasoned that he probably wouldn't have been able to drag himself out of bed for a week. McDower's behaviour was different, however.

The howling of sirens pierced the air. Moray appreciated that this always meant bad news for someone somewhere. That omnipresent London noise had become exactly what pain, misery and tragedy sounded like to Moray, an anthem of distress, an electronic wailing of misfortune. Ambulances, fire-engines and police cars rushing to the scene of somebody's bad luck.

A dark blue Ford Mondeo pulled up sharply next to the kerb, and Moray cursed under his breath. 'Here we fucking go,' he muttered with a sigh, pretending not to have seen it. He began walking, but only managed a few strides before a CID officer he didn't recognize began to match him pace for pace. He was in plainclothes, and seemed to have taken the description almost too literally. The logo-less jeans and ironed shirt screamed copper louder than any uniform would have.

'Care to come for a ride?' he asked.

Moray scanned the window of the car behind the officer. There was a figure he recognized in the back, and he knew the game was up.

'Aye,' he said, 'why not? My feet are killing me.'

Moray sauntered over and climbed in through the rear door. The plainclothes CID officer sat in the front, and the car pulled off. Moray looked over at DI Charlie Baker and smiled. DI Baker was in full uniform, the severity of his black jacket combining with the sharpness of his beard to formidable effect. He didn't smile back.

'You a football fan, Mr Carnock?' Charlie asked.

'Only the proper stuff.'

'The proper stuff?'

'Kilmarnock, you know . . .'

'And do many Kilmarnock players shoot themselves?'

Moray raised his eyebrows, thick folds of skin rippling his forehead. 'It would be no bad thing if they did.'

DI Baker stared back, impassive and deadpan. 'We found some very interesting documents at Mr Accoutey's place, documents that reek of you and Reuben Maitland.'

'Really?'

The car cut through the traffic and took a roundabout at speed. Moray realized that they had failed to spot Anthony McDower. For a second he felt put out that he had been followed while he was following someone else. He heard a clichéd Hollywood voice-over in his head: *And then the hunter became the hunted.* It was an amateurish mistake that might have proved costly under different circumstances.

'And how do you figure that out?'

'I think you'll find, Mr Carnock, that we're able to figure a lot of things out.'

'Now this is interesting,' Moray muttered. 'And is that all you have?'

DI Baker appeared to redden under his beard, an angry scarlet topsoil just about visible through the undergrowth. 'We are talking here about the violent deaths of two people. Have you seen what a twelve-bore does to a human face?'

Moray shook his head. He had seen a lot of unpleasant sights, but had been spared that particular one.

'It's not fucking pretty. This is serious and high-profile. A shock to the public. One of the tabloids is apparently about to print some very disturbing pictures. Don't know how the fuck they got them. But this ain't fun and games, Carnock.'

'I still don't see—'

'Now you tell Reuben that he'd better watch his back. Old loyalties are one thing, but the press are scratching this like the pox. And sooner or later they're going to want to see some blood. As you well know, taking DNA from people without their knowledge is an illegal activity.'

Moray turned away, scanning the streets. CID were on to them, and it had happened quicker than he had guessed. True, they didn't have enough evidence yet, but they were obviously close. He wondered for a second why DI Baker was warning them, and concluded that he wanted to watch them squirm, needed to see what they would do now, had been eager to witness their reaction. He also realized that they didn't know Reuben's current whereabouts.

'I wish I could help you,' he said, turning back to face him, 'but I haven't the faintest idea what you're talking about.'

DI Charlie Baker held his gaze for several long moments, the look cold and appraising, an intensity gained from years of cross-examining liars and deceivers. Moray tried not to flinch. The bastard knew something else. It was there in the thin smile lurking in his beard. Something that could conceivably sink them.

Moray turned away and chewed his lip. He needed to contact Reuben and let him know that his old unit was coming for him.

11

Sarah Hirst closed the door of the records room behind her. Had there been a lock, she would have gladly used it. The windowless subterranean room was one of only a handful which escaped the all-pervasive air conditioning of GeneCrime. The building, only three years old, had been constructed with security and biological safety in mind. This meant that none of its small number of windows opened, and the laboratories were kept at a slightly higher air pressure than everywhere else, to prevent the ingress of airborne contaminants every time someone entered through a door. However, the fine balancing act that the four-storey, hermetically sealed building had to maintain resulted in air-conditioned rooms which were perpetually too hot or too cold. Nowhere seemed to be just right. Her own office was ridiculously cold, no matter the time of day or year. Even in summer Sarah had to wear a jacket or a coat as she sat in front of her computer.

Walking through the floor-to-ceiling stacks of records, Sarah ran her index finger over the paper and cardboard files almost absently, enjoying the still, natural air. She had requested Michael Brawn's record the previous week, but hadn't pulled it herself. From now on, she decided that if the opportunity arose she would hunt out what she needed without requesting support staff help. Just getting out of her office for half an hour felt like a major escape act.

The records room housed all the case notes, files, general information and forensic evidence available, around a third of which wasn't housed on the GeneCrime server. Even in the hunt for a modern serial killer, Sarah was well aware that there was no substitute for the depth and sheer volume of knowledge that old-fashioned paper filing systems housed. Currently, she was cross-referencing witness statements from the three murders, and examining the last-known routes of each victim. Sarah pulled the files she needed and lugged them over to a small area which housed a number of chairs and a couple of desks. Again, she could have carried them back to her office, but the thought of staring into her computer screen and shivering herself towards another biting migraine filled her with dread.

Sarah was deep into the testimony of the man who had discovered the body of the second victim, DI Tamasine Ashcroft, when the door opened.

She looked up and saw the neat, crisp form of Commander Robert Abner. Sarah had vowed from day one not to be intimidated by him, and so far had been reasonably successful. There was something strong and paternal about him which she found somewhat difficult to deal with. Her own father had, even through the eyes of a devoted daughter, been weak and inconsistent.

He approached her desk, almost hesitantly.

'DCI Hirst,' he muttered, 'do you have a moment?'

'Of course, sir.' Sarah glanced down at the files strewn everywhere, the photos of the victims, the typewritten statements and the photocopies of evidence. 'Excuse the mess.'

'Sorry to disturb your work.' Robert Abner indicated a chair. 'OK if I park myself?'

'Sorry. Of course.'

Sarah detected the slight awkwardness in her boss's approach, and the automatic diffidence in her own behaviour. Since he had arrived to oversee the division and put it back on track, she had never spent more than a few minutes alone in his company. He was a remote boss whom she respected, and who in turn allowed Sarah to get on with her work. From this, she surmised that the commander trusted her, largely because he wasn't interested in her daily activities. And she was more than happy with the arrangement.

'I'll come straight to the point,' Commander

Abner said. 'When was the last time you saw Reuben Maitland?'

'Two or three days ago, sir.'

'Do you have a current whereabouts for him?'

''Fraid not.' A small voice inside told Sarah not to say anything daft. She had barely breathed since the first question. 'All I know is that he's away on a job.'

Commander Abner frowned, and Sarah noticed that the crease of his forehead and the wrinkling of his eyes made him almost handsome.

'What kind of a job?'

Sarah exhaled, hoping to God that she wasn't blushing. She had arranged Reuben's entry into Pentonville without her boss's knowledge. Maybe the commander knew more than he was letting on. But it was too late to tell him now. She decided to feed him a vague and unincriminating version of the truth.

'I'm not sure,' she answered. 'Just heard along the lines that it was something underground, you know, out of the way.'

'Out of the way,' Commander Abner repeated, partly to himself. 'Anything else?'

'Not that I know.'

'But you're in touch with him?'

'Sometimes, yes. I know he's not necessarily welcome around here, but his depth of forensic knowledge is legendary. And, of course, he still has access to predictive phenotyping. Plus he's given us some potential avenues in the hunt for DNA from what we think might be the first victim.'

Robert Abner tipped his head back and regarded Sarah for a moment, his eyebrows pulled so tight together that they almost met. 'Don't worry,' he said. 'It's no bad thing to have Reuben on our side. I dealt with him myself recently.'

Reuben had told her all about the meeting, and about Abner's assertion that he might soon be requiring his services.

'Just wanted to know where he was at the moment, and what he was up to. That's all.'

Sarah folded her arms in her lap, forcing them still so they couldn't betray her with a sudden twitch or scratch of the face, or any other of the subconscious tics of the liars she questioned on an almost daily basis. 'Like I say, some sort of job, I think, sir.'

Commander Abner stood up again and straightened himself, smoothing the creases of his uniform. 'Right.' He aimed a smile at her and turned for the door. 'I won't disturb you any more.'

When he had left, Sarah rubbed her head and stared down into the folds of her skirt. Lying to an area commander was not good. She rewound through the conversation, trying to gauge whether she'd left enough grey areas, and whether she'd been vague and noncommittal where it counted. Then she wondered whether she should just have come clean. After all, if Reuben was right, Abner was actually behind the internal investigation into Michael Brawn. Although this made a lot of sense, she had no direct evidence of it. But this was her case, and the fewer people she told the better. And when Reuben completed his mission in a couple of days' time, and they had the result she needed, she would take all the glory, and no one would ever care that she had gone behind Abner's back.

12

Reuben realized it was getting close. The time to take a sample from Michael Brawn was fast approaching. Every extra day he spent in Pentonville increased the chances of disaster. Twelve hundred inmates; surely someone would recognize him soon. He had to take an unambiguous DNA sample from Michael Brawn, and then get straight to the governor. But as he sat on the toilet seat of a flimsy cubicle, examining his Kinder egg and picking out its forensic contents, he knew he was going to have to be an opportunist. When the moment arrived, any moment, he would have to seize it quickly and without hesitation. And also without Michael Brawn or anyone else knowing.

In many ways, the SkinPunch weapon would have been ideal. Reuben had designed and built it for just such an eventuality. The anonymous and certain removal of a skin specimen, a few thousand fibroblast cells, pure and untainted DNA. But

Reuben knew he could never have smuggled the gun through the searches. And if he had, it would have been substantially less fun to remove than the Kinder egg. He continued to play with a small pair of tweezers and a short cottonwool bud, lost in thoughts of how and when. While he pondered, Joshua's face drifted in and out, lying in a hospital bed somewhere, the terrible word 'tests' hanging over him.

Reuben was about to pack his kit away when the door to the toilets opened and closed, and he heard a voice he half recognized, echoed and distorted by the high ceiling. He peered through one of the many deliberate gaps in the cubicle's structure. Standing in front of a long row of porcelain sinks, Damian Nightley was washing his hands quickly and hurriedly. Reuben sensed someone else in the toilets too. Damian turned his head towards the urinals, which were hidden from Reuben's view.

'Just leave me the fuck alone,' he said.

Reuben strained to see who he was talking to. Running water obliterated the reply, which was short and sharp.

'I'm connected,' Damian replied. 'You should think carefully about that.'

He turned the tap off and walked over to the hand-towel. From his movements, Reuben sensed he was acutely uncomfortable, but unwilling to back down and leave the toilets in a hurry.

And then the voice came again. This time Reuben heard it clearly. 'I've got my eye on you,' it said. It was a hard, dry Mancunian accent. It was Michael Brawn.

'And what's that supposed to mean?' Damian asked.

Reuben focused intently through the space between the door and its formica wall. The sound of footsteps. Not trainers, like most of the rest of the prison, but leather shoes, slapping the tiled floor, ricocheting around the hard surfaces. Then he saw him. Michael Brawn walking over to Damian, face to face. Peering slightly down, sneering and pale. 'If you don't know by now, son, you haven't been paying attention.'

A toilet flushed close to Reuben's, and its door banged open. A man Reuben didn't recognize walked over to the sink and began washing his hands. Reuben returned his attention to Damian, who remained motionless, staring long and hard at Brawn, before eventually walking out. Brawn lingered a moment, looking blankly in the mirror. He didn't smile or alter his expression. He just took it all in, his own mouth and hair and eyes, a statue facing a statue. Reuben wondered what the hell he was thinking. What would be on my mind if I was Michael Brawn? Reuben asked himself. And then Brawn spoke into the mirror. Three short words which Reuben strained to hear. But they were unmistakable.

'Not long now,' he hissed.

He turned and disappeared from view.

Reuben packed the forensic contents of his egg away. This could be it. The moment. He waited a beat, then flushed the toilet. If he could follow Michael Brawn to his cell, he would stand a chance. He slid the bolt back and pocketed the Kinder egg. All he would need were a few hairs or access to his toothbrush.

And then the door flew open and Michael Brawn stood in the door-frame, wide-eyed and bristling with violence. He shoved Reuben back, stepped inside the cubicle and locked the door.

'Let's have a look,' he said.

Reuben had no time to react. Brawn's long straight arm pinned him to the wall, his open hand pressing into Reuben's sternum. With his free hand he reached forward, still holding eye contact, and forced Reuben's right sleeve up. Then he licked his index finger slowly. A thousand fears flashed through Reuben's mind. Alone in a cubicle with a psychopath. Off balance and trapped. The porcelain of the toilet cold against his leg. Brawn ran his wet finger across the surface of Reuben's tattoo. A light seemed to go on in his eyes, sparkling in the gloom, never moving away from Reuben's.

He pulled a small penknife from his trouser pocket. Reuben tried to edge back, but there was nowhere to go. Brawn's strength defied the relative leanness of his torso. He lowered the blade until it touched Reuben's tattoo. He pushed it down, and Reuben felt the sharp nip of the cutting edge. Then, slowly and deliberately, Brawn sliced the blade across the tattoo. A cold sting, a tingle somewhere in his groin, a biting pain opening up along the line marking the knife's progress. The burning tear of skin, the spasm of slit muscle, the deafening scream of bisected nerves. Droplets of red pushing their way through the dark inky-blue epidermis, lining themselves up into an angry stripe, merging into larger drops, oozing over hairs, funnelling along the pattern of the tattoo, dropping on to the floor. Michael Brawn, his eyes enjoying the sight of blood.

'I don't know what you want,' he whispered, folding his knife in a quick, seamless movement. He slapped Reuben half seriously, half mockingly around the face. 'But you keep the fuck away from me.'

Michael Brawn unlocked the door, stepped out and walked smartly away, his footsteps echoing behind him.

Reuben clenched and unclenched his right hand, feeling for damage. His grip was fine, as were his movements. He looked down at the cut, straight and sharp, through the heart of his tattoo. Superficial damage only. Blood continued to fall on the tiles, and Reuben stooped to clear it up with some

13

Damian's cell, like most of the others in the block, was defined almost exclusively by the pictures stuck to its walls. The images reminded Reuben of tattoos. They were the visual story you wanted to tell, the parts of your life projected for public consumption. And whereas Narc's pictures were eclectic and virtually unreadable, Damian's were obvious and straight to the point. Reuben felt that he knew Damian's entire life story from one glance at his wall, and that Damian wanted it that way. Three children, two boys and a girl, at various stages of development; school mugshots in front of identically blurred backdrops; holidays on beaches and at campsites; a smattering of weddings, parties and family occasions. In some shots a squat, dark-haired woman stared bleakly into the camera, never quite smiling. Reuben wondered who had taken most of the photos. Damian had spent long years under detention, so it certainly hadn't been him. But the message was there all the same: this is my family, and this is what really matters to me.

Reuben couldn't help but wonder why, if that was the case, Damian had risked everything by being so deeply involved in the supply of firearms. He hoped Sarah was wrong, and that former associates of Kieran Hobbs wouldn't go straight back to their criminal ways. With a bit of luck, Damian would change careers when he was released in a few weeks. Certainly, Reuben wouldn't want to see him arrested by any of his ex-colleagues at GeneCrime.

Reuben decided to ask the question that had been refusing to abate for the last two hours, while the cut on his arm throbbed acutely and refused to stop bleeding.

'What do you two know about Michael Brawn?' he asked.

Damian caught his eye, a flash of hostility. 'What's it to you?'

'Just curious.'

'Best kept clear of,' Cormack answered, turning the page of his newspaper. 'He's got form and a half. Involved in a lot of not-nice things.'

'Like what?'

'Who knows? You just hear rumours. That's all you do hear in this place. Rumours. How someone bumped someone else, or is connected to the guts, or takes it in the greenhouse . . .' Cormack glanced up from his paper. 'Trouble is, you never get to know what's right and what isn't.' He smiled, a boyish, cheeky grin that Reuben imagined had saved him from the odd bollocking at school. 'Take Laughing Boy, for example.' Cormack jerked his thumb in the direction of Damian.

'What?'

'I heard the other day he accidentally smiled.'

Damian scowled at him. 'Cocksucker.'

'And that as well.'

Despite himself, Damian broke into a brief grin, which quickly faded. His characteristic apprehension returned with a vengeance. He stood up, smoothing the crease on the bed where he had just been sitting.

'Anyway,' he said quietly, pacing to the door.

'What?'

'Don't wreck my cell. Leave it tidy.'

'Where you going?' Cormack asked.

'Visiting time.'

'Who's coming?'

Damian's sigh was more visible than audible. His whole chest heaved up and fell back again. 'My old lady.'

He left the room, and Cormack raised his eyebrows at Reuben.

'What's the story?' Reuben said.

Cormack returned his attention to the paper. 'Some things are best left unasked,' he muttered.

Reuben lifted his sleeve a couple of inches, keeping it out of Cormack's view. The toilet paper was dark red, the blood dry and brittle. Between bouts of pulsing and throbbing, the wound had begun to itch. Reuben lowered his sleeve, ignoring the temptation to scratch it. As he did, an image hunted him down, sparked by two words Damian had said.

Visiting time.

Seated next to his brother Aaron, fidgeting, thirteen-year-old boys unable to sit still. A sparse room with empty tables and chairs. His mother Ina opposite, sharing her scolding looks between the two of them. Appreciating that his mother looked drawn, her fine features burdened by bags and wrinkles. Looking uncomfortable and out of place. Waiting and waiting, the room gradually filling up. The noise level rising, whispers turning to murmurs becoming chatter rising to shouts. And then Dad approaching, shuffling, his head down. Dressed in drab blue clothes, picking his way between tables towards them, gruff and awkward. Wanting to hug him, to hold him, anything. But something in his eyes holding Reuben back. His mother asking, so how are they treating you? His father replying, fine.

Oh, George . . .

I said, fine.

Aaron asking, when are they going to let you go?

And Reuben chipping in, soon, Dad?

His mum and dad exchanging quick glances.

Ina Maitland saying, we'll talk about this later, boys. But for now, give your dad a hug.

Reuben rubbed his face slowly, his eyes screwed tight with the memory. The place was starting to fuck with his head. This was the problem, he understood, the very thing that happens in prison. You fester. All the time in the world to sit and think does you no good at all.

Reuben stood up. 'I've got to get out of this place,' he muttered.

'Haven't we all,' Cormack replied laconically. After a couple of seconds he asked, 'What were you asking about Brawn for?'

Reuben rolled up his right sleeve and pulled the wad of tissue away. It clung to the wound, and congealed blood came away with it.

'He ran a knife through this.'

Cormack sat up on the bed and leaned forward for a closer look. He whistled through his teeth. 'You're kidding.'

Reuben shook his head, defiant and angry, something he didn't like the feeling of welling up inside him.

'And I'm going to make the fucker pay for it.'

He walked out of Damian's cell and back towards his own, where his small scalpel blade lay, ready to be used for something a good deal nastier than he had originally intended.

14

Laura Beckman, a petite female in a tight red cardigan and dark blue jeans, stands up and waits by the doors for the night bus to stop. The brakes grind and squeal and the vehicle shudders to a halt. There is the sharp hiss of pneumatics and the doors fold open. He stands up and follows her off.

She leaves the vehicle and turns down an empty street. On the other side to her lies a school. There are zigzag lines in the road, multiple signs and speed bumps. A white painted railing on a small wall runs almost the length of the two-storey building. He remains twenty paces back, blotting out memories of his own schooling, suppressing his own pathetic and ineffectual efforts inside the classroom and out of it, still seeing the playground fights, the crush of eager pupils chanting 'Scrap, scrap, scrap!' while on the inside he or someone else was pulverized by boys who knew they wouldn't lose.

He doesn't know what time it is, except that the pubs kicked out seemingly an age ago. They are on the other side of the Thames and moving away from it. It is warmer tonight than it has been, but is still by no means pleasant. He wonders momentarily whether the woman is cold, and why she isn't wearing a coat. He knows that if he had dressed more . . . nothingness. And back again. A short blankness. He shakes his head. He is still walking, on automatic pilot, the woman just about in sight. He quickens his pace. The black-outs are becoming more frequent and less predictable. He has no idea what happens or where he goes, but he knows they can't last more than a few seconds at a time.

The rules should have changed by now, but they haven't. He takes some reassurance from this, gradually closing in on the red cardigan ahead. There have been theories in the papers, but nothing more, no details. Besides, they have been consumed with the death of a footballer and his bimbo wife. But no official statement. No warning to stay off the streets. Just vague articles saying the police are still trying to link the death of this one with that one. And so the women of London continue to roam the streets, all dolled up, looking their best and remaining available.

He squeezes his fists tight, muscles hardening. She is ten paces ahead now, turning past a row of terraced houses. He glances around. The street is empty. There are no CCTV cameras and no cars. Most of the houses are unlit. The moment is coming. The surge, somewhere deep in his stomach. A tightness in his groin. Chewing his teeth hard. The show is about to begin. Time to make one more of them understand the truth about power.

The tablets from earlier are fully in his system now. He senses the energy they bring, expanding his chest, breathing deeply and quickly. The doctor talked again about side-effects, but that's all they are. It is the main effect that really matters, not the small and unimportant changes they smuggle along with them for the ride. And what a ride. He is, he firmly believes, unstoppable. What would it take to bring him down when he is in full flow? A van-load of coppers might be in with a chance. But a large proportion of them would end up with broken skulls and smashed-open noses.

The slag in front takes a left turn up a side street. The lighting is worse, the houses sparser and separated by commercial buildings and lock-ups. As she walks, she spins her head sharply round. Through the dark, he sees her face for the first time. It is pale, pretty and etched with concern. She is on to him. It is time to do it. Her pace increases, the heels of her shoes stabbing hard into the pavement. No black-outs, he says to himself. No black-outs.

He concentrates, the anger rising, the sick dread, the nervous anticipation. He starts to run, full tilt, leaning forward, his arms thumping through the air. She looks back again. He sees the fear, and it turns him on. He sprints faster, a lion in the chase, utterly focused on the kill. He feels light and strong, pounding towards her. Seven or eight paces back. Gaining with every stride. He can see she doesn't know what to do, other than run for her life. Again, this spurs him on, sends his excitement up a notch.

And then she stops. Turns round and faces him. She is breathing hard, mustering some defiance. He doesn't hesitate. She raises her hands, palms up. He leaps forward, lunging through the air. Flattens her, like at rugby. Her skull thuds into the pavement, a hollow sound, a coconut dropped on to concrete. He is on top of her, tearing at her clothes. She is dazed, maybe even concussed. He leaves her jeans and slaps her round the face. Come on, bitch, come on, he says to himself. Wake the fuck up.

There is blood in the back of her hair. He looks at the surgical glove on his right hand, which is smeared in red. He slaps her again in the face, shaking her body. Nothing. She is out cold. He glances around. The street is quiet. 'You have to wake up,' he growls. Her breathing is shallow, despite the chase. He feels the side of her neck for a pulse. It is difficult to detect through the gloves. This is no good. He screws his eyes up. It cannot be accidental. You have to know what I'm doing to you.

Suddenly he wonders, what if she doesn't come

round? What then? She dies outright from a head injury. He knows the excitement is ebbing. He has lost control of the situation. And with no control, there is no point to be made. He wipes the bloody glove across her breasts, still tightly wrapped in the cardigan. Slowly, he stands up. If he blacks out again now . . . He turns and walks away, angry, frustrated, upset. Not looking back and staying in the shadows now. A lesson learned. Sometimes showing a woman too much power can be a bad thing.

15

Reuben strode into the pool room, an unhealthy anger raging. It had refused to abate, just as his wound was refusing to scab over. Inside, fifteen prisoners were standing or leaning, quietly smoking, intent on the game in progress. Michael Brawn languished in the corner, holding a pool cue, his hands in front of his chest. By the look of him, Reuben guessed that he had just played his shot and missed. A well-built inmate with dreadlocks was leaning over the table, taking his time. The atmosphere was tense with the suggestion that this was more than merely a game of pool. Something was riding on this. Maybe money, maybe cigarettes, maybe favours, Reuben didn't know. But a couple of paces to the right of Brawn, Reuben noticed Aiden Boucher among the spectators, intense and wide-eyed, his beard sharp with hostility.

Reuben walked round the table and stood in front of Michael Brawn.

'I want a fucking word with you,' he said.

Michael Brawn surveyed Reuben. The room fell silent, Brawn's opponent slowly straightening from his shot. All attention transferred from the game and on to Reuben. Brawn passed his cue to the inmate closest to him and stepped closer to Reuben.

'I'm all ears.'

'You put a knife through my tattoo.'

Reuben pushed his arm towards him, the evidence in red, an angry slit five inches long, bleeding thin, watery fluid.

'You're lucky it wasn't your heart,' Brawn said.

A couple of the spectators wolf-whistled, and Reuben sensed that this was going to get nasty.

'Now I'm going to fuck *your* tattoo up,' Reuben continued.

Michael Brawn laughed, his face never changing expression, his mouth barely open.

Reuben darted his left hand forward and grabbed Brawn's forearm. He pulled the scalpel blade from his back pocket with his right.

'Still think it's funny?' he asked, burning into his eyes.

'Hilarious.'

'You're not so tough.'

Brawn snorted. 'Tougher than you.'

'You think so?'

'Come on, streak of piss. Do it.'

Reuben moved the blade closer to Michael Brawn's arm, holding it above one of his tattoos. It was a crude skull, the standard bluey green of prison tattoos. The orbits of the eyes were red and the lower jaw bone missing. The thickness of its lines spoke of a blunt needle and repeated puncturing of the skin.

Brawn fixed his stare. The spectators stood in rapt attention. Reuben was aware that this was a hell of a lot more important than the game they had been watching. He gripped the scalpel blade perfectly still, the fingers of his other hand digging into Brawn's wrist.

'Because, deep down,' Brawn taunted him, 'you ain't got the balls.'

Reuben held his nerve. 'Only one way to find out.' He lowered the blade until it was touching the fine dark hairs of Brawn's arm.

'That's it, new boy. Nearly there.'

Reuben scanned the room with his peripheral vision. In the prisoners' expressions he detected a hunger for blood. Aiden Boucher monitored him intently, almost quivering with expectation. Reuben glanced back at the blade. His fingers had started to tremble slightly. As he watched them, fighting it, they shook more obviously, almost as if someone else was controlling their movements.

Don't panic, he told himself. You can do this.

'I mean, fair's fair,' Michael Brawn sneered. 'I cut you, and now it's your turn.'

Reuben pinched the small blade hard. All around, prisoners craned their necks for a direct line of sight. Michael Brawn's eyes continued to bore into Reuben, willing him to dare. Despite gripping harder, Reuben failed to stop the shakes. The anger was still there, but it was becoming muddied by events and feelings beyond his control.

'Shut the fuck up!' he shouted.

Brawn raised his arm slightly. 'I'll make it easy for you, yellow boy.'

The blade touched skin, juddering on the flesh, making a shallow depression in the inky tattoo. Reuben was sweating, telling himself he was waiting for the right moment. He needed to do this.

There was suddenly something ablaze in Brawn's face. 'Come on, you motherfucker! Cut me! Cut me!' he screamed.

Behind him, Boucher shouted, 'Slice him, for fuck's sake!'

A few more spectators joined in the chorus. The words 'Slice him!' echoed around the walls of the room.

Reuben looked up from the blade and into Michael Brawn's psychopathic face. The pupils were huge, the pale cheeks filling with red, the stained and worn teeth clamped together. He sensed the sweat from his fingertips wetting the blade, loosening his grip. He held it tighter and ground his teeth. He closed his eyes and pushed deeper. Into Michael Brawn's tattoo, into Michael Brawn's skin.

And then he stopped. Something somewhere said, 'Enough!' There was nothing more to gain. He lifted the blade, pocketed it and glanced around the room, sensing the reaction. There was an instant outpouring of derision, inmates booing, laughing or making the universal 'chicken' noise. Reuben turned from Brawn's pitying grin and walked away. His chin dug into his breastbone, his head held low, his walk slow and dejected.

But as he turned the corner, Reuben smiled, his lips pulled back, his teeth bared. He punched the air with his fist. He brought the fingers of his left hand up to his face and examined them intently. A small dab of double-sided sticky tape was still in place on each fingertip, and each held a hair or skin fragment or some other microscopic part of Michael Brawn tightly to its surface. Reuben punched the air again. He had DNA-sampled Brawn in front of a room full of witnesses without anyone knowing. Including Michael Brawn.

Reuben made his way to his cell. Thankfully, Narc was elsewhere. He sat down on his bed, the door swinging shut behind him. Leaning forward, he took the Kinder egg out of a pair of socks under his pillow and placed it on top of the chest of drawers. He used the small pair of tweezers to remove the strips of tape from his fingers, manoeuvring them into the Eppendorf tube with the pink fluid. Then he carefully removed the scalpel blade from his pocket and rubbed a cottonwool bud along its surface, before snipping the bud into the Eppendorf tube.

Monitoring the door, Reuben unfolded a letter he had written the previous night. He carefully poured a few drops from the tube on to each corner of the page, wafting it for a couple of minutes to allow it to dry. Then he folded it back up and slotted it into an envelope.

He glanced up as the door opened, quickly hiding the contents of his forensic kit in a drawer. Narc entered, a rolled-up magazine under his arm, whistling contentedly.

'What time's the post?' Reuben asked him.

'Six,' Narc replied, between tuneless bars of a song Reuben didn't recognize.

Reuben licked the envelope and sealed it, leaving the cell at a brisk walk. The postbox, a hangover from the jail's Victorian days, was ornate and bore the embossed words 'Her Majesty's Prison Service'. Reuben hesitated a second, savouring the victory. Then he slid the letter into the sealed metal box. Job done. He sauntered down to the dining room where dinner was about to be served.

16

In the morning, Reuben ate breakfast then made his way to the governor's office, as agreed with Sarah. A weight had been lifted from somewhere and he walked with the easy nonchalance of someone about to be released. The only problem that remained was his son, who had been lying in a children's hospital the previous day having a series of tests. Lucy had been vague, but from what Reuben could tell, the GP was playing it safe. Lucy had that effect on men. But not, it turned out, on Reuben. Perhaps if she had, he conceded while queuing for a phone, he might still be a dutiful husband in a respected job.

As far as he knew from his restricted contact, Joshua had been unwell for around three months. Nothing more than a series of colds and other nursery-borne ailments, all of which had sapped his strength and slowed him down. But he was secretly pleased that Joshua was having the tests anyway. When he had the all-clear, there would be no more excuses for blocking access, no more being turned away from Shaun Graves' immaculate house to trudge back down that immaculate drive, Joshua supposedly too unwell to stand a day out with his father.

A phone became available, and Reuben went through the rigmarole of phone cards, of dialling through the prison operator, of waiting to be connected. When the call was answered, it was clear that Lucy was fighting her way through the early-morning traffic.

'I'll get straight to the point,' she said.

Her voice sounded deeply sincere. It was unlike Lucy to be anything else. In fact, this had been one of Reuben's favourite things about his wife when they were together. Just coming out and saying what was on her mind, with no agenda or prevarication. Although she had, of course, failed to mention the small matter of the affair she was having.

'What?' he asked.

'Joshua. The tests. Where are you, by the way? Maybe we should meet up.'

Reuben knew at that instant the news wasn't going to be good. Lucy suggesting that they get together hadn't happened since the day Reuben had moved out.

'I can't,' he said. 'What is it?'

'Look, the consultant implied that things have been going on a long time without us realizing.'

'What sort of things?'

There was a pause, an intake of breath. 'Reuben, they think it's leukaemia.'

Reuben stood motionless, the word freezing him to the spot. He appreciated what the disease was and what the implications were.

'Which type?' he asked.

'They're not sure. I've got to take him back tomorrow. He's booked in for more tests.'

'Fuck.'

'But things aren't great.'

'How do you mean?'

'Some of the things they said . . .'

'Like what?'

'He's failing fast, Reuben. He needs help. They said something about his white blood cells reaching the point of being overwhelmed.'

Reuben pressed the receiver into his face, as if this could bring him closer to Lucy. The background noises grew louder. But also, somewhere deep among the cacophonous sounds of London, he detected a change in Lucy's breathing. Long, broken inhalations, and sharp, sighed exhalations. She was crying.

'Look,' he said, 'it will be fine. We'll cope. We'll manage.'

'*We*?' Lucy asked quietly.

'You, me and Shaun.'

'Quite a trio.'

'You know what I mean.'

Lucy sniffled, the noise exaggerated by the

speaker. 'I guess so. I mean, until the next set of tests . . . But now I think of it, he hasn't been himself for so long now. I just hope it's not as bad as they made out yesterday.'

Amen to that, Reuben thought.

'Look, I've got to sort something, then I'll come and see you tomorrow. Which hospital is it?'

Lucy told him the details of the ward and Reuben wrote them down. He hung up, distracted and on edge, a heavy grey sadness tightening his brain. He walked slowly, thinking through the implications, wondering whether it would be acute myeloid leukaemia or some other variant, desperately flicking back through university lectures on medical biology and the immune system. Reuben realized his knowledge was patchy at best.

He turned out of the old high-ceilinged corridor of the telephone area and into a newer-looking block, with pastel walls and strip lighting. The governor's office was at the end of the hallway. Reuben knocked on his door and waited, shaking his head, trying to rouse it from its melancholy.

Inside was a small waiting area, with three seats and a couple of potted plants. A guard sat at a modern pine-effect desk in a blue swivel chair. His name-plate read Prison Officer Simms. He was thin and weaselly, and Reuben guessed that his moustache was an attempt to compensate for the fact. Officer Simms wore black trousers, a white shirt with black numbered epaulettes and a black tie with the HMP insignia. He was by far the smartest guard Reuben had encountered so far.

'And you are?' Simms asked.

'Reuben Maitland, prisoner 4412598.'

Prison Officer Simms regarded him keenly. 'And what do you want to see the governor about?'

'A private matter,' Reuben answered.

Simms wrote Reuben's details down, slowly and carefully, taking his time.

'A private matter?' he repeated.

'Something important.'

Simms sighed, then nodded sharply in the direction of a chair. Reuben walked over and sat down. He glanced at the door marked 'Governor', which lay to the right of Simms' desk, then scanned the clock impatiently.

'You're next,' Simms added a few seconds later. 'But he hasn't got much time.'

'I know how he feels,' Reuben whispered to himself.

Ten minutes later, Reuben entered through the door and sat down opposite the governor, who was studying a piece of paper. The governor was relatively young – early forties, maybe – and almost entirely bald. In fact, Reuben noted as he watched him, his scalp was so shiny it looked wet.

When he had finished reading Reuben's details, he looked up. There was, Reuben noted, an almost nervous air about him, which clashed with every mental image he had ever stored about prison governors.

'So, Mr Maitland,' he began. 'Remand, awaiting trial dates. What can I do for you?'

'My colleague Sarah Hirst has been in touch?' Reuben said.

'I'm sorry?'

'DCI Sarah Hirst, Euston CID.'

'Remind me again,' the governor said with a smile. 'It's a big prison.'

'I'm finished here. I need to be shipped back out to the courthouse. As arranged.'

'OK. I see the problem.' The governor raised his eyebrows sympathetically and offered Reuben a cigarette, which he refused. He took a long drag on his Marlboro Light, his words exhaled through a stream of smoke. 'Mr Harrison was taken ill at the weekend, suspected stroke.'

'Mr Harrison?'

'I'm the acting governor in his absence.' He flicked some ash into a small plastic ashtray. 'So there's been some contact with—'

'You mean you don't know who I am?'

'Not apart from what it says here on your charge sheet.'

Belatedly, the implications of the governor's words hit home. Reuben appealed for inner calm, the news of his son clouding his thoughts.

'Let me explain things to you,' he said quietly. 'I came in here to perform a job with the cooperation of the Met. I've now finished, and I need to be transferred back out.'

The governor's expression changed to one of suspicion, his eyes narrowing through the smoke. 'What sort of job?'

'I'd rather not say.'

'And now you'd like to be released?'

'Not released, exactly . . .'

'Well, form a queue, Mr Maitland.'

'But—'

'You may have noticed that most of the men in here are rather keen on being let out.'

'But DCI Hirst—'

The governor cut him short again. He appeared to be relishing his authority. 'Is there anything else I can help you with?'

'For fuck's sake!' Reuben stood up and banged the desk. 'This is a joke!'

'Sit down, please.'

'Look, ring the DCI, see what she says.'

'Calm it, Mr Maitland. And, for the second time, sit down.'

'My son is ill. I need to get the hell out.'

Behind Reuben, the door started to open. Reuben had to convince the governor, had to make him understand, had to get the fuck out of Pentonville.

'Sit down, Mr Maitland,' the governor repeated, his cheeks reddening.

Reuben spoke slowly and clearly, desperate to

get his point across. 'I'm an ex-police officer, for fuck's sake. Forensics section. All you have to do is make some calls.'

'Sir?' Prison Officer Simms asked from the doorway.

'Escort Mr Maitland back to his cell, please.'

Reuben banged the desk hard. 'Come on. For fuck's sake. My son—'

'Mr Maitland! In here you play by my rules. You don't come into my office and raise your voice. And until you understand that, I have nothing more to say to you.'

The governor stubbed out his cigarette and closed Reuben's file, swivelling to return it to a filing cabinet. Officer Simms stepped towards Reuben, one hand on the truncheon lurking in his belt.

'Don't make me use this,' he said.

Too many fucking films, Reuben thought, a large part of him wanting to see Simms try and swing at him before Reuben floored him. Instead, he walked out of the office and, slowly and dejectedly, back towards his cell, his shoulder scraping the wall, his anger subsiding, a sick feeling of defeat settling in his stomach.

17

'You should have cut me when you had the chance.'

Michael Brawn was standing in the doorway, tall, looming, intense. He pulled the door to behind him.

Reuben sat up on his bed, knowing the answer but asking anyway, 'What do you want?'

'To see a copper die.'

'I'm an ex-copper,' Reuben answered.

There was a glint in Brawn's eye. 'That's the general idea.'

Reuben stood up slowly, a couple of paces back from Brawn. He saw quick flashes of his final training session with Stevo. The wooden-lined gym, Kieran and his minders watching, things played out for real. Stevo saying, 'Let him come at you. Use his momentum against him.' Stevo swinging a punch, Reuben sidestepping it and grabbing his arm. Tugging smartly, pulling Stevo forward and on to a low body blow. Winded, Stevo trying to catch his breath.

'Word travels fast,' Reuben said to Brawn.

'The speed of sound, when it's important.'

'And why is it so important?'

'I think I remember telling you to leave me the fuck alone.'

'Fine. I'll leave you alone.'

'Oh, you'll do that all right.' Brawn took a step forward. 'Only people you're going to be bothering for a while work in the hospital wing.'

'Officer Simms,' Reuben said, partly to himself.

'See, information goes both ways when it needs to.'

Reuben tensed his body, subtly shifting position, readying himself. Brawn took another pace forward. His arms were by his sides. He was in utter control and knew it. His features were on fire, his eyes wide, his nostrils flaring, his teeth bared. Reuben didn't like what he saw in the face standing just a single step away from his.

'Had you figured from the outset,' Brawn sneered. 'Tattoo too new, hair too short, words too long.'

'Is that right?'

'Said to myself, this one doesn't belong.'

Brawn stared past Reuben, at the scratched metal mirror on the wall. Reuben sensed for a second that he was almost talking to himself.

'So what's your point?'

'Shall I tell you what every educated man's worst nightmare is?'

Reuben shrugged, his mind racing, knowing he was trapped in his cell, Narc probably in the weights room, lunch not for a couple of hours, no likelihood of anyone entering for a long time, the chances of being heard slim at best.

'Pentonville,' Brawn continued. 'And every forensic scientist's worst nightmare? Shall I tell you, Maitland?'

Reuben nodded almost imperceptibly, barely listening.

'Alone in a cell with a man like me. And *your* worst nightmare? Here. Now. With the door closed.'

Reuben's eyes darted quickly around his surroundings, confirming the extent to which he was trapped.

'But this is worse than that. Much worse than that.'

Without warning, and in one fluid movement, Michael Brawn grabbed Reuben's shirt and yanked him forward. His knuckles exploded into Reuben's nose. Reuben collapsed to the floor, blood streaming from his face. His nose was buzzing and on fire, an urgent stabbing pushing up through his sinuses. Brawn stood over him, mesmerized by the blood.

'Because this one needs to be shown.'

Reuben tried to stand, desperate to fight. Brawn kicked him in the face, an upward trajectory, snapping Reuben's neck back. Reuben knew he had to react now or he would be in serious trouble.

'This one needs to be told.'

Reuben lunged for Brawn's leg, but he jumped up, bringing his full weight down on Reuben's outstretched arm. Reuben cried out, his ulna and radius squeezing together, a marrow-deep ache burrowing into the bones.

'This one needs to be damaged.'

Brawn stepped back and kicked Reuben's prone form in the guts, causing Reuben to curl up like a fetus. He rasped for air, his diaphragm flattened, his lungs useless. His chest heaved quickly back into life, coughing up blood. Reuben rolled on to his front and tried to stand up and defend himself. Through the quick succession of blows, he realized that Michael Brawn was toying with him. He used the white formica chest of drawers to pull himself to his feet. He was breathing hard, bleeding through his nose, and his left arm was throbbing and numb. Brawn grinned at him, then headbutted him clean on the chin.

'How was that for you?' Brawn asked, upright, fists clenched, beginning to enjoy himself. 'OK?'

Bent double, blood gushing from his nose and mouth, Reuben steadied himself. There was no point in defending himself. Suddenly, he straightened and ran at Brawn, who sidestepped him and pulled him on to a torso punch. The name Stevo lit up in Reuben's screaming mind.

Brawn walked round to stand in front of Reuben, pulling his head up by the hair. Reuben sensed that

Brawn needed him to understand the full horror of what was about to happen.

'What say we step things up a bit?' Brawn said with a grin. 'Get this party started?'

He pulled out his small, sharp knife. Reuben pictured fragments of his skin still clinging to the blade, some dyed red, others blue. Brawn waited until Reuben was paying attention, angling the blade so that it glinted in the light.

'You ever had a tattoo removed?' he asked.

Reuben didn't answer, heavy rasping breaths all the noise he could muster.

'I don't suppose you have. But I warn you, it might sting a bit.'

Brawn pushed Reuben back into the corner of the cell. He thrusted the knife forward and Reuben parried the blow. Brawn brought his other fist round and socked Reuben hard in the solar plexus. As Reuben gasped for air, Brawn used his strength to pin Reuben to the bed, right forearm exposed, the tattoo facing up.

'Let's see what it takes to remove one of these completely.'

Reuben tried to thrash, but Brawn was strong and was pinning him down. Reuben scanned the cell wildly for a weapon. On the drawers was his mini-forensics kit, hidden in a pair of socks. He reached his other arm towards it, pushed it out and popped the egg open with his hand. The scalpel blade clinked on the hard surface. Reuben grabbed it between his forefinger and thumb. Brawn wasn't looking. He was staring down at the tattoo, lowering his knife slowly, mimicking Reuben's efforts the previous day. Finally, blade touched skin. Reuben felt the sharp bite of the contact, an inch to the right of the long, angry cut Brawn had already given him. He saw the pulsing on Brawn's twisted neck, slow and thick. The carotid artery. A quick stab and it would all be over. Reuben gripped the scalpel hard, fingers white with the effort. Brawn was still playing with the knife. He started to run it round the outside of the tattoo, a shallow cut growing deeper. Beginning to dig into the skin, excavating, levering up a deep layer of epidermis.

Reuben took aim. He pulled his arm back to lunge. There was a bang. The door flew open. Prison Guard Tony Paulers burst in, followed by Damian and Cormack. Reuben dropped the scalpel blade into the palm of his hand. He felt the pressure ease.

'That's enough for one day, Brawn,' Guard Paulers said, one hand on his can of pepper spray.

Michael Brawn straightened and stood up. He folded his knife slowly and deliberately, before tucking it away.

'Just a bit of fun,' he said, smirking.

Guard Paulers fingered the canister in his belt. 'Out. And don't let me catch you in here again.'

Michael Brawn sauntered slowly past the guard, winking at Damian on his way out. Reuben flopped on the bed, losing blood. He heard the voice of the officer requesting medical help on his radio. Most of his torso was in agony and his face felt battered. He closed his eyes and waited for painkillers to come and find him.

18

Judith Meadows carried the post through the hall and into what remained of the kitchen. The builders were late, but this was not unusual. She sat down on one of the two remaining stools and ran her eyes around the room. It had badly needed doing, had done since the day they moved in. But two public-sector wages didn't go far in London, and after the mortgage there was rarely the money for significant improvements.

She flicked through the letters. Two for her husband, one for next door, again, one from the bank. Judith didn't need NatWest to tell her how skint they were. She aimed the white envelope unsuccessfully at the bin, watching it somersault on to the brick-dusted floor. Although Reuben's money was helping, with a baby coming, financial matters were now more serious. And while the cash that Reuben gave her was an undeniable bonus, it was not the reason she helped him. She thought again about the bloodied photo of Kieran Hobbs, wondering whether Reuben would be able to make anything of it when he resurfaced.

The fifth letter made her raise her eyebrows. The envelope was stamped 'HMP Pentonville'. Quickly, Judith padded upstairs to the spare bedroom. Among several tins of paint was a box of nylon lab gloves. She had brought them home a couple of days ago to use for the cheek-swabbing of Kieran and his minders; now they would come in useful for the painting and decorating. She slipped one on to each hand, padded back down the stairs and returned to the kitchen. It felt early in the day to be putting her first pair of surgical gloves on, and incongruous in her small terraced house.

She opened the letter slowly and carefully, her index finger under the flap. Inside was a letter on ruled paper, faint blue lines running across the page. Scrawled in Reuben's barely legible lettering were two short sentences. 'I am safe, if a little cold. Put me out of sight.'

Judith paused, her brow furrowed. She examined the inside of the envelope again, even opening it and tapping it on the worktop, knowing it was empty but double-checking all the same. Then she examined the front and back of the envelope at an oblique angle, and performed the same careful examination of the letter.

'I'm safe, a little cold, out of sight,' she said to herself. Judith didn't imagine for a moment that he was safe. Pentonville may well be cold, and she was willing to put him out of sight, but she quickly appreciated that he was telling her something else. She repeated the words a few times, trying them on for size, imagining what they could mean.

Her husband entered the kitchen and Judith stood up. She gave him a stiff hug, and let him pat her belly. No signs as yet, nothing to show, but minute and invisible things were happening. Two parallel lines on a plastic stick the previous day had told them that. Inside, a switch had been flicked, a timer telling Judith that things were about to change. She swallowed the sick queasiness that was climbing her throat, and flicked the kettle on.

'How's today looking?' Colm asked.

'Not good. Plus I had a text request for another double shift tomorrow.'

'Really?'

Her husband, she noted out of the corner of her eye, gave her an unpractised look of concern. Two blue lines and his behaviour was already changing. The murmur of the kettle quickly became a roar, and Judith made him a cup of tea, her gloves still on.

'The extra cash will come in handy.'

'I don't want you working yourself to death. Not any more.'

'So it was OK before?'

Colm smiled in defeat. 'You know what I mean.'

'I'm not doing overtime for the sake of it. There's a killer on the loose.'

'There's always a killer on the loose. That's London. Eight million people; some of them will be psychopaths. Pure statistics.'

'Yeah, well. The difference is I get poorly paid in order to help catch killers. And when someone's actively murdering women—'

'Something sexual?'

'Yes.'

Colm lifted the mug of tea to his lips and blew across its grey surface. 'In what way sexual?'

'He rapes them after death.'

'Is that really rape?'

'How do you mean?'

'If you're dead, you can't say no.'

Colm was never interested in her cases, and Judith seldom divulged the details. It was against the rules to talk about them anyway, even with loved ones. She found Colm's curiosity unusual.

'Why are you so concerned?'

'I'm not,' Colm answered, risking a sip of his drink. 'I just thought I should take more interest in what you do. You know, now you're . . .' He tilted his mug in the direction of Judith's belly.

'Pregnant.'

'Yes.'

'Well, it's early days. And for the record, rape is rape, whether before death, during death or after it.'

Colm leaned against the counter, one foot on the bottom rung of a stool. He was silent except for an occasional slurp. Judith continued to watch him, wondering what the hell pregnancy did to the male mind. Those thoughts fought for space with the short sentences of Reuben's letter, which still rebounded around inside her head. If it was important enough to write down and send to her, it had to mean something.

Presently, Colm walked over to the dusty sink and placed his mug in it. 'Gotta dash,' he said. 'Good luck with the builders.' He pecked Judith briefly on the cheek, gently patted her stomach again and made for the front door.

After he'd gone, Judith opened the letter again and read it out loud. 'I am safe, if a little cold. Put me out of sight.' Safe. Cold. Out of sight. At last, she understood.

Judith folded the letter and replaced it in the envelope. She took a transparent plastic bag out of a drawer and slid the letter in. Then she opened the freezer compartment of her fridge. She widened the opening of a box of fish fingers and slotted the envelope carefully into it, closing it again and pushing it to the very back.

19

Narc's first few words of the day had been prophetic. When Reuben returned to his cell after a night in the hospital wing, Narc had announced gleefully, 'So, rumour has it you're a bizzie.'

'Ex-bizzie,' Reuben had muttered.

'Oh, you're in the wrong place,' Narc grinned. 'You are so in the wrong place.'

Reuben had shrugged, not wanting to give his cellmate the satisfaction.

'They're going to fucking eat you alive.'

Reuben had then examined himself in the steel mirror. His face was battered, his left eye half closed, the bridge of his nose swollen. Five uneven dark red stitches zipped two lips of cheek-flesh together. He touched the straight nylon thread poking out of the end of the wound. It was sharp and unbending, at odds with the soft numbness of the tissue it held together. The sutures had been administered by an unsympathetic male nurse without anaesthetic. Reuben grimaced. The whole hospital wing had reeked of desperation. Three prisoners who had hurt themselves just to be locked away where other inmates couldn't get to them. A failed suicide case having his wrists sewn back up. Two men who didn't speak English, weak with something viral. A butch female nurse ignoring a request for pain relief until she had finished her tea break. Reuben had almost been glad to be back in his cell. That is until he encountered Narc.

The rest of the day had been just as difficult. He had hobbled in to join the breakfast queue, and watched prisoners move away from him. The food server had dolloped a large spoonful of scrambled egg on his tray, half of which ended up on Reuben's shirt. When he tried to find somewhere to sit, it had been as difficult as it was on his first day. And when he did eventually pull out a chair to sit down, the two prisoners there had stood up and walked to a different table.

The TV lounge hadn't proved any better. Reuben had been spat at from behind, an obvious, hawked-up ball of phlegm landing on his shoulder. When he turned round, a trio of prisoners were sneering at him. And when he swivelled back, more spit began to fly in his direction. Reuben had stayed as long as he could bear. Don't let them see that any of this matters, he told himself. But still, with his shirt festooned with phlegm, he had been forced to leave eventually.

Reuben appreciated that most of the prison

would very quickly know who he was. Word had spread almost instantaneously from Officer Simms to Michael Brawn, whether directly or indirectly, and wouldn't stop there. The presence of ex-CID among the ranks, especially a forensics officer, was bound to cause a stir. Reuben realized that he had obviously been pointed out; relatively few people had known his name or what he looked like yesterday. Today, however, that had changed. It was there in the eyes of men he passed in the corridor, inmates he had no recollection of seeing before. Even the guards seemed to view him with a mix of pity and amusement.

What Reuben needed quickly were friends and information. He had to find Damian and Cormack, and had to talk to Sarah, to find out what the hell was going on. Every extra day was going to feel like a lifetime.

As Reuben turned into the telephone corridor and passed through a barred gate, he finally spotted Kieran Hobbs' men. He approached them, feeling the bruises beginning to freeze up, his walk almost mechanical, but optimism nonetheless in his stride.

'Look, about yesterday,' he said when he reached them, attempting to smile. 'Thanks for bringing the cavalry.'

'Forget it,' Cormack answered.

'I mean, if you hadn't—'

'I said, forget it.'

'Kieran said you'd help me, and he wasn't wrong.'

'Yeah, well.'

'I thought Brawn was going to kill me in there.'

Cormack's tone was harder than before. 'That's what you get when you overstep the line.'

'There wasn't a lot I could do.'

Damian turned directly to Reuben. 'From now on,' he said, 'you stay the fuck away from us.'

Cormack angled his head back. 'Kieran never told us you were an ex-copper. There's no fucking way we'd have agreed to baby-sit you.'

Reuben examined the graze on one of his knuckles, smelled the sour male odours of tobacco and sweat that pervaded the prison.

'Look, I used to be a copper, then I moved over to forensics.'

'Same fucking thing,' Damian answered.

'See, we keep hanging round with you, what's everyone gonna think?' Cormack's eyes were wide and angry. 'That we're giving you info, grassing them up. You think we're going to risk our lives for you?'

'Not a fucking hope. I got eight weeks left in this shit-hole. And I'll tell you this, Damian Nightley ain't going out in a fucking box.'

'So from now on, stay the fuck away. Whoever you are.'

Damian and Cormack pushed past Reuben, one on either side, their shoulders barging into him, re-igniting the pain of his bruises. Reuben watched them go, sensing the anger in the stiffness of their walks, the betrayal in their refusal to look back. He ran his fingers over the angry wound on his cheek. Now he was truly alone. And there were other issues to take care of.

He limped on to the huddle of corridor phones, and waited his turn. An image returned to him, awoken by the blankness of the walls. Eighteen years old, sitting on the cold leather seat of an ageing Renault 12, the car parked outside huge blank gates of steel. Rain cascading down the windows, distorting the view of the prison. The passenger-side door swinging open, his father climbing in. Surveying his dad, who was resting his face against the steamed-up side window, silent and distant, water dripping from his short hair and sliding down his face, another in a long line of custodial sentences coming to an anti-climactic end.

Reuben saying, freedom. So how does it feel?

His father replying, it doesn't feel anything.

Jesus, what did they do to you in there?

George Maitland continuing to stare out of the windscreen, his head leaning against the glass of the side window.

Reuben finding a gear in the notchy gearbox and pulling off in silence.

The queue shuffled forward. After a couple more minutes it was Reuben's turn. He dialled a number from memory, and drummed his fingers on the metal hood. When it was answered, he asked, 'How much longer?'

Rapid keyboard taps punctured the short silence, then Sarah said, 'There's been a hitch.'

'What do you mean, a hitch?'

'We kept this quiet.'

'So?'

'Maybe too quiet.'

'What are you saying?'

'Look, sit tight. I'll sort it, but it's going to take a few days to get official clearance.'

'You don't understand. I have to get out now.'

'It's not that easy. We've put someone in jail who shouldn't be there. The Prison Service will go ballistic if we don't handle this carefully.'

'I'm not particularly worried about upsetting the Prison Service. Sarah, my son is ill and I need to see him.'

'I'm sorry to hear that, Reuben, and I understand. But see it from my side.'

'Your side? There is no your side. Sarah, they know I'm an ex-copper. Twelve hundred fucking inmates know that one of their number is ex-force. Maybe even helped put some of them away. Michael Brawn almost killed me, and he's still roaming around free. So the only sides I'm interested in are me against the whole of Pentonville. You've got to sort this, and do it now.'

'OK.' Sarah breathed heavily down the line. 'I'm

doing what I can. But I have to warn you again, it's not going to happen quick. Abner doesn't know you're there. In fact, I told him I had no idea where you were. If I go to him now and request special assistance—'

'I'm not bothered about whether you've compromised yourself. I'm worried about getting out of here alive and seeing my son. Do something. *Now.*'

'Like I said—'

Reuben slammed the receiver down. He knew what she was going to say. Covert operations couldn't just be undone. There were toes that shouldn't be stamped on, torn-up protocols that had to be stitched back together. He wondered momentarily whether Sarah was dragging her stiletto-ed feet deliberately. Whether she was happy Reuben was isolated and cut off. She had done worse things before to win cases and further her causes. He dismissed the notion, knowing he was angry, sensing a burrowing desperation deep in his stomach. A few days might be too long.

He headed back to his cell, to the steel door and the thick walls, a prison within a prison.

20

Moray Carnock ran his foot through the sea of white Eppendorf tubes washed up on the floor. They made the sound of a brittle plastic shale. As he peered closer, he saw that each one was labelled with a letter or a number in fine black marker pen. Some were bar-coded, a short, thin strip of adhesive paper running down one side. Moray was no scientist, but he could tell that the tubes had been there for at least a few hours. Small, receding pools of water were dotted about, the Eppendorfs mainly dry to the touch. He turned to Judith.

'How long have you been here?' he asked.

'Half an hour,' she answered. 'I called you straight away.'

'Bit of a mess.'

Judith was perched half on and half off a lab stool. Behind her, three freezer doors gaped open, their drawers pulled out, their compressors desperately buzzing, trying to cool the yawning air. Thousands of tubes were scattered across the floor.

Solutions had been poured over benches, leaving them dripping and hazardous. Bottles lay empty on their sides, on shelves or on the work surfaces. The place stank of antiseptics, solvents and alcohols, as if a succession of pub optics had been poured into a bucket with a litre of toilet cleaner. It was, Moray determined, a scene of methodical carnage. He closed the front door carefully, and slumped down on the sofa.

'How are we going to tell Reuben?' Judith asked.

'Guess we'll have to wait for him to ring.'

'He's going to be distraught.'

'Aye,' Moray agreed sadly. 'He is that.'

'And there's another thing. The photo that Kieran Hobbs gave us, and the exclusion samples.'

'Thawed as well? Are they going to be any use?'

'Almost certainly no.'

'You going to tell Kieran?'

'No point till Reuben's had a chance to take a proper look. And even then it might take a bit of time. I guess we keep this quiet for now.' Judith glanced at the door, which had been open when she'd arrived. 'We've got more important issues. Who do you think got in here?'

'Fuck knows. But they came equipped.' On his way in, Moray had admired the use of subtle force which had breached the entrance. There were scratches around the hinges and a dent where a crowbar had been used. Other than that, there was remarkably little to see, and not enough damage to prevent it closing again. 'You don't get through anti-squatter doors with a screwdriver and a penknife.'

'So it's not kids roaming the estate?'

'Wouldn't have thought so. Besides, this place seems virtually deserted. How many other people have you ever seen on your way here?'

'A few. I think there's a couple of families on the second floor. But they seem to want to keep themselves to themselves, like they know they shouldn't be here.'

'Squatters. Just like our good selves. So where does that leave us in terms of suspects?'

Judith shrugged, a brief movement of her shoulders through her thin and stylish leather jacket. Moray suspected that when she had decided a scooter required protective leathers, she had interpreted the idea fairly broadly.

'Look, one thing's for sure. Whoever got in is used to breaking and entering. This wasn't the work of opportunist amateurs or bored youths.' Moray stood up, scratching his chin. 'But there is a more important question.'

'What?'

'Why did they break in? It wasn't to steal anything. The PCs are still here. So it's clearly about the lab, and its samples.' Moray paced around the floor, displacing ripple after ripple of white tubes. The soles of his shoes squeaked in the wetness. 'So they were looking for something. Now, the point is this. Did they find it and take it?'

'We should be able to work that out.'

'How?'

'All the samples are inventoried. Some of them are bar-coded. If you're feeling energetic . . .'

'Unusually, no.'

'We could pick all the tubes up and tick them off. See what's gone.'

'Or, option B, and the point I'm getting to, was simply destroying what they were looking for enough for them?'

Judith gently poked a low-heeled shoe into the carnage. 'Well, all the samples *are* ruined.'

'Is it definitely a quick process?' Moray asked.

'If you thaw them out, they die reasonably soon, yes.'

'How soon?'

'Depends what they are. But a standard DNA in water, a few hours at most.'

'So what I'm saying is that even if we catalogue all the specimens, we may well be wasting our time. Somewhere in all this might be the samples they were after. And if they were smart, they'd just have left them, among thousands of others, to quietly rot and become unusable.' Moray snorted, his bushy eyebrows flicking upwards. 'Perfect and undetectable.'

'Maybe you should inhale more solvents, Mr Carnock. It obviously suits your brain.'

'I'll bear it in what's left of my mind.'

Moray continued to pace around. Now that Judith had mentioned it, he did feel light-headed and a little dizzy. Maybe he would give the pub a miss on his way home.

'Just about the only thing they left,' he said, inspecting one of the shelves, 'was this cylinder.'

Moray reached forward to open a large metal container sitting imperiously on a widened shelf.

'Don't touch it,' Judith shouted.

Moray froze. 'What?' he asked, arm still outstretched.

'Liquid nitrogen. Minus one hundred and eighty degrees. Best not opened if you value your fingers.'

Moray withdrew his hand. 'Thanks. Now, remind me again what we've actually lost?'

'Most of the archived cases Reuben was pursuing. A lot of GeneCrime samples, things he shouldn't have had anyway. FSS specimens from eleven or twelve full investigations. All of them irreplaceable.'

'Surely they're just small portions of larger banked samples?'

Judith sighed. This really wasn't good, whichever way she looked at it. 'For some of the investigations, yes. I took a few microlitres of all the DNAs, labelled an identical batch of tubes, and passed them on to Reuben. No harm done. But for a proportion of the others, what you see dead on the floor is all that remains.'

‘Fuck.’

‘Exactly.’

‘So it’s safe to assume that whoever broke in wanted rid of DNA samples that were unique and irreplaceable.’

Judith was quiet for a second, her dark eyebrows knotted. Sometimes Moray still found it hard to believe that she was actually a scientist. She was light and easy-going, a pleasure to be with. But he saw it now. Her concentration, when circumstances demanded it, was absolute, her working through of a problem logical, careful and methodical.

‘Nope,’ she answered, ‘we can’t conclude that. Why tip all the solutions out? Why not trash the computers? Why not wipe the records off the equipment? And who really knows exactly what Reuben should and shouldn’t have? I can barely remember at times. If you really wanted to erase the past, you’d have burned the lab down.’

‘OK, Madame Curie, what’s your theory?’

‘That they were after something specific.’

‘Which was?’

Judith pictured the box of fishfingers lying in her freezer at home.

‘I’ve got a fair idea,’ she answered.

21

From his vantage point, a shallow kink in the corridor, Prison Guard Tony Paulers was able to monitor most of the telephones. As luck would have it, the phones were unusually empty, and he had an unobstructed line of sight to his target.

This time he wasn't talking in code. Tony couldn't make out the exact words, but there was a distinct lack of repetition about his few short utterances. The last occasion, a few days ago, Tony had called a friend in the Met, someone he could trust, someone he had been on a training course with over a decade back. Tony had told him all he knew: that a prisoner in Pentonville called Michael Brawn, a tall, sinewy psychopath with a propensity for sadistic cruelty, was passing coded messages out of the prison. His friend had been sympathetic and understanding, but said he needed more. Tangible evidence, specific information. He'd also asked why Tony hadn't informed the governor, and Tony had hesitated, and finally answered, because I want to do this my way.

Things had changed since then, however. The governor was recuperating at home, a heavy stroke having strangled his words and staggered his gait, and a new man, Robert Arnott, had been assigned to take his place. Tony had met Arnott twice, and was not impressed with what he had seen. Too young, too inexperienced, too eager. But with the sole advantage that, compared with the former governor, he was less likely to collapse into early infirmity. So, for now, Tony had resolved to keep an eye on Michael Brawn, and see what he was up to. And here, in the telephone corridor, Brawn was talking quietly, considering his words, and almost certainly doing something he shouldn't.

Tony strained his ears, flattening himself back out of view. He turned his head and monitored the corridor, eager not to be witnessed eavesdropping. It was lunchtime, and the vast majority of inmates were either eating or waiting to eat. Then a figure approached from the far end, taking his time through the gated double doors. Tony held his radio to his ear, pretending to be in conversation. The man came closer, and Tony recognized him. This is going to be interesting, he thought to himself.

The prisoner was a shade under six feet tall, relatively slender but with wide shoulders which were slightly hunched forward as he walked. Features that otherwise might have been considered fine were blunted by the swell of early bruising. The nose and chin, in particular, had taken a pounding. Despite his injuries, there was something undefeated about him. He had heard from guards and prisoners alike that Reuben Maitland was a former copper who had worked in forensics. Tony wondered how he had come to fall so low, on remand in Pentonville, accused of attempting to kill his wife. He tried and failed to picture the man in front of him in police uniform or in a laboratory coat. That was the problem with prison, Tony believed. Dress all the men in the same casual baggy clothes and you erased the subtle signs that existed on the outside which told you about a man's likely character and background. It was like a deliberate wiping of the slate to enable a whole new set of rules to be established from scratch.

As Tony watched Reuben Maitland walk past, Michael Brawn stood upright, the phone's metal lead dangling at his side, his head rotating almost robotically to follow his progress. Something in his demeanour spoke of unfinished business. Maitland glanced across at Brawn a couple of times, emotionless and unperturbed. Tony was prepared to bet that his heart was beating fast though. What he must have seen in Brawn's eyes wouldn't be difficult to interpret.

Tony knew he should have confiscated the

weapon the previous day. But without back-up, there was no way he was going to risk it. Brawn had been on fire with a psychopathic zeal, and Tony, if he was entirely honest with himself, had felt a crippling tremble of fear. It had been as much as he could do to order him out of the cell. Besides, Tony suspected that a small penknife was neither here nor there. If Michael Brawn really wanted to hurt someone, the lack of a blade would be only a minor inconvenience.

Tony watched Brawn return to his call, his eyes still burning into Maitland's back as he turned at the end of the corridor. Tony pressed himself back in the alcove, listening hard. Brawn still hadn't spotted him. He was drumming his fingers on the rounded metal hood and had resumed his conversation. After a few seconds, Tony heard the sound of the receiver being replaced. Still holding his radio, he waited, praying that Brawn wouldn't walk past him. When he knew he was safe, Tony stepped out. Brawn was near the far end of the passageway, heading in the same direction as Maitland. He wondered for a moment whether he should follow him, but decided against it. He had saved Maitland once already. He would have to fight his own battles from now on.

Tony counted the telephones until he arrived at the one Brawn had been using. The receiver was still warm, and it smelled of aftershave and coffee, a sweet and sour combination that Tony found unsettling. He dialled 0 for an operator, and waited impatiently until it was answered.

'This is Prison Guard Tony Paulers,' he began. 'Who's that?' The operator gave her name, and Tony said, 'Hey, Sandra, how's things? Look, can you do me a small favour? Could you get me the last number dialled on this phone?' Tony took out his small prison notebook, with its matching pencil. 'No, it's nothing official. Just double-checking something.' After a slight delay, the operator gave him the information, and he scribbled it down. 'Got it. And, the last thing, Sandra, remind me what number the prison uses for dialling out?' Tony entered a second number below the first. He thanked her and hung up.

When Tony dialled the first number, it was answered almost immediately.

'*Bargain Pages*.'

This wasn't what Tony had been expecting. 'Oh, hello,' he said. 'I wonder if you could help me?'

'What section are you after?' The voice was on the hard side of female. Tony pictured a middle-aged smoker.

'I'm not sure,' he answered honestly.

'Well, are you buying, selling or meeting people?'

'None. Look, my name is Tony Paulers, and I'm a police officer,' he lied. 'I'm chasing up a call that was made from this phone just a few minutes ago.'

'Oh yeah?'

'I could give you the number.'

There was a barely detectable sigh, a slight hesitation, and Tony knew his luck was in. 'What's the number?' she asked flatly. Tony read the second set of digits to her, a Pentonville line reserved for external prisoner calls, a number he knew to be occasionally and sporadically tapped. He heard the sounds of keyboard activity, and a couple of barely suppressed expletives. 'Just checking the calls-received folder. Yeah, hang on. That's the one. Eleven fifty-eight. Does that sound about right?'

Tony checked his watch. 'Bang on,' he said.

'So, what do you want to know?'

Good question. All he knew was that Brawn had made a call to *Bargain Pages* at a time when the phones were empty.

'What section did the call get put through to?'

'Looks like it went through to Personals.'

'Was an advert placed?'

'And you're from the police, right?'

'Oh yes. Yes I am.'

Another pause, another sigh. 'Well, makes no odds to me. Advert in the Men Seeking Women section. Let's see.' A smoker's cough, a smoker's laugh. '"*The time is ripe. Must act now. Share your feelings with me.*" Can't see him getting a lot of replies out of that one, can you?'

Tony wrote down the words quickly, before he forgot them.

'And that was all?'

'You want more?'

'It's just . . . When does the advert go out?'

'First thing tomorrow. He made the noon deadline by a couple of minutes. So, what station are you from, so I can log this?'

Tony hung up, his mind racing. A distinctly impersonal message in the Personals. Michael Brawn was putting a communication out there for someone. He read the words again. *Must act now. Share your feelings*. What the hell was he up to? he wondered. And what did the message really mean? He tried to figure out how the response would come, whether or not *Bargain Pages* had a phone line to pick up replies. He vowed to call back later and find out.

In the meantime, he picked up the receiver again, once more catching the lingering coffee and aftershave scent of Michael Brawn, almost as though he was still standing there. He checked the corridor was empty, and then he dialled his contact in the Met.

This time, he had something substantial to impart.

22

Reuben stuck to the edge of the corridor. It was safer that way. At least one side of him was protected. Things were going downhill fast, and he needed to be out of prison. Narc's verdict had stayed with him, his jarring Scouse accent lending menace to the prophecy. *You are so in the wrong place. They're going to fucking eat you alive.*

So far, he had been attacked only once by Michael Brawn, but more bloodshed was likely. Other inmates, ones he didn't even recognize, had whistled and jeered at him, or offered specific and gratuitous threats. The prisoner serving his breakfast had made a show of hawking and spitting into his scrambled egg. Reuben had walked over to an empty table and sat alone, and a plastic mug had been thrown across the room at him. Except for exercise periods, Reuben had stayed in his cell, lying on his bed and staring at the wall, wondering and waiting.

But nearly two days had now passed, and it

had got too much. He had to have answers from Sarah before Brawn came after him a second time, or some other psycho caught him in the semen-stinking showers, or his food was contaminated with something more dangerous than phlegm. And the question came to him again: what was Brawn waiting for? The right opportunity? A suitable weapon? The help of another prisoner? The way he had looked at him earlier in the telephone corridor told Reuben that something was imminent. Brawn would not be delaying for long.

As he scraped along the wide hallway, Reuben appreciated that the first three days of his incarceration had been fine. With a mission, and the support of Damian and Cormack, time had passed reasonably quickly. He had rediscovered the routines of his first sentence fifteen years ago, and had eaten, slept and watched TV in synch with the other twelve hundred inmates. Now, however, he was out of step, keeping himself hidden away, the minutes dragging by, cuts and bruises healing with slow reluctance, on guard and unprotected. He could see that his fight training with Stevo had been woefully inadequate. When a lunatic really wanted to hurt you, there wasn't that much you could actually do.

And thoughts of Joshua, pale and in hospital, cannulas in his veins, his blood being scrutinized, white cells being counted, diagnoses being discussed, treatments being debated . . . all of this attacked him with more ferocity than even Michael Brawn had mustered. He was alone and isolated, his son with suspected leukaemia, growing weak as his bodily defences were dismantled from within. Reuben shook his head as he walked. He needed to shout at Sarah down the phone. Hopefully this time Brawn would be nowhere in sight. He had to get Sarah to forget about protocol and procedure and going through the correct channels and just drag him the fuck out of Pentonville. There was no other option. The place was secure as hell. The bars to his window, the lock on his door, the height of the walls, the gates within gates, the cages within cages. Escape was a fantasy perpetuated by films. There was only one way out, and that was through high-level CID intervention.

The corridor widened and Reuben stayed to the right. Ahead and in the middle lay two pool tables, end to end. Reuben passed a guard and nodded. The guard was, he thought, called Tony, the man Cormack and Damian had alerted when they observed Michael Brawn entering his cell. He was early to mid-fifties, Reuben guessed, and looked to have spent most of his life incarcerated. He wondered whether Tony was as institutionalized as the lifers who surrounded him. Tony nodded back, a barely perceptible dip of the head which managed to be polite but not friendly. Reuben thought he detected a small hint of disappointment in Tony's face, but couldn't be sure.

He approached the first table, which was not being used. Seven or eight men were milling about. Reuben sensed that Tony might have been keeping a casual eye on them. He glanced over at the second table. John Ruddock, thick-necked and shaven-headed, was hunched down, ready to play his shot. Damian had told him that Ruddock, the only inmate to shout abuse at Michael Brawn during the Arsenal–United match, was serving time for the murder of two nightclub doormen, and ran a ruthless extortion ring in D Wing. His sidekick and opponent, he had also learned, was Clem Davies, similarly best avoided. Reuben looked away, eager not to catch their eye.

The phone corridor ran through two gated intersections, and into the newer section of the wing. Reuben fingered the phone card in the pocket of his jeans, composing his words to Sarah. As he drew close to the table, Davies, who was standing upright and staring past Reuben, said the barely audible word 'clear'. Reuben tensed. Out of the corner of his eye, he saw John Ruddock straighten, a pool ball in his hand. A dark, fast-moving object whizzed past his face, cracking into the wall and ricocheting off it at speed. Reuben kept walking. Ignore it, he urged himself. A flash of Ruddock's arm and a second ball hurtled at him. Reuben flinched, dropping his left shoulder. The pool ball grazed the surface of his shirt. There was a thump and a cry behind. Collateral damage.

Reuben turned and marched over to Ruddock. Without breaking stride, he picked up a pool cue and swung it, catching him across the head with its thick end. Davies rushed at Reuben and Reuben pulled him on to a punch. A quick-moving form darted round the back. A turbaned prisoner holding a pool ball. Throw this would you, you cunt? He stamped on the prone form of John Ruddock. Two other inmates rushed over to help him, kicking Ruddock in the head. Davies straightened and aimed another blow. The body shape. Watch the body shape. Stevo's words belatedly tracked him down. Reuben stepped into the punch, stifling it, and delivered a sharp uppercut.

Around him, the entire area sparked into uproar. Reuben punched Davies again, the last two days boiling over. The humiliation, the threats, the taunts. He saw the prison guard approach, then back away. Two or three more inmates rushed into the mêlée. Clem Davies caught him on the side of the head. Reuben's ear rang. He shook himself and reached again for the pool cue. Ruddock was struggling to his feet, aiming wild punches at whoever was closest.

The guard blew his whistle repeatedly and urgently as chairs and tables began to fly through the air. An inmate stepped up and punched the guard in the face, knocking his whistle out. Reuben knew things were getting very close to a full-scale riot as he swung at Davies with the cue. Scores being settled in the heat of the battle. Long-held tensions bursting out into the open. Blood pouring from Ruddock's shaven head. Inmates grappling and kicking, using whatever came to hand. Somewhere a bell ringing. Prison guards doubtless struggling into riot gear, their features hidden behind masks, revelling in the heavy poise of metal truncheons, holding them in both hands like baseball bats, ready to swing as they swarmed into the corridor. Reuben caught up in the fight, unable and unwilling to leave, a point needing to be proved to the scumbags who'd tried to damage him. Being punched in the back. Turning round and swiping at a prisoner he didn't recognize. Another plastic chair hurtling through the air, catching someone full-on. Wanting to walk away, but knowing that wasn't possible. That things had gone too far. That any second the hoses would come out and anonymous guards would burst through the corridor swinging their batons at whoever came to hand.

23

Seated opposite the governor, Reuben ran his tongue around the inside of his lip, which was bleeding again. The day's activities had burst the scab, the sweet metallic taste reminding him of Brawn's initial attack. The governor was taking his time, scanning a sheet of paper, letting the silence build. Classic intimidation tactic. Control the quiet and you own the conversation. Reuben let him play at junior psychology. He had been in enough police interviews to know the deal.

The governor opened his packet of cigarettes, and slid one out. He slowly put it to his lips and lit it, blowing smoke through his fingers. Reuben had a sudden urge to snatch the cigarette and stamp on it. But sudden urges, like swinging pool cues, was what had brought him to the governor's office in the first place.

Finally, the governor laid the piece of paper flat and looked up at Reuben. 'When you came to see me, you claimed to be, what was it, an ex-police officer on a covert mission.' His voice was high and pinched, a Home Counties accent.

'Yeah,' Reuben answered.

'Interesting. Because what I've seen of you so far hardly smacks of discipline.' He slanted the piece of paper up again and scanned it. 'A knife confrontation with a fellow prisoner. And then another incident with the same prisoner, in your cell—'

'When he attacked me.'

'Trouble in the dining room. A search which revealed that you'd smuggled certain contraband into the prison. Including, it says here, the scalpel blade used in the initial confrontation.' Another drag, a smoky pause before the punchline. 'You think we *approve* of prisoners smuggling weapons into Pentonville?'

'I guess not,' Reuben muttered.

'And now this. A riot. A long-serving warder in casualty, four inmates in the hospital wing.'

'It was hardly my fault.'

'You deny that you were wielding a pool cue?'

'No.'

'And that you assaulted a number of inmates, including' – he squinted at the names in front of him – 'prisoners Davies, Hussein and Ruddock?'

Reuben remained silent, pleading for calm. All of this was irrelevant. He had to get the hell out. His son needed him.

The governor took a deep, measured drag on

his Marlboro Light and blew the smoke out of the side of his mouth. 'No, I'm sorry, it's time to take action.'

'What are you going to do?'

'Only thing I can. Ship you off to the next rung on the ladder. I don't have the resources to monitor you twenty-four seven.'

'Where?'

'Scrubs.'

'Wormwood Scrubs?'

'They have a room in their Secure Unit.'

'Look, I appreciate that I've forced you into this. But it just isn't like that.' Reuben was desperate. Another prison would raise a whole new series of problems. 'Like I said, I was a CID officer before I transferred to the Forensic Science Service. I ran GeneCrime – you've heard of the unit?'

The governor stared back and shrugged. 'So?'

'I'm here to track a prisoner, to take forensic evidence from him. Now I've done it, and I need to be released. I'm not a criminal.'

'Like you said before. Although there is this, Mr Maitland.'

The governor opened a shallow drawer in his desk and pulled out a slim file. There was a sense of check-mate about his movements which Reuben tried to overlook.

'What is it?'

'Previous arrest record.' He leafed through a few of the fragile pages within. 'Let's have a look.

Possession of cocaine with intent to supply. Three months in Belmarsh.'

Reuben slumped in his seat. The bastard had been digging. 'How did you get that?'

'Wasn't easy, but I have some useful contacts. So you *are* a criminal, in fact, Mr Maitland. And also one who has covered up his identity at some point in the past, in order to work in the force.'

'So at least you know I was in the force.'

'Oh, you were. But now you're not. A covert mission? Don't make me laugh. Where's your evidence? Where's the paperwork? Why have no CID officers come knocking on my door and begged for your release? Shall I tell you?'

'Go on,' Reuben answered flatly.

'Because you're a fantasist, Mr Maitland. Nothing more, nothing less. After our last little chat, I cross-checked. You were sacked by the FSS for gross misconduct. No one I talked to knew where you were any more or what you were up to. None of my contacts in the Met are even aware of a policy for forensics officers entering prisons. Face facts, Mr Maitland. I know what you are and you know what you are.' He made a show of signing the piece of paper in front of him, briskly and irritably, and motioned Reuben to the door. 'Go and pack your stuff. I've booked a van. You're leaving tonight at eight p.m.'

'You're wrong,' Reuben muttered, defeated and powerless in the governor's office.

'And, for the record, don't mess the governor of Scrubs around. He really is the meanest governor in the whole prison system.' He allowed himself a sly smile as he finished his Marlboro Light. 'I look forward to hearing how you two get along.'

24

Reuben checked his watch. He didn't have much time. Things had moved so quickly, from seeing Michael Brawn at the phones, to the fight in the hallway, to being summonsed to the governor. He had just under two hours before they transferred him. Reuben had tried and failed to get through to Sarah. Her mobile was off. Her answerphone told him that she was attending a crime scene. She would be unaware of his movement to Scrubs until he could contact her. And that might take days. Secure Unit prisoners, he was well aware, had to earn luxuries like phone cards.

His second choice, however, was more helpful.

'They've fucked your lab,' Moray said, matter-of-factly.

'Who?' Reuben asked.

'Interesting question,' his partner answered. 'But they were good at it. We thought you might have some suggestions.'

Reuben closed his eyes. He was going to a

different prison, his son was sick and his lab had been done over. This wasn't a great day.

'Look,' he said, 'forget that for now. I need you to do something for me.'

'Name it,' Moray said.

'This is a big one.'

'Go on.'

'In fact, my fat friend, this is *the* big one.'

Moray didn't bother disguising his sigh. 'As I said, big man, name it.'

'And you don't have much time.'

'As in weeks, days or hours?'

'As in minutes.'

'I'm on it. When and where?'

Reuben told him what he knew and hung up. He glanced at his watch again. An hour and fifty-five minutes to pack his meagre possessions and say his goodbyes. An hour and fifty-five minutes to avoid a last-minute beating by Michael Brawn. If there was an up-side to his current situation, at least he would be leaving Brawn behind.

Reuben made his way back to his cell and slumped on the bed. He dozed for a while, then spent a long while staring at the eclectic series of images Narc had chosen to decorate his wall with. There he saw illustrated the conflicted state of mind brought about by incarceration. The pictures of freedom, of nature, of sexual possibility. A mental slide-show of denied opportunity, of self-imposed captivity.

The door opened and Reuben sat up. Narc eyed him almost triumphantly. Reuben realized that he had given Narc a new lease of life over the past week. He had become the copper's cellmate, his notoriety rocketing within the prison, a nobody who had suddenly become a somebody, with information and observations and stories to tell.

'So it's true?' Narc asked, looking down at him. 'You're off?'

''Fraid so.'

'Of course, they're gonna fucking *love* a bizzie in Scrubs.'

'That so?'

'You think this place is bad? I've heard stories about the secure wing would make you want to fucking die than go there. And that's normal prisoners. Not fuck-ups like you.'

Reuben stared up into his beaming face, his almost cheeky expression of joy. 'Narc, shut it.'

Narc changed instantly. 'You threatening me, copper?'

Reuben stood up. He opened his drawer and the clear plastic HMP bag he had been given and started to stuff his clothes into it.

'You threatening me?' Narc sneered again. 'Cos there's about a hundred cons in this wing would like to say goodbye to you properly. All I do is open this door and shout. You want that?'

'Like I said. Just shut your mouth.'

'The trouble with you, you don't know when

you're fucked. I mean, really fucked.'

Reuben grunted. Prison was starting to mess with his mind. He gripped the handle of his bag.

'Right now, people in this wing will be ringing their mates in the Scrubs, telling them there's a smart-arsed copper on the way over tonight, telling 'em what you look like, who you are, what you've done. And you know who's at the head of the fucking queue?'

Reuben tried not to meet his eye. 'Surprise me.'

'Your mate. Michael fucking Brawn.'

Reuben continued to round up his possessions, knowing that he had to stay calm. Out of the corner of his eye, he noted that Narc was visibly gaining in confidence.

'And an educated boy like you, delicate hands, pale eyes, could be very popular over there. Make someone a very nice wife.'

Reuben suddenly snapped. A lifetime of being in control had disappeared in just under a week. He wheeled around and grabbed Narc by the throat, pushing him hard against the wall.

'I've got you a leaving present,' he spat, pulling his fist back.

Narc's triumphalism only seemed to grow. 'At last! The educated man becomes an animal!'

'I'm warning you . . .'

'This is the system you send people into.' Narc was undeterred, despite the imminence of violence. 'And what does prison do?'

'Tell me.'

'It brutalizes you.'

And Reuben saw it. He knew he was right. His father, the rain pouring down, head bowed in the passenger seat, examining his knuckles, raw and wounded. Realizing that a barrier had been put up between them, a gruffness, a sadness, which had never been there before. His father increasingly withdrawn, given to depressions and fits of temper. A different man from the one who had gone in.

'Doesn't matter who you are. If you weren't brutalized before, you fucking are by the time you leave.'

Reuben slackened his grip and turned away. Narc was smiling slyly at him, his point made.

There was a rattle at the door, and then it swung open. Two guards stepped in, ones Reuben had seen in riot gear earlier, removing their helmets after the fun was over, wiping the blood off their metal truncheons with paper towels. One of them brandished a pair of handcuffs and sauntered over to stand uncomfortably close to Reuben.

'Who's been a naughty boy then?' he asked. His breath reeked, sour tobacco on top of wet halitosis.

'And naughty boys have to be punished,' his partner added.

The first guard grabbed Reuben's wrists and fastened the handcuffs tight.

'Time for a trip to hell,' he grinned.

25

The modified Ford Transit was a snug fit, designed to transport a maximum of two or three prisoners at a time. Its blackened windows were barred on the inside, invisible from the street. The driver sat in an enclosed compartment, sealed off in wood and metal, with a drilled plastic hatch at head-height to the side. Reuben sat between the two guards, his manacled hands in his lap, wrists already swelling and sore.

They were, Reuben appreciated, picking their way through quiet North London back-streets. He monitored their progress for a second through the tinted window. Some of the roads were familiar, well-worn routes across an area of the capital he and Moray had come to know well over the last few months. They were only a couple of miles from GeneCrime, not far from Kieran Hobbs' patch, and Judith's house was a handful of junctions away. The pavements were almost empty, the darkness unappealing, the cold keeping people inside. The van passed the Italian café where Moray had dropped him just over a week ago, Sarah Hirst sitting inside, drinking coffee, Michael Brawn's file resting on the table, a faked signature inside. Reuben pulled in a deep breath and held it. The guards fidgeted in their seats, bored and listless. Reuben sighed the air out again and slumped forward, holding his head in his hands.

'That's it,' the first guard said.

'Kiss your arse goodbye,' his partner added.

'Cos from now on, it's gonna belong to someone else.'

Reuben stayed where he was, long second after long second. The guards lost interest in him. The van slowed, the driver working through the gears, the brakes complaining as they reached a junction.

And then there was an almighty thump. A screeching, grinding aftershock of metal contact. A strangled shout from somewhere, maybe the driver. Out of the corner of his eye, Reuben saw events in slow motion. The two guards careering forward like crash test dummies, in flight, ramming into the seats in front. Papers and belongings hanging in the air. Reuben, in the brace position, staying still, his movement subdued by the rear of the next seat. Shaking his head. Standing up and turning to the rear of the van. Walking unsteadily back. The guards slumped in their seats, blood beginning to pour from their faces. Reuben kicking the buckled rear doors. Glass crunching under his feet. A smell of petrol in the air. The doors yielding on the third blow. Outside, Moray jumping down from the cab of a four-tonner which was leaking fluids from the impact. Moray grabbing Reuben's arm and leading him across the empty road to a parked car. Vision still blurred, senses running slow. Buzzing in his ears. Climbing into the car and driving off at speed. Looking back through the side mirror, pale and aching, sight and sound starting to cooperate. Watching the damaged prison van slowly recede into the distance. A guard emerging, bent double and coughing.

Out of prison.

A free man.

1

. . . and back again. He takes a couple of seconds, shakes his head. Gaps, holes, rips in the present tense. No way of knowing whether they're getting more frequent or whether it has been like this for months. Very difficult to tell. But they seem to happen under certain conditions. Excitement and anticipation, at night, when alone. Then during the day, hardly at all.

He glances quickly around, checking nothing has changed. The car park still has just three vehicles in it, the lights of the surgery burning bright behind vertical blinds. He clenches his fists and releases, repeating the move several times.

The noise of a car. He looks over at the entrance, a battered maroon Polo pulling in, spluttering past and parking. A young woman, nineteen or twenty maybe, climbing out. Just yards away. On another occasion, he tells himself. Not tonight. He watches her from behind the thick laurel hedge, her body slender through her coat. Dressed tight, exhibiting what she can despite the temperature. Wanting to be looked at, inviting his stare. But another night, another occasion.

He drags his eyes away, checking his watch. Almost seven p.m. Those general practitioners are putting in the hours. Late surgeries twice a week for office jockeys tied to their desks. He hunches his shoulders and pushes them back, laughing to himself. The police putting in the hours as well. Looking for him. Feeding wildly inaccurate descriptions to the newspapers. Coming up with half-baked theories and notions. And he is right under their noses, has been, all along. No one has twigged anything. It gives you faith. All that staring at computer screens and DNA sequences when a quick look around, a few questions here and there, could do the trick straight away.

There was nothing in the papers about the last one. He checked them all, reading and scanning, page after page, fingers grubby with ink. They obviously hadn't linked it. True, it was different. Could almost have looked accidental. A young woman in a red top lying on the pavement, having fallen and hit her head after a night out. But it had left him hungry. Being denied something has that effect. A missed opportunity. A reckless attack that didn't go as planned. The one that got away. He wonders whether she survived the cold, lying on the empty street, bleeding from her head, and suspects she didn't. He smiles to himself, the answer coming to him. If she had, the police would have tried to link it.

Somewhere a car alarm screams for a few seconds, before being terminated. It is cold, but not as bad as it has been recently. He guesses it is three or four degrees, about the temperature of a drink in the fridge. For a second, he wonders whether a chilled can of Coke would just feel normal if he drank it now. It's all relative, after all. How things relate to each other. How events are linked. How compounds interact. How you deal with those interactions.

Negative feedback, that was the problem. The doctor told him that. Although she'd said a lot of things. More long names and clinical conditions. What were her exact words? It increases the desire but inhibits the performance. Like alcohol or something. But what did alcohol ever do for you, apart from make you thirsty and sluggish? For a doctor, her knowledge was laughable. Two-dimensional textbook stuff. This alleviates this, but may cause this. This is associated with this, but rarely this. This interferes with this, and shouldn't be used with this.

But this, this is the stuff, this is life, proper life, as it is designed to be lived. Not scraping by, office hours, tired and bruised, weak and enfeebled, never quite catching up, never really being who you wanted to be, repressed and suppressed, unable to fight, just taking it from your corporation, your boss, your partner and your kids, a bloated punchbag, there for the kicking, waiting in the warm air of a doctor's surgery at seven p.m., praying to fuck that they'll put you on antidepressants.

But it is not enough simply to survive. You must exist. And you must demonstrate your power of existence. And if one part of your power is denied you, is lost as a by-product of who you are and what you do, you must find another way. A more gratifying way. A more permanent way. A way that shows the low-lifes and reprobates surrounding you that you are more alive than the rest of them put together.

An old man hobbles across the car park to his car, and makes a meal of pulling out and driving away. His exhaust gases stay in the air after he has gone, wafting through the cold, still car park. Seconds after he disappears, the young female returns to the safety of her Polo, a prescription in her hand. She leaves briskly, no seatbelt, tyres squealing slightly. He glances around. Just two vehicles left now. Nice ones, noticeably smarter than the patients'. One with four-wheel drive, the other Scandinavian and sleek.

A light in the top left of the three-storey building goes out. He reaches into his pocket and takes out a small plastic bag. Inside are two vinyl gloves, transparently thin and lightly powdered. He pictures her taking hers off as he puts his on. He is careful, not touching the outside of the gloves, wriggling into them as he has observed and practised again and again. The plastic bag is folded up and zipped into the inside pocket of his jacket. He pulls out a woollen balaclava and rolls it down over his face.

High heels, echoing along the alleyway. He is breathing hard through the coarse material, wet, excited breaths. And then he sees her.

He knows this one will be different. Away from the usual area. No point in dumping her in the Thames. Besides, it will keep those CID boys and girls busy. This is far too early in the evening to be driving around. And the plush upholstery could do without the blood. Just do it here. She will understand.

She approaches. Tired and relieved. A heavy black case with her. Fishing in her coat pocket for her car keys. Pushing the button, a flash of indicators on the four by four. Smaller than the one he drives, he notes, stepping out, staying in the shadows, skirting round. She pulls open the rear passenger door and slides her case across the seat. And he is there. Behind her. Gloved hands around her neck. Doesn't even have time to cry out. Babbling incoherent words through her crushed windpipe. He allows her to rotate a little, to see him. The shock in her eyes. But she is a doctor. Surely she knows about these things, and what to expect? With one hand pulverizing her trachea, he uses the other to lift his balaclava. Face to face. Red cheeks, eyes frozen wide, mouth in a silent scream.

Still alive. Just. He knows she will be thinking three minutes. Two words burned into her suspended consciousness. Three minutes of oxygen starvation before permanent brain damage.

He has a quick glance around. No one. He senses the rising panic in her movements. The tensing, then the thrashing, stiff and flailing, unnatural jolting of the limbs, jerky actions through suddenly engorged muscles. He rips her coat off her. 'Look at me now and tell me I'm impotent,' he grunts. Her terror is turning him on. She knows that three minutes is not a long period of time. He pulls the balaclava back down, and unzips his trousers. 'Call this erectile dysfunction?' The condom is already on. He lets her see it, allows her to make the leap, to understand what is going to happen to her. He thinks he detects it in her face. Revulsion amid the shock and the horror.

He squeezes harder, the soft cartilage of her neck yielding, windpipe and blood vessels closing. She is showing the first signs. Her three minutes are almost up. He pushes her into the back seat, so she is lying partially down. As he waits for it to end, patiently watching the colour ebb, the life slip away, he realizes that although it started out random, now there almost feels to be a pattern. He wonders whether it is always like that. Just like life. You drift into things, follow them where they take you, end up going in directions you had never thought about.

He releases his grip. The doctor, with her mocking manner and unsympathetic words, doesn't move. He opens her legs, knowing that after this one, the next is already sorted.

A female from GeneCrime, the forensics unit in Euston.

And not just any female.

2

Moray eased the car to a halt in the parking bay of the Children's Hospital. A large sign read 'No Waiting'. Reuben, stiffening up after the prison van impact, rubbed his neck and glanced up at the building. It was modern and new, all glass and steel, guaranteed to look awful in fifteen years' time. Moray killed the engine and swivelled in his seat to face him.

'You sure?' he asked. 'You've only just broken out.'

'And now I'm breaking in.'

Moray pulled a pair of bolt cutters from the side compartment of his door. 'Here, let me see those things.'

Reuben placed his hands on the steering wheel, which was still damp from Moray's grip. He knew the risk his partner had just taken on his behalf.

'Thanks,' he said.

'I haven't got them off yet.'

'I mean for the rescue.'

'Ach, it was wild. Wouldn't have missed it.'

Moray continued to work on Reuben's handcuffs, testing successive regions of the metal for hardness and ease of access, squeezing the handles of the bolt cutters together and then relaxing them again. Reuben watched him as he battled. He seemed to be getting fatter, if anything, and if Reuben didn't know better, he would have mistaken him for a lazy slob. But lazy slobs didn't rush out and hire commercial vehicles at short notice and slam them into prison vans, let alone steal cars and secrete them at pre-determined points. He had asked a lot of Moray – too much, in fact, for most – but he had planned it all and carried it off in less than two hours. Truly, despite his size, there was even more to Moray than met the eye.

Between grunts of effort, Moray said, 'As tactics go, this isn't the best.'

'It'll be fine. They won't think of looking here yet.'

Moray released the left-hand manacle, and using the same technique on the other, quickly broke through. 'There you go.' He took the various pieces of metal and glanced up at the front of the building. 'I managed to get hold of her, finally. She should be inside main reception, waiting for you.'

'Thanks,' Reuben said again, rubbing his wrists. 'What are you going to do?'

'I'll wipe the car clean and ditch it. Meet you by the entrance.'

Reuben smiled gratefully at Moray and climbed quickly out of the car. This was no time to be congratulating each other. He walked briskly to the rotating doors, a bitter wind rushing straight through his jumper. Hot air churned out to meet him as he entered. He was wary, glancing about, taking in the two security guards behind the front desk, the profusion of fake plants and vending machines, the concerned parents pacing about, the general air of sad and efficient ill health.

DCI Sarah Hirst was sitting on a plastic chair reading a magazine. She stood up as she spotted Reuben and walked straight over. Against the paleness of her blouse, Reuben sensed a flush of anger in her face.

'This isn't good,' she said, up close. 'On so many levels, this isn't good.'

'It's a fuck of a lot better than where I was before.'

'I mean, what the hell were you thinking?'

'That I was going to spend the rest of my days being buggered in Wormwood Scrubs.'

'But I could have got you out.'

'It was taking too long.'

'I thought I explained. I was making progress. Gently pulling strings. It would have happened in a couple of days, max.'

There was something in Sarah's eyes that suggested she didn't wholeheartedly believe what she was saying.

'By which time I would have been in a different prison.'

'But still—'

'Look, Sarah, my son is ill and getting iller. Plus, someone's smashed up my lab, and I need to know who. I'm not blaming you for the difficulties involved in getting a disgraced ex-copper out of a prison he wasn't officially in, it's just that time is of the essence.'

'This isn't good,' Sarah repeated, almost to herself. 'Come on, let's walk and talk.'

She guided Reuben through a set of double doors and up two flights of stairs. The corridors, like Pentonville's, like GeneCrime's, were low-ceilinged and strip-lit, with neutral colours and little warmth. Sarah turned to Reuben as she walked, her shoulders relaxing a touch, her face gaining a small degree of compassion.

'So, how was it?' she asked.

'Every bit as good as you might imagine.'

'And Michael Brawn?'

'Nailed. I guess this is where things start making sense.'

'Yeah.' Sarah gave him a once-over with her pale blue eyes and long dark lashes. 'Jeez, you look rough. And you could have smartened yourself up a bit.'

'I'll be fine. The plainclothes look.' Reuben glanced doubtfully down at his trousers and trainers. 'Besides, you think you can spot the difference between a con and a cop just by their clothes?'

'Generally, yes,' Sarah answered with a smile. 'Here we are.'

They came to a halt outside a door marked 'Acute Ward 4'. Sarah reached forward and pressed the intercom button. Reuben suddenly felt nervous. Until this moment, he had barely stopped. From his cell, into the van, into Moray's car and through the hospital. Now, standing still and picturing what he was about to see, Reuben inhaled a cold, deep breath, which seemed to drop like liquid nitrogen into the pit of his stomach.

Sarah pushed her mouth up to the speaker of the intercom and pressed the button again.

'Hello? This is Detective Chief Inspector Sarah Hirst. I called earlier.'

The door clicked, electromagnetic contacts moving apart. Sarah and Reuben pushed through. Inside, the ward was decked out in luminous colours. It had been Disneyfied, with approximately drawn cartoon characters having fun across the walls. Within a few paces, they were met by a nurse. Filipino, Reuben guessed, or possibly Malaysian.

'Can I help you?' she asked.

Sarah swiftly pulled her warrant card out of the front pocket of her trousers, as if she was about to start shooting. 'DCI Sarah Hirst,' she said. 'And this is DI' – Sarah glanced unsurely at Reuben, and then at the wall they were facing – 'Michael Mouse.'

Reuben nodded, his eyes wide at the name.

'The father of your patient Joshua Maitland has recently escaped from prison,' Sarah continued. 'We're concerned he might try to get access to his son. Myself and DI Mouse would like to have a look around, if that's OK. Maybe talk to one or two staff?'

The nurse remained impassive. 'He's over there – bed six.'

She turned and pointed towards a curtained-off section where the ward opened out, a new profusion of cartoon characters desperately trying to bring a sense of fun to acute childhood illness. Reuben walked slowly towards the veiled area of beds, excitement and nervousness fighting in his stomach.

'*Mouse?*' he whispered tersely to Sarah.

'It's all I could think of at short notice. And you're lucky it wasn't Donald fucking Duck.' She stopped, keeping her distance. 'You go in, I'll chat to the staff. But you've only got a few moments.'

Reuben steadied himself, swaying slightly on his feet, his eyes closed. Helplessness, fear, worry, love and sadness surged through him in consecutive waves. He listened for a moment to see if Lucy was there, then pulled back the curtain and stepped inside.

Joshua was sleeping on his front, his light brown hair ruffled, a tube intruding into his nose. Eighteen months old and beginning to lengthen, his arms and legs seemingly longer already than the last time. Reuben realized with shock that he was losing weight. Toddlers should be chubby and rounded, all puppy fat and soft, bowed limbs. Joshua, however, was getting thin. He must never have noticed it before, but here, naked except for a nappy, his sheets wriggled out of, there were sharp angles and prominent ribs. He bent down and kissed his hair, running his fingers over Joshua's skin, fighting his emotions, trying not to cry.

'You hang on in there, little fella,' he whispered, pulling the yellow sheets over Joshua and composing himself. 'Your daddy's going to do everything he can.'

Reuben reached over to the far side of the bed and grabbed the metal clipboard hanging there. He scanned Joshua's medical notes, flicking through the four pages of blood results, sodium levels, fluid pHs, white cell counts, temperatures and case notes. Seven words in large black capitals dominated the final page: 'Acute Lymphocytic Leukaemia. Scheduled chemo. Donor negative'.

Reuben screwed his eyes up. 'Just give me another day and a half,' he muttered, stroking Joshua's hair. 'Daddy's got to sort some nasty people out. And then I'll be back, and no one will be able to touch us.'

Joshua remained still, his breathing slow and regular, immersed in the dead sleep of children. Reuben replaced the notes and kissed his son again, this time on the shoulder. His skin was hot and smelled of the pure, innocent, undiluted love that cuts right through you and stops you breathing for a second. Truly, he thought, his face bent over Joshua's skin, the scent of a woman was a weak sensation in comparison. He stood up slowly, lingering in the close presence of his son.

'And then we'll be together,' he whispered. 'You and me. Fit and well. Happy ever after.'

The curtain was pulled back and Sarah poked her head through.

'Sorry,' she said, 'but it's time to go. I'll get my car, see you at the front.'

Reuben hesitated a long couple of minutes, burning the image of Joshua into his retinas, before reluctantly walking out. He returned the curtain to its position of privacy and headed sadly away, through the ward, along the hospital corridors and into the biting cold, silence hanging over him like a premonition.

3

The traffic was sparse, and Sarah carved through what little there was with her customary confidence. Reuben remained quiet, thinking things through, trying to catch up with the events of the last eight hours. The implications of his actions were starting to make themselves clear to him, and when Sarah began to talk, she merely voiced his misgivings.

'You're going to be high priority,' she said, taking a roundabout at speed.

'I can see that,' he responded, sliding around the back seat, Moray blocking most of his view through the windscreen.

'For all the force knows, you're a dangerous criminal who has murdered his wife, escaped prison, and is now on the run.'

'But you can sort it?'

'Wrong. I can influence specific officers here and there, but I can't protect you from a manhunt.'

'You can put the word out, though?'

'Look, even if I do break cover and tell my commanding officers what has happened, they're still going to want to see you brought to account. Since you and Brains here' – she jerked her thumb dismissively in Moray's direction – 'decided to smash up a prison van and injure its guards.'

Moray shrugged, unconcerned. 'Omelettes and eggs, Sarah. Omelettes and eggs.'

'No, your best bet is to lie very low. Let me do what I can do.'

'Where have I heard that before?'

Sarah's features hardened, her concentration fixed on the road. 'Fuck off, Reuben. You think it's easy, in the middle of a serial killer investigation, to be running round helping you out?'

Reuben stared forlornly through the rear passenger window, thoughts of Joshua darting in and out of his head. The words acute lymphocytic leukaemia played themselves over and over, bringing images of irregular white blood cells slowly dying in veins, arteries and capillaries and not being replaced.

'I guess not,' he said.

'The papers will be swarming all over you by now.'

'Yeah, I guess they will. Look, we're here. Take the next left and pull over.'

Sarah glanced in the rear-view, maybe to check on traffic, maybe to check on her passenger. She screeched across a junction and pulled smartly up.

With the engine idling, she swivelled in her seat to look at Reuben.

'You sure about this?'

'You can't lie much lower than here.'

'How long's it been since you saw him?'

'Year or so.'

Reuben pulled out his mobile phone and dialled a number. After a few seconds, he said, 'Aaron? It's me. I'm here. Right.' He flipped the phone shut, sad and slow in his movements, a resignation weighing him down. 'Said he'll be straight out,' he muttered.

Reuben monitored the street. Victorian terraces with white frontages. Cars parked nose to tail on both sides. The occasional tree, leafless and shivering in the cold. Streetlamps with their heads bowed in defeat. An OK place to live if you couldn't afford anything better.

Out of an alleyway between two blocks of houses a man dressed in baggy clothes appeared.

'We're on,' Reuben said.

Moray pointed at the man. 'That him? Jeez, he's the spitting image.'

'You know many twins who aren't?' Reuben asked.

'It's still uncanny,' Sarah said. 'Apart from the long blond ponytail, of course. What's he up to these days?'

'I dread to think,' Reuben answered, climbing out of the back seat. 'And I probably shouldn't say in front of a serving officer. I'll see you both later. And, Sarah?'

'What?'

'You know.'

Sarah raised her eyebrows at him. 'I know.'

Reuben shut the car door, then Sarah revved the engine and pulled away at speed.

Reuben ran his eyes around his brother's front room. He had often pictured what Aaron's squat would be like, and he could see now that he had been wildly inaccurate. Apart from the scruffiness of the furniture, and the slowly dying carpet, the room was like most of the country's living rooms: more cluttered than it might be, less clean than it should be, and with almost everything pointing in the direction of the television. A wooden table in the knocked-through dining room supported a mass of books and CDs, and looked never to have been used for its intended purpose. A couple of plants were forlornly wilting in the dry central heating. Full ashtrays and empty cans colonized any remaining surfaces. As squats went, though, this was fairly comfortable.

Aaron was silent, sitting on the sofa, rolling a joint. Reuben knew that too many things had happened for them to be entirely comfortable in each other's company. He saw his arrest file in the governor of Pentonville's office; he'd been stopped with over fifty grams of cocaine in

Aaron's car, and taken the blame for his brother to save him breaking his parole. Reuben realized he still hadn't truly forgiven Aaron. And there were other factors. The way they had ruthlessly explored opposing sides of the law; Aaron's decision to stay at home while Reuben went to university; the death of their father, a habitual and petty criminal whom Reuben had begun to distance himself from during his early years in CID. All in all, the family had fallen apart, Reuben and his mother on one side, Aaron and his father on the other. Legal and illegal, law making and law breaking.

Aaron lit the joint. After several deep drags, he offered it over. Reuben took it from him and pulled on it, stale air rushing through the papery structure, bitter smoke filling his mouth and entering his lungs. He held his breath for a couple of seconds, and as he exhaled, he said, 'You hear about Jeremy Accoutey?'

'Who didn't?'

'I kind of got involved in it, just before everything went pear-shaped.'

'In what way involved?'

'Forensic testing of his wife's lover.'

'Fuck.'

'Yeah.'

The image had stayed with him. A petite blonde with a large exit wound in her scalp.

'The tabloids had a field-day with the fact she

had a boyfriend. You know, *Footballers' Wives* and all that. And you were in on it?'

Reuben took another drag and passed the joint back to his brother. A warm tiredness began to wash through him, and he sensed a sudden weight to his skull.

'It's not something I want to talk about,' he said. 'People died in nasty circumstances, indirectly related to my activities.'

'Shit. That's scary stuff.'

'That's not the half of it. I needed to get away for a bit, and someone was very interested in a prisoner in Pentonville. Twenty-five grand interested. Only things didn't go as smoothly as I'd anticipated.'

'How?'

'I got myself in a very bad situation, isolated in Pentonville, people knowing my background.'

'And now you're on the run.'

'I guess so.'

Reuben swigged from a can of beer and massaged his aching neck. Generally, he preferred stimulants. Dope slowed you down, made you sluggish and unfocused. Alcohol didn't help either. But for some reason the two depressants mixed together seemed to warm him up and melt the tension that had been squeezing his insides for several days.

'And you?' he asked, moving the conversation on.

'Same old,' Aaron answered.

'No girlfriend?'

'Women aren't exactly my strong point.'

Aaron handed the joint to Reuben again.

'But what are you up to?'

Aaron flashed his half joking, half serious expression. Reuben knew it well. He had an almost identical one. 'That depends whether you're going to arrest me.'

Reuben sighed through a long, smoky exhalation. 'As I'm growing tired of explaining lately, I'm no longer a copper. So?'

'The odd car here and there. Spot of five-fingered discount. Small-time stuff.'

Casting his eyes around the squat, Reuben was suddenly struck by the realization that Aaron was thirty-eight, and still living outside the bounds of normal society. Squatting was, he believed, something you eventually grew out of, like spinning your wheels or doing handbrake turns.

'Hell, Aaron,' he said, handing the joint back, 'what happened to you?'

'What do you mean?'

'I mean, look at this squat. Look at you. Where did everything go wrong?'

Aaron dragged deep into the joint, his brow furrowed. 'You're the geneticist. You tell me.'

'You can't blame Dad for everything.'

'OK, let's start with genes and environment.' Aaron sucked back some beer and pulled on the remnant of the joint before poking it through the hole of the can, triggering a loud and angry hiss. 'Nature and nurture. What other blame is there? Either way, Dad's fucked.'

'But you're thirty-eight—'

'Exactly the same age as you. And where's *your* cosy life, suburban house, cushy job and faithful wife?'

Reuben glanced down at the carpet, with its small army of burn holes, noting how they were clustered towards one end of the sofa. He remained silent, biting his tongue.

'I may be a loser, Reuben, but I'm one by choice.'

'What are you saying?'

'That you, on the other hand, have fucked everything up without even trying.'

Aaron let his words do their damage, monitoring his brother keenly, antagonism and resentment burning bright across his features. Reuben stared into the pale green eyes of the face on the opposite sofa. The mirror image that belied a lifetime of perplexing differences. The same, but not the same.

'And now you come to me with the fucking police on your trail. Glass houses, brother.'

Reuben stood up, stinging and angry, the sedation evaporating. Pacing into the kitchen, fists clenched. Old scores unsettled. Rivalries resurfacing. Stitched-up wounds tearing themselves back open. Knowing that no one can cut you more precisely than your brother. Knowing that twin brothers are even more adept at it than normal siblings. And knowing that Aaron was right.

4

The usual bony hardness of Judith's hug was missing. Today, she was softer somehow, more gentle, less vigorous. Reuben wondered momentarily whether something was wrong, whether she was having second thoughts about working for him. He wouldn't blame her. A critical member of the GeneCrime forensics squad, his former loyal deputy, she was in an impossible position most of the time. But as she stepped back, he could see in her eyes that she was genuinely pleased to see him again, and this gave him some hope.

Judith walked over to sit on the sofa, and Reuben perched on a lab stool.

'So, the prisoner returns,' she said.

Reuben frowned. 'Something like that.'

When he had first entered the lab, he had been amazed at how little damage there was. The only visible signs were a front door that didn't close quite as well, and a faint smell of spilled chemicals.

Judith and Moray had obviously been busy, sweeping up Eppendorfs, replacing boxes, tidying everything to its usual state of uncontaminated efficiency. If Reuben was a gambling man, he would have bet that this was more down to Judith's efforts than Moray's.

'You think the police know about this place?' Reuben asked.

'Only Sarah. And she's OK.'

'No one at GeneCrime has mentioned its whereabouts?'

Reuben watched Judith intently. Not because he didn't trust her, just for any sign of hesitation or uncertainty. He needed to know that she was one hundred per cent convinced.

'Not to me.'

'You're sure you've never been followed?'

'As sure as I can be. You ride a scooter, you keep a very close eye on the cars around you.'

'I guess so.'

'Colm reckons it's a death-trap.'

'But a very pretty one.'

'Yeah, well.' Judith treated him to one of her distant half smiles. Reuben chose to overlook the fact that the dreamy look gave her an enigmatic beauty, an unknowable and demure distance. 'I guess you shouldn't spend too much time here if you can help it,' she said.

'Just a few hours, that's all. But you're right, we'd both better only be here for the minimum time we can. Even between procedures, we should bail out. I've made myself – what did Abner say a few days back?'

'Vulnerable.'

'That's the fella. Made myself vulnerable. Half the city's police hunting me down. Violent escape from custody. They're going to be coming for me, Judith. And we can't ignore the possibility that someone in the force knows where the lab is.'

'As well as Sarah.'

'You trust her, though?'

'You know what she's like. You've observed what she's capable of at work. It's not that she's dishonest . . .'

'What?'

'Well, to make something her own. To solve a case. To advance her career. We've both seen it. Trampling on people, messing them around, not being entirely open and honest.'

Reuben was silent. Beneath her occasional dreaminess, he knew that Judith's cogs turned with remarkable speed and accuracy. Sarah had been involved in all the events of the last week. Was it possible, Reuben wondered, that he was somehow serving Sarah's needs? Why the sudden offer to help with Michael Brawn? How did she gain such quick access to his arrest details, not to mention his DNA specimens? How had she managed to insert Reuben into Pentonville so easily, and then be so apparently powerless to pull him out again? What did Sarah have to gain, especially in the middle of a large manhunt? Reuben turned these thoughts over in his mind for a few moments. Sarah and Michael Brawn. How could she have stood to profit from Reuben's involvement? He scratched his face irritably, knowing that he was wasting time, and sensing once again that the longer he spent in the lab the more exposed he was.

Glancing around again at the tidied surfaces, he felt once more a rush of relief that Judith had understood his cryptic instructions, as she'd confirmed earlier on the phone.

'You got the sample?' he asked.

Judith patted her handbag. 'In here.'

'Smart girl. What about the rest?'

'Systematically ruined. Thawed and destroyed.'

Judith ran her eyes around the floor of the lab, as if pointing out to Reuben the last resting places of the thousands of DNA specimens which had died in the heat. Reuben saw the wasted hours of work, the irreplaceable samples of psychopaths and sociopaths, the meticulously labelled and inventoried investigations leaking away on a laboratory floor. Of course, some of them were just aliquots of specimens that were safely housed in the temperature-controlled store rooms of GeneCrime. But others, ones that Judith had taken in a rush, were all that remained. That was the obvious risk of taking fragile items out of their laboratories and into the wider world.

And you could have all the back-ups and security doors you wanted, but if someone truly wanted to destroy something then that's what would happen. Reuben found it suddenly perverse that DNA was happy at body temperature for a whole lifetime, yet extracted and placed at room temperature it fell apart in hours.

'Fuckers,' he said, mainly to himself.

Judith pulled Reuben's letter, still bearing the Pentonville postmark, out of her bag. It was sealed in clingfilm inside a clear plastic freezer bag, surrounded by frozen peas which were showing signs of thawing.

'This wasn't a bunch of kids breaking in,' she said. 'Most of the equipment was left untouched. But the samples . . .'

'What did Moray have to say?'

'He had a theory that the intruders may have left the very thing they were after. Letting it thaw out with the rest. Undetectable.'

'Well I have another theory.' Reuben took the freezer bag from Judith. 'They didn't find what they were looking for. Because this is it here, hidden among these few words.'

'Short and sweet. Who says the art of letter writing is dead?'

Reuben opened the bag, extracted the letter and held it up to the light, which was bright and blinding, the halogen bulbs of the industrial fittings almost piercing the thin prison writing paper.

'It all depends on the message you're trying to put across,' he muttered. 'And how good the recipient is at understanding.'

'I'll take that as a compliment.'

Reuben pushed his fingers into a pair of vinyl gloves and cut the corners of the letter into a tube, pipetting a series of fluids on top.

'Let's give these a while to soak,' he said, 'and then we'll begin.' He turned to Judith. 'We should get out of here. See you back here in three hours?'

Judith picked up her gloves and helmet, and Reuben followed her out, locking the damaged front door and making sure that no one was watching them.

5

'Look, just because you're on one side and I'm on the other, doesn't mean it has to be like this.'

'And what side are you on?'

Reuben shrugged, looking down at his empty hands. The conversation had been slow and awkward, with long, tense gaps. The question surprised him. Aaron saw the law as an arbitrary concept, a logical fallacy used to repress the timid and the weak. A discussion of its boundaries suggested he might finally be taking the idea seriously.

Reuben opened a fresh can of beer, pausing to think. The last week had reminded him that the law wasn't something you could just cross for fun. Every time you passed from one side to the other, you left a little piece of yourself. You ended up blurred. Bits of you abandoned on either side for ever. That's how Reuben felt, sitting in Aaron's squat – blurred, distributed, diluted, two identities, neither of which he was particularly comfortable with. And seated next to his brother, their elbows almost touching, tickly arm hairs occasionally meeting, Reuben sensed that Aaron saw it as well. But Michael Jeremy Brawn had had something that Reuben needed. His blood, his skin, his hair, anything would have done. Small fragments of a psychopath that Reuben had stolen and mailed back to his lab. Crossing from the legal to the illegal and back again.

'It's complicated,' he answered.

'Only this Jeremy Accoutey thing disturbs me.'

'Probably not as much as it does me.'

'I mean, what you did was illegal, right? Taking DNA from a woman without her knowledge, testing it, and then giving her husband the results. Not to mention stealing a sample from the team physio in a public place.'

Reuben shrugged.

'And those actions precipitate a murder. Then you enter prison under a false identity, before crashing your way out. So I ask you again, brother, what side of the law are you actually on?'

Reuben rubbed his face. He flashed through the undercover missions he had carried out during his career and after it. Pretending to be bad when he was good, lying to superior police officers to get jobs done, feeding criminals small truths to gain bigger ones. Reuben sensed his brother – sitting on the same tatty sofa, facing the same direction, avoiding direct eye contact – waiting for an answer.

'Difficult to tell these days,' he replied quietly. 'But the aim is always good.'

'Helping footballers kill their wives?'

'Channelling money into investigations that no one else carries out. Abuses of power. Misuse of technology. Tracking criminals the police can't touch. I mean, we put a CID officer away last year who had tampered with the DNA evidence of four nationwide manhunts. Cases collapsed, the real perpetrators remained at large, the victims were denied justice. A police officer taking short-cuts to manipulate convictions. It's murky, at times, but what we're trying to do . . .'

Reuben petered out, ill at ease, appreciating that things had become complicated. The TV was off, but he found himself staring at it, as if it would spring to life at any moment and save them from each other's company.

'OK. What you do these days is up to you. It's past events that really fuck me off.'

'Like what?' Reuben asked, suddenly angry and defensive and trying to hide it.

'Dad.'

'What?'

'When he went down the final time, you virtually cut him off.'

Reuben scratched his hair, fingernails finding skin through the crew-cut. 'What could I do? I pleaded with him to clean his act up. For his sake, for Mum's sake, for everyone's sake. I was a copper, catching the bad guys. And there's my own father, a career criminal, in and out of prison.' Saying the words out loud made his actions sound harsh and predetermined. Trading his father for his career. But it hadn't been like that. 'It was beginning to undermine me. The implications, the scenarios. "Squad, let me introduce you to Dr Reuben Maitland, lead forensics officer, section head of GeneCrime. Oh yeah, and son of a crook."'

Aaron sniffed. 'Didn't mean you had to abandon him.'

'I didn't. I just . . . stepped back a bit.'

'And let me pick up the pieces.'

'You make it sound like I wanted that.'

Aaron lit up, and pointedly kept the joint to himself.

'You're saying you didn't?'

'Of course not, Aaron. It just happened. Like families do. Things falling apart, people moving away, circumstances changing.' Reuben drank from his can, hoping the cold lager could extinguish the searing frustration. 'And I've more than served my debt to you, brother. You remember?'

Aaron blew a long stream of smoke into the living-room air. 'Yeah,' he answered eventually. 'Whatever.'

A fidgety silence closed in on them, oppressive and uncomfortable. Arm hairs touched again briefly, sending shivers through Reuben's body.

'Look, I've got to get back to the lab.'

'And then what?'

'It'll all die down as soon as I've run the lab test. Then I'll sort Joshua out, which is all that really matters at this moment. After that, I'll go back to my life, and you . . . well, you've got my number.'

Reuben stood up, draining his can and finding an empty surface to stack it. He double-checked his watch. Moray would be waiting, an anonymous car, a couple of streets away, the engine running.

'I guess this is it.'

Aaron got up slowly, his eyes narrow, his brow furrowed. For a second their eyes met, pale green to pale green, the same but different, staring at each other across a divide Reuben knew would never be bridged. He felt like hugging his brother, grabbing his arms and wrapping them around him, the twins reunited at last after years of sporadic contact and icy bitterness. Instead he turned and walked towards the door.

Aaron's voice stopped him. 'Here,' he said, 'take this with you. See what they're saying about you out there.'

He handed his brother a copy of the London *Evening Standard*. Reuben took it, the final contact between them.

'Bye,' Reuben muttered.

'You made page three,' Aaron said.

Reuben opened and closed the front door without looking back. The documentaries, the articles, the all-pervasive notions of society assailed him as he walked. Identical twins and spooky coincidences, being separated at birth and then discovering they had identical lives with identical partners and identical children. Twins who still lived together in their mid-eighties. Mirror-image brothers and sisters who dressed alike and finished each other's sentences. Pairs even their parents couldn't tell apart. Having the same thoughts, the same tastes, the same wants and needs. Being the other half of something which looked and felt exactly the way you did. And then there was Aaron. Perplexing, diffident, too clever for his own good, itching powder on Reuben's conscience. The closest person to him genetically, but seemingly the furthest away from him.

Reuben opened the paper at page three, annoyed and depressed in equal measure, Aaron once again having climbed under his skin, delved into the past and found conflict. Moray, a hundred metres away, flashed the lights of a car Reuben didn't recognize. But Reuben had seen something. Below the quarter-page article headlined MURDER SUSPECT FLEES SCENE OF CRASH. Underneath the byline proclaiming 'Former leading forensic scientist is hunted by police'. A smaller sister-article, bold font, just two short columns. The headline, PENTONVILLE INMATE FOUND HANGED.

'Fuck,' Reuben said to himself. 'Fuck.'

He scanned the article, double-checking the

name, making sure. This changed things. An idea was beginning to form. An idea he didn't like the feeling of. He pulled out his phone and dialled a number, his thumb quick across the keys, rising excitement and fear in his chest.

6

Sarah Hirst had been sitting with her hands cradling her head for the best part of ten minutes. The skin of her cheeks was pulled tightly back, her eyes fully open, her brow creased with a series of fine parallel wrinkles. DI Charlie Baker, his arms straight, continued to lean against her desk, giving her the impression that he was looking down at her. As he talked, a myriad of scenarios jumped and danced around inside her skull. She saw names and descriptions and wounds and motives and statements and violence and desperation. But mostly she saw empty database files; sequencing traces with depressingly irregular peaks; patchy stretches of coloured bands on profile read-outs; neutral blue DNA swabs; empty agarose gels; matching patterns which failed to match.

The fucker, she had recently decided, knew about forensics. He understood how to keep out of trouble. He appreciated how to avoid contaminating a body. And then Reuben's notion came to her again as it had done almost hourly since he mentioned it a week or so ago: whoever had put Michael Brawn away was still inside GeneCrime. And if they had doctored one investigation, what was to say they wouldn't alter others? Maybe they were tampering with evidence right now, swapping samples or muddying the truth while she sat and stared into the middle distance. It was only a hunch, with no facts to support it, but it was beginning to eat away at her with unsettling regularity.

Sarah glanced up at DI Baker. He was talking rapidly, his mouth barely seeming to open behind his sharply trimmed beard, his eyes dark and distant, as if he was visualizing something as he spoke. Sarah saw him as a threat. Twice recently she had seen him coming out of the secretary's office which buffered Robert Abner from the rest of GeneCrime. Prolonged contact with the big man was generally an event reserved for bollockings, sackings or promotions. She wondered momentarily whether Charlie was after her job, but quickly dismissed the notion. Commander Abner understood policing too well to mess his staff around in the middle of what could be their largest case for years.

Charlie was now quiet, staring down at her. Sarah lifted her head from the support of her hands and mumbled, 'Sorry, Charlie, you lost me.'

Charlie narrowed his eyes. 'I was saying, Path are still a bit fifty fifty about it. The other four women are definites, including Joanne Harringdon, killed, we think, in the car park of her surgery. All held down and strangled first, raped second. But Laura Beckman doesn't fit the pattern.'

'Except that she was killed late at night, on her own, half a mile from the Thames.'

'Half of London is half a mile from the Thames. Besides, Path can't confirm it as a murder yet.'

'Smashed cranium, broken ribs?'

'She could have been knocked down. Fallen off something. Whatever. No witnesses, just a young woman bleeding from the back of the head into the pavement. There's no way we can link it.'

Sarah sighed, showing Charlie without saying it that she was prepared to back down. 'OK. But if it's not our man, and it's not an RTA, then the likelihood is that we have another killer on the loose.'

'Nah, I don't see it,' Charlie said.

'Why not?'

'I just don't. No way.'

Sarah looked up at him. He could be irritatingly dismissive at times, a slamming of the door which endeared him to few. Before DCI Phil Kemp's sacking and arrest, Charlie had been one of his closest allies. Relatively new to GeneCrime, and making very few friends, but always there when Phil needed the support of a CID stalwart. And it was now, for the first time, staring into his eyes, seeing the mix of defiance, contempt and detachment which always seemed to dwell there, that the words came to her. *You're up to something, Charlie. You're involved in something you shouldn't be.* It was intuitive, illogical and without foundation, but it struck her with all the certainty of a stone-cold fact.

Charlie turned his head, glanced around the office, bit into his top lip through his beard. 'Either way,' he continued, 'it's irrelevant. It's unlikely to be our man, there's nothing to link him, and we need to be focused on the job at hand.'

Sarah flashed him a short, insincere smile. I've got my eye on you, she said to herself as she asked, 'So what now?'

'Fuck knows. Four definites in the morgue. We keep looking at what we've got, hope he makes a mistake.'

'Great.'

'Maybe he'll stop. Take a break.'

Sarah grimaced. 'I don't know. Our sick friend seems to have got a taste for it.'

'Yeah, well.' Charlie straightened, stretching, pushing his shoulders back. As he did so, his jumper lifted, revealing a mat of dark hair across his belly which Sarah tried to ignore, the thick primal blackness unsettling her. 'Look, I'm going to get Mina Ali and some of the forensics section together with senior CID later this afternoon. Kick some ideas about. You OK with that?'

Sarah nodded. Technically, it was her job to coordinate the disparate factions of GeneCrime, to make sure Forensics were updating CID, that Pathology was talking to SOCOs, to help IT and Technical Support integrate all areas of evidence collection. But she let it go. There were more important issues than protocol.

The phone rang, and Sarah picked it up.

'DCI Hirst,' she said.

'Sarah, it's me.'

Sarah looked at DI Baker, cupping the mouthpiece with her hand. 'Charlie, I need some privacy.'

Charlie sucked his cheeks in, lingering, taking his time. 'Now?' he asked.

'Now,' Sarah repeated. She watched her colleague leave the room, slowly and defiantly, and waited until the door was closed before putting her mouth to the receiver. 'What is it?'

Traffic noises and Reuben's breathing. Maybe the rustle of a newspaper held close to the phone. He sounded excitable, his words quick and direct.

'I don't know if I should tell you this, but what the hell. There's no one else.'

'What is it?'

'Damian Nightley has committed suicide, just weeks before his release date.'

'Nightley? Ten years for weapons trafficking, right?'

'Yeah. What can you find out about suicides in Pentonville?'

'In case you'd forgotten, I'm in the middle of a murder hunt here.'

Reuben sighed. 'Sorry. Any news?'

'Look, your advice on what we think was the first death – you know, the one with the oil and algae issues – helped, but not enough to say one way or another.'

'What's the problem?'

'We're getting DNA but it's more degraded than we'd hoped. And because we're still having difficulty purifying it, it's proving unreliable.'

'Is it good enough for matching?'

'We've got partial matches to four hundred profiles. But as you know, we don't deal in the currency of partial matches. So we're playing a waiting game. Testing and re-testing, and almost hoping he strikes again and makes a mistake.'

'So you'll help me?'

'I didn't say that.'

There was the sound of a car door slamming, and the background noise instantly disappeared.

'Look,' Reuben said, 'I've got a fair idea Nightley's suicide may turn out to be important.'

'Well it had better be, Dr Maitland. I'll get back to you later.'

Sarah replaced the receiver. She held her head in her hands again, feeling the weight, annoyed at the distraction, but interested anyway. Nightley had flagged up a couple of interesting issues when she'd run his file for Reuben. Contacts and acquaintances across the capital. And now he was dead. An alarm bell was ringing somewhere inside her but she couldn't quite track it down. Damian Nightley. Where else had she heard that name?

Sarah turned to her computer and began pulling records and requesting files, suddenly alive and animated, a new urge surging through her.

7

Reuben tried to make his troubles disappear into the protocols of forensic detection. The fact that Joshua was ill and fading fast; that the police had launched a manhunt for him; that Damian Nightley had committed suicide; that his lab had recently been ransacked; that a footballer and his wife were dead. All of these gnawing, seeping wounds were soothed by his utter concentration on the task at hand. It had to be done quickly, and done well.

Reuben pulsed Michael Brawn's dissolved DNA specimen in the noisy bench-top centrifuge, decanted off its supernatant and suspended the remaining pellet in 70 per cent ethanol. He labelled a series of sterile tubes, flicked them open and added minute quantities of colourless fluids to each. He then vortexed the tubes and set a hot-block to fifty-five degrees. The methods and procedures were imprinted in his brain, each step coming to him as he needed it, as if he was running a mental finger down a vastly elongated recipe. Amid the volumes, temperatures, ratios and molarities, thoughts of his son remained controlled and disciplined. By imposing order on one part of his consciousness, Reuben kept the rest in check as well.

While a PCR machine hummed through a pre-amplification step, Reuben pulled his gloves off and scratched his face, before biting into a sandwich. He was acutely aware that being in the laboratory was risky. It was more than possible that its location was known to CID. But Reuben needed to grasp the answer. Who the hell was Michael Brawn? Solve this and he could go straight to Commander Abner, who would be able to use the information to validate Reuben's mission and call off the manhunt. But without Michael Brawn, Reuben would be detained, maybe shipped on to Wormwood Scrubs, locked up while his claims were investigated, testimonies taken, evidence considered. All of which would take precious days, even weeks – time that Joshua didn't have. He swallowed his sandwich and pulled on a fresh pair of gloves. Until he could take his answer to Robert Abner, everything else was just about manageable, an unavoidable limbo from which he would soon be emerging.

Three hours into the process, Judith entered. 'Got a few hours between shifts,' she said, swapping her leather jacket for a cotton lab coat and joining Reuben at the bench. Just like the old days, Reuben thought with a smile. Side by side in the GeneCrime laboratory, pipetting samples and solving cases, Reuben occasionally cracking jokes, Judith quiet between bursts of laughter. They loaded the sequencer together, Reuben injecting the sample, Judith the controls. While it ran, they tidied up, scrubbing the bench with paper towels, returning reagents to freezers and restoring solutions to shelves.

Reuben then sat at the bench and doodled on a piece of paper, his drawing skills rusty, the faces he conjured rough and uneven. Throughout his career it had been his habit to restore some dignity to the dead, people who had met obscene and violent ends, penetrated, hacked and mutilated. He would paint them late at night in his study, picturing them as they were before the atrocity that drained them away. It had been therapeutic, a way of coming down from the adrenalin rush of each crime scene. He resolved to take up painting again. His hobby had bitten the dust of late, and Reuben suspected he knew why. Every face was haunted by the fact that he was somehow caught up in the death.

'You got access to the national database?' Judith asked, bringing him round.

'Sarah's ID and password.'

'You could have used mine.'

Reuben glanced down at the sketch he had

started. Lesley Accoutey, as she had appeared in the papers, blonde and effervescent, a toothy smile, a sparkle in her eye.

'Sarah reckoned it would be better this way.'

'Are we done?'

'Looks like it.' Reuben examined the sequence profile, scanning through the multicoloured lines on the screen. 'Quality fine, no bands maxing out, background low. A reasonable profile. You ready to find out who Michael Brawn really is?'

'When you are.'

Reuben copied the sequence file on to a memory stick, and inserted it into the networked PC which sat on a small wooden desk in the corner. He typed some commands, copy-pasted the information into a text-box and pressed a button on the keyboard to begin the database search. The computer murmured into life, its hard drive buzzing and crackling, galloping through the database and grabbing for similarities.

'What do you reckon, Rube?' Judith asked.

'Dead cert we find something. A match to someone already on file. And then we start closing in on whoever in GeneCrime put him away.'

'Why so confident?'

'Why else use a fake profile? I think we're about to find some surprises about Michael Brawn.'

Judith made herself comfortable on the couch. 'OK. I'm going to bet we draw a blank.'

'How come?'

'Because science is like that. Ten negatives for every positive.'

'The usual stake? Loser buys the beers?'

Judith hesitated for a second, before answering, 'Deal.'

Reuben and Judith remained silent, sensing the technology of detection, the algorithms and pattern matching, the invisible binary digits, the plundering of datasets held somewhere else, on ethereal servers, insubstantial and otherworldly, intangible processes they knew were happening but which they barely understood, the only evidence of any action the noise of a computer hard drive vibrating and humming. Human time passing slowly while unimaginably vast amounts of communication raced back and forth along telephone cables.

An insistent beeping broke the silence. Reuben and Judith rushed over to the computer. On the screen was a list of numbers and names and, by one of them, a small button marked 'Update'. Reuben glanced at his watch.

'Twenty minutes,' he announced. 'The searches are getting slower.'

'The databases are getting longer,' Judith said, through an elongated yawn.

'Well, moment-of-truth time. You ready to buy the drinks?'

Judith nodded. Reuben pressed the 'Update' icon, then double-clicked on a tab marked 'Classified'.

After a few seconds of rapidly scanning the information, he let out a slow, extended whistle.

'Last known address, telephone number, criminal record, the lot.'

'Is it unequivocal?'

''Fraid so. Stats of ten to the minus seven. You'd better have been paid this month.'

'Any chance of taking it out of my earnings?'

Reuben didn't answer. He was scrolling through records, arrest dates, background info, physical characteristics.

'And haven't we been a busy boy, Mr Cowley?' he said quietly.

'Who's Mr Cowley?'

'Michael Brawn. His real name. False genetic identity, false criminal identity. Michael Brawn doesn't exist.'

'No? What else does it say?'

'Here, I'll print you a copy. You pass a postbox on the way?'

'Several.'

Reuben pressed 'Print', and the printer hummed into life.

'If I pop this in an envelope, could you send it to the PO box number on the last note? Give the man his twenty-five grand's worth.'

'And then what?'

Reuben quickly jotted some of the details down on a yellow Post-It note and slotted it in his back pocket. As he wrote, his brow furrowed in concentration, and he said, 'The search gets called off and I can actually go and help my son.'

'How so?'

'We now have evidence that Michael Brawn has been using a false identity. Sarah will be able to use this to convince the Met that I was in Pentonville on police business, and that I don't need to be recaptured.'

Judith picked a copy off the printer and scanned it. 'Guess so. But this is interesting. A false profile gets him a false ID, which is convenient given the seriousness of his previous offences. Still doesn't add up though. Juries aren't allowed to know previous. Why go to the trouble of changing your whole identity, genetic and otherwise?'

'I guess that's the whole point.'

'Anyway, I've got to dash. Late for the next shift. It's brutal at the moment. You seen my helmet?'

'On the sofa.'

'I'd leave my head if it wasn't screwed on.'

'In which case you wouldn't need your helmet.'

Judith scanned the lab. 'I'm bound to have forgotten something.'

'As long as you post the letter.'

Judith picked up the envelope, slotted it into her upturned helmet, smiled briefly at Reuben and left the lab. Reuben barely noticed. He was absorbed, his eyes wide, sucking all the information in, the possibilities and the meanings. He stared into the screen, a summary view of Ian Cowley's previous convictions. Numbers and figures which told short, staccato truths: Agg Burglary, Conv. July 5 1988, 1yr susp 6mo. ABH/GBH, Conv. Aug 12 1989, 9mo. Manslaughter, Conv. Jan 23 1990, 6yr 6mo. ABH, Conv. March 19 1996, 2yr. Attmptd Murder, Conv. Feb 27 1999, 5yr 8mo. Reuben rubbed his face, thinking. He glanced at the newspaper that had announced his escape from the prison van. Dots were beginning to join, the truth starting to dawn.

Behind him, there were a couple of light taps on the door. He walked over, brow furrowed, swimming in ideas and notions.

'Judith,' he said, pulling the door open, 'I think I know the truth about Michael Brawn.'

He looked up. He was standing in the doorway, pushing a gun into Reuben's chest.

'Do you now?' he asked.

Reuben stared into the face, shocked, disbelieving, his brain fighting for sense. For a second he was blank. He looked into the eyes, cold and dark and wide. The name and the face suddenly merged.

Michael Brawn forced Reuben back into the lab and kicked the door shut.

'Should be interesting,' he said.

'But . . .'

Brawn gestured with the pistol for Reuben to sit down.

'Right, plod,' he spat. 'Let's sort a few things out. Man to man.'

8

Lucy Maitland loitered in front of a hospital vending machine, surveying its rows of multi-coloured snacks and chocolate bars, each assigned its own unique number and letter. She bent forward until her forehead pressed against the cold, isolating glass, her eyes screwed tightly shut. She needed sustenance – a cheap carbohydrate high or a greasy saturated fullness – but she had never quite trusted this type of machine. It reminded her of being six or seven, of school trips to the local swimming baths, of standing forlornly looking up, her money swallowed, the spiral not quite turning far enough, the bar of chocolate clinging sadly to its metal corkscrew, unavailable and unobtainable. Slowly, Lucy reached out and gripped the sides of the vending machine as if she wanted to shake everything loose, violently and desperately, a cascade of long-denied promises thudding into the empty catch-tray. She held still for a second, swamped by recollections, her own childhood summed up for her by chocolate bars that refused to drop.

A throat cleared behind her and she straightened, swivelling her head. The house officer, three or four years out of medical school, still slightly unsure of himself. She brought her body round to face him, looked him straight in the eye, saw his barely suppressed nervousness.

'What?' she asked.

'I just wondered whether you're ready to come back in,' he said.

Lucy frowned. Of course she wasn't ready to go back in, to stand beside the bed of her only child, who was failing by the day. She had needed to escape the gaudy colours, the hospitals-can-be-fun cartoon characters on the walls, the stifling air of cheerful efficiency, and had found herself irresistibly drawn to the vending machine. But the medic had already begun to walk, less a question than a request, and Lucy reluctantly followed him.

The house officer was positioned at the end of Joshua's bed, pretending to flick through a brown file marked Joshua Fraser Maitland. Lucy took her time. When she arrived, he glanced up from the notes with what Lucy took to be practised concern. For a moment, her legs trembled beneath her suit trousers, and her stomach seemed to leap and fall in the same instant. It was bad news. More bad news. She glanced down at Joshua, serene and sedated, lying on his back, blinking slow, heavy blinks.

Lucy regained her composure and asked, 'What is it now?', crushing the tremor from her voice, the uncertainty from her manner.

'As you know, Mrs Maitland, the latest batch of tests won't be back until tomorrow.'

'And?'

'Well, whatever the results, there is something we need to do with increased urgency.'

'Which is?' Short sentences, clipped words, holding it all together.

'What we need to find now is a marrow donor.'

'As you said before.'

'Ah yes.' The house officer opened the file again, giving the impression he was simply reading out facts and figures rather than having to impart the news himself. 'The blood tests from yesterday are back. And what they show is not terribly great news. The HLA types suggest that you are not, in fact, a good donor match for your son.'

'Fuck,' Lucy whispered. 'But I'm the mother. Surely—'

'It doesn't always work like that. In the meantime, we're trawling the databases, searching for potential matches.' He lifted his head, tried to engage with her. 'There is, however, another route.'

'Go on.'

'What about the father? Could he help?'

'There are issues there. Difficult, complicated issues . . .' Lucy Maitland stared down at Joshua, uncertainty and panic in her moist eyes, unable to fight it any longer, clumsy, sticky words getting caught in her throat. 'I told the other doctor the day before yesterday . . .' She pulled out a tissue and blew her nose, grinding to a halt.

'Right.' The young medic returned his attention to the file. 'The consultant will see you tomorrow morning, go through all the options with you. We're expecting the final test results by then.' He snapped Joshua's notes shut. 'OK?' There was the briefest of smiles before he walked quickly away, leaning into the corner of the corridor, tilting his whole body as if it would help him go round faster, escaping the awkward scene of a mother and her dying infant.

Lucy watched him go. She blew her nose again. Her stomach rumbled and she glanced through the double doors in the direction of the vending machine. She hesitated for a second, before taking out her mobile, dialling Reuben's number and waiting impatiently for him to answer.

9

Reuben knew enough about firearms to recognize that the gun was genuine. It was a revolver popular on both sides of the law. Its snub nose stared back at him, bleak and unforgiving, absolute and inarguable. This is what death looks like, Reuben thought. The black promise of the barrel of a gun.

Michael Brawn was smarter than before. A pale shirt poked out of the top of his black leather jacket, and his charcoal jeans had been recently ironed. The straight lines and folds lent him a further severity that had been lacking in prison. He continued to stare down at Reuben, gun arm steady, face waxen and unemotional.

Reuben fidgeted on the sofa. How the fuck had this happened? Michael Brawn escaping as well. Tracking him down and entering the lab. And all because Reuben had DNA-profiled him. A multitude of notions continued to swarm around inside his head, insect ideas that buzzed and teemed and crawled and stung. A cacophony of thrumming thoughts in a still and silent lab.

Brawn took a step closer. 'It's time for you to end your life,' he said. 'Get on your feet.'

Reuben stood up, scanning the lab, desperate for anything that could help him. Brawn wasn't fucking about. He had tried to kill him once already. Reuben knew that without intervention he would have died in his cell. And now there would be no help, no Damian or Cormack to alert anyone, no guard rushing in to save him. Just Reuben and a psychopath in a small series of rooms in a virtually empty building.

Brawn nudged a lab stool until it lay underneath the light fittings bolted into the ceiling. He pulled a plastic bag-tie out of his jacket pocket.

'Hands behind your back,' he instructed, 'wrists together.'

Reuben did as he was told. Brawn walked behind him, confident, in control, showing that if it came down to it, he would simply put a bullet through him. He wrapped the slim, stiff band around Reuben's wrists, slotted it through its aperture and tugged. He was obviously in no hurry. Reuben's forearms still had some movement, which he was happy about. Then Brawn grabbed the end and pulled hard, Reuben's wrists forced together, the tie burning into his skin. Brawn paced back round in front of him, reached into his other jacket pocket and pulled out a length of rope. Keeping the gun on Reuben, he climbed on to the stool and looped the rope around the brushed steel lighting attachment. He made a crude noose, yanking it to test its strength, the pistol momentarily under his arm. Then he jumped down and bared his teeth at Reuben.

'Poked your fucking nose in, didn't you?'

'How did you find me?'

'I know a lot more about you than you know about me.'

'I doubt it,' Reuben countered.

Brawn snorted, his nostrils flaring. 'I've got contacts, informants in the right places. If you know who to follow you can find a lot of people. Just like I found you.'

'So now what?'

'I finish what I started in Pentonville.' Brawn nodded his pistol at the stool. 'Now you have a go.'

Reuben stepped forward, taking his time, hoping to fuck he could think his way out of what was about to happen. For a second he longed for the police to come and find him, the manhunt actually getting the scent at last, tracking him down like it had failed to do so far. But Reuben knew he had been careful, staying in Aaron's squat, Moray driving him around in anonymous cars and staying out of sight of the police, Sarah keeping her mouth shut. As he climbed on to the stool, Reuben realized that Michael Brawn was watching him intently, his features almost gleeful. He had done this before.

Reuben's mobile vibrated silently in his pocket six or seven times. A call from who knew who that would never be answered. Brawn motioned with his pistol for Reuben to place the noose around his neck. He poked his head through it.

'You see how this thing works. Now, lean forward and tighten the fucker. That's it.'

Reuben did as he was told. Experience told him there was no benefit to antagonizing Brawn. What he had to do instead was talk his way out, sidetrack him, shift the balance. He recalled his early years in CID, learning about negotiating, looking for a route out. It was his only option. He knew Brawn wouldn't hesitate to fill him full of bullets. Reuben had to take the longest course he could that gave him time to think.

'Come on, Ian,' he said, feeling the rope against his skin, 'we don't need to do this.'

'Oh yes we do.'

'It is Ian, isn't it?'

'We're getting to know each other now, are we?' Brawn grinned up at him. 'Coppers. All the fucking same.'

'Don't you want to know what I've discovered about you? Your real name, and what you've been up to?'

'I'll have a look at your computer. While you're swinging.'

'But you escaped from Pentonville?'

Michael Brawn gave a gruff half laugh. 'You really don't know fuck all, do you?' He stepped one pace closer. 'None of this. What's going on. You know fucking nothing.' With his right leg, he measured up for a kick of the lab stool. 'And you never will.'

Reuben stared frantically around the lab. At the shelves beside him. At the scalpel lying on the bench. At the glass bottles on the side. One jolt of the stool and it was all over. A three-foot drop. Maybe enough to snap his neck. If not, a slow few minutes of strangulation, Brawn leaning against the bench and lighting a cigarette, smoking it down as Reuben thrashed away. He glanced up at the light fittings, bolted into the joists above, knowing they would hold his weight. Reuben had salvaged them from a gutted factory to give the lab the harsh white light it thrived on. He had never pictured himself hanging from them.

Brawn was sizing the stool up again. Reuben scanned the room with growing desperation.

'OK, tell me then. What is it I don't know?'

'Goodbye, copper,' Brawn growled, stepping forward.

Reuben swung his left leg round to the nearest shelf, aiming a kick, dislodging empty bottles. Brawn lifted his right leg up, bent at the knee. Reuben lashed out again, more solutions raining down on to the floor. Brawn kicked the stool hard, jolting Reuben back. He tottered forward, rocking on the balls of his feet. Fall off and he was dead. He regained his balance, and aimed his foot a third time.

Brawn steadied himself. Knocking a stool from under a fourteen-stone man needed the right amount of force. Reuben noted the split second of hesitation. His shoe crashed into the large, heavy cylinder of liquid nitrogen on the shelf beside him. It lurched and fell, its lid coming off, fluid cascading out, litres of volatility splashing over Michael Brawn's left arm and surging on to the floor, the metal drum knocking him off balance. Brawn slipped and went down with it, into a hissing, fizzing pool of liquid nitrogen vaporizing and lifting the floor tiles.

A second of silence, of nothingness. Reuben fighting to stay upright, Brawn on his back, staring at his hand lying in the fluid. Standing up. Dropping his gun. Then screaming. Brawn holding his arm in shock. Fingers whitening and glaciating. Reuben wriggling out of the noose, jumping down, picking up the scalpel and using it to cut his tie. Freeing his hands and grabbing the gun.

Still screaming, Michael Brawn lunged for him. Reuben smashed the pistol butt into his injured hand. An icy cracking, shattering sound. The tips of two frozen fingers snapping off, rolling on to the bench. No blood, just dead white flesh. Bone poking out, stripped of its tissue. Pointed, skeletal metatarsals under the harsh strip lighting. Brawn falling back to the floor clutching at his broken hand.

Reuben suspected he wouldn't be subdued for long. He picked up the lab phone and dialled the number of the one man who could help him, keeping the gun trained firmly on Michael Brawn.

10

Commander Robert Abner entered the lab warily and gestured towards the sofa. 'Do you mind?' he asked.

Reuben shrugged. 'Who's the back-up?'

Robert Abner raised his eyebrows in turn at the two men who had come in with him. 'Detective Superintendent Cumali Kyriacou, and Assistant Chief Constable James Truman.'

Both of them stepped forward and shook hands with Reuben. Senior brass. Thickset men who had seen it all before and had managed to come out the other side, as if their solid frames were resistant to the hurt and the damage.

'I know back-up is usually a little younger and fitter than this,' DS Kyriacou said with a smile, patting his plump abdomen, 'but we were with Commander Abner when you requested help.'

'And a bit of action is a rare treat these days,' Truman acknowledged, almost sadly.

Reuben glanced at Michael Brawn, who was silent and pale, shivering on the floor, hunched over, his ruined hand wrapped up in a lab coat. He held on to the gun regardless. Brawn was injured, but a wounded psychopath was an unpredictable entity.

'So this is the lab,' Commander Abner said. He cast his eyes around. 'Nice set-up.'

'Thanks.'

'And this, I guess, is the prisoner. Want to tell me what's going on, Reuben?'

'I called you because I think you're the one person who can sort everything out.'

'Let's see what I can do.'

'OK, here we go.' Reuben closed his eyes, getting everything straight in his head. 'Using the alias Michael Brawn, Ian Cowley here was sent down ten or eleven months ago for sexual misdemeanour. Pleaded guilty, among other things, to the attempted rape of a woman on a train. GeneCrime were called in to tie some of the strands together. However, for reasons I won't go into now, his DNA evidence – our GeneCrime evidence – was faked. Michael Brawn couldn't possibly have carried out those attacks.'

'You're saying our proof was bent?'

'Looks that way.'

Abner's forehead creased, thin folds of skin darting upwards. 'Not good. What else have you found out?'

Reuben glanced over at Brawn. 'He's been passing messages out of Pentonville.'

'Pertaining to what?'

'I don't know. He used some sort of code which I couldn't crack.'

Brawn stared over at him, brooding, the colour returning to his cheeks, slowly sitting up, a Dobermann beginning to take interest in an intruder.

'That's everything you know?'

'More or less.'

'And now you've nailed him. I guess we should call off the hunt, eh?'

Commander Abner nodded at DS Kyriacou.

'I'll phone it in,' the DS answered. 'We'll still need to clear it with Scotland Yard, and we'll have to do some face-to-faces. But yes, let's get the ball rolling.'

'I've got to see my son without being arrested and taken back to Pentonville.'

'As DS Kyriacou says, a few hours and we'll have it all wrapped up.' Abner scratched the short grey hair at the base of his neck. He cleared his throat, looking down at the floor. 'I heard about your lad. Sarah told me. She's been bloody evasive recently. But it's a bad business, Reuben.'

'He's beginning to get critical. Got a message from my ex-wife twenty minutes ago. She sounded pretty . . .' Reuben had been about to say the word 'hysterical', but let it go. 'Days and hours, that's all. I need to go and see if I'm a donor match so they can begin the chemo.'

Robert Abner glanced over at Brawn, who stared

back with palpable hatred. Reuben noted that Brawn was now poised, on one knee, ready.

'As I say, we'll sort something. Maybe get you a car down to the hospital.'

'Thanks.'

Commander Abner stood up and stretched, his large shoulders rising and falling inside his uniform. 'OK. Pass me the gun. I'll bag it up and send it for ballistics. You never know what stories it might tell.'

Reuben checked Michael Brawn one final time. Surely even Brawn wasn't going to try to attack four men, one of whom was armed. But he looked like he fancied his chances. Reuben gave his former boss the pistol quickly and handle-first, so that Brawn could be instantly subdued if necessary.

Commander Abner examined the gun with deft expertise, checking the safety catch and the number of rounds in the chamber. 'Nice weapon,' he muttered, walking over to Michael Brawn. 'Well, Mr Brawn, or Mr Cowley, or whoever you are. I think we have a few issues to sort out, don't you?'

Michael Brawn stared intensely up at the commander.

Robert Abner turned to his colleagues. 'Either of you have any questions for Mr Brawn?'

Both silently shook their heads.

Commander Abner then pushed the gun into Michael Brawn's chest. 'Sweet dreams, Mr Cowley,' he whispered. And then he pulled the trigger.

A loud, dull shot, muffled by proximity, boomed through the lab. Michael Brawn's body lurched back from the impact, and fell on its side. He groaned, breathing desperately through empty lungs, dying into the floor.

Reuben stared at Commander Abner in horror. The two senior officers remained silent and still, unmoved by what they had witnessed.

Robert Abner turned to Reuben. 'Let's go for a ride,' he said, a thin wisp of smoke trailing from the barrel. 'Turn your phone off and slide it into a drawer. You're not going to be needing it where we're going.'

Reuben sat in the front seat. DS Kyriacou drove. Commander Abner was in the rear, behind the driver, and next to ACC Truman. Reuben glanced quickly back, Commander Abner in his peripheral vision. A head-fuck was in the process of happening, a reappraisal of everything he believed, a spin cycle of feelings and truths and assumptions.

The Volvo D90 sped through a junction, joined a wider carriageway, negotiated a couple of roundabouts, cruised along an overpass in a built-up area, and merged effortlessly into the fast lane of the motorway. They passed knots of traffic, coagulated around slow, sticky lorries. Inside, the car was silent. From time to time DS Kyriacou licked his lips, a quick flick of the tongue, out and in. Reuben noted its sharpness, pointed and triangular, a dry pinkness to it.

Gradually, tarmac and concrete became trees and grass. Reuben stared out of the window, his breath on the glass. Most of life, he appreciated, we don't know the truth. We think we do, but we don't. And when something startling happens, that's the reason it hits us so hard. Because it is a yes or no, a black or white, a definitive certainty. And those moments are rare. Reuben's guts rumbled like thunder. He knew that a lot of his convictions about his existence were about to be challenged.

Before long they were driving on a bumpy stone surface bordered by tall hedges, and then they emerged into a clearing. DS Kyriacou skidded the car to a halt, tyres slewing across gravel. The three senior officers climbed out. Commander Abner opened Reuben's door and pointed with the gun. A few metres ahead lay a small concrete outbuilding, windowless and solid, with a rusted metal door. Reuben was escorted towards it. Robert Abner stopped just in front of the door and turned to him.

'Before you go in, I want you to think about something, Reuben. You know how leukaemia works. Your son has a cancer deep in his bones which is eating his immune system as we speak. Chomp. There goes another white blood cell. Munch. There goes another macrophage. Not that a toddler has much of an immune system to start with. You're the only person who can help your son now. And yet, and yet . . .'

Commander Abner ushered him forward with the gun.

'When he has succumbed to the cancer in his bones, we'll be back for you. You will die in the knowledge that you failed to save your only flesh and blood. We'll be monitoring Joshua's lack of progress keenly.'

'You sent me the notes, didn't you?'

'What notes?'

'About Michael Brawn. So you could get to him.'

'Way off beam.' Abner looked confused, his brow ruffled for a second. 'I'm the last person who would have sent you after Mr Brawn.'

'Then why kill him?'

'Do you think a man like Michael Brawn deserves to walk the streets?'

Reuben was consumed with questions, but he knew that Abner would tolerate his curiosity only so far.

'And, shit. It was you who forced me out of GeneCrime. Not Phil Kemp, not anyone else. It was you.'

'Nudged, Reuben, not forced. You made yourself vulnerable. And when you do that, you deserve all you get.' Abner flushed, losing patience. 'Now, inside. It's time to face your own personal hell.'

Reuben turned away from Commander Abner.

A kick from one of the senior officers plunged him into the darkness. Off balance, he fell to his knees. The door slammed shut and a key turned. A shaft of light poked between the roof and the top of the walls. There was a damp, human smell that Reuben didn't want to think about. Feet crunched over the gravel and car doors slammed. The large unmarked Volvo pulled away, kicking up stones.

Reuben got to his feet and rushed at the door, shoulder-first. It didn't budge. Leaning against it, he saw Joshua, pasty and listless, his eyes closed, eyelids so pale that a multitude of tiny blood vessels showed through. A rapid and insubstantial heartbeat leaving a faint green trace on a monitor. A nurse replacing the saline bag feeding his cannula. He saw days of confinement, of isolation, of helplessness and starvation. He knew that he had fucked everything up and that there was no way of fixing it.

Reuben pounded the door, over and over, slamming his fists into it, possessed and crazed, imprisoned again, the words of Robert Abner echoing in the din, knowing that he had it right.

This was his own personal hell.

11

The Thames Rapist. Who the hell had christened him that? Judith wondered, head squeezed tight inside her helmet. Rapist implied sex and nothing else. This was a killer, pure and simple. She zipped up her jacket and pulled on her gloves. The rape seemed to Judith almost incidental – a violent act among other more violent acts.

She pictured Commander Robert Abner writing names on a whiteboard, his crony Charlie Baker nodding his hairy face, or shaking his bearded chops. The still air, the squeak of marker pen cutting right through them. The Riverbank Murderer. The Thames Killer. The Riverbank Rapist. Give him a name, a tag for the papers. Something catchy, something that will lodge in people's minds. A moniker that tells a story all by itself. She thought of the pride involved in being the one to name the serial killer, to attach a sobriquet which would burn bright long after the details of the crimes or the victims' names had faded into obscurity. The

Yorkshire Ripper. The M69 Rapist. The Boston Strangler.

Judith blew air out of the side of her mouth, feeling it warm the foam interior of her helmet. Abner had stuck to the rules. First the geographical location, then the act. The killer had been christened, and now he was more than just a man: he was a public figure, with an appended personality, a household name. Finally, he existed. But still it rankled with her that the word 'rapist' had been chosen, as if rape was somehow more serious than having your windpipe crushed or your neck broken or your ribs snapped.

Judith pressed the start button on her scooter, the small engine catching first time. She remembered how, a few days before, Charlie Baker had approached her in the car park, asking her about Reuben and Moray. Something about him that always suggested more, his words only half of the meaning. Like there were two messages, one verbal, the other secreted in his tone, or in his body language, or in the way he looked at you.

Judith climbed on, revved hard and pulled off, the scooter almost sliding from under her. She was tired, her eyes blurred, her hands aching against the vibration of the handlebars. They were closing in, that's what she heard more and more. But Judith knew the final couple of pieces of evidence were still not there. Hundreds of potential suspects, but nothing to separate them. Vague vehicle makes, conflicting witness statements, poor physical descriptions, scant forensics. Without a positive DNA they were drowning in circumstantial quicksand. And despite double shifts and extra personnel, GeneCrime, the country's leading forensics unit, was basically going nowhere.

Judith swung out of the car park and down the long straight ramp, letting the engine hold her speed back. That was the problem with forensics. You could be as advanced as you wanted but if your killer knew what he was doing, or had some basic knowledge of science or police procedure, you were in trouble. Test after test was coming back negative, or unreadable, or outside the confidence intervals. Stretching the limits of detection to the point where they became inaccurate or unrepeatable. False positives, potential breakthroughs which couldn't be corroborated. It was hell. Mina Ali barking orders, feeling the strain. Bernie Harrison, Simon Jankowski and the others coming up with ideas, new approaches and incisive strategies, but no tangible data. The first body proving difficult, DNA possibly there, but of low quality and partially degraded. Reuben's suggestions helping, although the raw material remaining elusive in terms of progress. A whole unit tearing its hair out as women were raped and murdered and dumped in the river. Maybe Reuben was right after all. Maybe the killer had protection from within.

The air that penetrated the gap in her visor was cool and refreshing. At least it was real air, not the filtered, sterilized and recirculated version which permeated the laboratories of GeneCrime. Judith stopped at some traffic lights and raised her visor, breathing it in. There was no other traffic, sensible people in normal jobs having long since turned out their bedroom lights and drifted off to sleep.

The image caught Judith for a second as the red light burned into her. Colm would be asleep, spread across most of the bed, maybe snoring quietly to himself. He was still acting strangely, and Judith found the thought of not having to talk to him when she got home a positive one. Surely pregnancy was something that most men dealt with better than this. She sighed. And with the thought of her husband, and the red light pointlessly barring her progress to an empty road, Judith also thought briefly of Reuben. He had failed to return her last three calls. This was unusual. He was generally the sort of person who got back to you no matter what. Even in prison.

Judith revved the engine, hoping to wake the light up. Really, she should just jump it, but she had always felt—

Blackness. A ripping, tearing feeling. Off the scooter, the bike crashing to the ground. Being dragged head first. Arms and legs failing to grip anything. Shoes and gloves bouncing along the tarmac. Muffled noises through her helmet. A defeating strength. Scuffing along and then stopping. Silence. Fear kicking in. A slow realization. This is him. The man Abner christened the Thames Rapist. Photos in operations rooms. Dark strangulation marks. Brooding organ damage. Sick stomach contents. Fractured X-rays of broken ribs. She knows she is next.

A heaviness, dragging her down. Cold concrete through her tights. Pushed into the ground. An unbelievable pressure. A hand clamping around her throat. Two deaths, she realizes. One adult, one fetal. Everything quiet and stifled, her helmet covered with something. An incredible pain in the front of her neck. Helplessly crushed. Breathing stopping. The pain intensifying, the pressure clamping harder. Going. Not gently but violently. Smothered. An insect squashed. Pressed into the ground. Life squeezed away. An unanswerable force. The end of everything. Two lives slipping away . . .

12

Two metres by three metres. Barely room to lie down. Pacing back and forth through the pitch darkness. Stopping every now and then to attack the concrete. Intense and frenzied bursts of activity. A small silver coin scratching at the wall. Short, concentrated movements, side to side. Fingers bleeding, multiple grazes and cuts from the rough, sharp surface. Knuckles and fingertips stinging with the blood and the contact. Pausing to wipe the fluid away before beginning again.

The smell intensifying. Human and sour. Evidence that someone has been here before, locked up, isolated, for long periods of time. The stench of suffering. Not death, necessarily. Not the reeking fleshy nausea of corpses or rotting body parts. More a sharp acrid scent of wasting away, of fear or of torture. Instinctive odours that track you down and tell you a story you don't want to hear. But something else in there as well.

Another bitterness that lies silently in the darkness, waiting.

Feeling into the concrete, suspecting that it is hardened or reinforced. The coin making little difference, its edge flattened and becoming blunter. Continuing anyway, faster and with more force, knowing there is no other option. The floor is made from the same material, the ceiling also, the door utterly unmovable, with no handle or lock on the inside. A hollow concrete block with no obvious way out.

Slumping down on the ground, head in hands, the coin hot from the friction. Sucking at bleeding fingers, the sweet iron taste flooding in. Thinking and trying not to think. A world turned upside down. Events escalating beyond control. A son in trouble, a dead man in the lab, a senior policeman tying up all the loose ends. Breaking into prison and breaking out. And now locked up for good.

Attacking the wall again. The same place, a hand's width from the door hinge. Grunting and crying out with the effort and the pain. Skinning fingers, shredding nails. Feeling into the shallow gouge and knowing that it isn't working. But trying all the same. Refusing to quit or acknowledge the terrible possibilities. Just scratching and scraping and digging with utter desperation.

Stopping mid-stroke, breathing deep, lungs working hard. Suddenly understanding what the smell is. Not just urine or sweat or human terror, also something inorganic. A fluid from a laboratory hovering in the mix. A heavy, vaporous gas, hanging low, near the floor. Bending down and sniffing, mentally flicking through solutions and reagents. Alcohols, esters, phenols, hydrocarbons, acids, solvents, bases . . . an acid. A thick, noxious, stomach-churning acid. Getting closer to the floor, the sense of smell fatiguing, but knowing it is still there, hiding in the damp, pungent stench. The pitch blackness making the odours come alive, pure and undiluted by other sensory distractions.

Acetic, nitric, boric . . . sulphuric. A light bulb of recognition. Sulphuric acid. Concentrated sulphuric acid. Slightly yellowy, a whiff of vapour around the mouth of an open bottle, always attacking the air that dares come near it. Images of flesh and bones and clothes being sucked into the fluid and dissolved molecule by molecule, devoured and liquefied, melting into the hungry acid. And among the visions, a haze of questions. Who is next? Michael Brawn? Or simply anyone who stands in the way? What of, though? What do senior CID want? What are they after? What does Abner need? Who else has he brought here? Who has been liquefied on this very floor?

Standing up again, away from the floor, away from the horror, still gripping the coin. Feeling for the superficial hollow in the wall. Pushing the

13

She grabs at the plastic and pulls. It stretches and tears, streetlights spilling in through the hole. As she drags it away from her helmet, she sees that it is a black bin bag. She scrambles to her feet, panting, breathing through desperate lungs. She coughs hard, a dry, uncomfortable hack which won't go away. Bent double for a second, unsteady.

He is just standing there. Looking almost confused. Vacant and staring.

Sense returns to her. A stark clarity kicks in. She turns and sprints. Out of the walled car park, into the street. Her scooter is still ticking over. On its side, the handlebars twisted. She glances around. The roads are empty. Don't panic, she says. Decide. Quick. The long ramp up into GeneCrime. A street of metal shuttered windows. Vacant pavements. He is frozen. Still in the car park. Staring into the ground. Close to the only car in there. She has time. She grabs the handlebars and pulls. The scooter lifts up and drops again. It is very heavy, unexpectedly awkward. She tries again, getting lower, her back straight. It slides a few inches across the tarmac.

She looks up. He is shaking his head, rubbing his eyes through the gap in his balaclava. It is too dark to see him well. She curses. *This is him.* A positive ID, a clear description, and they will take a massive step forward. But all she can see is a shadowy form in baggy clothing with a balaclava over his head and white latex gloves. There is one detail, however. Light blue shoe covers. Used by forensic teams for contamination avoidance. The sort Judith wears half of every day.

Judith knows that her mobile is switched off, zipped into a pocket of her jacket, senses that there wouldn't be time. She crouches down, trying to push the handlebars up. She keeps her back straight and uses everything she has. The fast pulse, the rapid circulation, the glut of adrenalin sluicing through her body, all of it straining and wrenching, desperate to get the scooter up. Slowly rising, inch by inch, righting the machine in a gradual, controlled movement.

Behind the bike, she sees his body shape change. He is looking around, alert, back in the present. Judith tries to put it all together. He must have come up behind her, placed a bin bag over her head and dragged her into the car park. Then the crushing weight, the strangulation. He must have known that she was working late. He was waiting for her. Forensic scientists in murder hunts don't accidentally become victims. She coughs again, uncontrolled, her throat tight and sore, her breathing still laboured. A revelation: this is someone she has encountered before, or is even acquainted with. Accepting it is not random, it follows that he must know her. A name flashes through her mind like a neon light.

He is coming. Slowly at first, but now fifty metres away. Not running, just pacing. Leaning slightly forward, aiming directly at her. Large strides full of intent. Judith pushes with everything she has. The scooter is almost upright, but still as heavy as hell. She shifts her grip. The engine continues to tick over, oblivious. She is pulling it up now, rather than pushing. He is twenty metres away. She can see him more clearly, but doesn't recognize him.

As she puts her leg across the scooter, he starts to run. Powerful and quick. Nearly upon her. She opens the throttle. The bike lurches forward, not quite vertical. It takes off in an arc, passing close. He grabs for her but misses. Judith leans against the pull and gets it up. She ploughs through the intersection, starting to gain control. Swivelling her head, she sees he is running after her. Sprinting across the road. The scooter gathers speed and she knows she is safe. Both of her.

She twists the throttle as far as it will go, the engine whining and complaining, and looks back. He is giving up, slowing down. She unzips her

14

The Operations Room clock read 9.15, slender black hands lying prone across its centre, cutting the steel face in two. Commander Robert Abner monitored it for a second in silence, waiting for the stubborn hands to move. Out of habit, he glanced at his watch, and noted that its hands were horizontal as well. He sighed and ran his eyes slowly around the Operations Room table, naming names. Sarah Hirst. Charlie Baker. Mina Ali. Bernie Harrison. Helen Alders. An assistant pathologist whose surname he didn't know. Generally, he kept the hell away from operational meetings if he could help it. From now on, though, it was in his interest to know what was going on the second it happened.

Sarah Hirst cleared her throat, the usual signal she was about to say something he didn't want to hear.

'Sir?' she said. 'Shall I continue?'

Abner frowned. DCI Hirst. Young, ambitious

and dangerous. Difficult to judge, up to things she shouldn't be, exactly the kind of person Charlie Baker should be keeping an eye on.

'Go on,' he muttered.

'So, Judith is at home, shaken but OK, badly bruised neck, under twenty-four-hour guard.'

'Same kind of neck wounds as the corpses?' Abner asked.

'It appears so. Steve?'

The young pathologist with short cropped hair shuffled in his chair. Commander Abner noticed that he didn't look directly at him, which was good. Most of GeneCrime were still uncomfortable in his presence, which pleased Abner a lot. His large, imposing frame, the distance he kept, his terse pronouncements, all these had helped. And he knew that this might come in handy in the following weeks.

'I examined her a couple of hours after the attack. It's difficult to be one hundred per cent before the bruising develops more fully. But yes, I think it's probably the same shape of hand and angle of attack. From behind, finger marks along the length of the trachea.'

Sarah glanced at Commander Abner, then back at the scientists and police in front of her.

'We can't neglect the possibility that we are somehow the target now,' she continued. 'When someone working on a case is attacked . . . well, you know what I'm saying.'

'What about the other police officer?' Abner scanned his notes, double-checking the name and rank. 'Detective Inspector Tamasine Ashcroft. Did she ever have any dealings with GeneCrime?'

'We think she may have had some minor contact with the unit. Nothing unusual, and therefore hard to make a link. Plus, we haven't been able to find anything in her recent caseload that could have explained her death.'

'And the others?'

'Kimberly Horwitz, American citizen, working over here in banking. Laura Beckman, a post-graduate student – but remember, there was no sign of rape, just crush injuries to the ribs. Joanne Harringdon, a partner in a general practice. And our still as yet unidentified first one. Five women who seem almost entirely different, and in no specific way linked to Judith, who nearly became number six.'

'So these could still just be random attacks, women in the wrong place at the wrong time?' Abner bit hard into the end of his biro and grimaced at Sarah. 'I'm playing devil's advocate here.'

'I appreciate that, sir. And what you say is right, apart from Judith. I can't help but think the answer lies with her. It can't be pure coincidence.'

Commander Abner turned his attention to Mina Ali, senior forensic technician, who was sitting opposite. So far, he was pleased with Mina's appointment. She was entirely focused on one case at a time, and didn't go poking her nose where it wasn't wanted. Not like the previous incumbent. Commander Abner shut Reuben Maitland out of his thoughts and asked, 'Mina, how is the inspection of Judith's clothing panning out?'

Mina Ali beamed bright, as if she had been saving her news, letting CID waste their breath with half-baked supposition. She looked to Commander Abner like she had been up most of the night and would soon need some rest. But for now, she was obviously too excited to feel the fatigue.

'I have something,' she said.

Abner watched CID sit up, a couple of them straightening in their seats. Since Maitland had left and she had been appointed in his place, the pressure had seemed to grind into her. And with no definitive DNA from the five bodies, Mina had been tearing her long black hair out. But now he guessed she had something positive to say.

'We have DNA,' she stated. 'Two hairs caught in the zip of Judith's motorcycle jacket. We're extracting them at the moment. But we're sure they're his.'

'How?' Abner asked curtly.

'They don't match hairs from Judith, her husband Colm, anyone in the lab, or any other people Judith can recall spending time with yesterday. The hairs had to have physically got caught in the zipper; they didn't float there by accident. We're ninety per cent on this one.'

'Fine. We'll see.'

'But you know what we should do now?' Mina continued.

'What?'

'As soon as we have a profile and are throwing it through the searches, we should send a sample to Reuben Maitland.'

'Why would we want to do that?' Charlie Baker asked, suddenly attentive.

Abner peered over at him, still trying to sum the DI up, and decide whether he had made the right choice of informant within the division. Difficult to tell, but he seemed loyal enough so far.

'Get a visual, in case we don't get any matches.'

'You mean via his predictive phenotyping?' Baker said.

Mina blinked a couple of times and answered, 'Yes.'

Commander Abner bit the inside of his cheek. Here was the moment he had waited for.

'You reckon that will help, Mina?' he asked.

'It can't hurt us. Could save a few days, by which time—'

'Another strangled corpse in the morgue,' Robert Abner mumbled. He tried not to appear too keen on the idea. 'OK. Now this is tricky. Maitland is the subject of an ongoing manhunt by our colleagues in the wider Met. We know that he's clearly in hiding somewhere. But if we could get him to perform his specialist analysis for us . . . Well, you understand what I'm saying. The lesser of two evils and all that.' Abner turned his large hands over, palms upwards, as if illustrating the balancing act. 'And the Met don't need to hear that we've been in contact with someone they're actively pursuing. So, who's currently in touch with him? Anyone? Sarah?'

'Not recently,' Sarah answered.

Commander Abner's intuition told him she had replied too quickly. He stared hard at her, wondering what the story was, and knowing that Maitland was out of harm's way now.

'Well, ring him,' he said.

Sarah nodded, a stiff and rapid movement of her tightly pinned hair. 'I'll try him later.'

Robert Abner felt a surge of anger. 'Now.'

He watched Sarah take her mobile out, scroll through a long list of contacts and dial his number. He pictured Maitland's phone in a drawer in his lab, and Maitland himself in the forest lock-up. Once again, he cursed his luck that the fucking scientist had been led towards investigating Michael Brawn, digging into things he would never understand, stumbling into truths that must never surface. He remembered the feel of the Smith and Wesson, still warm from Reuben's hand, pulling the trigger, the heavy jolt, the dispatching of Michael Brawn, the solving of a problem. Nothing, Abner was well aware, solved a problem like a bullet. Small pieces of lead fracturing and ricocheting, tearing through flesh and ending disputes.

Sarah raised her eyebrows, showing that the number was at least ringing. Abner scrutinized the occupants of the room. Bright and serious coppers and forensic scientists. But none of them with the balls to truly make it. The guts to go all the way. The fight to get where he had got. He tried to hide his contempt, checking the clock again. Nine twenty. A series of meetings beckoned, press briefings, senior brass, liaising with other forces. A day of telling partial truths and careful lies.

'Answer machine, sir,' DCI Hirst announced.

'Keep trying,' Abner instructed. He visualized the inside of the concrete outbuilding, flashed through some of the previous events that had occurred there and tried to sound upbeat about Maitland, who was spending his last few days on earth in utter pain and misery. Shooting him straight away would have been too kind. Waiting until his son was dead, that was where the fun was. A nice touch which had kept him warm inside all the way back to London. 'Be good to get Reuben's input into this.' It was as much as he could do not to smile to himself.

Soon, it would be time to take DS Cumali Kyriacou and ACC James Truman back there, to sort out what needed to be done, to solve another problem, to close another door, to finish what needed to be finished.

15

At least this one probably knew what he was talking about. Lucy had witnessed enough medics, architects, accountants and other so-called professionals being cross-examined in court to know that even the most highly qualified of them was just two or three questions away from complete ignorance. Ask the right questions and you could trip anyone up. There was an art to it, a method of countering generalities with specifics, and specifics with generalities. Lucy yawned and shook her head, her dark bob swaying, a stiff movement signifying the liberal application of hairspray. Stop thinking like a fucking lawyer, she told herself. Listen to what he says, and what he can do to help you.

The consultant was standing unbearably close, a balding man, fit and clean-shaven, positively bristling with irritating good health. His name tag read Professor C. S. Berry. Lucy suspected he was on the young side to have progressed so far in paediatric medicine, and saw this as a good thing.

'So, then, Mrs Maitland,' he said, glancing up from his pager, which had just sounded, 'as my colleague intimated yesterday, this is serious. The diagnosis has come rather late in the day. You said he'd been ill for some time?'

'Just nursery stuff, you know.' Lucy stifled another yawn, her eyes watering, a restless night proving hard to shake. 'The usual random infection on top of random infection.'

'And for how long?'

'A few months. I don't know. We never thought it might be—'

'We're not here to play the blame game. But we're going to need to be aggressive. We now have all the bloods back from the lab, and are pretty sure of where we're at.'

'*Pretty* sure?'

Professor Berry smiled quickly, almost a twitch. 'OK, we're very sure. His best chance is an intensive course of chemotherapy coupled with marrow donation. Now we've been checking our database for matches and have drawn a blank. I understand the biological father is out of the picture?'

Not this again. Lucy grimaced. Did these medics not talk to one another?

'The biological father . . . it's not that simple.'

'I see.' Professor Berry's eyebrows raised, disrupting the smooth skin of his retreating hairline.

'I mean, there's a fair chance that Joshua's father . . .' Lucy took a deep breath, telling herself to lower her defences for once. 'Look, I don't feel good about this. But when Joshua was conceived, well, there was another man on the scene.'

The consultant flicked back through his notes, the same pages that had so occupied his junior colleague the previous day. 'And this would be Shaun Graves?'

'But his tests came back negative. So he can't be the biological father, right?'

'Just because he's not a good donor match doesn't mean he's not the father. But this other man . . .'

'Reuben Maitland, my husband. Technically at least.'

'He could be the father?'

Lucy Maitland dragged her high-heeled shoe along the shiny floor. This was verging on a cross-examination, and she was not happy to find herself on the wrong side of it. 'Yes. Yes, it's possible.'

'How possible?'

'Just possible. I don't know. I honestly don't know.'

'Look, without prying too much, you're saying that you aren't sure who the biological father of Joshua is? This could be important.'

'Do you think I don't know that?' Lucy snapped. 'Do you think I haven't obsessed about this since he was born? Do you think this doesn't matter to me?'

She peered over at Joshua. He was taking quick

shallow breaths, but other than that, other than the fact that he was hooked up to several machines in a ward full of sickly kids, you wouldn't know that he was so ill. And as for the other question, how did you tell? How did you really work it out, without resorting to the kind of methods even Reuben wouldn't perform on Joshua? After all, what parents could recognize with one hundred per cent certainty visible characteristics that had emanated from them? Particularly when children changed so quickly, when hair colour was a continuum throughout life, and eye colour could alter until two, and the gaining and losing of weight could bend and stretch your features so profoundly. Shaun had thankfully assumed that Joshua was his, in his seemingly black-and-white take on the world. But Lucy knew that Reuben was still fixated and that she couldn't rule the possibility out. She looked back at the consultant, who was chewing on a pen, frowning at the notes.

'I'm sorry,' she said.

'What really matters at the moment is getting him tested.'

'OK. I understand.'

'Then, if he is a good match, the treatment options we can pursue will be much more aggressive and likely to work. The percentages will shift dramatically from where they currently are. And where they are currently is not very good.'

'I'll do everything I can.' Lucy scratched her

scalp irritably, the thick stickiness of the hairspray fixing to her fingers. 'Trouble is, I haven't been able to get hold of him for a day or so.'

The consultant placed a hand on Lucy's shoulder, and she fought the urge to shrug it off. 'I'm sure you don't need me to tell you this, but time is marching on. You'd better find him. He's our best hope. Or else . . .'

'Or what?' Lucy asked, her eyes narrowing.

The consultant didn't answer. He squeezed her shoulder twice, let go and walked off, the warning in what he didn't say, the threat in the way he averted his eyes.

sites, testing them out, pursuing the ones where even the most negligible progress seemed possible. Digging around the door hinges, sensing for loose concrete or patches of damp. Urinating in the far corner of the shed, hoping his piss might soak into the surface and make it more vulnerable. Trying not to defecate, fighting it, placating his bowels, knowing that conditions would quickly deteriorate, that flies would find their way in en masse, that the task would become harder.

The third day saw an intensifying thirst, and a hunger that came and went on waves of tiredness. By the end of it he calculated that he'd gone seventy-two hours without food or water. His palms were cracked, his fingers blistered, his knuckles skinned. A cloud-burst beat down on the roof, making him shiver. He huddled against a wall, wrapping his jacket around him. When it had finished, Reuben crouched by the door. Its rust was immediately in his nose and in his mouth. He extended his tongue until it touched. A tingling metallic twinge, like licking the terminals of a nine-volt battery. But there was moisture, condensation from the rain. Reuben flicked his tongue across the surface. The dry flesh began to rehydrate, cracked furrows filling with the precious droplets. He swallowed, the taste making him gag, his throat sucking down the fluid. Not enough to keep him alive indefinitely, but water all the same.

Days were measured by thick, shadowy gloom

giving way to utter darkness, a browny greyness leaking inevitably into black, and back again. In the murkiness, he saw images, snapshots of the last three weeks. In Commander Abner's GeneCrime office, Abner with his arm around Reuben's shoulder, saying, 'One day, I'm going to come knocking.' Moray Carnock holding the tight bundles of fifties from the padded envelope, saying, 'Someone wants this guy bad.' Kieran Hobbs in the dingy restaurant, saying, 'My boys will look after you on the inside.' Flashes of moments and lives. Damian Nightley, hanging from a rope in his prison cell, silent and ended. Leafing through photos of the latest Thames Rapist victims in DCI Sarah Hirst's car. GeneCrime forensics trying and failing to isolate DNA. A severely wired Michael Brawn running a blade across his tattoo in a Pentonville toilet. Joshua lying asleep in his curtained-off hospital bed. Michael Brawn lying dead on the laboratory floor, staring at Abner in horror. Abner and his colleagues silent in the car, knowing where they were heading and what would happen.

Reuben paced the building, intense and angry. He muttered to himself, almost delirious. It had to be linked. Everything. There had to be something or someone. Too many people on both sides of the law crossing back and forth again at will. And whoever it was had wanted him involved. Why? To make him vulnerable? To go where they couldn't? To distract attention from something else? So that he ended up here, in a windowless prison, waiting to die?

And who would miss him? he wondered. Who would truly grieve for him? A son he hardly knew. An estranged wife who was edging him out of her new life. A brother who blamed him for the break-up of the family. A DCI who kept her feelings bound tight under starched white blouses and angular trouser suits.

Sarah.

Controlled and ruthless, but somehow always there. Holding him close, but not too close. Striking, when she smiled. Intoxicating, when she laughed. Sarah Hirst. Something in her eyes sometimes. Lingering a fraction longer than they should, her guard dropping, her cheeks alive with the faintest of blushes. Maybe Sarah would grieve, for a missed opportunity, for a man she could have loved under different circumstances. Reuben allowed the thought to grow, picturing them together, wasting time, wrapped up in each other, her exterior melting, her features blossoming in the summer. The thought held him for several hours as he sat in the dark, the moist air surrounding him and seeming to seep into his body, kept at bay by thoughts of Sarah Hirst.

The fourth day began as the third had. An early spring chill, his body damp, his mouth parched, his teeth on edge. Reuben dragged his coin back and forth along the wall for as long as he could, sensing the futility but refusing to give up on Joshua. I have to survive, he told himself. I have to get out of here and save my son. But the concrete remained sharp and impenetrable. He was suddenly overcome by the need to defecate. Just over three full days and his body was switching modes, from passive to active, from being controlled to taking control. Survival mode. Reuben knew that fat reserves had been burned, and that protein was turning to carbohydrate. He wasn't starving yet, but after about eighty hours and extended bouts of activity his metabolism was beginning to change. Decisions were being made on his behalf. Again, Reuben wondered who had been in this windowless cell before him, and how long they had been kept, and what had become of them.

The day was interminable. Long stretches of nothingness. Haunted by Abner's words. *We'll be back for you. You will die in the knowledge that you failed to save your only flesh and blood.* Seeing Abner checking on Joshua's progress. Using his police access. Sitting in Reuben's old office and dialling the numbers, explaining that it was relevant to the case of an escaped prisoner. Joshua silently fighting, but all the time being attacked deep in his bones, his immune system being eaten away, his tiny eighteen-month life ending before it really began. Reuben wiping streams of tears from his face, angry, upset, frustrated, helpless tears, the type only a parent can cry when a child is dying. Standing up and running headlong at the door. Gratefully taking the pain, running at it repeatedly, slamming into the surface.

Reuben awoke, stiff and aching, his shoulders throbbing. He paced back and forth, muttering and whispering, shaking the dawn from his bones. He didn't believe in Satan, but he knew that this was hell. Here, now, entombed, unable to save his child, with no food or water for four days, waiting to die. This was Reuben's Hades. Forget the clichéd scenarios of flames and torture, this very moment was what hell felt like.

Reuben stopped pacing. He placed his sleeve across his nose and mouth. The stench was unbearable. The caustic nip of sulphuric acid had been replaced by something far more immediate and overwhelming. Reuben had been forced to shit in the corner of the tiny concrete building the previous day. But something worried him. There were no flies. He was deep in a wooded area, and there were no flies. He listened intently. The buzz of curious insects was just audible. No rain had permeated, and now no bluebottles. If flies and water couldn't breach a building, then it was effectively sealed. The toughened concrete was standing its ground. Reuben was trapped, and he knew it. This was a fortress. No one got in, and no one got out. He realized with an even clearer certainty that he was fucked. He slumped against the wall, which scratched at his jacket as he slid down it and on to the floor.

A noise. The crunch of gravel, the rumble of an approaching engine. He screwed up his face and screamed. 'No, no, no! Joshua, no!' With his head buried deep in his hands, he whispered, 'What the hell have I done to you?' The tears came properly. Joshua was dead.

What he had to do now was make sure that the men who let this happen were punished. The rules had suddenly changed. This was no longer about survival. It was about revenge. He pulled himself together. A plan was needed. A strategy of attack.

Three car doors slammed in quick succession. Abner and his colleagues would be ready for him. But he would be more ready. Reuben stood up. He felt the coin in his hand, which he had spent half the night sharpening. It was like a razor. He paced over to the door and stood to the side. There was a series of scraping noises at the lock. Reuben summoned the energy he would need. He saw his fight classes with Stevo, recalled what he had learned from Michael Brawn.

There was a banging, echoing thud. The door flew open. A shotgun appeared through the opening. Then an arm, and then a shoulder. And Reuben leapt at it with every ounce of strength he possessed.

17

'Fuck off me! Fuck off!'

The large arm swung back and forth, the shotgun flashing through the gloom. Reuben dug the coin in, ripping flesh, blood seeping over his hand. He swung a punch with all his might, his fist connecting with jaw, the man reeling. Reuben brought his other arm round, a glancing blow which ricocheted off ribs.

'Reuben, Jesus!' A voice from outside. 'It's OK!'

Gruff and East End, something familiar in its grittiness. Reuben paused. The man with the shotgun righted himself. 'Easy, doc.' He came into full view. Nathan, Kieran Hobbs' minder. And behind, the man himself, grinning in the light.

'Shit. I thought—'

'Gotcha! My old mate Reuben. Gawd, you don't smell too good. You coming out, are you, or do you like it in there?'

Reuben stood still, blinking in the light for a second, before stumbling out. He glanced at

Nathan, who was running a hand over his right cheek.

'Nathan, sorry. I didn't realize it was you.'

'Quite a punch,' Nathan said with a grimace. 'You work out?'

'Not exactly. And sorry about the cut.'

Nathan followed the direction of Reuben's eyes, noticing the slash in his tracksuit sleeve, presumably for the first time. He dabbed at it with his fingers and said, 'No damage done.'

'All the same.'

'Just glad the boss stopped it when he did. I'll have to pass the good news on to Stevo.'

Nathan grinned, and Reuben tried to calm down, the adrenalin taking its time to subside.

'Look,' he said, turning to Kieran, 'I've got to get back to London. Now.'

Kieran turned and pointed to the silver Range Rover Valdek was leaning heavily against. 'Your carriage awaits.'

Wordlessly, Valdek climbed into the front passenger seat. Reuben followed Kieran into the back, and Nathan backed the large four by four out of the clearing.

On the motorway, Reuben turned to Kieran and said, 'So you wrote the notes to me about Brawn?'

Kieran frowned, taking a thoughtful time over his words. 'Let me explain a few things to you. Back where I grew up in the East End, a lot of people knew Ian Cowley. He's come from up north somewhere, Moss-side maybe. Starts getting a bit of a reputation. Hard bastard, but not in the normal way. Not like my boys in the front there. Although after what you did to Nathan . . . Anyway, Cowley just had something about him that told you not to mess, something that said this guy would fuck you over if it killed him doing it.'

'But why not just ask me to do it?'

'I'm coming to that, my friend.' Kieran span the bevelled dial on his Swiss divers watch, each click sounding slick and oiled. 'So this cunt Cowley is in and out of prison. Serious stuff. A lot of people in the know reckon he's bumped a few geezers for cash. And not just for the cash. For the love of killing. For the thrill it gives him. He's never banged up for any of this – just ABH here, attempted murder there. But as I say, word gets round.'

'So why would Commander Abner want to kill him?'

'Here's the thing with Abner. Before he joined Forensics, he was a tough bastard. Serious Crime Squad. Had a few run-ins with him over the years. Decade ago, mid-nineties, Abner's on Firearms. Always had a fascination for weaponry.'

Reuben took another swig from the bottle of mineral water Kieran had pulled from a chilled compartment in an armrest and pictured the plaques in the commander's office, the practised way he had checked Michael Brawn's pistol over before firing it at point blank.

'His squad track gun shipments, seize them, accept their commendations. Only their actual and declared seizures are very different beasts, if you get my drift. Bit by bit they start to get a stranglehold on the UK gun market.'

'They were selling them on?'

'Not directly. They're coppers. They've got to be careful. So what do they do? They approach one of my outfits, get them to do the distribution. And it's win fucking win. Abner's cronies seize the guns and take the glory. Then they pass the rest on to my outfit, pocket a hefty slice, and come down mercilessly on any other fucker trying to sell firearms to the public at large. None of the saps they arrest complains too much, because they only get done for the weapons Abner's lot don't cream off.'

'I can't believe Abner . . .' Reuben shook his head. 'Look, can this thing go any faster? I need to get to Joshua.'

Kieran leaned forward in his seat. 'Nathan, you heard the man.' There was no response from the front. Kieran jabbed a thick, stubby finger into Nathan's shoulder. 'Step on it,' he urged. 'Nathan!'

The bulky minder, still bleeding slightly from his right arm, sat suddenly up in his seat. 'Sorry boss, miles away.'

'You see? One bang on the jaw and you're

fucking useless. I don't know what I pay you boys for. Now put your foot down.'

'I'm nudging the ton already, boss.'

Kieran flushed, his pink cheeks reddening. 'Well fucking nudge it harder.'

The Range Rover accelerated gracefully, its bonnet rising, and Reuben returned his attention to Kieran.

'So, what changed?'

'What always happens. Politics. A new Home Secretary, gun crime out of control, a severe crackdown on the cards. Abner's gang are looking exposed, and need someone to take the fall for them. So they set my outfit up as the major supplier of weapons in the capital. A lot of accusations at the trial, but Abner's been clever. Saw what was coming and began supplying my boys with marked firearms. Passed off former dealings with them as entrapment. And who's a jury gonna believe? Decorated officers or . . . well, you've seen the state of some of my punters.'

'So this all happened ten years ago. What now?'

'It's obvious. My syndicate have served their time. They're on the verge of being released back into the community. Abner and colleagues start to panic. Their reputations, careers and lives are under threat. They've done well for themselves in the intervening decade. Hence they call on the services of Ian Cowley.'

Reuben glanced out of the window, willing the

vehicle to go faster but lapping up the information, and desperate to know more. 'Because he was already serving time?'

'Look, Cowley's presence in Pentonville was no accident. He was placed there to do a job.'

The penny was beginning to drop. 'The false genetic evidence . . .'

'He was given a clean identity, Michael Brawn, and set up for the sort of crime that could get him close to my boys. He was inserted there to kill them, how would you say, *in utero* – an abortion, ending them before they're spewed back into the real world.'

'Nice image.'

'You know what I'm saying. Brawn had been put into Pentonville to get a job done, slowly and without suspicion, and now he's done it. The strings are pulled and he's magically released. And who's going to lose sleep over two or three suicides during the course of a year in a suicide hot-spot?'

'Damian knew it was going to happen,' Reuben said, almost to himself. He slugged back the rest of the water, draining the bottle, seeing again the headline PENTONVILLE INMATE FOUND HANGED.

'I'd twigged all this months ago, I just didn't have the proof. I needed to know without ruffling any feathers. Abner had to be in the dark. And with your links to the Met, and to Abner, I couldn't risk it. But now with your help, it's all stitched together.'

Reuben span round, suddenly angry, implications catching up, his brain beginning to fire again. 'And now my life is a fucking mess.'

'Which is why I bunged you twenty-five large.' Kieran smiled appeasingly. Reuben pictured this smile sorting out arguments, papering over rivalries, placating policemen. It was practised and ruthless, eyes twinkling and teeth shining, and difficult to dislike. 'Not bad for a week's work. And as for your son, we're gonna get you to him fast as we can. Don't forget who's just saved your life.'

Reuben sighed. Kidnapped by coppers and rescued by villains.

'How did you find me?'

'Heard along the line that you were missing. Your fat Jock friend put the word out. Since then we've been combing known haunts and lock-ups of Abner and his colleagues.'

'You knew about that place?'

Kieran stared out of the side window. 'See, cops always think it's one-way traffic. They're monitoring us, and that's that. But they forget we spend just as much time watching them. Be professional suicide not to know what the fuzz are up to and how they do it.'

The Range Rover was now picking through the outskirts of London, houses becoming thicker, traffic heavier. Reuben felt a tight knot of apprehension in his stomach, his fists clenching and unclenching, his palms wet.

'And when I've dropped you at the hospital it's time to deal with Abner once and for all.'

'What are you going to do?' Reuben asked.

'The cunt who has faked the suicides of my friends is going to get sorted himself. No minders. Just me and him. Man to man.' Kieran fingered the shotgun lying upright between his legs. 'And that's all you should know.'

18

Reuben slammed the Range Rover door and sprinted into the hospital. The last time, Sarah had been inside. His neck had been stiff from the prison van impact, his heartbeat furious, a fugitive desperate to see his son. This time, things were different. He might be too late. As he pushed through the revolving doors, he asked himself, what if he is dead? How will I live with myself? How will I cope?

He ran to the large round reception desk. An auxiliary worker in a light blue uniform looked him up and down. Reuben ran a self-conscious hand through a week's stubble as she checked a list. Then she pointed towards the lifts. Reuben took the stairs. On the second floor he sprinted along an off-white corridor which reeked of antiseptic. A sign marked 'Acute Theatre 4'. Lungs cold and empty. A set of double doors. Heartbeat frantic. A gowned surgeon, his sleeves rolled up, his eyebrows raised. A blue door, with the words 'Hospital Personnel

Only'. Throat aching in anticipation. Pushing it partially open, peering through the slit, seeing them in there, lying side by side, motionless. His eyes welling, understanding coming almost instantly, his tired, traumatized brain making the connection. Closing the entrance again, ignoring the surgeon, walking slowly away, his head and stomach and heart and emotions seemingly all connected, his skin tingling, his lungs now breathing fast. Joshua unconscious, a tiny form on a special operating table. Deathly pale, tubes seemingly sucking the life out of him. And next to him, on a full-sized bed, a man, also unconscious. Reuben rubbed his eyes.

By the time he found the canteen, which was on the lower ground floor, Reuben had calmed down slightly. He was still amazed, but it was a composed amazement, restful and still, the aftermath of dissipated panic. Reuben took a tray and picked out a range of food and drink: chocolate and fruit, a bottle of Lucozade, a portion of hospital stew and chips. He had several days' nutrition to replace. He sat at an empty table, barely noticing his surroundings, making up for lost time.

His brother and his son side by side. Aaron. He could kiss him.

Reuben took a break, knowing he shouldn't bolt his food. He scanned the canteen, with its buzzing staff and its silent parents: doctors, nurses and support workers glad of the break, mothers and fathers knowing there was no break, eating only through necessity. Children's hospitals were truly harrowing places, regardless of the bright colours and cheerful personnel.

And then Reuben spotted someone who made him stop, mid-chew. She was carrying a chocolate bar and a can of drink, zig-zagging between close-spaced chairs, seemingly oblivious to everything and everyone. Reuben guessed she was making for a vacant table near the corner. He stood up and waved at her. It took her a few seconds before recognition dawned. And it wasn't, Reuben noted, a happy recognition.

'Where the hell have you been?' Lucy Maitland asked, pulling out a chair opposite. 'I've been trying your phone for days.'

Reuben pictured his mobile sitting in a laboratory drawer, switched off, Abner's fingerprints all over it. 'Away,' he answered.

'For Christ's sake. Where do you go, Reuben? Where is it that you disappear to?'

'Just away.'

'Well it doesn't seem to do you much good. I mean, I know you don't exactly thrive on being smart, but God, you look like shit.'

'Thanks.'

Reuben was well aware that four and a bit days of captivity would have done little to improve his personal grooming, and he suddenly craved a shower and a change of clothes. He scrutinized his ex-wife for a moment. She looked tired and vague, like she was running on empty. Her eyes were bloodshot, her normally rouged cheeks pale and flat. Only her hair maintained any vigour. Reuben suspected this was more down to whatever product she applied to it than its inherent condition.

'Well, while you've been enjoying yourself, I've been stuck here.'

Reuben picked at a couple of soggy chips.

'So,' he said, 'I guess this changes things.'

'This changes nothing.'

'My twin brother is a donor match.'

'So?'

'You now know that Joshua is my biological son.'

Lucy nodded her head slowly, and Reuben anticipated trouble. 'And I also know that you abused your position within the Forensics Service, placed Shaun's name on a sex offenders database—'

'That wasn't directly my fault.'

'So I don't see how this changes anything.'

Reuben rubbed his face. It was impossible to win an argument with his former wife. Even when you were right.

'Look, Lucy, I want more access. That's all.'

Reuben glanced at her and she quickly looked away. He wondered whether she had been secretly disappointed at the news. Maybe she had hoped all along that Shaun was Joshua's father. Things would have been simpler that way. But he could now afford a broad smile in the knowledge that the single question that had haunted him since the birth of his son, since he had discovered that Lucy had been having a long-term affair, had been answered. It was official. He was the biological father of a beautiful young boy. It had taken severe illness and a donor match with his brother, but he knew the odds against it were phenomenal.

'So how did you track Aaron down?'

'I didn't,' Lucy answered flatly. 'Some Scotsman with a pie habit came to me and put us in touch.'

Moray Carnock. The man who could fix just about any mess you cared to get yourself into.

'How long till they come round?'

'The nurse said the operation will last about four hours, then they'll keep them pretty much sedated until tomorrow morning.'

'And when will we know more?'

'Not for several days. They've begun the treatment now, so things are heading in the right direction. But he's not out of the woods yet.'

'I guess not.'

Reuben finished his drink. It tasted pure and beautiful, even though it was stacked with additives. Compared to water from a rusting door, it was wonderful.

'Look,' he said, pushing back his chair and standing up, 'there's something I've got to do in a hurry.'

'What?' Lucy asked.

'Something urgent. One last thing. I'll be back before Joshua and Aaron come round tomorrow.'

And with a sense of rising apprehension, Reuben left his ex-wife, strode out of the canteen and exited the hospital.

19

Judith's hug was shaky. A little stiff, a slight tremor in her chest, her arms wrapped tight for a couple of seconds before letting go and stepping back.

Behind her, Moray said gruffly, 'I don't do hugs. And I will fight you if you try.'

Reuben grinned. 'Not a problem,' he said. 'Now, this might sound like a daft question, but what have you done with the body?'

'You're right,' Moray answered, his face serious.

'What?'

'It does sound like a daft question.'

'Really, though.'

'What body?' Judith asked.

'Michael Brawn. You're telling me there was no body here?'

'Afraid not.'

'And the lab door?'

'Unlocked.'

'So they came back and tidied up.'

'Who?'

'Robert Abner and friends. After they took me for a ride and put me away.' Reuben retrieved his mobile from the drawer and turned it on. It vibrated, indicating that he had messages to view. 'Look, this is all fucked up. Brawn was working for Abner, deliberately placed in prison, executing a gang of inmates one by one before they could be released.'

'Why?'

'Abner was bent. He ran London's gun market in the nineties, made a mint out of it, and then needed some scapegoats to do his time. But he made the mistake of crossing Kieran Hobbs. Who, at this very moment, is exacting his revenge.'

'What's Hobbs going to do?' Judith asked.

'I don't know. Even Hobbs isn't big enough to take on senior Metropolitan brass. Christ knows what he's hoping to achieve.' Reuben paced over to the lab bench that Brawn had lain under, his fingertips ruined, a gun exploding in his ribs. There was no obvious sign now, the floor wiped, probably even fingerprints cleaned away. 'But I guess we'll find out soon.'

He thought of Brawn, and whether he had already been disposed of, melted down, poured away. The damp sulphuric smell of the concrete outbuilding seemed to be burned deep into Reuben's nostrils. So much life and menace seeping into the ground somewhere. But at least with no corpse in his lab, one serious problem had been averted.

'So, what else has been going on?' he asked.

There was a pause, Judith looking into the floor, Moray finding other things to occupy him.

'So?' he asked.

Judith cleared her throat. 'I . . . he attacked me. The man.'

'Who? The Thames—' Reuben didn't say the rest of the name.

Judith nodded quickly, her eyes fixed on the floor. 'After work. Late. Near GeneCrime.'

'Fuck.' Reuben walked over and put his arm round her. 'Are you OK?'

'Fine,' she said.

Reuben glanced at Moray, who shook his head.

'But what—'

'I'm fine,' Judith repeated. 'I got away. I was lucky.'

She started to cry, and Reuben held her close. Soon, her breathing became slower and less jerky, as if she was trying to control her tears, fighting to stem the outpouring.

'But there was something good.'

'What?'

'They finally got DNA. A couple of hairs caught in the zip of my jacket in the struggle.'

'Really?'

'No matches yet. But they have a sample.'

Judith said this triumphantly, as if she almost believed her ordeal would have a positive outcome. Almost. Reuben noted a pair of dark red marks on her neck, just visible above the collar of her white blouse as she moved her head.

'What are they doing?'

'Just prelims at the moment. A crude run, plug it through the database. When we found it was negative, yesterday morning, Mina decided we should do it properly, which will take another few days.'

'How are they certain they're his,' Moray asked, 'and not some random hairs you picked up along the way?'

'Fragments matched the sample from what we think was the first victim, the one Reuben helped with. Just a couple of loci, but enough to get stats on.'

'And what do you guys do when you've confirmed that the murderer's DNA doesn't match anything in your database?'

Reuben was quiet. Excited, thinking through the possibilities.

'We start screening. You know, working our way through the hundreds of suspects we've identified from witness statements, car registrations, descriptions. The net begins slowly to tighten. But of course there is another way, now Reuben's back with us.'

'Which is?' Moray asked.

'Predictive phenotyping,' Reuben answered slowly. 'So we can see his face. But we'd need access to the DNA.'

Judith smiled. 'Catch,' she said, tossing an Eppendorf tube through the air. 'Dried down, desiccated and ready to go.'

Reuben caught it and brought the tube up in front of his eyes. The DNA of the Thames Rapist. Molecules of the man who had been terrorizing London for weeks. Fragments of the psychopath who had tried to kill Judith, microscopic pieces she had carried with her in her pocket. He flicked a hot-block on and began programming a thermal cycler. The last time, predictive phenotyping had shown him that Michael Brawn was a black man. This time, there would be no mistakes.

Reuben took a breather, leaning against the bench, a phosphoimager scanning two thousand spots which were crammed on to a nylon membrane the size of a postage stamp.

'Who wants a cuppa?' he asked.

Moray, who was slumped on the sofa reading the paper, answered 'Aye' without looking up.

'If you're offering,' Judith said, pulling off a pair of lab gloves.

Reuben slid a clear bottle marked 'Ethanol' from the shelf above him. He poured a slosh into three Pyrex beakers and handed one each to Judith and Moray.

Judith eyed the liquid suspiciously. 'You drink this stuff?'

'Why not?' Reuben asked, taking a swig.

'Management always told us that laboratory ethanol was spiked with meths.'

'And why would they do that?'

'To stop us drinking it.'

'Exactly.'

Moray straightened slightly and raised his beaker in front of him. 'To scientists. Who'll believe anything except the obvious.' He took a healthy gulp, then his cheeks reddened and his eyes widened. 'Fuck me,' he muttered. 'Not exactly single malt.'

'One hundred per cent pure alcohol,' Reuben answered. 'An acquired taste. Don't you think, Judith?'

Judith placed her beaker on the bench. 'I've changed my mind. Look, I'll get the wash steps ready.'

Reuben watched her pull on fresh gloves and busy herself. She had come through a head-fuck of an ordeal. The only one to survive. The only one to get away from him alive. He knew that she would have made the same deduction he had: that the killer had already met Judith, or was familiar with GeneCrime's personnel. This was not coincidence. He marvelled that she was coping so well, but then, she had always been tough. It was one thing you never suspected of Judith. She might be petite and demure, but she was as gutsy as hell.

Reuben took another swig, savouring the warmth, wondering what the predictive phenotyping would show him. Faces and names flashed through his mind. He glanced at his watch. In three more hours, he would know for sure.

20

There was a noise, a scratching and scraping sound, and the front door swung open. Kieran Hobbs was standing in the doorway, brash and bold, grinning from earring to earring. He walked in, nonchalant and relaxed. Reuben pressed the 'Start' icon on his laptop and turned to face him.

'Kieran,' he said, slightly taken aback.

Kieran extended a smile around the room. 'Reuben. Mr Carnock. The lovely Judith.'

Moray and Judith smiled back.

'You make any progress with that mugshot of mine?'

'We've had a few technical problems,' Judith answered.

'You win some, you lose some.'

'So you haven't found Abner?' Reuben asked.

'Oh yeah, I found him all right. Do you mind?' Kieran gestured towards the sofa, then lowered himself down.

'What happened?'

'Went straight there. Sorted a few things out. One to one. Just me and him.'

Reuben pulled his gloves off and put them in the bin. His laptop was busy, grinding through algorithms, beginning to construct the human face responsible for weeks of subhumanity.

'Such as?'

'You know how these things work. Revenge being served cold and all that.'

'Yeah?'

'Trouble is, sometimes you don't have the stomach for cold food. Sometimes you fancy something from the dessert trolley instead. You know what I mean?'

'Can't say I do.'

'See, the thing is, no one, no matter how big, kills three senior coppers to get what they want. Am I right?'

Reuben took in the winning smile, the expression of quiet, forceful bonhomie. 'Obviously.'

'These days, you have to be smarter than them.'

'And how do you do that exactly?'

'You have to ask yourself, what's more use, owning a dead copper, or owning a live one?'

Out of the corner of his eye, Reuben noted the scaffolding, the contours, the 3D outlines. A mesh of intersections steadily gaining texture, depth and colour. A network of coordinates being mapped and re-mapped until the software was happy with itself. 'So what happened?'

'What always happens. We cut a deal. In return for silence, certain activities of mine will gain immunity from prosecution, while the Met comes down hard on my competitors.'

'But he killed your men,' Reuben said.

Kieran stood up, edgy and menacing all of a sudden, the smile gone, the mouth tight. 'A lot of people kill my men. It's dog eat dog out there.' He slid a pistol out of his jacket. 'And now there's only one problem left.'

'What?' Reuben asked, appreciating that the rules were about to change for good.

'I want my twenty-five grand back.'

'Why?'

'Plus all the other money I've given you recently.'

'We had a deal.'

'And now I have a different deal. I've got the boss of GeneCrime in my pocket.' Kieran waved the pistol about with practised detachment. 'I hardly need some two-bit forensic scientist to sort my problems, do I?'

Reuben straightened, ready. He eyed Moray and Judith, sensed where the door was, flicked through his options. Kieran Hobbs with a gun was not good news.

'See, by my estimates you've had the best part of twenty grand from me over the last few weeks, plus the twenty-five I sent you . . . we're looking at forty-five large. *Please*.'

Kieran pointed the gun directly at Reuben's head.

Reuben paused a second, again glancing at Moray and Judith. Then he paced over to a chemical bin in the far corner.

'And don't try anything silly,' Kieran said.

Reuben opened the metal bin slowly. It held half a dozen nasties: phenol, mercaptoethanol, sodium hydroxide, glacial acetic acid, ethidium bromide. And sulphuric acid. Reuben paused, his fingers close to the brown bottle. A label marked 8N H_2SO_4. Highly concentrated. To be handled with utterly paranoid care. Brooding among liquids of lesser evil. The smell from the concrete building. A fluid that melts bones for fun.

Reuben glanced over his shoulder at Kieran. The gun was pointing at Judith. Reuben reached his hand in slowly, changing direction at the last second. He felt for a padded envelope sellotaped next to the sodium hydroxide. It came free with a small ripping sound, and Reuben stood back up. For a second, he had been tempted. Until he'd seen the weapon aimed at Judith.

'Here,' he said, holding the thick envelope out.

Kieran snatched it from him and nosed through its contents with the barrel of his pistol.

'Look, there's other money in there,' Reuben said dejectedly.

'How much more?'

'Three or four grand.'

'What a fucking bonus! Interest on my investment.'

Kieran slotted the envelope into an outside pocket and slapped Reuben around the cheek. 'You over-educated mug,' he said with a smile. Standing toe to toe with Reuben, he pulled out a fat cigar and lit it with a gold lighter. 'B.Sc.' He blew a long stream of smoke into Reuben's face. 'Ph.D.' Kieran chewed his cigar, grinning at Reuben. 'M.U.G.' He waited a second, letting the message sink in. 'You mug.'

Reuben stared back at him, his eyes narrowed, utterly powerless. Behind him, the face on his laptop was taking shape, colours and tones subtly shifting, features beginning to stick.

Keeping the pistol trained on Reuben, Kieran edged back towards the door. 'See ya,' he said, before heading out and away, his footsteps echoing along the concrete walkway, nearly fifty thousand pounds richer.

Judith and Moray slumped on to the sofa almost simultaneously. Reuben stayed where he was, his head bowed, focusing into the vinyl floor. He had been used, a scientific pawn in a game with secret rules, where the good guys and the bad guys swapped sides for fun. And what had he achieved? A senior police officer had covered his tracks, and a well-known gangster had bought immunity from prosecution.

'Fuck,' he said. 'My enemy's enemy—'

'Has a new friend,' Judith muttered.

Moray glanced up at Reuben. 'And it ain't you.'

'Ever get the feeling you've been taken for a ride?' Judith asked.

'Not until now,' he answered, dejectedly.

Reuben walked over to the computer. If he squinted, the face almost looked like a photograph. In a few more minutes it would be ready; 3D, with texture and depth, a pheno-fit face of the Thames Rapist.

Reuben knocked back the remnants of his ethanol and paced to the rear of the flat. Below, he watched Kieran Hobbs climb into the driver's seat of his silver Range Rover. Reuben looked more closely. There was someone in the passenger seat. Commander Robert Abner, in uniform, even his hat on. A folded copy of what appeared to be the *Bargain Pages*. Noticing Reuben and waving with the folded newspaper. Reuben watched the vehicle pick its way across the rubbled car park, and shook his head sadly.

'I've got to get back to the hospital,' he said.

Moray stood up, between Reuben and the door. 'I don't know, Reuben,' he said. 'You're going to have to watch yourself.'

'What are you saying?'

'Things have changed. Abner knows you've seen too much. And Hobbs, his new best buddy, isn't averse to having Nathan and Valdek beat people to a pulp. Not to put too fine a point on it, you, me, Judith, the lab . . . it's finished.'

Judith didn't look at him. 'Face it, Reuben,

they're going to come for you. Maybe not today, but it won't be long.'

'And don't forget, all the archived samples have been ruined.'

'Moray's right. There's not a lot left, and now you've made yourself dangerous and vulnerable.'

'Again.'

Reuben ran his nails over an impenetrable section of lab bench. Fuck. Fuck. Fuck. He had been used up and spat out. Too quick to follow his hunches, too eager to take the bait. Sensing cover-ups and impropriety but missing the point. Entering prison on a whim and paying for it now. The detective urge strong, the obsession for the truth almost overwhelming him at times. Reuben bit deep into the inside of his cheek. Defeated, lied to, taken for a ride.

The face on the screen stared back at him, deadpan and indifferent. Reuben pressed 'Print' and waited for the photo to emerge, thinking, glancing hard at the patch of floor where Michael Brawn had been slumped in death. He frowned at Moray and Judith, took the picture, paused for a quiet moment and then made for the door.

It was a long shot, but an idea had just come to him. Maybe the laboratory was not what it seemed. Maybe he had been wrong about events. Maybe, just maybe, his eyes had deceived him. He slid a folded yellow Post-It note out of the back pocket of his jeans. As he left the lab he pulled out his mobile phone and dialled a number, praying after every ring that it would be answered.

21

Sitting between them, listening to their breathing, one long and slow, the other quicker and more shallow, both peaceful, almost serene. Reuben glanced back and forth, holding their hands, Joshua's tiny and unblemished, Aaron's larger and rougher. Watching them gradually return to him, a closed circle of father, son and brother. In the background, two sets of monitors fired green traces from left to right, digital numbers ebbing and flowing, varying around fixed constants. The blank, windowless ante room magnified the noises and images of recuperation around its walls. His two closest relations sleeping off the effects of the operation, lying on adjacent beds, their cardiac traces duetting.

Reuben wondered what his own heartbeat would look like. It seemed to have raced for days, with little let-up. Maybe it was used to it, he reasoned – the days of amphetamine, speeding through crime scenes, concentrating for sixteen-hour stretches, pupils wide, consuming each scrap of information, understanding everything, making the case stick. The last week had been different though. Breaking out of Pentonville, the Met launching a manhunt, Michael Brawn turning up, being driven to the woods by Robert Abner and locked up for four days and nights. Reuben asked his pulse for calm, begging it to slow to normal speed, trying to persuade it that all the bad stuff was over.

While his heart continued to ignore the request, he took out the pheno-fit and stared grimly at it. Who the fuck are you? he asked. The face stared back impassively. There was something in the eyes, maybe, or in the shape of the ears that spoke to him. Fragments of someone he knew or had met. But the visage as a whole drew a blank. It was not a man he recognized. Reuben pondered this for a second. It was like identifying the windows and wing-mirrors of a car, but not being able to discern the actual model. He replaced the pheno-fit, deep in thought.

And then he had a sudden urge to feel his brother's skin, to see if it was the same as his own, or smoother or hotter or somehow strange to the touch. He hesitated, and then reached forward and placed his fingers on Aaron's forehead. It was cool and sticky, verging on the wet. Aaron opened his eyes, stared at Reuben for a second, and then closed them again.

'You think I'd let you down?' he muttered.
'You want me to answer honestly?'
Aaron managed a drowsy smile. 'Probably not.'
'You OK?'
'Tell the nurse I need more drugs.'
'Nice try.'
Aaron tried to force his eyes open. 'There has to be an up-side to this.'
'There is,' Reuben said. 'You just saved your nephew's life.'
Aaron's heavy eyelids slid shut again, the anaesthetic dragging him back under. Reuben closed his eyes as well, the last few days catching up. He was overtaken by an overwhelming heaviness, a desire to be where Aaron was, semi-conscious, and all the world's problems irrelevant.

A noise outside brought him round. He had been asleep. His neck ached, his hands still intertwined in Joshua and Aaron's. He yawned, massaging the back of his shoulders, which were tight, as if he'd just come off a long-haul flight and had stiffened up. He watched the door open, surgical staff checking up, or a nurse taking notes. Aaron stirred, mumbling something under his breath, finally starting to come round. But it wasn't a nurse or a medic. It was a senior CID officer. Behind him, lurking in the corridor, two uniformed officers standing with practised stillness.

'Hello, Reuben,' the CID officer said, walking over and standing in front of him, staring down.

'Hello, Charlie,' Reuben answered. He rubbed his neck. 'It's been a while.'

'Word is you've developed a taste for prison food.'

'Yeah?'

'And that you want some more.'

Charlie Baker pulled a pair of handcuffs out of the back pocket of his jeans. Reuben glanced down at his wrists, fingers still holding Joshua's hand. Charlie's forearms appeared contrastingly hirsute, broader than Reuben's, a dark width to them, magnified by the hair.

'I'm arresting you on suspicion of perverting the course of justice in the murder of Jeremy Accoutey's wife Lesley, and Mr Accoutey's subsequent suicide.'

'Learn that off by heart?'

'You can have the full caution, if you need it.'

Reuben grunted. 'This you, Charlie?' he asked.

DI Baker shrugged, glancing back at his supporting officers. 'Abner sanctioned it,' he said.

'Really?'

'He's got a hard-on for you all of a sudden.'

'Sounds about right.' Reuben nodded at Joshua. 'You've got family, Charlie. Just give me a few minutes here. For old times' sake.'

Charlie Baker hesitated, winding the handcuffs around his index finger, his brow creased. He scanned the room.

'Ten minutes to say your goodbyes.'

'Right.'

'Then I'm coming back in.'

'Great.'

'And these two will be outside.' He took out his mobile phone and waggled it in front of his ear to show Reuben what he would be doing. 'I've got to make some calls. Some important calls. Don't do anything daft.' DI Baker motioned his head in the direction of the static coppers, who were staring evenly at Reuben. Then he turned on his black heels and walked back out of the windowless ante room, a police radio crackling away, echoing into the corridor.

Reuben saw that Aaron was awake. He checked on Joshua, who was still under, his heart-rate steady, his features beautiful and calm.

'You heard all that?' he asked.

Aaron nodded. 'Unfortunately. Looks like you're fucked.'

Reuben didn't answer. He pulled out the pheno-fit again and scrutinized it. Ten minutes and it was all over. Abner would have him questioned, charged, sent back to Pentonville, or on to Wormwood Scrubs, the place he had been heading to anyway. In prison, possibly for a few years. Perverting the course of justice. Precipitating the deaths of two public figures. Sports-mad tabloids screaming for blood.

For a second, he saw himself and Aaron as twenty-five-year-olds, dressed in identical black suits, at their father's funeral, standing in front of the freshly dug grave, an intense rain with fat, penetrating droplets cascading over the few mourners. Between them, their mother sobbing quietly. Reuben wrapping an arm around his mother, accidentally touching Aaron's hand as he did so, and recoiling. He stared at his brother now. The brother whose bone marrow was inside his son, helping him live.

Reuben checked his watch and returned to the pheno-fit, bending it back and forth. As he did so, the face became convex and concave, wide and narrow, fat and thin. Reuben stopped. He held it in the convex position and scanned its features again. An image was starting to crystallize, an idea, a series of interlinked events. Gathering speed, falling into place, times and places and actions. He stood up excitedly and paced the floor, checking it through, making sure it fitted, examining and re-examining the picture. Whispering 'Fuck' under his breath over and over. The murders, the rapes, the lack of DNA evidence until now . . . It wasn't that Abner or someone inside GeneCrime had been subverting the Thames Rapist investigation. No, the truth was much closer to home.

'What is it?' Aaron asked, propping himself up.

Reuben stopped in front of Aaron's bed.

'Brother, I need one final favour from you. And it'll be just like the old days.' He glanced over at a pair of scissors on a tray of bandages and syringes. 'But it has to be now.'

22

A silver Range Rover idles. The alleyway is narrow and blocked at one end. Ahead, a small sign reads 'Private Property of the Forensic Science Service'. Dual exhaust gases slink low to the ground, the sweet, heady pinch of petrol thick in the air. Two men in the front seats shake hands and make muffled assurances.

A figure approaches quickly and from behind, close to one wall, ducking low, under the side mirrors. He waits a couple of moments, inhaling the fumes, listening to their quiet words. The fumes make him slightly giddy, a light-headedness he doesn't like. He stands up quickly, jacket sliding against the polished metal of the over-sized vehicle. He pushes a gun through the window and smiles briefly at each man in turn. Then he fires two silenced headshots. The noises are quick and muted, but there is still a small echo through the dead-end alley. Both bullets enter through the men's foreheads, almost dead centre.

Their mouths remain open in surprise.

He grips the pistol hard in his right hand. Waiting. Ready to shoot again. He sights down the slim barrel with its wider silencer. A couple of rasping breaths, small choking noises, and then nothing. Standing and looking, he replays the last few moments. The heads turning, the eyes widening, the jaws slackening. And then afterwards, a pause of nothingness. Fine sprays of red catching the light. Small bits of blood and bone and brain appearing on the cream leather. One of the rear windows shattering. Two heads slumping, neck control gone, final gagging breaths, life over. Pitching forward towards the dash, seatbelts tensing and catching them. A slow-motion crash.

He smiles and reaches a bandaged hand into the car. He flicks open the glove box. A folded copy of the *Bargain Pages*, a pistol and a padded envelope. He leaves the weapon and takes the package. Peering inside, he smiles again. Then he glances left, up towards the road, forty metres away. A couple of cars pass, a woman hurries by with shopping. The noise of the silenced shots play themselves again in his brain. One. Two. Not like in the films. Louder and duller, less whistle. But pleasing anyway.

He looks back inside the Range Rover, double-checking. The key in the ignition, the engine purring away. Everything else is still. No twitching, no writhing, no futile, desperate spasms of life. Just nine-millimetre pieces of metal ricocheting around inside skulls, fragmenting and tearing, setting up shockwaves, ripping through, hot and excitable. One piece of metal obviously escaping the cranium, continuing on its way to crack the back window. Thick cherry blood starting to appear, running over an earlobe, dripping on to a shoulder.

He pulls his head back out and checks the road again. He tucks the padded envelope inside his jacket. His mobile is in his trouser pocket and he thinks about making the call. The one person he had never expected to contact him. The man who gave him this job. The man who had helped him do what otherwise would have been almost impossible. He changes his mind. He will ring in a few minutes, when he is clear, out of the vicinity and away from the bodies.

He scrapes his way back along the wall, slow and unhurried, just another person in the capital going about his business. The pistol is still in his right hand. He savours the warmth of the barrel through his gloves, unscrewing the silencer slowly and carefully, wincing as he does so. He slots each piece into separate pockets of his jacket as he nears the end of the alleyway. The pavements are half full, the road a mess of bikes, cars and buses. He turns right and allows himself to be swamped by office workers and shoppers.

There are now just two more cunts to deal with. A couple of minders. Valdek and Nathan, scum who protect Kieran Hobbs. And then all ends will have been tied. No trace back to him, no vested interests to make him vulnerable. He heads for his car, ready to sort the final duo out.

In the alleyway, the five-litre petrol engine continues to idle as Commander Robert Abner and Kieran Hobbs bleed into the luxurious interior of the Range Rover.

23

The old fish-gutting factory. A dampness that reminded him of the days he spent locked up in the woods. The kind of building that wore its history on its walls like tattoos. Faded patches where signs had once hung, unfilled holes where shelving had been attached, speckled stains where innards had clung stubbornly to the interior. The sluicing channels in the floor, the drains every five paces, the large metal tables with their gleaming plumbing and elongated taps still intact. It was unnervingly similar to the GeneCrime morgue, all designed to get unwanted flesh and unneeded fluids out of sight as quickly as possible. He wondered where the drains led. At GeneCrime, there were strict rules on blood and tissue disposal. But here they could go anywhere, even direct into the Thames. Reuben pictured Ethan de Groot, leaking into gullies, flowing along pipes, dripping into the river.

He made his way across the floor, his shoes

echoing against the concrete, wanting to announce his arrival. Kieran might well be in the building and Reuben had no intention of creeping up on him. That could give out the wrong signals entirely. But he had no way of knowing for sure where Kieran was. Or if Kieran was still alive. He hadn't answered his phone, but that wasn't unusual.

Reuben recalled him leaving the lab, the smirk of it's-only-business across his face, a thick wad of fifties in his pocket. He was nervous. This went beyond money. This was serious. He saw the recent terror in Judith's features, her pale nervousness, the hangover of being attacked and nearly killed. Across the capital, women in fear, a psycho on the loose. In his pocket, the pheno-fit, its picture suddenly crystallizing in the hospital ante room, the implications still buzzing away at him. And then, for a second he allowed a pleasant memory in, almost laughing under his breath. Swapping clothes with Aaron, trimming his brother's hair, Aaron being taken away by Charlie Baker's henchmen while Reuben lay on his hospital bed next to Joshua. Waiting and then leaving, relishing the change of identities as they had done a thousand times as adolescents.

Halfway across, and a door in the wall opened slowly. It was a room originally used, Reuben guessed, for cold storage. He stopped, surprise blowing the reminiscence away, suddenly awkward and on edge. This wasn't in the game plan. Valdek

Kosonovski striding over to him, iron bar in his hand, flushed and angry.

'What the fuck do you want?' he growled.

Reuben took in the dark matted hair, the large rounded forehead, the threat of violence that emanated from his wide-shouldered bulk.

'Kieran,' he answered.

'We don't deal with you any more.'

'No?'

'So fuck off.'

'Where's your boss?'

'Out somewhere.' The eyes blazing, the mouth tight. 'Business.'

'Whereabouts?'

'Like I said, business.'

'Because he came to my lab and then went off with Commander Abner.'

'So?'

Reuben knew he was pushing it, but kept going regardless. 'So, did he say where he was heading?'

'He rang a while back. Said you might come sniffing around. Had a few things to take care of.'

'How long ago?'

'A piece of advice round here.' Valdek held the iron bar horizontally with his left hand, tapping it into the palm of his right, emphasizing his strength, his superiority, his command of the situation. 'Don't ask me any more questions. Turn round, forget all about it and fuck off.'

Reuben's phone rang. He ignored it.

'OK. But before I go, one final one. When did you see your boss last?'

Valdek blew air out of the corner of his mouth, just about keeping his cool. 'He dropped Nathan and me, and then went to do what he had to do.'

Reuben decided to change tack. 'Doesn't really matter. It wasn't just Kieran I came to see.'

Despite himself, Valdek said, 'No?'

The phone burst into life again, and Reuben fumbled for the 'Decline' button.

'No. After him, I wanted to talk to you.'

'What about?'

Judith's words echoed in his head. A big man. Strong enough to lift her clean off her moped. Holding her down and crushing her with his weight. And then the Path reports Sarah had shown him from Tamasine Ashcroft, from Kimberly Horwitz, from Joanne Harringdon. Broken ribs, collapsed windpipes, deep tissue bruising.

'About the rape and murder of several young women.'

'I don't know what you mean.'

Reuben frowned at the large man in front of him, realizing that if it came down to it, Valdek would tear him apart, or turn him to pulp, like Ethan de Groot. That is, if it wasn't for Reuben's hidden weapon. Ten minutes in the laboratory on his way over, and he had rounded up what he needed.

'I think you do.'

Valdek Kosonovski scanned the factory floor,

checked the two entrances and flicked his eyes from the iron bar to Reuben and back again.

'Let's say I do,' he snarled. 'What are you going to do about it?'

For a third time, intrusive as hell, vibrating with urgency, Reuben's phone interrupted him. Cursing, he pulled it out and checked the incoming number. Staring evenly at Valdek, he said, 'We'll get to that. But first I've got to answer this.' Reuben pressed the button, cleared his throat and asked, 'You finally got what they owed you?'

'Some of it.'

'And Abner?'

'Finished.'

Reuben turned partially away from Valdek and lowered his voice. 'Hobbs?'

'Finished.'

'Finished?'

'As in brains rearranged.'

Reuben let this information sink in. It was queasy news, the stuff that made you question your motives and wonder whether there could have been another way, while at the same time exciting. His stomach surged and fell in waves.

'So what now?'

'You get your tattoo removed, copper, and I get another one done.'

Reuben nodded, despite being on the phone. He hoped to fuck that Valdek wasn't understanding this. As a confirmed weight-lifter and user of steroids, Reuben thought his chances were good. But if he twigged, picked through the implications and realized what Reuben's role had been, Reuben was fucked.

'Fine,' he muttered.

'And if I ever see you again, I'll rearrange your brains as well. From now on, stay the fuck away from me.'

'I'll see what I can do.'

There was a noise behind him. Footsteps, a double echo in his ear. Reuben span round. A man making his way in through the factory door. Tall and lean, walking quick, head bent forwards. One hand bandaged, slotting his mobile into his leather jacket, taking out a pistol.

Michael Brawn.

'You don't seem to be trying very hard,' he said to Reuben.

Valdek lowered the iron bar and took a few steps back. Brawn stopped five paces in front of him, sneering.

'Valdek Kosonovski,' he said with a smile. 'I've heard a lot about you.'

24

Reuben senses the pounding of his heart. It is so strong he can almost hear it. Two psychos, two men with a confirmed taste for killing. Both armed. In Reuben's pocket, the only thing that can help him. But against a pistol or an iron bar . . . He watches Valdek closely. No glimmer of recognition as he stares back at Brawn. Reuben surmises that Valdek doesn't know who is standing in front of him waving a gun about, or that this man has just killed his employer.

As Brawn takes a cigarette out and lights it, slowly and calmly, revelling in the moment, Reuben wonders how he has found the factory, and whether he has been here before. It is possible, but from what Kieran Hobbs said, Brawn was not someone he had associated with. And then, as Brawn blows a long stream of smoke out of the corner of his mouth, a more pressing question comes to him.

Why is he here?

'How did you know?' Brawn asks.

'What?' Reuben says.

'That I was still alive.'

'Just a hunch. No blood residue anywhere in the lab, no stains anywhere, the bulky jacket you were wearing at the time. And then, of course, the fact that you answered your mobile.'

'I was sincerely hoping never to set eyes on you again. But now we find ourselves in the same place at the same time, well, that changes things.' Brawn gestures with his gun. First Reuben, then Valdek. 'Walk backwards,' he says. 'Both of you.'

Reuben glances over his shoulder, stepping back, short paces. In his jeans pocket, he still carries the folded yellow Post-It note. Brawn's address, phone number and likely haunts, copied from his arrest file. Getting hold of him had been straightforward. Guessing he was still alive and unleashing him was the easy bit. Standing in front of him again now, backing up and staring into the short, brutal nose of his gun, is another matter. Reuben rewinds to his cell in Pentonville, the merciless blows, Brawn waiting for him to get up before knocking him down again, the jarring of teeth and the tearing of skin, the knife ripping into his tattoo, the utter control, the purest sadism widening his eyes and making him grin.

Reuben sees that Brawn is backing them into an enclosed section of the factory. Two large counter-sunk tables section off an area the size of a small dining room. Reuben retreats as far as he can, his back touching the clammy wall. Valdek stays in front of him, standing closer to Brawn, still holding his weapon.

'Before we start,' Brawn says, 'there's something you need to know.' He turns to Valdek, the gun pointing at Reuben. 'Kieran Hobbs is dead. Killed him myself a couple of hours ago.'

Valdek stares blankly back at him.

'He had some money a copper called Abner owed me. And Abner had tried to end me with a bullet to the guts. So, like I say, Hobbs and Abner are both finished.' Brawn takes a long, deep drag. 'Business, that's all, Valdek. Just so you don't hear it from someone else first.'

Valdek holds his gaze, unmoved by the news. And then, after a few more seconds, he says, 'Appreciate that.'

Brawn returns to Reuben. 'So, here we are.' He spits on the floor, taking a couple of paces forward. 'No guards, no rules, no nothing. Just you and me and some unfinished business.'

Reuben takes in the wide eyes, scanning around. They are cold and glassy, a distance to them. That is, until they turn on you. Then they suck at your features and rip at your composure, dazzling you till you squint, reading you as you squirm. Reuben again detects the unorthodoxy which slices clean through the normal rules of engagement. He battles flashbacks from Pentonville. Brawn is peeling back the bandage of his left hand, blood seeping into the gauze, the white bones no longer visible.

'Got a mate to round the ends off. Fingers in a vice, electric saw, clean off. Took about ten seconds per bone. Any idea how that feels?'

Reuben gives a small shrug.

'Not fucking good. Think about it. The bone sticking out, being ground through by a power saw. Whining and screaming. The smell. The burning . . .' Reuben notices a fine perspiration on Brawn's forehead, as if reliving it hurts as much as the event. 'Then casualty. Had these nice bandages put on. Bit easier to explain than some fucking scientist took the tops of my fingers off with liquid fucking helium.'

'Nitrogen,' Reuben mutters.

'You see my fingers?' he screams. 'They're fucked. And now it's your turn. I don't want this to be quick. A gun's no good for what I've got in mind. Valdek, pass me the iron bar.'

Valdek stands still, his muscular frame twitching.

'It's OK,' Brawn says, 'my problem's not with you. It's with this cunt.' He waves his gun at Reuben. 'We're on the same side here. I actually came to discuss some business with you and Kieran's other minder. Ex-minder now. Is Mr Bardsmore around?'

'Nathan's got a hospital appointment,' Valdek answers.

'Home address Colmore Garden Towers. Flat 113, isn't it?' he asks. 'I'll catch up with him later. But pass me the bar and you take the pistol. It's time to start the fun.'

Valdek sums him up for several long moments. He is taller and wider than Brawn, and as mean as they come.

'Gun first,' he says.

Brawn turns the weapon round and passes it to him. Reuben again pictures Valdek beating Ethan de Groot to death, repeated body blows with the iron bar, and is almost glad when Valdek hands it over in exchange.

'Right,' Brawn instructs. 'Keep that fucker on him. If you have to shoot, make it somewhere painful.'

Reuben watches them both, edgy and alert. The low ceiling of the factory presses down. He is fucked, and he knows it. Brawn winks at him.

'You see, if you really want to damage someone, a gun is useless. Doesn't hurt enough. And if you're wearing a Kevlar vest, just feels like a bad punch in the guts. Bruises, that's all, even when Abner shot me from point blank. Couple of cracked ribs at worst. But half an hour with an iron bar, that's different. There's no vest for iron bars. You just fucking take it, and your body falls apart. Ain't that right, Mr Kosonovski?'

Valdek nods, gun hand dipping with each movement of his head. Stupid, violent and very strong. A bad combination.

Reuben has one chance, but it won't be enough. His chemical weapon will only disable one of them. The SkinPunch gun in the right-hand pocket of his jacket. The tiny probe holding a minute amount of aqueous potassium cyanide. Enough to kill a man in seconds. But he will only have a single shot. Reuben hasn't banked on facing more than one maniac.

Michael Brawn raises the iron bar, running his eyes along its surface, enraptured for a second. Seeing the damage it will do, the bones it will crack, the flesh it will mash. 'Nice weight,' he says, almost to himself. 'And the edges . . .' He turns to Valdek. 'The edges are what makes it.'

Valdek stares back, impassive.

Reuben hopes he will pass out before his limbs are crushed. He moves his hand into position, gripping the SkinPunch weapon in his pocket. And then Brawn spins round in an instant flowing move and crashes the bar into the side of Valdek's head. Valdek drops to the floor, poleaxed, out cold. Reuben struggles to pull out the SkinPunch. It snags as he rips at it, catching on the lining of his pocket. Brawn spinning back round. Reuben levelling the gun, aiming. One shot. Sighting along its thin aluminium body, the hammer cocked, the probe and its poison ready. Brawn lifting the bar, a glint of metal. Focusing on his face, his tight, pale, psychotic face. Pulling the trigger, feeling it click, the whizz of the probe through the air. A crashing, grinding explosion in his arm, bones cracking. The SkinPunch falling. Reuben dropping to the floor, breathless with agony. Trying to focus on Brawn's face, desperate to see where the probe hit. Reuben's arm a funny shape. Bent where it shouldn't be. Through his jacket, a throbbing, swelling bump urgently pushing to the surface. His right forearm, beneath the tattoo. Grinding his teeth, shock giving way to incredible bursts of pain. Vision narrowing. Looking up. Brawn lighting a fresh cigarette, his eyes on fire, reflecting the match. Calm and measured, seeming to stand taller. If the probe hit, he would be dying now. Choking and writhing, coughing his guts up. Reuben knows it must have missed.

He watches Brawn take the gun from Valdek and slowly load it with six rounds from his pocket. The smell is ground into the floor. No matter how many times it has been mopped. Death. Gutted fish and violent death. He wonders where the hell the Skin-Punch probe ended up. Reuben looks at Brawn again and knows for certain it didn't hit him.

Brawn turns around and walks away, quick and purposeful. 'Got something in my car,' he calls back over his shoulder. 'Meant for Valdek and Nathan, but you can have some too.'

Reuben stares at Valdek. He is motionless. Reuben wonders whether his skull is cracked. Thick redness is starting to pool under his hair. Reuben sits up, unable to stand for the time being.

He senses instinctively that bones have breached skin. He is bleeding into his jacket, ulna and radius poking out. He grits his teeth. A wave of nauseous agony burns deep in his arm. He feels cold. The fracture is disabling, making his whole body feel shivery and useless. He knows this is just one blow with the iron bar. One heavy blow. For a second time he prays he will pass out rather than be beaten to a conscious death. And he wonders what the fuck Brawn has brought for Valdek and Nathan.

Reuben cannot see Brawn or hear him. He looks through the steel legs of the nearest table. He is nowhere to be seen. 'Valdek,' Reuben gasps. 'Valdek. For fuck's sake.' There is no answer. Valdek remains motionless, his breathing hard to detect. Reuben scours the floor around him for the probe. If he can find it and reload it, he has a chance. Blood drips out of the cuff of his denim jacket. It is running inside his sleeve. Crashing waves of sick torture, making him weak. He grabs at the table with his good arm and tries to pull himself up. He has to get out. Every movement is paralysing agony. He makes it to his feet, dizzy for a second. The table is thirty centimetres deep, almost like a sink. He grabs hold of its chrome plumbing and uses it to steady himself. Then he starts to walk.

As he reaches Valdek, there is a noise, a scraping sound, punctuated by grunts. He swivels his head. Michael Brawn lets go of the large metal cylinder he is dragging and takes his gun out.

'One more fucking step and I'll fuck your other arm.'

Reuben stops, rocking on his heels. He forces himself to focus, knowing he could go into shock. A bad fracture, losing blood, locked in a factory with a killer . . . it is more than possible.

He watches Brawn struggle to lift the cylinder on to the table. Brawn is gripping it with his right arm, his left there more for balance and support, wounded fingers kept well away from the lifting, but the gun kept pressed in the palm, safe and ready. Reuben guesses the barrel is forty or fifty litres, weighing roughly the same in kilos, and again appreciates Brawn's wiry strength. Sweating and manic, he positions it on a firm base under the taps. He appears energetic, excited, up, as if he is on drugs. A dangerous high. Reuben pictures Ian Cowley's charge sheet, the multiple convictions for wounding, and remembers Kieran's prophetic words in the back of his Range Rover. *Cowley just had something about him that told you not to mess, something that said this guy would fuck you over if it killed him doing it.*

Reuben peers at the cylinder. His first instinct is liquid nitrogen. But there is no way Brawn could have got access. It is a chemical of some sort, though, its markings removed, a round, silver barrel with an aperture in the top for pouring.

'Come here,' Brawn instructs, breathing hard. 'I want you to watch this.'

Reuben takes an unsteady pace forward, knowing that something very bad is about to happen, something worse than being beaten to death. Brawn pushes the gun against Reuben's broken arm, feeling along its length, finding the spot. Then he slams the butt of the pistol hard into the exposed bones.

'Next to the sink, just there,' he says. 'Let's run you a little bath.'

Reuben is almost paralysed with pain, his vision blurring for a second, fighting the urge to cry out. He smells the distinctive odour as Brawn carefully unscrews the top of the metal container. He watches him slot a large plug into the gutting table. Brawn tips the metal cylinder, right arm around it as if he is propping up a drunk, his injured hand still nursing the pistol. Reuben listens to the glug as the fluid spills out, thinking, I should lunge at him, this is the moment, right now. But he is unable to move, the gun telling him not to, his arm gushing out blood, its shattered bones grating against the denim of his sleeve.

The countersunk table begins to fill, five centimetres, ten centimetres, fifteen. Deep enough. And now Reuben is certain what it is. Fizzing, burning, scorching. Attacking anything in the gutting table it can get its acid teeth into. Snarling like a dog, hungry for flesh. Brawn tips it up, shaking out the dregs of the sulphuric acid, using his left hand as well, now that the weight has gone. He has done this before, Reuben realizes. Maybe not here, but somewhere. He wonders where Brawn has been able to get hold of the stuff, and comes up with the name Abner. Laboratory grade, highly concentrated, used for making buffers and solutions. But never without very careful dilution and protective wear.

Reuben's arm is cold, and he is trying not to shake, his body wanting to go into shock, Reuben refusing to let it.

'You fucker,' Brawn snarls, nodding his head. 'Stand fucking here.'

Reuben steps slowly forward. The gun or the acid? he asks himself. The gun will be quicker, but he knows what will happen. Brawn will shoot him somewhere disabling, a knee or an elbow, then throw him in anyway. The table is low, a metre off the ground. Reuben could easily step into it.

He scans the factory desperately, thinking, clutching, knowing he is about to die. With his last broken breaths, he sees Joshua, coming round from his operation, the chemotherapy commencing, and longs to be there. He pictures Judith, deep bruises in her neck, passing the pheno-fit of her attacker to Sarah Hirst. He sees CID and Forensics running the picture through their databases and drawing a blank. He imagines Charlie Baker realizing he has been duped, and that Aaron, with his freshly cut hair, is of no use to him. He sees frantic, pointless endeavour across the capital. GeneCrime, CID,

Forensics, all missing the point. He flashes through years of laboratory work, of lessons and lectures, of academic progression. Formulae chalked on blackboards. Scratchy white letters copied down into his school book. Basic chemistry, the beginning of his scientific journey. He grits his teeth, ready, still dizzy and numb with pain.

'Now, I shoot you first, in the bollocks. Then I take the tips of your fingers off. And when you're paying attention, I put you in.' Brawn bares his teeth, alive, on fire, a zealous excitement igniting his face. 'Or you just get in yourself. This can be easy or difficult. Your decision. But you've only got five seconds.'

Brawn steps closer to the table, ready.

'One.'

He nudges the empty cylinder out of the way with his leg.

'Two.'

He aims the gun at Reuben's groin.

'Three.'

His finger tightens on the trigger.

'Four.'

He sights along the barrel, one eye closed.

'Five.'

He pulls the trigger.

25

Reuben hears the word 'five' and dives forward, through the air, muscles launching him, bones grinding, reaching and lunging, his fist punching the flat paddle of the tap, knocking it fully open. A shot being fired, the echo in his head, Reuben crashing down and hitting the floor hard. Above him, the one reaction that should always be avoided – pouring water into a concentrated acid. Water continuing to gush out of the taps and into the volatile liquid. A pause, the reaction spreading and intensifying, unstable molecules unleashed and on the rampage. Sudden oxidation on a massive scale. A deep whooshing noise. A volcano of boiling acid tearing through the air. A sharp, stinging burn in his nostrils. A scream from Michael Brawn.

Reuben is lying on his shattered arm. He turns on to his back, grunting with pain. Brawn is grasping his face, still shrieking. He has the gun. He turns blindly and fires at the floor. The shot misses Reuben and ricochets off the second gutting table.

Brawn is clawing at his eyes with one hand, the other waving his pistol around. Reuben drags himself under the table. Another bullet randomly fired, this time closer. He glimpses Brawn's face as he spins wildly round. It is red and blistered, patches of chemical burns. Reuben glances over at Valdek. He is starting to come round.

A stinging burn in his hair. A screaming man firing shots at the floor. It takes a minute, and then Valdek remembers. Michael Brawn.

Valdek's head is ringing and buzzing and bleeding. He feels into his hair and inspects his fingers. A lot of blood. He sees the iron bar lying on the floor and shudders. A weapon for psychos. Fine as a visual warning, but actually using one . . . He thinks of Nathan, the iron bar his favourite plaything, and shakes his aching head.

Valdek pulls himself slowly up, blurry and disorientated. He spots Maitland sheltering under a table. Fucking copper. Not to be trusted. And just because he isn't in the force any more is no reason to let up. All coppers are cunts, never to be helped in any way. But compared to Brawn . . .

Valdek is on his feet. He rolls his head, his thick neck clicking as he does so. The vision in one eye is blurred and his hearing is patchy. But he is OK. Good enough to take care of business. He walks slowly towards Maitland and Brawn. Brawn spins round but doesn't see him. He is swearing and spitting and screaming, deep red craters in his face, fingers rubbing his eyes. Valdek watches Brawn shout Maitland's name and fire another shot. This one is not far away, inches at best. The copper, to give him his due, doesn't flinch.

Valdek stares at the back of Brawn's head. He flexes his biceps and his lats, and tenses his abs. He reaches slowly forward, grabs the left arm that Brawn is shielding his eyes with, pulls it back hard, and instantly snaps it to the right. Brawn doesn't have a chance. The movement is too quick, the shoulder having no strength in that position. Valdek pictures his sessions in the gym with Nathan, working on the shoulder groups, smaller weights used in awkward positions to build tone rather than mass. Brawn screams, louder this time, his arm going slack, dislocated at the shoulder. He twists round with the gun but Valdek catches his other arm. Brawn is strong, but he is no match for Valdek. Day after day in the weights room, legal and illegal supplements, years of bulking up and working out. For just such a moment.

Valdek performs a similar movement on the left. It is more difficult, Brawn now aware of what he is doing, the element of surprise gone. Up, back and out, rotating at the end. Ten seconds of struggle before Brawn is off balance, hurting from the first one, with no leverage or means of protection. He feels a satisfying pop through the sleeve of Brawn's jacket, the gun falling down, his arm hanging loose at the shoulder. Brawn is unable to rub his eyes. His coat hangs long, his arms closer to his torso, his hands lower down his body than normal, his shoulders baggy at the sides. Double dislocation. A move that has proved useful to Valdek over the years. No need to tear people to pieces. With both arms out of their sockets, very few men persist in lying to you.

Valdek strides over towards Maitland. He looks pretty bad, a lot of blood, an arm almost at right angles to where it should be. Maitland grimaces up at him, and Valdek fights the urge to make eye contact. Kieran is dead, and the ex-copper is involved somehow. He wonders for a second what to do to him, whether to dislocate his undamaged arm, or whether to leave him alone. Cunts like that who come round asking questions deserve everything they get. And then the words from earlier eat into him, washing around his ringing skull. The rape and murder of young women in the capital.

Valdek ponders his options. Brawn is shouting and screaming, blindly pacing around, yelling Maitland's name, still desperate to destroy the fucker. Valdek walks up to him. He glances at the gutting table. It is boiling and alive, a whitish vapour hovering over it. Valdek guesses it is acid or something similarly nasty. Part of him wants to grab Brawn by the hair and push his face into the liquid, hearing it fizz, listening to him drowning and choking. Instead, he pulls his fist back and punches Brawn clean in the face, watching him fall to the floor, no arms to stop him, crashing into the concrete with a thud, the screaming instantly over.

He glances down at Maitland again, fighting old loyalties and ingrained suspicions. With Kieran dead, Valdek realizes the rules have just changed. He could stamp on the copper's head, throw him into the bath, see what it did to him. But something tugs at Valdek, something strong and new. Maitland is pulling himself up, surveying Brawn's unconscious form, picking up a small aluminium object shaped like a gun and slotting it into his pocket. He straightens to face him, eyeball to eyeball. The ex-copper looking at him, emotionless and calm. This time, Valdek returns the gaze.

'That address,' Valdek says quietly. 'You remember it?'

Maitland nods. He taps the side of his head with his good hand. 'Up here,' he answers. 'You got a phone?'

'Don't push it,' Valdek answers.

He watches Maitland struggle to get his mobile out of his pocket and make a call, listens to his short description of events, clenches and unclenches his fists, telling himself he is doing the right thing.

When Maitland has finished, Valdek says, 'He won't be there for a while.'

'It's OK. They'll pick him up when he gets back.'

'What about that fucker?' He kicks his leg towards Brawn.

'They're on their way. A couple of ambulances as well. Get that head sorted.' Maitland scowls, supporting his broken arm. 'So, what made you suspect?'

Valdek is quiet. The left side of his vision is closing in around the edges. Fucking coppers. Can't help themselves but ask questions. He chews his teeth, angry, but not knowing what else to do but spit it out. If the copper wants the truth, that's what he's going to get, like it or not.

'It's all been about you, helping Kieran. Giving him ideas, learning the ropes. Without you, he'd have been caught a long time ago.'

'How do you mean?'

'He sees your gloves, your shoe covers, what you look for on a body and where you check. He watches you, talks to you . . . I reckon he learned how not to get caught from you.'

Maitland stares at Valdek, almost sad, as if he already suspects this. 'But what did he actually do that made you think—' He winces in pain. 'I mean, you beat Ethan de Groot to death.'

'Nathan, not me. Always had a bit of a temper. Kieran called me to come in and clean up. He went crazy at him before you got there. Sent him out to cool off, get his act together.'

Valdek falls silent. The factory as he had seen it that day less than three weeks ago. The Dutchman lying ruined on the floor, Nathan gripping the bar tight, red with someone else's blood, Kieran asking Valdek to tidy up. Nathan. His weights partner and buddy for six years. Calm, popular, well liked. But getting stranger and more erratic. Flying off the handle, pounding fuckers to death, Valdek having to come in and mop up the pieces, dispose of the bodies. Talking about night-time black-outs. The things he let slip, seeing the way he was around women, the interest he took in the Thames Rapist story, the nights he went missing.

'You know, a lot of gym guys do stacking, but Nathan's been taking it even further. Oral and injections. He's been obsessed. And there are side-effects. I don't need to spell it out.'

Maitland nodded. 'Increased desire, decreased performance.' He made eye contact to force his point across. 'And sexual aggressiveness.'

Valdek heard the sirens coming. He was dizzy on his feet, a lot of blood loss, aware that he was rambling slightly, his thoughts coming and going in snatches, but letting it out anyway.

'And see, Nathan's missus, I've only met her a couple of times, she's a bit of a one. Big girl, if you know what I mean. Not averse to giving Nathan a tongue lashing, putting him in his place. I just—'

Valdek stops. Something tells him that he has said enough. The far door opens. There is a sense of relief, of things coming to a head, of difficult decisions being broached, of a bottled suspicion finally out in the open. He glances back at Maitland. Less cuntish than most police, but still . . .

'Look, nothing personal,' he says. 'I just fucking hate coppers.'

A female officer approaches. She is pretty, dressed in jeans and a tight jumper. She ignores him and goes straight to Maitland. Valdek is unsteady on his feet again. He knows he needs treatment. The back of an ambulance, some stitches, maybe a couple of units of blood. He thinks again of Nathan and Kieran. One about to be put away, the other dead. Valdek stumbles towards a medic who is running into the factory, and wonders where the hell his life goes from here.

26

Three hours in casualty, in the sister hospital to the one Joshua was in. At least there had been gas and air. So much, in fact, that he had almost begun to hallucinate, his voice coming out in a deep echo, the pain not so much eradicated as floating away somewhere just out of reach. But Sarah had sat with him the whole time, sometimes quiet, other times pressing him for information. And then the phone call had come through, Nathan Bardsmore returning home, and Sarah had left in a hurry. There had been an anxious look in her eye as she walked away, glancing back over her shoulder. As Reuben waited for someone to examine his X-ray, he had allowed himself to imagine that the concern was for him.

Later, after the bones had been set under general anaesthetic, Sarah had returned. A small part of Reuben enjoyed the quiet, coming round from the operation, lying in a pastel-coloured room, surrounded not by gangsters, minders or policemen but by slowly convalescing people leafing through magazines and waiting for relatives. Reuben had been told he could leave when he felt up to it, the plaster on his arm shielding the damage beneath, but he was in no hurry. For the first time in as long as he could remember, everyone around ignored him, wanted nothing from him. The anonymous health service. There was no substitute.

Judith had come then, quickly followed by Moray. They felt like his family, the closest thing he had, aside from Aaron and Joshua. Judith was quiet and reticent, Moray talking too loudly, asking about the food, wondering if Reuben wanted a bottle of something smuggling in. And then Judith finally said it, softly and without fanfare.

'I'm pregnant. Five or six weeks, early days. If it's a boy we're going to call it . . .'

She stared down at Reuben's face.

'What?' he asked.

'Anything but Reuben. We want him to have a quiet life.'

The old Judith was breaking through, and Reuben sensed that given time she would recover from the attack.

'Are you sleeping any better?'

'A little. In a funny way it's a comfort knowing it wasn't just a random attack. Nathan knew I had a swab and was going to DNA-test him for exclusion, because of the photo of Kieran Hobbs they found on Ethan de Groot.'

'And then he panicked that you might make a connection to the case?'

'A psycho is a psycho. But that's my best guess at why he chose me to . . .' Judith smiled sadly. 'Well, you know.'

Reuben held her hand for a moment. 'I know,' he said.

When Sarah arrived again, she was grinning, a warm, toothy smile that normally spelled danger. Now, however, Reuben didn't care. He was officially an invalid for the time being, and no good to anyone.

'Charlie's fuming,' she said as she perched herself on the bed. 'You should see him. The oldest trick in the book, and he fell for it. I mean, did he not think, I'm about to arrest a man whose twin brother is in the same room, I should be slightly careful?'

Reuben allowed himself a grunt of laughter. 'Good old Aaron. Quickest haircut he's ever had. And without him—'

'You'd be fucked. Wormwood Scrubs and no way out. Disappearing for a long time.'

'But what is it with Charlie?'

'You should try working with him.'

'I mean, do you think Charlie and Abner were in collusion?'

Sarah put her index finger to her lips and shushed him. 'I don't think anything.' She glanced in the direction of the bedside cabinet. 'No one send you a card? Flowers? Nothing? For helping me catch the Thames Rapist?'

'Mail me an invite to your promotion,' he muttered.

'I'll see what I can do.'

Reuben sat up.

'So, how did it pan out?'

'Fairly routine, in the end. We spent a couple of hours staking out his flat, waited for him to finally turn up and go in, then we were straight through the door. Heavy back-up, you know, some of the larger boys from CID, and a lot of them. I was expecting a fight, and he's a big man.'

'And there wasn't?'

'Not at the beginning. He just stood there, staring at us, grinding his teeth. We got him cuffed and out. Ankle restraints as well, just in case. Then I heard he kicked off in the van, went mental and butted a couple of the arresting officers, put them both in hospital. But with his limbs tied, even a man like Nathan Bardsmore is up against it in a van full of coppers.'

Reuben tried to picture the scene. Nathan raging, unstable and erratic, twenty stone of muscle fighting right to the end.

Sarah waggled her mobile phone, sweeping a strand of blonde hair from her eyes. 'You know, I've had some interesting calls today.'

'Oh yeah?'

'I wondered if you could help me sort a few

things out.' The coldness was back, the smile gone, almost as if it had never existed. 'Abner's dead. Hobbs is dead. Probably, Michael Brawn got shot by Abner but was wearing a bullet-proof vest. Right so far?'

Reuben shrugged, patting his pillows and propping himself up in bed. Really, he should be out and about, but he was enjoying the rest too much.

'Which means you've got a lot of explaining to do.'

'If you've got the time, I've got the explanations,' he replied.

'I'm all ears.'

Reuben scratched at his stubble and sighed. 'Abner made sure I was fired over the Shaun Graves case by leaking the details to the press. Then, when he was supposed to be fixing GeneCrime, he used his position to get Michael Brawn inserted into Pentonville, to erase the only witnesses to his past.' Reuben slid open a bedside drawer and pulled out the pheno-fit and the folded yellow Post-It note. 'Using the DNA from Judith's attack I performed predictive phenotyping on the Thames Rapist. Only the pheno-fit wasn't immediately apparent. Bits of it were. When I bent it, though, it suddenly began to click. Widening of the face. Altered musculature. Years of steroid abuse. Classic coarsening of the features. And then I began to think. What does excess testosterone do?'

'Make you drive like an idiot?'

'I'm being serious.'

'So am I.'

'Come on, basic biology. Reproduction 101. Negative feedback. It switches off your sex hormones FSH and LH. Stops testicular function. Makes you impotent. The great irony of becoming more masculine is you actually head the opposite way.'

'Sex after death?'

'That's what I began to think. All that desire, but a profound lack of performance.'

'We just interviewed Nathan Bardsmore's wife. They've been having what she will only describe as marital problems.'

'So he's impotent, can't perform, his wife doesn't understand, maybe mocks him. He's stacking steroids, oral and injections, brain all over the place—'

'But why each victim? Joanne Harringdon, for example, or Judith?'

'Judith had recently swabbed Nathan for exclusion. Long story, probably not for the ears of a DCI. But he must have guessed there was a chance that Judith could have run his sample through the national database. As for the GP, presumably he had some medical contact with her at some stage . . . The others are down to you guys to clear up now.' Large gaping holes had been ripped in families that would never heal, daughters or mothers or sisters destroyed and violated.

'Believe me, we're working on it.'

Reuben fingered the Post-It note. 'Anyway, I had Michael Brawn's phone number and last known address from his police record.'

'Ian Cowley's?'

'Whichever. Realized he might not actually be dead. Judith and Moray had found no evidence of a body and when I looked closely I couldn't see any blood residue at all in the lab. Tried his number, and guess what? The evil fucker answered.' Reuben frowned, biting his lip. He wasn't proud of what he had done. It had been impulsive, the kind of fighting you do when your back is against the wall, and when all other options are gone. 'I saw a way of straightening things out. For him, for me, for everyone. And then I was going to hand his details over to you guys so you could arrest him. Only things didn't quite work out that way. And when this all shakes out, you didn't get any of this from me, OK?'

Sarah's face hardened, taking it all in but struggling to understand exactly what Reuben had done.

'Look, how did you do all this?' she asked. 'We're still trying to work out where everything fits. Dead gangsters, police commanders, acid baths, psychos with dislocated arms. What exactly was your role?'

'Maybe I should call my brief.'

'You wouldn't be concealing something, would you?'

'That depends.' Reuben sighed, and scratched a fingernail along the blue surface of his lightweight cast, vainly attempting to address the underlying itch. 'Look, Sarah, you're either on my side or you're not. You either arrest me or you don't. Let's say we stop beating around the bush we've beaten around all these years.'

Sarah ran a finger along the delicate curve of her eyebrow.

'Are you propositioning a senior Metropolitan officer?' she asked.

'Are you with me or against me?'

'Let's say I'm with you. Then what?'

'My son is alive. Everything else is just icing.'

Sarah stared long and hard into Reuben's face.

'And me?'

Reuben took it all in. The light blue irises with the deep blue borders. The pale face with colour leaking into its cheeks. The pink unpainted lips, pouting slightly, a hint of concern. Sarah Hirst, feelings emerging from hibernation, revealing themselves just for a second, maybe about to run away and hide again for ever. Years of building to this one single moment, a short question, two small words saying more than a decade of working together ever had.

'Maybe,' he said, slow and unhurried, revelling in the moment, 'you could be the candles.'

'You know, I might just have you arrested after all,' she smiled. 'Prison seems to have done you some good.'

Reuben closed his eyes. In a while, when he had the strength, he would walk out of the ward in his stockinged feet, through the hallway, up the stairs, along a link corridor, across an internal walkway which traversed a road outside, through another passageway, into a lobby, past the reception area and into the heart of the other hospital. He would smile at his ex-wife, raise his eyebrows at Shaun Graves, bend down and hold his son, his own flesh, blood and DNA.

THE END

DIRTY LITTLE LIES
by John Macken

The truth can kill you . . .

Reuben Maitland runs the UK's most elite crime squad, working only on the highest-profile cases, tracking down the country's most vicious criminals. At the cutting edge – controversial, ruthless, effective – the squad have always made enemies. But now they're in danger. A killer is using their own techniques against them. The hunters have become the hunted.

Reuben must find the killer before his team is eradicated. But the more questions he asks, the more complex the answers become. And as the case unravels, so his own personal life collapses. Not only is he fighting to save the lives of his colleagues, he is fighting for his own professional and personal survival. The choices he makes will determine his future. And when he makes the wrong one, he finds himself alone on the outside of the law, at the mercy of a seemingly unstoppable killer.

'A terrific forensic thriller, with real flesh-and-blood characters and a plot that never lets up'
Peter Robinson

9780552154468

CORGI BOOKS

DEADLINE
by Simon Kernick

'We've got your daughter.'

It's evening, you're back late from work – and the house is in darkness.

You step inside, and the phone rings. You answer it – and your world is turned upside down.

Your fourteen-year-old daughter has been taken, and her kidnappers want half a million pounds in cash. They give you 48 hours to raise the money. If you call the police, she will die.

Trying desperately to remain calm, you realize that your husband – the man you married two years ago – is also missing.

But he can't be involved in your daughter's abduction, or can he?

As the nightmare unravels, you can be certain of only two things: that you will do anything to get your daughter back alive – and that time is running out . . .

'Simon Kernick writes with his foot pressed hard on the pedal. Hang on tight!'
Harlan Coben

'Great plots, great characters, great action'
Lee Child

9780552156608

CORGI BOOKS

A KILLING FROST
by R.D. Wingfield

A DI Jack Frost Investigation

A human foot has been discovered in Denton Woods, a multiple rapist is on the loose, the local supermarket has reported poisoned stock and a man claims to have cut his wife up into little pieces yet can't recall where he hid them. Then two young girls are reported missing, and the Denton crime wave reaches terrifying heights.

As DI Jack Frost staggers exhausted from case to case, something nasty arrives at the station in the form of Detective Chief Inspector Skinner. The scheming, slippery Skinner clearly has his eye on the Superintendent's office, but his first job is to manipulate the transfer of the unorthodox Frost to another division.

Will Frost find the missing girls before his new nemesis forces him away from Denton once and for all?

'With more twists than a bucket of eels, this is a fitting climax to an incredible series. I can't believe there won't be any more'
Stuart Macbride

9780552156899

CORGI BOOKS

BANGKOK HAUNTS
by John Burdett

'Few crimes make us fear for the evolution of our species. I am watching one right now . . .'

Detective Sonchai Jitpleecheep has seen just about everything in Bangkok's crime-riddled District 8. But the terrifying snuff movie he's been sent is something else: the person who dies is Damrong, the beautiful women he once loved and whom he still dreams about.

And there's more: slayings turn the ensuing investigation into a murder enquiry, and Sonchai into an obsessed and haunted man.

Sonchai's enquiries form a dizzying route from his own apartment, where he sleeps next to his pregnant wife while his fantasies deliver him up to Damrong; to the backstreets of Phnom Penh where street gangs are only the most visible threats; to the gilded rooms of the most exclusive men's club in Bangkok, whose members will do anything to explore their darkest fantasies . . .

'A wonderful mystery series that is at once sprightly and densely layered, like the Thais themselves'
Washington Post

'Spellbinding . . . unique'
Boston Globe

9780552153591

CORGI BOOKS

THE STRANGLER
by William Landay

Boston, 1963. A city on the edge. A mysterious killer has claimed a dozen victims – already his name is indelibly linked to the city: the Boston Strangler.

For the three Daley brothers, crime is very much the family business:

Joe – a tough-talking cop whose bad habits – fast women, slow horses – drag him down into the city's gangland.

Michael – a Harvard-educated lawyer, assigned to the embattled Strangler task force.

Ricky – the devil-may-care youngest son, leads a charmed life as an expert burglar.

But when the Strangler strikes too close to home, all of them are forced to look into their family's own lethal secrets and the one death that has changed them for ever . . .

'A dense and satisfying novel of crime and retribution'
Independent on Sunday

'A gripping, grown-up tale, that leads to a shattering conclusion'
Evening Standard

'Compulsive reading'
Daily Telegraph

'A meaty, ambitious book'
Guardian

'A complex mystery that builds to an unpredictable climax'
Maxim

9780552149457

CORGI BOOKS

THE DARK RIVER
by John Twelve Hawks

You cannot escape the past – *or the future*

Fear stalks our lives, in the press, on the television, over the airwaves, across the internet. Everywhere you go, someone somewhere is always watching. Waiting for the mistake that will reveal secrets, truths, lies, the real story or what they want to believe. No longer is anonymity a given right. And small freedoms are sacrificed daily, never to be returned.

There are some who will fight to the death to protect those freedoms. They live off the grid. Gabriel Corrigan is one such man. But the system says that you cannot opt out, that you have to participate. And it will do whatever it takes to return Gabriel to the fold – alive or dead. It will pursue him to the ends of the earth. From the underground tunnels of New York and London to ruins hidden beneath Rome and Berlin to a remote region of Africa that is rumoured to harbour one of history's greatest treasures, Gabriel will fight his running battle for freedom against the forces that even he cannot see . . .

'Take some Orwellian undertones, add a dash of Philip Pullman and sprinkle with a few lines of Dan Brown'
Metro

9780552153355

CORGI BOOKS

THE WARRIOR'S BOND

The Fourth Tale of Einarinn

JULIET E. McKENNA

www.orbitbooks.co.uk

An *Orbit* Book

First published in Great Britain by Orbit 2001

All characters and events in this publication are fictitious and any resemblance to real persons, living or dead, is purely coincidental.

A CIP catalogue record for this book
is available from the British Library.

ISBN 1 84149 065 2

Typeset in Ehrhardt by Palimpsest Book Production Limited,
Polmont, Stirlingshire
Printed and bound in Great Britain by
Mackays of Chatham PLC, Chatham, Kent

Orbit
A Division of
Little, Brown and Company (UK)
Brettenham House
Lancaster Place
London WC2E 7EN

Dedication

For Mike and Sue, always there.

Acknowledgements

Another year, another book and as always, I couldn't do it without those who know a friend can't be a flatterer – and when to offer unconditional support as well as bracing criticism, interesting facts, curious books and cunning notions. My thanks as ever to Steve, Mike, Sue, Helen, Liz, Lisa, Penny and Rachel, with particular gratitude to Andy G for providing inspiration at a crucial juncture by suffering concussion.

Michael S R merits special mention for his help with the ever-vexed title question on the Hammersmith and City Line, and Pete C did me a considerable service with his question about the arm ring. Also, thanks to the non-fictional Burquest family for allowing me the use of their name. In translating my work into Dutch, Richard H has made me pay close attention to several aspects of my writing, for which I am most grateful. I am also indebted to those, too numerous to mention, who have helpfully answered some downright bizarre email queries at first or second hand.

For constant help with the practicalities of life as author and mother, I thank Sharon, friend and neighbour without peer, and Margaret, for taking home one extra at key points. Ernie and Betty remain vital props and my thanks to Mum and David for the lads' summer holiday (and thereby, child-free writing time).

Time brings change and at Orbit I am most ably supported by Simon, Ben and Tamsin, while Tim remains editor without equal. The unstinting efforts of Adrian and his colleagues are very much appreciated, as is the enthusiasm of so many booksellers and reviewers, such essential links in the chain between author and booklover. My final thanks go to all those readers who have passed their appreciation of our efforts back up the line.

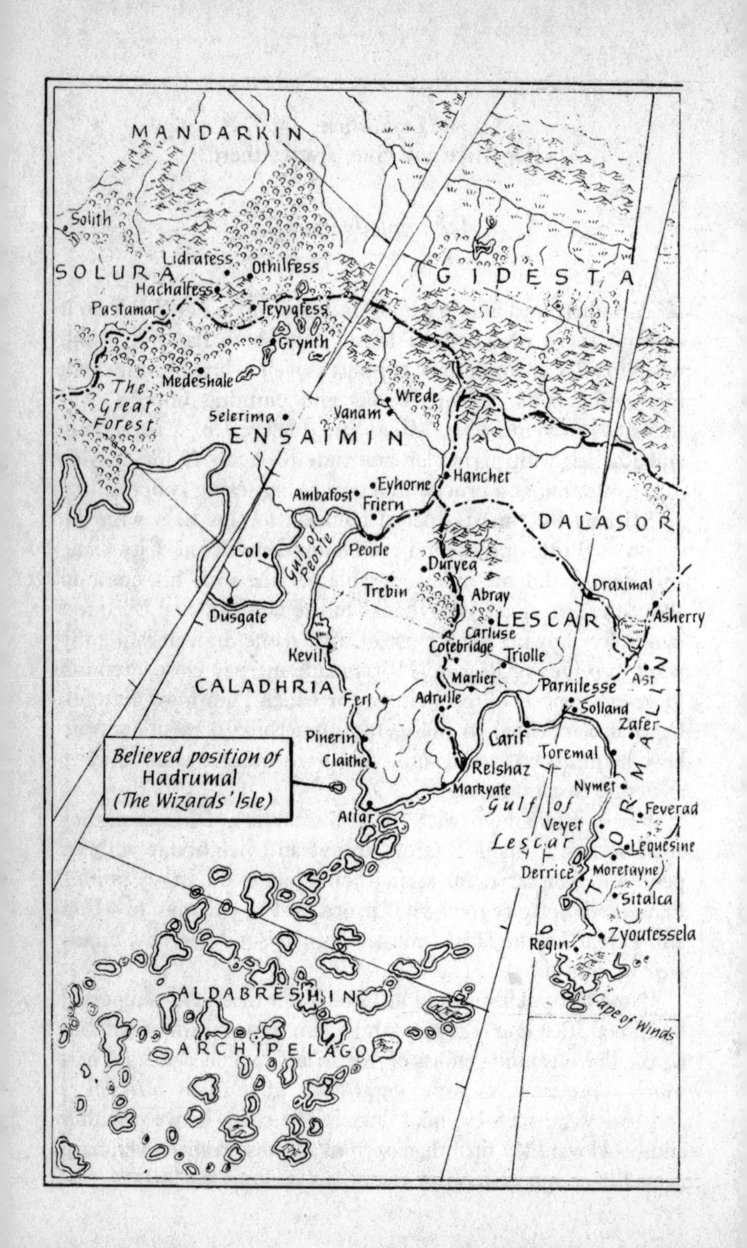

MANDARKIN
Solith
SOLURA
Lidrafess
Othilfess
Hachalfess
Pastamar
Teyvafess
Grynth
Medeshale
The Great Forest
GIDESTA
Wrede
Vanam
Selerima
ENSAIMIN
Hanchet
Eyhorne
Ambafost
Friern
DALASOR
Peorle
Col
Gulf of Peorle
Duryea
Trebin
Abray
Draximal
Asherry
Dusgate
LESCAR
Carluse
Cotebridge
Kevil
Triolle
Marlier
CALADHRIA
Parnilesse
Ast
Ferl
Adrulle
Solland
Zafer
Pinerin
Carif
Toremal
Claithe
Relshaz
Nymet
Believed position of Hadrumal (The Wizards' Isle)
Markyate
Gulf of Lescar
Feverad
Attar
Veyet
Lequesine
Derrice
Moretayne
TORMALIN
Sitalca
Zyoutessela
Regin
Cape of Winds
ALDABRESHIN
ARCHIPELAGO

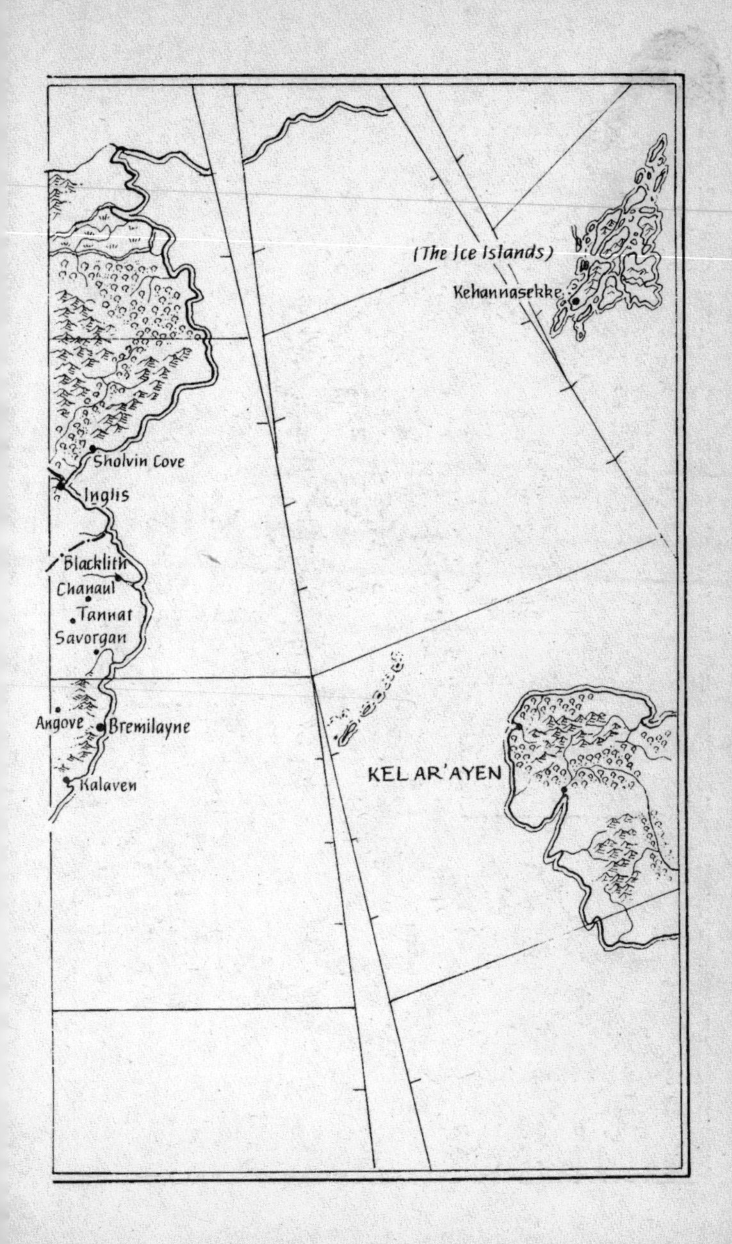
(The Ice Islands)
Kehannasekke
Sholvin Cove
Inglis
Blacklith
Chanaul
Tannat
Savorgan
Angove
Bremilayne
Kalaven
KEL AR'AYEN

CHAPTER ONE

The Sieur's Frontispiece to the D'Olbriot Chronicle, as Written by Messire Guliel in His Own Hand at This Winter Solstice, Concluding the Second Year of Tadriol the Provident

There are years when I swear it takes me as long to compose this short summary of notable events as it does for all the clerks and archivists, the stewards and chamberlains to abridge their ledgers and records for the posterity of the House. There have been times when I wonder if any Sieur in later generations will even read my carefully chosen words detailing important alliances, significant births or sorely mourned deaths. This year and last, my fear is that some future guardian of D'Olbriot's interests will treat my record with the same amused condescension I have been wont to feel when reading the more fanciful entries made by my forebears.

But as a rational man I must accept I can do nothing to counter whatever beliefs or prejudices might influence subsequent readers of this annal. By that same token, I can only relate the startling dealings of this past year and ask that my words be accepted as the unvarnished truth, on my oath as Sieur of this House.

The first year of our new Emperor's reign concluded with the discovery of islands far in the eastern ocean, inhabited by a race of men hostile to Tormalin and backed by inimical magic entirely unlike conventional wizardry. These men of the Ice Islands – or in their own tongue, Elietimm – were pursuing some arcane purpose of their own that led them to attack vulnerable members of this and other Names, robbing them of heirloom jewels and artefacts. As this year opened, I was persuaded by Planir, Archmage of

Hadrumal, to assist his search for answers to this puzzle by granting him the service of Ryshad Tathel, sworn to this House for ten years and more. Ryshad had already done much to track these villians to their remote lair, as he sought justice in my Name for a victim from our House. I also acceded to the wizard's suggestion that I reward Ryshad with an ancient sword the Archmage had recently returned to me.

Believe me as I declare here and for perpetuity that I had no notion what this seemingly innocent gesture might demand of Ryshad. But as my honour binds me, I confess I might have yet done the same, even had I known what would befall him. My duty as Sieur of this House demands I must look to the wider interests of all, even at severest cost to any one individual.

These Elietimm pursued Ryshad and the wizards he had been sent to protect, seeking the sword I had given and other artefacts held by the mages. By some foul connivance, the Elietimm encompassed Ryshad's enslavement by the Aldabreshin, and it was only by virtue of his resourcefulness and courage that the man escaped alive and whole from the savagery of those southern islands. His first safe landfall beyond the Archipelago was regrettably the island of Hadrumal. There, Planir determined the sword Ryshad carried held vital knowledge, locked within it by archaic enchantments. I do not pretend to understand by what means but the Archmage had learned that this blade and other treasures sought by the brutal Elietimm had come from that supposedly rich and fertile colony founded by Tormalin nobles in the final years of Nemith the Last, and lost thereafter in the mists of the Chaos that toppled the Old Empire.

Thus far I can picture your astonishment, unknown reader, but hereafter I am concerned lest you dismiss my words as incredible. Do not; I charge you by whatever beliefs you hold dear. There will be other records to attest to this, as I have declared all that follows before the Convocation of Princes in my capacity as Adjurist.

The information Archmage Planir retrieved by his magics led him and mercenaries backed by D'Olbriot gold, carried on D'Olbriot ships, to the far side of the ocean, where they found the long-buried ruins of that lost colony. More astonishing yet, they discovered nigh on a thousand of those who had crossed the ocean in the distant past still living, if it could be called living, held in ensorcelled sleep through all the generations that had intervened. Enchantment was finally used in service of Tormalin blood to revive these unfortunates.

It is now clear that the Elietimm had been seeking these hidden sleepers intent on their utter destruction, determined to claim this vast, unfettered land. Seeing by whatever arcane means they had been outflanked, the Elietimm attacked and Ryshad Tathel again distinguished himself as the first assault was successfully driven off. Wizardly magic was also vital in countering fell Elietimm enchantments, so, of necessity, I continue my association with Planir. This will entitle me to call on his assistance, should any Elietimm magic be used against Tormalin. I am also taking steps to have every ancient record and archive of the House and the shrines under our protection searched for lore that might explain the mysteries of Artifice. Knowledge of such enchantments could prove critical in some as yet unforeseen struggle. When all else fails, one must fight fire with fire.

At this close of the year, I am relieved beyond measure to state we have seen no more ships come out of the north to harry coasts on either side of the ocean. The sole surviving noble patron of the original colony is Temar, Esquire D'Alsennin, and accordingly we are working closely with him. The colonists are even now attempting to rebuild their livelihoods, and as soon as the Spring Equinox brings surcease from winter's storms we will send them all the assistance D'Olbriot can offer. However, it remains to be seen how close our two realms can grow, given these ancients are still so dependent on religious beliefs that we in this present generation have long since discarded as superstition. I foresee it will fall to D'Olbriot to guide these innocents to a more rational understanding of the world and their place within it.

The Shrine of Ostrin, Bremilayne
9th of For-Summer in the Third Year of
Tadriol the Provident, Afternoon

'It's raining darning needles out there.' That's what we say in Zyoutessela when a summer storm brings fine, piercing rain sweeping in from the ocean. Drizzle content to hang as mist on more sheltered shores is whipped by merciless winds to sting skin and soak clothing, leaving a lingering chill long after the sun has returned. Not that I had any concerns, watching the weather's vagaries from a comfortable lodging high on a hill above the bustle of the harbour.

'Do you get storms like these in Hadrumal, Casuel? You must face heavy weather off the Soluran Sea.'

My companion acknowledged my remarks with a sour grunt as he snapped fingers at a candle stand. The wicks flared with surprise at being called into service, but the louring skies made the room too dim for reading. Today Casuel was fretting over his almanac, a tide table and a recently acquired set of maps. I suppose it made a change from the ancient tomes he'd been scouring for the last two seasons, hunting hints of lost lore from one end of Toremal to the other, garnering clues that might unravel the mysteries of the past. I admired his scholarship, but in his place I'd have taken these few days to draw breath, waiting to see if those on the ship we so eagerly anticipated could supply some answers.

There was a rattle behind me. I turned to see Casuel had pushed aside my game board. The trees of the Forest had toppled over to knock into apples thrushes and pied crows, sending the little wooden birds skittering over the scarred wooden surface. I held my peace; I didn't particularly want to finish the game and Casuel wasn't going to learn anything from another defeat to add to the three he'd already suffered. The wizard might be learnèd in his abstract arts but he was never going to win a game of Raven till he overcame the spinelessness that inevitably hamstrung his hopelessly convoluted plans.

I squinted into the gloom, trying to distinguish between the ripples in the glass and the torrents of rain blurring the vista. Black squalls striped the swags of grey cloud, dragging curtains of rain across the white-capped, grey-green swells. 'Is that a sail?'

Casuel shot an accusing look at the timepiece on the mantelshelf. 'I hardly think so. It's barely past the sixth hour and we don't expect them before the evening tide.'

I shrugged. 'I don't suppose they expected Dastennin would send a storm to push them on.' That darker shape in the turmoil of the water was too regular to be shadow or swell. That fluttering white was too constant to be wind-driven spume. Was it the ship we'd spent two days of idle comfort awaiting? I took up the spyglass I'd bought that morning, one of the finest instruments the skilled seafarers of the eastern shore could supply. Opening the upper light of the window, I steadied the leather-bound cylinder on the sill, ignoring the flutter of paper riffled by an opportunist gust darting inside.

'Saedrin's stones, Ryshad!' Casuel slapped at uncooperative documents, cursing as his candles were snuffed.

I ignored him, sweeping the brass circle over the roiling surface of the sea. Where was that fugitive shape? I checked back with my naked eye – there, I had it! Not a coaster; an ocean ship, with steep sides, three masts and deck castles fore and aft.

'Are there any ships due in from the south?' I asked Casuel, minutely adjusting my glass to keep the tiny image in view.

Pages rustled behind me. 'No, nothing expected from Zyoutessela or Kalaven until the middle of the season.'

'That's according to your lists?' I didn't share Casuel's faith in inked columns of names and dates. My father may be a mason but I'd known plenty of sailors growing up in Zyoutessela, an isthmus city uniquely favoured by Dastennin with ports to both east and west. This could well be some ship whose captain had risked a profitable if unscheduled voyage. I find seafarers a curious mix of the bold and the cautious, men who plan obsessively for every eventuality they might face once out of reach of harbour but who throw caution to the winds to seize some unforeseen opportunity winging past.

Casuel came to stand at my shoulder, a sheaf of documents in his hand. 'It could be from Inglis.'

The metal ring cold in my eye stopped me from shaking my head. 'I don't think so, not coming in on that course.' I leaned forward in a futile effort to see some identifying flag.

'What is it?' Casuel demanded.

I was hissing through my teeth as my concern for the vessel grew. 'I think they're carrying too much sail.' The masts were trimmed with the barest reef of white, but even that was enough to let the winds make a plaything of the ship. I looked up from the spyglass and out at the ocean. The captain's choices were going from bad to worse. A run for the sheltering embrace of the massive harbour wall would mean letting the storm batter broad on the beam, with seas heavy enough to sink the ship. Turning the prow into the weather risked being driven clear away from the safe anchorage. Taking his chances on the open ocean might save the ship but the captain had wind and tide against him and the Lord of the Sea hones this ocean coast to a razor's edge with the scour of wind and water. I could see the unforgiving reefs tearing the rolling waves into fraying skeins of foam beyond the sea wall. 'Dastennin grant them grace,' I murmured.

Casuel raised himself on tiptoe to look out of the window where my few fingers of extra height saved me the effort. A spatter of rain made him duck and look through the lower pane, brushing wavy brown hair out of his dark eyes. I wiped drops from the end of the spyglass and took a moment to study the sky. Slate-coloured storm clouds threw down rain to batter the bruised seas, crushing the crests of the waves into flat smears of spume. I savoured the sharp salt freshness carried on the wind but then I was safe ashore.

The bowsprit dipped deep into a mountainous sea, wrenching itself free a breath later but the whole ship seemed to shudder, embattled decks awash. Imagination supplied the cries of the panicked passengers inside my head, curses from hard-pressed crew, the groan of straining timber, the insidious sound of water penetrating stressed seams. Pale canvas went soaring away from the masts like fleeing seabirds. The captain had opted to cut loose his sails but the ocean was fighting him on every side now, contrary wind and current confusing rudder and keel.

'Are they going to sink?' the wizard asked in a hesitant voice.

'I don't know.' My knuckles were white on the spyglass, frustration hollow in my gut. 'You said there'd be a mage on board. Can't you bespeak him, work with him somehow?'

'Even assuming this is the colonists' ship, my talents are based in the element of earth,' said Casuel with habitual pomposity. 'At this distance, my chances of influencing the combined power of air and water that such a storm would generate . . .' His voice tailed off with honest regret.

The storm-tossed ship slid across my field of view and I cursed as it escaped me. Looking up, I exclaimed with inarticulate surprise. 'There's another one.'

Casuel scrubbed crossly at glass fogged by his breath. 'Where?'

'Take a line from the roof of the fish market and out past the end of the harbour wall.' I turned my glass on the newcomer and frowned. 'They're rigged for fair weather.'

'They can't be,' said Casuel with arbitrary authority.

'I'm the one with the spyglass, Casuel.' I forced myself to keep my tone mild. Irritating he might be, but I had to work with the wizard and that meant civilized manners from me, even if Casuel couldn't manage common courtesy.

Time enough for idle thoughts later. I focused on the

second boat, a round-bellied coastal craft with triangular sails plump and complacent when it should have been fighting for its life in those surging seas. Heedless of raging swells fighting to ram it on to the rocks, it was sweeping serenely towards the harbour.

'Oh.' Casuel's tone was heavy with displeasure.

'Magic?' I hardly needed mystical communion with the elements to realise that, when I could see the ship defying all sense and logic.

'An advanced practitioner,' Casuel confirmed with glum envy.

I looked for some telltale of magic, a crackle of blue light or a ball of unearthly radiance clinging to the masthead. Deepwater sailors talk of such things, calling it the Eye of Dastennin. There was nothing to see; perhaps this unknown wizard considered it enough to set the ship riding high in the water, untouched by the storm.

I looked back abruptly to the first vessel, now heeling dangerously. It had moved a full length or more closer to the seething rocks, its plight ever more perilous. As we watched, helpless, a great wave plunged over the deck, the waist of the ship vanishing completely, deck castles alone resisting the insatiable seas. We held ourselves motionless until the ship struggled up to ride the surface once more. But now it had a dangerous list; cargo must have shifted in the hold, and that had been the death of many a crew.

'They're going to help.'

The breath came easier in my chest as I realised Casuel was right. The little coastal vessel veered toward the reefs.

'Dast's teeth!' I took an involuntary step backwards as lightning split the darkness like a rip in the very fabric of the sky. A shimmering spear lanced down to the mast of the struggling vessel and I expected to see the burning blue-white light set ropes and spars ablaze, but the incandescent arc floated free from the clouds, reaching over to the bobbing coast boat and fastening itself to the stern. The ocean ship was pulled up short with a visible jerk, prow wheeling round like some toy tugged by exuberant hands. For an instant it seemed storm and sea froze in mutual amazement. I watched with equal astonishment. The ocean ship should have been pulling the coast boat in to share its doom on the saw-edged reefs but the magic was proof against the pull of the bigger vessel. The little vessel barely slowed its pace towards the harbour, triangular sails full-bellied and ignoring winds that should have ripped them to rags.

Casuel made a sudden grab for my spyglass, making me bring it up so fast I nearly blacked my own eye. In the brass circle I saw figures emerge on to the sodden decks of the ocean ship, even at this distance their gestures eloquent of bewilderment and relief. A flash of green and gold defied the all-encompassing grey of the storm as a pennon was run up the foremast. The lynx's mask was no more than a yellow blur above the chevron, but the ancient pattern of the D'Olbriot insignia was plain enough to me.

I slapped Casuel on the shoulder. 'It's them! Let's get down to the dock.' Rival emotions jostled my thoughts. Relief for the sake of all on board barely masked hollow realisation that all Messire's current ambitions had nearly been sunk along with the vessel. Then I would have lost all, committed to the Sieur's service for no hope of the reward that had persuaded me to renew my oath to the House. Elation crowded out such pointless worry. The ship and its precious passengers were here. Now I could promote my patron's interests in good conscience, while also settling those obligations that touched my honour. Once such debts were settled on either hand, I could hope for future independence with Livak at my side. Exhilaration carried me as far as the door before I realised Casuel was still standing at the window, arms crossed over his narrow chest and with a scowl so black it threatened to tangle his brows in his hair.

'Come on,' I urged. 'They may need help.'

Casuel sniffed. 'Any mage who can wield that kind of power is going to have little use for my assistance.'

There's a widely held belief in Tormalin that wizards are

so air-headed they're no earthly use. Casuel confirmed this more thoroughly than any other mage I'd met. Before Messire's command and Dastennin's whim had tangled me up in these arcane complexities, I'd had no cause to meet mages. Like most folk, I vaguely assumed studying the mysteries of magebirth conferred wisdom, as always seemed the case in ancient tales. In reality I'd not met anyone quite so small-minded as Casuel since the dame-school where I learned my letters. Always fretting over what other people might think of him, suspicious that he was never given his due, he was a tangled mess of petty ambition. I'd been born to a family of no-nonsense craftsmen, and had chosen a life among soldiers in service to a noble House, so I'm used to men straightforward to the point of bluntness and confident in acknowledged skills. Casuel tested my patience sorely.

But he's a dedicated scholar, I reminded myself, a talent you can't claim. Just as important, Casuel was Tormalin born and bred, so knew and respected the ranks and customs of our country, which undoubtedly made him the most fitting wizard to act as link between Hadrumal and Toremal. It was just a shame he wasn't easier to work with.

'We're here to greet the Kellarin colonists on behalf of the Sieur and the Archmage, aren't we?' I held the door open. These past few seasons shepherding Casuel around the byways and bridleways of Tormalin in search of ancient tomes buried in ancestral libraries had taught me that arguing simply set the wizard digging in his expensive boot heels. Calm assumption of his cooperation soon had him picking up his cloak, grumbling under his breath as he followed me.

I drew my own cape close as we stepped out of the superior guest house into the extensive grounds of Ostrin's shrine. The flighty wind snatched at my hood and I let it fall back rather than struggle to keep my head dry as Casuel was doing. The porter at the main gate opened the postern for us with a friendly smile to lighten his grimace as he left his sheltered niche. The wind slammed the heavy oak behind us.

Catching Casuel by the arm, I pulled him out of the path

of a sled skittering down the hill on gleaming metal runners. We placed our feet on the slick blue cobbles with care but locals ran down the notoriously steep streets of Bremilayne with the practised abandon of goats from the mountains rising up behind the city. Rain poured from the slate-hung eaves of houses stepped on foundations obstinately defying the slope, the door of one often nigh on a level with the upstairs windows of its neighbour. The wider-spaced houses of the upper town gave way to cramped and dirty lanes. By the time we emerged on to the broad sweep of the quayside, a crowd was assembling, drawn from unsavoury harbour taverns. Dockers were eager to earn their ale money unloading the new arrivals, hawkers and whores keen to take any advantage. I forced a way through those just avid for spectacle and Casuel scurried close behind me.

'I've never seen the like, not magic used like that.' One man spoke across me, awe mixed with uncertainty.

'And won't do again, I'd say,' agreed his friend, sounding relieved.

'I'll grant it was novelty enough but if they'd gone down, we'd have had some wreck-sale.' A third was looking with greedy eyes at the tilted masts of the ocean ship. 'Think of the salvage that would have washed ashore.'

I elbowed the would-be scavenger gull aside. With the list on the ship still severe, the crew and dockers were fighting to secure sodden ropes running slick and uncooperative round battered bollards. I wrenched on my own gloves and added my weight to steady a hawser that two men were struggling to make safe. 'Casuel! Lend a hand, man!'

The double-headed bollards lining the quayside suddenly glowed and amber light crackled in the air, startling profanity from the man beside me. I clutched the cable in surprise myself; I hadn't intended Casuel use magic. Immobile metal twisted and ducked beneath the ropes, black iron arms questing blindly then looping themselves round the straining hemp before drawing back to stand upright once more. Reeled in like a gaffed fish, the great ship lurched, rolling upright to smack hard into the side of the dock with a crash that reverberated round the harbour. The vessel shivered from bow to stern with an ominous sound of splintering.

'Nice work, Cas!' I dropped the rope and hurried along the quay, scanning the crowded deck. 'Temar!' A sparely built young man by the stern castle looked round at my hail, acknowledging me with a brief wave. 'We need to get your people off, quick as you can.' The ship hung low and unbalanced in the water and the damage Casuel had just done might finish what the storm had started. Cargo could be recovered from the bottom of the harbour but I didn't want to be dragging the dock for bodies.

A gangplank was hastily thrown out from the ship's rail but a flare of golden radiance sent the dockers reaching for it recoiling in surprise. I turned to see Casuel gesturing at the hovering wood, face pinched with pique. A path instantly cleared between the mage and the ship and the crowd around Casuel thinned noticeably.

Temar ignored the last remnants of magelight fading from the gangplank as he hurried down to me. 'Ryshad!'

'I thought we were going to be fishing you out of the rock pools.' I gripped his forearm in the archaic clasp he offered, noting that his fingers were no longer the smooth white of the idle noble but almost as weathered and calloused as my own.

His grip on my own arm tightened involuntarily and I felt the pressure of muscles hardened by work. 'When that last wave hit, I did wonder if we would surface on some shore of the Otherworld. Dastennin be thanked we made landfall safely.' The accents of ancient Tormalin were still strong in Temar's voice but I heard more modern intonations as well, mostly Lescari. I looked up to the ship to recognise various mercenaries who'd chosen to stay on the far side of the ocean after the previous year's expedition had discovered the long lost colony of the Old Empire. They were getting the people off the vessel as fast as they could.

'Dastennin?' Casuel came up, frowning as he struggled to

understand Temar. 'Tell him he has modern magecraft to thank rather than ancient superstition.' Casuel had been born to a Tormalin merchant family and this wasn't the first time I'd heard echoes of his Rationalist upbringing. It must cause him some confusion, I thought with amusement, since that philosophy denounces elemental magic just as readily as it reviles religion.

'Casuel Devoir, Temar D'Alsennin,' I made a belated introduction hastily.

'Esquire.' Casuel swept a bow worthy of an Emperor's salon. 'Your captain was relying on his own seafaring skills? I thought it was clearly understood an ocean crossing can only be safely managed with magical assistance.'

'Quite so.' Temar bowed in turn with a deference to the wizard nicely combined with hauteur. 'And one of your colleagues was performing admirably until he took a fall that broke both his legs.' Fleeting disdain in Temar's ice blue eyes gave the lie to the measured politeness of his words. He indicated a figure being carried down the gangplank by two burly sailors, injuries solidly splinted with spars and canvas.

'I'm sorry?' Casuel spared his injured colleague a scant glance. 'Please speak more slowly.'

I decided to turn the conversation to less contentious matters. 'When did you cut your hair?'

Temar ran a hand over the short crop that replaced the long queue I'd last seen him with, hair as black as my own but straight as a well rope. 'Practicality is now the watchword of Kel Ar'Ayen. Fashion is a luxury we cannot yet afford.' I was glad to see a smile of good-humoured self-mockery lightened the severity of his angular features.

'We'd better get this lot under lock and key, Temar, over yonder.' I pointed to the warehouse I'd bespoken when we first arrived in Bremilayne. Sodden sacks and battered casks were being swung on to the dock in capacious slings, stacked anyhow as everyone hurried to lighten the stricken vessel. I caught an avid expression on more than one onlooker's face.

'I will direct the men aboard ship.' Temar returned to the gangplank without further ado.

'I'd better see to whoever that mage is,' Casuel said hastily as he watched the injured man being lifted on to a litter.

'Absolutely.' Casuel could deal with wizardly concerns and I'd see to my own responsibilities. Noticing D'Olbriot insignia on the cloak of a thickset new arrival by the lofty warehouse, I hurried over and ushered the man inside the shelter of the echoing building, speaking without preamble.

'This arrival's going to be the talk of the taverns, so who do we have to secure the place if the wharf rats come sniffing around?' I ran fingers through my hair to shed the worst of the rain, damp curls clinging tight to my fingers.

'I've a double handful of newly recognised and four sworn and loyal.' The man's grizzled and wiry hair ran unbroken into a full beard framing a prominent nose and bulbous eyes, leaving him looking like an owl peering out of an ivy bush. 'Sorry we're so behind hand. We'd have been here day before yesterday if a horse hadn't gone lame.'

'It's Glannar, isn't it, from the Layne Valley holdings?' His rich, rolling voice helped me place him, sergeant-at-arms to those most isolated holdings of the House of D'Olbriot.

The man's face creased into a ready grin. 'You've the advantage of me. I recall you came up when we had that trouble in the shearing sheds but I can't put a name to you.'

'Ryshad.' I returned his smile. 'Ryshad Tathel.'

'Done well by the House, I hear,' Glannar observed with a glance at the shiny copper circling my upper arm. He spoke with the self-assurance of a man who'd earned chosen status long enough since to let his own arm ring grow dull with the years.

'No more than staying true to my oath.' I kept my tone easy. Glannar was only making conversation, not fishing for secrets or better yet salacious detail, like some I'd met since half-truths about my adventures in the Archipelago had escaped Messire's orders for discretion. 'You've got your lads well drilled?' I'd spent my share of time training raw recruits with wits blunter than a plough handle.

Glannar nodded. 'They're lead miners' sons, all bar one, so won't stand any nonsense. We'll keep this lot safe as a mouse in a malt heap.'

'Good.' I turned my head as the great doors swung open to let a row of wet and laden dockers enter. I curbed an impulse to shed my cloak and make myself useful; getting my hands dirty wouldn't have been appropriate to my shiny new rank or to Glannar's consequence as sergeant-at-arms hereabouts. So I watched as he sent the sworn men about their business with brisk gestures. They in turn were visibly diligent in organising the recognised men, lads newly come to the service of the House, on the lowest rung of the ladder and keen to prove themselves worthy of invitation to swear the oath binding them to D'Olbriot interests.

I watched the well-muscled youths set to with a will. I'd sworn that same ancient oath with fervent loyalty and believed in it with all my heart until the events of the last year and a half had shaken my faith to its roots. I had come within a whisker of handing back my oath fee and abandoning my allegiance to the Name, believing the House had abandoned me. Then reward had been offered, the rank of chosen man as recompense for my anguish, and I had taken it, more than a little uncertain but not sure enough of my other choices to abandon what I'd known for so long. But I had taken other obligations on myself as well, where once my oath had left no room for other loyalties.

Glannar's genial commands rang to the rafters behind me as I went out. The rain was slackening but the sky stayed grey and sullen. About as sullen as Casuel, who was standing in the meagre shelter of the dockside hoist being addressed by a tall figure wrapped in a bright blue cloak. I let a burdened sled scrape past over the cobbles before making my way over.

'Ryshad Tathel, this is Velindre Ychane, mage of Hadrumal.' Casuel looked as if he were sucking a lemon. 'Her affinity is with the air, as you've no doubt guessed. It was her on the other ship.'

'My lady.' I bowed low. 'We are deep in your debt.' I doubted Casuel had shown any gratitude but the House of D'Olbriot owed this woman a full measure of thanks, and for good or ill I was its representative here.

'It's lucky you were there,' chipped in Casuel.

'Luck had nothing to do with it.' She made a plain statement of fact out of words that could so easily have been arrogance, rebuke or both. 'I've been making a study of the air currents off the Cape of Winds this past half-year. When I heard Esquire D'Alsennin would arrive around the middle of the season, I decided to work our way up the coast. I scried his ship as well as the likely impact of the storm and thought it best that we make landfall together. Given Urlan's accident, it's as well we did.' She addressed me directly, leaving Casuel tugging impatiently at the ties of his cloak. Her voice was low and a little husky, as self-assured as her stance. For all her Mandarkin name, the regular accents of Hadrumal were unshaded by any older allegiance and I guessed she had been born on that distant, secretive island.

'You want to meet Temar? Esquire D'Alsennin, that is?' This was setting a new piece on a game board already well into play. I'd want to know more about this unknown lady before letting her loose among the complex concerns of the colony and the House I served, whatever Casuel might have to say about the unquestioning cooperation a mage was entitled to as of right.

'When he has leisure from more pressing matters.' Velindre's smile lent a sudden feminine air to her almost mannish features. She would never be considered a beautiful woman but her striking appearance would halt any eye and that impact would outlast more conventional charms. A few wisps of fine blonde hair escaped the confines of her hood and she brushed them away from pale lashed hazel eyes. 'So you are Ryshad,' she mused. 'I've heard a lot about you.'

I decided to match her directness. 'From whom?'

'Initially, from Otrick.' As she spoke sadness seemed to

darken the heavy storm clouds above us. 'Latterly from Troanna.'

'What has Troanna to do with your studies?' Casuel was fidgeting from one foot to another anxious lest someone else's manoeuvrings escape him.

'She's been keeping me supplied with all the news from home, Cas,' answered Velindre easily. 'Shall I tell her you were asking after her?'

Casuel blinked, caught off balance. I've yet to fully understand the formal and informal ranks and authorities of the wizards of Hadrumal, the ill-defined and often overlapping functions of their Council and their Halls, but I knew enough to know Casuel wouldn't want the acerbic wit of Troanna, acknowledged as pre-eminent in water magic, sharpened up at his expense. If Cloud-Master and Flood-Mistress kept her informed, Velindre had powerful friends.

'How might Esquire D'Alsennin be of assistance?' I asked politely.

Velindre smiled again. 'He's crossed the ocean and sailed unknown shores with currents and winds that no mage has ever sensed. No wizard ever passes up the chance of new knowledge.'

Which was certainly true, but if that was the whole story I was a Caladhrian pack mule.

'I'll see if we can accommodate you,' said Casuel with fussy self-importance.

Velindre's eyes hardened, and I thought for a moment she was about to challenge his pretensions, but a new arrival spared him any rebuke.

'Mage Devoir.' The newcomer bobbed a nervous curtsey that edged the hem of her rose pink dress with the muck of the dockside.

'Allin?' Casuel sounded both surprised and displeased.

'You're entitled to call him Casuel, just like anyone else,' said Velindre drily. 'So how is Urlan?'

The girl Allin looked up, blushed and dropped her gaze to study her folded hands intently. 'Both legs are broken and the bosun was saying he'd seen splinters of bone through the skin of his right shin. He's been taken to the infirmary at the shrine.'

Where Velindre was scarcely shorter than me, Allin barely came up to Casuel's shoulder. Even allowing for the heavy cape bunched round her, I guessed her figure would be as round as her plain snub-nosed face. But her boot-button eyes were bright with intelligence and good nature, attributes lacking in many a prettier girl.

'Do you have lodgings arranged?' I asked.

'The man from the shrine said we could probably stay there as well.' The girl peeped up at me from beneath her dun-coloured fringe. Her Tormalin was fluent but of unmistakable Lescari origin.

'If there's any difficulty, refer it to me. We're in the upper guest house,' said Casuel officiously.

'We'll join you there for dinner.' Velindre turned on her heel with a final smile and before Casuel could shut his protesting mouth her long stride took her out of earshot.

'So who's she?' I asked the wizard.

Outrage was slow to fade from his well-made features. 'Velindre is a mage of some standing in Hadrumal but she's always claimed to prefer focusing on her studies rather than engaging herself with the wider concerns of wizardry.'

I wondered just where the sneer in his tone was directed but decided his prejudices weren't worth pursuing. 'So she hasn't been privy to any of Planir's intrigues over the last year or so?'

Casuel bridled. 'I hardly think intrigue is the right word for the necessary care Planir takes of Hadrumal's interests.'

'Could you bespeak the Archmage, please? To let him know she's here and apparently interested in the colony.' I made my request with a politeness calculated to soothe Casuel's ruffled feathers.

'I was intending to do so, naturally.' Of course Casuel had been planning to tell Planir about Velindre; telling tales was another dame-school habit I'd observed in the man over the past half-year. 'I wonder if he knows Troanna's been in touch with her.'

'Shall we do it now? Planir might have an opinion on Velindre's reasons for being here, and he'll certainly want to know what's happened to Urlan.' I wanted all my birds in a row before I encountered Velindre again and there was little enough for me to do here.

'Yes, I should see what news the Archmage has for us, shouldn't I? Let's get out of this rain.' Those notions sent the wizard scurrying eagerly up the hill, clutching the hood of his cloak tight beneath his handsome chin.

Once we were back in the guest house chamber he'd appropriated as a study, Casuel set about his wizardry. I'd seen him work various spells over the last season or so, and, oddly, he was at his least objectionable when working magic. The wizard took a seat at the table, setting a steel mirror on the table with a candle before it, lighting the wick with a snap of his fingers and a flourish of the lace at his cuffs. He laid his hands flat on the chestnut wood, eyes fixed unblinking on the reflected flame of the candle

I sat in a corner, content to watch and listen; Casuel could do the talking. What I wanted was Planir, who presumably had the power to curb this Velindre, told of her arrival here, just in case she had some private ambition that might threaten all I was working for. I had no reason to suspect her, but then again no reason to trust her. I didn't particularly trust Planir either, having suffered the charming ruthlessness of Hadrumal's Archmage on my own account, but I knew he would always defend his own interests and for the moment those marched in step with mine and those of the House of D'Olbriot.

The candle flame burned yellow then darkened to a bloody orange, the colour tainting the reflection. Shimmering across the mirror, magic began to slowly revolve like water stirred with a rod. Where a hollow might have appeared in swirling liquid, a hole in the very fabric of the air spread across the metal surface, elements yielding to the arcane influence of the mage-born. Casuel was frowning, jaw set in utter concentration, the barest movement of light reflecting from a gold ring on one taut finger. Even after all the times I'd seen Casuel do this, I felt my spine tense at such an inexplicable manipulation of the natural order.

An image appeared in the mirror, magic reflecting the Archmage sat at a table in his study. I recognised it from my own unwilling visit to Hadrumal, a room of elegant furnishings and deadly purpose. Some instinct lifted his dark head and he looked directly across the countless leagues down through Casuel's spell, fine black brows lifted in surprise. 'Yes?'

'The colonists have arrived,' said Casuel, speaking rather rapidly. 'They had trouble making landfall because Urlan injured himself in a fall.'

'Badly?' Planir leaned forward, face intent. 'Have you seen him?'

'Not yet, it's his legs you see, he's been taken to the infirmary.' Casuel sounded like a slack apprentice trying to excuse himself to my father.

Small in the mirror, the Archmage's image nodded abruptly before gesturing in unmistakable dismissal. 'Go and see him for yourself and then bespeak me again at once.' My father had no time for underlings coming to him with tales of a task half done either.

Casuel cleared his throat. 'Velindre arrived in Bremilayne on the same tide. It seems she's eager to speak to D'Alsennin.'

'Is she?' Planir's tone was noncommittal, but even at this distance I could see his lean face was unsmiling.

Casuel was nonplussed. 'So what should I do? What should I say to her?'

Giving her some credit for saving the stricken ship would be a good start, I thought silently.

'You make the introductions she seeks.' Planir sounded faintly surprised that Casuel needed to ask. 'And you make note of her questions, whom she asks them of and the replies she receives. Then you tell me.'

Casuel preened himself visibly at the idea of being thus taken into the Archmage's confidence. It looked more like a fool's naivety being used against him to me as Planir's mouth curved like the merciless smile of a shark.

'Is she seeking some advancement?' persisted Casuel. 'She always says mastery of her element is more important than rank within the halls or recognition by the Council.' His bemusement was plain; that someone might disdain the status that he so ineffectually craved.

I heard Planir drum his fingers on the table in an uncharacteristic betrayal of tension. 'I've heard her name mentioned as a possible candidate for Cloud-Mistress,' he said lightly. 'I'd be interested if she were to say anything that suggests her own thoughts turn that way. Though you're not to raise the subject yourself, Casuel, understand?'

'But Otrick is Cloud-Master,' frowned Casuel.

'Indeed,' Planir replied flatly. 'And will remain so, whatever Troanna might say.'

But that old wizard was locked in enchanted unconsciousness, laid low by aetheric malice along with so many others in the fight for Kellarin the summer before, souring the triumph I'd shared with Temar, the mercenaries backing him and the mages who'd paid them. Finding some means of restoring those unfortunates ranked high among the obligations prompting me to continued service to Messire D'Olbriot. Fortunately, as a leading Prince of the Empire, the Sieur was foremost among those backing the search for lore to counter Elietimm enchantments. That's why I had spent the first half of the year shepherding Casuel round distant dusty libraries while my beloved Livak had taken herself clear across the Old Empire on a quest for knowledge held by the ancient races of wood and mountain.

Planir's next words diverted me from wondering how she might be faring. 'Ryshad, good day to you.'

I couldn't prevent a faint start of surprise; I'd been thinking the spell wouldn't reach to my distant seat. 'Archmage.' I gave the amber-tinted reflection a nod but moved no closer.

'I heard from Usara a few days ago,' Planir continued in friendly fashion. 'Livak's keeping well. They're heading north to see what Mountain sagas might teach us all.'

'Did they find anything of note in the Great Forest?' asked

Casuel anxiously. He'd been voluble in his contempt for Livak's theory that archaic traditions could hold unknown wisdom, so any success on her part would make him look a mighty fool. Armed with a book of old songs she insisted held hints of lost enchantments, Livak had set off determined to prove him wrong.

'Nothing conclusive has come to light.' The Archmage raised his hand again and the glow in the mirror flared bright. 'If there's nothing else, I've much to attend to here, as you know.'

'Give Usara my regards the next time you bespeak him.' The shimmering void closed in on itself, leaving no more than an after-image burned on the back of my eye. I blinked, not sure if Planir had heard me or not. Still, at least I knew Livak was in good health and I hugged that knowledge close. She was with Usara, and I reminded myself that it wasn't magic I mistrusted, just certain mages. Usara was competent and honest and that weighed heavy in the scales against Planir's deviousness and Casuel's mean spirit.

'I'd better see how Urlan is.' Casuel was looking abstracted. 'Then I'd better review my notes, to get questions for D'Alsennin clear in my mind.' And to remind himself of those few fragments of possible knowledge he'd pieced together from scraps of unheeded parchment and books faded with age. He'd want something of his own to mention casually to Planir, to counter anything Livak might find in the Forest or the Mountains. She'd certainly crow loud and long over him if she returned successful, so I could hardly blame Casuel for that. I stifled my recurrent longing for her exuberant company by reminding myself I'd agreed to her trip, so I should hardly be complaining about her absence. And her quest was only one half of the two-handed plan we hoped would secure us a future together, and Casuel wouldn't be the only one feeling the lash of her tongue if Livak returned to find I'd failed to play my part. Smiling at that thought, I recovered my damp cloak from its hook. 'I'll go and see how they are getting on at the dock.'

Casuel was already deep in his books; so much for his concern for his fellow mage. I left him to it and went back down the hill to the harbour. Seeing Glannar's men at their ease in front of the barred warehouse door, I looked for Temar. He was standing amid burly dockers, counting out coin into the gang-leader's calloused palm.

'A fair rate for the day,' I observed, calculating the Tormalin Crowns bright in the man's filthy hand. The docker grunted noncommittally.

'But with the weather hardly fair, I think something over for the cold and the wet.' Temar dropped a couple of silver Marks on to the gold and a grudging smile lifted the docker's lip to reveal stained brown teeth.

'Pleasure to do business with you, Esquire,' he nodded before stowing the coin securely in a money belt and whistling up his crew with a gesture towards a nearby tavern.

'You don't want to get a reputation as an easy touch,' I warned Temar.

He shrugged, unconcerned. 'If the ships of Kel Ar'Ayen are known to pay well, we will never lack for labour to get them unloaded.' He nodded towards the ship that had brought Velindre. 'So who is this wizard that I owe my life? How does she arrive in so timely a fashion?'

'Her name's Velindre, but that's all I know of her,' I admitted reluctantly. 'She says she's interested in the winds and currents of Kellarin's coast, but Planir thinks she may have ambitions to make a name for herself in Hadrumal.'

'If she hopes for a salvage due, she had best get in line behind those others looking to make a claim on the colony,' said Temar lightly.

I looked at him, assessing the hint of seriousness in his words. With an easy assumption of D'Olbriot authority over Kellarin running through the idle gossip of sworn and chosen over the last season, I'd been the only one suggesting the game might play out differently.

'Temar!' A thin woman came striding over the cobbles towards us, hood falling back from brown hair liberally streaked with grey and concern deepening the lines of age in her face. Though the rain had all but ceased, she was wiping her face in unthinking, repetitive gestures, speaking rapidly to Temar. Her speech was too thick with the intonation of Old Toremal for me, but I recognised her as the Demoiselle Tor Arrial, one of Kellarin's few other surviving nobility. Temar nodded and looked at me. 'Avila wishes to know where we are to lodge. Most of the crew and other passengers are claiming rooms in these inns.'

'We have everything you need made ready at the Shrine of Ostrin.' I spoke slowly in my most formal accent. Avila Tor Arrial looked at me sharply, one chapped hand clutching a cloak pin set with rubies and pale rose diamonds at her throat. After a pause she nodded and her gesture needed no translation, so I led the way, leaving behind the ramshackle dockside for the more regular streets around the circle of Ostrin's walls.

'I thought there were supposed to be more of you,' I remarked to Temar.

He shrugged. 'When it came to it, they all found reasons to stay. The more we talk to the sailors, to the mages, the more we learn how our world has changed. At least in Kellarin we know what we are dealing with.' He fell silent and we walked without speaking until we reached the embrace of Ostrin's walls.

'It's this way.' I waved Avila through the gate welcoming all comers into the stone circle. The broad gravel sweep inside was busy with new arrivals, two coaches unloading a vociferous family presumably taking ship to north or south.

'Perhaps they were right to stay,' murmured Temar, eyes wide as he looked back out of the gate at the thriving town. 'It is all so different, nothing as I remember it.'

'Let's get you warm,' I urged, seeing a pallor I didn't like in his face.

He followed me without protest to the comfortable guest house behind the main shrine to Ostrin. Maidservants were busy about the hospitality that is ever the god's chief concern, offering soft towels, ewers of warm water and hot tisanes to stiff and chilled arrivals, porters discreetly depositing battered luggage in bedchambers.

'There are rooms reserved here for you and the Demoiselle Tor Arrial.' I led Temar up the broad stairway, wooden panelling gleaming with years of dedicated polish. 'The sailors and mercenaries can shift for themselves in the inns but Messire thought you would welcome some privacy.' The exaggerated tales of the mariners and freebooters could supply sufficient grist to satisfy the rumour mill, so there was no need to expose Temar to intrusive curiosity.

That thought sparked another as I opened the door to the room I'd chosen for Temar. 'The mage Velindre has invited herself to dine with me and Casuel this evening. Why don't you and Avila eat in the upper parlour?'

Temar halted on the threshold to give me a narrow look before shrugging. 'As you see fit.'

'There's clean linen, shaving soap, razor.' I nodded at the washstand. 'I'm next door if you need anything else.' I hesitated, wondering whether to offer companionship or allow the lad some solitude to gather his thoughts. A footfall behind me heralded a maidservant with a steaming jug of water so I stepped aside to let her pass.

'You must want to change.' Temar nodded at my sodden leather boots. His tight smile didn't quite meet his eyes so I took the hint and withdrew, pulling his door closed.

A quick trip to the kitchens housed across the courtyard meant I could leave my cloak in the drying room and once I was satisfied that my orders for the evening's meals were clearly understood I hurried back to the guest house. I found Casuel and Allin squaring up to each other in the main hall. Her high colour was cruelly unflattering but her folded arms were braced with resolve. Casuel, clutching a folded bundle of white, looked more baffled than annoyed.

My arrival gave Allin the chance to escape. 'I'll see you both at dinner.' With her curtsey a touch too hurried, she walked away just fast enough to betray her eagerness to flee.

'I only asked her to do some mending,' said Casuel crossly.

'I'm sure one of the maids would be glad of the extra work,' I suggested. 'It'll only cost you a few pennies and I don't suppose a wizard's linen is any different to anyone else's.'

The realisation that he was standing there holding his small clothes for any passer-by to see sent Casuel scurrying up the stairs. Following at a more leisurely pace, I shed my soaked clothes gratefully, getting my blood flowing again with warm water and vigorous towelling before having a contemplative shave. I needed to know what Temar hoped to achieve on this visit, I decided, and some clue as to Velindre's business would be useful. Concluding that it wouldn't hurt to remind her of my standing with D'Olbriot, I dressed in the elegant attire my new status entitled me to claim from Toremal's finest tailors at Messire's expense. The price to me was wearing a mossy green that I didn't particularly care for. A knock on my door came as I was buttoning my shirt. It was the Steward of the Shrine with a query about how long we were staying and just how many rooms were required, so I took up my more prosaic duties once more.

The Shrine of Ostrin, Bremilayne, 9th of For-Summer in the Third Year of Tadriol the Provident, Evening

Temar lay down on the bed and hid his head beneath a down-filled pillow. Clamping it tight over his ears shut out the noises of the guest house: a man passing his door with a shouted query, someone else's demands for fresh towels, the rough bumping of heavy burdens dragged up the wooden stairs. But he couldn't banish the memories assailing him, the agony of the injured mage, the frantic prayers of his companions that Dastennin calm the sea, that Larasion quell the winds, that Saedrin spare them. The foul and desperate curses of the sailors echoed in his memory, the groans of ship's timbers stressed beyond endurance, the wicked crack of snapping rope and the scream of someone lashed by the vicious ends. After all they had been through, after all they had endured, he and his companions had nearly drowned, so close to shore, within very sight of safety, all their hopes and those of the colony they had left behind sunk beneath Dastennin's malice to feed the scavenging crabs.

Time passed unnoticed until loud disagreement from the room above forced itself into Temar's misery. He emerged red-faced from beneath the pillow, tears and dirt smeared on his face. One shrewish voice rose indignant, prompting a harsh response that rang through the floorboards.

Temar couldn't make out the meaning. How was he ever going to make good his bold boasts to Guinalle when it took all his concentration just to comprehend what people were saying? Albarn, Brive, all the others, they'd turned back from this insane attempt to revisit the world they had lost and no one had thought the worse of them. Why couldn't he have done the same?

Because his rank denied him that freedom: Temar could almost hear Guinalle's terse reply, for all that she was half a world away. Because he had a duty to his people and the only way he could fulfil his obligations was to risk the ocean crossing and all that he might find in this strangely changed Tormalin. For whatever reason, by whatever means, Saedrin had entrusted those people to his care, and if he failed – Temar shivered. He would have no words to excuse his failure when he came to knock on the door to the Otherworld and seek admittance from the god who held the keys. And what would Guinalle think of him hiding his head like a child afraid of Eldritch-men creeping out of the shadows?

Temar went numbly about the business of a much needed wash, oblivious to the luxuries of the room. Raising a blade to his face was beyond him, he realised, finding his hands shaking so badly that he spilled soapy foam all over the marble washstand. Scowling fiercely, he forced himself to concentrate on mopping up the trivial mess and the dread oppressing him faded a little until a knock on the door set his heart pounding. 'Enter,' he managed to say before his voice cracked.

The door opened and Avila slid into the room, her faded eyes hollow in a face grey with fatigue. 'So, are you comfortable?' It was a meaningless question, Temar realised, just an excuse to come and find him.

'After the privations of Kel Ar'Ayen?' He gestured at the snowy linen of the bed, the polished floor and the curtains embroidered with Ostrin's faithful hounds. 'I'll sleep through the chimes and back again, given half a chance.'

'I doubt we'll get that.' Avila summoned a faint smile. 'Are there any others from the ship lodging here?'

'No.' Temar tried to mask his own regret. His friends among the sailors and mercenaries might have been little more than casual acquaintances but he'd rather spend the evening sharing a flagon of ale with them than dining alone with Avila. This trip was going to be trial enough without her bracing criticism constantly at his elbow.

The great bell of the shrine broke into the awkward silence

with its unexpected peal. As the master note struck eight times, Temar realised Avila's eyes were edged with white, her taut face reflecting his own myriad anxieties. Perhaps he wouldn't have to spend the evening trying to deflect her usual challenges after all. Seeing the normally assertive woman so subdued put perverse heart into Temar.

'A true sound of home, which must mean it's time to eat.' He forced an encouraging smile, but Avila looked askance at him. 'Try something sweet, or a little wine, just to settle your stomach?'

'Your appetite's not suffered then.' Her sceptical tone was a faint echo of her normal forthrightness.

Temar held out his arm, and as Avila took it they walked downstairs. His boots fell heavy on the floorboards, in contrast to the whisper of Avila's soft shoes, and abruptly the fleeting confidence buoying him fled. All at once Temar felt weary to his very bones and complex qualms filled his belly, leaving him no wish for food. But a lad in what must be a livery of the shrine bowed to them as he arrived with a tray of covered dishes and Temar followed him to a south-facing room furnished with simple elegance. If old ways still held true, all this was gifts from those grateful for Ostrin's hospitality, Temar recalled. As Avila released his arm, he went to stand at a broad bay window looking out across the ocean. A bright blue sky was streaked with white clouds tinged with gold, the sun making some amends before retreating behind the mountains lifting a dark shadow to the west. Temar shoved clenched fists deep into breeches pockets to stop their trembling as he looked at the sea, sparkling and serene with no hint of the fury that had so nearly been the death of them all.

'Here you are, Demoiselle, Esquire.' The lackey was laying out dishes on the table as he spoke. 'There's pease with leek and fennel, sheatfish in onion sauce, mutton with rosemary, and mushrooms in wine. Now, ring if there's anything else you need.' He placed a little silver bell next to the place he was laying for Temar and startled him with a quick wink before going on his way.

Temar's battered spirits revived a little. Perhaps he and the other folk of Kel Ar'Ayen weren't too far removed from their long-lost relatives. That thought set him wondering where Ryshad might be.

'Now what do you suppose those two want?' Avila ignored the food, joining Temar at the window and looking down on the paths and lawns of the shrine. 'I'm more than a little tired of these wizards treating us like some freak show.'

Temar watched two women emerge from another guest house and found he shared Avila's weary annoyance. 'Probably hotfoot with the usual curiosity about Kel Ar'Ayen and its fate.'

'These so-called scholars don't appreciate we've a new life to build, as surely as when we first made landfall,' said Avila tartly.

'They are helping, most of them,' Temar protested, forcing himself to be fair. 'Without the mages of Hadrumal, we'd all still be locked in enchanted darkness.'

'Are we expected to repay that debt forever?' sniffed Avila.

Temar didn't know how to answer that, but she turned away to pour herself a goblet of rich red wine from a crystal jug. 'Please give my apologies to the servants, but this is all too rich for me to stomach.' She took a piece of fine white bread from an ornate silver basket. 'I'll see you in the morning.'

Temar watched her go with mingled relief and dismay. It wasn't as if he particularly liked Avila, still convinced she'd some hand in Guinalle's refusal to accept the love he offered, but the acerbic Demoiselle was the only person he knew on this side of the ocean.

He lifted the lid on one of the silver dishes but his gorge rose at the spicy scent of the mutton. He poured himself some wine. No, Avila wasn't the only person he knew here. There was Ryshad. Was the sworn man going to prove the true friend he'd seemed the year before? Temar sipped the excellent vintage and tried to ignore a mocking memory of his self-assured boasts to Guinalle before sailing. It was his duty to serve Kel Ar'Ayen by presenting their needs to the nobility gathered for Solstice in Toremal, and he'd surrender that to no man, he'd told her.

Now he wondered just what he would find there, seeing how this one little town was so fearfully changed.

He needed Ryshad's help, that much was certain. Setting down his wine, Temar opened the parlour door, but as he did so a hall lackey opened the main door to the two lady mages and Temar hesitated, pushing the door to.

'You owe Casuel a certain duty of gratitude. He recognised your affinity and brought you to Hadrumal. That does not entitle him to treat you as his personal maid.' Velindre sounded a worthy match for Avila at her most abrasive.

Temar smiled a little as he held the parlour door open a crack and watched the lackey usher the women into a dining salon.

'My lady Velindre Ychane and my lady Allin Mere.' The grace titles seemed entirely appropriate as the taller mage swept elegantly into the room, Allin at her heel visibly unsure of herself. Temar sympathised ruefully.

'Good evening.'

Temar clicked his tongue in annoyance as he heard Ryshad's courteous greeting. There would be no chance to speak to him in private now. As he wondered what to do, the other mage, Casuel Something-Or-Other, bustled down the stairs, all ill-disguised curiosity and smoothing a full-skirted coat of rich tan velvet as he hurried into the dining room. The fool was going to be uncomfortably hot in that, thought Temar uncharitably. No, Guinalle was always rebuking him for that kind of rapid judgement. Temar rubbed a hand over his long jaw. If he was ever going to make Guinalle change her mind about him, he had to succeed in this voyage. Unknown wizards intent on their own concerns could be a real thorn in his shoe. Temar walked softly down the hallway and listened at the dining salon door.

'Are the colonists not joining us?' That was Velindre. An artless question, Temar thought, but why ask when she could plainly see they weren't?

'Not tonight.' Ryshad was courteous as always. 'So, what's your interest in Kellarin?' Courteous but blunt when need be. Temar grinned.

'A passing one,' the mage replied readily enough. 'I'm only

interested in so far as it relates to the Elietimm threat.'

Temar felt his skin crawl and fancied the chill silence filling the room was nigh on palpable through the door.

'We have no reason to suppose they have abandoned their ambitions to territory beyond their own islands,' Velindre continued easily.

'And you saw no need to seek Planir's permission or guidance before involving yourself in concerns that reach as high as the Emperor himself?' asked Casuel waspishly.

'Not for a few general enquiries, no,' Velindre said coolly.

Casuel cleared his throat. 'The Elietimm were comprehensively rebuffed when they tried to seize Kellarin last year. It's clear enough their scheming in Tormalin before that was part of their search for the lost colony. They'll know they are overmatched now and abandon such adventures.'

Temar shut his eyes on vivid recollection; black-hearted Elietimm raiders shattering their dream of a new life over the ocean, murdering friends and mentors, forcing the trapped survivors to insane trust in the half-understood enchantment that was their only hope of refuge. Bloody visions of carnage hovered at the edge of his mind's eye while the screams of the slaughtered sounded silently in his ears.

'We held our own in the fight for Kellarin only because Temar and I were able to kill their enchanter.' Ryshad contradicted Casuel and Temar opened his eyes. 'Fortunately Elietimm troops are so in thrall, be it through enchantment or simple terror, that once their leaders are dead the rest surrender. As long as their enchanters survive, they are a lethal foe.'

'Their earlier crimes in Tormalin first got you involved?' Velindre evidently wanted Ryshad to confirm what she had already learned. Wizards were all like that, Temar mused, never taking anything on trust.

'A nephew of Messire D'Olbriot was attacked, robbed and left for dead. I was pursuing those responsible when I met Darni, the Archmage's agent, and learned of his interest in the matter.' Ryshad's voice was emotionless, but Temar knew the truth of the swordsman's desperate battles for life and liberty as he sought his master's revenge. He wondered bleakly if he'd ever match Ryshad's self-possession.

'Which is when these people were first traced to islands in the far ocean,' Casuel hurried to fill the silence Ryshad had let fall. 'And we first identified their peculiar magic.'

And the men of those ice-girt islands were descendants of the self-same Elietimm who massacred the first colonists of Kel Ar'Ayen, who forced them into enchanted sleep as the only means of saving themselves. Waking so many generations adrift from the world they'd known still to be assailed by the same foul enemy was a torment worthy of Poldrion's own demons. Temar set his jaw. Common foes meant common cause and, with the Elietimm already enemies of princes such as D'Olbriot, the colonists could look for help this time. Whatever else had changed in the endless years of their sleep, the fundamentals of honour were untarnished.

Velindre was speaking again, her voice hard and low, and Temar strained to hear. 'Aetheric magic, some sorcery that the mage-born cannot comprehend, let alone wield.' As with most wizards Temar had encountered since waking to this strangely changed world, Velindre clearly felt this a personal affront to her own curious powers. Was that her reason for being here?

'Which we now know to be the magic of the Old Empire?' That safe contribution had to be from the younger woman, Allin.

'What the ancients called Artifice,' Ryshad confirmed, an encouraging note in his voice. 'But when the Empire fell into the Chaos, nearly all such knowledge was lost.'

'Meaningless superstition peddled by priests and shrines,' said Casuel tartly. 'Not worthy to be called magic.'

How dared this overdressed fool judge something he knew less than nothing about? Artifice had held together a greater Empire than any this age would ever see. Temar reached for the door handle but someone unexpected was setting Casuel right.

'Elietimm enchantments rend minds and twist wills. Worse, mage-born working their own spells are peculiarly vulnerable to attack,' snapped Velindre. 'Cloud-Master Otrick lies in a deathless sleep thanks to these scum. Until we can counter their sorcery, the Elietimm are a potent threat to wizardry, whether they cross the ocean this summer or in a generation hence.'

'They're just as much a threat to Tormalin,' Ryshad pointed out in moderate tones. 'I wouldn't wager a lead penny against them crossing the ocean again inside a couple of seasons. I've visited the barren rocks they call home. No one would live there given a choice. That's why Planir and Messire D'Olbriot sent last year's expedition in search of the lost colony. Finding some knowledge of Artifice to combat Elietimm enchantment was reckoned worth the risks.'

No, it hadn't been some selfless bid to rescue those unfortunates lost in the toils of ancient magic, thought Temar glumly. He was tired of hearing Kel Ar'Ayen always discussed in terms of its utility to other people.

'The colony's rediscovery must have tongues wagging from the Astmarsh to the Cape of Winds,' ventured Allin.

'Hundreds of people hidden in a cavern over countless generations, bodies uncorrupted by time or decay while the very essence of their being was locked in some inanimate artefact.' There was unmistakable challenge in Velindre's tone. 'I still find it incredible.'

That was quite enough. Temar opened the door. 'Incredible or not, I am living proof that it is so.' There are scant people you owe a bent knee to, he reminded himself, summoning all the poise he'd learned as a nobleman in the final days of the Old Empire.

'Temar, may I make known Velindre Ychane, mage of Hadrumal, and Allin Mere, also a wizard.' Ryshad fetched an extra chair from the side of the room without comment. 'Ladies, I have the honour to present Temar, Esquire D'Alsennin.'

'The honour is all mine.' Temar made a low bow.

'Wine?' offered Ryshad. 'We have a white from the western slopes of Kalavere, which should be good, or a Sitalcan red, which I'm afraid I don't know.'

'White, thank you.'

Ryshad saluted Temar with the goblet as he passed it over and then rang a small silver bell. Temar took his seat.

'So what was it like?' Velindre fixed Temar with an intent look. She wore a plain, round-necked gown of fine indigo wool, her face free of any cosmetic and her only jewellery a chain of silver around her neck carrying no pendant or jewel. Long blonde hair was braided in a plait with tidily trimmed ends sun-bleached nearly to white. Temar guessed her a handful or more years Ryshad's senior.

'Like sleeping, mostly, with some dreams like those of a fever,' Temar replied with bland composure. He wasn't about to elaborate on his turbulent visions of those who'd unwittingly borne the sword holding his consciousness locked deep within it.

Velindre was about to pursue this but a maid entered with a tray. Ryshad alerted her to lay an extra place in front of Temar with a quick gesture and everyone sat in silence, watching the lass set down a sauceboat alongside a dish of pork braised in wine and green oil.

'Superstition or not, you can trust those serving Ostrin to keep their vow of discretion,' Ryshad said with some force as the girl departed with an uncertain backward glance.

'You were caught up in this enchantment, weren't you?' Velindre challenged him.

'Thanks to the contrivance of Archmage Planir.' Ryshad leaned back in his chair, rolling rich red wine round in the engraved glass he had cupped in one hand. 'He ensured I was given Temar's sword. I dreamed of Temar and the colony as it had been so long ago. That gave the final clues to finding the cavern.'

Temar managed to meet the older man's half-smile with a nod of his own. The terrors of madness both had suffered, the struggle for identity and mastery over Ryshad's body as Temar, all unwitting, had struggled to break free of the enchantment: that was no one's business but their own.

Velindre was patently not satisfied and turned back to Temar. 'I hear you have an Adept of Artifice with you?'

'Avila Tor Arrial,' replied Temar, striving for Ryshad's self-possession. 'The Demoiselle wishes to learn what has become of her House in the generations since we slept. She also wants to see if anything remains of the lore this very shrine was founded to husband.' Temar doubted that, now he'd seen the place so altered.

Velindre frowned. 'I thought Guinalle Tor Priminal was the foremost practitioner of this Artifice?'

'She is,' agreed Temar. 'Which is why her first obligation remains to the colony she originally crossed the ocean to succour and support.' The endless frozen years hadn't changed that; whatever love he might one day win from Guinalle would never outweigh her sense of duty.

'We all have our responsibilities.' Velindre let slip a smile of considerable charm. 'But I feel she could clarify so many of the mysteries that plague us.'

'Guinalle is working with scholars of Col and Vanam,' pointed out Ryshad mildly. 'Those that are prepared to cross the ocean, at least.'

'We are finding much of interest within the archives of the great Houses of Tormalin,' remarked Casuel loftily, anxious not to be kept out of the conversation. 'My colleagues and I are daily identifying new aspects of aetheric magic.'

'You always had an aptitude for searching through dusty documents, Cas.' Velindre nodded at the table as the maid reappeared with a laden tray. 'I think we should eat, don't you?' She helped herself to chicken breast and green herb dumplings.

'More wine, Allin?' Ryshad proffered the carafe.

'White, please, just half a glass.'

Temar thought about teasing the lass with some remark about such decorous abstinence; they were much of an age, a clear double handful of years younger than either Casuel or Ryshad. Remembering she was a wizard, he decided against it. The table was well supplied with food and Temar noticed the dishes he'd abandoned had been brought in. To his surprise he realised his stomach was threatening to growl like a beggar's dog. He passed Ryshad a dish of lobster in lovage and cider sauce and reached for the plate of boiled ham and figs that caught his eye. Whatever it was Velindre wanted to know, she seemed satisfied for the present, and Temar was content to eat and listen as the mages swapped news of people he didn't know. Velindre and Ryshad compared their experiences of the southern ports of Toremal, and Casuel tried to interest people in his theories on the political situation in Caladhria.

Allin made few contributions to the conversation, and none without blushing, but when the maids were clearing the table she turned to Temar with a shy smile. 'Are there many differences between this meal and those – before?'

'Not so many,' he replied with some surprise at the realisation. 'But there can be only so many ways of cooking, and meat, fish or fowl remain the same.' A maid reached past him with porcelain bowls of sweetmeats while a steward set out decanters of sweet wine and cordials.

Allin nibbled a little pastry stuffed with nuts and raisins. 'You sound quite Lescari, did you know that? Do you know people from there?'

Temar nodded. 'Most of those who came to fight for Kel Ar'Ayen last year were from Lescar. Many chose to stay on and help in our rebuilding and they hope to bring friends to start a new life with us. I have doubtless picked up something of their tongue.'

Allin drew so sharp a breath she choked on her mouthful. Temar hastily offered her glass but she pushed his hand away as she struggled to control her coughs. 'Mercenaries!' she spat. 'Nurse a wolf cub at your hearth and it'll still eat your sheep. Be more careful whom you trust.'

Temar looked a frantic question at Ryshad, mortified to have caused offence.

'Your family has suffered in the fighting, I take it?' Ryshad asked Allin sympathetically.

'We used to live just north of Carluse.' The girl was scarlet to the roots of her hair but managed a hoarse reply. 'Sharlac mercenaries burned us out and we fled to Caladhria.'

'Which is where I identified the girl's talent,' piped up Casuel. 'And now she is your pupil?' He looked at Velindre with ill-disguised annoyance.

'Forgive me,' said Temar soberly to Allin. 'I know nothing of modern Lescar. In my day it was a peaceful province of the Empire.' But he should have remembered it had been rent by civil war for ten generations or more. He saw his own thoughts reflected in Ryshad's alert brown eyes. How would Temar hold his own among the Princes and courts of Toremal, so ignorant of politics within and beyond the Empire's reduced borders? More important things had changed than the way people spoke or sauced their dinners.

'So, Velindre, will you be travelling to Toremal with us?' Casuel persisted, his voice loud in the awkward silence. Ryshad silently passed Allin a dish of honey-soaked sops of toasted bread to give her time to recover her composure.

Velindre inclined her head towards Ryshad. 'I take it you are going to the capital for the Solstice Festival?'

He nodded as he filled small glasses from a decanter of white brandy. 'Messire D'Olbriot is keen to introduce Esquire D'Alsennin to the Houses of the Empire.'

'I should like to meet the Demoiselle Tor Arrial before you go,' Velindre said firmly. 'To learn something of Artifice and its uses. You'll be sparing a few days to rest?'

Ryshad looked at Temar who shrugged uncertainly. 'It may be a day or so before Avila's recovered from the voyage.'

'We'll most certainly wait,' Casuel frowned. 'The moons aren't fit for travel! The lesser will be past the half in a few nights and the greater is nigh on full dark.'

'I'd rather keep days in hand to rest the horses along the way,' Ryshad disputed. 'Solstice doesn't wait for Saedrin or anyone else.'

'How do we travel?' Temar enquired.

'By horse,' Ryshad stated firmly.

'Coach,' contradicted Casuel, looking obstinate.

'I'll risk saddle sores over coach sickness, thanks all the same,' Temar said lightly. 'But Avila may think otherwise.'

'Well I intend to drive, even if no one else does,' Casuel snapped.

'I never cease to be thankful for the magecraft that saves me from such choices,' Velindre smiled. 'I'll see Urlan safely back to Hadrumal, Cas, and after that I imagine we'll see you at the Festival. For the present, we'll leave you with your wine. Come on, Allin.' Temar watched as Velindre made her exit with the poise of a noble from any age of the Empire.

Casuel looked after her with some irritation. 'I was about to say I would bespeak assistance for Urlan. It's just—'

Ryshad spoke over the mage with a wicked smile as he refilled Temar's glass. 'In Toremal, we swap indecorous stories once the ladies have left.'

Temar laughed as Casuel drew an indignant breath. 'Something else not changed, for all the generations I have missed.'

'But there are many things you do need to know.' Casuel leaned forward, face eager. 'I made some preliminary notes, but we need to identify particular areas of concern—'

'Not tonight, if you please,' Temar pleaded.

'Give the lad a chance to catch his breath,' Ryshad chided Casuel genially.

Temar suddenly felt exhausted. He set down his half-finished glass with an unsteady hand. 'I'll gladly learn all I may from you and you'll have my thanks, but for now I'll bid you good night.'

'Arimelin send you pleasant dreams,' said Ryshad.

Temar looked sharply at him but saw nothing but good will in the man's face. 'And to you,' he stammered before hurrying from the room.

The Shrine of Ostrin, Bremilayne,
10th of For-Summer in the Third Year of Tadriol the Provident, Morning

It's such a commonplace to wish the goddess send someone refreshing dreams that the words were out of my mouth before I'd realised what I was saying. Temar's startled look set nervous fingers plucking at the back of my own mind and, once I'd bid Casuel good night, I climbed the candlelit stairs of the guest house with uncommon reluctance. I'd thought nigh on a year of being alone in my own head had cured me of the horrors of having my mind invaded by another's, but it seemed not. I even considered going back for a flask of some liquor to drown any dreams but sternly reminded myself I'd found such remedies ineffective enough in my callow youth. Uncomfortably aware of Temar's presence in the next room, I resolutely diverted my thoughts by speculating what Livak might be up to and listened to the chimes of the shrine sounding well into the night.

Arimelin must have been busy elsewhere. When I finally fell asleep I didn't dream of my red-haired beloved or anything else and woke to a clear sunny morning. Washed, shaved and dressed in short order, I was downstairs early enough to startle a servant girl sweeping the hall floor.

'We're done in the dining salon, sir.' She sent a cloud of dust out of the open door billow in a golden haze. 'You can make yourself a tisane or I can fetch you something from the kitchens?'

I shook my head. 'I'll breakfast with everyone else.'

The sideboard in the salon was laid with delicate ceramic cups and an array of jars with silver tags around their necks identifying the herbs and spices within. A kettle sat on a small charcoal stove set in the fireplace, puffing gentle wisps of steam up the chimney. I was finding a spoon when the door opened behind me and I turned to see Temar looking much better for a good night's sleep.

'Tisane?' I dangled a pierced silver ball by its chain.

Temar gave a brief smile but his wolf-pale eyes were still wary. 'We use scraps of muslin in Kel Ar'Ayen.'

'Like most people this side of the ocean.' I clicked the little sphere open and spooned in some lemon balm. 'But noble guests are accustomed to their little luxuries.'

Temar made some noise that could have been agreement or not. He studied the crystal jars before helping himself to some red-stemmed mint. 'Back in my day, this shrine was a place set aside for the contemplation and study of Artifice.' A broader smile cracked his rather solemn expression. ' "Back in my day"; I sound like some grandsire lamenting his lost youth.' The smile faded. 'Well, it's certainly lost, along with my grandsire and everyone else I ever knew.'

'But you have new friends,' I said encouragingly. 'And the House of D'Olbriot will welcome you as warmly as one of their own.'

Temar was staring out of the window, tisane forgotten. 'I knew it was all gone, that they were all gone, but in Kel Ar'Ayen things aren't so different, not to how it was when we first arrived. We'd lost all we'd worked for but we knew that, with the Elietimm destroying everything as we fled—' His voice trailed off into uncertainty.

I took the tisane ball from his unresisting hands and added some bittertooth, my mother's specific for low spirits. 'And now you're here?' Fetching the kettle, I poured water into both cups, hoping no one would interrupt us.

Temar sighed, lacing his long fingers round the cup's comforting warmth. 'I don't know where I am. Bremilayne was a fishing village, a few boats pulling crabs from the rocks.' We both looked down at the sizeable fleet returning from the night's fishing, seabirds wheeling within the massive curve of the harbour wall. 'The adepts founded their sanctuary here because the place was so isolated, of no use or interest to anyone else. That has certainly changed.' He gestured at the imposing houses set around the equally impressive precincts of the shrine.

'The port deals with all the Gidestan trade,' I explained. 'Goods from the mountains come down the river to Inglis and are shipped down here.'

'To be carried over the mountains to the west?' Temar nodded at a shallow cleft in the looming ridge. 'Even the skyline has changed. When did that landslip close the old route?'

As he pointed I saw a hollow where a great mass of stone and earth had fallen from the heights in some past age. The sprawl of broken ground wasn't immediately obvious as trees tall enough to make ships' masts dotted the scrub. 'Not in my lifetime, or anyone since my great-grandsire's, I should think,' I admitted.

'Perhaps I should ask your friend Casuel,' Temar suggested, and his half-smile encouraged me.

'I know something of what you're feeling,' I reminded him.

Temar sipped his drink and looked up with frank scepticism. 'How so?'

'The Aldabreshin Archipelago was as foreign a place to me as all this is to you,' I pointed out. 'I found my feet there. It'll take us a good while to cross the country, and I warn you Casuel's determined to teach you all you need to know, and more besides, I'll wager. In any case, Solstice Festival is only five days, and once it's over you can take ship back to Kellarin whenever you like.'

Temar suddenly set his cup down. 'I have not asked your pardon for my part in your enslavement.'

I was taken aback. 'You were hardly to know what was happening, caught up in the enchantment as much as me. What's done is gone and we need to be looking to the future, not turning over last autumn's leaves.' I managed to make something of a joke of it and in any case I blamed Planir far more than I'd ever blame Temar.

Temar studied my face and some of the tension left him.

'And as far as we can tell, it was the Elietimm setting their claws in my mind that woke you in Relshaz and set you searching for your lost companions,' I reminded him. Temar's fellow colonists had been sleeping like him, their enchanted minds held in seemingly innocent artefacts. Once roused, Temar's consciousness had overwhelmed my own, starting a frantic quest for one of those trinkets that had landed me in chains. Taken for a thief, I'd been condemned to be sold into slavery to repay my so-called victim's losses. 'That Elietimm enchanter we killed in Kellarin was the one who got the Aldabreshin woman to buy me. He was after the sword that was linking me to you and the secrets of the colony.' Even my anger with the wizards didn't blind me to the true enemy here.

'True enough.' Temar's face hardened. 'I have no doubt the Elietimm will attack us again, whatever Master Devoir may say. We must have means to defend ourselves. I refuse to stay reliant on the Archmage for protection.'

'So what do you need?' I prompted.

'First and most important we must recover the artefacts to restore those still held in enchantment,' said Temar firmly. 'Several of our most adept are still lost to us.'

'How many are still asleep?' I stifled a shudder at the memory of that vast, chill cavern, dark beneath the weight of rock as unchanged through the years as those frozen bodies beneath it.

'Some three hundred and more.' Temar sounded surer of himself. 'That is why I came for Solstice. It has to be the best time to trace the missing artefacts, with all the great families gathered in the capital.'

I nodded. 'And Kellarin has gold, gems, furs, who knows what else to trade. Messire D'Olbriot has the contacts to help you earn the coin to buy in tools, goods, skilled men, everything you need to rebuild. He was saying Kellarin goods could rival the Gidestan trade inside five years.'

'How much can I accomplish in five days?' Temar looked a little daunted.

'I'll be there to help,' I pointed out.

'You are D'Olbriot's man. You will be busy with your own

duties,' he protested, but with evident hope I was going to contradict him.

'You'll be D'Olbriot's guest,' I reminded him. 'I'll be your aide, at Messire's direct order.' Which was fortunate, since I'd have been doing all I could for Temar, with or without the Sieur's permission.

Faint sounds of the guest house rising for the day came from the rooms above us. I savoured the sharp tang of lemon from my cooling cup.

'You were not so keen to return to your patron's service the last time we spoke,' Temar said cautiously. 'You were talking of striking out on your own with that girl of yours. Are you no longer together?'

'Livak?' I hesitated. 'Well, yes and no. That is, a future together's easier wished for than found.'

'She seemed very independent.'

I wondered what prompted Temar's interest in my love life. I hoped he wasn't expecting advice on salvaging something from the disasters of his own romance with Guinalle. 'Independent to the point of criminal at times, which is certainly not a road I can take, any more than she'll settle to life in a grace house sewing her seams while I attend Messire.'

'So what are you to do?' Perhaps Temar was just looking for some distraction.

'If I can render Messire some signal service . . .' I faltered. 'I've made the step to chosen man. The top of the ladder is proven man. As such I'd warrant a commission to manage an estate for D'Olbriot, or to act as his agent in some city like Relshaz. I'd be looking out for D'Olbriot interests, but no longer at the Sieur's beck and call. Livak and I think we could live with that.' As with so many plans, it sounded less likely spoken aloud than it seemed in the privacy of my own head.

'Oh.' Temar looked blank. Of course, the oath-bound traditions of service that I was committed to meant nothing to him. That had all grown up after the Chaos, the bloody anarchy that had brought the Old Empire low, when ties of loyalty had gone for nothing as the Princes of the great Houses turned on the feckless Emperor who'd brought ruin on them all. The ordered fealty of tenants to their Liege-Lords that Temar had known was as foreign to me as this new Bremilayne was to him.

'So what is this signal service to be?' Temar challenged.

I grinned. 'Helping you set Kellarin fair for a glorious and profitable future, to the mutual benefit of the Houses of D'Olbriot and D'Alsennin?'

Temar grinned but with a humourless curl to his lip. 'If those Elietimm scum permit it.'

'Messire has people searching for enchantments to be used against the Elietimm, in defence of Kellarin and Tormalin.'

Temar looked hopefully at me. 'How so?'

'Livak's travelling in the Sieur's name, hunting aetheric knowledge among the ancient races of wood and mountain,' I explained. Casuel might have scorned Livak's theory about her song book, but the Sieur had thought it worth wagering a little coin.

'Saedrin make it so,' murmured Temar, and I nodded fervent agreement. After the best part of a year without their black ships on the horizon, I was certain the summer would see renewed Elietimm attack. One small consolation for Livak's absence was knowing she'd be as far from any fighting as possible. Her finding something powerful would also be a signal service to weigh in our favour when the time came to ask Messire for my freedom.

Urgent steps sounded on the gravel outside and rapid hammering at the door brought a hall lackey running up from the cellars.

Temar and I looked at each other startled and Glannar burst in, face like thunder. 'The warehouse's been robbed!'

'Sit down.' I urged him to a chair, not liking the florid colour beneath his beard.

'No,' Glannar waved me away breathlessly, 'I need the Esquire D'Alsennin.' He looked uncertainly at Temar.

'At once.' Temar moved to the door.

'Don't you want to know what happened?' Glannar looked from Temar to me and back again.

'We will see for ourselves.' Temar was already out of the room and I hurried Glannar to the gate of the shrine.

'A little slower, I think,' I said quietly as we reached the road. 'Or we'll have every eye in town turned to our business.' Temar on my near side gave me a sharp look while Glannar on the off hand scowled ferociously, but they both slackened their pace a little.

The town was still quiet, some women scrubbing front steps with a few men about nameless tasks in the morning cool. Slate and cobbles shone blue and silver in the sun, mimicking the sparkling sea below. There was bustle on the quayside, all hands busy unloading the fisher fleet, scavenging birds raucous above the shouts of the labouring men and women.

We ignored everything apart from the warehouse, where two of Glannar's sworn men stood guard, swords drawn and jaws clenched on humiliation. Inside the recognised lads were attempting to tidy the shambles made of the previous day's neat stowage while the other two sworn propped a ladder beneath a gaping skylight letting cheerful sunlight into what should have been secure gloom. A rear door beyond had its locking bar tossed aside.

'No need to ask how the wharf rats got into your malt heap,' I commented to Glannar.

'Get moving before I take a horsewhip to you!' he snarled as three of the recognised stopped working to stare at us. One looked angry enough to give Glannar a back answer he'd regret, the second dropped his gaze, shamefaced, while the third and youngest was close to unmanly tears. He was right to fret; this night's work had dropped his chances of an oath right down the privy.

Did we have honest watchdogs here, or had Glannar set a fox to watch the geese? It happens, let's be honest, and even in the best-regulated barracks – someone bribed to look the other way and stay deaf as well as blind, tarnishing the honour of everyone sworn to the Name. 'When did it happen?'

'Any time between midnight and sixth chime,' said Glannar tightly. 'I know the recognised are green but I was sure the sworn were seasoned.' He was about to elaborate but I stopped him with a raised hand. 'I'll see what they've got to say for themselves.'

The newly recognised and would-be sworn were busy with scattered bales and broken chests. Pelts sewn tight into oilcloth and canvas to withstand the sea crossing spilled out across the floor, dust dulling the bright fur.

'So what happened?' I demanded of one lad half-heartedly picking up the skins.

'Our watch was for midnight onwards,' he began, eyes sliding away from me. 'Damage was done when we arrived.'

'But we didn't get here until nigh on the sixth chime.' The second had the wit to see only honesty would redeem their situation.

I kept my anger reined in for the moment. 'Why?'

'It wasn't our fault,' began the first, looking this way and that for some excuse.

'We went to find a quiet tavern,' said his pal glumly.

'We meant no harm,' protested a third, man enough to come and stand by his fellows.

'So what kept you from marking the chimes?' I asked harshly.

The youths exchanged sheepish glances. 'We got into a game of Raven,' admitted the newcomer. 'More than one.'

'Some stranger who lost invited you to make a small wager then suddenly showed some talent for the game?' I guessed. 'You played on in hopes of winning your losses back?'

'No,' said the second with scornful anger. 'It was Rasicot, sworn to Tor Bezaemar.' He looked to Glannar, who grunted grudging support.

'All the sworn and chosen mix freely hereabouts, Chosen Tathel. With none so many of us beholden to any one Name, we help each other out.'

I shook my head. 'So you just lost track of the chimes?'

'We came straight here when we realised,' protested one forlornly. 'Sent the early duty to their beds.'

'So where were they when you arrived?' I asked. 'Asleep?'

'No,' said one, outraged. 'We were guarding the front, just like we should.'

'While thieves got in round the back,' I pointed out. 'How did you miss that?'

Guilty looks were traded between lowered eyes. 'Well?' I demanded.

'Danel was round the back,' said the first one to own up to being on early duty. 'He got a clout that knocked him clean into the Shades.'

'They dragged him inside and tied him up,' volunteered someone at the rear.

'Didn't anyone go looking for him?' I demanded.

'We did,' objected another youth. 'Only when we couldn't find him we reckoned he'd gone off with Brel.'

'Who's Brel?' I asked.

'Brel and Krim, senior sworn men, they both went off to find the second watch.' The lad nodded towards the two still struggling with the ladder.

'Let's see what they have to say.' Leaving the lads with a look conveying the full depth of my contempt, I walked over to the skylight, Glannar with me muttering a blistering denunciation of the man Brel's parentage and sexual tastes. The two sworn sighed as one man.

'What happened?' I demanded

'It was past midnight and the relief hadn't shown,' one began, a thick-necked man with a crooked nose and a missing eyetooth. 'We knew our lads were losing their edge.'

'So we went looking,' agreed his colleague, a wiry type with features somehow too small for his face, close set eyes either side of a questing nose.

'Both of you?'

'There's been trouble before now, between our men and the dockers,' said the senior belligerently. 'I wanted someone to watch my back.'

'You're too cursed fond of a fight, Krim,' spat Glannar.

'Which is why I wasn't about to let him go off on his own!' The thin man's protest rang with complacent truth.

I raised a hand to silence Krim's indignation. 'So where were the relief? The sworn that is; I know where the lads were.'

'Torren says they'd agreed to meet at the end of the rope walk, Ardig says it was outside the chandlery,' spat Glannar. 'They were both late and each thought the other must have rounded up the lads and gone on. Seems neither was in any hurry on their own account.'

'Did you find either of them?' I demanded of the two sworn men before me.

'Only Ardig,' muttered Krim. 'By then midnight had come and gone.'

'Torren sniffs round a pretty little slattern up in Rack Row any time he's in town,' said the rat-faced one. 'Seems he'd headed there to poke up her hearth on a cold night.'

'So what did you find when you got back here?' I snapped.

Krim sneered. 'Torren's lads sitting out front, no more use than tits on a boar, the back open wider than a whore's legs.'

'None of yours had the wit to worry where the lad watching the back had got to,' I reminded him. 'Torren can answer for the shit on his shoes and you can answer for yours. Tidy this mess up and see if you can find any scent. Glannar, let's get some fresh air.' I wanted to escape the musty atmosphere thick with recrimination and justification.

Glannar walked with me to the door, red-faced embarrassment struggling with fury at his men. 'All right, you don't have to tell me. All four wheels came off this cart, good and proper. I'll kick their arses from now until Solstice for not sending me word when the relief didn't show. But in all justice, Raeponin be my witness, I never thought there'd be theft, not with a decent watch set for all to see. Bremilayne can be rough, I'll grant you, but it's a small place for all that. There are too many trading interests here for wholesale thieving to go unchecked! One warehouse gets robbed, every sworn and chosen turns the town upside down. We catch the bastards and they get a flogging to warn off any others thinking of trying their luck. That's as long as we get the goods back, mind. If they've nothing to trade for their lives, it's the gibbet on the end of the seawall.' He fell silent, out of words as well as breath.

'Start turning over rocks and see what crawls out,' I told him tersely. But I was as cross with myself as I was with Glannar. I should have realised a tarnished arm ring was a bad sign; you have to keep the talents that warrant it polished up along with the copper.

'Ryshad!' I turned to see Temar wave a parchment at me.

I left Glannar without a word. 'What's all this?' I shifted a splintered scrap of deal with one boot.

'We brought mostly woods unique to Kel Ar'Ayen,' explained Temar. We both looked at the cords of logs untouched in their ropes. 'But our joiners made prentice pieces, to show how it can be worked.' He passed me a tiny drawer scarcely the length of my hand, one jagged scratch marring the smoothly waxed front. 'Those pieces were all boxed together. My guess is they broke open the case thinking it was something valuable.'

I looked inside the shattered top of the rough wooden box to see miniature copies of fixtures and furniture like the ones Messire's craftsmen make for the Sieur's approval when some residence or other is being refurbished. 'Have any been taken?'

Temar shrugged. 'I think not. Some of the furs are gone though, the small pelts, the finest ones.'

I bent to retrieve a torn sheet of parchment. 'What's this?'

'Notes from our artisans.' Temar frowned. 'Nothing important, but everything is unsealed.'

'Thieves looking for information more than valuables?' I mused

'Anything valuable has gone,' scowled Temar. 'There was some copper, but it is nowhere to be found.'

'We all grew up with tales of the riches of Nemith the Last's lost colony.' I looked at him. 'Gold and gems. Were there any?'

Temar smiled grimly. 'All still safe in my personal baggage back at the shrine.'

'Along with any maps or charts that might give away

Kellarin's secrets?' I hazarded, relieved to see him nod. 'But whoever broke in here wasn't to know that.'

'So was this just sneak thieves taking advantage?' Temar wondered aloud.

I sighed and nodded towards the door. 'I don't suppose the inns down here serve tisanes, but I'll buy you ale if you want it this early.'

Temar shook his head as we walked out into the sunshine and both drew thankful breaths of clean, fresh air, crossing the dock to sit on a baulk of timber.

'Glannar's men have got a sorry tale of thoughtlessness adding to mishap piling on stupidity.' I scrubbed an irritated hand through my hair. 'It could just be some bright-eyed lads taking the chance they saw offered, certainly. A ship from unknown lands, all but dragged off the rocks by wizardry, the whole town would have heard the tale before their dinner yesterday, and a fair few would have been curious to know just what you'd unloaded.'

'Curious enough to search through every scrap of parchment?' Temar was as keen as me to find an innocent explanation but equally alert to more sinister implications.

'There are plenty of sailors keen to know the currents and winds between here and Kellarin,' I mused. 'Some might be foolhardy enough to risk the crossing without magic if there's enough profit to be had.'

An unwelcome voice hailed us in a strangled shout.

'What has been going on?' puffed Casuel as he reached us, hair unbrushed and mismatched buckles on his shoes.

'Some of the Kellarin cargo has been stolen,' I said flatly, hoping his precipitate arrival might go unnoticed.

'By whom?' he demanded, outraged.

'As yet, we don't know,' I replied calmly.

'Why aren't you out looking for them!' Casuel looked around the harbour, presumably for some slow-footed miscreant draped in stolen pelts.

I turned my attention back to Temar. 'It could have been pirates. They'll be interested in knowing what comes from

Kellarin and how it might compare to the Inglis trade.'

'And they would certainly be interested in looking for charts,' agreed Temar.

'Thieves or pirates, what's the difference?' Casuel folded his arms abruptly, scowling.

'Otrick was keeping Velindre informed, hadn't he?' I took a step closer to Casuel, using my greater height to force him back a pace. 'Otrick was well liked by pirates all along the coast, wasn't he? If Velindre has similar friends, perhaps she let something slip?'

'Impossible,' snapped Casuel, affronted.

'From her manner last night, I hardly think the lady would be so careless,' Temar said cautiously.

'Unlikely,' I agreed. But not impossible, and anyway the notion had Casuel too distracted to interrupt again.

'But what if it's neither?' I said to Temar.

'Elietimm?' He nodded, expression dour. 'People forgetting what was agreed, forgetting to mark the time, that could be Artifice at work'

'What?' Casuel looked from Temar to me and back again, eyes horrified. 'There's nothing to suggest Elietimm, is there?'

'No, but nothing to suggest it wasn't, as yet.' I heaved an irritated sigh. 'But how by all that's holy can we tell? Could Demoiselle Tor Arrial tell if these men had been enchanted?'

'I am afraid not.' Temar looked thoughtful. 'But she can look for anyone working Artifice hereabouts.'

I stared at the warehouse. 'Copper is copper, and melted down it could have come from anywhere, so I don't think we'll see that again. But furs are too easily identifiable to risk selling them here, if our thieves have any wits.'

'So they ship them out with goods honestly bought and paid for?' Temar guessed.

'Organise a search!' cried Casuel. 'There's only one road out of here, so anything going overland can be stopped. Isn't there some chain to close the harbour to pirates? Get that in place and turn every ship inside out!'

'On whose say-so?' I enquired mildly. 'Planir's? Archmage

he may be, he has no authority here, not over Tormalin citizens when nothing's been proved against them.'

'Is Messire D'Olbriot's word not good enough, even by proxy?' Temar asked hesitantly.

'No, not for a general search.' I tried to recall the little I knew of Old Empire law. 'A Prince's power is still absolute over his own tenants and property, but that's as far as it goes. Houses on good terms with D'Olbriot would cooperate, but those that aren't would refuse, whether or not they had anything to hide. Self-governing traders and artisans will hardly compromise their independence by yielding to D'Olbriot influence like that. Forcing the issue will set them appealing in every court up to the Emperor himself.'

Temar was looking puzzled. 'Are many people living outside the security of tenantry?

'A great deal changed as a result of the Chaos,' said Casuel officiously. 'The autonomy of sufficient men of business is an important check on the influence of Princes.'

'Casuel's father is a pepper merchant,' I explained. 'Anyway, even where someone's officially beholden to a Name, the ties may be no stronger than ribbon sealed on a parchment.'

'But who safeguards their interests?' Temar looked genuinely concerned.

'The Emperor and the justiciary, naturally.'

I interrupted as Casuel's drew breath to explain twenty generations of precedent and custom. 'The best way to be sure we've no Elietimm creeping in the shadows is to find those stolen goods. I'll call in the few markers I have hereabouts and see if the strength of the D'Olbriot name can get the most likely places searched at least. Temar, go back and have your breakfast, then see if Avila can find any sniff of aetheric magic. Casuel.' I gave him a warm smile. 'Go and ask Velindre if she has any contacts among the free-traders.' I raised my voice over his incensed protests. 'I don't suppose she was involved in anything, but free-traders are most likely to be offered unusual goods at half their market value. We might get a scent that way. If she refuses to help, that might be worth telling Planir.'

Casuel's indignation subsided as Temar managed to control a smile I could see tugging at the corners of his mouth.

'Feathers!' the mage said suddenly.

'Of course!' I snapped my fingers. 'Why didn't I think of that?'

'I don't suppose your lady has much time for the heights of fashion,' Casuel smirked.

I let the jibe go as I saw Temar looking at me and the mage as if we'd both taken leave of our senses.

'Feathers, bright ones in bold colours are worth, oh, I don't know how many times their weight in gold,' I explained.

'No lady would dream of going out without a fan of plumes carefully chosen to match her dress or in the colours of her House,' Casuel broke in. 'And then there are the combinations that signify—'

'If someone thought you'd brought back exotic feathers unique to Kellarin, that would definitely be worth a break-in.' Much as I hated to give Casuel any credit, his suggestion made simple theft a far more likely explanation.

'I must tell Guinalle to send hunters out with some nets,' said Temar with well-bred amusement. 'Strange that none of the mercenaries or mages mentioned this.'

'Well, mercenaries just sweat and I don't suppose wizards have much time for the heights of fashion either.' I nodded with mock politeness to Casuel, but baiting the mage wasn't going to get us anywhere. 'I'll see you back at the shrine at noon and we'll share anything we've found out. If there's any hint it's something more sinister than thievery, then we get on the road to Toremal where we've got the Name and the men to back us.'

'But what if we're attacked on the road?' Casuel bleated.

'Then you show us some magic, Master Wizard,' smiled Temar.

CHAPTER TWO

Appendix to the D'Olbriot Chronicle, Winter Solstice Concluding the First Year of Tadriol the Thrifty, As Written by Esquire Fidaer, Castellan of the Tailebret Estates

Solstice celebrations have seen some relaxation of the austerity enjoined on us in the immediate aftermath of the new Emperor's election, much to the relief of tradespeople the length and breadth of Toremal. But all the gowns and furbelows adorning our ladies must be paid for with solid coin this year, now merchants have Imperial sanction to refuse open-ended credit to even the noblest of Houses. Well, Tadriol's strictures may be unpopular with giddy girls obsessed with fashionable competition and Esquires keen to cut an elegant figure, but I write this after submitting my annual accounts to the Sieur of my Name with the best set of balances for some years. With Messire's approval, I plan to use these funds firstly to support the tenantry who suffered in the recent floods around Nymet, and thereafter to expand whichever of our enterprises will benefit from sustained investment.

On the Sieur's insistence, all branches of the D'Olbriot House heeded the retrenchments urged by Tor Tadriol earlier than most. Thus, the increased coin taxes levied on our strong rooms have not hit us too hard. It is also consolation to see Tor Tadriol's thrift does not fatten his own coffers under the threadbare guise of Imperial necessity. This winter has seen a wide extension of Imperial munificence to the commonalty, even without unduly harsh weather, and Tadriol used the occasion of Convocation to announce that the Emperor's Dole at Summer Solstice will be a substantial gift for the truly indigent rather than token silver for notables of shrine fraternities and craft guilds.

Speaking purely for myself, I am relieved to report no return to the costly, stifling ceremonial so beloved of the Name so lately gracing the throne. The Convocation of Princes was a brisk affair, the Adjurist's rod duly broken after the briefest of addresses by the Emperor thanking the Sieur Tor Sylarre for his many years of loyal service to Tor Bezaemar. The Sieur Den Thasnet echoed these sentiments in florid terms but was soon caught by the Imperial gaze and wound up his eloquence. Tadriol may not have that knack of making friends that so characterizes the Esquires of Tor Bezaemar, but the man has undeniable presence in debate.

My Sieur D'Olbriot proposed Messire Tor Kanselin for the now vacant office, and once Den Murivance and Den Gennael had backed him with patent enthusiasm the other Houses voted accordingly, led by Den Janaquel. Tor Priminale held aloof, but that is hardly remarkable, given the extensive bonds tying that Name to Tor Bezaemar. The Sieurs Tor Sauzet and Den Ferrand then acknowledged new Designates before Convocation. Each is a younger son, but both can claim established friendship with the newly elevated Tadriol, and, of course, our new Empress was born Tor Sauzet.

Marital propsects for the ladies now entitled to style themselves Tor Tadriol have been understandably enhanced by their Name's accession. Within the privacy of these pages, I wonder if his superfluity of daughters influenced Messire and the Sieur Den Murivance when Den Tadriol proposed this particular scion as candidate for the Imperial throne. Alliance by marriage has to be the speediest way for a new dynasty to secure its position among the preeminent Houses, after all. As I write this, my wife sits across the library, studying cadet lines of Tor Tadriol in hopes of finding some younger son or daughter who might be amenable to a match with us, while the lesser lines of that House still remember we were both of equal standing so recently. I hope I have some success to record in these pages next year.

Betrothal of the Emperor's eldest legitimate girl to a senior line of Tor Kanselin was announced at the dance concluding the

Festival, and I imagine all five younger Demoiselles quite wore the feet out of their slippers, they were so much in demand. The illegitimate girls are being similarly courted among the upper echelons of merchantry, prompting Esquire Den Muret to tactless jokes that Tadriol's enthusiasm for spreading his seed before marriage was all part of some long-held plan to endear himself to the commonalty. In my experience, youth needs no encouragement for such exuberance and, while such large a posy of byblown children is unusual, it is hardly unheard of. More importantly, there is no hint that Tadriol has dishonoured his vows since his marriage, whereas we can now openly condemn the late Bezaemar's scandalous profligacy with his favours.

As we wait for the new year to open tomorrow, I find myself full of optimism. Tor Tadriol is a young man with an open mind and considerable intelligence, ready to look beyond the confines of his House, with an astute eye to the wider interests of Tormalin. After nigh on a generation of rule by that Bezaemar called the Generous but whose largesse was so often confined to those of his own circle, I am confident we cadet lineages will benefit from all manner of new opportunities over the next few years. The first of these will be playing our part in deciding what epithet to bestow on our new Emperor; I fully intend to make sure we lesser voices are heard.

In the Archive of the House of D'Olbriot, Summer Solstice Festival, First Day, Morning

I was none too keen on lessons as a boy and watching someone else learning their Emperors was truly boring. I stifled a yawn and leaned back in my chair to stare up at the long barrel of the wooden vault high above us. The lynx and chevron badge of D'Olbriot was repeated all along the top of the wall, interspersed with insignia of Names allied in marriage to the House over the years, and I squinted as I tried to identify them. At least when Casuel had been burying himself beneath parchments in libraries the length and breadth of Tormalin, I'd been able to idle the time away with other chosen men once I'd delivered any messages from the Sieur to whatever Esquire of the Name managed that particular estate. Officially I'd been advising my counterparts on their training regimens, but in practice we'd usually spent more time swapping fighters' tales, all the while cosseted by housekeepers and stewards impressed with my new status. It had certainly made a pleasant change from my days as a sworn man, when, visitor or not, I'd been expected to take my turn at all the duties customary for my rank.

The yawn escaped me and a clerk laden with ledgers spared me an indifferent glance on his way past. We were sitting about a third of the way along a long line of identical tables running from one pair of vast double doors to another, hemmed in by serried ranks of bookshelves reaching out from the walls, dark leather bindings of close-packed tomes enlivened here and there as a flash of gilt caught sunlight filtering through narrow windows to remind us of the morning outside. In the few scant stretches of unshelved wall, niches held statues and a few ignored curios forlorn in polished glass cases.

'Do you have it straight?' Casuel demanded curtly.

'I think so.' Temar ran a cautious finger down a parchment.

'Then recite the rote, if you please,' ordered the mage.

I tried to look interested. Temar did need to know such things if he wasn't to embarrass himself and his hosts, and the first of Festival's social gatherings was after noon today. When Casuel had insisted on reviewing Temar's lessons, we'd reluctantly had to agree it was a sound notion.

Temar dutifully shut his eyes, brow furrowed. 'Modrical the Ruthless, Modrical the Hateful—' He broke off. 'How in Saedrin's name could the Princes pick a title like that for their Emperor? Calling Nemith the Reckless was the worst slap in the face the Convocation could think of for him! What *did* this second Modrical do?'

I shut my mouth at a glare from Casuel. 'No one is really sure,' said the wizard tightly. 'The Chaos was still raging. Indeed, he was assassinated at the Summer Solstice Festival of his second year, when he was acclaimed as Hateful.'

'Presumably when he was already dead?' Temar opened his eyes, grinning at me.

'And who was elected to replace him?' asked Casuel.

'Kanselin.' Temar sighed. 'Kanselin the Droll?'

'Kanselin the Pious, then Kanselin the Droll,' the mage corrected.

'Then Kanselin the Rash, Kanselin the Blunt, Kanselin the Confident, and lastly Kanselin the Headstrong, who presumably had not the talent of his father and uncles,' Temar suggested.

'When you have the leisure to study the period, you'll find it rather more complicated than that.' Casuel visibly curbed his impulse to explain. 'And the next House awarded the throne?'

'Decabral,' Temar ventured slowly.

Casuel took the parchment from the younger man's hands. 'And the first was acclaimed as what?'

'Decabral the Eager. Then the Patient, the Nervous,'

Temar smiled again. 'The Virtuous, the Pitiless, whom the Houses deposed after a couple of years, and lastly the Merciful. But do not ask me who was whose brother, son or cousin, I beg you.'

'Getting the rote correct is sufficient.' Casuel tried to sound encouraging.

'Sauzet next, the Worthy and the Quiet.' Temar ticked the names off on his fingers. 'They were shoved off the Imperial cushions by Perinal the Bold, who found himself edged out by Leoril the Wise.'

'I see no need for flippancy,' commented Casuel. 'Next?'

'Leoril the Dullard.' Temar looked at me but the question died on his lips as he caught Casuel's sour expression. 'Leoril the Eloquent, Leoril the Affable. Then Aleonne the Valiant.' He fell silent.

'Acclaimed the Valiant when the Lescar Wars rose to such a pitch they spilled over our western borders,' I prompted. 'So we needed Aleonne the—?'

'Sorry.' Temar drew a sudden breath. 'Aleonne the Defiant, the Resolute and then Aleonne the Gallant.'

'You need to know more detail of events after that.' Casuel sorted through books stacked neatly before him, sparing a disapproving glance for the untidy array by Temar's elbow. He handed one over with evident reluctance. 'Annals of Tor Bezaemar. Read as much as you can, and do be careful, it's my own copy and such things are expensive.'

Temar turned the pristine tome in his hands. 'I thought Inshol the Curt succeeded the last Aleonne.'

'Correct.' I nodded my own approval at Temar. Once we'd left Bremilayne behind us and travelled without incident for a few days, Casuel's fears of being called on actually to make magic had faded. Then he'd applied himself to teaching Temar everything he might conceivably need to know for a visit to Toremal and plenty he'd have no use for as well. I was impressed to see how much the lad had learned. After long days in the saddle on our interminable journey across the highlands, the last thing I'd have wanted was a tutor like Casuel, his charmlessness woefully exacerbated by leagues jolted along in a carriage shared with Avila Tor Arrial. Temar and I had stuck to our horses.

'And when he died, his relict married the Sieur Den Bezaemar, who became?' The wizard wasn't about to give up.

'Bezaemar the Modest,' said Temar after a pause. 'His son was Bezaemar the Canny, who must have seemed like a permanent fixture after reigning for nearly fifty years. His grandson was Bezaemar the Generous, then the Princes wanted someone less free-handed with their coin and chose Tadriol the Thrifty. Thrifty but none too healthy, so his brother soon stepped up as Tadriol the Staunch. He stepped down after a handful of years, but Convocation picked the wrong nephew because Tadriol the Tireless dropped dead in under a year. They had better luck with his brother the Prudent, who ruled for eleven years and was already well provided with children, including your current Emperor Tadriol, his third son, acclaimed the Provident last year!' He grinned at Casuel.

'The rote is correct but please keep facetious comments to yourself.' Casuel shot me an indignant glance. 'I imagine that's your interpretation?'

'We had to talk about something as we rode,' I shrugged. We'd used the time to review the previous day's lessons and to talk about family, friends, life in Kellarin and in Tormalin. With Casuel sitting on his dignity in his coach, we'd reaffirmed our tentative friendship and incidentally smoothed the most jarring archaisms out of Temar's speech.

'Well, I hope you took note of the insignia of the Imperial Houses as I told you to, Temar.' Casuel reached across the table for a roll of parchments laced together across their top with scarlet ribbon. 'You need to study this as well. I've asked the Archivist for a copy but he says all the scribes are too busy with the courts sitting, so you'll have to make your own.' He handed over paper and a charcoal stick in a silver holder.

Temar looked blankly at the tightly drawn columns of names and figures, little heraldic symbols heading each entry. 'What is this?'

'Last year's Land Tax register.' Casuel stared at Temar.

'There was no such thing in the Old Empire,' I reminded the wizard. 'Each House and Name pays an annual charge to the Imperial coffer, based on its holdings and assets.' I explained to Temar. 'The old system of levies for specific wants was abandoned generations ago.'

Temar shook his head. 'I wonder my grandfather's shade did not return from the Otherworld and kick me awake at such insult to Princes' privileges.'

He stood up abruptly, pushing himself away from documents, ledgers, leather-bound volumes and screeds folded within sealed ribbons. I watched as Temar turned slowly on his heel, looking grimly at the racks of rolled parchments, shelves of bound tomes, flat cases holding maps, charts, records and plans. The only sound was the susurration of turning paper, broken by the muted rasp of the ladders attached to each set of shelves being pushed along its rails. Every day must bring some new shock to remind the lad just how much life had changed on this side of the ocean, I thought.

'Sit down,' Casuel hissed as curious heads peered down from shelf-lined bays in the galleries above. High windows transmuted golden sunbeams into reds and blues, greens and browns, the alchemy of stained glass spilling blurred jewels across the dun matting.

Temar shook his head as he slowly resumed his seat. 'My grandfather kept all deeds of grant and records of tithe in one locked chest. Granted, it was as long as a man and an armspan deep but—'

'Remember just how much time has passed,' Casuel interrupted. 'This archive holds the record of twenty-five generations, twenty-five years to each one.'

'I allow I am ignorant of much, Mage D'Evoir, but I know how many years to a generation,' said Temar acidly.

I hid a smile behind my hand as Casuel paled. Temar's unconscious aristocratic inflexion belatedly reminded the mage of their relative rank.

'I only meant—' said Casuel hastily, 'oh, never mind.

Documents became far more important after the Chaos. In the Old Empire everyone knew which House held what lands, whose service was owed to whom. Things had stayed constant for so long, after all. When the rule of law was re-established, rival claimants arose to land and property and written proof of title was invaluable.' Casuel tapped the taxation roll sharply. 'Please apply yourself, at least to the first two or three leaves. Names are listed in order of taxes paid, so it's a good indicator of the wealthiest. The first fifty or so are Houses you're likely to visit or meet but it wouldn't hurt to have at least read through the first few hundred.'

Temar ran a thumb over the unbound edge of the stack of parchments. 'In my grandfather's day all the Sieurs of all the Houses sitting together wouldn't have filled these tables.'

'I'd advise you to get your bearings in Toremal as it is rather than repine for what is past.' Casuel lifted his chin defiantly as I gave him an icy look.

Temar bent over the close-written list. 'I do not see why we cannot have ink in here,' he muttered as he smudged his notes.

'Because the Archivists forbid it and quite right too. Who knows what accident or mischief might be done.' I noticed Casuel glance at the floor by his feet as he spoke. He'd done that several times today. 'The right document can make or break a family.'

'Half the Names I knew are gone and many of these mean nothing,' said Temar at length, rubbing a hand round the back of his neck. 'Where are Tor Correl, Den Parisot? What about Den Muret? Who in Saedrin's name are D'Estabel, Den Haurient or Den Viorel?'

'Many Houses fell into ruin during the Chaos.' Casuel couldn't resist another glance at the floor by his chair and I shifted myself to see what he'd got there. 'It's nigh on unheard of for a modern Name to fall extinct in the male line, but when warfare racked the Empire there were many casualties. New grants of nobility were made later, or indeed simply assumed.'

'Nemith has much to answer for,' spat Temar. 'Poldrion grant demons drown him yet in rivers of sorrow.'

'Of course – you knew him.' Casuel blinked. 'Forgive me, this is merely history to us.' As he leaned forward, a leather satchel resting against his chair slid flat to the floor unnoticed by the fawning mage.

'I knew him, so far as a cadet of a minor House had anything to do with an Emperor,' said Temar grimly. 'Enough to learn he was a whorestruck drunkard wasting the gold the Houses sent for troops to defend the Empire on debauchery and enriching his favourites.'

'In all justice, Nemith's folly wasn't the only evil blighting the Empire,' countered the wizard.

'True, Raeponin forgive me.' Temar sighed and reached across the table for another of Casuel's books. 'Your man Minrinel, in this so-called *Intelligencer*, he doesn't even mention the Crusted Pox.' Temar's mouth yielded to a brief grimace of grief. 'Three other sons of the House of Nemith might have been elected Emperor had they not been ashes in their urns even before their grandfather the Seafarer breathed his last.'

I looked up from trying to reach the strap of Casuel's satchel with my toe as the wizard scribbled notes eagerly in the margin of his own papers. 'Do you know what went on at the Convocation of Princes when the Imperial throne fell vacant? Why did they make such a disastrous choice?'

'I have no notion.' Temar's eyes were distant with a memory of mourning. 'I was not of age and my grandfather didn't attend, too busy with the affairs of House and tenantry. The Crusted Pox killed all the men of my father's generation and my own brothers and sisters besides.' Temar bent suddenly over the taxation list, scribbling furiously. I shut my own eyes on an echo of my own remembered grief, the death of my only sister.

'Indeed.' Casuel twisted his fingers together uncertainly. 'I'm sorry, I didn't want to distress you. But all the weeping in the world won't uncrack an egg, that's what my mother always says.' He coloured slightly.

'Just how powerful is D'Olbriot?' Temar asked me suddenly, curt words echoing in the hush.

'Please lower your voice,' Casuel begged in muted entreaty.

I nodded at the list before Temar. 'At the last taxation, Messire D'Olbriot was reckoned to control a twentieth part of Tormalin revenues and commerce.'

'Add in about seven or eight other families and those Names are responsible for just less than half the entire commonalty of the Empire?' Temar pursed his lips.

'Which is why you must learn due courtesy,' said Casuel severely.

'Life was very different before your Chaos, Mage D'Evoir, but we were taught a modicum of manners,' Temar said icily.

I wasn't about to let Casuel get away with that patronising attitude either. 'From everything those scholars working with the Archmage said, the last days of the Old Empire probably have more in common this present age than with any era between.'

'Why are you so well read in such things, Casuel?' Temar asked unexpectedly. 'The mages who come to Kel Ar'Ayen would be hard put to list the provinces of the Empire, let alone the Imperial Names. They spend all their energy on study of their element and think Hadrumal is the centre of the world.'

'My family has a particular interest in these matters,' Casuel stammered with uncharacteristic nervousness. He looked down for his satchel but I'd managed to hook it over to me.

I grinned at the wizard as I opened the flap and lifted out a folded bundle of parchment tied with faded ribbon. 'What's all this?'

'The House of D'Alsennin was not the only one to disappear in the Chaos.' Casuel snatched the documents from me. 'You call me D'Evoir, Esquire, but that's not really an honour I'm entitled to, not yet, anyway.' He gave me an indignant look before unknotting the ribbons and spreading the top parchment out for Temar to see. 'The last D'Evoir attested in the historical record was a Governor of Lescar. He was murdered in the final year of Nemith the Last's reign, but other than that I can't find anything about him, not even if he had a family or sons. I've managed to trace my own family back nineteen generations but the evidence before that is scarce and contradictory. If I could find any other D'Evoir from the Old Empire, I might find some threads to tie my own family back to the Name.' The mage shut his mouth but not before we'd heard a definite note of pleading in his voice.

Temar lifted fine black brows. 'If the Name is gone, the property of the House scattered to the four winds and tenantry claims lapsed, there can be no obligation to answer nor indeed coin to do so.'

'It's not a question of wealth but of status,' said Casuel stiffly. 'It would mean a great deal to my family, to my mother, to establish a tie. Then we can use the style D'Evoir, adopt the badge of the House.'

'I see.' Temar's face was a well-schooled blank. I bit down my own opinion of such middle-ranking, jumped-up ambition. So the wizard fancied himself descended from noble blood, did he? I wondered if his merchant father would consider the cachet of rank sufficient recompense for Casuel's snobbery raising his family to the Land Tax register.

Soft steps made us all look round and Casuel hastily tucked his parchments beneath a ledger marked with ancient fingers. 'Not that it's of any real importance. No need to mention it to Messire D'Olbriot or his nephew.'

I was already on my feet as Esquire Camarl D'Olbriot approached from the southern door. I bowed and Camarl's answering bend from the waist was constrained both by his close-tailored coat and incipient portliness. His dark hair was brushed into a careful affectation of disorder but eyes and mouth showed resolution at odds with the season's fashion.

'How go your lessons, D'Alsennin?' he asked humorously.

'He's a most diligent pupil,' Casuel smiled ingratiatingly.

Temar shrugged wryly. 'There is a great deal still to learn.'

'We can't expect you to master the complexities of the modern Empire in a scant half season of study at inns along the high road.' Camarl grinned suddenly. 'Don't worry; you'll be with me at most social occasions and Ryshad's to be your escort elsewhere.'

'Planir has asked that I make myself available,' interrupted Casuel hopefully. 'To offer assistance.'

'Indeed.' Camarl nodded graciously at the wizard. 'But I beg your pardon, Temar, we're disturbing you. It's Ryshad I came to see.' Camarl led me adroitly into a book-lined alcove. 'Can he hold his own in company without looking an utter fool?' the nobleman asked bluntly, turning his back on Casuel's ill-disguised curiosity.

'I think so,' I said slowly. 'And as you say, either you or I will be with him, to smooth over any difficulties.'

Camarl looked thoughtful. 'We have more pressing concerns than stopping Temar frying himself in his own grease with a thoughtless remark. Kellarin has potentially enormous resources.' His amiable face hardened. 'A great many people want Temar to grant Master So-and-So rights over such-and-such. Someone else will want exclusive licence to this, that or the other, while their rivals will be falling over themselves to offer a supposedly better deal. He's a bright lad and has acquitted his responsibilities admirably this past year, but the Sieur and myself, we're worried that he'll find his rooster's cooked and eaten before he knows it. Then all he'll go home with is a feather duster.'

I spared a brief smile. 'So you don't want him overwhelmed with demands?'

'We've had invitations from half the Houses in the city; Festival's only five days long and every hostess wants Temar to decorate her revelry,' Camarl nodded. 'Don't let him commit himself to any invitation without checking with me. Saedrin only knows what might be asked of him, and surely he deserves some leisure after his rigours in the wilderness.' Camarl looked a little anxious. 'It's safest for everyone if he stays within our House's circles. The Sieur can manage all the to-and-fro of negotiating Kellarin's trade, then Temar need only put his seal to finished agreements.'

I nodded slow agreement. 'The Sieur will secure the best for D'Alsennin's people.' Temar nailing his own foot to the floor through some entirely understandable ignorance would serve no one's purpose. 'Anyway, Temar's main concern is recovering the artefacts needed to revive the rest of the colonists. I imagine he'll be happy to leave trade to Messire.'

Camarl grimaced. 'I suppose he can ask people about their heirlooms without causing too much offence, but don't let him make a nuisance of himself. There'll be plenty of time for such things after Festival.'

'Indeed,' I said neutrally.

'I knew you'd see sense. Oh, and I have these for you.' Camarl handed me three neatly folded and sealed letters.

'My thanks,' I said in some surprise. It's not the place of the Sieur's Designate to be running errands.

'I needed some excuse to bring me here,' Camarl smiled with a shrug. 'No need to mention our other discussion.' He turned away, bowing to Temar and acknowledging Casuel with a brief wave. 'If you'll excuse me, Esquire, Mage.'

Temar grunted absently, lost in the taxation list. Casuel watched the Esquire D'Olbriot walk away before dragging his attention back to Temar's notes. He clicked his tongue with annoyance. 'The likelihood of you meeting any scion of Den Cascadet is so remote as to be laughable.'

'Why?' Temar demanded.

'They're nobodies!' Casuel fumbled for a fuller answer as Temar stared at him unblinking. 'They'll spend Festival ringing the loudest bell in Moretayne, but hereabouts they'd make a very tinny rattle.'

'They're a provincial Name running cattle in the downlands near Lequesine,' I volunteered.

'Two artisans beholden to that Name lie insensible in Kel Ar'Ayen.' Temar's lips narrowed. 'The artefacts to revive them may have been passed back to the family. I must contact the Sieur or his designate.' He ran a charcoal-dusted finger down the taxation record. 'I will not let those who entrusted their lives to my hands spend a day longer in that stifling enchantment than is absolutely needful.'

'Saedrin make it so,' I said with feeling.

'Do please take care.' Casuel gently rubbed at a grubby mark with a kerchief from his pocket. 'That's all very well, Esquire, but you'll hardly have the leisure to call on every fifth-rank Name in the city, and no one will have time to spare searching through their archive to accommodate you. Every clerk is busy preparing for the assizes.' He gestured at a sombrely dressed man climbing a ladder to a high shelf stacked with deed boxes.

Temar looked at me. 'How much time do these assizes take up?'

I grimaced. 'Strictly speaking, cases raised at Solstice should be settled before the following Equinox or penalties are levied. Few Houses avoid such censure.'

'It'll be the turn of For-Autumn before anyone can spare attention for your requests,' said Casuel with some satisfaction.

'That's true enough, as far as the archives go, but I could make a start while you're at this afternoon's reception,' I said slowly. 'If you tell me what you're looking for and what Names might have the pieces, I could at least visit the Houses here in Toremal and see if anyone knows anything.' Even slight progress towards rescuing those unfortunates from the enchantment that had so nearly killed me would be a sight more productive use of my time than kicking my heels in some gatehouse with all the other sworn brought along to add to their liege's consequence.

'I hardly think you'll be invited in to poke round any House you please, Ryshad,' protested Casuel. 'Can we please concentrate on the matter in hand?'

I ignored the mage as Temar wrote industriously on a fresh sheet of paper. 'We are mostly looking for pieces of jewellery and small trinkets.'

'And well-bred Demoiselles will let you make free with their jewellery caskets?' Casuel scoffed.

'No,' I agreed, 'but I can ask valets and ladies' maids about heirloom pieces, can't I?'

'You'll be the one risking a whipping.' Casuel took the paper from Temar and slapped it down in front of me. 'Can we please concentrate on the taxation lists. We've precious little time as it is.'

Temar and I exchanged a rueful glance and he bent over his notes once more. I tucked Temar's list inside the breast of my jerkin and sorted through the letters the Esquire D'Olbriot had brought me. I recognised the writing on the first: my brother Mistal, one of those lawyers who earn their bread spinning out litigation between the Houses until the very eve of the following Festival. He wanted to meet for a drink, asking me to send the letter straight back telling him where and when tonight. I smiled briefly but wasn't about to waste time on his raptures over some lady-love or whatever ripe scandal he'd unearthed. The next letter was creased and stained with sweat and dust, the direction simply to Ryshad Tathel, House of D'Olbriot, and written in an unpractised hand. I snapped the wax seal and slowly deciphered spidery writing that looked to have been written in treacle with a blunt piece of stick.

'Temar.'

'What is it?' He looked up.

'It's from Glannar.' I'd made the man swear on his arm ring to write and tell me what he found out. 'They've not turned up any of the stolen goods and there's still no scent of any culprit.'

'Any trace of the Elietimm?' demanded Casuel.

I shook my head. 'No sign of any strangers at all.'

'That's no proof,' snapped Casuel. 'They use Artifice to conceal themselves.'

'You can see all the Eldritch-men you want if you stare into a chimney corner long enough,' I retorted, 'but they'll still only be the shadows from the lamp stands.'

Temar looked at Casuel and then to me. 'So what does that tell us?'

'That we know no more than we did when we left Bremilayne.' I didn't bother concealing my own annoyance. I wasn't about to blame the Elietimm or the Eldritch-men, not without proof, but it would have eased my mind to know the theft had just been wharf rats taking a tasty morsel.

Temar returned to his list and Casuel started leafing through his books, marking places with slips of paper and stacking the volumes in front of Temar. 'These are significant events in the annals of the leading families that you must know about.'

I opened my third letter: good-weight paper precisely addressed in an elegant hand using sloping Lescari script in regular lines and faintly perfumed with something my memory told me was expensive. 'Will you excuse me, Esquire D'Alsennin?' I asked formally. 'It seems I have some business to attend to.'

'What?' demanded Casuel.

I hesitated; best not to raise Temar's hopes until I knew if this speculation had paid off. 'A lady I know is visiting the city.'

Casuel sniffed with censure but Temar laughed. 'Can I come?'

'Not this time.' I winked at him.

'Well, you can hardly read these things for me, so by all means call on the lady.' Temar shrugged a little unconvincingly.

'Then I'll see what I can do with your list.' Temar's expression lightened at that thought so I left him to his studies, abandoning Casuel to his disapproval.

Once outside, I looked both ways along the road before leaving the broad portico sheltering the wide steps of the building. The D'Olbriot archive is housed in one of the Name's many ancestral possessions scattered throughout the city. While the nobility have long since left the lower town to tradesmen and hereabouts to worse, the archive has stayed put. The contents are just too unwieldy to move to more salubrious surroundings and, valuable though the yellowing parchments are to advocates preparing their interminable deliberations, they're reckoned safe enough here. Thieves prefer real gold more readily spent and the clerks are backed by watchmen big enough to deter casual destruction or fire setting. I tossed a copper to an old man sitting on the steps with two shock-headed puppets dancing lifelike at his deft command. He'd been there for years and always alerted the Archivist to anyone threatening his pitch.

The close-packed houses all around had been long since broken up into squalid lodgings, four or five families now cramped beneath roofs sheltering one household in better days. The crumble-edged yellow stone was marred by stains of water and filth poured from narrow mullions below old-fashioned steep gables. Here and there intricate oriel windows stood out below the vanity of the little turrets that had been so desirable in the days of Tor Inshol, their conical caps of ochre tiles broken and patched.

A gaunt girl staggered out of a nearby alley, green-tainted eyes vacant. I could smell the sickly sweet sweat of the tahn enslaving her clean across the street. I ignored her outstretched hand and hurried on, clapping a hand over my mouth and nose as I passed a dead dog motionless but for the seething of maggots. Even with the sun riding high, shadows were held captive by tall buildings three and four stories high, and I kept an eye out for anyone lurking in hopes of cutting a purse to pay for whatever vice had them in its claws.

I was heading for the tongue of higher land that forms the northern side of Toremal Bay. When I'd first come to the city, little older than Temar and proud of my newly sworn status, it wasn't a district D'Olbriot's men would go to in anything less that threes, daylight or no. Any Name with property thereabouts balanced the rents they might collect against the blood it would cost them, and most reckoned the game not worth the candle. Then a new storm had blown up in Lescar's interminable wars and the ebb and flow of battle washed fresh flotsam up on to Tormalin shores. This was the only place the dispossessed wretches could get a foothold, and they'd dug in their heels, refusing to be knocked on their arses again. It's easy to despise the Lescari, to mock their dogged persistence over claim and counterclaim, their obsession with land title and vengeance, but there's no denying that single-mindedness serves them well at times.

I walked along streets where broken shutters had been replaced with new wood, bright with paint. The children might be grubby from playing in the dust but had started their day with clean if patched clothes and lovingly brushed hair. The clack and creak of working looms floated out of open windows high above, and women chatting as they kept an eye on their offspring sat on balconies with distaffs busy in their hands. The Lescari may have arrived without half a lead Mark in their pockets but they had skills in their hands and knowledge in their heads. These days more than half the noble dwellings in the upper city have North Bay tapestries gracing their walls.

I pulled the perfumed letter from my jerkin and realised I had missed a turn. Retracing my steps, I found the narrow flight of stone stairs. Counting doors along the soiled walls, I saw I wanted the one marked by an earthenware pot bright with scarlet flagflowers. I knocked, wondering how long the brilliant splash of colour would last before some drunken reveller kicked the blooms down the steps, either from accident or exuberant desire to see how far they might fly.

The door opened a scant hand's breadth and I saw a shadowy figure within. 'Yes?'

'Ryshad Tathel.' I held up the note. 'For my lady Alaric.'

The door closed as the wedge securing it was kicked aside. It opened to reveal a gawky youth whose nervous energy kept his hands in constant motion. He was no stripling though, much my height and with shoulders broad enough to promise strength when he filled out. He wiped sweat from his forehead before running a hand over the beard so many Lescari affect. His beak of a nose and wide set eyes reminded me of seasons spent about Messire's business along the border with Parnilesse. I'd had a friend from there, Aiten, whose death was a score I vowed to settle with the Elietimm.

'This way,' the lad said curtly. Tormalin was much his mother tongue as my own so some earlier brush with Lescar's recurrent catastrophes must have swept his wretched forebears here.

I followed him up uncarpeted stairs dimly lit by an inadequate skylight. The lady I had come to visit proved to rent the entire first floor. A demure maid in an expensive silk dress sat on the landing and rose to greet me.

'I'll let my lady know you're here.' Her accent was unmistakably Relshazri, seldom heard in Toremal for all the trade plied across the benign waters of the Gulf that separates the two great cities.

She disappeared and the lad clattered noisily down the stairs to his kennel. I ran a contemplative finger over the inlaid swags of flowers decorating a table where the maid had put her sewing. This piece would grace the boudoir of any wife of D'Olbriot.

'My lady bids you welcome.' The maid ushered me into the front room. I swept a bow fit for the Imperial presence.

'Good day to you, Master Tathel.' The woman seated serenely on a richly brocaded daybed gestured me to equally costly cushions gracing an immaculately polished settle.

I stifled an impulse to check my boots for filth from the streets. 'My lady Alaric.'

She smiled demurely as the maid reappeared with a tray carrying a crystal jug and fluted goblets with white spirals frozen in their glass stems. My hostess studied me openly as the girl served us both water, as is Lescari custom, so I returned the compliment.

There are many women who look perfection at twenty paces but fewer than half look so enthralling at ten, when the counterfeits of powder and paint, cut and drape are revealed. This was that rarest of beauties, a woman who would still be flawless when you were close enough to taste the scent adorning her graceful neck. Her complex coiffure, not a hair out of place, was the deep rich chestnut of a prize horse. Her lightly powdered skin glowed like the palest ceramic, broad high forehead and elegant nose above lips with the colour and velvet softness of rose petals. Her eyes were a blue-violet deep as an evening sea and dark and wise with experience, one of the few things giving a hint of her age. I guessed her older than me but couldn't have said whether by two years or ten, and that suggestion of superiority made her allure both more tempting and more daunting. She smiled slowly at me as the maid left the room and the heat I felt round the back of my neck had nothing to do with the weather.

'You can call me Charoleia,' she said, lifting her glass in a brief salute.

'Thank you.' I raised mine but didn't drink. A man might wish to drown in the depths of those peerless eyes but I wasn't about to risk water from any north side well. 'That's how I think of you,' I admitted. 'Livak told me your various travelling names but I don't think I kept them straight.' I hadn't imagined I'd ever have business with a woman Livak said had a different guise for every country and another for every complex scheme she devised to separate fools from their gold.

'No matter. And you can drink that.' Her smile widened to betray an entrancing dimple in one cheek. 'I send the boy to buy water from the Den Bradile springs every morning. You won't spend your Festival stuck in the privy because of me.'

I took a sip. The water was cool and untainted, black fig sliced in it for freshness. 'I trust you had a good voyage?' I wasn't quite sure how to get to the point of my visit. Charoleia was one of the many friends Livak had scattered across the Old Empire, all living on the outside of law and custom. I'd met a few of them and had found them mostly shabby, straightforward to the point of bluntness and be cursed to the consequences. But Charoleia was a lady fit to adorn an Imperial arm.

'The trip was uneventful.' She set aside her glass and smoothed the skirts of her pale lavender gown. Fine muslin was appropriate for the heat, but it's cruelly unflattering to so many women. On Charoleia the delicate cloth simultaneously enhanced and discreetly blurred the sensuous curves beneath. 'How is the young D'Alsennin? I hear you had some trouble in Bremilayne?' Her musical voice was as beautiful as her face but I couldn't hear the ring of any particular city or country.

'Some goods were stolen but we don't know who was behind it,' I said frankly. 'Could you help find out?'

Charoleia arched a delicately enquiring eyebrow. 'What makes you ask that?'

I leaned back against the cushions and matched her gaze for gaze. 'Livak says you've a network of contacts in every city between the ocean and the Great Forest.' Livak also openly admired this woman's intelligence and my beloved isn't given to empty praise of anyone. 'I imagine you'll get news from places no Sieur's man would get a welcome.'

That enchanting dimple fleeted in her cheek. 'I'll expect to be paid for my trouble.'

I nodded. 'That would be only fair.'

Charoleia rose with consummate grace and crossed to a stout cupboard set in a far corner. She unlocked it with a key on a chain at her wrist. 'And there's my courier's fee for this to settle.' She removed a small wooden box and opened it to show me a battered copper armring. So she had it.

Similar to the one I wore in form only, this one had been made in the last days of the Old Empire, had crossed the ocean on the arm of one of Temar's still sleeping companions and by whatever route had come back to end up in a Relshazri trader's strong room. When Elietimm enchantment had overwhelmed my waking mind, Temar's sleeping consciousness had woken and gone in search of this ancient piece, whoever was trapped within it calling out in a voice only he could hear.

'What is your usual fee?' I kept my feelings hidden behind an expressionless face. Truth be told, they were a fine mixture of satisfaction and apprehension.

Charoleia smiled with feline grace. 'How much is this trinket worth to you?'

I pursed my lips. What would be a fair price, for me and for her? Living this elegant didn't come cheap after all, and I had some personal resources to draw on before I'd need to make an appeal to Messire's coffers, but there are rules to every game. 'Its value's not so much a matter of money.'

'No,' she agreed. 'It's far more important.' She spun the ring on one perfectly manicured forefinger. 'This holds the essence of a man in thrall to enchantments generations old.'

'If it's the right piece.' I've played out games of Raven from hopeless-looking positions and won them before now.

'It's the right piece,' she assured me. 'I got every detail from Livak when she passed through Relshaz at Equinox.'

'I do hope so.' I raised a hand in demur as she offered it to me. I wasn't about to lay a finger on the thing.

'So what is it worth to you?' she repeated softly.

'What's your price?' I countered.

She took her time replacing the armring in the battered box before leaning back against the cupboard, her face lively with mischief. 'A card for the Emperor's dance on the fifth day of Festival.'

I blinked. 'You don't want much! Half the Demoiselles in the city would sell their little sisters for that.'

'That's my price.' Charoleia laid a hand on the little box and smiled sweetly. 'I'm sure Esquire Camarl would oblige.'

'You want an introduction?' I'd been expecting to haggle over gold but this wrong-footed me. 'What would your name be?'

'Lady Alaric will do,' she shrugged. 'Dispossessed and orphaned in the battles between Triolle and Marlier, she's here to try and build a new life for herself, you know how it goes.' Now her accent was flawlessly western Lescari.

'Why does she warrant invitation to Imperial entertainments?' I asked a little desperately.

'Isn't her matchless beauty sufficient?' she enquired, wide-eyed. 'Then again, perhaps she has some family secret, some key information to assist Imperial efforts to halt the warfare brewing between Carluse and Triolle?'

'Do you?' I demanded.

'What do you think?' She dimpled at me.

'I think you've a scheme in hand that'll leave some poor goose well plucked,' I told her bluntly. 'If half what Livak's told me is true, you'll be gone by the first day of Aft-Summer, leaving empty coffers and shattered dreams littering the city. That's your affair and Dastennin help all fools, but I've no intention of being your whipping boy. I'll be the first person the Duty Cohort would come asking after if I'm seen introducing you to D'Olbriot.'

Charoleia's laugh was surprisingly hearty, a full-throated chuckle with a sensuous edge to it. 'I see you have something in common with Livak. But you're right to cover your own flanks.' She lowered luxuriant lashes for a moment. I let her take her time and drank my water.

'I've no game in hand, Halcarion be my witness. I'm here playing a speculation.' She resumed her seat on the daybed, tucking her skirts demurely around sculpted ankles white above silken slippers. 'Your Esquire D'Alsennin, his ancient colony, this new land across the ocean, it's the talk of Relshaz, Col and every other city between Toremal and Solura. All the runes are in the air at present and I want to see how they fall. Half the mercenary commanders in Lescar are working with understrength corps because every third mercenary is hanging round Carif hoping to take ship for the rumoured riches of Nemith the Last's final folly.'

She wasn't about to share any more than that, I realised as I watched her drink her own water. 'So you're waiting to see how the game plays out?' Livak had told me information was more precious than gold to this woman.

Charoleia nodded. 'All the major pieces will be on the board at the Emperor's dance. I want to see their moves for myself.'

'I'll see what I can do,' I said slowly. 'I make no promises, but Dastennin's my witness, I'll try.'

'Livak tells me your word is a solid pledge.' Charoleia smiled amiably.

'How was she when you saw her?' Charoleia's charms

notwithstanding, it was a future with Livak that my own game aimed to win, I reminded myself sternly.

'She was well,' nodded Charoleia. 'Tired from the sea crossing, but then she's never a good sailor. They rested for a few days and then took the Great West Road for Selerima.'

I didn't envy Livak that journey, clear across the old provinces. I frowned. 'Usara said they'd be heading for Col.'

Charoleia shrugged. 'Livak said she was looking for Sorgrad and 'Gren. I knew they were going to be in Selerima for Equinox.'

I stifled a qualm. Livak had told me precious little about that particular pair of long-time friends and I suspected that was because she knew I'd take against them. Livak stealing to keep food in her belly as an alternative to earning her keep lifting her skirts – that was something I'd come to terms with. These brothers had no such justification, and when me and Livak had been fighting for the lives of Temar and the colonists they'd been robbing the Duke of Draximal's war chest, that much I did know.

Charoleia was studying me with interest and I kept my face impassive. 'Do you know if she found them?' If so, Livak might well be finding ancient lore to earn us the coin to choose our own path together. Then again, going back to a life of travelling and trickery with old accomplices might be tempting her astray.

'I haven't heard.' Charoleia shrugged.

I'd have to go and soothe Casuel's ruffled feathers, I realised with irritation. I needed a wizard to bespeak Usara and get me some news.

'Are you taking the armring with you?' Charoleia nodded at the battered box.

I hesitated, like a dog seeing a bone in the hearth but remembering a burned mouth.

'It should be safe enough locked in the box,' said Charoleia softly. 'But I'll send Eadit with you to carry it, if you prefer. Livak told me that you'd been used against your will by enchantments woven round such things.'

I set my jaw against her sympathy. Used against my will scarcely began to describe being held captive inside my own head, unable to resist as some other intelligence used my body for its own purposes. My stomach heaved at the memory.

'No, I'll take it.' I took the accursed thing from her, my hands slippery with sweat against the scuffed wood. Nothing happened. No frustrated consciousness came scratching round my sanity, no desperate voice howled in the darkest recesses of my head, and I let slip an unguarded sigh of relief. 'I'll take my leave then, and I won't forget about the dance card.'

Charoleia rang a little silver bell and I realised she was nearly as relieved as me. That was understandable; she'd hardly want a man-at-arms losing his wits in her elegant boudoir. 'Call yourself. You'll always be welcome.'

The maid opened the door and I wondered how much she'd heard from her post at the hinges. Her serene face gave no hint as she showed me down to the street door where the lad playing watchdog was desultorily polishing his sword.

I tucked the box under one arm as I stepped out into the heat of the day now building to its peak. The sun rode high in the cloudless bowl of the sky, glare striking back from white-washed walls of new brick repairing ancient, broken stone. Sweat soon beaded my face, soaking my shirt as I took the circular road that skirts the shallow bowl of the lower city, keeping an eye out for broken slabs or curbstones that might trip me into the path of the heavy wagons and heedless drays lumbering along. I hurried past genteel merchant houses and between ambitious traders' yards, ignoring the rise and fall of the land over the hills that ring the bay for the sake of the quickest route back to the D'Olbriot residence.

Paved roads branched off the stone flagged highway and led up to the higher ground where the Houses had built anew in search of clean water and cool breezes in the peace of the Leoril era. A conduit house stood in the corner where the route to the D'Olbriot residence joined the high road. The stream running beside the road sparkled in brief freedom between the spring behind the D'Olbriot residence and the conduit house diverting it into the myriad channels and sluices serving the lower city and giving D'Olbriot tenants one more good reason to pay their rents on time. But the Sieur still maintains the public fountains and wells for the indigent, and one stood here, an eight-sided pillar rising high above me, each spout guarded by god or goddess in their niche above a basin.

I dipped grateful hands into the clear water, splashing my head and face and feeling the heat leaching from my body. I drank deeply and then looked up at the blue marble likeness of Dastennin, impassive beneath his crown of seaweed as he poured water from a vast shell, gathering storm clouds looming behind him. You spared D'Alsennin's life in Bremilayne, Lord of the Sea, I thought impulsively. Let him achieve something with it. Help us release those people still sleeping in that cave. Turning to the gods seemed in keeping with a tale of enchantments from a time of myth.

'If you're done, friend—' A groom in Den Haurient livery was waiting, the horse he was exercising gulping from the trough for thirsty beasts.

'Of course.' I walked more slowly up towards the D'Olbriot residence. The usual stifling stillness hung over the ever narrowing strip of parkland clinging to the bottom reaches of the hill and tiny black flies danced in swirling balls beneath fringed leaves. But the shade trees offered welcome respite from the heat, and as I reached the top of the rise a breeze freshened the air. A well-tended highway winds between the spacious preserves of the upper city. No cracked slabs are allowed to trip the privilege of the oldest noble Houses – Den Haurient, Tor Kanselin, Den Leshayre, Tor Bezaemar. I walked past tall walls protecting extensive gardens surrounding spacious dwellings served by more lowly lodgings clustered close by. At this time of day there was little traffic, the only cart already nearly out of sight as it headed for some distant House built in more recent generations to escape the ever increasing pressures of the lower city.

As I drew closer to home I saw sentries walking slowly

along the parapets of the walls. The watchtowers added in the uncertain days under T'Aleonne were fully manned and the D'Olbriot standard flew from every cornice. All customary pomp was displayed for Festival, to remind any visitors just which House they were dealing with and to bolster far-flung family members with pride in their Name.

'Ryshad!' The man sitting in the gatehouse hailed me, a thick-set, shaven-headed warrior with a much broken nose. He'd trained me in wrestling when I'd first come to D'Olbriot service.

'Olas!' I waved an acknowledging hand but didn't stop or turn up the stairs to my new room. Elevated rank warranted privacy and that meant I was sleeping in the gatehouse rather than the barracks that filled one corner of the enclosure. Though I'd found privilege could have a sour aftertaste. With so many of the D'Olbriot Name arriving for the Festival, the noise of the gate opening and closing late into the night had disturbed me far more than the familiar bustle of the watch changing at midnight in the barracks. Still, with any luck most of the family would have arrived by now.

Turning sharply on to the gravelled path I hurried towards the tall house at the heart of the precisely delineated patterns of hedges and flowers. Temar had this reception to attend and I wanted to show him some small progress towards our shared goal before he left. Then I reckoned I'd earned half a chime out of the merciless sun for a meal and more than one long, cold drink before I went to see what I could discover from the Names on his list.

Leaving the grand reception rooms behind me, where the ladies of the House were catching up on half a season's gossip by the sound of it, I passed lackeys bringing laden trays of refreshments up from the lower levels. I hurried up the first flight of stairs leading to the private salons reserved for the Sieur and Esquires of the Name. They were as busy talking as the women, open doors revealing older men deep in serious conversation, sons and nephews in attentive attendance, news and promises for later discussions exchanged on every side.

I bowed my way down the hallways and gained the second storey, where the corridors became narrower, with softer carpets underfoot and the intricate painted patterns on the walls giving way to plain plaster sparely stencilled with leaves and garlands to complement the ornate tapestries. Visiting servants were busy with trunks and coffers, some calmly hanging dresses and setting out favourite possessions while others went flustered in search of some missing chest. Resident maids and lackeys went steadily about their business with arms of lavender-scented linen and vases of flowers to make ready rooms for unexpected arrivals who'd changed their minds and accepted the Sieur's invitation at the last moment.

I turned down a side passage to see a page was sitting on a cross-framed chair by the door at the end. He jumped up but I waved the child back to his hornbook. He'd spend enough of his day on his feet without me insisting on due deference and I could knock on a door myself. 'I'm here to see Esquire D'Alsennin.'

'Enter.' Temar answered my knock at once and I opened the door. The Sieur had decreed Temar was to be treated with Imperial courtesy and thus warranted the finest, coolest quarters available. Windows broadened when this northern façade had been rebuilt filled the room with light and Temar was standing by one, arms folded crossly over his creased shirt and looking distinctly mutinous.

'Good day to you, Chosen Tathel.' Demoiselle Tor Arrial sat on a gilt-wood stool upholstered with damask that matched the curtains of the old-fashioned bed dominating one half of the room.

'Demoiselle.' I made a low bow, mindful of her Imperial heritage.

Her bark of laughter made me look up. 'I am in no mood to be flattered by a title more suited to those coveys of maidens cluttering up the place. Avila will suffice.'

'As you wish,' I said cautiously. Informality was allowable on the road, but I wasn't going to call her by her given name in Messire's hearing. 'Are you fully recovered from the journey?' She'd looked fit for her pyre the previous day, every year of her age weighing heavy on her head.

'I am quite restored,' she assured me. 'A good night's sleep works its own Artifice.'

'Ryshad, I really should come with you this afternoon,' Temar appealed to me. 'This is my responsibility and my Name will lend weight to our requests.'

'How so, when no one knows your face?' demanded Avila acidly. 'You need to assert the dignity of your House with these lately come nobles before you can claim the right to speak for Kel Ar'Ayen. That means exchanging the usual courtesies, just as Festival always demanded.'

'I was never any good at such things,' the youth objected.

'Because you never applied yourself and there was your grandsire to do the duty for you. You cannot escape the obligations of your rank now,' challenged Avila.

'Making yourself known will certainly smooth our path, Temar,' I interjected. Messire D'Olbriot would hardly thank me if Temar absented himself this afternoon. 'And I've made a start on tracing the artefacts already.' I placed the box on a marble-topped table and opened it with hesitant hands to reveal the armring within.

Temar reached out an eager hand but then withdrew it.

'What is it?' Avila asked with a curious look at us both.

As one man Temar and I glanced across the room to a scabbarded blade resting on a walnut cabinet by the dressing room door. Artifice had confined Temar's essential self within that sword through nine Imperial eras. No, he was no more about to risk handling an artefact holding a similarly imprisoned mind than I was.

'Let me.' Avila came to pick up the armring and turned it to examine an engraved device, dark lines blurred with age in the tarnished metal. 'Ancel fashioned this badge when he and Letica married.'

'Maitresse Den Rannion, as was,' Temar whispered hastily to me. 'Her sister, you know.'

I nodded. I'd made it my business to know all the long-dead colonists regardless, but I also seemed to have Temar's own memories lurking in the back of my head supplying such answers. I wasn't sure I liked it, but it was undeniably useful.

'This belongs to Jaes, the gate ward. He helped Letica plant her herb garden.' Avila ran a creased finger over the incised sea eagle's head and tears shone briefly in her faded eyes.

'One more will be rescued from the darkness,' said Temar hoarsely.

'We can spread our efforts this afternoon,' I suggested. 'I'll take your list and try to talk to servants, men-at-arms, people like that. You make yourself known to the nobility and charm a few likely Demoiselles.'

He rubbed a hand over his hair, leaving it in unruly black spikes. 'I might manage that.'

'Who is to keep this safe?' Avila put the armring back in its box and looked at us both.

I held up my hands in demur. 'I've nowhere to keep it.'

'It is not staying in here,' said Temar hastily.

Avila gave us both a scorching glare as she got stiffly to her feet. 'You would-be warriors can be remarkably chicken-hearted. Very well, I will keep it in my room. Temar, dress for this afternoon's folderols.'

I opened the door so as to avoid her gaze but nearly betrayed myself when I saw the face Temar was pulling at her departing back. I grinned at him. 'We'll see who's made most progress after dinner tonight.'

The D'Olbriot Residence,
Summer Solstice Festival, First Day,
Early Afternoon

Temar watched Avila and Ryshad go with some regret, then realised the page was staring hopefully at him. 'I need clean clothes and I have yet to see my own luggage,' he said bluntly. 'Whom do I ask?'

'I'll get Master Dederic,' said the boy hastily and before Temar could say anything further he disappeared towards the backstairs.

Temar went back to staring out of the window, looking down on the complex interlacing of hedge and blooms that hemmed this enormous dwelling. The grounds of his grandfather's modest hall had nourished deer and cattle, useful animals, not some empty display.

A discreet tap on the door drew him back to the present. 'Enter.'

'Good day to you, Esquire.' A dapper man bowed into the room with aplomb.

'Forgive me, I do not believe we have met . . .' Temar apologised.

'I'm Dederic, tailor to the House.' The man clapped his hands and two liveried lackeys hurried in, arms full of garments. A hesitant youth with a ribbon pierced with pins tied round one wrist followed clutching a two-handled coffer. There must be more servants in this house than mice, Temar thought. In fact, there was probably some underling specifically dedicated to removing mice, and a separate one for the stableyard rats.

'Send the page for hot water. The Esquire will wish to shave.'

Dederic dismissed one of the lackeys before producing a length of knotted silk thread from one pocket. 'I made up a few outfits for you overnight. I took measurements from your old clothing, so the fit won't be all we might wish, but if I measure you now we can make the necessary adjustments tonight.'

The apprentice with the pins produced a small slate from his coffer and both tailors looked expectantly at Temar.

He stopped running a hand over his chin to judge for himself whether he needed to shave and stood still as Dederic moved rapidly round him. 'Two fingers less in the back. If you could just raise your arms – thank you. Half a handspan long in the sleeve, Larasion help me. And your feet a little wider apart – thank you.'

The man took an impertinently intimate measurement and Temar was about to ask just what in Talagrin's name Dederic thought he was doing when he noticed the close fit of the breeches everyone else wore. He swallowed his curt enquiry.

'It's the Tor Kanselin reception this afternoon?' Dederic raised a fine black brow.

'It is? I mean, yes, it is,' Temar nodded firmly. 'Who exactly is to be present, do you know?' he asked cautiously.

'Just the younger nobility from the better Names, mostly those from cadet lines who are visiting for Festival,' said Dederic, measuring the width of Temar's shoulders with an approving murmur. 'It's a chance for everyone to catch up with the gossip while the Sieurs are occupied with assizes business.'

That didn't sound too bad, thought Temar, determinedly quelling unwelcome nervousness. 'What would you advise me to wear?' The last thing he wanted was to be embarrassed by his appearance.

Dederic ran a thoughtful hand over precisely pomaded curls. 'Perhaps the pewter? Where is your valet?'

Temar blinked. 'Camarl's servant saw to my needs when we arrived. I have no attendant of my own.' And the struggle to convince Camarl's valet he didn't require anyone's help washing had put Temar right off having one.

'I'll assist you just this once.' Dederic's narrow nostrils

flared a little. 'Speak to the Steward about a valet and don't let him tell you everyone's so busy you'll have to share with some minor Esquire.'

One of the ubiquitous pageboys arrived with a steaming ewer. 'I can shave myself,' said Temar hastily.

'Very well, if you wish.' Dederic glared at his apprentice, who was exchanging a smirk with the pageboy. 'Huke, lay out linen and the pewter coat and get back to the seamstresses.'

Temar shut the door of the dressing room on the man's continuing instructions with a sigh of relief. He pulled his shirt over his head and poured precisely warmed water from the ewer. Lathering his face, he looked at his reflection in the mirror of the ornate fruitwood washstand. The face in the glass looked irresolute, hollow-eyed, and Temar set his jaw beneath the soft luxury of the scented soap. Remember the uncompromising civility of real court life, he told himself silently, forget the easy camaraderie of Kel Ar'Ayen. He looked at his reflection again; people had often said they saw his grandfather in his eyes, hadn't they? Temar shaved with firm yet careful strokes of the expertly honed blade, summoning up a host of memories of the stern old man. That was the example to keep in mind. None of these modern Sieurs could have matched his grandsire.

'Can I be of assistance?' Dederic peered round the door.

'Thank you, no.' Were these nobles incapable of doing anything for themselves? Temar stifled his irritation with a last wipe of his face with a soft white towel, remembering his grandsire had little use for men who needlessly rebuked their servants. He ignored the scented unguents arrayed along the washstand and went back into the bedchamber. 'So what am I to wear?' He looked dubiously at close-tailored breeches and a full-skirted coat laid on the bed.

'Your shirt, Esquire.' The tailor held up the garment and Temar shrugged it on. 'Oh, no, not like that.' Dederic raised frantic hands as Temar tugged brusquely at the fine frill around the neck.

'Camarl's shirts are plain-collared.' Temar tried to conceal his dislike of the starched linen brushing his chin.

'For everyday wear.' Dederic smoothed the fabric with deft fingers. 'For Festival, we fancy a little more elegance.'

More idiocy than elegance, Temar thought to himself as he buttoned cuffs hampered by lace falling to his knuckles. 'At least hose have not changed that much.' He sat on the bed to roll pearly knitted silk over one foot and then realised the stockings were a handspan shorter than he expected and had no laces, and in any case there were no points on his drawers to tie them to.

Dederic smiled briefly. 'The buttons at the knee secure the hose, like so.'

Temar pulled on the breeches, shoving his shirt in all anyhow before fumbling with unfamiliar fastenings at one side.

'Please, Esquire, allow me.' Dederic looked so pained that Temar reluctantly let the man pleat the linen neatly around his waist before smoothly securing the fine woven wool. Temar grimaced at the unaccustomed snugness.

'And now the coat.' Dederic held it up proudly, light grey wool with smoky watered silk showing where the cuffs were folded over and where buttons caught the fronts back for ease of movement. Temar was relieved to find it wasn't as heavy as he had feared but immediately felt uncomfortably restricted beneath the arms and across his shoulders.

Dederic took his chance to sort out the confusion of lace at Temar's cuffs and arrange the frill of his shirt within the stiff upright collar of the coat. 'Most pleasing, Esquire.'

Temar managed a strained smile and turned to a long looking glass in a fussy ormolu frame. He clenched fists unseen beneath the absurd lace. The colonists of Kel Ar'Ayen had worn practical shirts and functional jerkins, serviceable breeches of leather or sturdy cloth, clothes little different to those of the mercenaries who'd rescued them. If women's gowns had changed in cut, length or neckline over the generations, that had been of little interest to Temar.

Seeing himself dressed up like this was as forceful a reminder as any yet of just how far adrift he was from his own age. Qualms knotted Temar's belly so tight he half expected to see his stomach squirming in the reflection. He moved his arms; no wonder these sleeves were so constricting, sewn tight to the body of the garment rather than laced in, as he had always been used to. What he wanted, Temar decided, was to rip off these stupid clothes, hide in that ludicrous bed and pull that absurd coverlet over his head until all these fawning servants and this whole incomprehensible Festival had gone away.

'A house shoe will suffice for this afternoon,' Dederic continued. 'But the cobbler will take your pattern for boots at your earliest convenience.'

'I have boots,' said Temar curtly, turning to the chair he'd kicked them under. But Dederic was already kneeling before him with what looked like a girl's slipper. Temar sighed and reluctantly eased one foot into the square-toed soft grey leather.

'I have plain buckles or—'

'Plain,' interrupted Temar.

Dederic reached into the box for an unembellished silver fastening. As the tailor fussed around his feet, Temar scowled angrily at his reflection. He could run back to Kel Ar'Ayen, couldn't he, but what would he say when he got there? How could he excuse himself when everyone was trusting him to bring home the artefacts to restore loved ones to life and light? Ryshad was right; the chosen man could talk to servants and men-at-arms but it was Temar's duty to deal with nobility.

'Don't you have any jewellery?' Dederic asked plaintively as he stood. 'Something with your own badge on?'

'Just this.' Temar raised the hand bearing his father's sapphire signet ring.

Dederic looked doubtful. 'It's not quite the colour for that coat. Some diamonds, perhaps?'

Of course, Camarl always wore rings and pins, some collar or chain. No matter. Temar had no wish to show off like some cockbird flaunting fine feathers. His father's ring was sufficient for him. 'I see no need for anything more.'

'Perhaps a little pomade?' Dederic offered Temar a brush.

'No, thanks all the same.' Temar dragged the bristles through his hair and gave Dederic a warning look as the man made a move towards a scent bottle. 'This will suffice.'

'I'll see if Esquire Camarl is ready,' offered the tailor and bowed out with a practised smile.

Temar was examining his sword thoughtfully when Camarl came breezily into the room some time later. 'Oh, we don't wear blades, not indoors, not at a social gathering.'

'There's no way anyone could fight in these clothes.' At least his own spare frame was more flattered by close tailoring than Camarl's stoutness, Temar thought. He slid the gleaming steel back into the scabbard.

'You look most stylish.' Camarl ushered Temar out into the corridor. 'Though this afternoon will be quite informal, just a chance for you to meet a few people before the real business of Festival begins—' Camarl broke off and clicked his tongue against his teeth.

'What?' Temar looked sidelong at the other man, noting jewelled clasps securing the turned-back cuffs of his amber coat, rings on every finger glinting beneath the lace at his wrists.

'I was going to say you'll be able to recognise people's Names by their badges but I don't suppose you will.'

Temar frowned. 'We have – we had insignia, for seals and battle standards, but from what Master Devoir said your business of badges is rather more complicated. But he did his best to drill me in the important ones.'

'I've been meaning to ask what would the D'Alsennin emblem be,' grimaced Camarl. 'People will be asking. The Archivist set his clerks looking, but there's not one recorded, not as such. Formal insignia were mostly adopted after the Chaos and your Name—'

'Had died out by then,' Temar supplied sadly.

'Quite so.' Camarl coughed to cover his discomfiture and for some moments they walked in silence down to the bustle of the lower floors. Camarl smiled at Temar as they turned down the final flight of stairs. 'But even in the Old Empire, most Houses favoured some theme for their crests?'

'D'Alsennin mostly used leaves.' Temar closed his eyes on childhood memories of the silver clasp that had secured his father's long hair, one of the few things Temar remembered him by. But he'd left that treasure safe with Guinalle.

'Leaves are certainly traditional, but you'd need to decide on something distinctive.' Camarl's hand strayed to the enamelled lynx mask fastening his shirt collar. 'Opting for your own badge would be a good notion, though. It'll give us an ideal opportunity to introduce you to the Emperor.'

Temar halted on the bottom step to let a giggling trio of girls trip lightly past. 'How so?'

'All grants of emblem have to be approved by the Emperor.' Camarl raised his voice above the excited buzz of conversation. 'Well, that's the formality. What's important is our Archivist making sure any new device is sufficiently clear not to get confused with someone else's.' He raised a hand and two stripling Esquires halted to let him and Temar pass ahead of them through the crowded hallway.

'We all just chose our own insignia,' grumbled Temar as they walked out into the sun. 'No Emperor had a say in such things.'

'Life in ancient times was freer, perhaps.' Camarl stopped to look thoughtfully at Temar. 'But after the Chaos, when the time came to rebuild, the Names surrendered freedoms for safeguards all would abide by. That's why the Emperor rules on things like badges, since he's pledged to enforce them.'

Temar was trying to find something to say to that when a new thought diverted Camarl. 'Where's Ryshad? He should be attending you.' He looked around the thronged gatehouse with growing displeasure.

'I had errands for him.' Temar met Camarl's frown with a challenging look. 'I have that right, do I not? To set him small tasks?'

Camarl sighed. 'We have plenty of servants for such things.

Ryshad really does need to appreciate a chosen man has quite a different status to the merely sworn.'

Temar dutifully followed Camarl through the crowd waiting in the gatehouse as a succession of small carriages and gigs were brought round from the stable yard at the rear of the residence. 'Is everyone going to Tor Kanselin's reception?' He smiled faintly at a young girl who was white with suppressed excitement.

'Oh, no.' Camarl snapped his fingers and the next gig drew up smartly in front of them. 'The first day of Festival's very informal. People mostly visit old friends and call on relatives in other Houses.'

He urged Temar into the open carriage and they were carried along the highway. Temar looked down the hill, trying to work out exactly where the D'Olbriot residence was in relation to what he remembered Toremal to be. So far he'd seen nothing of the walled city he had known, arriving after dark and then being jolted through seemingly endless crowded streets in the coach that had taken them to the archive. He'd seen nothing he recognised and found this lack of any bearings disconcerting. But the trees blocked any view of the land sloping down to the bay, so Temar turned to looked with some interest at a knot of buildings tight inside an ancient bank and ditch incongruous beside the square-cut wall of the residence. 'What is that?'

Camarl smiled. 'Grace houses, workshops, that kind of thing.'

Temar recognised a frail, silvery carillon of traditional bells. 'You have a shrine there?'

'Sacred to Poldrion,' nodded Camarl absently. 'A D'Olbriot priesthood for generations. The Sieur granted it to one of my cousins at Winter Solstice, I believe.'

So much for the hallowed observances the god expected from the Head of a House, thought Temar indignantly.

Their carriage halted as a wain loaded with freshly cut blocks of stone negotiated an awkward little bridge over the stream. Temar turned to watch it heading for a building as yet no more than a promise of scaffolding poles beyond the shrine enclosure.

'Here we are.' Camarl stepped lightly down from the carriage.

'Already?' Temar wouldn't have bothered harnessing the horses for this distance.

Lackeys in bronze and beige escorted them through the gatehouse. 'As you see, the late Sieur Tor Kanselin rebuilt in the Rational style,' Camarl told Temar in an undertone.

Temar only just managed to stop himself stumbling on the steps to the gravel walk when he saw the edifice before him. While later wings had clearly been added to the D'Olbriot residence, Temar had approved the new building as a sympathetic mix of old and new. It was evident Tor Kanselin had scorned such compromise. A square, unbroken frontage was pierced by regular windows, longest on the lower floors, graduated in size to the small garret rooms half hidden by the pediment topping the wall. Every line was straight, every corner exact, the pale stone ornamented with precisely parallel carving framing rigidly geometric designs. These angles were reflected in the sharply delineated gravel walks and hedges of the gardens, the potential unruliness of flowers banished and patterns of coloured gravels laid out instead. Where trees were permitted, they were clipped into tightly disciplined shapes, not a sprig out of place.

'What do you think?' chuckled Camarl.

'It is rather startling to my eye,' Temar said cautiously.

'It's a fine example of Rational architecture,' Camarl commented, 'and yes, it's a bit severe for my taste. But the old Sieur was one of the first, so it's one of the strictest examples you'll see. Styles have softened around the edges these days.'

He smiled to a waiting lackey as they walked up to the door precisely in the centre of the frontage. 'Fair Festival, Getan. No, don't trouble yourself. I know my way.'

As the retainer bowed low, Camarl immediately turned down a long corridor leading to the rear of the building. Mock pillars of polished golden stone were set in the white plaster of the walls, supporting a complex frieze running above the tops of doorways and blending into the ornate decoration of the coffered ceiling. 'That looks a bit more lively,' Temar remarked.

'Yes, Rational style is all very well, but you do have to recognise the heritage, don't you?' Camarl sounded amused. 'Watch your footing.'

The glassy marble floor caught Temar unawares as he tried to identify the mythic figures among the intricate detail.

'When we were children we'd get a hearthrug and slide along here if we could escape our nursemaids,' grinned Camarl, gesturing at the white expanse inlaid with mottled tawny lines.

Temar laughed but thought all those choice ceramics set on spindly tables must have been horribly vulnerable to rampaging children. There had been no such hazards in the halls of his youth, where plain panelled walls were only relieved by stern-faced statues on plinths it took three men to shift. Banners hung overhead from dark hammer beams and plain silken drapes only framed the long windows to baffle drafts from ironbound shutters. But he liked the idea of the staid Camarl causing havoc hereabouts.

A florid platter displayed on a side table caught his eye. Arimelin sat weaving dreams in her bower and the trees reminded Temar of the tracery engraved on his sword, his grandfather's gift before he sailed for Kel Ar'Ayen. The blade had been made for the uncle expected to be the next Sieur D'Alsennin before the Crusted Pox blighted all their lives.

'Holm oak,' Temar said suddenly. 'Could I take the holm oak as my badge?'

Camarl cracked his knuckles absently. 'I can't think of a House using it, not anyone of significance. The Archivists would have to check the lesser Names but we could argue for D'Alsennin precedence.'

Would that help put him on an equal footing with these nobles always flaunting their finery, wondered Temar. His grandfather had never needed such display; face and Name were enough to command respect from equals and subordinates alike.

'Here we are.' Camarl nodded to the waiting lackey as they reached the end of the corridor. The leaves and flowers of the plasterwork frieze framed a marvellously lifelike swan, wings bating in defiance and neck arched with its head hovering right above the lintel as if it might peck at those passing beneath. Temar laughed.

'Just to remind people who they're dealing with,' smiled Camarl.

The lackey flung open the double doors with the efficiency of long practice and Camarl strode casually through, Temar rather more stiffly by his side.

'People will call in through the afternoon, then go on to other things,' murmured Camarl. 'We're here to socialise, not talk trade, so don't let anyone press you on colony business.'

Temar wondered just how exactly he was to manage that without giving offence, but he followed Camarl obediently down the vast room. This high ceiling was another triumph of the plasterer's art, swags and garlands framing flowers, knots, beasts and birds, too stylised and too fantastical to be anything but insignia, Temar decided. The plain walls, by contrast, were a mere backdrop to an imposing array of gilt-framed paintings. Glazed doors in deeply recessed bays in the three outer walls gave on to terraces where Temar saw tempting glimpses of green foliage. The inner, southern wall had bays to match the doors furnished with intimate circles of chairs upholstered in deceptively plain silver brocade. Fireplaces of clean-cut white marble held vast arrays of lilies, while bowls of golden roses scented the air from fruitwood side tables.

Two young ladies occupied one of these bays, prettily pink but appropriately demure in dull silk gowns of honey gold and jessamine yellow, collars of diamonds and pearls around their necks.

'Demoiselles.' Camarl's dark eyes warmed with affection.

'May I make known Temar, Esquire D'Alsennin. Temar, I have the honour to present the senior Demoiselles Tor Kanselin, Resialle and Irianne, two of my dearest friends.

Both swept elegant curtseys, first to Temar, then to Camarl. 'You're horribly early,' accused the one in the honey-coloured gown, hazel eyes charming in a strong-featured face.

'Lady Channis arrived just before you. She's calling on our lady mother,' piped up her younger sister, light brown gaze fixed on Camarl.

Resialle, the elder, stepped past Temar towards the empty length of the gallery. 'Let's walk a little, before the room becomes too crowded. I'm sure you've been wanting to see the pictures.'

Temar could take a hint as plain as a kick in the shins. 'Demoiselle.'

She led him briskly out of sight of Camarl and her sister, silken shoes whispering on the woven rush matting. 'This is the Sieur Tor Kanselin who was uncle to Inshol the Curt,' she said brightly, indicating a portrait of a balding man, chin on chest and arms folded, swathed in a black robe barely distinguishable from the vista of storm clouds dark behind him.

'He looks half asleep to me,' said Temar critically.

'That's a pose of earnest contemplation, I believe. In a time of uncertainty, a show of wisdom helped maintain confidence in the Name.' Resialle stole a glance at Temar from behind a raised hand. She adjusted a discreetly jewelled comb pinning a long fall of lace to the back of her high-piled black hair before folding her hands demurely at a trim waist girdled with a heavy golden chain with a pomander and a fan hanging from it.

Temar winked at her. 'You need not play the tutor just to get your sister and Camarl a little privacy.'

Resialle looked a little abashed. 'He said you weren't stupid.'

'Festivals were always a favoured time for match-making.' Temar smiled, resolutely looking her in the eye rather than letting his gaze fall to the low circular neckline of her gown.

He did permit himself a brief glance at her cleavage, where a jewelled swan fashioned round the body of a single, splendid pearl hung on gold and white-enamelled chains linked by a diamond clip.

'Oh, the deal was done at Equinox, but they'll be more than just a match.' Resialle caught up her fan and smoothed the pristine white feathers clasped in a golden handle set with fiery agates. 'Irianne's adored Camarl since before we put up our hair or lengthened our skirts.'

'Since he slid down corridors with her?' hazarded Temar.

Resialle laughed. 'He told you about that? Yes, and shared sweetmeats with, and consoled over lost cage-birds – and teased mercilessly about her hopeless singing.'

'So when will the wedding be?' Temar asked idly.

'Mother's doubtless planning it as we speak, but she'll keep it to herself until the very last minute,' Resialle shrugged.

Temar was puzzled. 'Why so?'

Resialle looked askance. 'We hardly want people claiming a marriage entitles them to some handout from the Name. It can cost a small fortune to stop that kind of nonsense turning into a riot.'

So the nobility no longer celebrated a wedding by rewarding their faithful tenantry with feasting and gifts. Trying to conceal his disdain, Temar turned as the double doors opened for a handful of richly dressed young men and women.

Resialle laid a hand on his arm. 'You could drop Camarl a hint, you know, that Irianne's a grown woman. She's threatening to have herself painted by Master Gerlach if he doesn't at least kiss her soon.'

Her laugh, half scandalised, half admiring, plainly told Temar some response was expected. Unfortunately he had no idea what it should be. 'That would make him realise?'

'You don't know Gerlach's work?' Resialle's colour rose a little. 'Of course you don't.' She led Temar to the gallery's most remote recess. 'That's one of his, our mother, painted as Halcarion, you know, in the allegorical style.'

Temar's jaw dropped. He couldn't decide what was more

shocking, that any woman could be so impious as to have herself portrayed as the goddess or that she would do so in diaphanous gauzes clipped negligently over one shoulder leaving one glorious breast all but naked to be rendered in loving detail by the artist.

'It's very good, isn't it?' said Resialle admiringly. 'But Mother would have five kinds of fit if Irianne suggested it before she was married.'

How was he ever supposed to meet this Maitresse Tor Kanselin without dying of embarrassment? Temar turned hastily to look for something more familiar, walking rapidly and gratefully towards a clutch of smaller pictures hung close together on the far wall. 'This is more the style I remember,' he said inarticulately.

Resialle wrinkled her nose at the stiffly formal figures. 'We consider that kind of thing very old-fashioned.' Her attempt to make light of her opinion fell as flat as the faces in the ancient portraits. 'But there aren't many families with pictures from before the Chaos, so we keep them on display.'

Awkward silence hung in the air until a steward broke it with ringing declaration. 'Esquire Firon Den Thasnet and Demoiselle Dria Tor Sylarre.'

Resialle let slip a glance at the girl who looked back with avid curiosity.

Temar didn't think he could cope with two of these girls and hurried to start some conversation to forestall introductions. 'So how do we get from these to that?' Temar waved vaguely in the direction of the scandalous picture.

Resialle managed an uncertain smile. 'Tastes change gradually, naturally. These old styles, the figure on a plain background, they were to convey presence, power, weren't they? That square stance is all about strength.' She was clearly repeating something some tutor had drilled into her.

Temar shrugged. 'I suppose so.' He'd never really thought about it, but then there'd never been anything different to look at.

Resialle moved down the gallery to some smaller canvases.

'These are from just after the Chaos.' Her tone became more animated. 'That's the Sieur D'Olbriot whose cousin was wife to Kanselin the Pious. It's the old pose, but see the map beneath his feet. There's Toremal with the sun's shining on it, to show hope and renewal, while the lost provinces are all still in shadow.'

Temar studied the ominous darkness behind the solemn figure, broken only by a single shaft of light edging the clouds with gold. 'I see,' he said politely.

Resialle's smile betrayed relief. 'Even when the backgrounds stay plain, the people become more natural-looking.' They walked slowly down the length of the room, gazing at the portraits increasingly viewed from an angle or the side, some looking away from the artist, clothes painted with soft realism.

'Later you have to look at what they're holding,' explained Resialle as they halted in front of a hollow-eyed man with a forked, greying beard and an odd-shaped hood to his enveloping cloak.

Temar obediently studied the silver-banded staff in the old man's hands. 'And that means—?'

Resialle looked faintly disconcerted. 'It's the Adjurist's rod.'

'Of course.' Temar hoped he sounded at least half convincing. He'd better remember to ask Camarl what in Saedrin's name that was. No, he'd ask Ryshad. He looked up at the long-dead old man and realised this sombre elder's father's grandsire hadn't even been thought of when Temar had left Toremal behind.

Resialle retreated behind noncommittal remarks as they continued their slow progress and Temar didn't dare venture any comment of his own. A lackey brought crystal glasses of sparkling wine, which at least gave them both an excuse for silence. More people were arriving now, mostly much of an age with Resialle, but Temar noticed a few older ladies whose satin gowns were overlaid with lace from throat to hem. Resialle was casting longing glances at her friends so Temar stared at the pictures to avoid catching her eye. That was how sensible clothing had drifted into this nonsensical attire, he realised, seeing lengthening jerkins becoming ever more full cut. At least he'd not been woken to some of the more ludicrous excesses of fashion, he thought, gaping at a bloated lordling in a puff-sleeved coat, shirt poking through slashes in the fabric caught together with jewelled clasps. And if breeches had turned too close-tailored for Temar's liking, at least that was better than the bagged and frilled style that cursed some earlier generation.

'Tiadar, Tor Kanselin as was, who married into the D'Olbriot Name nine generations since.' Resialle was beginning to sound bored, Temar realised. He studied the painting, desperate to find something intelligent to say about it. 'That jewel!' He stared at the swan pinned to the scalloped neckline of the painted lady's gown, faithfully rendered in minute detail. 'That's the one you're wearing, isn't it?'

'Oh yes,' said Resialle, brushing it with a finger and a touch of smugness. 'It came back to our House with a daughter in the next generation but one. It's been a Tor Kanselin heirloom piece since the Modrical era. It's in all the portraits.'

'Are many jewels handed down like that? Do people make a point of having them painted?' Temar leaned forward to study the swan but remembered himself just in time.

'Yes,' Resialle said slowly. 'The lately ennobled buy things and then break them up for new settings, but decent families have a proper sense of history.'

Temar startled her with a beaming smile. 'Most of those still sleeping in Kel Ar'Ayen entrusted themselves to their choicest jewels, rings and lockets. Vahil, my friend, Vahil Den Rannion brought them back to the Name that gave them leave to go,' he explained. 'Do you think we might find them in a House's pictures?'

Resialle looked nonplussed. 'I don't see—'

'Hello, Ressy. Doing your duty by Camarl's poor relations, are you?' A spotty youth dressed in startling purple with silver edging to his lace appeared at Temar's shoulder. 'You want to be careful. Leeches are cursed hard to shake loose.'

'Esquire D'Alsennin, may I make known Firon Den Thasnet,' said Resialle without enthusiasm.

Den Thasnet favoured Temar with a curiously close-mouthed smile that betrayed acrid tainted breath. 'White feathers, is it, Ressy? But your Sieur refused to discuss Tayven's suit with our designate, he said you weren't open to offers.'

'If you're going to be offensive, you can go away,' snapped Resialle.

'We'll see you sniffing round any girl showing a white fan, will we, D'Alsennin?' Den Thasnet's raised voice turned nearby heads and several people drifted closer, faces animated. 'Looking to restore the family fortunes with a good match is all very well, but you'll need something to back an ancient Name if you're going to dance the measure hereabouts. Have you any property this side of the ocean?' He sneered at Temar, showing unattractively stained teeth.

'Of course, your brother's up before the assize, isn't he?' A newcomer just beyond Resialle interrupted the youth. 'So you're honour bound to be the loudest arse in the room, if he can't be present.' He inclined his head to Temar. 'Maren Den Murivance, at your service.'

'That's a spurious claim and you know it,' retorted Den Thasnet angrily. 'That was our mother's settlement. Den Fisce only wants it back because we've doubled the rents.'

'By rebuilding and reletting to lately come tradesmen with more money than lineage,' countered Den Murivance. 'Perhaps Den Fisce's concerned about the tenants you threw on to the streets when you tore down their houses.'

Temar kept his mouth shut and wondered who these families were, what their quarrels might be and whether or not he should make some effort to find out. A girl on the edge of the group tittered behind a fan shading from black to palest grey and Den Thasnet coloured unpleasantly. 'At least I'm not begging charity round the coat hems of my betters. You've made quite the fool of old D'Olbriot with your nonsense, haven't you?'

He thrust his face belligerently at Temar, who realised everyone close by was waiting with interest for his response. He wondered if punching the lout in the mouth would split the seams in this tight-sewn coat.

'Believe me, friend,' he laid ironic emphasis on the word 'with the wealth of Kel Ar'Ayen behind me, I need no one's charity.' He smiled winningly at Den Thasnet but his heart was pounding. Was someone going to challenge that idle boast?

'Surely you've heard of Nemith the Last's colony?' said Resialle sweetly.

'I doubt it,' chimed in Den Murivance. 'Firon's as ignorant of history as he is of manners.'

'Is it truly as rich as they say?' breathed the girl who'd been giggling behind her fan.

Saedrin save me from clever ideas, thought Temar with a sinking feeling, realising all eyes were fixed on him.

'This is hardly a very edifying display of your breeding.' The entire group started like children caught in mischief and parted in front of Temar to reveal a stout woman well beyond her middle years. Her rose gown, covered with a grey lace overdress, belied its cost with simplicity of cut. But there was nothing simple about her heavy necklace, bracelets and rings, and her hazel eyes were as bright as her diamonds, her plump and kindly face taut with displeasure. 'When will you grow out of making cheap taunts to show how clever you are, Maren? As for you, Firon, if you must indulge in stableyard habits you should stay there till the effects wear off.' Den Thasnet's hand moved involuntarily to his mouth.

'Temar, Esquire D'Alsennin, may I make known Dirindal, Relict Tor Bezaemar,' said Resialle nervously.

'Esquire, I've heard a great deal about you.' She linked her arm through Temar's unresisting one and led him inexorably away from the group. 'Were they being very childish?' Her voice was sympathetic but loud enough to be heard by the abashed group.

'They all know each other and I do not. Awkwardness is inevitable.' Temar realised he was still the centre of attention.

The Relict smiled at him. 'You got Firon's measure soon enough. He chews thassin of course, which addles the little wits he was born with and gives him a quite unwarranted confidence in his attractions. You can load an ass with gold but he'll still eat thistles, won't he?'

Temar laughed. 'My grandsire used to say things like that!'

The Relict patted his arm with a comforting hand. 'Doubtless a great deal has changed in all the time you slept, but some truths remain constant.' She looked beyond Temar's shoulder and nodded to someone he couldn't see. A moment later a trio of double pipes struck up at the far end of the long room and curious heads turned away. 'Let's take some air.'

She led Temar out on to a smoothly paved terrace where precisely trimmed trees in elegant pots shaded two couples sitting not quite close enough together to be in an actual embrace. 'As the sun moves, we move from terrace to terrace,' the Relict explained to Temar in a deliberately carrying voice. 'This northerly one for the afternoon, to the west for the morning, to the east for the evening. That way we always have shade, a most rational scheme. Zediael, Tayha, Fair Festival to you.' She smiled benevolently on the closest couple who nevertheless took themselves inside, quickly followed by the other pair.

'Do sit down, my dear.' The Relict tucked a cushion at her back with a sigh of pleasure. 'My ankles swell if I have to stand for long in this heat.' She waved at a lackey peering anxiously out of the door. 'We can have a quiet glass of wine and get to know each other a little better.'

Temar perched on the edge of a bench. 'You have the advantage of me, my lady Tor Bezaemar.'

'Call me Dirindal, my boy, she urged him. 'Ah, there's Demoiselle Tor Arrial. Avila, my dear, do join us!'

Temar wasn't sure if he was relieved or not to see Avila emerge on to the terrace but he found himself grinning as she manoeuvred the train of her overdress past a table. Creamy lace laid over dove grey satin suggested Avila had found a maid well informed as to the colours of the Tor Kanselin gallery.

Temar bowed. 'You look most elegant, Demoiselle.'

'I must be wearing a year's worth of work for a lacemaker.' Avila sat next to the Relict. 'But at least it covers me up. I would look like a plucked chicken in a neckline like those girls are wearing.'

'Which is why we matrons have set the fashion thus,' chuckled Dirindal. She smoothed a hand over her discreetly draped bosom, where a little black bird held her lace secure in golden claws. 'Now, my dear, has Lady Channis been introducing you to the people you wanted to meet?'

'Indeed.' Avila smiled with unfeigned pleasure. 'I had a most interesting conversation with the current Maitresse Tor Arrial.'

'Did she introduce her brother?' Dirindal twinkled. 'Esquire Den Harkeil is quite a charmer, so be on your guard against his flattery.'

'Camarl did say Tor Arrial was a House that survived the Chaos.' Temar wasn't sure that he wanted Avila to find herself a whole new array of family, leaving him as alone as he had ever been.

'We have come down in the world, Temar,' Avila told him without visible regret. 'Tor Arrial's little more than a minor Name around Zyoutessela, but the Sieur has hired a house here for Festival. He has invited me to dine tomorrow and says he will invite Den Domesin's designate.'

'Another minor Name but well enough esteemed,' Dirindal said judiciously. 'You've a son of Den Domesin over in Kellarin, I believe?'

'Albarn.' Avila nodded. 'But he decided to stay behind and help with the harvest.'

'Well, I don't suppose he wanted to come and see all the changes reminding him of everything he's lost,' said Dirindal shrewdly. 'And I don't suppose that's any too easy for either of you. If you need to ask who's who, what they warrant by way of notice or caution, don't be afraid to call on me. That's doubtless one of the reasons I was invited here today. I'm usually quite idle these days.' She looked from Temar to Avila and back again. 'And I don't suppose you came all this way just to make merry at Festival. '

Temar and Avila exchanged a glance. 'That is very good of you, my lady Tor Bezaemar—' began Temar.

'Dirindal, my dear,' she chided him gently. 'We're related, so I think I can allow it.'

Temar was startled. 'Related?'

Dirindal smiled, delighted. 'Of course, my boy. My grandmother on my father's side was born Tor Alder.'

Temar stared, his mind scrambling frantically to make sense of her words. 'My mother? She married Rian Tor Alder not long before we sailed—' His voice cracked.

'Oh, now I've upset you.' Dirindal took his hand between her own soft beringed ones and held it tight. 'How thoughtless of me. I'm so sorry, my dear.' She snapped her fingers and a lackey with a glass appeared at Temar's elbow.

A long swallow of wine did much to restore his composure. 'So it's a marriage connection of how many degrees?'

'A blood connection, my dear,' Dirindal assured him. 'Your mother bore Rian Tor Alder two sons. She was widowed very young, after all.'

Temar choked on his wine. 'I had no idea!'

'Well, I don't suppose young Camarl's had a chance to discuss such matters with you. But it's true, you have plenty of connections you can pursue if you want to settle fools like Firon.'

'Been getting yourself into quarrels, Temar?' asked Avila with a touch of asperity.

'Not of my making,' he retorted.

'One of Den Thasnet's sons was making himself offensive.' Dirindal defended Temar.

'Saying I am here to beg charity or steal property from D'Olbriot,' said Temar grimly. 'And no one contradicted him.'

Dirindal looked at him, eyes alert in her plump face. 'It's a fact you'd have a legal claim on your mother's dower, even after all this time. Tor Alder would be honour-bound to grant you something, and that would undeniably give you some standing, some independence from D'Olbriot. But no matter, everyone knows Firon's a fool.'

'But we do have some begging to do,' said Avila with the first hint of embarrassment Temar could recall seeing in her. 'There are valuables we need to trace if we are ever to bring the remaining sleepers of Kel Ar'Ayen back to themselves.'

Temar explained as briefly as he could while the Relict's eyes grew round with astonishment.

'Vahil, Sieur Den Rannion as he became, he brought all these back?' Dirindal nodded slowly. 'Yes, as heirlooms such things would be all the more precious.'

And these modern nobles see no higher duty beyond conserving their coffers of gold, thought Temar sourly.

'How do we request such things without causing offence?' Avila asked hesitantly. 'If we are seen as making some improper request—'

'You certainly need to be discreet.' The Relict looked pensive. 'Would you be willing to make fair recompense?'

Avila shared a grimace with Temar. 'Kel Ar'Ayen is a rich land but more in resources than minted metal.'

'But Camarl will be spending his Festival arranging the very best returns for your trade,' Dirindal encouraged them both. 'That'll soon bring the coin in. The first thing is to find these things you're seeking. You don't want to risk an approach until you're certain where some piece is.'

Temar sat up straight. 'I have an idea about that. Heirloom jewels are often shown in portraits, Avila.'

Dirindal nodded. 'Indeed they are.'

'If we visit families we believe hold artefacts, we might be able to find them in their paintings,' Temar explained. The uncertainty shadowing Avila's eyes lifted slightly.

'Let's see what invitations you and I can accept together over the next few days, my dear.' Dirindal patted Avila's knee. 'At my age, I know everyone. No one will think anything of me showing you round a House's gallery, to explain dealings between the Names in the generations you've missed.' She held up a forefinger. 'Let's find Channis. She can wheedle invitations out of anyone not holding some Festival gathering.'

She got to her feet with a little puff of exertion and Temar hastily offered his arm. Dirindal waved him away with a smile. 'No need, my dear.' She rustled ahead of them, small feet in high-heeled shoes tapping on the terrace.

'Who's this Lady Channis?' Temar hissed with a hand on Avila's arm. 'Camarl's mentioned her, but I can't figure out her standing.'

'She's the Sieur's paramour.' Colour rose on Avila's sharp cheekbones. 'But it's not the same as in our day. She's a Den Veneta with widow's rank in her own right. She and the Sieur don't marry for inheritance reasons but they've been acknowledged lovers for years. She has her own apartments at the D'Olbriot residence and acts as his hostess for things like this. Don't make a fool of yourself when you're introduced.'

'And this isn't scandal to set the ashes of the dead rattling their urns?' gaped Temar. 'And have you seen that painting of the Maitresse Tor Kanselin?'

'And several others just as startling.' Avila fixed Temar with a steely gaze. 'We must take the realities of this new order as we find them, my lad. Refusing to acknowledge a truth that's biting your ankles has always hampered you.'

She shook off his hand and Temar watched her go with rising annoyance. He was about to pursue her, to finish that conversation to his own satisfaction, when he saw the Relict Tor Bezaemar with the original of that scandalous painting, a statuesque woman whose iridescent lace overdress was pinned back to her shoulders. The golden silk of her gown barely covered the milky swell of her breasts, but little could be seen beneath an inordinate display of opals. Her dark hair was piled high with jewelled combs above a face expertly masked by cosmetics, lips painted in a sharp blood red line. Dirindal was introducing Avila, who certainly looked the poor relation beside that wealth and beauty, Temar thought with some satisfaction. It was short-lived. If Avila wove herself into the web of gossip and cooperation that women of every age seemed to perpetuate, she'd be the one returning in triumph to Kel Ar'Ayen. How was Temar supposed to impress Guinalle then?

The music ended with a flourish and muted conversation burst into renewed life on all sides. Temar realised he was the focus of covert attention from more than one group of giggling girls and lifted his chin in defiance.

One maiden, bolder than her companions, moved closer and, catching Temar's eye, made a low curtsey, her cerise dress whispering on the woven matting. 'The musicians are very fine, don't you agree, Esquire?'

'Most pleasing,' he smiled hopefully at her.

'Do you prefer the traditional style or the more Rational composers,' she asked artlessly, but her eyes were sly behind a fan of frivolous magenta plumes.

'I know nothing of either mode, Demoiselle, so am unable to judge.' Whatever game she had in mind, Temar wasn't about to play it.

The girl looked disappointed before tossing her head with elaborate unconcern. 'No matter.' She turned a dismissive shoulder on Temar, returning to her friends without acknowledging his bow.

He gritted his teeth, seeing expressions of faint derision pass between the girls. He hardly had time for music lessons, not with everything else he was supposed to accomplish in these scant five days. Were there any familiar faces in this room? Did he know anyone here who might help him achieve something to equal Avila's undoubted successes?

As he looked round the room a knot of girls in a far corner drifted apart for a moment and Temar was surprised to see a familiar face. It took him a moment to place the little mage girl from Bremilayne; Allin, that was her name. He frowned. She had her back to the wall while the other girls pressed round, faces clearly malicious. Temar feared the mage girl was close to tears, face scarlet and hands pleating the front of what even he could tell was a hopelessly unfashionable gown. He made his way though the busy room and arrived without attracting undue attention.

'We were surprised to see you here,' one girl was saying sweetly.

'But you could hardly expect to go unnoticed in that dress,' said another, not bothering to honey her malice.

'I don't know how these things are done in Lescar,' began another, and from the contempt in her voice she clearly had no wish to know. 'But here it's accepted that wizards leave the concerns of the Names well alone.'

'My father only hopes D'Olbriot is making that clear to you people,' added the one who'd criticised Allin's dress.

'No House would dream of meddling with Hadrumal's affairs,' chipped in the first.

'My lady mage!' Temar put all the pleasure he could into his greeting. 'How delightful to see you again.'

He bowed low and Allin managed an abrupt curtsey. 'Esquire D'Alsennin.' Her voice was steadier than he had expected and he realised it was anger rather than upset colouring her round face.

'Someone else who doesn't know when he's not wanted,' murmured one girl behind a canary yellow fan. A sudden lull in conversation all around left her words clearly audible.

Temar inclined his head at her. 'You would be Demoiselle Den Thasnet?' A silver and enamel trefoil blossomed at her freckled neckline, twin to one the odious Firon had worn. 'I recognise your House's style.'

'You should be careful with that fan, Demoiselle,' Allin remarked. 'You don't want to get that dye on your gown.'

Satisfied to see the young women all disconcerted, even if he didn't know why, Temar decided to leave before someone launched some jibe he'd no defence against. 'Allin, shall we take some air?'

'Thank you, Esquire. It's more than a little stale in here.' Allin took his arm and Temar escorted her out on to the nearest terrace. It turned out to be the western-facing one so there was little shade but the sun had spent the worst of its heat.

Allin fanned herself with one hand. 'I wish I didn't blush so much,' she said crossly.

Temar wasn't quite sure what to say. 'Do not let them upset you.'

'I don't,' snapped Allin.

Temar looked around the terrace. 'What did you mean about that girl's fan?' he asked after an awkward pause.

Allin bit her lower lip. 'You know how Demoiselles fuss over getting the best feathers, making up their fans with hidden messages in the colours?'

Temar didn't but he nodded anyway.

'Well, no one would dream of admitting they dyed old feathers to get the colours they needed rather than buying them new from the most expensive merchants,' Allin explained with contempt.

He really must find out if Kel Ar'Ayen had any birds with suitably lucrative tails, Temar decided. 'I see. Anyway, what brings you here today?'

'I'm here with Velindre,' Allin answered in a more moderate tone. 'She's over there.'

Following Allin's gesture, Temar saw the willowy wizard elegant in unadorned azure silk and deep in conversation with Avila and the Relict Tor Bezaemar. 'What is she doing here?'

He was thinking aloud rather than asking, but Allin answered him anyway. 'We're wondering what the other Houses think of D'Olbriot's links with the Archmage.' She sighed. 'I imagine you heard.'

'They were just a gaggle of silly girls.' Temar shrugged.

Allin shook her head. 'They're parroting the prejudices they hear at their own firesides, and if they're any guide the Sieur's association with Hadrumal does him no credit at present.'

'What is Hadrumal like?' Temar's curiosity got the better of him.

'Rather inclined to see itself as the centre of the world and look down on everyone else,' said Allin bitingly. 'A bit like here.'

Temar didn't know how to answer that so squinted uncertainly at some bird perched on a balustrade confining a distant pond. Music, laughter and vivacious conversation spilled out on to the terrace from the animated gathering within and Temar felt very lonely.

'I'm probably not being fair,' said Allin after a while. 'I'm tired of new places and new people and being so far away from my home and my family.'

Temar glanced back at her. 'You and me both.'

Allin smiled briefly. 'And there's no going back for either of us. Magebirth separates me from mine as surely as the generations have cut you off from your roots.'

Silence fell heavily as a lively new tune struck up inside the house.

'But we just have to get on with it, don't we?' said Allin bracingly. 'What progress have you made so far?'

Temar offered her his arm. 'I am developing an interest in art. Let me show you.'

The Tor Kanselin Residence, Summer Solstice Festival, First Day, Late Afternoon

Casuel hesitated on the threshold. 'No need to introduce me.'

'Are you expected?' The door lackey looked uncertainly at him. 'Sir?' he added as an afterthought.

The wizard bridled. 'My name is Devoir, my title Mage. I assist the Sieur D'Olbriot on matters of vital importance to the Empire. There are people here I need to consult.' He peered into the long gallery, searching for Velindre. How had she managed to insinuate herself into such a gathering? He really was unfashionably late but he'd barely had time to dress fittingly for such a House as it was. Velindre might at least have had the courtesy to let him know where she'd be rather than just sending that offhand note saying she'd arrived in Toremal. If he hadn't got the address of her lodging off the lad, if he hadn't gone to call, hadn't demanded the landlady tell him what Velindre was up to, he'd never have found out she'd be here.

The lackey was looking at him with interest. 'Are you related to Amalin Devoir?'

Casuel drew himself up indignantly. 'He has the honour to be related to me. May I pass?'

The door lackey moved aside with a low bow. Casuel looked at him suspiciously for a moment. Was the fellow just being a little overservile or was that some sarcasm in his gesture? Deciding it wasn't worth pursuing, he hurried into the broad room, taking a glass of straw-coloured wine from a passing footman's tray.

He sipped it as he walked to look out on to the terrace.

No, Velindre wasn't there. The excellence of the vintage brought a smile to Casuel's face. Perhaps he should take a little time for himself now Festival was here. He'd worked ceaselessly since the turn of the year, after all. A few days socialising with the educated and influential was no more than he deserved. He edged his way through the assembled nobility, careful to bow to anyone looking in his direction, waiting politely until anyone in his way stepped aside.

Temar was deep in conversation with a youth some years his senior, a handsome man in coat and breeches of rough silk as black as the martlet badge repeated on every link of a heavy chain looped around his shoulders. 'Yes, it's an heirloom piece, cursed heavy of course, but one has to dust these things off for Festival.'

'I would swear Den Bezaemar as was favoured an ouzel in my day,' Temar was saying thoughtfully.

'These things doubtless change over the generations. One little black bird is much like another, after all.' The Esquire Tor Bezaemar was sharing his attention between Temar and the rest of the room with practised ease. 'I believe someone wishes to speak to you, D'Alsennin.'

'Casuel!' Temar turned to greet the mage with a flattering heartiness that was a little uncultured in present company. 'Oh, forgive me, may I make known Esquire Kreve Tor Bezaemar. I have the honour to present Casuel Devoir, mage of Hadrumal.'

'We are honoured,' Kreve said politely. 'I can't imagine when any Festival reception last entertained three wizards.'

'Good day,' Casuel said stiffly. 'Hello, Allin.'

'I'm here with Velindre.' The girl blushed, as well she might. What did she think she was doing, aping her betters in her ill-styled dress?

'If you'll excuse me,' Kreve Tor Bezaemar bowed deftly. 'There are other people I must speak to.'

Casuel bowed to his departing back before turning on Allin. 'And what is Velindre's business with Tor Kanselin?' he demanded. He looked around the room again. How could such a gawky, ill-favoured woman be so hard to find among elegant ladies?

Allin smiled sweetly at Casuel. 'She's here at the personal invitation of the Maitresse. They met at a feather merchant's.'

'Quite by chance?' Casuel's sarcasm made it clear what he thought.

'Hardly,' Allin shrugged. 'Velindre made it her business to fall into conversation.'

'Does Planir know what she's up to?' snapped Casuel.

'You'd have to ask her that,' said Allin with a touch of spirit. 'She's talking to the elder Demoiselle Den Veneta at present but I'm sure she'll give you a few moments.'

'I have too many calls on my time to wait on Velindre's convenience,' said Casuel sourly. 'Tell her to call on me later and explain herself.'

'So what did you come here for?' asked Temar brightly. 'Apart from showing everyone your new haircut.'

Casuel raised an involuntary hand to wiry brown hair cut and brushed in a close approximation of Camarl's style. 'Naturally, as Planir's envoy to D'Olbriot, I have a duty to represent Hadrumal to the nobility during Festival.'

Temar laughed loudly, the hearty chuckle turning curious heads. So much for archaic noble manners, Casuel thought crossly. Didn't the boy realise he was letting down the dignity of Kellarin just as surely as Allin was disgracing Hadrumal in that frumpy gown? How was wizardry ever to achieve due recognition in Toremal if it couldn't even manage to dress decently?

Allin was looking over at the other side of the room. 'Excuse me, Velindre wants me.'

Casuel watched the close circle of lace-covered shoulders in the far bay open to admit the girl before closing against curious glances from a fair few people. 'What are they talking about?' the mage wondered, frustrated.

Temar hesitated.

'You know something?' Casuel narrowed his eyes. 'What

is it? Keeping something from me could have serious consequences, Esquire. I don't think you realise—'

'I believe they are discussing someone's betrothal,' said Temar.

'Yours?' gasped Casuel. That would be something to report to Planir. But what if the Archmage disapproved? He quailed at the thought of conveying unwelcome news.

'No,' said Temar scornfully. His expression turned rueful. 'I hardly think these Demoiselles would entertain my suit, not for all the gold in Kel Ar'Ayen, not as long as I know nothing of their fashions and fancies.'

'I could have told you such things,' sniffed Casuel. 'But it was rather more important to teach you at least the barest bones of all the history you slept through.'

'True enough,' agreed Temar. 'I owe you an apology for my inattentions.' He waved aside Casuel's hasty demur. 'But it seems which Emperor reigned when and the badges of all these Houses is merely the start of what I need to know. Can you explain all this business with feathers and fans to me?'

'Oh, yes,' Casuel assured him. 'My sisters—'

Temar smiled. 'Good. Let us go back to the D'Olbriot residence and we can go over it together.'

Dismay had left Casuel's mouth hanging open and he shut it hastily. 'But I only just got here.'

Temar fixed Casuel with an unblinking stare. 'Unless you have some means to force your way through that rampart, you are hardly going to find out what Velindre is discussing.' He gestured at the intimate circle in the far bay. 'But I asked Allin to call on me this evening, to share a supper or something. If you are helping me with my studies, you can see what you can get out of her then?'

'You don't want to encourage her,' said Casuel bitingly. 'She's of no consequence in Hadrumal, and hereabouts she's quite below your notice. If Velindre had any sense, she'd never have brought the girl. That Lescari accent alone—'

He saw Temar wasn't even doing him the courtesy of listening. 'Let us make our farewells.'

Casuel wondered how Temar's expression could seem so warm while those pale eyes stayed as cold as ice. 'But I only just got here.'

'I have been here since just after the sixth chime of the day,' said Temar crisply. 'Which is quite long enough for these girls to treat me as if I were missing half my buttons and for these elegant Esquires to hint tactfully I have no real business here as long as I have barely a copper to scratch my stones with.'

'There's no need for mercenary vulgarity,' Casuel said plaintively. 'Where's Esquire Camarl?' He'd make Temar see sense, the wizard thought.

'Making the better acquaintance of the younger daughter of the House out in the grounds.' Temar smiled thinly. 'Interrupting would hardly be tactful.'

'We can't leave without him,' Casuel protested uncertainly.

'Everyone keeps telling me how informal this gathering is,' insisted Temar. 'We will make our bow to Resialle and she can inform Camarl. Come, Master D'Evoir.'

'Don't call me that,' Casuel hissed urgently. 'It's not appropriate.'

'What's not appropriate?' asked an unwelcome voice. 'Some beggar the ocean washed up pretending to rank and title, or D'Olbriot infesting the place with wizards?'

'And who might you be, sir?' Casuel turned indignantly. 'Ah, Den Thasnet, I see.' He tried for a more conciliatory tone. 'I think you mistake the nature of magic—'

'Esquire,' Temar interrupted. 'Do as my shirt tail does.' He caught the wizard's elbow in a grip like steel pincers and moved him forcibly away.

'What did you mean by that?' asked Casuel in confusion.

'You prefer I tell him plainly to kiss my arse?' Temar let go of Casuel's arm and glanced back at Firon, who was frowning as he tried to work out Temar's insult. 'And I will not play lickspittle to some fool who puts an afternoon of wine on top of a morning of thassin. I wager his head will collapse when he next visits the privy.'

'We'd better make our farewells.' Casuel shuddered at the spectre of such coarseness being overheard, leaving him to excuse Temar to Planir or the Sieur D'Olbriot. 'And I think you're spending too much time with Chosen Tathel if that's your notion of politeness.' Casuel stopped to let a stout youth past him and had to hurry to catch Temar up. How was the boy to learn decent manners if he never listened to anyone, the mage thought crossly.

'Demoiselle,' Temar was bowing low before the eldest daughter of the Name. 'I thank you for a most pleasant afternoon and regret that other duties call me away.'

Naturally Casuel recognised Resialle Tor Kanselin. He'd spent several days of Spring Equinox walking outside those Houses closest to the D'Olbriot residence. The wizard made his most respectful bow to the pretty girl. He hadn't actually managed to fall into conversation with anyone of rank, but he should be able to do so, if he was Temar's guide over the next few days. 'Casuel Devoir, my lady, mage of Hadrumal.'

She nodded a polite acknowledgement. 'You're Temar's tutor, I believe?'

Casuel smiled. 'More of a friend, really.'

Resialle's mouth quirked prettily and Casuel smoothed the front of his coat with some satisfaction. He'd certainly made an impression there, and if Temar could only recall D'Evoirs of his own day Casuel would have rank to socialise in these circles as of right, not merely through association with D'Olbriot. This business of feathers could wait until he'd jogged the lad's memory about more important matters.

'Please make my farewells to your mother and to the Relict Tor Bezaemar,' Temar was saying. 'And let Esquire D'Olbriot know I have gone home.'

Out in the cool of the marble corridor, Casuel hurried to catch Temar up. 'You met the Relict Tor Bezaemar? I hope you were polite!'

'She was the nicest person there,' said Temar with some force. 'And she and Avila look set to be firm friends.'

'That is good news,' Casuel said with satisfaction.

'How so?' Temar looked at him. 'I mean, I take it the title Relict still means she is the widow of the late Sieur, but is there more to her rank than that?'

'You really must study the annals I lent you,' said Casuel severely. 'She's the widow of the late Sieur who was brother to Bezaemar the Generous. If the Convocation of Princes hadn't opted for Den Tadriol, she'd have graced the Imperial throne. No one's better connected in Toremal.'

Temar smiled. 'A useful ally to have won.'

When they got outside Casuel looked appreciatively at the methodical design of gardens and house. 'My father has rebuilt in the modern style,' he remarked. 'We have rather less space, obviously, but the effect is very much the same.'

The boy still wasn't listening, the mage realised with irritation, seeing Temar's curious face turned to rising noise beyond the gatehouse. 'What's to do?' he asked Casuel.

'It's beggars and hawkers hoping to wheedle coin out of the nobility.' The wizard drew Temar aside beneath the broad arch as the gate-wards opened to a coach. 'Riff-raff always comes flocking up from the lower town at Festival.'

'I have no coin with me.' Temar looked regretful. 'Do you?

'Not for the likes of these,' retorted Casuel.

Temar peered through the barred and studded double gates and saw people thronging the broad road outside. Liveried men-at-arms cleared space for a portly Esquire and his lady to depart in their carriage and Temar saw two scrawny girls entertaining the crowd with a pair of battered wooden puppets, hands deft on sticks moving jointed wooden limbs. 'Come on.'

'We'll send word for D'Olbriot's carriage, if you please,' said Casuel indignantly.

Temar raised his eyebrows. 'We kick our heels while a boy runs to D'Olbriot's stables and wait still longer for the coach to be readied and arrive? We can walk back in less time.'

'Persons of rank do not walk in the common road,' Casuel told him severely.

'As several people have told me this afternoon, my rank is by no means established,' said Temar sarcastically. 'And I would like to get some exercise.' He nodded to the sworn man on the gate, who looked rather doubtfully at Casuel.

'Let's at least keep out of the dirt.' He guided Temar towards the welcome shade of trees that edged the road, scowling fiercely at a tattered ne'er-do-well who raised a grubby hand to Temar. White and yellow flowers dotting vines that were threaded round the trees perfumed the air but Casuel's nostrils still twitched, apprehensive of some stink of poverty. 'What are you doing?' he exclaimed as Temar accepted something from a tousle-headed child in ragged motley.

Temar studied the coarse piece of paper. 'What is a rope dancer?'

'Some foolish mountebank risking life and limb to entertain the uncouth.' Casuel tried to take the handbill off Temar.

'Exotic beasts can be seen at Vaile's Yard, birds of the Archipelago and a great Aldabreshin sea-serpent,' Temar peered at the crudely printed text, smudgy promises of delights cramped close together. 'Or there are any number of puppet shows, a wine-drinking contest, a display of tumbling and feats of strength, it says here. I see the Houses still put on plenty of entertainment for their tenantry.'

'None of this has anything to do with the nobility.' Casuel pushed away the arm of a lass trying to give Temar some other piece of rubbish stamped out with lamp black on a woodcut. 'The rabble amuse themselves gulling each other out of their coin with such stuff.'

Temar had taken one anyway. 'An infallible cure for green wounds, yellowing of the eyes, disorders of the brain and the scald. What is the scald?'

Casuel coloured to his hairline. 'Not something you're likely to encounter if you steer clear of the brothels.'

'A tincture formulated according to the most recent Rational principles to combat the effects of summer heat by promoting effective perspiration.' Temar whistled mockingly as he studied the apothecary's list. 'As opposed to the ineffective sweat we manage without its help.'

Casuel beckoned to a crossing sweeper as they reached a sandy lane leading off the main highway to the rear of the Tor Kanselin residence. 'You might as well throw your coin in a pond.'

The grubby boy brushed the debris on the road aside with his battered broom and they crossed, the mage forging ahead with a forbidding expression for hopeful beggars pressing closer.

'Casuel!' Temar's indignant rebuke turned the wizard's head.

'What now?'

'It must be customary to pay the lad?' Temar was waiting by the woebegone child who hugged the handle of his brush with arms scarcely thicker than the wood.

'Of course,' Casuel fumbled in the inner pocket of his breeches for some pennies. 'There you go.'

The child's pitiable expression turned rapidly to scorn and he spat at Casuel's highly polished boots before disappearing into the crowd.

Casuel raised an indignant fist but Temar's astonished expression halted him. 'Oh, let's just get home.'

People crowded close on the strip of flagway skirting the huddle of houses that served Tor Kanselin. Carts forced a determined path in the late sun, drivers shouting curses at a handful of tumblers spilling out of an alleyway between two tall storehouses, but the weary horses simply plodded on, blinkered to the clamour all around.

'Are those masqueraders?' Temar turned to Casuel with delight. 'The mercenaries speak highly of them.'

'I'm not surprised; after all it's Lescaris we've to thank for bringing them here.' Casuel scowled at the tatterdemalion figures with battered wooden masks covering the upper half of their faces. 'The better troupes can be quite entertaining if you're used to nothing better, but what you want to see are proper Tormalin marionettes worked with real skill.' He looked up from trying to identify the soft foulness he'd just stepped in. 'Temar? Esquire D'Alsennin?'

Stolid faces met Casuel's searching gaze, some with faint question, more uninterested and turning back to the masqueraders' impromptu display of dance and song.

'D'Alsennin?' Casuel yelled, voice cracking on a sour taste of dust and just a little panic tugging at his coat tails.

Commotion suddenly stirred beside a portico jutting out from one of the larger houses of the hamlet. A low-voiced murmur of shock and surprise ran beneath the high-pitched clamour of the throng.

'Send to Tor Kanselin!' A shout went up close by the pillars topped with improbable stone leaves that held up a flat stone slab. The lone voice was soon joined by others and a confused surge of people nearly knocked Casuel clean off his feet. He struggled for balance; this was no time to get caught up in some disturbance, and where was Temar? Anger tightened Casuel's lips. If the foolish boy had gone off after futile amusements offered by some inky-fingered pamphleteer, noble birth or not, he'd tell him—

The mage's indignation tailed off into incoherent horror as the crowd in front of the portico cleared. A prone figure lay beneath the protecting arm of a doorkeeper. The man wore a pewter coat dark with dust. As the prostrate figure lifted his head for a moment, he realised it was Temar! Hard on the heels of that horror-struck realisation, Casuel saw an ominous stain spreading across the lad's back. 'Here, let me through, let me pass!'

Most of the bystanders were following the masqueraders who'd packed up their instruments and props as soon as they realised a bigger drama was overtaking their own. Those looking to watch it were only too happy to let someone else take charge of the calamity but the doorkeeper glared ferociously at Casuel. 'Are you an apothecary? A surgeon?'

'What?' Casuel stared at the man. 'No, I'm a wizard and—'

But the doorkeeper was leaning over Temar, who was deathly pale in the shadows. With a surge of relief, Casuel saw the lad's eyes were open and he knelt hastily. 'What's this mishap? Did you trip?' He strained to understand Temar's mumble, his archaic accent thick.

'I hurt myself.' His eyes were disorientated and vague. Casuel was appalled to see a huge bruise on Temar's temple, the swelling a finger thick and the colour of a ripe plum. He was shocked to realise the brutal lines mimicked the moulding at the base of the pillar.

'Bide still, boy,' instructed the doorkeeper, blunt face concerned.

'What happened?' demanded Casuel.

'I hurt myself,' repeated Temar in puzzled tones. 'How did I hurt myself?'

'Temar, what happened?'

'I hurt myself.'

'Can you hear me?' Casuel reached for Temar's shoulder, thinking to shake some sense into the boy, but snatched his hand back from blood soaking the outstretched sleeve. Where was that coming from?

'Has someone gone for Tor Kanselin's sergeant?' the doorkeeper bellowed, scowling bushy black brows at Casuel, stark contrast to his shaven, balding head.

'We must get him to D'Olbriot's surgeon.' Casuel snapped his fingers in front of Temar's wandering eyes. 'Temar, answer me, what happened?'

'It hurts,' the boy mumbled again. 'How did I hurt myself?'

'No one's moving him,' the doorkeeper growled at Casuel. 'You lie steady, boy.'

Casuel fumbled nerveless fingers beneath his shirt for the D'Olbriot amulet he wore as a courtesy to the Name. 'I have the authority to insist.'

'No one moves the lad till Tor Kanselin's surgeon says.' The burly man looked hard at Casuel while one gentle hand stroked Temar's head in mute reassurance, thick fingers light on the fine black hair. 'I'll not answer to my Sieur for letting you kill him with mishandling, whoever you are.'

'Kill him?' Casuel sat back on his heels, aghast.

'There's a knife in his back, you fool!' The doorkeeper moved his protective arm slightly.

Casuel saw the dagger, unadorned hilt shuddering and catching the light as Temar drew a shallow breath. 'We should press something to the wound to stop the blood.' Cold sweat beaded Casuel's brow and he felt sick to his stomach. Screwing his eyes shut he fought to quell the nausea and terror threatening to overwhelm him.

The doorkeeper looked at the wizard, puzzled. 'Are you all right?'

Casuel was ashamed to find himself trembling like some mute animal. Who'd done this? Some low-born scum out to rob their betters, treacherous knives greedy for coin they couldn't bother to earn like honest men. That would be it, surely? No need to fear anything more sinister.

The rhythmic tramping of heavy boots distracted the grateful mage from the terrifying possibilities forcing themselves upon him. Casuel scrambled to his feet. 'Stand aside! Clear the road!'

'Let's find out why you're making this your business, shall we?' The doorkeeper's grip on Casuel's arm was like a watchdog's bite and he barely needed to tighten the muscles in his broad shoulders to hold the helpless mage immobile.

Casuel's indignant protests went unheard as ten men in Tor Kanselin livery forced the crowd back with staffs held level to make a solid ring of iron-bound oak, swan medallions at their throats proclaiming their unquestioned right to do so. The sergeant strode towards the portico, uncompromising in metal-plated hide. 'What's happened here?' He looked down from well over Casuel's height, black hair cropped above a mobile, pockmarked face, dark brown eyes intense.

'I thought the lad had just stumbled,' explained the doorkeeper. 'Then I saw he'd taken a blade in the back.'

'By the looks of that bruise, someone was out to break his head on the pillar.' The sergeant knelt to study Temar, whose repetitive mumbles had faded to faint whispers, eyes vacant.

'Don't touch the dagger!' yelped Casuel when the chosen

man drew a knife and carefully slit the back of Temar's coat. He shut his mouth, horrified to hear shock forcing his words into a girlish squeal.

'Who's this?' The sergeant glanced at the doorkeeper.

'Says he's a wizard.' The doorkeeper gave Casuel a shake of unconscious emphasis. 'Seems to know the lad.'

'Who's he to you?' The sergeant carefully cut Temar's shirt to reveal skin white beneath scarlet smears, blood pooled in the hollow of his spine.

Casuel swallowed hard on his nausea. 'He's my – my pupil. I am Casuel Devoir, mage of Hadrumal.' He wondered why that sounded so inadequate.

The sergeant peered beneath the fold of linen and wool held fast by the blade. 'So this lad's a wizard?'

Casuel tried to shake off the doorkeeper's hand to no avail. 'His name is Temar D'Alsennin, a guest of Messire D'Olbriot, recently arrived from Kellarin.' His indignant words carried through the rapt silence to the onlookers and a buzz of speculation took flight.

The sergeant gave Casuel a sharp look before getting to his feet. 'Anyone with something useful to say, make yourselves known,' he shouted at the crowd. 'Otherwise, be on your way before I call you to answer for blocking Tor Kanselin's highway!'

This uncompromising declaration had people hurrying away immediately, scattering as a second detachment of armoured men arrived with a curtained litter carried shoulder high. A slightly built man with a shock of hair like grizzled sheep's wool followed. His deeply lined face was jowled with age but his brown spotted hands were deft as he knelt to peel back the bloody cloth on Temar's back.

'You have to staunch the blood!' insisted Casuel.

The surgeon ignored him. 'Are you still with us, lad?' After a cursory examination of the wound he seemed far more concerned with the bruise still swelling at Temar's temple.

'I hurt myself. How did I hurt myself?'

'Get him back to the barracks, quick as you like,' the

surgeon said briskly. Casuel protested weakly as four well-muscled men lifted Temar to lay him gently in the padded litter. For all their care, Temar let out an agonised cry that broke into racking sobs. The surgeon tightened a strap to hold him secure before drawing the curtains close and nodding to the men to pick up the poles.

Hot distress blurred Casuel's own vision. 'Where are you taking him? I want him taken to the D'Olbriot residence, at once, do you hear? He's a guest of Messire D'Olbriot, the Sieur himself! I want him informed, at once, and I want your names. Your Sieur will hear about this, I assure you.'

The wizard hurried after the litter, repeating himself in futile fury.

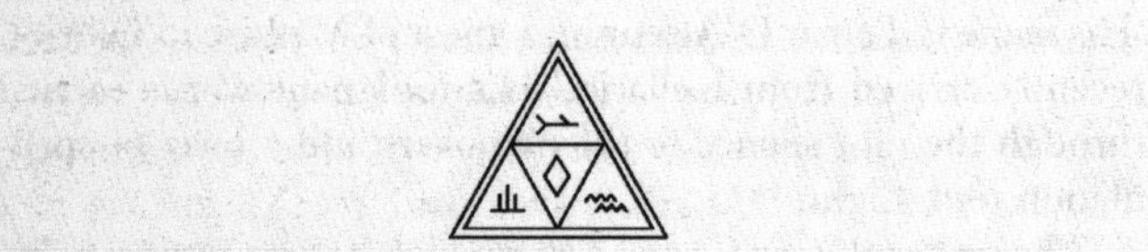

D'Olbriot Font Lane,
Summer Solstice Festival, First Day, Evening

I hold a good collection of markers of one kind or another after twelve or more years spent in Messire's service. Most of my duties in recent years have taken me away from Toremal but I've still got favours owed and small debts never repaid clear across the city. Spending this credit against redeeming Temar's people seemed the best use I'd ever find for it, and as I walked up past the conduit house satisfaction with my afternoon's work warmed me like the sinking sun at my back. There was a chosen man of Den Cotise I'd sparred with over the years; we'd shared a superior flagon of wine at the Popinjay inn down on the Graceway. Intrigued by the puzzle, he'd introduced me to a giddy under-dresser to the Demoiselles Tor Sylarre. Once we'd worked out which women of Den Rannion and Den Domesin had married into Tor Sylarre over the generations, we reckoned upwards of twenty artefacts could well be safe within that family's jewel coffers.

I'd left word in a myriad other places that might bring back useful answers and had a double handful of chance remarks to follow up besides, so I was wondering whether to go out again that evening or to wait until morning as I began the long haul up the hill towards the residence. A tailor who'd been grateful to D'Olbriot since a troop of us sworn had stopped some chancers robbing his sewing room had introduced me to an elderly valet raised in Den Muret's service. That Name had long faded into obscurity but the daughters of the House had married widely and well and with the help of the tailor's ledgers, and the valet's memory, we'd identified where. Better yet, the valet was now serving the newly nominated Sieur Den Turquand and pointed out several judicious marriages that had bolstered that Name's rise. He reckoned the young Sieur would be delighted to ingratiate himself with D'Olbriot and Kellarin for the price of a few discarded antiquities.

Shadows beneath the fringed trees cloaked the road, oppressive rather than cooling, and a heaviness seemed to hang in the air. I looked up but saw no sign of the thunder in the deepening blue of the sky. Walking faster, I still found myself unable to shake a sense of foreboding.

It's all very well Livak teasing me about feeling responsible for everything and anything, I thought, but Dast's teeth, I'm the closest thing Temar has to family on this side of the ocean. Perhaps I should have stayed close at hand; something might have upset or confused him. After all, he was new to the city, and there are always a few young nobles we men-at-arms privately agree would improve after a thorough kicking round the back of some stable block some dark night.

Outright dismay hit me like a slap in the face when I saw the commotion outside the D'Olbriot gatehouse. Sentries who'd been idly displaying their crossbows to impress passing maidservants now stood stern-faced and vigilant. The vast travelling coach the elder ladies of the House used was being wheeled round from the stables, a full contingent of sworn men ringing it, swords drawn. As I ran towards them I drew my own blade, elbowing through the confusion as I saw a familiar face. 'Stoll! What's going on?'

Stolley was sworn long before me and chosen a few years since. One of Messire's most effective sergeants-at-arms, he's a well-muscled brawler whose ears still stick out like mill sails, even after the punishment they've taken over the years.

'Rysh, get over here!' He shoved a gawping vagabond aside, and raised swords admitted me within the ring of steel. I swung myself on to the running board of the carriage as the horses were whistled into a trot.

'Your boy's been stabbed,' said Stolley shortly, jogging beside the carriage with the rest of the troop.

'D'Alsennin?' I looked down on him in disbelief. 'At Tor Kanselin's reception?'

'Dunno.' Stolley shrugged massive shoulders beneath a coat of plates. 'Stabbed and needing the gentlest ride home, that's all we're told.'

'How bad?' I demanded, feeling a catch of apprehension in my throat.

'Rumour's got him on the threshold to the Otherworld,' growled Stolley. 'But then they'd be saying that if he'd grazed his knees.'

As soon as the coach reached the sweep of gravel inside Tor Kanselin's gates, I jumped down. It was quieter inside the walls but the air still crackled with suppressed curiosity, little knots of wide-eyed servants speculating behind raised hands.

I sheathed my sword and kept walking, not about to add grist to the rumour mill before I had a few solid facts to chew on myself. A sentry nodded the D'Olbriot badge on my armring into the residence and I looked around the lofty hallway for someone who could tell me what had happened. The best I could come up with was Casuel, forlorn on a side chair, velvet coat and shirt ruffle in disarray, his wiry brown hair hanging lank at his temples.

He jumped up as soon as he saw me, eyes hollow with fear. 'What's happened to the boy?' Miserable uncertainty lengthened his face in place of the self-importance that habitually tightened his weak chin.

'That's what I'm asking you.' I tried to restrain my anger.

'It wasn't my fault,' stammered Casuel. 'The fool insisted on walking back. He wouldn't wait for a carriage. He wouldn't stay close to me—'

The sharp click of a lady's shoes turned my head to the marble stairs. Abandoning Casuel to his ineffectual self-justification, I hurried to meet the Demoiselle Tor Arrial with a perfunctory bow. 'How is he?'

'Temar?' Avila tried for her usual terse manner but her heart wasn't in it. 'The morning will most assuredly bring him an aching head and a sore shoulder but a day or so in bed should see him well enough.' I gave her my arm and she leaned heavily on me.

'I thought he was dead.' Casuel struggled for a further response; the relief in his face would have been comical if the whole matter weren't so serious. Then the mage's knees gave way and he landed gracelessly on his chair.

'They said he was stabbed?' I enquired as gently as I could.

Avila rubbed her face with a hand that trembled in spite of herself. 'Talagrin be praised, the blade went awry. It hit the shoulder blade.'

'I've been waiting for the courtesy of some word.' Casuel managed to look both woebegone and petulant.

I wasn't about to waste time consoling Casuel's imagined grievance. Anyone with a pennyweight of common sense would have gone looking for news.

'The head wound had me most concerned,' Avila continued, 'but the House surgeon deems it none too serious.'

A sober-faced man coming down the stairs in his shirt sleeves, fastening cuffs that had rusty smears.

'Chosen Man Ryshad Tathel,' I introduced myself politely. 'How's Esquire D'Alsennin?'

'You'll have seen worse on the training ground,' the surgeon sniffed. 'He'd his wits knocked clean out of him, but that'll pass, and the knife wound looked worse than it was.'

I nodded my understanding, relief closing my throat too tight for words.

Avila nodded. 'A little blood goes a long way.'

'The Demoiselle here says there's no crack in the skull, according to her arts,' continued the surgeon with a slightly wary look at Avila. I remembered with relief how healing was a major part of her Artifice.

'If he'd waited for a carriage, we'd have got home without mishap,' protested Casuel with a mildewed expression.

'You were with him?' The surgeon fixed the wizard with a look as sharp as his scalpels. 'Proven Man Triss will need to speak to you.'

'This wasn't my fault,' said Casuel hastily. 'Why does he need to see me?'

The surgeon ignored him, turning to me. 'Take him along

to the barracks, will you? Esquire Camarl left word you were to talk to the Cohort Captain.'

Finding I could speak again, I looked at Avila. 'I'll be at your disposal when you wish to return to D'Olbriot's residence, Demoiselle.'

'Go on,' she said a little wearily. 'I will be with the Maitresse and Lady Channis.'

'Come on, Casuel.' I caught the visibly reluctant wizard by the elbow to urge him along.

'I wish people would stop doing that,' he exploded, shaking off my hand in sudden rage.

I grabbed him again and had him out of the residence with his feet barely touching the steps. 'Stop behaving as if you've no interest in what's going on!' I rounded on him. 'You tell the guards whatever you saw and we might get some idea who did this. I want to know, even if you don't!'

Casuel's objections withered under my scorching glare but his back stayed rigid with protest as I escorted him to the barracks on the far side of the enclosure.

'Take a seat in the bower,' the sentry replied to my explanation of our arrival. 'I'll send word to Proven Triss.'

I nodded and turned on my heel, Casuel hurrying after, muttering crossly. Luckily for him he'd run out of indignation when we reached a vine-covered bower shading a ring of low benches. At least that meant my continued good reputation was safe because I couldn't have stood much more of his nonsense without shutting his mouth with a fist.

With evening drawing on, cool, dark leaves swathed the little yard with moist, green fragrance. I sat and closed my eyes and forced myself to take slow, even breaths as the blood pulsed in my head. Noises from the stable yard over in the distance and from the crowd in the road just beyond the wall contrasted with the stillness within the empty bower.

It didn't last. Casuel started talking again. 'I want a runner sent to D'Olbriot, to the Sieur himself. Ryshad, I want paper and ink, do you hear? And sealing wax, at once. No, wait, Esquire Camarl must still be here? Yes, that's it. I need to see him. No, you need to ask if he'll see me. Ryshad? Are you listening? Esquire Camarl will vouch for me, won't he? But what will the Sieur think? Why did that foolish boy go dragging the D'Olbriot Name into some needless turmoil?'

Just as I was thinking I'd better sit on my hands I heard boots falling in measured tread on the gravel.

'Good evening to you.' A scar-faced man with sharply receding hair stepped into the bower, face impassive as he bowed to the wizard and gave me a brief nod of acknowledgement. 'I'm Oram Triss, proven man to Tor Kanselin and by the Emperor's grace Captain of the House Cohort.'

I hoped Casuel knew enough to realise this was Tor Kanselin's most senior soldier, the man who would answer to the Emperor if the Cohorts were ever summoned to fight a war for Tormalin. Judging by his strangled murmur, the wizard did.

'Raman Zelet, chosen man,' continued Triss, indicating his companion. The tall man had skin tanned a deep copper brown and I noted leather oil deeply ingrained around his fingernails as he set a lacquered tray on a broad stone trough planted with bright summer flowers. He poured wordlessly from a jug of water beaded with condensation and Triss handed Casuel a greenish glass. The wizard drank in hasty gulps, hand shaking to spill cold drops that spotted his shirt.

The proven man smiled reassurance at Casuel. 'May I know your name?'

'Fair Festival to you.' Casuel cleared his throat with a creditable assumption of ease. 'I am Casuel Devoir, mage of Hadrumal, at present envoy from Archmage Planir the Black to Messire Guliel D'Olbriot, Sieur of that House.' He brushed at the droplets bright on his shirt front but still spilled more water as he put his glass back on the tray.

Zelet raised an eyebrow as he passed me some welcome water. 'You're a wizard.'

Casuel lifted his chin defiantly at the faint distaste in the other man's face. 'And a rational man of good family and disciplined habits.'

Proven Triss laced long fingers with work-hardened joints together. 'So what happened?'

'I really have no idea,' Casuel protested. 'We got separated in the crowd. I'd been telling him to stay close—' he reached for his glass and took another sip of water. 'Then I saw the commotion by the portico. When I got through the mob, I saw Temar had been stabbed.' He appealed to the expressionless Zelet. 'You saw that for yourself.'.

'The doorkeeper reckoned someone smashed the lad's head against the stonework deliberately,' Zelet said to Triss.

The proven man ran a pensive finger along a fine cicatrice beneath his cheekbone. 'If this was some cutpurse losing his head and using a knife that's straightforward enough. We've sent word to every barracks, and with Raeponin's grace someone'll string the cur up on the nearest gibbet before he uses his blade again.' He turned to me. 'But who'd want to dash your boy's brains out? If this is some private quarrel, some personal grudge, it's D'Olbriot's right and duty to deal with it. Tor Kanselin shouldn't interfere.'

'Why would some cutpurse stab him?' Zelet's dark eyes bored into Casuel. 'In that crowd he could've taken the lad's money and been gone before you drew breath. Why break the lad's head? Do you know more than you're saying, master wizard?'

'Your companion certainly seems apprehensive,' Triss remarked to me.

'The sight of blood distresses me,' Casuel's eyes darted between the two men, making him look more weaselly than ever. 'I'm a mage and a scholar, no swordsman.'

What to do for the best, I wondered. 'It's just possible that an enemy already known to the Sieur D'Olbriot might have attacked D'Alsennin,' I said slowly.

'Who?' demanded Zelet.

'Blond men, shorter than common height, enemies of the Empire from across the Ocean,' I began.

'Then it was them ransacked D'Alsennin's goods in Bremilayne? Why didn't you warn me? But they're killers, merciless, evil—' blurted out Casuel before I silenced him with a glare.

'Yellow-haired men?' Zelet's dark eyes were fixed on me. 'Mountain Men?'

'Not as such, though perhaps they were once of the same blood,' I said slowly. 'Elietimm they call themselves, Men of the Ice. They live on islands far out in the northern ocean and they've ambitions to better themselves by kicking the colonists out of Kellarin or maybe even grabbing land in Dalasor.'

'How would killing Esquire D'Alsennin help them?' Proven Triss wasn't going to unleash his men until he was good and satisfied this was a true scent.

'He's the closest thing Kellarin has to a leader.' I'd been thinking about that. 'There were precious few nobles on the original sailing, just D'Alsennin, Den Fellaemion and Den Rannion.' I wasn't about to complicate matters by mentioning Guinalle and Avila. Both were noble born but primarily valued for their skills in Artifice. 'Den Fellaemion and Den Rannion were killed, so D'Alsennin's the only one left with rank to deal with the Names on this side of the ocean.'

'What happens if someone gets a blade through his heart next time?' asked Zelet with frank curiosity.

I shrugged. 'I don't know, and I don't suppose anyone else does. But the Elietimm will take full advantage of any confusion, Dastennin curse them to drowning.'

'But you don't know this was these Elietimm,' Proven Triss reminded me.

'Who else could it be?' cried Casuel. 'They use knives all the time, lurking in corners to leave innocent men bleeding in the dust.' As the mage clutched unconsciously at his stomach I remembered he carried a twisted line of vivid scarring on his soft pale skin, memento of an Elietimm attack that had left him for dead. Perhaps I should have more sympathy for his panic.

'Did anyone see anything out of the ordinary?' I asked.

Zelet shook his head, acknowledging my grimace of frustration. 'The streets were packed like a market stockyard.'

'Of course no one saw anything! Elietimm use enchantments to baffle and deceive.' Casuel turned on me with a weak man's fury born of fear. 'You should've pursued them in Bremilayne when you had the chance! They got away! They followed us here! Saedrin's stones, it could have been me with a knife in my back—'

He threw out a hand in emphasis, sending the tray crashing to the ground where jug and glasses broke into glittering shards, the water spreading dark on the pale gravel. Zelet grunted with faint disdain as he knelt to pick up the pieces.

'Permit me,' said Casuel tightly. The mage snapped his fingers and emerald light flared in every drop of water. The shattered glass glowed golden along each broken edge and the fragments slid noiselessly over each other, fitting themselves into their remembered places. Whole, the jug righted itself as a tracery of magelight glowed with a furnace intensity that seared the eye before suddenly blinking into nothingness. Trickles of spilled water were gathering themselves around the base and rolled into a glistening braid that twisted up and around the swollen belly of the jug. The water reached up and poured itself back over the lip, swirling into an aquamarine spiral, bubbles of green fire sparking from the surface. Casuel plucked a newly mended glass from the floor, refilled it with surprisingly steady hands, and toasted the two liveried men. 'Perhaps the reality of my magic will make you take the possibility of Elietimm sorcery more seriously.'

Triss and Zelet looked steadily at the mage without answering.

'I'll see you back at the D'Olbriot residence, Chosen Tathel.' With a tide of colour rising from his collar, Casuel got to his feet. 'I expect your full report since I have a duty to keep the Archmage informed.'

Triss nodded to Zelet. 'Get Master Devoir a carriage. If there are knives with a purpose out there, I don't want a second D'Olbriot guest stabbed on my watch.'

I stood too, ready to be dismissed, but Proven Triss waved me back into my seat as Zelet escorted Casuel away. 'I'm not asking you to break confidences, but there are all manner of rumours about this supposed colony D'Alsennin's from. Are we really supposed to believe enchantments held this people in sleep over countless generations after some unholy magic wrecked their hopes in Nemith's day? But there's no question the Archmage took an interest last year, and D'Olbriot's had mages like your friend there in his confidence ever since. Now I'm a rational man; I don't believe a tenth of what I hear, but there's no denying the truth of magic. I'll hunt thieves and bandits from one side of the Empire to the other, but I won't send my men up against fire called to melt the flesh from an honest man's bones. If D'Olbriot chooses to, that's for him to justify to his oath-bound.'

'The Elietimm have a style of magic all their own.' I picked my words carefully, thinking rational probably described Proven Triss's philosophy as well as his character. 'It's not fire and lightning but tangling the wits inside your head. But wise women among the colonists can match it; one's here with D'Alsennin, the Demoiselle Tor Arrial. She's been using her skills to heal his wounds.' If Avila could demonstrably cure illness and mend injury, the sooner we'd persuade men like Triss that Artifice wasn't some dark enchantment to be either feared or banished. I looked him in the eye. 'If it was Elietimm did this, we can use mages and Artifice both to draw their teeth without any of yours or D'Olbriot's risking their neck.'

'If they're in the city at all,' commented Triss.

'Do you recall Esquire Robel D'Olbriot being attacked the year before last?' I said slowly. 'That was the work of those whore-begotten Elietimm.'

Triss scowled. 'I heard they didn't even kill him cleanly.'

'Left him blind and helpless as a swaddled infant.' Anger sharpened my voice. 'That was the first of their offences against the Name and they've earned our enmity thrice over since. The Sieur D'Olbriot wouldn't be dealing with wizards otherwise.'

'D'Alsennin wasn't carrying a purse,' mused Triss. 'The knife could just have been spite because there wasn't any coin.'

'I'll buy wine for your whole Cohort if you find me some cutpurse with the boy's blood on his cuffs,' I assured him.

'It'll empty your purse,' Triss warned me with a grin.

'Coin well spent,' I replied. 'Of course it could be happenstance, I know that. It's Festival after all, there's always trouble in the lower city, and it wouldn't be the first time vermin climbed higher.' And the way Casuel's luck ran, my mother would say he'd get hit by a bowl if it was raining soup. 'Does the knife give some hint?'

Triss drew a blade from his belt with a private smile.

'So do you owe Zelet or is he buying the wine tonight?' I turned the cheap blade in my hands, feeling a peculiar frisson at the dark lines of Temar's blood caught in the binding of the handle.

'I said you'd want to see it,' admitted Triss. 'Zelet called no wager.'

'Let me guess, half the Festival hawkers are selling these?' If this were a puppetry tale, I thought ruefully, the blade would be unique to the knifeman and some innocent bystander would helpfully recall seeing him with it. But real life is never that straightforward.

'Three peddlers out of five.' Triss shrugged. 'I expect we could find whatever back-alley smithy is knocking out that particular style by the barrel full, but we'd learn no more than that.'

'Of course,' I said lightly, handing the useless blade back.

'I'll send word if I hear anything, but frankly I doubt there'll be news.' Triss pursed his lips.

'You and me both.' I nodded ruefully.

'Keep your eyes and ears open, though. Let me know if you learn anything.' Proven Triss got to his feet and I followed him out of the little bower. 'We'll catch the cur if we've a scent to follow, and I take it very personally when a guest of my Sieur can't walk hereabouts in safety.'

'You and me both,' I repeated curtly.

Movement by the residence caught my eye and I saw a blanket-covered litter being gently carried down the steps.

'Permit me to take my leave, Proven Triss?' I said formally.

Triss nodded and turned towards the gatehouse. Avila was walking beside the litter and beckoned to me. 'On the other side, if you please, Ryshad.'

I helped steady the burden as Tor Kanselin's servants and D'Olbriot's footmen eased the unconscious Temar inside the wide-bodied coach. His face was white as bone in the dim interior and I saw an angry bruise at the edge of a poultice strapped to his temple.

I turned to Avila. 'Is he going to be all right?' I asked with a qualm at his stillness.

'He sleeps deep in the shades, by grace of Arimelin's Artifice,' said Avila calmly. 'That will do much to restore him. Tor Kanselin's surgeon knows his herbs well enough, so I have everything I need for the night.'

'You'll be sitting with him?' I'd been wondering if I should do that; head injuries can turn nasty in a hurry.

Avila nodded. 'So you can find out who did this,' she ordered sternly.

'Casuel thinks it must be the Elietimm,' I said, still looking at Temar.

'Just because the master mage is one part flash and nine parts foolish, do not assume he must be wrong,' Avila commented brusquely.

'True enough.' And if the wizard were right he wouldn't let me or anyone else forget it this side of the Otherworld.

'Ryshad!' I turned to see Esquire Camarl standing by the door at the top of the steps. He summoned me with a snap of his fingers.

'Esquire.' I bowed as I arrived on the step below him.

'Where were you, Ryshad?' he demanded without preamble.

I hesitated. 'Temar wanted me to make some enquiries around the Houses he thinks may have these artefacts he's searching for. We thought it would save time if I made a start while he was here.'

'D'Olbriot holds your oath, Ryshad, not D'Alsennin.'

There was an edge to Camarl's voice. 'Your place was at his side.'

'He should have been safe here. Tor Kanselin's men are on a par with our own,' I said before realising I was sounding like Casuel trying to excuse himself. I shut my mouth.

'He was hardly safe outside, was he?' snapped Esquire Camarl.

'No.' I admitted with honest regret. 'Your pardon, Esquire. I was at fault.'

'There's more than enough blame to go round, Ryshad. I shouldn't have spent so much time listening to Irianne's plans for her wedding dress.' Camarl sighed and his face relaxed a little. 'And Temar needs to understand the dignity of his rank these days, that he can't just do wandering around like some junior son of a cadet line. He should've taken a carriage or at least requested a proper escort.' He raised a reprimanding finger at me. 'And you need to understand chosen duties a bit better. I know you're used to using your own initiative when the Sieur sends you on a task halfway across some backward province, but this is Toremal. You send sworn men out on errands, five at a time if you need to, and when they bring back the word you come to me with what I need to know. You're an upper servant now, and it's time you acted like one.'

'Esquire.' I waited a moment before speaking again, trying to strike that fine line between dutiful respect and the assertion that would get me my own way. 'But we have no sworn men who know anything about the Elietimm. Surely the most important thing now is to look for any trace of them in the city? I'm the only man you can send to do that.'

Camarl looked at me with narrowed eyes. 'I suppose that's true enough. But if you get any sniff of them, you come back and rouse the entire barracks, do you hear?'

'I won't take any Elietimm on without a full Cohort at my back, on Aiten's oath,' I promised him.

Camarl smiled sadly. 'You learned that lesson the hard way, didn't you? He was a good man, Aiten, too good to lose to those bastards, and the same is true for you, Ryshad. Be careful.'

'I will,' I assured him. 'Do you want me to report to you as soon as I get back?'

'Whatever the chime,' Camarl confirmed. 'Wake me if you need to.'

'Watch your back,' Stolley called as I passed him on my way through the gatehouse. I spared him a wave and broke into a jog trot, ignoring the protests of my weary feet. If anyone in the lower city had the answers, I'd take them on the point of my sword if need be.

CHAPTER THREE

Preface to the Chronicle of the House, As Given by Sieur Loedain D'Olbriot, Winter Solstice of the 50th Year of Bezaemar the Canny

It has fallen to few Sieurs of this House to record any Emperor completing a second full generation on the throne, but I find myself thus honoured. Indeed, as I look over the Imperial Rote, I see we have been blessed with more long-lived rulers over the last handful of generations than at any time since the Chaos. The world is a very different place since the days of Decabral, when the Eager, the Nervous and the Merciful all died by the sword. I wonder if Bezaemar the Canny will equal Aleonne the Gallant's fifty-six years of rule; he has certainly faithfully followed the wise man's example in using diplomacy to bring us peace instead of the warfare that once so often drained our resources of coin and youth.

As Tormalin fares, naturally so does D'Olbriot. How stands Tormalin at the end of so momentous a year? I can declare without hesitation that concord extends clear across the traditional domains of our Old Empire. We are seen again as the natural leaders of all lands bordered by mountains, forest and sea. Even the distant kingdom of Solura bows to our supremacy. Tormalin culture reaches once more to the very gates of Selerima. Our fashions are worn as far afield as the streets of Col, and learning from the antiquarian scholarship of Vanam enriches our libraries, restoring much that was lost in the Chaos. With accredited ambassadors in every Dukedom of Lescar and sitting as honoured observers in the Caladhrian Parliament, we are no longer at risk of unheeded anger boiling up into unexpected attack. Gold once spent like water to service the cohorts and galleys that guarded borders and coasts now enriches our dwellings with paintings and sculpture, ceramics and furniture. As noble wealth supports our craftsmen, so our traders carry their goods ever further along the peaceable high roads, even to the Great Forest and beyond. Long seasons of patient negotiation mean the Archipelago is no longer a source of fear and danger but a ready supplier of muslins for the poor and silks for the wealthy.

As ceremonial rivalry replaces contests of arms, D'Olbriot stands as of right in the first order of nobility. The niceties of rank are ever more finely codified to guide those visiting from lesser lands, and D'Olbriot reputation grows with every year that passes. I have extended D'Olbriot patronage beyond our own tenantry to those lesser Houses whose distance from Toremal or lack of resources hamper them in this race for status. Our daughters are eagerly courted and our sons are received with hopeful civility wherever they pay their addresses to a lady. D'Olbriot lands and enterprises flourish from the Ast Marsh to the Cape of Winds and our tenantry benefit daily from the enhanced position we have secured for all beholden to our Name.

So why do I not rejoice? Is it simply that I too am an old man, tired of bearing my own burden? I am in truth weary and let this document thus record my own decision to step down at this close of the year, bidding my Designate, my grand-nephew Chajere, take up the oath of the Sieur. But wisdom is a blessing of age, and it may be that I see within with clearer eyes, for all the webs clouding my outer vision. As Bezaemar has celebrated the longevity of his rule with lavish pomp, precious few of the commonalty have seen him do so and none too many of the nobility at whose pleasure he supposedly rules. Even Esquires of my own Name find themselves endlessly delayed in anterooms where tedious games of precedence are played out before they are admitted to the Imperial presence. Bezaemar has always been noted for his intelligence, but how can even the wisest of men make sound judgements when all his information comes from so small and so limited a circle of advisors? I am minded of a pond, peaceful and still, thus pleasant to look at but after time smelling rank with decay. After so long without anything to stir us, does not Tormalin risk similar stagnation?

Perhaps I am unduly pessimistic. The recent celebrations have naturally prompted renewed speculation as to who might succeed Bezaemar the Canny and those old Sieurs supporting him will soon be replaced in their turn by younger men looking to make a mark on their House. The Tor Bezaemar grandson most often mentioned is a lively, good-humoured lad, well known and liked among all who will vote on the question and with a wide circle of friends among the junior Esquires of our Houses. If I am spared, I pray that I might see such a man take up the mantle of the Emperor with new vitality.

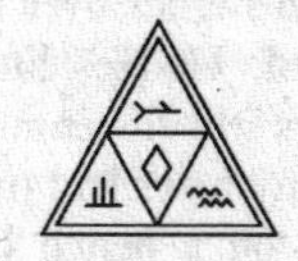

The D'Olbriot Residence Gatehouse, Summer Solstice Festival, Second Day, Morning

I woke to one of those moments when your cares haven't raised their heads and you can savour a comfortable bed, crisp linen and the promise of the new day. All that was missing was Livak curled close beside me and waking to my kiss. That fancy lasted about as long as it took me to fling aside the single coverlet that was all these sultry summer nights needed. Washed, shaved and out of the gatehouse before the early sun had risen a hair's breadth higher over the roof tiles, I found the day outside still cool. Hedges lining the walks of the grounds cast long shadows still glistening with dew as I hurried to the barracks to see if any news had turned up while I slept.

Stolley was lounging on a bench by the barracks door. 'Morning, Rysh, I've some messages for you.'

'Thanks.' I took two letters from Stolley. 'Did anything else I should know about turn up last night?'

'Maitresse Tor Kanselin sent a bowl of crystal berries from her personal hot-house.' Stolley shrugged. 'A lad from Tor Bezaemar came offering their Sieur's personal physician. Sirnis Den Viorel sent him a tisane casket this morning.'

'Anything else?' I persisted.

Stolley sucked air through the gap where he'd lost three teeth in a fistfight. 'You're expecting some growling rough with a nail-studded club asking for a private audience, are you?'

'Or a mysterious beauty claiming to be an old friend, maybe some down-on-his-luck musician begging for a hearing?' I nodded, mock serious. All these characters and more were dusted off each year for puppet shows to tempt our Festival pennies. 'How about the genial old man just looking for an honest game of Raven? I could do with winning a few crowns.'

'Don't go looking in the barracks,' Stolley warned me. 'All the new blood has been warned about you.'

'Spoilsport.' So nothing out of the ordinary had caught Stolley's eye.

'Did you get any scent last night then?' Stoll was as keen as me and everyone else in the barracks to see whoever had stabbed Temar strung up from a gibbet.

'Nothing, and I checked in with every sergeant between the hills and the sea.' I shook my head. 'I'd best get some breakfast and start calling back on them.'

'It's the lower hall for upper servants,' Stoll reminded me with a pointed nod at the main house.

I groaned. 'Why do housemaids have to be so cursed shrill in the morning?' But I crossed the grounds to the main house, mindful of Esquire Camarl's rebuke. A hall servant I knew slightly was sweeping briskly around the door as I took the steps at the run.

'Ryshad, good morning!'

'And to you, Dass.' Not inclined to stop and chat, I took the backstairs down to the whitewashed lower hall, a long basement with shallow windows high in the walls bringing light from outside. Heavy, scarred tables with backless benches were crowded with ladies' maids, housemaids, valets and lackeys, all talking at once and all trying to make themselves heard by speaking louder than their neighbour. The babble echoed back and forth from the limewashed stone, battering my ears. I knocked at the servery built between two massive pillars that once supported the undercroft of a D'Olbriot residence built and demolished generations since.

'What can I get you?' A freckle-faced child tucked a wisp of chestnut hair back behind her ear, wiping hands on her coarse apron.

'Bread, ham, whatever fruit's left and a tisane with plenty of white amella.' I smiled at the lass.

'Something to keep you awake?' she chuckled as she assembled my meal from the plates and baskets to hand.

'Fifth chime of midnight was sounding as I got back last night,' I admitted.

'I hope she was worth it,' she teased, suddenly older than her years.

'And Fair Festival to you,' I retorted

She laughed. 'It will be once I've served my turn today and fetched my dancing slippers.'

Sipping my tisane with a smile puckered by its bitterness, I found a seat at the very end of a table. A few of the maids and footmen spared me a glance but were more interested in sharing their gossip with the visiting servants. I knew most faces, even if I couldn't put a name to them, and the few newcomers were visibly escorted by resident servants. Messire's steward wasn't about to have the smooth running of his household disrupted by some valet not knowing where to go for hot water or how to find the laundry.

The first note was another from Mistal, wanting to know where I'd got to yesterday, so I ignored it in favour of the salt richness of dark dry-cured ham against soft white bread still warm from the oven. The second simply had my given name scrawled clumsily on the outside. I cracked the misshapen blob of unmarked wax and unfolded the single sheet as I savoured the perfumed sweetness of a ripe plum.

'What in Dast's name is this?' I was so startled I spoke out loud.

'Sorry?' The girl beside me turned from discussing southern fashions with a maid from Lequesine. 'Did you want something, Ryshad?'

'No, sorry, but Fair Festival to you anyway, Mernis.' I smiled up at her with all the charm I could muster after shock on top of a late night. 'Do you know if the breakfast trays have gone upstairs yet?'

'The hall lackeys were taking them up as I was coming down.' Mernis nodded. 'You're supposed to be shepherding the young D'Alsennin, aren't you? Didn't do too well yesterday, from what I hear?' She wasn't being offensive, just curious, but I wasn't about to give any gossip to share with her friends inside the House and beyond.

'Is he awake, do you know?' I wiped my sticky hands on a neatly darned napkin before tucking the letters inside my jerkin.

'I saw the Demoiselle Tor Arrial going in to him,' volunteered a lad some way down the table, the tailor's apprentice as I recalled.

'Many thanks.' Everyone at this end of the long table was paying keen attention now, so I gave them all a bland smile and took the backstairs to the upper floors. I took them two at a time, varnished oaken boards underfoot softened only by a strip of woven matting and limewashed walls an unadorned yellow. There was no page outside Temar's door this morning, but a newly sworn man, sufficiently flattered by the assignment not to pine for festivities he'd be missing.

'Verd.' I nodded a greeting. 'Has anyone asked after D'Alsennin?'

'A few of the maids,' he shrugged. 'Always after any excuse to dally.'

'Or flirt.' I grinned. 'If anyone does come sniffing around, don't set their hackles up, but I'll be interested to know their names.'

Verd's pouchy eyes were shrewd. 'And what do I tell them?'

'Just shake your head and look dubious,' I suggested. 'See if they look like that's good news or bad.'

I knocked and hearing a muffled summons, opened the gilt-latched door. Temar was sitting up in the massive bed, an old-fashioned piece but still monumentally impressive. Hung with valance and curtains of scarlet and ivory damask, the ornately carved posts were matched by a deeply incised headboard. Temar sat against a bank of pillows looking uncomfortably self-conscious, a tray with the remnants of a good breakfast by his knees.

'When can I get dressed?' he grimaced in frustration, looking faintly ridiculous in a frilled nightshirt.

'When I am satisfied you are fit to do so.' This crisp response came from the Demoiselle Tor Arrial, who was sitting over by the window, hair confined in a silver filigree net this morning, a touch of elegance to offset her austere mauve gown.

'Ryshad, tell them to let me out of bed,' Temar appealed. I noted the appalling bruise had faded to a purplish smear and dark stains under one eye.

'How is he?' I turned to Avila. This healing was her handiwork so she was the best judge.

'Well enough,' she allowed after a pause.

'Can I get up?' demanded Temar.

'You lost entirely too much blood for my peace of mind,' said Avila repressively. 'You must not do anything strenuous for at least another full day.'

'Getting out of bed is hardly strenuous,' the youth objected. 'And I cannot spend half the Festival sat here. Inside a handful of days, the leading Names will leave for country properties with cleaner water and cooler air. There are people I need to see!'

'If you overreach yourself today you risk lying flat on your back for another three.' Avila met Temar's challenge with equal force. 'How will that help us recover the missing artefacts?'

'Talagrin's haste is Poldrion's bounty.' Temar and Avila both looked blankly at me. 'Hurrying now risks more delay in the long run? Never mind. You feel fit enough sat in your bed, Temar, but you can't rush a head injury. I've seen enough novices knocked senseless on the sparring floor to know that. What about your wound? You must be feeling that cut every time you breathe?'

'Avila healed it with Artifice,' said Temar scornfully. 'She took the stitches out just now.'

'Oh.' There wasn't much I could say to that.

'But we do not want another blade wasting my efforts,' Avila said waspishly. 'Were you able to run any assailant to earth last night, Ryshad?'

'Not a one.' I shook my head. 'Every man sworn to D'Olbriot and every other Name that owes us will be picking up the hunt, but until we get some scent you really shouldn't go beyond the walls of the residence, Temar, not today certainly.'

'Have you found any hint of Elietimm within the city?' Avila demanded.

'Nothing.' I shook my head. 'And Dastennin be my witness, I've looked. Have you felt anyone else working Artifice?'

'Not a trace,' she replied. 'But I will continue to search.'

Temar looked as if he were about to speak, his thin face sulky, but he quailed beneath Avila's steely gaze.

I pulled a letter out of my jerkin. 'This morning's bad news is someone wants to put a knife in me next. Whoever's behind this, Temar's not their only target.'

Avila recovered first from her astonishment. 'Explain yourself.'

'This is a declaration of challenge.' I unfolded the anonymous note I'd received and read the crisply printed pronouncement aloud. 'Be it known to all men duly sworn to the service of a Prince of Toremal that Ryshad Tathel, lately sworn to D'Olbriot and newly chosen to honour that Name, stands ready to prove his merit with sword, staff and dagger. According to custom, he will meet all comers in formal combat at the noon of Solstice on the practice ground of the D'Olbriot Cohort.' I folded the sheet carefully along its creases. 'All quite according to form, as you see. The only problem is, I didn't declare for trial.'

'I am sorry but I do not understand,' said Avila testily.

'Raising a Cohort was an uncommon event in your day, wasn't it? Tenants were called up to serve for some specific emergency?' They both nodded slowly. 'Well, during the Chaos the nobility needed standing troops to defend their people and their property. That's when the first men were sworn, as soldiery to the Houses. By the end of the Kanselin era the formal structure we use today had developed. Recognised men are the bottom rung; they wear the livery of the House and if they show themselves trustworthy the Sieur offers them his oath and they swear to him in turn. Sworn men wear the amulet to symbolise those oaths. For those who make a mark, there's promotion to chosen man, and then proven are at the top of the ladder, those few most highly regarded by the Sieur and his Designate.'

'At this business of challenge?' Avila gestured at the paper I held.

I looked at it. 'There's not so much need for warriors these days, but sworn men serve as bodyguards when nobility travel. Each House takes its turn supplying the Cohort keeping Toremal's peace in the Emperor's name, season by season and festival by festival, so we all have to be useful in a fight. Only a handful of Houses still maintain sword schools.' I ticked off the names on my fingers. 'D'Olbriot, Tor Kanselin, Den Haurient, Tor Bezaemar and D'Istrac, but they all take men from the other Houses and train them up.

'When a recognised man comes to take his oath, he must prove he's a competent fighter, so he issues a challenge with letters like this posted on all the sword school doors and sent to every House's Sergeant-at-Arms. He has to fight everyone who turns up – any sworn man that is, not just ruffians off the streets – or he forfeits the honour of being offered an oath.'

'A test of endurance as well of skill.' Temar was looking interested. 'You are also supposed to do this?'

'A sworn man elevated to chosen or a chosen man raised to proven always used to issue a challenge. Those already holding the rank would test his worth for promotion.' I rubbed a hand over my chin. 'But it's seldom done these days, only if the sword school wants to put on an extra display at the end of the recognition bouts or to honour a noted swordsman.' I shook my head. 'And in any case, I didn't issue the challenge. But now it's posted I'm honour bound to answer anyone who turns up to meet it.'

'What is the person responsible hoping to achieve?' Avila wondered.

'Beyond killing Ryshad, if they get the chance,' commented Temar with a faint grin.

I smiled humourlessly back at him. 'They won't get that

chance, but humiliating me out on the sand would be a major embarrassment for D'Olbriot.' Just as injuring Temar had humiliated the Name.

'If this challenge is nothing to do with you, why take the risk?' objected Avila.

'It is a question of honour,' Temar retorted swiftly.

I was glad he'd said that. 'I'll go down to the sword school this morning, shed a little sweat getting my eye in. It's been a season or more since I did any serious training. I can ask a few questions while I'm there.'

'I had best take up the work you were doing yesterday.' Temar threw aside the coverlet, very nearly upsetting his breakfast tray.

I looked at Avila and saw my own doubts reflected in the Demoiselle's eyes. 'You really should stay within the walls today. Until we know more, we can't risk you.'

'You need at least a day's more rest, my lad,' Avila told him with a quelling look. 'If someone truly wishes you dead, they will not send a man to face you with an honourable blade but with a dagger to hide in the shadows again. What am I to tell Guinalle if all I return to her is your ashes in an urn?'

I looked at my boots. That was a low blow from Avila, playing on the lad's hopeless devotion for Guinalle. I happened to know she'd been keeping company with Usara, pupil and friend of the Archmage. His scholarship and intellect were far more to her tastes than Temar's exuberance these days. Which reminded me – I still had to ask Casuel to use his wizardry to bespeak Usara to find out what Livak was up to. I couldn't shake the suspicion that those brothers she was so fond of might lead her astray again.

'What am I supposed to do then?' Temar demanded crossly.

I hastily concentrated on the matter in hand. 'There must be useful records in the library here. Not as many as at the archive, but the Sieur's personal clerk will be free to help you. Messire will be at the Imperial Palace all day.'

Temar was still looking mutinous.

'At least you can get dressed,' I told him with a grin.

'I am invited to gossip over tisanes with Lady Channis and Dirindal Tor Bezaemar this morning,' announced Avila, a determined glint in her eye. 'We can compare what we learn at lunch.'

Temar subsided on to his pillows. 'I suppose so.'

'Please excuse me.' I bowed out of the room and caught up with a pageboy delivering carafes of spring water to the bedrooms along the corridor. 'Do you know if Esquire Camarl has risen yet?'

The child shook his head. 'He's still in his bed, master, not even sent down for hot water or a tisane.'

Which meant Camarl's fiercely devoted valet wouldn't let anyone disturb him. I wasn't surprised; when I'd reported my lack of progress to Camarl last night it had been well past midnight and the Esquire had still been working in the library, surrounded by parchments and ledgers. Better to go and see if anyone at the sword school could shed any light on this fake challenge, I decided. Then I could report to Camarl with more than half a tale.

I headed for the gatehouse, where I made sure Stolley knew not to let Temar go out without firstly getting Camarl's express permission and secondly surrounding the lad with a ring of swords. A heavy wagon bearing the D'Olbriot chevron on its sides was lumbering past as I walked out on to the highway and I swung myself up on the back, nodding to the lugubrious carter.

'Chosen man, now is it?' He gave my armring a perfunctory glance and spat into the road. 'You should know better than come borrowing a ride from me.'

'Where's the harm, this once?' I protested with a grin. 'Everyone does it, surely?'

'Everyone sworn, maybe.' He turned to his team of sturdy mules with a dour chirrup.

I swung my legs idly as the cart ambled round the long arc of the highway little faster than walking pace, but I was content to save my energies for the exertions a morning at the D'Olbriot sword school promised. The mules needed no prompting to take an eventual turn towards the sprawl of warehouses, chandleries and miscellaneous yards that sell everything and anything brought in from the towns and estates of the Empire or ferried from overseas in the capacious galleys that ply their way along the coasts from Ensaimin and beyond. As the carter began a series of stops to fill his wagon with sacks and barrels to supply D'Olbriot's festivities I got off and waved my thanks.

It wasn't far to the sword school, a rough and ready cluster of buildings inside a paling fence. It's an old joke that our Sieur's sacks of grain are housed in more luxury than the men who'll defend his barns. But these austere barracks are where recognised men have their mettle and commitment tested; newer accommodations up at the residence reward those sworn to the Name with more comfortable lodging. I walked inside the weathered and gaping fence, a boundary more for show than defence. If anyone was foolish enough to think there was anything here worth stealing, he'd soon find fifty swords on either hand ready to explain his mistake.

But the sandy compound was empty today. All those who usually spent their days here training and sweating were either in attendance on the Names who'd recognised them or were off taking advantage of all the distractions Festival could offer. Those who drank themselves senseless would regret it soon enough when the first day of Aft-Summer had them back on the practice ground.

I headed for the simple circular building dominating the compound, rough wooden walls built on a waist-high foundation of stone and holding a shingled roof twice the height of a man. The wide doors stood open to welcome in any breeze that might relieve the summer sun, even for a moment. Squinting in the gloom I went in, grateful for the shade, even though the full heat of the day was yet to come.

A shove sent me stumbling forward, barely keeping my feet. I broke into a run, partly to save myself from falling, partly to get away from whomever was behind me. I whirled round, drawing my sword all in one smooth move, blade arcing round to gut anyone trying for a second blow.

My sword met the blade of the man attacking me in a harsh clash of metal. My blade slid down his and the guards locked tight. Our eyes met, his gaze on a level with mine. I threw my assailant away with a sudden heave, my sword ready for his next move.

The tip of his blade hovered a scant hand's width from mine. He moved with unexpected fury, brilliant steel flashing down to cleave my head like a melon waiting for the knife. But I wasn't waiting. As soon as his shoulders tightened I brought my own sword up, with a sliding step to the off hand to take me out of danger. I swept my blade down on his, forcing it away, the same movement taking my own sword up and into his face, threatening to slice his throat to the spine. He stepped back, balanced on light feet, raising his sword first to protect himself and then slashing up and round to scythe into my upper body. I ducked, moved and would have had the point of my sword into his guts but he changed his strike to a downward smash. Our swords caught fast again, both of us leaning all our strength into the blades, muscles taut.

'So what was she like, your Aldabreshin whore?' He tried to spit in my face but his mouth was too dry.

'Better than your mother ever was.' I blinked away sweat stinging my eyes and running down my nose to drip on the sand. 'You're getting old, Fyle.'

'I'll be old when you'll be dead,' he sneered. 'You can stake your stones on that.'

'First time I heard that I laughed so much I fell out of my crib.' I shook my head. 'A lot of dogs have died since you were whelped, Fyle.'

We broke apart and moved in a slow circle, swords low and ready. I looked him in the eyes, seeing implacable determination. In the instant he brought up his blade I stepped in, rolling my hands to lift my sword up under his arms, the edge biting into his shirt sleeves. As he flinched, retreated and recovered to continue his downward stroke, all inside a breath, I stepped out and around, bringing a sweeping cut in from behind to hack off his head.

I rested my blade gently on his corded neck, between grizzled, close-cropped hair and his sweat-soaked collar. 'Yield?'

He dropped his sword but only so he could rub the tender skin above each elbow. 'That cursed hurt, Rysh.'

'Good enough?' I persisted, turning my face vainly for a cool breeze but the air was heavy and warm inside the rough wooden circle.

Fyle nodded, easing broad shoulders in a familiar gesture. 'Good enough, unless someone unexpected turns up to answer the challenge.'

'So you've heard about that.' I sheathed my own sword and picked up Fyle's blade, returning it to him with a bow of respect. 'Any notion who might be interested?

'In taking you down a peg or two? His laughter rang up to the crudely shaped rafters. 'They'll be lining up!'

'Anyone I know in particular?' I wiped sweat from my face with my shirt sleeve.

Fyle paused, shirt open at the neck, breeches patched and sweat stained. He had more than half a generation on me, the chest hair tangling in the laces of his shirt greying, but he was still impressively muscled. 'It was D'Istrac men you got into that fight with, you and Aiten.'

I sat on a plain wooden bench to ease the laces on one boot but looked up at his words. 'Which fight?'

'Well, there were so many, weren't there?' Sarcasm rasped in Fyle's voice.

'Not so many,' I protested. 'And we didn't always start them.'

'You started that one with D'Istrac's men though.' Fyle shook his head at me. 'When you were ringing a bell about the way men raised to chosen and proven should take their turn at challenge, same as the rest, same as it always had been done. Debasing the metal of the amulet, wasn't it?'

'But that was ten years ago,' I said slowly.

'You'd forgotten?' Fyle laughed. 'Well, throw shit in the sea on the ebb and the stink'll come back on the flow, you know that.'

'Can't a man say stupid things when he's young, drunk and stupid?' I pleaded, shucking my jerkin and hanging it on a peg.

'Of course,' Fyle assured me. 'But older, wise and sober, you admit your mistakes.' He looked at me sternly, the scant space between his bushy eyebrows disappearing. 'That's what I reckoned when I saw that challenge posted. If you'd come to me to get my warrant, I'd have told you to forget it and just buy enough wine to sink the insult if you felt that bad about it.'

'But it's not my challenge,' I told him. 'That's what I came to see you about. Who might have posted it in my name?'

'I've no idea,' said Fyle, voice muffled as he scrubbed at his face with a coarse towel.

'What about the other sword provosts?' I persisted. 'Maybe someone came to them looking for a warrant?'

'No, and I went asking, ready to take a piece out of anyone's hide who thought he could give warrant for a D'Olbriot challenge.' Fyle shook his head.

I managed a rueful grin. 'So D'Istrac will be sending every chosen man they can muster, will they?'

'All those who don't mind risking a bloody nose or a few stitches to put a crimp in their Festival rutting.' Fyle shoved wide bare feet into loose shoes. 'You've a face like the southern end of a northbound mule! There's no malice in it, Ryshad, but you've done well for yourself, got the Sieur's ear these last few years, been sent off on Raeponin knows what duty. So you got chosen when men you trained with are still polishing up their scabbards in the barracks, and the higher a cat climbs a tree the more people want to tweak its tail.' He slapped me on the shoulder. 'I'll get us something to wash the dust out of our throats and you can tell me all about that Aldabreshin woman of yours. I've been wanting to hear the full story.'

Fyle went to the open door and whistled. An eager lad appeared; there are always a few hanging round any sword school, watching, learning and hoping one day to be recognised.

Fyle gave the boy coin and he ran off to fetch wine from one of the many nearby inns and taverns making their money by quenching swordsmen's thirsts.

Young men drinking deep on empty stomachs say some brainless things. Was it that simple? Were my own foolish words coming back to mock me? Dast be my witness, I'd completely forgotten that quarrel so long past. I couldn't even recall exactly where or when I'd been laying down the ancient law of the sword schools, intoxicated with all the vigour of youth and not a little wine. I didn't relish explaining this to the Sieur or Camarl, admitting this challenge wasn't some ploy to deprive the House or D'Alsennin of a valued defender but just muck trailed in from the days I'd been too dimwitted not to foul my own doorstep.

Who else would have remembered that evening? Who would care enough, after all this time to want to set me up for a fall? Why now? I'd spent a lot of time away from Toremal these last few years, but there'd been other Solstices for anyone wanting to settle that score to set their little game in play.

Aiten would have laughed, I thought gloomily. If he'd been here, he'd have been the first I'd have suspected of posting the challenge. He'd have thought it a glorious prank and then would have trained with me every waking moment so I'd walk off the sand as victor at the end of the day. But he was two years dead, all but a season and a half. Dead at Livak's hand, but his death was owed to Elietimm malice. I knew she still fretted about the appalling choice she'd made, to kill my friend to save my life and hers when his wits had been taken from him by foul enchantment. I only hoped this distance between us wouldn't have her doubting my assurance that I never blamed her.

Fyle returned swinging leather beakers in one hand and a blackened flagon in the other. 'We'll drink to your success tomorrow, shall we?'

'I hope there's plenty of water in that,' I commented, taking a drink. Aiten was dead, Livak was away and I had to deal with the here and now. Someone had set a challenge and I had to meet it. If I was paying debts run up in my foolish youth, so be it. If someone planned to leave me bleeding on the sand, I'd make sure he was the one needing the surgeon. Then I'd want to know whose coin had bought his blade in defiance of every tenet of oath-bound tradition.

'We'll lift the good stuff tomorrow,' Fyle promised, seeing my expression as I sipped. 'When you've seen off whatever dogs come yapping round your heels.'

'You think I'll do?' If he didn't, Fyle would soon tell me.

'You're the equal of any sworn man I've had here in the last five years,' he said slowly. 'You're young for a chosen, so you'll face men with more experience than you, but on the other side of that coin they'll be older, slower.' He smiled at me, the creases around his dark eyes deepening. 'You were a loud-mouthed lad, but you were saying nothing we sword provosts don't mutter among ourselves over a late night flagon. Too many chosen and proven polish up their armring and let their swords rust.'

Like Glannar, I thought sternly. 'So you'll be putting down coin to back me, will you?'

'You know I'm no man for a wager.' Fyle shook his head. 'I only take risks I can't avoid, like any sensible soldier.'

We both drank deep, thirst gripping us by the throat.

'I'd have thought you'd have had a few more tricks up your sleeve,' remarked Fyle as he refilled our beakers with the well watered wine. 'Didn't you learn anything in those god-cursed islands down south?'

'You're not going to let that go, are you?' I laughed.

'One of our own gets sold into slavery by those worthless Relshazri, taken off into the Archipelago, where even honest traders say disease takes three men for every two the Aldabreshi kill. He fights his way out with wizards behind him and then turns up on the far side of the ocean, unearthing Nemith the Last's lost colony, untouched by time?' Fyle looked at me, mock incredulous. 'You don't suppose I'm going to swallow that, do you? What really happened?'

I let go a long breath as I thought how best to answer him. 'I was arrested in Relshaz after a misunderstanding with a trader.'

'And they claim to have a law code equal to ours,' scoffed Fyle.

I shrugged. I could hardly claim the trader was being unreasonable when he'd objected to Temar taking over my hands and wits to steal that unholy armring. 'Raeponin must have been looking the other way. Some mischief loaded the scales so I got bought by an Elietimm warlord looking for a body slave for his youngest wife.' Elietimm mischief had been behind it but I wasn't about to try explaining that to Fyle. 'I did my duty by her for a season or so, jumped ship, and headed north when I got the chance.' A chance offered me by the warlord, since I'd done him the favour of exposing the treachery of another of his wives, a vicious stupid bitch being played for a fool by those cursed Elietimm. 'I got caught up with the Archmage and his search for Kellarin when I took a ride on a ship to Hadrumal.' I shrugged again. 'After that, I was just looking out for the Sieur's interests.' Discovering he'd sacrifice me for the greater good of the Name without too much grief.

Fyle leaned back against some cloak left hanging on a peg. 'So what kind of service does a warlord's wife want?' From the way he loaded the word, he meant it in the stableyard sense.

I laughed. 'Oh, you've heard the stories, Fyle.' As had I and every other man in Tormalin. The Archipelago was ruled by vicious savages who used their women in common, slaking blood lust and the other kind in orgies of cruelty and debauchery. Crudely copied chapbooks with lurid illustrations periodically circulated round the sword schools, those who could read entertaining their fellows with the titillating details. When one particularly unpleasant example had come to light in a provost's inspection, Fyle's predecessor had made a fire of every bit of paper in the barracks.

'Well?' Fyle demanded. 'Come on! Half the lads here were expecting you to float up dead on the summer storms and the rest thought you'd be cut two stones lighter if we ever saw you alive again!'

'Luckily eunuchs have gone out of fashion in this generation.'

Fyle laughed, thinking I was joking. I leaned over to him, keeping my voice low. 'Fyle, you haven't heard the half of it.'

'Master Provost?' A shout from the far door saved me from any more questions. It was the Barracks Steward, a thick ledger under his arm.

'Duty calls.' Fyle groaned. 'But I'll have the truth out of you, Rysh, if I have to get you drunk to do it.' He pointed a blunt, emphatic finger at me.

'You can buy the brandy to celebrate my success tomorrow,' I offered.

Fyle laughed as he left. 'Yes, Master Steward, what can I do for you?'

I wandered out of the far door, squinting in the bright sunlight. A few lads sat in the dust, playing a game of runes with a battered wooden set discarded by some man at arms. White Raven's more my game; I never have that much luck with runes, unlike Livak. But then, she makes her own luck if needs be. I wandered past the long, low-roofed barracks where narrow windows shed scant light on the cramped bunks inside. The shrine was at the far end of the sword school compound, a small round building in the same pale sandy stone, ochre tiles spotted with lichen on an old-fashioned conical roof.

I went inside and sneezed, old incense hanging in the air having its usual effect. The ancient icon of Ostrin had a fresh Festival garland around its neck and the bowl in front of the plinth was filled with the ash of more than one incense stick recently burned in supplication. Fyle took his duties as nominal priest of the place more seriously than Serlal, sword provost through my early training. He'd left the place to dust and cobwebs that made a greybeard out of the youthful Ostrin, holly staff in one hand and jug in the other.

I looked up at the statue, carved in some smooth soft grey stone I'd never been able to identify, much to my father's amusement. Ostrin has many aspects endearing him to fighting men: god of hospitality, legends tell of him rewarding faithful servants and even taking up arms to defend dutiful folk being abused by the unworthy. When taking up arms leads to bloodshed, then we can beseech the god's healing grace. These days I'd be more likely to see what Artifice could do for me, I thought irreverently.

Taking incense, steel and flint from the drawer in the plinth, I lit a casual offering in remembrance of Aiten. I'd failed to bring his body back, to be burned on the pyre ground behind this little shrine. I hadn't even returned with his ashes, purified in some distant fire and safe in an urn to join in the serried ranks lining the curved walls, mute remembrance of all those men who'd died in D'Olbriot service and now took their ease in the Otherworld. I hadn't even brought back his sword or his dagger, to lay in one of the dusty chests tucked behind the altar. But I had his amulet, sewn in my sword-belt, the token in earnest of our oaths. I'd lay that to rest here, I decided, when I'd taken suitable revenge, some day, somehow, when I'd won a price in blood with all the interest accrued out of some worthless Elietimm hide. Ostrin, Dastennin and any other god who cared to listen could be my witness, the Elietimm wouldn't lay hands on Kellarin, not while I was still breathing.

Would Ostrin care for Laio Shek, the warlord's wife? I smiled. What did the gods think of those who never even acknowledged them? But Laio had looked after me, according to her peculiar customs. No, Fyle hadn't heard the half of life in the Archipelago. I couldn't speak for every warlord, but Shek Kul wasn't merely a barbarian. An astute man, he walked a difficult path in a dangerous world of shifting alliances and armed truce. He was capable of unholy cruelty; I'd seen that when he'd executed his errant wife, but by the stars of the Archipelago that had been justice. His other wives were no mere ornaments subject to his lusts and abuse either, but intelligent women who managed more commerce and underlings than the Sieurs of many a minor House.

But trying to convince the assembled swordsmen of Tormalin that everything they'd always believed was false would be as pointless as shouting defiance to Dastennin in the teeth of a gale. Fyle and some of the others might listen if I told them a few new truths along with a circumscribed tale confirming the Archipelagan reputation for erotic expertise was no exaggeration. Aldabreshin women certainly took many men besides their husbands to their beds, but that was their choice, not some dictate of brutal masters. Not that I'd sully the memory of my intimate dealings with Laio by laying every detail bare to salacious view.

I smiled. Next time I accompanied my mother to Halcarion's shrine, on her market day visits to polish up my sister Kitria's urn, I'd light another scrap of incense in hopes that the Moon Maiden would look favourably on little Laio.

I frowned. I'd have to watch my tongue if Fyle did ply me with white brandy. Laio had sent me on my way with enough gold to buy a sizeable tract of the upper city. Truth be told, I still wasn't certain if she'd meant that as payment for services rendered.

Enough of this self-indulgence; I had more important things to occupy me without wasting time in idle reverie. I turned my back on the feathery wisps of blue smoke and walked briskly back to the sword school, remembering I'd left my jerkin by the door.

When I entered the echoing building I saw someone going through my pockets. I caught him by surprise and had him face down on the ground before he could draw breath. 'Turned thief, have you?'

'Get off, Rysh!' My brother Mistal spat out a mouthful of dust.

'Not earning a living at the law, so you come picking my pocket?' I had his arms behind him and a knee in the small of his back. 'Come on, get up. A soft lot, you lawyers.'

He struggled ineffectually. 'Let me up and say that, you bastard.'

'Now that's really worth a slapping, sullying our mother's

honour.' I let him go and stood, ready for his move.

He didn't make one, brushing pale sand from the dull grey of his law court robes with one hand and waving two crumpled notes at me. 'Is there any pissing point sending you letters?'

I was surprised at his anger. 'I've been busy, Mist. You know what Festival's like. I've no time to go admiring masquerade dancers with you.'

'This isn't about god-cursed dancers!' Mistal thrust a letter at me. 'Nor's this one. I needed to see you!'

'Chain up your dog.' My pleasure at seeing my brother was fading fast. 'I'll write a reply while the wax is still warm on your letter next time, good enough? Dastennin help you if all you want is to show me is some curly lass who's been flirting her skirts at you.'

Mistal opened his mouth then shut it with a sheepish grin. 'Fair enough. But this is serious, Rysh.'

I was starting to realise it must be for him to leave the court precincts during daylight. If Mistal just wanted to enjoy the Festival's entertainments with me, he'd have waited until the tenth chime of day ended all business with sunset.

'Not here.' A sword school is no place for a confidential discussion.

'Let's take some air on the rope walk.' Mistal reached into his pocket for chewing leaf. I waved away his offer.

The sword school's not far from the docks and we took a short cut through an alley lined with brothels doing good business with both seafarers and men-at-arms. Not that combining such trades was without its hazards; Stolley had lost those teeth of his somewhere hereabouts.

'What are you doing down here?' Mistal asked. 'Shouldn't you be dancing attendance on your Sieur instead of sparring with your friends?'

I smiled without humour. 'Someone thought it a good joke to post a challenge in my name. Given young D'Alsennin nearly had his skull cracked like an egg yesterday, we think someone's out for D'Olbriot heads to hang from their walls.'

Mistal looked sharply at me before scowling blackly in thought.

We came out on to a broad quayside, a few galleys tied up but quiet decks empty of all but a solitary watch. All their goods had been unloaded days earlier in good time for Festival buying sprees. This stretch of the sea front was owned by D'Olbriot, bollards and warehouse doors marked with the lynx for a good distance in either direction. Some whores were enjoying a brief respite on the paved walkways, plenty of room for them to stroll while the ropemakers were away enjoying their Festival along with everyone else. They'd be back on the first of Aft-Summer, stringing hemp between frames and posts, walking up and down as they turned handles twisting yarn into cables strong enough to hold the broad galleys secure in this wide anchorage and ropes for every lesser task. But for now we had space to walk and talk and not be overheard.

Mistal was looking with interest at a fetching little slattern with improbably auburn plaits. She was glancing back from beneath her painted eyelashes. He's a handsome man, much my height and colouring but with the finer features our mother has given him, whereas I have inherited our father's forthright jaw. But his looks would be of less interest to the whore than his dress; advocates are noted for their heavy purses. I nudged Mistal. 'You had something important to say? Or do you want to try a rush up her frills?'

'She can wait.' He gripped the fronts of his robe in a pose lawyers seem to learn in their first season around the courts. 'It's this colony of yours, the one D'Olbriot's mixed up in. Some people are looking very greedily out over the ocean.'

'Lescari mercenaries.' I nodded. 'I've heard those rumours.'

'Lescari mercenaries?' Mistal looked incredulous. 'They don't know sheep shit from dried grapes. Rysh, your Sieur is going to walk into a hailstorm of law suits tomorrow and I don't think he knows a thing about it.'

I stopped in my tracks. 'Who's bringing suit?'

'Tor Priminale for one.' Mistal raised one finger then a second. 'Den Rannion for another. They're claiming rights in this Kellarin colony on account of ancestral due.'

'How so?' We started walking again.

'As the Houses who originally backed the colony. They claim a share of the land, the minerals, timber, animals. Whatever's been turned into coin already, they want a penny in the Mark paid up prompt.'

'Can they do that?' I wondered.

'They can make an argument for it,' Mistal said grimly. 'I don't know how strong, but regardless, it'll tie your Sieur up in parchment tapes until Winter Solstice.'

'How do you know all this?' Lawyers are bound by oaths they hold no less dear than we swordsmen, oaths of confidentiality and good faith, sworn to Raeponin and enforced with crippling penalties if respect for the God of Justice doesn't keep them honest.

'I was asked to submit a reading on the question,' replied Mistal scornfully. 'Along with every other advocate who's ever argued a case on rights in property. Not because they wanted my opinion but to make sure that if D'Olbriot came looking for my services I'd have to cry off on account of prior interest.' He laughed without humour. 'Not that a Name like D'Olbriot is ever going to come looking for representation in the stalls where lowly advocates like me ply our trade.'

'But whoever's behind this didn't want to leave any rabbit hole unnetted before he sent in his ferrets.' I was getting the measure of this now. 'Tor Priminale is bringing suit? But the Demoiselle Guinalle is still alive, over in Kellarin. If the Name has any rights over there, she'd be their holder. Den Fellaemion was her uncle, and I'm sure he'd have willed his portion to her.' I'd have to ask Temar about that.

'Who's to say it's really her?' Mistal demanded. 'Who's to say she's still in her right mind after Saedrin knows how long under some cursed enchantment? I'll bet my robes against Mother's ragbag that someone's drawing up arguments like that to set aside her claims.'

'D'Olbriot can bring any number of witnesses to vouch for her wits,' I said scornfully.

'D'Olbriot witnesses?' queried Mistal. 'Anyone impartial? Wizards, perhaps? Mercenaries?'

'She'd have to present herself, wouldn't she?' I said slowly. 'Stand up in a court she's never seen, subject to laws she knows nothing of, harried with questions she'll struggle to understand. If she does answer, that ancient accent'll make her sound half-witted regardless.'

'She might well prove herself competent,' Mistal allowed, 'but she'll be spending Aft-Summer and both halves of Autumn in court to do it.'

'When she's one of the only two people with any real authority in Kellarin. How are they supposed to manage without her? I'm sorry.' I shook my head. 'I should have come to see you.'

'I could have made myself clearer,' said Mistal in some regret. 'But I didn't dare put this down on paper.' He looked round but there was no one within earshot. Even the pretty little whore had found some other amusement.

'I'll keep your name out of it when I tell the Sieur,' I promised soberly. If word of this got out no one would ever trust Mistal again and that would be the end of the legal career he's spent so many years pursuing.

'There's more.' Mistal sighed. 'Even allowing for Justiciary oaths, there are whispers in the wind. If Tor Priminale or Den Rannion get so much as a hearing, Den Muret will bring suit at Autumn Equinox and probably Den Domesin as well.'

I gaped at him. 'Both of them?'

He nodded firmly. 'And you were saying your Demoiselle Tor Priminale's so important to Kellarin? I take it Esquire D'Alsennin's just as significant?'

'Temar?' I stopped again, boot heels rapping on the stone.

'Tor Alder are bringing suit to have the D'Alsennin Name declared extinct,' said Mistal flatly. 'Apparently your Temar's mother married some Tor Alder back in the last days of the Old Empire. She bore him two sons and when the old Sieur

D'Alsennin died he left what remained of his holdings to that Tor Alder line, in trust against Temar or his sons ever coming back.'

'All signed and sealed and locked in a deed box for generations?' I almost laughed at the irony.

'You know what those ancient Houses are like,' Mistal nodded. 'They save every inky scribble down from the days of Correl the Potent. It's been Tor Alder's title to some of the best lands around Ast and a tidy stretch of property on the south side yonder.'

I looked out over the wide bay of Toremal, iridescent sea sparkling in the sunlight, ruffed here and there with white foam. The shore came sweeping round from distant northern headlands to the far-flung sandy stretches of the southern reaches, arms spread wide to welcome ships into a safe embrace. I'd no idea what land over there had been worth in Temar's era but nowadays the rents would likely pay for a fleet of ships to serve Kellarin and all the supplies he could load on them.

'How can they declare the Name extinct?' I demanded. 'Temar's still alive.'

'Only just, from what I heard yesterday in the tisane houses,' Mistal pointed out. 'And even if some dark sorcery brought him back from the brink of death—'

'Sadrin's stones!' I objected.

'That's what they're saying,' insisted Mistal. 'Anyway, even if he is alive with all his wits under his hat, there's only the one of him, an Esquire, no Sieur, no badge, no nothing as far as law codes written after the Chaos are concerned.'

'Anything else?' I hoped for a shake of Mistal's head.

He smiled. 'Just Den Thasnet arguing that D'Olbriot Land Tax should be assessed against the entire extent of Kellarin henceforth, given that House is the only beneficiary of all those resources.'

'They can go piss up a rope,' I said before I could stop myself.

'Quite possibly a case to argue.' Mistal struck a lawyerly

pose on the clean-swept cobbles. 'The sons of that House have been splashing their inheritance all over their boots since they could stand straight enough to hold out their pizzles, my lord Justiciar.'

I laughed briefly. 'Shit, Mist, this is serious.'

'It is,' he agreed, letting his grey robe fall back on his shoulders. 'And clever, because if Den Thasnet's argument is dismissed, that just strengthens Tor Priminale and the rest.'

'If Den Thasnet's upheld?' Was there some legal point to counter the obvious conclusion?

'Then D'Olbriot has the choice of bankrupting the House to pay the taxes or acknowledging Tor Priminale and all the others in a counter suit.' Mistal confirmed my worst suspicions.

We'd reached the far end of the quay by now, where a collection of little boats had been left high and dry by the tide. We turned back, both walking in silence, arms folded and brows knotted in thought, strides matching pace for pace.

' "Clever" and "Den Thasnet" aren't words you often use in the same breath,' I said after a long pause.

'Indeed not.' Mistal looked down at his hands, twisting the ring that signified his pledge to the Emperor's justice. 'They're puppets in this, I'll lay my oath on that.'

'So who's pulling their strings?' I demanded angrily. 'This stinks worse than cracked shellfish.'

'Which is why I wanted to warn you,' said Mistal grimly. 'My oath's supposed to protect those dealing with good faith, not shield someone using the law as a stalking horse for their own malice.'

'How long have you known about this?' I asked.

'I was asked to draw up an opinion on Festival Eve,' Mistal answered. 'Which is what made me suspicious. There's no way anyone could come up with a winning argument in that time. It had to be a tactic to spoil the spoor for anyone else.'

'But someone's willing to pay sound coin to do that,' I pointed out. 'If you're saying every clerk and advocate got the same retainer, that's a fair sack of gold someone's spending.'

'And they don't mind risking word leaking out, not at this stage,' Mistal commented. 'They're sure of themselves, which means someone's had archivists and advocates working on this for some while.'

'Lawyers won't break a confidence, but where do archivists and clerks go to wash library dust out of their throats?' I wondered.

'Who put the notion of a legal challenge in the Sieur Tor Priminale's head?' queried Mistal. 'And Den Rannion, Den Domesin and Den Muret, all at one and the same time? One bright clerk coming up with the idea, I could believe. Two? Perhaps in closely allied Houses, but the last time Tor Priminale and Den Rannion worked together on anything must have been your cursed colony. Four Names all going to law at the same time, every clerk in the town sent scurrying round the archives and every advocate retained? You'd need that gambler girl of yours to work out the odds against that being happenstance.'

I felt a pang at Mistal's dismissive reference to Livak. I'd expected our older brothers Hansey and Ridner to take against her, but I'd hoped Mist would like her. I looked at him. 'You say word of this will be getting out?'

'That D'Olbriot's going to be hip deep in horseshit tomorrow? You know what this town is like, Rysh.' Mistal shrugged. 'Some clerk, some advocate's runner will reckon that's too ripe a morsel to keep to himself.'

'Dast's teeth,' I cursed. 'I owe you for this, Mist, and so does the Sieur. Will I see you round the courts tomorrow?'

He hesitated. 'I can be seen with my brother but only if you're alone. Whoever's behind this won't waste a breath before accusing me of bad faith if I'm seen talking to anyone representing D'Olbriot without good reason.'

I nodded. 'Then you can walk back to safer streets with me. I can't leave you here in your nice clean robes for any passing footpad to club.'

'Just remember who's the oldest here,' Mistal warned me.

'Just remember what Mother said the last time she found

a cure for the scald in with your dirty linen. I'm not leaving you near all these brothels.'

We bickered amiably enough all the way back to the lower end of the Graceway, where Mistal turned off to head back to the warren of crumbling stone and worm-ridden wood that makes up the Imperial Courts of Law. I hailed a hireling gig and told the driver to get me back to D'Olbriot's residence as fast as his whip could manage.

The Library, D'Olbriot Residence, Summer Solstice Festival, Second Day, Noon

'And we may find something of interest here, Esquire.' An eager young man deposited yet another stack of dusty parchments in front of Temar.

'Thank you, Master Kuse.' Temar managed to sound grateful.

'Call me Dolsan,' said the saturnine youth as he leafed intently through the pile.

'Then you must call me Temar,' he said with feeling. 'Esquire D'Alsennin is over formal.'

'The Sieur likes formality.' The clerk brushed a cobweb from the front of his jerkin. 'Come to that, shouldn't you be the Sieur D'Alsennin by now?'

Temar sat back in his round-armed chair. 'Should I?'

Dolsan continued sorting documents. 'You're the elder male of the Name, so you're entitled to propose yourself in the absence of any others.'

Temar managed a shaky laugh. 'As far as I'm concerned my grandsire will always be the Sieur.'

'But what about everyone else's concerns?' Dolsan asked, head on one side.

'What has it to do with everyone else?' demanded Temar.

Dolsan raised hands to deflect the irritation in Temar's words. 'It's such an unusual occurrence, a Name reduced to one man. We've been trying to find precedent in the archives.'

'We?' Temar queried.

'The Sieur and myself,' Dolsan explained. 'And clerks from other Houses have commented in passing. We meet at the law courts, at archives and so on, sometimes share a few bottles of wine after a long day.'

Conversation over those cups must be mind-numbingly

boring, thought Temar. But then again, perhaps not. 'Have you friends in other Houses who might help us trace these people on my list?'

'Almost certainly,' Dolsan nodded. 'But it'll be easier if we can pinpoint the era and Name we're interested in.'

'Of course.' Temar bent over the creased and dingy parchment he'd been studying and Dolsan turned over tattered leaves he'd fetched from a dusty chest. Their soft fall was the only sound to disturb the graceful room. The walls were shelved from floor to ceiling, with only lavishly embroidered curtains hung at long windows to soften the all-encompassing severity of the thick leather tomes. A carpet richly patterned in gold and green carried a wide table polished to a glorious sheen surrounded by stylish chairs with cushions in D'Olbriot colours and several lamp stands stood ready to shed illumination if needed. A black marble fireplace with a gold-framed mirror over the mantel claimed the only expanse of wall not given over to books, fresh summer flowers bright instead of flames in the grate. The only incongruous note in all this sophistication was the stack of dark, dusty record chests inconveniencing anyone wanting to move around.

'We may have something here,' Temar said after a while. 'This inventory of the Maitresse Odalie's jewels mentions a silver brooch set with malachite. It came to her as part of an inheritance from a Tor Priminale aunt who died childless. We are missing a brooch like that and the woman it belonged to was from a family owing duty to Den Fellaemion.'

'Who were subsumed into Tor Priminale during the Chaos,' agreed Dolsan. 'The fact you can read archaic script makes this so much easier, you know.' He reached for a vast sheet of parchment covered in fine writing. 'Here we are, marriages under Kanselin the Droll. Odalie had four daughters, two of whom married within the Name, one married into D'Istrac, and the youngest married into Den Breval.'

Temar glanced up. 'Do you know anyone serving either Name?'

Dolsan leaned on his elbows, cupping his face in his hands.

'I know a couple of clerks working for D'Istrac, but Den Breval's a northern House; their archive's in Ast. I know Den Breval had to defend in an argument over grazing rights a few years back. They'd have hired Toremal help for that and I might find someone who knows something, at least where any copies of Den Breval records might be lodged. Remote Names often leave things in the Toremal archives of allied Houses.'

'Ryshad was right when he said you were the man for this job.' Temar shook his head. Would he ever get all these Names and their relations straight? It was doubtless all very well if you imbibed such things with mother's milk but this flood of information all at once threatened to choke him. 'But I admit I expected a sober old man with a long grey beard.'

Dolsan smiled as he returned to his ancient records. 'That sounds like my grandsire.'

'He was a clerk? You followed his trade?' Temar nodded; of course that would be the way of it.

Dolsan looked up. 'Oh, no, he just had the beard. He was a cobbler, and my father after him. But we're D'Olbriot tenants and that means the chance of better schooling than most. My teachers said I had a talent for words and recommended me to the Sieur's Archivist.'

'Do you enjoy your work?' asked Temar curiously.

'Very much,' laughed Dolsan. 'And anything's better than spending the days pricking my thumbs with a leather needle.'

'You must meet the scholars we have in Kel Ar'Ayen.' They shared this bizarre, intense determination to tease the truth of history from faded records and partial accounts, Temar recalled.

'Perhaps, one day,' Dolsan said politely.

A tap on the door made them both turn their heads. 'Enter,' called Dolsan when it was clear Temar wasn't about to respond.

'Good day to you, Esquire, Master Clerk.' Allin slid into the room, closing the door behind her. ' I was looking for Demoiselle Tor Arrial?'

'Avila?' Temar shook his head. 'She has gone out with Lady Channis.'

'Oh.' Allin looked uncertain. 'Oh dear.'

'Why did you want her?' Temar seized this welcome distraction from the documents stacked before him.

'It wasn't anything important,' said Allin in unconvincing tones. 'Don't let me disturb you.'

The gatehouse struck the five chimes of noon and Dolsan let slip a sigh of relief. 'My lady, I think we've earned a break, so you're not interrupting us.' He got to his feet. 'If you'll excuse me, Esquire, I'll go and eat. How soon would you like me back here?'

'Take your time, have a decent meal and some fresh air.' Temar turned to Allin. 'May I escort you to the upper hall?'

'Oh, no, thank you but it's not really—' stammered Allin.

Temar looked at her pink cheeks. 'Dolse, would you do us a small service?'

The clerk turned on the threshold. 'Esquire?'

'Could you send word to the kitchens. We'll eat in here, nothing too elaborate.' Temar turned to Allin with a faint smile. 'I am hardly in the mood for formality either.'

Dolsan hesitated. 'You won't get food or drink near any documents?'

'Of course not.' The door closed behind the clerk and Temar began folding parchments along their dusty creases. 'Please, do be seated. So, why did you want Demoiselle Tor Arrial?'

Allin took a chair, reached for a skein of faded ribbon and began tying documents into neat bundles. 'Oh, nothing important.' She blushed when she saw Temar's raised brows. 'Well, Velindre said it wasn't.'

'May I be the judge of that?' Temar didn't see why Allin should always have other people telling her what to do and what not to do, even he must.

Allin fumbled in the pocket of her skirt. 'Velindre's come to the Festival to find out what the Tormalins think of magic these days.' She unfolded coarse paper. 'So we've been picking up handbills, to see if any wizards are earning money from magical displays.'

Temar read the blocky letters aloud. ' "Saedrin locks the

door to the Otherworld to mortals but a few favoured ones may listen at the keyhole. Poldrion charges mortals the ferry fee he judges his due but brings visions back across the river of death without charge. Many questions may be answered by those with the sight to see them. Seek your answers from Mistress Maedura at the Fetterlock Inn, from sunset on every day of Festival. Suitable payment for services rendered must be made in Tormalin coin." The style falls off a little at the end, I think?' He looked at Allin. 'You suspect this is some magical charade?'

Allin shifted uncomfortably in her chair. 'Velindre thinks it's just some confidence play to trick gullible Lescaris out of their coin.'

'Why Lescaris?' Temar was puzzled.

Allin sighed. 'Trying to see something of the Otherworld, it's rather a Lescari obsession. Everyone's lost so many friends, families get split up, sons go off to fight and never return. People use all manner of divinations to try and find out what happened to loved ones; rune-telling, Soluran prediction, Aldabreshin omens.'

'I am confused.' Temar rubbed a hand over his hair. 'What has this to do with Demoiselle Tor Arrial?'

'I wondered if it might be aetheric enchantment if it wasn't elemental magic.' The plump girl set her jaw, giving an unexpected strength to her round face. 'I wondered if the Demoiselle might come with me?' Allin raised hopeful eyes to Temar.

He didn't think it fair to tell her the scathing response she'd probably get. 'Will Velindre not accompany you?'

'She has a dinner engagement,' said Allin regretfully. 'Tormalin mages gather for Festival like everyone else and there are wizards she wants to ask about the status of magic hereabouts.'

Temar was diverted by sudden curiosity. 'What do wizards do in Tormalin?'

Allin looked at him with faint surprise. 'They earn a living, same as everywhere else. Those with fire affinity help metal-workers and foundries, those linked to water find work with shipbuilders or something like that. But there's still a lingering suspicion of wizards in Tormalin, so they're only ever given short-term work, for a specific project usually.'

'The mages in Kel Ar'Ayen are none too ready to lend magical aid to such mundane tasks. They always make it out to be some great favour.' Temar shook his head. 'But why are mages so suspect on this side of the ocean?'

'After the Chaos?' Allin looked puzzled. 'Hasn't anyone told you this?'

Temar smiled appealingly at her. 'We are generally too busy with the day-to-day business of living in Kel Ar'Ayen for idle chatter.'

'Oh.' Allin looked round the room for a moment before visibly making a decision. 'I don't suppose it reflects very well on wizardry, so that's probably why no one's mentioned it. Some warfare in the Chaos was backed with elemental magic. Fire and flood, lightning, they were all used on battlefields. Other magic was wrought against encampments, armies found themselves mired in bogs where they'd been riding through pasture, that kind of thing.'

'So Houses backed by wizards had a significant advantage,' nodded Temar with interest.

Allin grimaced. 'Magic's a powerful ally in the short term, but in the longer term it's not that crucial. You can drive an army off a battlefield with waves of flame but magic won't help you hold the land you win. A single spellcaster soon exhausts himself; Cloud-Master Otrick makes sure every apprentice mage learns that. In any case, there were never that many wizards willing to turn their talents to warfare and once other Houses started banishing any mage-born – or doing worse – there were even fewer. But prejudice against magic in Tormalin persists.'

'But Artifice held the Empire together.' Temar frowned. 'Adepts in aetheric magic were highly respected. Everyone acknowledged that their work served the greater good.'

'And the magic went away and everything fell into Chaos?' Allin raised her eyebrows. 'Who do you suppose they blamed?'

'If what Guinalle says is true, they were right to do so.' Temar bit his lip. 'It seems the struggles of the Kel Ar'Ayen

Adepts against the ancient Elietimm somehow undermined the whole aetheric balance underpinning Artifice.'

'I heard some scholars visiting Hadrumal from Vanam arguing about that,' Allin nodded. 'Wizardry did some truly dreadful things, before Trydek brought the mage-born under his rule, and the tales are still told, doubtless exaggerated with each repeating. It's small wonder all most people believe is magic is magic and it's suspect, whatever its hue or origin. There are precious few people outside Hadrumal who even know about aetheric magic and its role in the Old Empire. The world has moved on, more than you know.'

'More than I am allowed to know, it would seem,' said Temar lightly, but anger sparked a gleam in his eye.

Allin looked at her hands. 'Perhaps I shouldn't have said anything.'

'I will not tell anyone you did.' Temar looked thoughtfully at Allin. 'The wizards I know mostly want to live in Hadrumal pursuing their scholarship. You are not much like them.'

Allin hesitated. 'Scholarship's important. Velindre spends her life trying to understand the work of the winds, what happens to air when it is warmed by fire or cooled over water. The more she understands, the more precise her magic can be, the more exact her control over the element of her affinity. It takes little more than instinct to raise a gale if you're mage-born, but to use air to cool a sick child's fever, to carry a word across a thousand leagues, that takes a depth of understanding that only study can give. That's the whole reason for Hadrumal's existence.'

'But such study is not for you?' guessed Temar.

Allin blushed. 'I want to learn enough to make my magic useful, but I'm no scholar.'

'Then what will you do with your useful magecraft?' asked Temar, teasing a little.

'I'd like to go home but magic's even more suspect in Lescar than anywhere else.' A hint of tears shone faintly in Allin's eyes. 'Each Duke's afraid someone else will enlist a wizard to fight on their side.'

'Which might at least bring all that sorry warfare to an end,' said Temar curtly. He waited a moment for the girl to regain her composure. 'Forgive me. So, if you can not go home, what would you do?'

'There are Lescari in exile all over what you knew as the Empire, mostly in Caladhria or Tormalin.' Allin looked at the paper lying on the table. 'Some do very well for themselves, settle and grow rich, but others struggle. There must be some way to use magecraft to earn a living from the wealthy and to help the weak better themselves.'

Temar studied the handbill himself, the silence in the room like a held breath.

'But Velindre dislikes you associating with other Lescari?' He set his jaw.

'Oh, no,' said Allin, flustered. 'She just doesn't think this is worth pursuing, and in any case she has other calls on her time.'

Temar looked at the handbill again and clicked his tongue absently against his teeth. 'This could be Artifice, used to read minds, tell people what they want to hear. There would be a value in determining that.'

'Whoever's doing this might have some way to find people, maybe even people sleeping in an enchanted artefact,' suggested Allin tentatively.

Temar looked searchingly at the girl. 'Are there not people you wish to find?'

Allin knotted her hands on the table before her. 'I'm luckier than most,' she said determinedly. 'I know where my parents are, my brothers and sisters. When the fighting finally rolled our way at least we managed to stay together. But I had uncles, aunts, cousins in and around Carluse. They were scattered to the four winds when our new Duke decided it was his turn to claim the Lescari throne and his Grace of Sharlac slapped him down.' She cleared her throat but said nothing further.

Temar felt a pang at the thought of his own family, long lost to him beyond Saedrin's door. 'What if this person can really contact the dead?' he wondered aloud. 'What if I could speak to Vahil? To Elsire?' What if he could speak to his mother, his grandsire, ask their advice once again?

'Vahil was the Sieur Den Rannion that came back from the colony?' Allin leaned forward.

Temar laid his long-fingered hands flat to stop them trembling. 'What if I could ask him where the artefacts were sent, who got the pieces we are missing? It will take an army of clerks a full round of seasons to worm such secrets out of these archives. What if Vahil could save us all that work?'

'So you'll speak to the Demoiselle?' Allin laid an unthinking hand on Temar's.

'We do not need her.' Temar gave Allin's fingers an encouraging squeeze. 'You said you were no scholar. Well, neither am I, but I have learned enough of Artifice to know if someone is working it in the same room. I will come with you. If we learn something to our advantage then we can share the pleasure of telling Velindre she was wrong. If it turns out we are looking for wool in a goat shed, then no one need ever know.' He hesitated. 'Except Ryshad, he had best come with us. Meet me at the gatehouse at sunset and we can all go together.'

As Allin nodded, the door opened. A curious lackey moved to one side to let two maids carry trays into the room. Allin blushed scarlet and pulled her hands free of Temar's.

Temar looked at the maids with a fair approximation of the blank aloofness he found so irritating in these latter-day nobles. All three servants kept their eyes lowered, but as the door shut behind them Temar clearly heard a giggle overlaying a murmur of hushed speculation. Both were hastily cut short by a curt enquiry in a familiar voice.

'Master Devoir,' Temar greeted Casuel courteously as the wizard stuck a suspicious face round the door. 'We were just about to have some lunch.'

'Allin? What are you doing here?' Casuel came in carrying two tall stacks of books carefully secured with leather straps, cloth padding protecting the covers against any injury to the binding. 'Esquire D'Alsennin isn't supposed to have any visitors today.'

'Oh, you were hurt, weren't you?' Allin's eyes were wide

with concern. 'Are you all right? But I did send word from the gate, to ask the Sieur's permission.'

'Thanks to the Demoiselle's Artifice, I am fully healed.' Temar smiled at her. 'So, Casuel, what have you there?'

'More clues for your search, if you can tease them out,' said the mage loftily.

'Velindre was saying you must have a source of information second to none,' said Allin unexpectedly.

Casuel smiled a little uncertainly as he began unstrapping the books. 'There are few wizards in Tormalin in these rational days and fewer who are also antiquarians.'

'She was talking about your brother?' Allin looked innocently at him. 'Velindre says he must hear all manner of news and opinion.'

Casuel's smile turned sickly. 'I hardly think he'll have anything useful to contribute.'

Temar looked from Allin to Casuel, carefully hiding a smile. 'Pardon me, but I did not know you had a brother, Casuel.'

'Amalin Devoir is a noted musician, a composer of considerable skill and innovation,' Allin explained with artless admiration. 'His works are played right across Lescar and Caladhria.'

'Another talented member of your family.' Temar smiled as Casuel inclined his head with ill grace. 'Surely it could not hurt to see if he could help us?'

'I could call on him, I suppose,' the wizard said reluctantly. 'But I think we'll get far more out of these books. So, if you'll excuse us, Allin, we've important work to do.'

'Allin is staying for some lunch,' Temar said firmly. With his face turned he could wink at her without Casuel seeing, and she bit her lower lip to hide a smile, cheeks pink as she studied a parchment in front of her with hasty intensity.

Esquire Camarl's Study, the D'Olbriot Residence, Summer Solstice Festival, Second Day, Afternoon

'I came straight here to warn you.' I concluded my explanation of Mistal's news and waited for the Esquire's reaction, hands behind my back and feet a quarter-span apart. The calm stance belied my inner agitation, my desire to be out running rumour and suspicion to ground.

Camarl was sitting by the window, a small table at his side piled high with correspondence. He turned a carved ivory paper knife slowly in his hands. 'This is certainly ominous news, as is this business of someone posting a challenge in your name. You should have told me about that this morning, before going off to the sword school.' He looked up at me, raising the ivory knife even though I'd made no move to speak. 'I'm not going to bandy words with you. Chosen or not, Ryshad, you have to keep me informed. Is there any other news, anything about the attack on D'Alsennin?'

I sighed. 'Last night I went round every barracks where I've friends, every Cohort I've shared duty with, asked every watchman hired for Festival that I could find. If any of them knew anything or even suspected, they'd have told me by now. I'll wager my oath fee there are no Elietimm in the city, but I can't swear any more than that. I've still got a few people to check back with, but I don't think they'll have anything different to tell.'

'You can send one of the sworn from the barracks to fetch and carry messages. I want your help looking for answers in different places.' Camarl smiled to take any rebuke out of his words. 'I'm going to a meeting of my art society this afternoon.' Camarl indicated the discreet elegance of his sober clothing with a hand bearing a solitary silver band enamelled with the D'Olbriot lynx. 'I meet men of all ranks there and I'll hear a certain amount of the gossip about D'Alsennin, Kellarin and the rest, but everyone knows my Name, so most will guard their tongues. I think you should come with me, Ryshad. No one knows you, so you might catch some indiscretion.'

'If I ask the right questions,' I agreed slowly. It wouldn't be the first time I'd kept eyes and ears open for the House's benefit. There was far more to being a sworn man in this day and age than simply swinging a sword. 'But are you sure I won't be recognised?' I spent a good few years serving in Toremal before the Sieur sent me out on his various commissions to ride the vast D'Olbriot estates.

'No one looks at a sworn man's face,' Camarl said carelessly. 'You'll just have been another nameless body in livery.'

'Am I dressed for the part?' I was in plain breeches and a nondescript jerkin, good-quality cloth and well cut but nothing special.

'Quite appropriate, for a mason from Zyoutessela, wouldn't you say?' said Camarl with an approving smile. 'There'll be other artisans there, as well as traders and nobles. It's one of the reasons I joined, to widen my acquaintance beyond my own rank.'

'What does the Sieur think of that?' I asked.

Camarl wrinkled his nose. 'He agrees it's a regrettable necessity of this era.'

I laughed, hearing the Sieur's dry wit in the words.

'I have letters that need an answer.' Camarl nodded to his personal scrivener, who was sitting patiently in a corner of the room. 'I'll see you at the gatehouse shortly, Ryshad. Get something to eat if you need it.'

The lower hall was full of kitchen maids and scullions now, drab in washed-out gowns and shirts shapeless with repeated boiling. They gossiped idly, enjoying some respite before embarking on the myriad preparations for a series of private dinners in the smaller salons and the more ceremonial banquet that the Sieur would host that evening. Lady Channis always made sure no formal lunches were planned for days when the House entertained in the evening. The pot-washers and vegetable-peelers cast envious glances at the cooks, everyone plainly ranked by their chapped hands. The lowest slaveys from the scullery were scarlet to the wrist; the premier pastrycooks and the Master of the Kitchens could afford discreet lace at their cuffs and scrupulously manicured nails.

I took bread and cheese from platters on a table and went out to the gatehouse, where I knew I could cadge a glass of wine from Stoll. We had scant moments to wait before Camarl's personal gig arrived, and the Esquire wasn't long in coming.

The groom jumped down and swung himself up on the back step as the Esquire took the reins. As Camarl drove us down to the lower city with habitual competence, I turned to the groom on the perch behind us. He was staring ahead, face as impassive as the carved cats' masks on the side panels, and he wouldn't meet my eye. I really was going to have to get used to being one of those served rather than serving.

The bright sunlight was touched with the faintest hint of salt on a breeze from the distant harbour as Camarl turned off the encircling road down the main highway that runs clear across the lower city to the bay. The ancient walls of Toremal soon appeared between the rooftops, once mighty bastions in their day but now hemmed in all around with buildings nearly as high. Camarl got his horse in hand as we went beneath the sturdy arch of the Spring Gate and we emerged into the sunshine gilding the Graceway. Great mansions had been packed close within the old city walls in the uncertain days of earlier generations and the Names had guarded their privileges jealously. Nowadays the iron gates, with their badges of gilded bronze high above the heads of the crowd, stand open but rank still counts for something. It's only those with a genuine amulet bearing recognised insignia that may use the wide, well-made street marching straight to the sea. I saw a woman trying to saunter past the duty guard with a beribboned basket held high in her arms and smiled as she was turned back to take the longer route through the tangle of lesser roads spreading ever wider beyond the walls. We were passed with a curt nod from the Den Janaquel man standing sentry, pike butt resting by one hobnailed boot.

'Do you know anyone sworn to Den Janaquel?' Camarl asked as we whipped the horse to a trot in the comparatively empty road. 'They're providing the Duty Cohort for the Festival, so they'll hear more news than anyone else.'

'I've never had dealings with the House but I'll see if I can get an introduction through the sword school.' Stoll probably knew someone, or if he didn't Fyle would. Fyle knew everyone.

Out of long habit I noted changes to the buildings lining the Graceway. What had once been a Den Bradile mansion was being refaced with pale new marble; trim, rational lines replacing the curlicues of an earlier age. The handful of shops now sharing the façade were getting broad new windows with deep sills for the better display of elegant trinkets for ladies, costly feathers and expensive lace. Further along a seamstress who'd been a tenant of Den Thasnet since before I'd come to Toremal had given up her lease to be replaced by some hopeful new tailor owing duty to the Name. His frontage was brightly decked to attract both year-round residents and those eager to buy the latest fashions on their once-yearly trip to this hub of sophistication.

This wasn't Bremilayne, where I had little local knowledge and few contacts. This wasn't chasing backwoods rumour in a fruitless quest for Elietimm sneaking into Dalasor to rob and maim. Whoever had attacked Temar had stepped on my ground. They had to have left tracks. Someone would get a scent, sooner or later.

'And here we are.' Camarl's words broke into my thoughts. We were outside a tisane house, once a wing of some long-vanished residence. Now it boasted a brightly painted sign telling all and sundry that Master Lediard could supply the finest aromatics and spices and the most luxurious premises in which to enjoy them.

Camarl handed the reins to his groom. 'Call for me at eighth chime.' He pressed a negligent silver Mark into the man's palm but all I could offer was a smile so I hurried after the Esquire. I prefer wine to tisanes as a rule but I could get used to drinking them in these surroundings. This was no futile attempt to drag a failing tavern up the social scale by offering hot water and stale herbs in place of ale.

Comfortable chairs ringed sturdy tables set just far enough apart to stop people hearing other conversations. Most tables were spread with parchments, ledgers and counting frames, since tisanes have always been popular with men of business, who might lose more than the cost of the flagon if they let wine blunt their acuity. Some men bent solitary over their documents, some sat in twos and threes deep in talk, others relaxed with one of the latest broadsheets, plentiful copies racked by the door. A baize-covered panel beside it was criss-crossed with leather straps holding letters tucked securely beneath. A lad was emptying folded and sealed sheets out of a box below it. The nobility have the Imperial Despatch to carry their letters but the middle ranks have to rely on these more informal arrangements between tisane houses and inns.

I overhead a snatch of intense discussion as Camarl let a lass in a dull blue gown slip past with a tray laden with little bowls of spice.

'I'll take a fifth share in the cargo, against covering you if the ship's lost.'

'Toremal value or Relshaz value?'

'Relshaz value at Equinox's best prices.'

'But what if they're delayed by bad weather? Prices could be falling by the time they arrive.'

'That's your risk, friend. Mine's the ship sinking.'

The man beside us selected some ivory tags from a shallow tray in the middle of his table. He handed them to a girl who took them to a sharp-eyed woman behind a long counter.

'We're upstairs,' said Camarl back over his shoulder.

As I followed him, I noticed the woman spooning the required herbs from the vast array of canisters on the shelves at her back. As the maid delivered the tisane ingredients to her waiting customer, another arrived with cups, tisane balls and a jug of steaming water, carried carefully from the far end of the room where a red-faced man tended an array of kettles on a vast range that greedily consumed the coal shovelled into its open maw by an ash-stained lad.

I followed the Esquire up a panelled staircase to find the whole first floor of the building was opened into a single room. Tables and chairs ranged around the walls were largely ignored by the busy crowd all talking at once in the middle. Plain coats, everyday jerkins and practical boots were the order of dress, though the discerning eye would see Camarl's clothes were a cut above the rest in both cloth and tailoring.

'D'Olbriot!' A burly man in an ochre coat strained at the buttons waved at Camarl.

'Fair Festival, Master Sistrin,' he replied cheerfully.

'Let's hope so.' Sistrin planted hands on hips as he jutted his chin at a younger man wearing the brooch of a minor House on his jerkin. 'What does D'Olbriot think of some of us traders setting up our own academy with our own funds?'

'Endowing schools has always been the honour and duty of the nobility,' the young man said politely. I managed to place the badge; a cadet line of Den Hefeken.

'But we have more sons wanting places than the established colleges can supply,' commented a third man, accents of the merchant class ringing in his voice. 'Learning letters and reckoning in a dame-school may have been enough for our fathers and forefathers, but times have changed.'

'If we endow a school, we have a say in what they teach.' Sistrin jabbed an emphatic finger at Den Hefeken. 'Rhetoric and precedence in Convocation and what House holds which priesthood aren't much use to my boy. He needs mathematics, geography, drawing up a contract and knowing which law codes back it up. Come to that, we've daughters who'd do well to learn more than sewing a seam or playing a pretty spinet.'

'With all D'Olbriot's mining interests, you could do worse

than teach your Esquires some natural science,' sniffed the third man.

'I quite agree, Palbere,' Camarl nodded. 'Our tutors having been doing just that since the turn of the year, assisted by some newcomers from Hadrumal.'

'Wizards?' Sistrin laughed heartily. 'That'd be unnatural science, then would it?'

Did I feel an unusual disapproval chill the air at the mention of wizards? Den Hefeken's face was a well-bred blank but Palbere was scowling

Camarl continued, unconcerned. 'I'd prefer my cousins learned their lessons alongside your nephews, Sistrin, rather than see schools divided by rank or trade. They'll pick up some understanding of your glass trade, and shared knowledge is always a road to common prosperity.'

Palbere sipped at a steaming tisane. 'Talking of roads, is it true D'Olbriot plans on digging a canal to cut the loop of the Nyme around Feverad? Will you be bringing wizards in to do the work of honest labourers there?'

'Feverad merchants first mooted the plan,' said Camarl cautiously. 'They've suggested D'Olbriot might care to back the project and magical assistance makes such tasks considerably faster and safer.'

'So you'll be taking the revenues off the rest of us when it's built?' Den Hefeken asked with careful neutrality.

'If it's built, and surely we'd be entitled to recoup our outlay?' Camarl looked at each man in turn. 'Of course, those costs would be considerably reduced by employing wizards' skills.'

Sistrin drew breath on some further argument but Camarl raised an apologetic hand. 'Forgive me gentlemen, I have a guest with me today. May I make known Ryshad Tathel, stone mason of Zyoutessela.'

Several nearby heads turned away from their conversations to note my name and I smiled as benignly as I could.

'Are you sponsoring him to the society?' Sistrin asked belligerently.

'If he decides it's for him,' smiled Camarl before drawing me politely away.

'That's one man won't leave you wondering about his opinions,' I commented in a low voice.

'Which makes him very useful, because what he says ten men more discreet are thinking,' agreed Camarl. 'And he's usually first with any hint of scandal, while Palbere has a nose for business second to none.'

'Do you do anything even vaguely connected to art here?' I grinned.

'Over here.' Camarl kept pausing to greet people but we finally edged our way through to the far end of the room, where tables in the better light under the windows were covered with books of engravings and single sheets of inked and coloured paper. 'Boudoir art is over there,' indicated Camarl with a smile, 'next to the satires and lampoons. We pride ourselves on being an open-minded society.'

Both artwork and model would doubtless be a considerable improvement on the grubby woodcuts that circulated round the barracks but neither interested me when all I had to do was shut my eyes and think of Livak. I picked up a small portfolio. '*Plants of the Dalasor Grasslands*?' I opened it on a beautifully detailed painting of a yellow heather.

'Several of our members are natural philosophers,' nodded Camarl. 'And as a mason, you might be interested in the architectural drawings over there.'

'Esquire, might I have a word?' A long-faced elder with depressed dewlaps framing a downturned mouth appeared at Camarl's shoulder. 'Master Ganalt, of course.'

I noted the old man wore the silver-leaf collar of a shrine fraternity, something you don't see so often these days.

'It's the shrine to Talagrin on the Solland road,' Ganalt began after a hesitant glance at me. 'It's on Den Bradile land and the priesthood's in their family, naturally, but the local people have always been faithful to the Hunter—' The old man fell silent.

'Is there some problem?' prompted Camarl.

'There's rumour Den Bradile intend making it a private cinerarium, even planning to removing urns already consecrated there unless they're linked to the Name in some way.' He lifted an unconscious hand to his silver rowan leaves, emblem of the Lord of the Forest. 'We might use our funds to build another shrine, but we're pledged to helping the poor . . .' He broke off with another dubious look at me.

'Excuse me, Esquire, I'd like to look at some of those plans you mentioned.' I nodded as much of a bow as I could in the confined space and slid past two men chuckling over a vivid satire. The architectural drawings included a series of maze designs, something increasingly fashionable in recent years, and I studied them with interest.

'The trick is matching suitable mathematical complexity with the tenets of Rationalism,' commented a man coming to stand next to me.

'And finding shrubs that grow fast enough to make a maze worth having before the whole thing goes out of fashion?' I suggested.

'There's that,' he agreed. 'Which is why this year's innovation is patterns laid out in bricks between little raised banks. I believe a Den Haurient gardener suggested it but the Rationalists will tell you it's so the logic of the whole can be better appreciated by seeing the whole design.'

I laughed, picking up an interesting perspective on new alterations to an old frontage.

'I hear you're a mason?' remarked my new companion. 'From the south?'

'Zyoutessela,' I kept my tone as casual as his.

'Is there plenty of work?' he asked with interest.

'The city's thrice the size it was in my grandsire's day,' I nodded. 'He hired himself from site to site with little more than a bag of tools and rock-hard determination to better himself. When he died, he left my father a sizeable yard and me and now my brothers work three sites.'

'They say a good block of stone rings like a bell,' remarked my would-be acquaintance with studied idleness.

'If you strike it right, and there's a tang to fine stone, like rotten eggs.' Hansey and Ridner were welcome to all the smells, the dust, the noise and headaches that went with the trade.

'Redvar Harl, Master Carpenter.' He bowed and I returned the courtesy. 'I saw you arrive with Esquire Camarl? Are you D'Olbriot tenants?'

He was very interested in me for a complete stranger but I didn't think he was about to stab me in an entire room of witnesses. 'We are.'

'There must be all manner of opportunities in the south, what with D'Olbriot sponsoring this colony overseas,' my new friend mused.

'It offers some intriguing possibilities,' I said in neutral tones.

My companion stared out of the window. 'D'Olbriot will want to do the best for their tenants, but if this land's as big as rumour has it Esquire Camarl might do well to think in rather broader terms.'

I nodded silent encouragement.

'I'm from Solland. I take it you've heard about the fighting in Parnilesse, after the old Duke's death?'

It wasn't hard to see my next step in this dance. 'Down in the south, we don't hear that much about border matters.'

'D'Olbriot has holdings around Solland, so the Sieur will be fully aware of the Lescari land question.' Master Harl turned to look intently at me. 'The Lescari still cling to their foolish system of all land going to the eldest born. Then they breed like the rabbits that infest their hills, whelping useless younger sons left landless and looking for a quarrel. Poldrion knows how much grief could be saved if those surplus spawn could be shipped across the ocean, to make their way in a new land by their own efforts.'

'That's an interesting notion,' I said slowly. 'I'd be interested to know what Esquire Camarl might make of it.' I could guess Temar's reaction.

Master Harl's eyes shifted to a point behind my shoulder.

'Excuse me, there's someone I must wish a Fair Festival.'

I turned to see whom he meant but Camarl stepped into my line of sight, a carefully constructed expression of amusement on his face. 'Now, Ryshad, what do you make of this?'

He handed me a crisp sheet of paper printed with a hand-coloured satire. A wedding carriage was being drawn through the streets of Toremal by the D'Olbriot lynx on the one hand and the Tor Tadriol bull on the other. This wasn't the robust animal of the Emperor's badge but a sickly calf with a foolish expression and comical spotted hide. The high-stepping lynx topped it by a head, looking down with avid eyes and sharp teeth exposed in a hungry smile. The Emperor himself was in the carriage, an unexceptional portrait but plainly recognisable. I tapped the face of the girl beside him, a vapid beauty with an unfeasibly large bosom. 'Is this anyone I should know?'

'No one in particular.' Camarl shook his head, fixed smile still not reaching his eyes. 'But I've a full handful of cousins of an age and breeding to make a good match for Tadriol. Most are here for Festival, naturally enough.'

I studied a capering fool in the foreground throwing handfuls of fire and lightning up into the air, stunning a few thatch birds in the process. The onlookers were barely sketched in but a few eloquent lines deftly conveyed expressions of contempt, ridicule and dissatisfaction. 'Do you reckon that's Casuel?'

The Esquire's smile widened and did reach his eyes. 'He'd hardly be flattered to think so. But few people know him and those that do find him inoffensive to the point of tedium. That's one of the reasons we agreed to him being Planir's liaison; no one could possibly see him as a threat.'

'Whoever drew this certainly doesn't like the idea of magic.' I pointed to a hooded figure in sooty robes stalking behind the carriage, people drawing back from his ominous shadow. 'Would that be Planir the Black, do you suppose?'

'The name's a gift to satirists, isn't it?' muttered Camarl with irritation.

'An apprentice joke, as I understand it,' I explained, 'on account of him being a coal miner's son.'

'We all have to take jokes in good part, don't we?' Camarl's eyes were cold and calculating once again. 'Why don't you see what other people here make of the jest?'

I weighed the paper in my hand and studied the detail of the picture. Engraving a plate to that standard was no overnight task. 'There's coin backing this artist.' I looked for a signature but couldn't find one.

'An unusually retiring satirist, now there's a novelty.' Camarl was clearly on the same scent as me. 'Why don't I see if someone can point me in his direction? After all, a talent like that deserves encouragement.'

'I'd say he's already got some noble patron,' I observed.

'Quite likely,' agreed Camarl. 'And perhaps he'll be prepared to say who, in return for a commission to create as handsome a joke at their expense, along with some D'Olbriot gold.'

Several heads close by turned at the Esquire's words, expressions eager. Genteel dispute between two great Houses would certainly liven up Festival, with scurrilous pictures to snigger over for a few coppers and discreet hints of scandal spicing up the usually stodgy fare of the broadsheets.

I'd track down the printer, I decided. There was no hope of stopping such things circulating: with books so costly, printers with mouths to feed need every copper they can tempt folk to spare on a sheet of gossip or a lewdly entertaining picture. But a few crowns might buy me some clue as to this tidbit's origin.

'Let's see what we can find out,' I said softly. I wasn't about to forget the Elietimm but I reckoned we had more serious concerns now, enemies closer at hand, enemies who knew how to use oath-bound ritual, the law courts and the thriving social networks of the city against us. And they weren't above knives in the back either, I reminded myself.

'Have you seen this?' I tapped a stranger on the arm in friendly fashion, introduced myself and we shared a chuckle over the satire. He offered an unsubtle depiction of some recent excesses by the younger Esquires Den Thasnet, which prompted his companion, a linen draper, to warn me against working for that House, claiming they were notorious bad debtors.

By the time I'd worked my way round the gathering and drunk more tisane than I usually do in a season, I was well up to date with the latest scandals, intrigues, births, deaths and marriages of Houses from the highest to the most lowly. I also shared in plenty of conversations where the nobility barely warranted a mention, an unaccustomed reminder of the life I'd known before I'd sworn myself to D'Olbriot, when the Name was merely a faceless rent office and a vague promise of help should some crisis strike our family. It was an interesting way of spending an afternoon but what I didn't hear was any particular malice directed at D'Olbriot, D'Alsennin or Kellarin. There was plenty of speculation, but most of these solid men of business were more interested in debating the potential opportunities and hazards of a new trading partner on the far side of the ocean.

Esquire Camarl signalled to me from the far side of the room and I made my excuses to an apothecary who'd been displaying considerable if completely ill-informed interest in Artifice.

'I have to go, I'm expected at Den Haurient for some discussions and then dinner.' Camarl was looking just a trifle exasperated. 'I have to go back to dress.'

'I've not heard anything significant,' I told him with regret.

He let out a slow breath. 'Stay for a while longer. People may let some indiscretion slip if I'm not here.'

'I'll keep my ears pricked,' I promised.

But the Esquire wasn't the only one engaged to dine elsewhere and his departure prompted a growing number to make their excuses. The determined core who remained began pulling chairs into comradely circles and called for wine rather than tisanes from Master Lediard's obliging maidservants.

I was going to look conspicuous if I tried to inveigle myself into those tight groups of long-standing friends, I decided.

These men might not realise I was one of D'Olbriot's chosen, but they knew at very least I was a tenant of the House. The casual atmosphere where someone might let slip a hint by accident or design had evaporated.

I made brief farewells to a few of my new acquaintances and left. Standing out on the flagway, I wondered what to do next as leisurely couples went strolling past arm in arm now the heat of the day had faded and the rich and elegant came out to admire each other in all their Festival finery.

I could go back and kick my heels in the gatehouse, waiting to tell Camarl I'd learned nothing new, I thought, or I could do something more useful with my time. It was all very well the Esquire telling me to send sworn and recognised about my errands but I could hardly expect them to explain all the complexities of Temar's search for his lost artefacts, could I? I had enough trouble making that tale sound convincing, and I'd been part of it.

I made up my mind and turned down the Graceway. Revellers were spilling out of taverns and inns with their goblets and beakers of wine and ale, so I stepped into the roadway. There was little enough traffic and, armring or not, most people hereabouts looked for me to step aside for them. I worked my way down to the heart of the old city. Here the Graceway crosses the Primeway, the ancient highway running parallel with the shore and leaving Toremal by the gates that guard the highroads to north and south. A fountain stands in the centre of the vast square formed by the crossroads, Saedrin looking to the east, Poldrion to the west and Raeponin with hands stretched to north and south, eyes raised to the skies. Years ago, word was, it had been a shrine dedicated by some long-dead Emperor in the days before the Chaos, now it was merely an inviting display of cool water where people could meet. Open coaches circulated round it, moving slowly for the better display of Festival finery.

The Popinjay is one of the bigger inns on the edge of this square, dominating the corner to the north and east. The ninth chime of the day was sounding from a variety of bell towers as I forced my way past the exuberant youths heedlessly blocking the doors. That earned me some hard looks but no one was bold or drunk enough to try taking me on. A glance at my armring was enough to make most clear my path.

'Banch!' I yelled over the clamour of people trying to catch a potman's eye or a maidservant's apron. 'Banch!'

The burly tapster surveying the tumult with the calm eye of long experience turned his head. He waved a hand the size of a shovel at me and I pushed my way through to the counter. 'Ryshad.' He handed over a tall flagon of ale, tucking the silver in a pocketed apron belted below his barrel of a gut.

'Have you seen Yane? Sworn to Den Cotise? I was here with him yesterday.' I leaned over the scored and puddled wood, lowering my voice to a muted bellow. Yane would be on duty again tonight, as soon as the first chime of night sounded, but he'd said he'd be meeting his sweetheart here and her mistress was usually done with her by the last chime of the day. She was the dresser to Tor Sylarre, who'd found the whole tale of Temar's quest so romantic.

'Out the back with Ezinna.' Anger darkened Banch's pocked moon of a face and he slammed up the counter top to come out and grab a couple of lads by the scruffs of their expensive coats. I don't know where people found the room but everyone stepped aside as he threw the two offenders out into the gutter. One started to argue so I left Banch to explain the error of his ways and ducked through a far door.

Even with pot lids clanging, knives and cleavers hitting boards and the dog turning the roasting spit yelping in its treadmill, the kitchen was still quieter than the taproom. A handful of girls were busy on all sides, a pause for more than a breath earning them new instructions from the stout woman ruling her domain with a gesturing iron spoon.

'Cut more bread and then baste that beef before it dries out!' Ezinna cuffed a pinch-faced lass lightly round the ear to emphasise her orders. I stepped hastily aside as the gawky girl yelped, burning her fingers on the ladle resting in the dripping tray beneath the meat, splashing hot fat as she dropped it.

'Where's Yane?' I asked Ezinna.

She tucked a wisp of hair dyed raven black behind one ear, the rest drawn back with a spotted kerchief that might once have been yellow to match her faded dress. Grey showed at the roots. 'Out in the scullery.' Ezinna's habitual smile vanished.

'What's happened?' I frowned.

'It's Credilla.' Ezinna shook her head in resignation. 'Go on with you, you're in the way. Have you eaten?' Ezinna grabbed a crumbling slice of bread from one girl's passing basket and wrapped it round a thick slice of beef. She sent me on my way with a shove before turning to give the hapless bread girl a lesson in how many a loaf was supposed to serve if the inn wasn't to be ruined by the baker's bills.

Soiled crockery was stacked high in the scullery, waiting for two little girls standing on rough boxes by deep stone sinks. Neither was working very fast, round eyes in round faces gawping at Credilla sobbing into Yane's shoulder.

'Credie, flower, Credie.' He looked over her head at me with a mixture of relief and stifled rage.

'What's happened?'

Credilla's sobs shuddered into a whimper and she turned around, chestnut hair tangled over her pretty face. It didn't hide the ugly bruise disfiguring her, a great welt of purple and black high on one cheekbone, swelling half closing her eye and blood crusted around a cut that must have come from a ring.

'What happened?' I repeated, handing the bread and meat to a scullery girl who was eyeing it hopefully.

'Demoiselle Lida Tor Sylarre.' Yane managed to get a rein on himself, but he still looked like a man desperate for someone to hit and plainly fancying me as a target. 'The Maitresse came in just after noon, all fired up, ordering all the daughters to turn out their coffers, checking every casket against every inventory and deed of bequest.' He shook his head, baffled. 'The Maitresse starts taking pieces, telling Lida to hold her noise when she says she'll need some necklace or other for her dress tonight.'

'She was in quite a rage,' Credilla managed to quaver. 'I didn't say anything, not really.'

'But you recognised the pieces the Maitresse was taking?' I guessed.

'Demoiselle Lida saw I was surprised.' Credilla clutched the tear-sodden front of Yane's jerkin. 'She wanted to know why. All I said was I'd met a D'Olbriot man who's interested in old jewellery but Lida said there must be more to it for her mother to be so fussed. When I couldn't tell her anything, she hit me.'

Yane folded protective arms around her as the recollection prompted fresh weeping. 'You keep your head down when there's a storm brewing, Credie, you knows that.'

I nodded. Volunteering knowledge is never wise for a servant; it only leads to questions and then more questions about where you got the answers you give.

'I'm sorry I mixed you up in this, petal. Can you go back?' If she'd been turned out by Tor Sylarre, I'd have to find another place for her. Not with D'Olbriot though; that would just confirm whatever suspicions Tor Sylarre might be nursing.

Credilla nodded, dabbing her battered cheek with a scrap of damp muslin. 'Maitresse would lock Lida in her bedchamber till the end of Festival if she knew what she'd done. She gave me three gold Marks to keep my mouth shut and said I've got to work with the seamstresses until my face's better.'

'That's something at least.' I bit down on curses the little girls shouldn't be hearing.

'What's it all about, Rysh?' Yane looked up from brushing hair away from Credilla's tear-stained face.

'Just keep your head down, both of you,' I advised. 'There's a storm brewing, but I don't know where it's going to break.' I hesitated as I turned to go. 'Artifice, the healing magic from Kellarin could do something for that bruise.' Demoiselle Avila could surely repeat whatever she'd done for Temar.

Yane shook his head. 'Best you can do is leave us well alone.' He didn't mean it unkindly and worse; he was probably right.

The sun was sinking with its accustomed rapidity as I left

the Popinjay, the fading gold of the skies darkening to rich blue dusk over the rise of the land ahead. The Graceway was bright with lighted windows, tradesmen returning to the homes above their shops for their own entertainments now while private parties celebrated Festival in the upper rooms of inns and tisane houses. Linkboys had their candle lanterns already lit and bobbing on poles to show people their footing for a few coppers.

Once out of the Spring Gate I waved down a hireling gig and pondered Credilla's unexpected suffering. So Tor Sylarre had somehow got wind of Temar's search for those ancient jewels and treasures that might restore his people, and the Maitresse was none too pleased. Did that mean the Name was somehow involved in these connivances against D'Olbriot? It was certainly an ancient House, dating well back into the Old Empire. I frowned. Hadn't Demoiselle Avila been betrothed to some long-dead scion of the Name, some lad who'd died in the Crusted Pox? Had Tor Sylarre had anything to do with Kellarin's first colony?

The gig was turning up the long incline back to the residence. Temar would be able to answer some of my questions, but I tapped the driver on the shoulder with a new request.

'Den Haurient, quick as you can, friend.'

I'd best report this new finding to Esquire Camarl before I did anything else. He might find himself facing some Tor Sylarre over the dinner table, or forewarned might be able to see some significance in an otherwise innocuous remark. Temar could wait, after all.

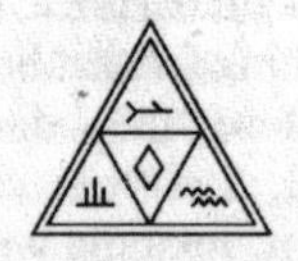

The D'Olbriot Residence Gatehouse, Summer Solstice Festival, Second Day, Evening

Temar drummed impatient fingers against the scabbard of his sword.

'So where's Ryshad?' Allin asked from the concealing shadow of the hedge.

'I certainly expected him to be back by now.' Having to concede Ryshad wasn't with the latest flurry of arrivals at the gate, he took a pace back.

Allin hunched her shoulders inside a light cloak. 'Perhaps we should just forget it.'

'You wanted to go,' said Temar firmly. 'It may be nothing, true enough, but if it is something I will have that something to show for today.'

'But can we go without Ryshad?' enquired Allin meekly. 'It's not too far. I've directions if you're able to walk.'

Temar looked at her with some indignation. 'My lady mage, I could walk from the springs to the sea inside a chime when I was last in Toremal. Granted, though, half this city was fields back then.'

'But you were wounded,' faltered Allin.

'I am fully recovered, and I am certainly not one of these lately come Esquires who cannot walk the length of a street lest they muddy their shoes.' Temar resolutely ignored the tender pull of the scar on his back and the ache lurking behind his eyes. 'All we need is some means of getting out of here unremarked. We can hardly keep this little adventure quiet if we call up a carriage to take us, and the gate ward this afternoon said he'd orders not to let me leave unaccompanied.'

'Unseen?' Allin bit her lip nervously. 'I could do that.'

'You know a back gate?' Temar turned to look back past the shadowy bulk of the residence towards the stables.

'No, but I could hide you?' Allin offered.

Temar looked at her. 'With your magecraft, you mean?'

'Velindre's been telling me I need to learn to take some initiative.' The quaver in Allin's voice rather gainsaid her bold words.

'Is it safe?' Temar shook his head. 'Forgive me, I do not mean to insult you.' He resolutely thrust away the freezing fear of submitting to any form of enchantment.

'I wouldn't dream of trying if it wasn't,' said Allin hastily.

They stood, hedged round with silence, faint noises from gatehouse and residence floating past on the cooling evening air.

'By all means weave your magic,' Temar said abruptly. He took a deep breath as Allin closed her soft hands tight around a faint spark of unearthly blue light, an expression of utmost concentration dignifying her round face.

Magecraft is a practical art, Temar reminded himself, *well-understood means of manipulating the stuff of creation that generations of wizards have studied and codified.* Casuel had told him all about it. Temar didn't have to understand, it was sufficient that these wizards did. *It's not Artifice*, he thought, gritting his teeth. *It's no enchantment wrought inside a man's head and working its will, holding him helpless to resist.*

'There,' Allin breathed.

Temar opened his eyes. 'Everything looks much the same,' he said for want of anything better.

'What about your hands?' giggled Allin.

Temar raised one, seeing only a dim outline of his fingers. He looked down and the rest of his body was no more than a faint suggestion in the gathering dusk. Gripping his sword hilt hastily, he was relieved to feel that as hard and reassuring as ever. He realised Allin was looking him straight in the eye. 'You can see me thus?' He'd be hard pressed to sneak through the gatehouse if he were no more than an Eldritchman's shade.

'You look like a shadow to me, and to any other mage, I'm afraid, but no one not mage-born will see anything.' Allin looked a little downcast. 'It's the best I can do.'

Temar nodded decisively. 'It is a marvel, my lady wizard.'

Allin ducked her head to hide a pleased smile. 'Stay close behind me, and hope we don't run into Casuel.'

Temar laughed. 'He went out to invite himself to some gathering of mages. It is wherever Velindre is going, I believe.'

'Be quiet,' Allin hushed him as they stepped out on to the empty sweep in front of the gatehouse.

Temar chewed at the inside of his cheek, carefully matching his steps to Allin's, especially when they reached flagstones where his hard boots could make far more noise than her soft shoes.

'Good evening, my lady,' called the Sergeant reading his broadsheet in the lodge.

Startled, Allin stopped. Temar promptly bumped into her. Allin managed to stifle her exclamation, but as she moved her cloak pulled her up short. Temar realised he was standing on the hem and hastily lifted his foot.

'Fair Festival, my lady,' said one of the recognised men guarding the postern. Temar found his sly suggestiveness faintly offensive.

Allin nodded curtly to the two youths. Temar pressed close to her, holding his breath and keeping arms and elbows close, lest he nudge someone.

As he stepped through the postern his sword caught against the wood and dragged round. Balancing it on his hip took Temar a moment and he caught a brief exchange on the inside of the door.

'Been visiting the young D'Alsennin, hasn't she?'

'What's he see in that dumpling? He's got his pick of the Demoiselles.'

'To marry maybe, but what about a little Festival jig? I'll bet a wizard wouldn't have cold hands for your fiddlestick.'

Temar strode hastily after Allin, feeling his cheeks burning with a colour every bit as fiery as her habitual blush.

She had halted to look vaguely at a gig trotting round a distant corner. 'Are you all right?' she whispered.

'Quite, yes.' Temar gratefully realised the invisibility hid his embarrassment.

'You'd better stay behind me,' she murmured as she walked slowly down the long slope towards the conduit house.

Temar did as he was bid, careful he didn't step on Allin's cloak again. At least there were precious few people out walking and those mostly looked to be liveried servants intent on their own tasks. The last daylight was fading now, and the dusk beneath the shade trees made Temar's feet even more indistinct to his straining eyes. He stopped, rubbing his eyes, taking a deep breath then hurrying after Allin.

Turning at the conduit house, she headed north and west along the circular road. Coaches swept past them, but hardly anyone else was on foot. Allin strode on, ignoring superior glances from passing carriages until she finally turned down into a busy thoroughfare. The air was cooling now but the stone buildings all around were casting the remembered heat of the day back into the night sky along with the exuberant clamour of the crowd.

Temar had to press close behind Allin, their progress increasingly awkward, Temar looking up and down at every other step, searching for his feet no darker than wisps of smoke. The lesser moon rose over the rooftops, golden circle all but full and unchallenged by the merest arc raised by her greater sister. But Temar had no time for such fancies as the moonlight cast queasy shadows through the hazy darkness that was all he could see of himself. Something in the back of his mind was protesting ever louder that what his eyes were telling him couldn't possibly be the truth.

He caught Allin's elbow, steering her irresistibly into a noisome alley. 'You have to undo the magic, else I will be sick.' He swallowed hard on nausea thickening his throat.

Allin immediately spread her hands in a decisive gesture. Sapphire light came and went at the edge of Temar's vision like a jewelled memory of the day and he could see his hands again. 'My thanks,' he said with heartfelt sincerity.

'If you're done, move on, will you?' A man about Temar's age shifted impatiently from one foot to the other at the entrance to the alley, a slightly older woman on his arm, eyes cynical in her painted face.

'Did they see anything?' whispered Allin.

'There's nothing I've not seen, blossom,' said the woman with a coarse chuckle.

Temar drew a mortified breath, uncertain how to respond. Allin giggled and slid her arm inside his. 'We're nearly there.'

As the road forked either side of an ancient shrine, Allin led Temar up an avenue of lime trees spreading a moist green scent. Mismatched buildings jostled a run of tall, narrow houses with proudly precise gables looking down on the six-sided chimneys of lower dwellings with narrow leaded windows and uneven rooflines.

'It should be down there,' said Allin uncertainly. Bright lights beckoned at the bottom of a small entry, too short to be a street, too wide to be an alley. Lively chatter lilting with unmistakably Lescari accents echoed from an open window.

'Yes, look.' Allin pointed with relief at the great half-circle lock hanging from a sturdy chain above the door. It was all that distinguished the building from its neighbours, each with irregular windows beneath a dishevelled roof of stone slates, oaken beams set for no readily apparent reason in walls crumbling with age and inattention.

Temar drew his arm close to his side to shield Allin with his greater height. 'I have not spent any great time in taverns,' he said cautiously. Not this side of the ocean, not since waking from enchantment, he amended silently to himself. Riotous evenings carousing with Vahil so long ago, not a care between them, counted for nothing now.

But they'd never have come to such a sober house, little changed from the dwelling it had once been. Two casks of ale were set on trestles in a parlour furnished with cast-offs from people who could have had precious little to start with. There were no potmen or maids that Temar could see, just an unhurried matron filling a steady flow of jugs brought by men and women in sombre, well-worn clothes who either sat near by or disappeared into the back of the building.

Four newcomers pressed past Temar and Allin as they hesitated on the threshold. Greeting the mistress of the house in Toremal-accented Lescari, two lads took tankards from a rack beside one door for their ale while the others helped themselves to glasses and a flat-bottomed greenish bottle, dropping silver and copper coin into an open box. A crone sewing a slow seam by the table nodded, her smile shrunken around toothless gums.

'Can I help you?' The woman drawing the ale looked over at Allin, polite but cool. Her clipped words carried echoes of the mercenaries Temar knew in Kel Ar'Ayen.

Allin fumbled beneath her cloak for the handbill. 'I was looking for Mistress Maedura?' Her own accent was stronger than Temar had ever heard it.

The woman nodded, indifferent. 'Out the back.'

Allin smiled uncertainly. 'May we see her?'

The woman glanced, incurious, at Temar. 'Please yourself, lass.'

'Come on,' he encouraged Allin, doing his best to sound like the Lescari mercenaries he knew back home. Digging a few coins from the purse tied to his belt, he pointed at a bottle of wine inky dark inside emerald glass. 'How much?'

The old woman chuckled, revealing a baby pink tongue, and said something Temar didn't understand. Allin held out some silver of her own, talking hastily in Lescari.

'She says we should wait our turn through here,' she said tightly to Temar.

He picked up a bottle and two thick glasses with uneven rims. 'What did I do?' He was used to struggling with the indecipherable mysteries of female disapproval from Guinalle and Avila, but had thought he'd made a fresh start with Allin.

'Tried to pay her about ten times what that wine's worth.' A faint smile was tugging at the corners of Allin's mouth. 'I said you thought she was taking money for the seer.'

People were waiting on chairs beneath an unshuttered window and by a door opening on to a small yard. A second door, cut through the wall to give access to some afterthought of an outbuilding, was firmly closed, though faint sounds of conversation filtered through to the expectant room. Everyone looked at Allin and Temar, some curious, a few defensive, but all with unspoken determination to protect their place in the line.

'We have some time in hand.' Temar rattled the coins in his hand absently.

'Don't do that,' Allin reproved him. 'Hasn't anyone told you what an Empire Crown buys?' She moved two rickety chairs to a small table with a dull, much wiped surface.

'No.' Temar looked at the thick white-gold coin. 'Camarl only gave me a purse today. I remembered what that hand-bill says, so I asked.'

'Did he ask why you wanted it?' Allin looked like a child caught in mischief.

Temar grinned. 'I said it was because Tor Kanselin's surgeon said I probably only took that knife yesterday by way of payback for having nothing to steal.'

Allin frowned. 'Don't you use coin in Kellarin?'

'Odd copper and silver, but the mercenaries brought most of the coin, so it comes from all manner of places.' Temar set down the glasses and wondered how he was supposed to get the cork out of the bottle. 'They only seem to use coin for gambling anyway. We mostly deal between ourselves by swapping work on a man's barn for a share in his corn, half a sheep for a side of beef and suchlike.'

Allin took a small knife from her purse and chipped at the wax sealing the wine. 'Camarl doubtless thinks an Old Empire Crown is a trivial enough sum, but round here three of those would feed a family for a week and leave table scraps to fatten the pig.' She worked the cork out of the bottle with the point of her knife. 'Get Ryshad or someone to change those Crowns for some common coin if you don't want everyone eyeing your purse.'

'How does common coin differ?' Temar took the bottle from Allin and poured them each a measure of wine.

'I'm not surprised they don't want you going out on your own.' Allin narrowed her eyes. 'Old Empire coin is noble coin, purer metal than anything minted these days, less of it to be had. Common coin is what we commoners use, what the various cities and powers mint for themselves.'

Temar fell silent for a moment. There was still so much he didn't know, wasn't there? 'Why would Camarl give me Old Empire money?'

'I don't suppose he thought you'd be spending it in places like this.' Allin was unconcerned. 'And you're a noble, aren't you? If you can get it, it's the best coin to carry.'

'Four copper pennies still make a bronze?' Temar looked for some reassurance. 'Ten bronze pennies to a silver and four of those make a silver Mark?'

Allin shook her head. 'No one's used bronze pennies since the Chaos. Ten copper to a silver penny and when six silver Marks make a gold Crown that's an end to it. Only the Old Empire used gold Marks.' She smiled but this time without humour. 'Don't take Lescari Marks off anyone. If any of the Dukes mint a coffer of coin, they add enough lead to roof a moot hall.'

She paused as a young woman carrying a baby on her hip came out of the far door, her expression half hopeful, half puzzled. The low murmur of conversation stopped and all eyes turned to the girl. The only one not looking was an old man in much mended homespun who hurried in, heavy boots clattering on the floorboards. The girl lifted her chin, hoisted the child more securely inside her shawl and strode out of the room.

'She looks as if she got something for her coin,' commented Temar in low tones.

'I don't think she's quite sure what she's gained though.' Allin drank her wine. Silence hung heavy between them for quite some moments.

Temar rolled a sip round his mouth thoughtfully. 'This is far from—'

A cry from the seer's room silenced him, a hoarse sob hastily stifled. The old man came stumbling out, one shaking hand hiding his eyes, the other groping blindly in front of him. Four of those waiting jumped to their feet, a sturdy woman in serviceable maroon offering resolute comfort in fast, unintelligible words. A gaunt man with one empty sleeve to his coat reached his good arm round the old man's shaking shoulders, while a pretty girl with haunted eyes supported an elderly female in rusty black, whose face had gone as white as her shabby lace cap. At brisk words from the stout woman, the family walked out with fragile dignity.

Everyone avoided everyone else's eyes as an apprehensive youth walked slowly through the door.

'What are we going to say to this seer, whoever she is?' Allin turned beseeching eyes to Temar.

'Have you some question you already know the answer to?' asked Temar thoughtfully.

'I could ask about someone still alive.' Allin nodded reluctantly. 'If she gets that right, I ask about someone I know to be dead?'

Temar looked at her in some concern. 'Does this distress you?'

Allin looked down, her hands knotted in her lap. 'We'd best find out, now we've come all this way.'

New arrivals prompted Allin to move hastily to one of the vacated seats, to claim their place in the queue. Temar grabbed the wine and moved after her. Hemmed in on either side, they exchanged silent glances over their glasses. The second chime of night was sounding by the time the portly man who'd been before them came back out, face dark with stubborn resentment.

Allin stood up, brushing decisively at her skirts. 'Let's see what's to see.'

Clutching the wine bottle for lack of anywhere to put it, Temar followed the mage girl into a bare room. All they saw was an iron-bound chest set on an unwieldy table in the middle of a rug woven from strips of threadbare cloth, two females sitting on stools beyond it. Tallow candles in sconces lit damp stained walls, smoky flames briefly fluttering to add more soot to the dirty lath ceiling.

Allin said something courteous and the older woman stood up. Her white hair was all but invisible beneath a pale blue kerchief, and she wore a full, shapeless skirt and sleeveless bodice of the same material laced over a loose linen blouse. No one in Tormalin dressed like this though Temar had seen some of the mercenary women in Kel Ar'Ayen wearing such garb. Poldrion's touch had whitened this woman's hair unduly early, he decided. Her firm face suggested she was still in her middle years but the lines that furrowed her brow hinted those years had been hard.

'Mistress Maedura.' Allin gestured to Temar. 'My companion, Natyr.'

'All who seek answers are welcome,' said the woman in passable Tormalin. Her shrewd eyes rather unexpectedly lacked the hard calculation Temar expected from a trickster. They were also the colour of a rain-washed sky and he realised how seldom he'd seen anyone with light eyes since arriving here.

'Your questions?' Mistress Maedura prompted.

'Of course,' said Allin nervously.

Temar looked at the younger woman sitting silent beside Mistress Maedura. She had the same pale eyes but hers were as empty as a summer noon, staring fixedly at the wall behind Temar. She was dressed in a soft green weave, skirt spotted with spilled food, and her sparse dull hair was cut short in a ragged crop. The laces of her bodice pulled unevenly over a mature figure yet her face had the unlined vacancy of a child.

'My daughter was caught between the realms of life as a babe,' said Maedura without emotion. 'Lennarda's mind wanders the shades, but from time to time she encounters those crossing the river with Poldrion. When Saedrin opens the door to admit them to the Otherworld, she glimpses what lies beyond and hears some small snatches of lost voices.' Despite her rehearsed words Temar nevertheless felt she genuinely believed what she said.

Maedura gave Allin a handful of three-sided bones and gestured her to the single stool facing the chest. 'Set out your birth signs on the lid.' Allin fumbled through the bones, finally picking out three separate runes.

Temar took a step closer, recognising the Deer, the Broom and the Mountain. 'You draw three separate bones?'

Allin shot him a piercing look of rebuke. 'But your father would have insisted on the Tormalin way, wouldn't he, just the one bone?' She turned to Maedura, speaking in rapid, offhand Lescari. Temar would have preferred to know what was being said about him but whatever yarn Allin was spinning, the suspicion flaring in Maedura's eyes faded to an ever present watchfulness.

Allin turned to Temar again. 'Your grandmother favoured the runes, didn't she? She swore there was *art* to casting them.'

Temar nodded hastily. Holding his wine glass up to shield his mouth, he began whispering under his breath, reciting one of the few charms Guinalle had managed to drill into him. If Artifice was being worked here, it would echo in his hearing with unmistakable resonance. He forced himself to concentrate despite the faint dizziness aggravating his lurking headache, reluctantly realising he wasn't as recovered as he'd boasted.

'Ask your question,' Maedura commanded.

'Where's my cousin Chel?' Allin demanded abruptly. Temar could see the tips of her ears going scarlet.

Maedura took her daughter's hands and laid them on the runes. Aversion flitted momentarily over Lennarda's blank face then her shoulders sagged, head drooping to show a scabbed and sore scalp. Temar nearly lost the rhythm of the enchantment he was attempting as he realised someone had been pulling the girl's hair out in handfuls.

'I see a river.' Lennarda sat bolt upright, startling Allin into a muted squeak. Temar's fingers tightened on the neck of the bottle.

'I see a river curving over a plain.' The girl's voice was deep, firm and assured. 'A big river, wide-mouthed as it enters the sea. The water is brown, bringing goodness down from the high land. Then this will be fertile ground. There are marshes, saltings full of white birds. No birds I ever saw before, but we should try bringing down a few, to see if they make good eating. See, there is a fair landing yonder, open grass above the tide line. We can build a wharf along the bank. There is plenty of timber for shelter too, goodly stands of trees.'

Lennarda stopped dead, pulling away from the coffer and folding her arms awkwardly against her chest. She hunched over, rocking back and forth with incoherent whimpers.

Allin turned to Temar, her face an eloquent mix of embarrassment and disappointment. 'Shall we go?'

'Your payment?' Mistress Maedura held her daughter's hands down as they hooked into impotent claws.

'Your fee?' asked Allin icily. She stood and pulled her cape around her.

'Whatever you think the information is worth.' Maedura got to her feet as Lennarda subsided into her earlier vacant stillness.

'Not very much, to be truthful.' Allin drew a resolute breath.

'No, wait,' Temar broke in, blood pulsing behind his eyes. 'Allin, ask again, about anyone.'

Allin looked doubtfully at him and Maedura laid a protective hand on her daughter's uncaring shoulder. Temar held up one of the Tormalin Empire Crowns. 'My payment in advance.'

'If this is your question, you must set out your runes,' said Maedura in some confusion.

'Here.' Temar pushed at the single bone bearing the Salmon, the Reed and the Sea. 'I was born under the greater moon, does that make any difference?'

Maedura shook her head as she lifted her daughter's hands with their chewed, split fingernails towards the rune and Temar hastily withdrew, flesh crawling at the thought of touching the unfortunate.

'I seek a little girl.' He coughed and forced his voice to

stay level. 'A little girl wearing a yellow dress with red flowers sewn around the hem. I do not know her name but she has an older brother and a sister. They all sleep together wrapped in a brown cloak.' His throat closed with emotion and he couldn't say any more.

Lennarda's low, unintelligible noises of distress were abruptly cut off as she slumped forward. Even forewarned, Temar still jumped as Lennarda suddenly reared up again. Allin clutched at his arm and he reached for her, grateful for her hand warming his fingers, which felt suddenly chilled to the bone.

'Where am I?' This time Lennarda's voice was light and wondering. She looked around, hands held to her cheeks in a parody of childishness. 'Where am I? It's all dark. Where am I? Mama?'

As she lifted her eager, searching face to him, Temar felt his heart miss a beat. For an instant Lennarda's empty eyes shone a vibrant grassy green in the candlelight. 'Can you hear me? Mama? Is it all right now?'

After a moment of utter silence, Lennarda began an ugly keening, empty face crumpling, rocking backwards and forwards again but faster this time, with a growing violence. Her hands clawed and she began tearing at her own head.

'Hush, hush.' Maedura tried to gather her child in her arms, fending off the raking nails with difficulty.

'Let's just go.' Allin tugged at Temar's arm.

He resisted. 'How many questions does that gold buy me?' he demanded roughly.

Maedura's expression was a turmoil of desperation and self-loathing. 'As many as you need to ask, what do you think? But only for tonight.'

'I will be outside,' said Temar with sudden decision. 'When you are done with everyone else, we will speak further.' He pulled Allin out of the room so fast she nearly stumbled on top of him.

Ignoring the covert curiosity of the people waiting, Temar strode rapidly into the front room. 'Do you have spirits?

Strong liquor?' he asked the serving woman curtly.

'White brandy, if you have it,' Allin shoved Temar towards the inglenook by the fire. His knees gave out as he reached the low bench so he waited while Allin brought over a black bottle and two small glasses fetched from the cupboard behind the crone's chair. She watched the pair of them with considerable interest in her watery old eyes.

'What was that all about?' demanded Allin, handing Temar as large a measure as she could safely pour. 'Aetheric magic?'

Temar swallowed the colourless liquor in one breath, gasping as it jolted him out of the shock numbing his wits. 'Not being worked in the room,' he said hoarsely. 'Neither of them have any notion of enchantments.'

'That girl doesn't look as if she's a notion in her head,' commented Allin with pity, sipping cautiously.

'Not unless she catches some echo from some other mind,' said Temar slowly.

Allin looked confused. 'But she didn't know anything about Chel. I know for a fact he's alive and well and trading leather from Dalasor to Duryea. I had a letter from his mother at Equinox and you can't get much further away from the sea than that.'

'What she saw was Kel Ar'Ayen.' Temar leaned forward intently.

'A big river, a wide empty plain? Couldn't that be, oh, I don't know, anywhere from Inglis to Bremilayne?' said Allin doubtfully. 'And I suppose Chel might have gone travelling.'

'What she saw, what she thought, we all thought the same when we made landfall in Kel Ar'Ayen.' Temar laid his hand on Allin's in unconscious emphasis. 'I remember looking at that river, wondering if the land would be fertile, picking out the best place to build and noting timber we might build with. Believe me, Allin, for Saedrin's sake!'

'Then how does that unfortunate know?' She extricated her hand, flexing her fingers with a slight grimace. 'Could it be something to do with the runes? Isn't Ryshad's friend Livak looking for an aetheric tradition hidden in old rune lore in the Great Forest?'

Temar shook his head crossly, regretting it instantly as pain lanced through his temples. 'No Artifice is being worked here. I can detect that much with the charms I know.' He looked up at Allin. 'I would give all the gold Camarl can spare me to look inside that chest.'

'They've got an artefact?' Allin nodded slowly. 'And that unfortunate child has somehow become linked with it, like Ryshad and your sword?'

'More than one,' said Temar with rising certainty. 'That second voice, that was a girl I saw Guinalle lay beneath the enchantments. I saw the child's green eyes, eyes from the northern hill country, I saw them reflected in the imbecile's face.'

Allin frowned. 'Where did that woman get a chest full of Kellarin artefacts?'

'Cannot such questions wait?' Temar demanded impatiently. 'We must secure that chest!'

'How?' countered Allin. 'Fraud or folly, that masquerade's their only means of earning bread. The woman at least must know the coffer's vital to the girl's supposed powers. They're hardly going to give it up to you.'

Temar chewed at his lower lip. 'What if we offered her the weight of the chest in gold?'

A startled laugh escaped Allin. 'Are you serious?'

'Entirely.' Temar kept his voice low, face grim. 'I would pay that to bring only one back from enchantment. I would pay the same time and again to bring every single sleeper back to themselves.'

Allin sipped her brandy with a faint shudder. 'So the rumours of Kellarin gold are true, are they?'

'For now, Camarl can advance me the coin,' Temar said with a confidence he didn't entirely feel. 'There are riches to be had over the ocean in time and we can repay him then. Perhaps I should pursue those claims the Relict Tor Bezaemar mentioned as well,' he added thoughtfully. 'That would at least give me means to buy any other artefact we find.'

'First we have to look in that chest and make sure there are artefacts in it.' Allin shifted to look through to the back room and the outbuilding beyond. 'Then we have to make some deal with the woman tonight. Otherwise she'll take to her heels, coffer and all. I would like to know just how this business of linking to an artefact works.'

It was Temar's turn to laugh. 'Do you always have to have the answers?'

'First, I'm Lescari, and secondly, I'm a mage.' Allin smiled a little guiltily. 'Both mean you never take a thing on trust. You ask all the questions you can think of and only go on when you've all the answers.'

Temar glanced into the far room still full with hopeful suppliants. 'What's it like, being mage-born? No wizard I have met will ever spare time to talk about it.'

'We're not encouraged to, not once we've been to Hadrumal.' Allin coloured slightly. 'I told you, there's a lot of mistrust.'

Temar shook his head. 'Granted, it is sorcery of some different nature, but I grew up with aetheric enchantments. All right,' he amended hastily, 'perhaps not used every day, but everyone knew Artifice was there, for healing and truth-saying, for sending urgent word across the provinces. So what is it, Allin, to be mage-born?'

'Oh, I don't know how to explain it.' She blushed pink. 'Imagine oil spilled on water but you're the only one who can see the rainbow when the light strikes it. Imagine hearing some counterpoint to music that everyone else is deaf to. You touch something and you can sense the element within it, like feeling the vibration in a table when a timepiece strikes the chimes. You can sense it, you can feel how it affects things around it. Then you realise you can change it, you can shade that rainbow to light or dark, you can mute that note or make it sound twice as loud.' Allin's face was animated in a way Temar had never seen before.

The slam of the outer door shattered the calm of the room.

'Where's this charlatan hiding out?' A thickset man in everyday Tormalin garb marched into the centre of the room. 'Seer she calls herself? I'll teach the bitch to take honest coin off a stupid girl!' He glared at everyone, sharp-featured and furious.

'Well? What's the fakery?' A younger man, unmistakably slurring his words through drink came in to the tavern. He was dragging a struggling girl, fingers biting into her arm as he forced her along. A frown gave his angled black brows a predatory air.

'Let me go! It's no business of yours!'

The second man gave the girl a vicious shake. 'Shut your mouth, you stupid slut.' She tried to hang on to the doorjamb and he slapped her hand away with a brutal oath. More men crowded round the doorway, some intent and indignant, others brought along by casual malice or idle curiosity. Many still had wine flagons in their hands.

Temar realised the girl was the one they had seen earlier carrying a baby.

'Masters, this is a quiet house.' The woman minding the ale casks stood a prudent distance from the thickset man. 'We want no trouble.'

'You get trouble when you let some trickster use your place,' spat the man, taking a step forward to shove the woman back with one broad, calloused hand. 'Where's this seer?'

'It's an insult to all rational thinking,' piped up someone from the back of the crowd at the door. An ominous murmur of assent backed his spite.

'Superstition. Falsehoods. Preying on an idiot girl's folly.' The man emphasised each assertion with another shove, backing the woman hard up against her ale casks. 'Taking her coin and telling her to go off Saedrin knows where after some feckless Lescari tinker we thought we were rid of?'

'Well rid,' the younger man panted, still struggling with the girl, who was trying to kick him, her face contorted with tears. 'Until her belly swelled. Got his irons hot in your hearth, didn't he, you whore?'

'I loved him,' screamed the girl in hopeless rage.

As the man gave her another vicious shake, she stumbled over a chair. Stretching her free hand out to save herself, she encountered a jug of ale. In one swift move, she smashed it on her tormenter's head.

The crash of breaking crockery acted like a war horn on the mob outside. Men surged through the door, shoving tables and chairs aside.

'You Lescari are all the same, cheats!'

'Never set to and earn honest coin if you can steal it!'

'Go swallow yourself, you dripping pizzle!' A man who'd been sitting quietly over his ale stood up. Others braced themselves, ready resentments rearing their heads.

'Rational men have a duty to combat pernicious superstition,' one voice from the back of the mob rose in a sanctimonious bleat.

'Rationalists are soft in the head,' an incensed Lescari voice called out to considerable agreement.

'Soft as shit and twice as nasty,' shouted someone from the back room.

The rapid accents of latterday Toremal and sharp Lescari lilts left Temar struggling to understand but the mood of mutual hostility needed no explanation. He realised Allin was clutching his arm, trembling with fear. With a spreading mêlée at the outer door and indignant Lescari pushing through from the inner room, getting through the throng was going to be no easy task. Temar tucked Allin close behind him, keeping firm hold of her hand.

'Is there a way out through the yard, do you think?' she asked nervously.

Temar used elbows and boots to force a way into the back room, ignoring the protests of those few still seated. 'There will be no more answers from the lady tonight,' he told them as he pushed Allin through into the outbuilding.

He looked at the door doubtfully. It wouldn't take much to break down that single thickness of warped plank. The first sound of splintering furniture came from the front of the tavern, a startled yell and someone crying out in pain. Temar pulled the latchstring through, tying it as tight as he could.

'What's going on?' Mistress Maedura was white and frightened but trying to calm Lennarda, who was rocking on her stool, moaning like an animal in pain.

'You saw some girl earlier, with a child,' Allin told her curtly. 'Whatever you told her, it's got her relatives all fired up.'

Maedura spread helpless hands. 'It's just what Lennarda sees and hears, echoes from the Otherworld.'

'You really do believe that, don't you?' Temar paused on his way to look out of each window. Maedura stared at him in confusion.

'Never mind that,' Allin snapped, voice taut with anxiety. An outraged scream cut through the rising turmoil beyond the door and made Lennarda wail in confusion.

'We will help you leave here.' Temar strode to the door in the far corner of the room but opening it only revealed a large closet, two strides wide and less deep. His jaw dropped before the thud of something heavy against the painted planks of the door brought him swinging round. The noise outside sounded like a full-blown riot. Temar drew his sword, wondering what to do with growing unease.

Lennarda began shrieking, eyes wide and staring at the silvery steel. She backed into the corner, grabbing at her ragged hair.

'Put the blade away, you fool!' Maedura had tears on her cheeks. 'She thinks you're going to hurt her.'

'Into the closet, all of you – and that chest.' Allin ordered suddenly. She tried to lift the heavy coffer from the table.

Temar stepped forward to take the other rope handle. 'Get her inside,' he yelled at Maedura, who was struggling with the frantic Lennarda. Once he had Allin and the chest inside he dragged the frenzied imbecile bodily towards the closet, Maedura following, nearly as hysterical as her daughter.

As the door to the outbuilding splintered and broke, Temar pushed the closet door shut, doing his best to brace himself against the frame. Barely a glimmer of light made its way through the cracks around the door and Temar felt the breath tightening in his chest. Was the darkness deepening, pressing in on him, threatening to steal away all sensation, as it had done before?

'You wanted us in here, Allin,' he panted. 'Now what?'

'Now this.' She brought her hands together on a flash of incandescent scarlet that changed in a heartbeat to azure flame that danced around the four of them like a silken veil. Maedura's mouth was a silent gape of terror but Lennarda's pitiful cries stopped to Temar's inexpressible relief. The unfortunate girl put forward one bitten finger to touch the radiance but the teasing light retreated from her groping hand.

There was a crash as the table in the room outside was thrown over, stools clattering in its wake. 'As quick as you can, Allin.' Temar struggled to hold the door closed as someone gave it an insistent shove.

Allin took a deep breath. The intensity of the blue light all around grew rapidly more intense, reflecting back from the whitewashed walls. Maedura and Lennarda faded into nothingness before Temar's astounded eyes. Everything faded, vanishing into the brilliant flare of power. Heat enveloped him, the dry warmth of a furnace hearth. The light flashed incandescent and he had to shut his eyes but the radiance still beat against them, printing the pattern of the blood vessels against the back of his eyelids. His face began to sting under the searing ferocity of the heat and just as Temar thought he could not stand it an instant longer the light dimmed as suddenly as it had arisen. He shivered and coughed on an acrid smell of burned wool.

'What the—'

Temar opened his eyes as Ryshad remembered his manners and swallowed whatever barracks obscenity he'd nearly let slip.

'Hello, Ryshad.' Temar couldn't help an idiotic grin. They were in the D'Olbriot library he realised, carried right into the heart of the residence by Allin's magic. The chest was cooling gently beside his feet as it seared a black mark into the costly carpet. Ryshad sat at the table with the Sieur D'Olbriot, an array of papers in front of him, a penknife in one hand and a half-mended quill in the other. The Sieur was leaning back in his chair, his expression quizzical.

'My compliments, my lady mage!' Temar turned to Allin and swept a low bow, unable to stop himself laughing.

'What in the name of all that's holy do you think you are doing, girl?' Casuel was standing on the far side of the mantel, a book open in his hands. His savage question overrode Allin's nervous giggle and Temar saw all the delight in her achievement instantly wiped from her face.

'How dare you intrude like this – and how can you have been so stupid as to try such a translocation unsupervised?' Casuel strode forward. 'Raeponin only knows what saved you from your folly. Planir will hear of this, my girl! This is the care Velindre takes of her pupils?'

Temar wanted quite simply to hit the wizard. 'Allin has distinguished herself this evening by leading me to a vital collection of lost Kel Ar'Ayen artefacts.' Temar spared a breath for a fervent prayer to Saedrin that the chest did indeed contain something of real value. 'Please do inform the Archmage of that, with my sincerest compliments.' At least he had the satisfaction of seeing his words strike the mage like blows. 'When some mob of Rationalists attacked the place, she brought us all safely here.'

'May I ask who your companions are?' As Casuel subsided in confusion, the Sieur D'Olbriot sat forward, pushing a counting frame to one side, an inkstand to the other. Dolsan Kuse hovered at his elbow, clutching a roll of tape-tied parchments.

'My pardon, Messire.' Temar bowed low. 'Forgive the intrusion; it was a matter of some urgency.'

'Doubtless,' said the Sieur drily. His faded eyes were shrewd in his plump face. 'My lady mage, we meet again. An unexpected pleasure, in every sense.' Dapper despite his informal shirt and breeches, he smiled at Allin, who managed a curtsey of more elegance than Temar might have expected.

'You're looking well, Messire,' she replied politely.

D'Olbriot ran a hand over his receding grey hair. 'For a fat old man, my child.'

'Oh you're hardly that, Messire,' fawned Casuel.

D'Olbriot ignored him. 'And who are these other two?'

'Mistress Maedura and her daughter, a natural simpleton.' Temar shot a hasty glance over his shoulder but Lennarda seemed in some stupor within her mother's protective embrace. Maedura was all but frozen with apprehension. 'They had Kel Ar'Ayen artefacts in their possession, all unknowing,' Temar added hastily. 'We had to rescue them, else they would have been beaten or worse.'

The Sieur D'Olbriot raised a hand. 'Beyond question a complicated tale. Tell it tomorrow, D'Alsennin.' He snapped his fingers and Dolsan moved instantly to tug a bell pull hanging by the chimney breast. 'Ryshad,' the Sieur continued. 'See these women comfortably lodged and Temar may tell you his tale. Report to me before I retire.'

Ryshad was on his feet at once, shepherding them all towards the door. Maedura made a futile move towards the chest but Ryshad shook his head. 'It'll be safe enough there.'

Casuel touched a hand to it and hissed with surprised pain. 'You really must work harder on controlling your elemental affinity,' he said spitefully to Allin, words indistinct as he sucked burned fingers. 'There's far too much fire in your working. Who's been teaching you anyway? Velindre?'

'And Kalion,' retorted Allin with some spirit. 'I'm sure the Hearth-Master will be delighted to hear your criticisms of his technique.'

'Enough.' Ryshad ushered them all into a small withdrawing room across the hall from the library, where a page was hastily lighting lamps. 'The Sieur requests the Demoiselle Tor Arrial join us here,' he ordered the lad. 'Now, Temar, explain yourself.'

'Allin and Velindre have come to the Festival to see what Toremal makes of magic.' Temar spoke rapidly, ignoring Casuel's suspicious gaze. 'They have been looking for hints of magic in any entertainment offered and Allin came across mention of this woman.' He indicated the still overawed Maedura. 'She was claiming to have some means of contacting the Otherworld, getting word from the dead.' Temar hesitated. This was all starting to sound ridiculously implausible. 'We wondered firstly if somehow it might be Artifice and I know you are interested in lost lore. Beyond that, if it proved true, I thought it might give us means to contact Vahil, Esquire Den Rannion that was.'

'I remember him,' Ryshad said softly, eyes dark in the golden lamplight.

Recalling how Ryshad had shared his life in dreams prompted by Artifice knocked Temar off his stride. 'There was no enchantment,' he said simply. 'But they have this chest and I'll swear by Poldrion's demons it has artefacts within it. The girl, the natural, hears echoes of the sleepers.'

'Where did you get the chest?' Ryshad demanded grimly.

Maedura clutched Lennarda to her. 'A shrine to Maewelin, on an island in the Drax. The goddess looks kindly on the simple. They said it was a miracle, the priestesses, when my girl spoke. She'd never said a word before, not one.'

'And you repaid their kindness by stealing that coffer?' sneered Casuel.

'Mercenaries went raiding into Dalasor from Draximal,' Maedura said bitterly. 'They sacked the shrine and everything for leagues around. Lennarda wouldn't leave the chest, wouldn't leave her voices, so I had to take it with me.'

'No one is calling you to answer for anything,' said Temar with a scowl at Casuel.

Maedura ignored him, her fear and fury fastening on Casuel. 'You'd have had us stay to be raped and murdered? If the goddess chooses to speak through my poor child, who am I to deny her? Maewelin was a mother; she'd never grudge me earning coin to buy bread. We never took more than folk were willing to pay. We never feigned or deceived or—' She broke into dry, angry sobs that set Lennarda whimpering.

Temar looked helplessly at Ryshad, who clapped his hands

together. 'Cas, you see Allin home. Go on, lass, we'll untangle this coil.' The swordsman gave Allin a kindly smile before turned a stern look on Casuel.

'Oh, very well.' The mage stalked crossly to the door. 'We'll call for a coach, shall we? A safer way to travel in your company, I think.'

Temar caught Allin's arm as she meekly followed Casuel. 'I am deep in your debt, my lady mage.'

She managed a faint smile before Casuel snapped an insistent summons over his shoulder.

Ryshad beckoned in two doubtful maids hovering outside in the hall. 'See these two settled for the night in a garret room. They're guests, but they're not to leave the residence without my say-so, do you understand? Send word to Sergeant Stolley.'

'What's all this?' Temar turned to see Avila rolling up the sleeves of her elegant gown as she appeared at the turn of the corridor. He raised his voice above the anguish of the two women now locked in desperate embrace. 'They had artefacts—'

Avila snorted. 'Some other time, my lad.' She laid a gentle hand on Maedura's skewed kerchief. 'Come with me. I can offer some respite from your grief.'

As Maedura looked up, wondering, Avila took Lennarda's hand with irresistible gentleness. Gathering up the maids with an imperious glance, she led everyone out of the anteroom and Temar shut the door gratefully on the fading commotion.

'Remind me about that the next time I find Avila's self-importance intolerable, will you?' he asked Ryshad lightly.

His high spirits sank beneath the stern look in Ryshad's eyes. 'If I even so much as suspect you're thinking about going off on your own again, after something like this, I'll chain you to your bedposts myself. Are we clear on that?'

Temar braced himself. 'I wanted your help. I waited for you by the gates as late as I could. You did not return and this was too important to ignore.'

'No, it wasn't,' Ryshad said bluntly. 'Not then, when you'd

no idea if this was all moonshine in a mustard pot.'

'It is the second day of Festival and I have achieved all but nothing,' Temar retorted. 'I will try raking moonshine if there is any chance of finding gold. Anyway, I came to no harm.'

'Thanks to little Allin,' Ryshad pointed out.

Temar opened his mouth to deny this but thought better of it. 'Thanks to Allin,' he agreed stiffly.

'I'd still rather you'd had a swordsman at your back.' A reluctant smile finally cracked Ryshad's severity. 'There's no doubt you were born under the greater moon, my lad. Halcarion certainly polishes up your luck nice and bright.'

Temar grinned. 'As the mercenaries keep saying, he who plays the longest odds wins most. Shall we take a look in that coffer?'

'We won't disturb the Sieur, not if we don't want to feel the sharp edge of his tongue,' said Ryshad with feeling. 'We'll have to make time in the morning, and that's going to be plenty busy enough to satisfy you, believe me. Someone's setting up D'Olbriot and D'Alsennin both for a whole new game, and if you're not to lose your boots and breeches you need to know all the other moves played out today.'

CHAPTER FOUR

Preface to the Chronicle of D'Olbriot, As Recorded on the Authority of Maitresse Sancaerise, Winter Solstice of the 9th Year of Aleonne the Valiant

It falls to me to give this testimony to the year now past in the absence of my beloved husband, Sieur Epinal, and with his Designate, his brother Esquire Ustin, incapacitated by wounds received in battle. It is my sorrowful duty to record that the surgeons now despair of his recovery. On behalf of all the women of the House, I beseech Drianon to watch over our sons and grandsons, brothers and nephews as they take up their swords to repel the Lescari from our borders as a new year of struggle opens.

None could argue with the Emperor's decree that all those under arms remain in their camps through the Festival. Aleonne has truly won his epithet of Valiant and vindicated time and again the trust of those who saw in him the military leader Tormalin so desperately needed. After the treacherous attacks launched by Parnilesse at Autumn Equinox, in direct spite of agreed truce, Winter Solstice celebrations in Toremal have been accordingly muted. I am pleased to report no word as yet of any such perfidy and the Imperial Despatch continues to bring regular reports from the battle lines, so we need not lament the uncertainty of silence.

The common purpose that unites us in these dark days perversely served to give those of us here a Festival of considerable harmony. When the coarsening effect of soldiering has of late been apt to give the court a masculine and oftimes uncouth atmosphere, so we ladies were pleasantly surprised to find ourselves in the ascendant with so many men away serving with the Cohorts. We were able to restore our spirits somewhat with peaceable diversions of music and dance.

As we remember Poldrion's care of the dead at this season, let us be thankful D'Olbriot and the House of my birth, Den Murivance, have suffered such minor losses compared to some Houses. The twin scourges of war and camp fever have reduced Den Parisot to such a pass that the Name may never recover. On the other side of the scales, the year has seen two more Houses ennobled, by letters patent sent by Aleonne the Valiant with the endorsement of those Princes serving in the field, for the confirmation by those Sieurs remaining to gather in Convocation.

The only Sieur to declare against the proposals was Tor Correl, but that was to be expected and no one took any heed of his vicious insults to the Emperor. I confess myself amazed that the foolish old man sustains such malice and that the men of the Name do nothing to force him to stand down. It is ten full years after his abortive attempt to snatch the throne by force of arms was so comprehensively rebuffed. That Sieur's continued claims to primacy solely based on ancestral military skills in legendary eras merely make his Name ridiculous. A House already so damaged and even stripped of its right to train men in arms cannot afford further injury.

I have paid my respects to the newly created Maitresse Den Viorel and the Sieur Den Haurient and find both worthy of rank and privilege. In this darkness that surrounds us, let us find some consolation in the way bright courage is bringing new Names to the fore. Let us hope that the Emperor's belief in rewarding military merit, be it from never so lowly a station, will be vindicated with rapid victories and surcease from this suppurating war.

I find it perplexing that the financial records of the House show a far healthier situation than I might have expected. While the warfare in Lescar has entirely disrupted our links with Dalasor and Gidesta, our galleys continue to ply their routes to the burgeoning seaport of Relshaz and thus to Caladhria. Aldabreshin pirates whom all expected to increase their predations have turned instead to dealing with any and all entangled in the fighting, presumably finding greater returns for fewer risks. This western trade proves crucial in maintaining a continuing market for the finished wares

The D'Olbriot Residence Gatehouse,
Summer Solstice Festival, Third Day, Morning

I woke with the dawn chatter of eaves-birds on the gables. My first half-conscious thought was regret for past Festivals. More generous Solstice rosters usually mean a chance of lying abed. But I couldn't get back to sleep, not with that coffer of Kellarin artefacts waiting. A wash and a shave helped clear the weariness fogging my thoughts and, once outside, the cool morning air refreshed me. Gardeners' boys carried buckets of water past me, silent maids were dusting the front hall of the residence and a heavy-eyed footman set some Festival garlands to rights.

'Ryshad!' A hiss from an upper landing stopped me and Temar ran lightly down the main staircase.

'On your way to the library?' I enquired.

'Indeed.' Temar strode through the house, oblivious to discreetly curious servants sliding past, an unobtrusive girl with an armful of fresh flowers, a shirt-sleeved valet with a pile of pressed linen. 'Arimelin be blessed, we are finally achieving something!'

I waited until we were in the corridor to the library and no one else was within earshot. 'I meant what I said last night, Temar.' He looked at me as I laid a warning hand on his arm. 'If you go off without me again, I'll take you round the back of the stableyard and beat some sense into you, Esquire or not! It all turned out well, but that's no answer, not to you risking your neck. You've responsibilities to more than yourself now. How would Kellarin fare if Guinalle had to drop everything and come over here because you'd got yourself skewered in some back alley? I'm not saying you shouldn't have gone, but you sure as curses shouldn't have gone alone.' I'd lain awake long into the night, chilled by the thought of what could have happened to the lad and the mage girl.

This morning Temar had the grace to look faintly ashamed of himself. 'I understand your concerns.'

I nodded. 'Just don't do it again.' But I'd finally slept when it had occurred to me that Temar had probably been as safe in the Lescari quarter, where no one knew his Name or face, as he would have been among Houses where Dastennin only knew what malice lurked behind the tapestries. Not that I was about to tell him that.

We reached the library and Temar rattled the handle with more irritation than was strictly necessary. 'Locked, curse it!'

I knocked cautiously on the bland barrier of polished panels. 'Messire? Dolsan?'

'Ryshad?' I heard Demoiselle Avila's firm tread. 'And Temar?'

'Of course,' he said crossly.

The key turned with a swift snap. 'You took your ease this morning, did you?' There was a spark of laughter in her dry face as she opened the door.

'I should have realised you would scarce let the dew dry off the grass,' Temar retorted.

I followed him in and we both looked rather nervously at the coffer open on the library table. Gold, silver, enamel and gems gleamed lustrous on a broad swathe of linen.

Avila made some uninformative sound. 'Since you are here, you can help.' She handed us each a fair copy of the list of artefacts so eagerly sought by the waiting folk of Kellarin.

Temar and I shared an uncertain glance.

'Oh get on with it. You need not even touch anything.' Avila picked up a distinctive ring, wrought with two copper hands holding a square-cut crystal between them. This morning she was wearing a plain brown dress, hair braided and pinned in a simple knot, looking more like one of my mother's sewing circle than a noble lady.

'Can you tell which ones carry enchantment, Demoiselle?'

I tucked my hands behind my back as I bent over the array of treasures.

'Sadly, no.' Avila sounded more irritated than regretful. 'We would need Guinalle for that.'

Temar made some slight noise but subsided under Avila's glare.

An elegant pomander caught my eye. Shaped like a plump purse tied with cord, the gold was cut away around a circle of little pea flowers on either side, blue enamelled petals undimmed through all the generations even if its perfumes had long since perished. I searched the list in my hand, where five artefacts were still untraced for every one with a note of success beside it. Temar's stomach growled, the only sound to break the silence.

'There's bread and fruit.' Avila nodded absently to a side table.

'Can I bring you anything, Demoiselle?' I offered politely.

'Thank you, no. So Temar, what are your plans for the woman and her child?' Avila asked in that deceptive tone women have, the one that sounds so relaxed when in fact the wrong answer will bring the ceiling down on your head.

'We will recompense her,' Temar said cautiously.

Avila reached for a pen laid across an inkstand. 'Hand her a heavy purse and send her on her way?'

Temar hesitated. Agreement would plainly be the wrong response but he was struggling for the right one. I kept my eyes firmly on my list.

'You take no responsibility for their fate?' Avila noted something with a decisive flourish of her quill.

'Perhaps the mother could be found work within the residence?' hazarded Temar. 'Some menial task?'

I glanced up to see him looking hopefully at me. 'The House Steward won't be interested,' I said slowly.

'If the Sieur instructs him, as a charity?' Temar suggested with a hint of pleading.

'Messire won't do that,' I told him reluctantly. 'The Steward earns his pay and perquisites by taking all responsibility for servants' concerns, and the other side of that coin is the Sieur doesn't interfere.'

Avila sniffed. 'In a properly regulated House, master and mistress know all their servants by name and family and treat them fittingly.'

Hearing an echo of loss beneath her tart words, I kept quiet. I found the pomander and ticked it off my list with an absurd sense of achievement. One more to be woken from the chill of enchantment; Master Aglet, a joiner, according to the record.

Temar took the quill from me and dipped ink for his own note, our gazes meeting for a moment. 'Sheer luck or not, you've made a success of your trip with this haul alone,' I commented.

'Grant Maewelin her due,' said Avila in quelling tones. 'The goddess surely took charge of these hidden minds, just as she holds seed and bud sleeping through the dark days of winter.'

'Which would explain how the pieces came to her shrine,' Temar nodded thoughtfully.

He was convinced, no question, but few people I know give Maewelin more than a passing thought beyond the close of Aft-Winter. Hunger in the lean days after Winter Solstice prompts some to cover all options with an offering to the Winter Hag, but even then it's a cult mostly limited to widows and women past any hope of marriage. That reminded me of something.

'The shrine to Maewelin in Zyoutessela is a refuge for women without family or friends. I know the Relict Tor Bezaemar makes donations to all manner of shrines, Demoiselle. You could ask if there's any charitable sisterhood in Toremal that might take in the woman and her daughter?'

Avila's severe expression lightened a little. 'I will do so.'

'I have one,' said Temar with relief as much to do with my answer to the question of Maedura as with identifying an artefact. He pointed to a ring, modest turquoise set within silver petals. An inexpensive piece in any age but for some reason

I knew beyond doubt it had been given with love and cherished with devotion.

'The woman with three children.' I shivered on sudden recollection of a little group still lost in the vastness of the Kellarin cavern. The sorrowful wizards hadn't wanted to wake two children to the news that their sister and mother couldn't yet be revived.

'The boy had my belt, with the buckle you recovered from the Elietimm.' As our eyes met I saw the lad through Temar's memory, wide-eyed but determined not to show his fear, clinging to the buckle of Temar's belt and to the promise that everything would be all right.

'This was for the youngest child.' Avila held up a tiny enamelled flower strung on an age-darkened braid of silk, her voice rough.

'Then we can wake them all.' Tangled emotions constricted Temar's voice.

Avila looked down on the motley collection of valuables and trinkets. 'But so many of the men held to knives or daggers,' she said softly. 'Where are those?'

Sudden inspiration mocked me for a fool. 'Weapons would've been laid in sword school shrines! I'll wager my oath on it!'

I'd have explained further if Messire's clerk hadn't come in.

'Oh.' He stood in the doorway, nonplussed.

'You have something to say, young man?' Avila asked with all the confidence of rank.

'Surely you should all be getting ready to attend at the Imperial Law Courts, my lady.' Dolsan bowed respectfully but there was no mistaking his meaning as he looked at Temar's creased shirt and Avila's plain gown.

'In my day, substance counted for more than show among persons of high birth,' said Avila with a stern glare.

'In this age, my lady, show and substance are often one and the same.' Service to the Sieur made Dolsan equal to this challenge. 'Chosen Tathel, Esquire Camarl's valet was looking for you.'

I excused myself hastily to Avila and Temar and hurried upstairs. The Esquire was still in his shirt and an old pair of breeches, sorting through his own jewels for suitable ornaments for public appearance. 'You weren't in the gatehouse or the barracks, Ryshad. How's my valet supposed to find you if you don't leave word where you'll be?'

'I was in the library.' I apologised. 'That coffer looks to hold a lot of the pieces Temar's hunting.'

'That's fortunate.' Camarl's expression was uncompromising. 'That could well be all the spoils D'Alsennin wins from this Festival.' He set down a broad collar of curling gold links and tossed a letter at me.

'I learn you are interested in acquiring certain heirlooms of my House,' I read. *'Certain others have also expressed a desire to acquire these pieces. Accordingly, I intend to have three jewellers unbeholden to any Name appraise the items in question. Once I have established their value, I invite you to make an offer. From Messire Den Turquand, given at his Toremal residence, Summer Solstice Day.'*

'His man must have been waving it in the breeze to dry the ink on his way here,' muttered Camarl. 'What do you make of it, Ryshad?'

'Den Turquand got wind of the value of Kellarin artefacts,' I said slowly. 'And he'll sell to the highest bidder, no question. Some of the Names offering argument to D'Olbriot before the courts will be only too glad to pay thrice their value to use them as bargaining counters.' I couldn't contain my anger. 'But these are people's lives! Hostage-taking belongs back in the Chaos.'

'How did he get wind of this?' Camarl demanded.

I looked him in the eye. 'I've been asking various of my acquaintance if their masters or mistresses have heirlooms that might date from the loss of Kellarin.'

'Perhaps it might have been wise to discuss that with myself or the Sieur,' Camarl said bitingly. 'Servants gossip and share titbits with their betters, Ryshad.'

'I'm sorry. I'm accustomed to use my own judgement in

service of the Name.' I managed a fair appearance of regret. That all the Demoiselles and Esquires gossiped just as eagerly among themselves and Camarl learned all manner of valuable things from his own valet was neither here nor there.

'This is just not a priority.' Camarl screwed up the letter, hurling it into the empty hearth. 'These people under enchantment – let's be honest, a few more seasons, even years, would make no difference, not after so many generations. Setting the colony on a sound footing, stopping interest in Kellarin degenerating into an ugly scramble for advantage – that's what's important. This business of artefacts, it's simply a complication. What's the Sieur to do, Ryshad, if someone comes demanding concessions on trade in return for one of these cursed things?'

I kept my eyes lowered, expression neutral. I'd spent long enough in the service of the House to realise the Esquire's anger wasn't really directed at me. Although everyone treated him as such, Camarl wasn't yet formally confirmed as the Sieur's Designate. If all the black crows hovering round the House this Festival came home to roost, the Sieur's brothers and all the other men bearing the D'Olbriot Name would be looking for someone to blame.

'Go and get yourself liveried,' Camarl said after a moment of tense silence. 'Attend us to the law courts before you go off to answer that challenge.'

I bowed to the Esquire's turning back and closed the door softly behind me.

Back in the gatehouse I dug my formal livery out of the depths of my clothes press. Dark green breeches went beneath a straight coat of the same cloth, more a sleeved jerkin in style really. Banded with gold at the wrists and around the uncomfortably constricting upright collar, it had a gold lynx mask embroidered on the breast, eyes bright emeralds among the metallic thread. There'd be no doubt that I belonged to one of the most ancient and wealthy Houses of the Empire as we travelled through a city gaping for a glimpse of nobles they only knew through gossip, scandal and broadsheet tales.

I scowled into the mirror and went to wait in the gatehouse. This was evidently a day to show I knew my place.

'Not going to be fighting in that?' Stolley laughed from the seat where he was reading the most recent broadsheet. It was his privilege as senior Sergeant to be first to see the tittle tattle culled from rumour, venal servants and indiscreet clerks.

I smiled humourlessly. 'Hardly.'

'Got up and trod in your chamberpot, did you?' He shook his head. 'At least your livery still fits. I need a new one every year.'

'Master Dederic must love you.' I ran a finger round inside my collar. 'I don't suppose I've had this thing on more than ten times since I swore to the Name.'

'Lucky bastard,' said Stolley with feeling. 'Oh, and my wife says you're to come to supper when Festival's over. I warn you, she's inviting her niece, saying it's time you found a nice girl to court, now you'll be settled in Toremal.'

'Married to you and she still wants to shackle her niece to a chosen man? They say misery loves company.' I tried for a smile to take the sting out of my words. 'Any word this morning, anything on who attacked D'Alsennin?'

Stolley stood up to pin the broadsheet to the door for the men on duty during the day to read if they had the skill. 'Just Tor Kanselin's men saying the lad only got off his leash because Esquire Camarl was busy dallying in the gardens with Demoiselle Irianne. There was a bit of nonsense when one of our lads wondered if the Esquire had got round to plucking a petal or two.'

'And that's supposed to get Tor Kanselin off the hook?' I retorted, annoyed. 'And when their esquire got married last Solstice, didn't I hear they were whispering in corners about Camarl never having a girl on his arm? Hinting he might take a less than rational view of women?'

'They can't have it both ways,' Stolley agreed. 'Yes, Demoiselle, how can I serve?'

He turned to deal with the first of a flurry of visitors arriving for a lunch party and then with a series of coaches drawing up to take cadet members of the Name to engagements all around the city. I dutifully assisted, holding fans, offering a supporting hand, closing doors, careful not to crush expensive silks or feathers as I did so. In between I watched the toings and froings outside the open gate. Several women from grace houses went past, Stoll's own wife among them. If I was to make the step to proven man, the Sieur had to see my face, and I had to be on hand to do him some service. That meant buckling down here for a good few seasons, fetching, carrying and proving my loyalty day in and day out. I tried to imagine Livak among the placid wives and decided she'd be as out of place as a woodlark in a hencoop.

Messire's coach finally rattled up outside the gate just as the fourth chime of the day rang out from the bell tower. The bay horses were matched within a shade of colour, the woodwork and leather shone richly in the sunlight and liveried footmen jumped down to attend to door and step. The Sieur arrived with the echoes barely died away, Esquire Camarl, Temar and Demoiselle Avila with him. For all the fullness of his figure, the Sieur moved with brisk determination, twinkling eyes keen.

Temar was looking stubborn about something. He carried his sword, and as he approached held it out to me. 'I thought you might use this, for this afternoon.'

'My thanks, Esquire.' I took the scabbarded blade and bowed first to Temar and then to Camarl, who watched with distant annoyance as I unbelted my own sword and gave it into Stolley's keeping. Camarl had given me that new blade at Winter Solstice and I'd accepted it gladly, all the more so since I knew both smith and the smithy where it had been made and would wager my oath that no unquiet shades hung round it. But I couldn't throw Temar's offer back in his face, could I?

'At least you'll get some fresh air down at the sword school,' the Sieur remarked genially. 'Put an end to this nonsense of a challenge as soon as you can, Ryshad. Let them have their fun, but don't risk your skin trying to prove a point.' He favoured me with a warm smile.

Another carriage pulled up and the Sieur's elder brother appeared behind us, several clerks laden with ledgers with him, Messire's youngest son hovering at the back. The Sieur turned. 'Fresil, send Myred to find me if there's any nonsense over the Land Tax assessment. And I want to know at once who's behind any application to sting us over Kellarin for the year to come.'

The brother nodded, face uncompromising beneath his bald pate. We all made our bow as Esquire Fresil climbed into his coach, a ribbon-tied document clutched in one age-spotted hand that would summarise the House's finances to the last copper cut piece.

'Your uncle will make sure no one rolls up this House in parchment, won't he, Camarl?' The Sieur smiled with satisfaction. 'If Fresil can teach Myred half his skills, he'll make a worthy successor to assist you.'

Which was as close as Messire ever came to telling Camarl he favoured him as Designate.

'I don't think we need fret unduly about proceedings in the Imperial court today,' Messire continued easily. 'We've been looking into potentially contentious areas for most of For-Summer, Dolsan and myself. We've plenty of strings to our bow.' His expression turned cold and I turned to see Casuel hurrying down the residence steps. 'But we don't want people wondering about anything underhand. Ryshad, tell that importuning wizard to keep his distance today.'

I walked hastily over to Casuel. 'We're off to the courts, Master Mage, so the Sieur has no need of your services.' I tried to keep my tone light.

Casuel looked crestfallen and suspicious at one and the same time. 'Surely reminding people D'Olbriot has Archmage Planir for an ally will strengthen his position?'

'You know what folk are like, Casuel.' I shrugged. 'An advocate might see you and raise the question of magic just to confuse the real issues.'

'Planir should deal with this nonsensical prejudice once and for all.' Casuel flushed with irritation. 'So what am I to do today? Sit on my hands?'

'You could go and see what Velindre thinks of Allin and Temar's little adventure?' I suggested.

The Sieur snapped his fingers at me and I bowed. 'I'll see you later, Casuel.'

Messire was first into the coach, nodding me into a seat opposite. I tucked Temar's sword in hastily as Avila arranged her skirts to her satisfaction. As Temar joined us the Sieur sat back against the mossy velvet upholstery. 'Thank you, Ryshad. This is no time to be associated with magic in the public eye.'

'That is surely a little difficult,' said Temar with barely restrained indignation, 'when the Demoiselle Tor Arrial is the foremost practitioner of Artifice in this city.' Temar was richly dressed in the latest style, in dark russet silk, the clasp at his throat a complex knot of gold set with small faceted stones. Gold chains secured with garnet studs looped around the cuffs of his coat. Borrowed wealth it might be, but after today none of the commonalty thronging the streets would believe any rumour claiming the Esquire D'Alsennin was just some washed-up pauper. His only ring was the sapphire signet I remembered, a jarring touch of colour that must have had Master Dederic tearing his well-cut hair. I was glad to see Temar wearing something of his own among all this borrowed finery.

Avila was laughing. 'I am the only practitioner, as far as I can tell. But the boy has a point, Guliel. That Artifice cured his wounds was widely discussed yesterday.'

Messire nodded. 'True, but that's not elemental magic. In time, with care, we can make people understand the difference.'

'So what is our purpose in displaying ourselves at court today?' Avila asked politely after a short silence.

'To show young D'Alsennin alive and well and ready to uphold his rights. To show we have nothing to hide and stand ready to answer any mean-spirited accusation.' The Sieur beamed with a charm that won an answering smile from Avila.

In bellflower blue brocade she looked every measure the

noble lady. A collar of pearls and sapphires circled her neck and silver rings adorned every finger, two set with diamonds that flashed fire in the sunlight. Her hair was dressed high and, as she leaned forward, I saw she had a striking jewelled ornament pinning on her veil of lace. The spray of emerald fronds had a blue butterfly nestling in the centre and it took me a moment to recall this was the badge of Tor Arrial. Did this mean Messire has secured the alliance of the current Sieur, or was he putting the Name on notice that Avila was not about to yield any of her claims?

'Cheer up, Ryshad,' chuckled the Sieur. 'I'm sorry you have to be liveried up but it's as well to remind everyone where your loyalties lie. Have you heard the rumours running round about your adventures in the Archipelago?'

His tone was familiar, intimate, with all the sincerity that had convinced me Messire's oath bound him to me as securely as mine to him. But he'd handed me over to Planir without hesitation when that best served the wider ambitions of his House. I sat back in the shadows as we swept between the shade trees lining the road to the lower city.

As we passed the conduit house, the bowl of the lower city spread out before us beneath the cloudless sky. The vista was a chequer pattern of myriad roofs, packed as close as the tiles they were made from, dappled with all shades of colour from the rawest new orange to ancient faded umber. Here and there a taller tower of golden stone looked down on less favoured neighbours, a gatehouse or some other remnant of a noble edifice now given over to more mundane uses, yet still keeping mute watch over a Name's interests. Chimneys that took no rest for the Festival breathed faint plumes of smoke that thickened the air as we left the green freshness of the upper city and the fitful breezes from the distant, hidden sea were baffled by cornices and façades turning them this way and that.

The carriage rattled over the cobbles, coachman keeping the horses trotting at a steady pace, a footman using a long horn to clear the commonalty off the road. It sounded ever more frequently as we drew nearer to the sprawling mass of the law courts.

'The walls!' Temar exclaimed. He twisted in his seat to peer out of the window. 'That is the Toremal I remember!'

'How the city is grown,' murmured Avila, mouth set in a bloodless line.

'Shall I lower the blinds?' Camarl forced a smile as he waved to acknowledge some loyal tenants cheering the D'Olbriot lynx on the door.

'No, I don't think so.' The Sieur clapped silent hands to show his admiration for a puppet in D'Olbriot livery held up for his amusement. The crowd was swelling with fervent excitement, the noise almost painful to the ears by the time we drew up beneath the looming shadow of the Imperial Courts.

'This is the palace,' said Temar suddenly.

Camarl frowned. 'No, that's over yonder.'

Temar shook his head impatiently. 'No, I mean it was the palace, in Nemith's day.'

'That's right,' I agreed. Even with the mighty walls protecting the city, the men who'd built Toremal's defences had prepared for every contingency. The palace had been set apart as a final bastion, impregnable within its own walls, a last redoubt where the Emperor could gather the Cohorts entrusted to him by the Names and strike out if ever the city itself fell. But the days when armed men could threaten Toremal were long since past and the palace had been rebuilt, extended and adapted through every era. Where once it had been the stronghold of Emperors charged with defending Tormalin through force of arms, now it served the law courts where Emperors of this era ruled on the rights and duties of the Houses of Toremal.

Messire's coach drew up before the western frontage. High overhead a sweep of ruddy tiles rolled down to a pierced balustrade of interlaced stone fronds. Oriel windows below were ornamented with carved foliage worn soft and indistinct by generations of rain. Statues weathered to anonymity stood in niches just above head height, and on the ground men sworn to Den Janaquel colours formed a line either side of carpet laid to save noble shoes from the dust of the streets. The crowd waited in benign enough mood, no need for the Duty Cohort to link arms just yet, or worse, use staves to reinforce their barrier. None of the cases heard today would have any impact on the common people, so they could just relish the spectacle.

'Out you get,' the Sieur prompted Camarl as the footman opened the door.

He brushed at the skirts of his sage green coat and stepped down to polite if not fulsome applause. The Sieur nodded to Temar, who was greeted with appreciably louder cheers above an undercurrent of avid gossip. When Messire himself appeared, he stopped to acknowledge a roar of approval, one hand on the doorpost, the other waving in elegant response. He wore darker green silk than Camarl, unbrocaded but shot with gold. The cut of his coat was fuller in line than fashion dictated, far better suited to his stoutness and comparative lack of height.

Judging the ebbing enthusiasm of the crowd to a nicety, Messire stepped down and turned to offer his hand to Avila. Her appearance incited the ebullient mob to fresh cheering and I heard a new note of speculation as the Sieur offered her his arm. I got out of the coach completely ignored by everyone.

'Where do we go?' Avila's smile was gracious but I saw nervousness darkening her eyes.

'In a moment,' said the Sieur, bending towards her with a smile that won renewed interest from the avid faces closest. 'These people have come to offer their duty, after all.'

'Smile, Temar.' Camarl turned to give people on the far side a look at his finery. 'If you're looking cheerful, satire artists and gossipmongers can't make up anything too dreadful about you.'

'Apart from drawing me grinning like a half-wit,' Messire laughed. 'Do you remember that dreadful picture doing the rounds last summer, Camarl?'

He laid a proprietorial hand on Avila's fingers as she held his arm close and walked slowly beneath the great arch. Camarl strolled behind with a relaxed air that Temar made a creditable attempt at matching. I followed with a few curious eyes sliding my way before returning to the far more interesting spectacle of highest nobility almost close enough to touch.

As we came out into the open sunlight of the courtyard a rattle of hooves and harness behind us prompted shouts of welcome for some new arrival. When Temar would have looked to see who it was, Camarl dissuaded him with the faintest shake of his head. 'Ryshad, who's behind us?'

A half-turn showed me the crest emblazoned on the carriage door. 'Den Murivance.'

Knots of clerks in lawyerly grey thronged the shadows of the colonnade ringing the courtyard, looking intently as the Sieur D'Olbriot escorted Demoiselle Tor Arrial. Two put their heads close for a moment and then one went hurrying off, the long sleeves of his robe flapping. I wondered if Messire really had an interest in Avila or if this was simply another move on the game board. Whichever, I'd bet my oath fee some hapless advocate would be guttering the candles writing up the implications of a D'Olbriot match with Tor Arrial.

Temar slowed, looking around at the five storeys of the palace, now all given over to archives and records and quarters for advocates rich enough to pay for a foothold in their battleground, spare rooms in garret and cellar divided and divided again for rank and file. 'I did not recognise that façade, but this is much as it was.'

I looked at the pitted and stained columns, the cracked flagstones and the mismatched shutters of the windows. Trying to imagine it as pristine as Temar's memory of it was disconcertingly easy. 'It's been the law courts since the days of Inshol the Curt.'

'Shall we proceed, Messire?' Camarl raised snapping fingers and an advocate hurried to his side.

'Indeed.' The Sieur followed the lawyer through the colonnade to a great double door opening on to an anteroom where lawyers milled around like a flock of banded pigeons.

'Demoiselle Tor Arrial, Esquire D'Alsennin, may I make known Advocate Burquest?' The Sieur introduced one of Toremal's most prominent lawyers with easy familiarity. Burquest was a broad-shouldered man with a round, kindly face and a deceptively amiable air. He wore his thinning hair brushed straight back and long to his collar, a style going out of fashion when I'd been a youth. But Burquest wasn't concerned with fashions. His whole life was arguing before the Imperial courts, and his reputation was formidable.

Temar did his best to bow despite the people pressing all round. Avila favoured Burquest with a tight smile, but I could see she was uneasy, hemmed in by unknown bodies.

The Sieur noticed as well. 'Are we ready to go in?'

Burquest nodded. 'This way, sirs, my lady.'

A burly warder in Den Janaquel colours was guarding the door to the court proper but drew his silver capped staff aside to let us pass. As Camarl stepped forward to hear what the advocate was saying to the Sieur, Temar fell back beside me.

'This was the Imperial audience room,' he said in an undertone, staring around the broad hall. Stone vaults high overhead were supported by intricate stonework springing like carved branches from massive faceted columns. Narrow windows of clear glass rose tall between the pillars and sparkling sunlight floated down to us. Down at our level the surroundings were not nearly so grand. The long tables and benches were sturdy and functional but no more than that. The floor had been swept, but some Nemith had probably been the last one to order it polished. There was nothing in the plain, undecorated furnishings to distract anyone from the business of the law, an Imperial decree dating back to Leoril the Wise.

'Up there?' Temar frowned as the Sieur headed for a broad gallery built around three sides of the room.

'Only advocates and their clerks appear before the Emperor.' I indicated a row of lecterns set in a line before a fretted screen.

'Where is he?' Temar looked around, puzzled.

I nodded at the screen. 'He'll be behind there.'

We took our seats in the second rank of the gallery, the Sieur and Avila in front, close to the dais so we could see everyone else in the gallery and almost all of the people below.

Camarl was on Temar's far side and he leaned forward to include me in his remarks. 'The Emperor sits screened so that no one can see his reactions, try to catch his eye, or make some move to influence or distract him.'

'But he can see us?' Temar looked thoughtfully at the black-varnished wooden lattice.

'More importantly, so can all these people. So look relaxed and unconcerned, no matter what's said below,' Camarl advised, turning to nod and smile as the gallery filled up. There were no formal divisions, but people separated regardless in tight huddles of mutual interest.

'Den Thasnet,' I murmured, my pointing hand hidden by Avila's shoulder. 'Tor Alder.'

'Dirindal thought I might find friends in that House,' said Temar a little sadly.

The Sieur half turned in his seat. 'It's easy enough to be friends until the cow gets into the garden. They think you're here to eat them out of House and home.' He looked at Camarl. 'Note which advocate speaks on each count and we'll set Dolsan to looking up any other suits they've been involved in. We might get some hint as to who's orchestrating this.' He turned to look at the rearmost gallery and waved to someone. 'I see we have a good turn out of the richer commonalty.'

The men of trade and practical skills were easily identifiable. Their clothes were as fashionably cut of cloth as rich as any noble, and plenty of silver and gold shone bright in the sunlight, but none of them wore any ornament set with gemstones. Perinal the Bold's law might be archaic and often disregarded, but no one was going to risk challenging it in the heart of Imperial justice.

Down on the floor of the court the advocates were standing in a loose circle behind the row of lecterns. Their grey robes were distinguished by various knots of gold on each shoulder and cord in differing colours braided around the upright collars. Mistal had tried explaining their significance to me more than once, but I'd never really listened.

Temar leaned forward. 'I see no insignia on anyone down there.'

'That was one of Tadriol the Staunch's reforms.' Camarl leaned back with every appearance of ease. 'No House may retain any permanent advocate. We sponsor clerks, train them up in our archives, but once they start offering argument to the court they're their own men.'

'A justified claim of bias can get a judgement reversed,' I explained to Temar.

'Which has happened to Den Thasnet more than once,' murmured Camarl. 'So it'll be interesting to see who their mouthpiece might be over in the Land Tax court.' He smiled warmly at a pretty girl with a Den Murivance portcullis picked out in spinels on the silver handle of her white-feathered fan. 'Have you been introduced to Gelaia, Temar?'

'No.' Temar looked momentarily startled but gave the girl a polite wave. The gesture stirred a faint ripple of interest on far side of the court, among a sizeable number of Den Rannion Esquires. I looked for any resemblance to Temar's long dead friend Vahil, vivid in my memory, but found none.

Temar stirred on the hard wooden seat, returning the hostile gazes levelled at him in full measure. 'I think we could take them on, the three of us, do you not agree?' He was only half joking.

'We don't dirty our own hands fighting among ourselves nowadays,' said Camarl in mock reproof. 'That's what law courts are for.'

'Whoever started this will soon find they've a battle on their hands,' remarked the Sieur. He wasn't joking.

A bell rang a sharp summons to order behind the imperial screen. We all stood, waiting in silence as unseen feet sounded on the dais and chairs scraped and settled.

'That's more than just the Emperor,' Temar said in the softest of whispers.

'He always has Justiciars from the lower courts to advise him,' I explained. 'Experts in property, inheritance, whatever suits are being brought.'

A brisk Justiciar whose coppery head clashed horribly with his black-braided scarlet robes appeared out of a door in one end of the screen. The advocates promptly took their places at their lecterns. Behind them, on backless benches, their teams of clerks sat alert.

'In the name of Emperor Tadriol, fifth of that name and called the Provident, I beseech Raeponin to give his grace to all who hear me. Be warned that the god's scales weigh the justice of every man's word within this court. All who speak freely may do so with truth as their witness. All who dissemble will be compelled to reveal what they hope to hide. All who lie will be marked by the god's displeasure. Any man shown forsworn will be whipped and flung naked beyond the city walls at sunset.' He rattled through words we'd all heard plenty of times but his face was uncompromisingly stern as he looked at each advocate.

I saw Avila's back stiffen and Temar shifted in his seat. Camarl laid a silencing hand on his arm.

The redheaded man nodded to the first advocate. 'You may proceed.' The others all took seats at the tables with their respective teams of clerks and the justiciar disappeared below us.

'May Raeponin hold me to my oath.' The hook-nosed advocate took a calm breath. 'I'm here to present the arguments of Den Rannion. The House declares an ancient interest in the land of Kellarin, by virtue of the investment in goods, coin and people made by Sieur Ancel Den Rannion in the days of Nemith the Last, even up to the cost of his own life. His son, Sieur Vahil Den Rannion, did not relinquish his claim. Even on his deathbed, he had his sons swear to uphold it. We have records and deeds to support our contention and ask that due disposition of that unknown land be made, fully respecting these ancient rights.'

He turned with a smile to the next advocate who stepped up to his lectern, one hand smoothing his close-trimmed beard. 'May Raeponin hold me to my oath. I argue for Tor Priminale in the Name of Den Fellaemion, now subsumed into that House. Messire Haffrein Den Fellaemion was first discoverer of Kellarin, in voyages backed by Nemith the Seafarer. He was the instigator of the colony, its leader and guide, and at the last died in its defence. The House of Tor Priminale begs leave to claim its rights and complete the work of so illustrious an ancestor in opening up this new land and making best use of its resources, in open cooperation with Den Rannion and any other interested Houses.'

The Sieur and Camarl exchanged a look of mild interest at the revelation that Den Rannion and Tor Priminale had so readily abandoned generations of antagonism.

The next advocate was on his feet almost before Tor Priminale's man had stopped speaking. 'May Raeponin hold me to my oath.' He straightened the fronts of his gown nervously. 'I speak for Den Muret, by reason of the great number of tenants of that House who travelled to the Kellarin colony. Their work and the rights due Den Muret in consequence should be recognised.'

He sat down quickly, taking the next man by surprise. I tried to see Camarl's face out of the corner of my eye, but Temar was in the way. Everyone was sitting motionless, all attention fixed on the court, the gallery silent as a shrine at midnight. I looked at Den Muret's man and recalled Mistal saying they wouldn't bring suit until they knew Tor Priminale was successful. Now Den Domesin had a man on his feet, arguing for rights in Kellarin by virtue of ancient investment. What reason did they have to be confident?

Temar was shifting in his seat again, his indignation plain to see. As I glanced sideways, I saw the Demoiselle Den Murivance watching him with speculative hazel eyes above the fan hiding her mouth as she whispered to her companion.

'May Raeponin hold me to my oath.' Down in the court a tall advocate with hair and face as greyly neutral as his robes spoke briskly to the impassive screen. 'I argue for Tor Alder that ancestral rights over inherited properties be respected. Those properties were conveyed to that House by bequest from the last Sieur D'Alsennin in the expectation that the last Esquire of the Name might reasonably be expected to return within the lifetime of his remaining parent. Since this did not happen, we contend the care with which those lands have been administered in the intervening generations must outweigh claims made by some pretender to an extinct Name.'

So they weren't going to argue D'Alsennin was a dead House, they were just going to invite the court to accept it as fact. I looked down to see Temar's hands tightly interlaced, long fingers bloodless beneath the pressure.

'May Raeponin hold me to my oath.' A stout lawyer with an unhealthily high colour was stepping forward, leaning on his lectern with the air of a man settling in for a long stay. 'I am here as a friend of the court.' Even Messire couldn't restrain a start at that and a hiss of surprise ran round the gallery.

'What does that mean?' Temar whispered urgently.

'It means we don't know who's behind him,' I answered softly. Camarl leaned forward, face a mask to hide his anger.

'I am here as a friend of the court,' the advocate repeated as the noise subsided into expectant silence. 'I am here to argue that the House of D'Olbriot has acted with grievous bad faith ill befitting such an ancient and illustrious Name. When scholars of the House realised the fabled colony of Nemith the Last was reality rather than myth, the Name did not share the opportunities becoming apparent. D'Olbriot has sought to keep all to itself, to its sole advantage and enrichment. Rather than seek help from the other Houses of the Empire in crossing the ocean, D'Olbriot turned to the wizards of Hadrumal. D'Olbriot has further invited them into the counsels of the House, even giving one house room.' The advocate paused to accommodate a hint of amusement from the gallery at his little sally. 'Rumour has it that marriage with a wizard is even now being contemplated by someone within

D'Olbriot walls, though not, at least, by someone of the D'Olbriot Name.

'But let us not speak of rumour,' he continued smoothly after pausing just long enough for everyone to look at Temar, who was plainly outraged. 'This court is only concerned with facts. It is a fact that now that the remnants of Kellarin's colony have been unearthed D'Olbriot continues to be the only link across the ocean. Whatever information is so vital to making such a voyage remains locked behind D'Olbriot lips. Just as the only living claimant to D'Alsennin rights is hidden behind D'Olbriot doors. D'Olbriot has installed this young man as leader of the colony. But what does this leader do? Does he speak for his people? Does he negotiate trade agreements, does he invite merchants and artisans to bring their skills to make a civilisation in this savage land? No, D'Olbriot's word is final on all such matters. All such concerns are most definitely a D'Olbriot monopoly, as is all the wealth that will result.'

The advocate turned his back on the dais momentarily to glance up at the rearmost gallery, where the merchants were listening with interest.

'Even if Kellarin has only a fifth the riches of tradition, it is most assuredly a wealthy land. We don't even know how far it extends, what resources might be found over its distant horizons. Small wonder that the House of D'Olbriot covets it all. But all the wealth of Kellarin pales into insignificance when we consider other advantages that might accrue to D'Olbriot as a result of this exclusive association with D'Alsennin. We've all heard the rumours, haven't we, ancient enchantments safeguarding these lost colonists and arcane magic sustaining them?' He laughed for a moment with delicate scepticism. 'Well, much of this may be mere fireside fancy, but no one can deny the presence of young Esquire D'Alsennin here today.' This time he turned to look full at Temar and everyone in the court and the gallery above did the same. About half looked envious while the rest seemed faintly repelled.

'Esquire D'Alsennin,' the advocate repeated, 'who was

stabbed, beaten and left for dead in the dirt of the road. Not two days later he sits before us, hale and hearty. Does the House of D'Olbriot propose to share the esoteric arts that make this possible? Will we be spared the death of our loved ones in childbed, our sons and daughters saved from pestilence? Such magic supposedly safeguarded the Old Empire and wrought more wonders besides. Can one truly send word back and forth across hundreds of leagues in the blink of an eye? Does D'Olbriot propose to share such knowledge, or keep the advantages for himself while the rest of us are limited to the Imperial Despatch?' The advocate looked apologetic. 'I do not mean to disparage those excellent couriers, but it is undeniable fact that a horse can only cover so much ground in one day.'

He turned briskly on his heel, walking up and down before the screened dais. 'That a mighty House might succumb to the temptations of selfishness and greed is understandable, if regrettable. But such base emotions cannot go unchallenged, lest they unbalance the compact of mutual respect that knits our Empire together. That's why we're all here today. My esteemed companions advance the most basic claims of those other Names with legitimate interest in Kellarin. I argue in defence of common justice and against abuse of noble privilege. As always, it falls to the Emperor to redress the balance.'

Bowing first to the faceless screen, the advocate turned to walk back to the table where his clerks were sitting. I saw a suitably modest smile as he lifted his face to the gallery, guileless warm brown eyes inviting everyone to agree with his entirely disinterested speech.

Messire's advocate, Master Burquest, was walking to his own lectern, smoothing the grey silk of his robe over his plain blue coat sleeve. He looked up at the centre of the screen. 'May Raeponin hold me to my oath.' He spoke simply, as if he were talking directly to the Emperor. 'I'm here to argue for D'Olbriot. I'll show that the House's interest in Kellarin was an unforeseen consequence of attempts by men sworn to the Name to uncover the reasons for robbery and attack suffered by a son of that House. Surely no one will deny D'Olbriot the right to protect its own? I'll argue that it's hardly reasonable to complain the free flow of commerce is being restricted when trade with Kellarin is still barely a trickle. I can show that with the briefest survey of the Name's accounts.' He waved a dismissive hand before voice and face turned serious, still focused on the unseen Emperor.

'I will show that magecraft is used to cross the ocean from simple necessity. Surely no one would suggest that the perils of the open ocean be needlessly risked when there are ways to lessen the dangers? That would hardly be reasonable – or should I say rational?' Everyone in the gallery was hanging on Burquest's words now, a smile here, a nod there approving his dry, unhurried delivery.

'It is just as reasonable for Esquire D'Alsennin,' Burquest raised a finger, 'in the absence of a Sieur of that Name for the present, just as reasonable for him to turn for advice and support to the Sieur of the House that risked so much, both materially and in reputation, to help those lost across the ocean. Perhaps, had Den Domesin and Tor Priminale shared in those initial expeditions, rather than dismissing D'Olbriot's folly, those Houses might have been able to make themselves known to their distant cousins. Esquire Albarn and Demoiselle Guinalle might well have been grateful for their aid and counsel. We'll never know, because they have been entirely ignored by their erstwhile Names. Tor Arrial, on the other hand, have shown us all a better way, welcoming their long-lost daughter and undertaking to work with D'Olbriot in supporting the colonists in Kellarin in their future endeavours.'

Burquest didn't look at Avila, which was probably just as well because I could see her neck going pink from where I was sitting. So the Sieur had got Tor Arrial on his side; that was good news. But even a hundredth share of the Kellarin trade would go a long way to restoring the Name to its former status. Diminished as it was at present, Tor Arrial didn't have a lot to lose.

Burquest leaned his elbows on his lectern. 'Of course, any

actions or circumstance can look good or bad, depending on your point of view. Which is why we trust this court to listen to all the arguments, to take a wider perspective and give judgement without fear or favour.' He smiled warmly at the fretted screen and turned to walk calmly back to his table.

There was a muted bustle of activity behind the screen and a small bell sounded. At that signal the clerks all burst into activity, some scribbling furiously, others sorting through ledgers and notes. Conversation hummed round the gallery, low-voiced speculation ringing with anticipation.

'Is that it?' Temar looked at me in perplexity. 'What now?'

'Each advocate presents his argument in detail, point by point, calling evidence as he goes.' I pointed to the deed boxes and stacks of ledgers piled high down the middle of each table. Burquest sat at his ease, chatting with a smile for his clerks and idly fanning himself with a leaf of parchment. Den Domesin's advocate on the other hand was frantically concentrating on a closely written sheet of paper and Den Muret's man looked positively unwell. Each had a much smaller team of clerks, some of whom looked barely old enough to shave.

'When does D'Olbriot's man get a chance to answer?' demanded Temar.

'Every time the Emperor thinks the point in question has been made and he wants to hear from the other side.' I nodded at the screen. 'You'll hear the bell.'

'What good will any of this do?' Avila hissed with irritation. 'You people mouth the words that should secure your justice and yet you all remain free to lie and dissemble.'

The Sieur, myself and Camarl looked at her in confusion.

'Forgive me but I don't understand,' Camarl apologised for all of us.

Avila turned in her seat, face hard. 'The invocation, what does it mean to you?'

Camarl raised uncomprehending brows. 'It's a reminder to all involved to act honestly.'

'Penalties are imposed, for any found forsworn,' Messire assured her.

'Those words once invoked Artifice proof against any forswearing!' Avila took a breath and forced herself to speak more quietly. 'Enchantment should make it impossible for anyone to speak a lie within this court.'

'It was ever thus, in our day,' Temar agreed grimly.

'What happens to someone lying?' frowned Camarl. I knew what he was thinking; we've all heard the nursery tales of the fox who'd lied to Talagrin about who'd eaten the plover's eggs. His tongue turned black and shrivelled up, but I couldn't see any advantage to D'Olbriot if that happened to some opposing advocate. The House's associations with magic were clearly going to be used against us and any overt display would just condemn the Sieur further.

'Do me the courtesy of listening,' snapped Avila. 'No one can lie. If they attempt falsehood, they simply cannot speak. Silence is all the proof needed of ill faith.'

I exchanged a bemused glance with Camarl and the Sieur. 'Could you make it so, here and now, if you repeated the rite?' I asked Avila.

She shook her head crossly. 'Not without each advocate invoking Artifice in his response, citing his oath to bind him.'

'So their oath was once enchantment as well?' asked Camarl.

'All oaths were,' said Avila coldly. 'Artifice bound all who exchanged them.

'So much has changed since the Chaos.' Messire looked at me with a faint smile. 'This is very interesting, but we just have to rely on eloquence and argument, don't we?'

Avila gave him a hard look through narrowed eyes. 'Yet another loss your age has suffered, Guliel.'

As she spoke I heard a faint carillon from outside. The Sieur nodded to me and I stood up. 'Now you know what Houses are drawn up for battle here, see if they've sent any skirmishers down to the sword school,' he ordered.

Temar made to stand as well but Camarl laid a heavy hand on his shoulder. I nodded a farewell to them both. 'Your fight's right here, Temar,' I said lightly. 'Look amused if Camarl's smiling, and you can look hurt if the Sieur turns round to commiserate. Don't ever look angry, don't look triumphant or smug. I'll find out who posted that challenge, if Raeponin wields any justice at all, and we'll hold a council of war this evening.'

Avila turned, face indignant. 'I'll thank you not to use the god's name so lightly, Ryshad.'

She would have said more but the Sieur stood up, setting renewed interest busy around the gallery. 'Defend the honour of our House.' He held both my hands between his, looking deep into my eyes. 'And take every care you can, Ryshad.'

Making my way out of the courtroom, curious faces on all sides, I felt I had some invisible advocate at my shoulder asking silent questions. Surely the Sieur wanted me safe for my own sake, not merely because my defeat would reflect badly on the House? In any case, wasn't Messire entitled to both concerns? Had he abandoned me to Planir and the wizards of Hadrumal out of callousness, or had he been forced by simple expediency? Were the resentments I'd been struggling with any more justified than the half-thought-out arguments of Tor Priminale and the like?

I ripped open the constricting collar of my livery as I strode out of the courts and headed for the sword school. I'd find time to look for answers to all that later. For now I had to fight whoever turned up to prove my fitness for honour or take a piece out of my worthless hide. If that was all there was to this challenge, I'd meet it head on, but if there was more to it, if I faced swords paid for by some noble dissatisfied with the proxy battles of the law courts, I wanted to know who was behind it all as much as Messire.

The Imperial Court,
Summer Solstice Festival, Third Day,
Late Morning

Temar shifted on the hard wooden bench. Feeling an ominous twinge of cramp in one calf muscle, he tried to point his toes inside his highly polished boots. The bell behind the screen rang briskly and Den Muret's advocate sprang to his lectern, clutching yet another parchment with writing faded nigh to invisible. Then a man in scarlet opened the door to the screen hiding the Emperor, exchanging a brief word with the Justiciar who'd administered those meaningless oaths. Temar looked eagerly at this first distraction in he couldn't recall how long. This man's robe had black trim to sleeves and hem and a loose cord around the neck rather than the advocates' circles of braid. Wasn't that cord made into a noose? No, that couldn't be right. Temar wondered why these two wore red when everyone else was in grey. What was the Emperor wearing?

Den Muret's advocate cleared his throat nervously and resumed his rapid mumble. Taking a deep breath, Temar restrained an impulse to rub his eyes and stifled a yawn. Even so vast a room was growing stuffy as the sun rose towards noon outside, and all the doors and windows stayed closed. He tried schooling his face to a bland mask of interest like Camarl's. Plenty of people in the close-packed gallery were looking his way, some merely curious, some plainly hostile. The Den Murivance girl kept glancing at him, fanning herself thoughtfully. It was a shame he wasn't sitting next to a girl, Temar thought, to get the benefit of a fan.

A discreet nudge startled Temar out of this inconsequential reverie. Camarl was smiling with rueful amusement, the Sieur turning to look at them with a mingled regret and enjoyment. Temar did his best to match their expressions, wondering what he'd missed. He was lucky to understand one sentence in three, given the pace and fluidity of the advocates' language.

What had Den Muret's man done to gratify Camarl and the Sieur? Faint discomfort was plain on more than one Den Rannion face in the far gallery. Temar glanced at their advocate, but the man's ascetic face was all unreadable bony angles. He sighed softly to himself. He'd never have imagined he could find himself facing Vahil's family in a court of law, with all these people squabbling over Kel Ar'Ayen like dogs tearing at a fat carcass.

The little bell sounded three sharp notes and everyone in the floor of the court instantly sprang to life, clerks gathering up sheaves of documents, advocates leaning close in urgent conversation. Temar looked down to see Master Burquest walking towards the door, chatting with someone in scarlet robes.

'What is happening?' Temar got hastily to his feet a breath after everyone else.

'The Emperor has called a recess.' Camarl sounded puzzled. 'Come on, we need to clear the stairs so everyone else can leave.'

Temar felt annoyed. It was all very well for Camarl, but no one had bothered to tell Temar the rules of this game.

With spectators crowding down from the gallery and clerks still busy around their tables, a considerable press of people were milling around in the floor of the court. Avila was looking pale by the time they had emerged into the anteroom and Temar was ready to curse the next clerk that jostled him.

'This way.' Camarl led them down a narrow corridor lit only by inadequate lancets. Temar felt panic rising in his throat, at the gloom, at the confinement, at the noise echoing incomprehensibly around high-vaulted ceilings. They turned a corner, and to Temar's inexpressible relief a door at the far end opened on to real sunlight.

'I must have some air.' He walked briskly, heedless of Camarl's directions to Master Burquest's chamber, almost running by the time he stepped through the door. Blinking with the shock of the brightness he heaved a huge sigh of relief, leaning against the wall, feeling the heat the grey stone had soaked up all morning on his back.

'Esquire D'Alsennin, isn't it?'

Temar squinted at a new arrival closing the door carefully behind him. He realised they were in a small courtyard tucked away among the intricacies of the palace buildings. Well, no one was going to stick a blade in him again. Temar's hand moved instinctively before he remembered he wasn't wearing his sword.

'Esquire D'Alsennin?' Temar realised the man was wearing an advocate's robe as yet unadorned with knots or braid. 'I'm Mistal, Ryshad's brother.'

'How do I know that for the truth?' Temar was alert for any sign of hostile intent.

The lawyer looked nonplussed. 'Rysh'll vouch for me.'

'But he is not here,' retorted Temar. 'What do you want?'

The man shoved hands into his breeches pockets, bunching his robe inelegantly. 'I wondered if you're going to see Rysh fight. I came to ask if you needed a guide.' Perhaps this man was Ryshad's brother. There was some resemblance around the eyes, and he certainly had the same irritated forthrightness.

'I would like to support Ryshad,' Temar said slowly.

Mistal nodded at the great bell tower just visible over a floridly curved gable. 'If you're coming, you'd best tell the Sieur D'Olbriot now.'

Temar hesitated. 'I am hardly dressed for anything but this charade.'

'I'll be swapping this for a jerkin.' Mistal grinned, brushing at one front of his gown. 'I can lend you something. Now, are you coming or not?'

'The Sieur will be with Master Burquest.' Temar opened the door and wondered where that might be.

'This way.' Mistal slid past him with faint amusement.

The door to the advocate's chamber stood open. The lawyer was hanging his robe carefully over the back of a chair while Avila sat on a daybed, sipping a glass of straw-coloured wine, her pallor receding. A lad in shirt and breeches handed Camarl and the Sieur full goblets.

'So Premeller reckons he's a friend of the court now,' Master Burquest mused. 'He's no friend of anyone else's and, more to the point, he can't afford to do this for love of justice. Someone's paying him, and we'd do well to find out who.'

'How are you going to answer these accusations over Artifice?' Messire D'Olbriot demanded.

'To be frank I was hoping to avoid the whole topic.' Burquest looked thoughtful. 'Premeller's little to lose, that's why he brought it up. Any explanation risks sounding like apology, and whatever we reveal, that'll just set everyone's imagination running riot. People will either fear you've your finger on excessive powers to rival the worst of the Chaos, or that we're concealing some underhand means of putting D'Olbriot ahead in any negotiation.'

Avila snorted derisively into her glass as everyone turned at Temar's arrival.

'The Emperor's judgement is the most crucial inside the court,' Burquest continued, with a smile at Temar. 'But we must also consider the judgement of the people. The nobles and the merchants will be listening to every word and they're the people you'll be dealing with every day outside the court.'

'Something to drink, Temar?' Camarl held up a crystal carafe. 'The Emperor wishes to break for a meal, so Master Burquest's clerks will be bringing food.'

'Half a glass, thank you.' Temar filled it to the brim with water. 'It would seem this is Ryshad's brother.' He turned to the young lawyer who was waiting politely in the doorway.

'I recall you visited him at Equinox.' The Sieur held out a hand. 'Mistran? No, Mistal, forgive me.'

Mistal bowed over the Sieur's signet ring. 'I'm honoured, Messire.'

'Mistal is going to watch Ryshad meet his challengers at the sword school,' Temar said. 'I wish to go, if it can be permitted.' He did his best to imitate the tone his grandsire had always used to quell argument.

Camarl looked inclined to forbid it but stayed silent as the Sieur pursed thoughtful lips. 'Burquest, is anyone actually bringing a suit against D'Alsennin?'

'No.' The advocate shook his head. 'No one wants to give the Name any hint of validity by doing that.' Burquest chuckled. 'Perhaps we should bring some suit in the Name ourselves, just to test the waters.' He nodded to Mistal, who was still waiting with quiet deference. 'You're getting a reputation for quick wits, Tathel. Write me an outline argument for the D'Alsennin's right to be recognised as Sieur of the Name by the end of tomorrow. We'll see if we can get something laid before the Court of Prerogative before the close of Festival.'

'Very good, Master Advocate.' Mistal bowed low, but not before Temar saw elation and apprehension chasing across his face.

'It might be as well to have D'Alsennin show his face unaccompanied, Guliel,' Burquest continued thoughtfully. 'Show he's his own man, which is what we need to establish, after all. I don't suppose he'll come to harm surrounded by men sworn to you.'

'I wish to support Ryshad,' said Temar rather more forcefully than courteous.

'A valid and worthy aim, my boy,' smiled Burquest. 'But there's no reason your actions can't serve more than one purpose.'

Avila set down her glass. 'Does that mean I can also be spared an afternoon of your eloquence?'

Burquest looked at the Sieur, who shrugged. 'It would keep them all guessing if she weren't there.'

'If you keep talking as if she were not even in the room she might well disappear all together,' snapped Avila.

Messire D'Olbriot had the grace to look abashed. 'I beg your pardon. Shall I call for the coach?'

'Thank you.' Avila stood up. 'No, continue planning your campaign with your marshal here.' Her tone was sardonic. 'These young men can escort me.'

Temar hastily finished his drink as Burquest sent the lad

running off with word for the coachman waiting in the stableyard. The half-train of Avila's dress rustled along the hollowed flagstones as Temar followed her out of the room, falling into step beside Mistal.

Avila turned her head, eyes glacial. 'If I wanted pages shadowing me, I would find some pair far better trained than you.' She fixed Mistal with a piercing look. 'Look after D'Alsennin, or you'll have me to reckon with.' She whipped her head round to catch Temar grinning. 'And you need not look so pleased with yourself, I could have used your help with that coffer this afternoon. But we owe Ryshad a pledge of support. Keep your wits about you. If I use my Artifice to reach Guinalle about those artefacts, I will not have energy to spare to piece you back together again.'

They reached the main courtyard to find it packed with people.

'Where did everyone come from?' Temar wondered aloud in his bewilderment.

'Court of Prerogative, Court of Estate, Court of Property, Court of Pleas.' Mistal nodded his head at different corners of the courtyard. 'The various assizes are held over in the next set of halls, and the Courts of Warrant are beyond that.'

Avila sniffed. 'What of a Sieur's duty to administer justice for his own people?'

'Justice is an imperial obligation nowadays, Demoiselle.' Mistal said politely. 'To leave the Sieurs free to manage all their other responsibilities.'

'You seem to have made everything unnecessarily complicated to me,' snapped Avila.

Fortunately the D'Olbriot carriage arrived with commendable promptness. Temar saw relief to mirror his own on Mistal's face as they watched the driver whip the horses into a brisk trot.

'My mother had an aunt like that,' Mistal remarked with feeling. 'We were always glad to see the back of her.'

Loyalty prompted Temar to defend Avila. 'The Demoiselle is not so stern when you get to know her.'

'That's hardly likely. She's a bit above my rank.' Mistal grinned. 'Come on, let's get rid of these masquerade costumes. I don't want to miss Rysh's first challenge.'

'You do not seem overly awed by my rank.' Temar followed Mistal down a dingy alley way.

'You're different.' Mistal headed for a wooden stair clinging precariously to the side of an old-fashioned building. 'You're a friend of Ryshad's. Chewing leaf?'

'No, thank you.' Temar waved away the proffered pouch as they climbed weathered steps. 'He has spoken of me?'

'Oh, yes.' Mistal rummaged in a pocket for a ring of keys. 'Highly, for a wonder.'

Temar found himself smiling with unexpected pleasure as Mistal unlocked a door set in what had plainly been a window frame. The room within was small and oddly shaped where later walls had been built between the vanes of the original wooden vaults. Mistal hung his robe carefully on a hook and then pulled a chest from beneath the narrow bed with its much darned coverlet. 'We'd best put your finery out of sight. Ragpickers round here would give their eye teeth to get their hands on that much silk.' He pulled out a pair of dun breeches and a long brown jerkin, throwing them on to an undersized table where stacks of books further reduced the limited surface.

Temar changed, delighted to be free of the constricting coat. Mistal dragged a faded blue jerkin over his own plain breeches and locked Temar's elegant tailoring and borrowed jewellery safely away. He looked at Temar's sapphire signet. 'What about that ring?'

'This I always wear,' said Temar firmly. 'Anyone who wants it is welcome to try taking it.'

'It's your coin to toss.' Mistal looked a little uncertain.

'Shall we go?' Temar nodded towards the door or window, whichever it was.

'I'm hungry.' Mistal locked his door securely and led Temar down into the street. 'Can you eat common food like sausage, Esquire?'

Temar laughed. 'I have eaten whatever mercenaries can

trap in the woods for the last year. Sausage would be a rare treat.'

'Smoked or plain?' Mistal spat the leaf he'd been chewing into the gutter before crossing the busy road. An old woman sat beneath a rack hung with sausages tied in circles, as wrinkled as if she'd been smoked over a long fire herself.

'Plain.' Temar accepted a plump sausage glistening with oil and bit into it cautiously, rewarded with a pungent mouthful redolent of pepper, savory and rue. 'This is what you call plain?'

Mistal paid the woman before tearing a small loaf apart. 'You've got to have a few spices to liven up a sausage.' He handed Temar half the bread. 'Do you like it?'

Temar nodded, mouth full. Mistal's face cleared and they both ate hungrily as they walked rapidly through the bustling city.

'This is better than wasting my time in that tedious courtroom,' Temar said with feeling.

'Enjoy your freedom while you can,' advised Mistal. 'You'll be spending long enough in the courts for the next few seasons, until those arguments are settled.'

'Me?' Temar frowned. 'Messire D'Olbriot's trials are nothing to do with me.'

'I must have misunderstood.' Mistal looked sharply at Temar. 'Rysh said you weren't stupid.'

'Then tell me what I am failing to see, Master Advocate,' retorted Temar, stung.

Mistal wiped greasy hands on the front of his jerkin. 'Rysh told me about this colony of yours, said you'd been attacked from some northern islands?'

'The Elietimm.' Temar shivered with sudden revulsion. 'They'll destroy Kel Ar'Ayen given half a chance.'

'But you've wizards to hold them off, haven't you?' Mistal demanded. 'Fire and flood to scorch or drown them? That's what Ryshad was saying. Well, if you think these northern islanders are a threat, they're nothing compared to the people setting their advocates against you back there.' Mistal waved an airy hand somewhere in the direction of the courts. 'It's a different kind of danger, but it's just as real for your colony. Your little settlement can't survive without trading for the things you can't make for yourself. Without a market for your goods you won't have the coin to buy them either. If you're to expand from whatever scant land you hold, you need new blood. But you need the authority to control who comes and who settles, otherwise you'll find competing townships springing up all along your coast before the turn of the year. If that happens, Elietimm assault will be the least of your worries.' Mistal's lawyerly delivery in his casual dress struck Temar as incongruous, but his words were too serious for laughter.

'If the Emperor upholds your rights, then every House must respect them. More than that, Tormalin will consider the colony as part of itself and thus something we'll all defend against greedy Lescari or Dalasorians.'

'The Sieur D'Olbriot supports our rights,' said Temar slowly. 'And he has the Emperor's ear.'

'For the moment.' Mistal looked stern. 'That influence lasts only so long as D'Olbriot is a Name other Houses can respect. If D'Olbriot's discredited, if these accusations of bad faith are upheld, then the Emperor won't hear the Sieur. He can't afford to, for the sake of his own credibility. Imperial authority is only effective as long as all the Names consent to obey it.'

'That much I do understand,' Temar replied crisply. 'I was there when Nemith the Last's insanities alienated every House in the Old Empire.'

'Which precipitated the Chaos,' nodded Mistal without missing a step.

'The collapse of aetheric magic caused that,' Temar contradicted him with growing irritation. 'Why will Burquest not mention the part Artifice played in the discovery of the colony? Listening to him you would think we had been merely mislaid for a few years, not cut off by generations of enchantment!'

'Because that would almost certainly lose him the argument,' retorted Mistal. 'No one would want to believe him.'

'Your courts take no account of the truth?' Temar was getting really cross.

'All too often the truth's whatever people want to make it.' Mistal shrugged. 'You and Ryshad, the Sieur, even Master Burquest, you all understand the aetheric aspects of your story, but there's neither time nor opportunity to convince people who've grown up with different history. Bringing aetheric magic into legal argument can only cause confusion. Worse, you risk getting tarred with the same brush as wizards, and no one in their right minds trusts a mage the moment they're out of sight.'

Mistal stopped to point an emphatic finger at Temar. 'As far as the world and his wife is concerned, Nemith the Last's bad governance caused the Names to turn their backs on him, and that's what caused the Chaos. Which is something no Emperor will ever risk happening again. Even the hint of a decision threatening the unity of the nobility will be enough to see the House of Tadriol lose the Imperial throne. Tadriol won't back D'Olbriot against all the other Names, whatever the truth of the matter. He can't afford to. That's what's at stake back there in the law courts, my friend. If Burquest can defend D'Olbriot's position, then the Emperor can continue to take the Sieur's advice and support your claims against all the other Houses who want their turn at the well. If not, Tadriol will drop D'Olbriot like a hot brick. If that happens, Kellarin will be a prize for the first House who can seize it and you'll be nowhere in the hunt. Until you've established a Name for yourself and you've got some judgements in the courts to back your claims, the House of D'Alsennin lives or dies with D'Olbriot.'

'Then I should look beyond D'Olbriot walls?' Temar looked uncertainly at Mistal. 'Make some contacts of my own?'

'How?' the advocate demanded. 'How will you know who to trust? How will you know if you're offered good coin or Lescari lead? Tell me, will you draw up contracts under Toremal or Relshazri law codes? Will you apply the same scales of premiums as Inglis, or adopt Zyoutessela equivalent compensations?'

Temar gaped for a moment before responding angrily. 'When I know what those things might be, I will be able to decide.'

'But what if I'm a merchant only here for Festival and I want an answer now?' countered Mistal. 'If you go off to find out what I'm talking about, I'll likely use my money on established trades offering a safer return, Aldabreshin spices, Gidestan metals, Dalasorian hides. Whatever you're offering from Kellarin has to be something special to convince anyone to risk their gold across the open ocean.'

'The Sieur D'Olbriot thinks we have excellent prospects for trade,' said Temar stiffly.

Mistal nodded ready agreement. 'With his Name to back you, most certainly. There'll be half a hundred merchants in Toremal ready to give you the benefit of their considerable doubts just because they trust D'Olbriot. But if the House is discredited in the courts, they won't touch you with someone else's gloves on.'

Temar relieved his feelings by kicking a loose cobble with an angry boot. They were walking briskly through a distinctly down-at-heel area of the town now.

'So it's a good thing you've got Master Burquest arguing for D'Olbriot and all the resources of the Sieur's archivist,' said Mistal bracingly. 'He'll have handfuls of clerks turning up with parchments from the days when Correl the Stout was a lad. And Master Burquest is well worth his fee; he hasn't lost an argument in the last nine seasons. Raeponin may favour the just, but coin by the sackload can tilt his scales all the same.' He turned down an alley between two low-roofed, modest terraces. 'But that's a different fight. Here's the sword school, and let's hope Rysh's got his wits about him today.'

Temar saw splintered paling fencing off a sizeable patch of land. Men in D'Olbriot colours stood either side of a sturdy gate with pails in their hands where Temar saw bills of challenge pasted up, just like the one Ryshad had shown him.

Mistal was rummaging in a pocket. 'Something for the widows and orphans.' He dropped a silver Mark into a proffered bucket.

'Good to see you, Mistal,' grinned the man-at-arms. 'So what's Rysh think he's playing at?'

'Can't say,' shrugged Mistal.

'Can't say or won't, Master Advocate?' The man shook his pail meaningfully at Temar. 'Something for charity, Esquire?'

So much for going unrecognised, Temar thought, digging in his purse. At least he had some small coin today, thanks to Allin.

Inside the compound women in modest gowns were selling bread, meat and miscellaneous trinkets from baskets and barrows. Two long trestle tables displayed swords and daggers guarded by muscular men whose forbidding frowns turned quickly to smiles of welcome if anyone approached with a purse. Runes were being cast over to one side and wagers made, to the considerable interest of onlookers, while a silent ring watched two men sitting deep in contemplation on either side of a White Raven board. Beyond, long, squat buildings flanked a lofty circular structure. A roar went up inside it, followed by enthusiastic feet stamping approval.

'Have many challenges have been met?' Mistal caught a passing man-at-arms by the sleeve.

'They're just rounding off the sworn.' The man lifted a jug of dark red wine, smiling broadly. 'My brother won his day, so I'm off to get the little shit so drunk he can't stand!'

Mistal laughed, nodding towards an open door. 'We've a few moments yet, Temar. Do you want a drink?' A girl wearing a scarf in D'Olbriot colours round her waist came out to stack empty bottles in a discarded wine barrel.

'Mist! Temar!'

Temar turned round to see Ryshad, loose shirt over faded breeches and soft shoes laced tight on bare feet.

'It's good to see you both.' Ryshad looked keenly at Mistal. 'So you introduced yourself. Turn it to any advantage?'

Mistal grinned. 'Master Burquest has retained me to research D'Alsennin's claim to be Sieur.'

Temar looked at his boots, all dusty now, and wondered if anyone in this age ever did anything without some ulterior motive.

'Then no one's going to wonder at you being with Temar.'

Ryshad sounded relieved. 'How's the Sieur faring at court?'

'They've a fight on their hands, but Burquest's equal to it,' Mistal said with judicious confidence. 'As long as Camarl doesn't lose his temper if he's goaded and provided your Sieur doesn't get too cocky after an easy victory. A bit like you here today.'

'I don't need advice on fighting from some soft-handed bookworm,' said Ryshad with faint derision.

'You get yourself killed and I'll argue Saedrin into letting me cross to the Otherworld, just so I can tan your arse,' warned Mistal.

'You and what Cohort?' challenged Ryshad with a grin. 'You haven't been a match for me since your seventeenth summer.'

Temar felt a pang of envy at this easy camaraderie. Turning away he saw a youth being led out of the sword school, one arm swathed in bandages stained with bright scarlet. That put an immediate end to feeling sorry for himself. 'I thought these contests were a matter of form.'

The wounded boy was screwing up his face in a futile effort to stem tears of pain and humiliation.

'They're to prove a man's fitness to serve his Name,' Ryshad said soberly. 'A few fall short of the mark.'

'Oh, there's always blood to get the crowds emptying their purses,' said Mistal with obvious disapproval. 'Otherwise they'd be spending their coin watching mercenaries slice lumps off each other up in the Lescari quarter.'

Ryshad rounded on him. 'There's no comparison, and you know it. Any blood shed here is down to bad luck in a fair fight. Lescari fights are little better than masquerades.'

'At least the Lescari use blunt blades,' challenged Mistal.

'Which is why they end up with broken bones and blood all over the floor,' Ryshad retorted. 'A fool thinks a blunted blade can't hurt him and goes in hard. A swordsman worth his oath treats a real weapon with due respect!'

Temar felt uncomfortably excluded from what was plainly a long-standing argument, never mind by the deepening southern accents both men were slipping into. He watched the lad slump by a barracks door, arms around his drawn-up knees, face hidden and shoulders shaking. Temar felt a pang of sympathy; he knew that bitter taste of defeat, though at least a sword fight was more straightforward than all these legal and social battles besetting him.

'What is the form of the contest?' he asked when Mistal took a breath.

Ryshad spared Mistal a glare. 'Each challenge is a formal bout, best of three touches.'

'Do you know who'll be answering the challenge?' asked Mistal.

Ryshad grimaced. 'I've seen Jord from Den Murivance around, and Fyle says Lovis from D'Istrac and Eradan from Den Janaquel are definitely up for it. But I know them, have done for years. They'll try and raise a bruise or two, just to keep me humble, but I can't think there's any malice there.'

Mistal mouthed the names silently to fix them in his memory. 'It won't hurt to ask a few questions, find out who's been buying their wine.'

'You advocates suspect everyone, don't you?' laughed Ryshad, but Temar found his air of unconcern a trifle unconvincing. 'It's the ones I don't know about that could be the problem.' There was no doubting the sincerity of those words.

Five chimes rang out from some heavy brazen bell.

Ryshad grimaced. 'If they've got all the boys off the sand, I'd better go and see who turns up. Keep an eye for the crowd, will you? If this is some scheme to leave me dead or injured, someone might give themselves away if I take a bad touch or their man goes down hard.' He grinned at Temar. 'It won't be the first time you've watched my back.'

Mistal guided Temar inside the echoing training ground. 'What did Rysh mean by that?'

'Oh, nothing,' Temar shrugged. He wasn't about to try to explain how he'd broken through the enchantment binding him, finding himself in what felt like some insane, waking dream, facing an Elietimm enchanter trying to bash out his brains with a mace. With aetheric malice unravelling Ryshad's wits, Temar had been the one guiding his limbs in that frantic fight far away in the Archipelago.

The memory still made him shudder, so Temar looked around the practice ground with determined interest. Old battles had no place here. He watched as men much his own age and dripping with sweat came walking off the sand, elation brightening their exhausted faces. Older men congratulated them, some struggling to moderate their pride in their protégés. Temar found the palpable air of common purpose and good fellowship more than a little familiar. This wasn't so far removed from his own training for service in the Imperial Cohorts, he decided. A few seasons spent fighting for the lands and privilege they assumed as their due might improve those pampered nobles who sneered at him so.

'Mistal!' A heavy-set man in D'Olbriot colours came over, arms wide in expansive welcome.

'Stolley,' Mistal nodded politely, and Temar belatedly recognised D'Olbriot's Sergeant. 'How's the morning gone?'

'All our lads acquitted themselves worthy of their oath,' said Stolley with pride buoyed by wine on an empty stomach. 'Esquire D'Alsennin.' His bow was studied. 'An honour to see you here. Are you looking to recruit for your Name?'

That remark and Stolley's carrying voice turned plenty of interested heads.

'The Esquire's just here to support my brother,' Mistal answered smoothly.

Temar's smile was guarded, but the idea intrigued him. Kel Ar'Ayen needed fighting men, didn't it? They'd given the Elietimm a bloody nose the second time round but they'd needed wizards and mercenaries to do it. Wouldn't Tormalin men, sworn to him be better? He'd see what Ryshad thought.

'I'll have silence or I'll clear the place!' A grey-headed man muscled like a wrestler strode out on to the sandy floor.

'That's Fyle, sword school provost,' Mistal whispered hastily.

Temar nodded; that explained the unmistakable air of authority.

'All challenges posted by recognised men have been duly met, as you all bear witness. Now we have a final challenge.' Fyle paused for some latecomers hurrying in. 'A challenge posted without the knowledge or consent of the man named, which is an abuse of all our practice. When I find out who's responsible, they'll answer for it at the point of my sword.' He scowled at the assembled onlookers standing in tense silence. Clapping his hands together with a crack that made everyone jump, Fyle turned to the far door of the practice ground. 'Ryshad Tathel, sworn man to D'Olbriot and newly chosen, stands ready to defend his right to that honour!' The belligerent shout echoed back from the empty rafters and even silenced the hum of noise outside.

Temar watched as Ryshad walked slowly forward, naked blade in hand, light catching the engraving on the metal. Looking at his calm face, Temar wondered if he'd ever have the experience to justify such iron self-control.

'Grisa Lovis, chosen for D'Istrac.' Robust cheers followed a man stepping forward from the far side of the crowd. Somewhat older than Ryshad, his sparse black hair was cropped so short as to be almost shaven.

'You're going bald,' observed Ryshad, mocking. 'Getting old?'

'Getting stupid?' Lovis countered, drawing his own sword. He unbuckled the scabbard and threw it to some supporter, an orange and red sash belted gaudily round his waist. 'What possessed you to call a challenge?'

'Not me.' Ryshad shook his head. 'Must have been a man with something to prove. Sure it wasn't you?'

Lovis was circling round now, sword held low in front of him. Ryshad moved on light feet to keep his opponent always in front, a handspan's distance between the hovering points of their swords.

'I've got nothing to prove.' Lovis looked as if he were about to say something more but stepped forward instead, blade coming in hard and level at Ryshad's belly. Temar's breath caught in his throat, but Ryshad angled his sword in a blocking move. In the same movement he was stepping sideways, sweeping his blade up and around as soon as he was out of danger. Lovis met the scything stroke with a counter strike that sent a clash of steel shivering through the intent crowd. Ryshad yielded to the downward pressure, but only by sliding his own blade round and out, drawing Lovis forward. The other man was too experienced to be tempted into compromising his balance, Temar noted with regret. He brought his blade up to counter Ryshad's turning stroke and the guards of the two swords locked, holding the men almost nose to nose.

As they broke apart, Temar remembered to take a gulp of air and realised everyone else had been holding their breath. All eyes stayed on the two men circling warily again.

Ryshad made the first move this time, raising his sword for a downward strike that tempted Lovis into a direct thrust. Ryshad moved off the line, sweeping his cut down at an angle, but Lovis was already moving sideways, bringing his own sword up in a parry. He slid from counter to strike, steel whipping round to bite into Ryshad's shoulder. But Ryshad had his blade there to block, and as Lovis stepped back to try a second cut in from the other side Ryshad swept his own sword across to leave a smudge of scarlet spreading through the sweat-soaked sleeve of his opponent's forearm.

Stolley's shout of triumph nearly deafened Temar and every man in D'Olbriot colours joined his exultant yells. Less partisan onlookers shouted their approval too as Mistal nudged Temar. 'D'Istrac's men are ready enough to applaud a good move.'

Temar saw men in the same orange and crimson as Lovis nodding their approval of Ryshad's skill.

Steel smacked on steel as the contest resumed. The two traded blows, each strike parried, each parry sliding smoothly into attack, swords flickering from side to side, gleaming metal always turning biting edges away from vulnerable flesh. Then, in a move that escaped Temar, Lovis curled the point of his sword over and round Ryshad's blade, darting forward to leave Ryshad recoiling back with an oath, clapping a hand to his upper arm.

'Is it bleeding?' asked Mistal anxiously.

'I cannot see.' Temar shook his head.

This time it was D'Istrac's men cheering while Stolley and the others yelled consolation and advice to Ryshad. Temar folded his arms, hugging anxiety to himself as Ryshad rubbed at his arm, Lovis waiting patiently, the tip of his sword lowered. Mistal groaned softly as Ryshad wiped his hand on his shirt front, leaving an obvious smear of red.

'He does not look overly concerned.' Temar tried to reassure Mistal and himself.

Mistal shook his head. 'He'd have that stone face on him if he was bleeding to death.'

Temar watched anxiously as Ryshad took up a ready stance and nodded to Lovis. D'Istrac's man came in hard and fast with a sweeping sideways cut but Ryshad smacked it away with a ringing strike. Lovis didn't miss a step, drawing Ryshad round as he turned the parry with a vicious downward blow. Ryshad deflected the slice but Lovis followed up hard, sliding his guard down Ryshad's blade until the hilts locked. Ryshad was the first to move and Lovis slammed his pommel on to Ryshad's hands as they broke apart. One of Ryshad's hands came away from his sword and Temar's heart skipped a beat. In the next breath, as Lovis tried to follow up his advantage with a hasty downward stroke, Ryshad moved, half turning his back in a seemingly fatal error. Mistal gasped, but Temar saw Ryshad reaching between Lovis's hands to take hold of his opponent's weapon. Lovis struggled to pull free, but Ryshad was already moving, driving his shoulder into the older man. Once he had Lovis unbalanced Ryshad brought all his weight to bear, sending D'Istrac's man stumbling headlong across the sand. As Lovis scrambled hastily to his feet Ryshad levelled the man's own blade at his face, grinning.

'Yield?'

Lovis spread submissive hands, smiling as broadly as Ryshad. 'I yield, Chosen Tathel, and with good reason.' The warriors around the practice ground yelled their approval, stamping on the hard-packed earth.

'Rysh, here!' Stolley's yell left Temar's ears ringing.

Ryshad walked slowly over, taking a leather jug of water from Stolley and drinking with careful restraint. 'What moron calls a challenge at noon on Summer Solstice?' he said with disgust.

'One who wants you exhausted and wrung out before he steps on to the sand,' said Mistal, looking suspiciously round the crowd. Temar followed his gaze but could only see keen-eyed swordsmen in animated discussion, empty hands rehearsing moves.

'How is your cut?' asked Temar urgently.

'That's all ready clotted, as good as.' Ryshad grimaced, spreading his fingers and flexing them. 'But I feel like Lovis slammed a door on my knuckles. This hand'll be swollen like a pudding cloth tomorrow.' He accepted a towel and wiped at sweat dripping down his face.

'Eradan Pradas, chosen by Den Janaquel.' A second challenger strode on to the sand. A wiry man with sandy brown hair and a distinctly Lescari cast to his eyes, he was the tallest man Temar had seen in Toremal.

'Who is this?' he asked Ryshad anxiously. 'Do you know him?'

'Oh, yes, long since.' Ryshad was unconcerned, raking a hand through curls sticking to his temples. 'He's always thought he's better than me, and I don't suppose he could resist trying to prove it. It shouldn't take long to send him about his business.'

Temar watched him go before turning to Mistal. 'Where can we find bandages hereabouts? To strap his hand?'

If that were the only support he could give Ryshad, it would have to suffice.

The D'Olbriot Sword School, Summer Solstice Festival, Third Day, Afternoon

'Yield?' I twisted the edge of my blade into Jord's neck, scraping thick black bristles with an audible rasp. We were face to face, my sword resting point up and over his shoulder, the guard digging into his chest and my arm braced to keep him off me. I had his sword arm in my off hand, twisted away and useless. He struggled, tendons taut, face and neck darkening with effort. I leaned in hard to make best use of my hand's width more height, but he was easily as broad in the shoulder as me and barrel-chested with it. He'd better yield because getting out of this without letting him mark me was going to be cursed difficult. He shifted his feet, and so did I. This wasn't a move you'd find in any manual of sword art and I'd face Fyle's derision for getting myself tied up like this.

'I yield,' said Jord with disgust. 'But you've got the luck of Poldrion's own demons, Ryshad.' He had the sense not to move until I'd carefully taken my blade away from his neck.

'I've some salve for that, if you want.' I didn't want to find myself in that position again, I decided. Drawing blood was one thing, but cutting a man's throat by accident wouldn't do much for my standing.

'I've had worse when the wife's been feeling passionate.' Jord rubbed the raw scrape on his neck. 'But you've the skills to ride your luck, so I suppose you're worthy of being chosen.'

I held out a hand. 'My thanks for helping me prove that, to myself as much as everyone here.'

The avid crowd were hanging on our words, just as they'd hung on every move of the gruelling fight. Cheers for us sounded above stamping feet, making the ground tremble beneath my boots. Jord turned for the applause of D'Istrac's men and I headed wearily for Fyle, who was standing with Temar and my brother. Fyle had the water jug.

'Some of us have other plans for Festival,' Fyle growled with mock severity. 'I thought you were going to take all afternoon.'

I spread my hands. 'Got to give a good show. We can't have people thinking you're the best this school has to offer, now can we?'

Fyle made as if to cuff me round the head as I drank. Dast's teeth, I was thirsty. 'Is that the last of them?' I'd fought four men through the fiercest heat of the day now, drinking only as much as I dared to replace the sweat I'd been shedding.

Fyle nodded. 'No one's come near me since Jord gave you that first touch.' And that bout had taken as long as the previous three together, so anyone wanting to step up to the challenge had had his chance. I sighed with relief and drank deep.

'Everyone probably thought you were done for.' Mistal's pallor was slow to fade, betraying his own doubts.

I managed a smile, water dripping down my chin to add to the sweat soaking my shirt. 'Jord did, which is how I got him.'

'I saw barely a feather weight's difference in your skills.' Temar moved closer. 'But that was enough for Raeponin's scales.'

'Listen to D'Alsennin, Mist, he knows what he's talking about.' I felt the first leaden weariness heavy across my shoulders now my blood was cooling. 'Here's your sword, Esquire, and many thanks for the loan.' I handed back the antique blade with faint regret. Now I'd managed to use it without Temar's disembodied presence trying to guide my limbs, I'd rediscovered the superb balance of the sword. When Messire had made a Solstice present of it to me, it had truly been a Prince's gift. But had he known enchantment would make it such a two-edged boon?

'I'll fetch the scabbard.' But before Fyle got halfway round the dusty circle, we saw a handful of belligerent men in Den Thasnet colours accost him.

'What's to do?' Stolley came over, face bright with a fair few goblets of Festival cheer.

'Not sure,' I said slowly. All I wanted was to get towelled down and into clean, dry clothes.

'No!' Fyle shouted, taking a pace forward to emphasise his refusal, but Den Thasnet's man failed to step back, leaving them nose to nose.

'I'll go and find out,' murmured Stoll, clenching his fists unconsciously.

'Is there a problem?' Mistal was staring, puzzled.

I rubbed at my aching knuckles. 'Temar, can you strap this up again?'

'Let me,' offered Mist.

'No offence, Mist, but you can't truss a chicken for the pot.' I hoped my light tone softened my refusal.

'If you would hold this.' Temar handed the blade to Mistal, who held it like a snake he expected to bite him.

Temar deftly unwound straps of linen binding, rerolling them as he did so. 'A sizeable number with Den Thasnet trefoils have suddenly appeared.'

'More than the D'Istrac men and the Den Janaquels together.' I looked round idly to tally the D'Olbriot men here to cheer me on. There were a fair number, but most had been taking full advantage of the Sieur's Festival wine.

'Do you think there's going to be trouble?' Mistal looked concerned.

I was watching Fyle; Stolley was beside him now, arms folded and one foot tapping as he listened to Den Thasnet's man. A murmur of anticipation laced with disquiet was spreading round the practice ground. We couldn't hear what was being said but Stolley shoving Den Thasnet's man full in the chest was clear enough.

'Strap it up, Temar.' I held out my tender and unpleasantly discoloured hand.

He nodded. 'This is only storing up trouble. You need cold water, ice if we can get it. Does the Sieur keep an ice house?'

I nodded absently, still watching Stolley and Fyle as Temar

made an efficient herringbone pattern of bandaging up my wrist. Fyle came striding rapidly across the sand, leaving Stolley facing down Den Thasnet's man with a sneer of disgust.

'What's to do, Provost?' I asked with mock formality.

'Den Thasnet have someone to answer your challenge,' replied Fyle without humour. 'Mol Dagny. Ever heard of him?'

I shook my head. 'No, but I've spent a lot of time away, you know that. How do you rate him?'

Fyle looked angry. 'I don't, because I've never heard the name, and I'll wager my oath fee that none of the sword provosts have. No one knows him.'

'Den Thasnet are putting him up as a chosen man?' I looked past Fyle to see Stolley squaring up to Den Thasnet's spokesman with an ugly face. 'Without a provost to justify him?'

'He's from Den Thasnet lands near Ast, shown himself worthy and the Sieur himself offered him his oath,' sneered Fyle. 'He saved some son of the House from a wolf and was chosen on the strength of that just after Equinox.'

'If there's no provost to vouch for him, aren't you entitled to refuse the challenge?' asked Mistal. He'd doubtless been reading up all the legal niceties of sword bouts.

'That story would make a fine puppet show, Fyle,' I commented. 'Which one is he?'

'He's outside,' said Fyle with rising ire. 'Waiting to hear if you're man enough to meet him.'

'He certainly doesn't know me if he thinks he'll rile me by pecking at my tail feathers like that.' I rubbed a thoughtful hand over my chin.

Mistal gave Temar back his sword, his hands on his jerkin in unconscious courtroom fashion. 'Give me a day and I'll prove Messire Den Thasnet's been nowhere near the House's lands near Ast, let alone offering oaths. His cousins hold those properties and they can't stand the man. He's not been north inside the last year and a half.'

'I don't think we have a chime to spare, Mist, still less a day.' A handful of D'Olbriot men had come to back Stoll. Den Thasnet's men were spreading out around the practice ground.

'Are they looking for a fight?' Fyle scowled. 'Right here in D'Olbriot's own sword school?'

'Which would do your Sieur's case in the courts no good at all,' Mistal pointed out with growing concern. 'With the right advocate, it could do him considerable harm.'

'Either I meet this so-called chosen and risk dishonouring the House by losing or we all dishonour the name by being dragged into a fight.' I tried my bruised hand carefully. 'We've been set up for knocking down like bobbins on a loom, haven't we? I'll have to meet this challenger. No, Mist, hear me out. There are too many women and children around, and too many men all but drunk to risk a brawl.'

I turned to Temar. 'I'll borrow your sword again, if I may? If trouble does start, get him out of here.' I nodded at my brother. 'Mist's no use with a blade, and if there is a mêlée someone could finish the job that dagger started on you.'

Temar's nod was grudging but that was good enough for me. I wouldn't trust him not to try some half-arsed heroics on his own, but with Mistal to protect the odds were better than even he'd keep himself out of danger.

'Right, Fyle, tell Den Thasnet they've got an answer.' I swung my arms to get the blood flowing again, refusing to acknowledge the fatigue threatening to blunt my edge, wondering if I had time to go for a piss. Whoever was behind this had timed their move very cleverly, the bastards. 'Mist, have you got any leaf on you?'

'Since when do you use it?' He held out his wash-leather pouch.

I grimaced at the bitter taste overlaid with sickly sweet honey spirit soaking the leaf. 'Does this stuff really wake you up?'

'It keeps me awake through both halves of a night reading legal precedents.' Mistal smiled but his heart wasn't in it.

I mastered the impulse to spit out the revolting pulp and wondered how long it took to warm the blood. I daren't delay, not if we were going to avoid a free-for-all. Stolley was puce with anger and Fyle virtually had to drag him away from Den Thasnet's man. I walked out on to the sand.

The so-called chosen Dagny appeared, walking straight past Fyle without even greeting him. Fyle took a step after the man, furious. It's the provost's privilege to grant permission to fight on his ground to anyone answering a challenge. I waved him back. The discourtesy meant Fyle was quite within his rights to stop the fight but there'd be more blood on the sand if he did. The Den Thasnet trefoil was dotted in threes and fours all round the practice ground by now and a worrying number of men who'd shown no badge earlier now turned kerchiefs to reveal that same flower at their throats.

Dagny stood in the centre of the practice ground, sword eager, a crooked grin lifting one side of his mouth. Walking round him in a slow circle, careful to stay beyond reach of his blade, I kept my face open and friendly.

'So Den Thasnet chose you because you're good against wolves?' I spoke as I was directly behind Dagny and he took the bait, wheeling round. Good, now he was reacting to me.

'That's right—'

I cut him off. 'How about real men?' I levelled my sword and he matched it immediately. I thrust at his chest, stepping to the side to avoid his counter thrust, rolling my blade hard over to force his down. I took a pace back, but he kept coming. He was fast, barely older than Temar, with all the fire of youth and a cocky smirk. Let him grin; I had years about the business of fighting behind me.

But this Dagny was suspiciously fast on his feet. He thrust, leaving himself open, but his attack was so furious all I could do was get clear, parrying as I did so. We circled each other and I studied his eyes. They were hazel, not so unusual in a man from Ast, where Tormalin blood meets exiled Lescari and wandering Dalasorians. But Dagny's pupils were mere pinpricks of darkness. That might have looked normal enough in the noon day sun, but here in the shade I was chary.

I thrust and Dagny parried with a move the very echo of his first riposte. I turned his blade, but this time I stepped in close, getting inside his guard as he left that self-same opening. I let go my sword with my off hand and grabbed his, crushing his fingers brutally against the hilt as I used my own blade to turn the edge of his away. Dagny stumbled in surprise, his grip broken, and I rolled my arm over his, twisting his body until I locked his captive elbow tight against my chest, his blade pointing impotently at the sky. He had to bend from the waist to keep his feet so I kicked some dust in his face. He spluttered and coughed.

'Do you yield?' I asked genially.

'Never,' he spat furiously.

I twisted his wrist, ignoring the protests from my swollen hand. 'You yield or I break your arm off and shove the bone end up your arse.'

That won a laugh from everyone close enough to hear, everyone but the one Den Thasnet's man in the corner of my eye.

'Yield!' I repeated with menace. Dagny's only response was to claw at my feet with his free hand so I stamped on his fingers. Whoever had trained up this animal hadn't taught him the first thing about formal bouts.

'First touch to Ryshad Tathel!' Fyle came out on to the sand, face like thunder. Den Thasnet's men raised a storm of protest but shouts from everyone else drowned them out. I held Dagny until Fyle had taken both swords and then I sent the boy sprawling in the dust.

'When you're called on to yield and you've no hope of a counter, you cursed well yield, you ignorant turd! Doesn't Den Thasnet train his dogs?' Fyle laid both swords down well apart before storming off, snarling abuse at Den Thasnet's spokesman. 'You call that chosen, shitting on my school with behaviour like that?'

I was watching Dagny, back on his feet as soon as the provost's back was turned, dirty face twisted with resentment.

'Didn't want Fyle to smell your breath?' I taunted him.

'I'm not drunk,' he scoffed.

'Better for you if you were.' Dagny hadn't wanted Fyle to smell the sweet piquancy of tahn hanging round him. No wonder he'd stayed outside, surrounded by Den Thasnet men presumably bribed to lose their sense of smell. Fyle would have thrown Dagny off the sand and clean out of the sword school if he'd realised the boy was flying high on the little berries.

Dagny was no chosen man; I doubted he'd ever been sworn. The best a recognised lad could hope to get away with was a taste for chewing leaf or thassin, and I knew from personal experience that Fyle and all the provosts reckoned to break any man of a thassin habit before he was sworn.

I picked up my sword without ever taking my eyes off Dagny. I could call off the fight, accusing Dagny of coming on to the ground drugged. I'd have the support of every man here, bar those of Den Thasnet. But the air was growing thicker with tension and hostility and it was grapes to goat-shit that every man here would want to kick some humility into Den Thasnet hides if I showed their man was doped with tahn. Then whoever wanted a brawl here would have one, wouldn't they?

Dagny turned his back on me as he went to retrieve his weapon, too focused on doing me harm to think about his own safety, I realised. The tahn was doing that, pinning his will on the one thing he'd had suggested to him, buoying him up with exultant confidence in his own abilities.

'Have at him, Rysh!' A voice shouted, one I vaguely recognised from D'Olbriot's barracks.

Dagny whirled round, sword flailing. Derisive laughter burst out all around and Dagny looked at me with sudden hatred burning with tahn-induced paranoia. Now it was my fault he'd shown himself up as an ignorant yokel, not realising no man of honour would attack an opponent's unknowing back.

He came at me, blade sweeping from side to side, over and

under, the tahn giving him speed and strength far beyond mine. I moved back, fending him off, too busy saving my own skin to attack the repeated holes Dagny left in his defences. My hand ached abominably every time I put any weight in a blow, hot pain spreading from my knuckles up my arm and down to weaken my fingers. Mistal's leaf was doing me no cursed good at all.

Our swords locked on their guards; we held together for a tense moment while everyone fell silent. I managed to throw him away, muscles hardened by years of hard toil on my side, to balance the energy of youth and intoxicants driving Dagny on. I backed away, keeping a safe distance.

'Come and fight,' he taunted. 'D'Olbriot's man, all hair oil and no poke, that's what they're saying.'

So tahn made him talkative. 'Who's saying?' Was it the person who'd put him up to this? I'd pay good coin to know who that was. 'Some whore trying making you feel better because you couldn't show her the eye in your needle?'

Dagny thrust at me, that same direct stroke of his. I tried to roll his blade over to stab at his forearms but he swept the sword out and away, swinging it round his head to scythe it back at me. I had that instant of choice again, to go for his open chest or to save my own skull. Prick him with the point of my sword and I'd have the bout won, I'd take his blade in my ear all the same. I could tell from his glazed eyes that Dagny wasn't about to pull his blow.

I countered the sideswipe with a block that sent splintering agony through my injured hand. I ignored the pain as I forced his sword down to the side. But he kept coming, turning his sword over and around, sliding a sweeping strike in over my guard, and this time I couldn't block it. The throbbing in my knuckles was momentarily dulled by the icy fire of a slice biting into my forearm.

Dagny cheered himself, hands high in a self-congratulatory display. Even Den Thasnet's men looked embarrassed and everyone else just yelled their contempt. Dagny hurled abuse back at the gesturing men, threatening those closest with his bloodied blade in defiance of all custom. The noise was deafening.

I let him strut like a dunghill cockerel, tearing at the rip in my shirt sleeve to look at the cut. Deep enough for stitches, Dast curse it, no mere token like the scratches Lovis and I had exchanged. No matter, I'd had worse, even though it stung like a father's sorrow, and Temar's strapping would soak up any blood that might otherwise foul my grip. I'd had enough of Dagny, I decided. After all, I'd my reputation and D'Olbriot's to consider.

How could I end this without killing him? Because that would give us a brawl and dishonour both. It'd take a bad wound to disable a man with tahn masking any pain and that was an interesting notion, wasn't it? Den Thasnet's men couldn't simply bundle him off if he was bleeding badly and Fyle's wife was the best nurse hereabouts. With a potent dose of tahn tea on top of what he'd already taken, Dagny would yammer louder than a pig hearing the slop bucket. Then we might well learn something interesting.

I walked slowly to the centre of the ground as Dagny exchanged insults with the crowd. I kept my face impassive but for faint disdain. Stolley started D'Olbriot's men on a rhythmic chant of my name, D'Istrac lending their voice, soon joined by Jord and other Den Murivance men.

Den Thasnet's men shout for their own man was soon drowned out. Dagny turned to me, the boldness in his eyes fading beneath the onslaught of hostility from every side. What replaced it was all the vicious cunning of a privy house rat. He took up a ready stance, two hands on his sword, blade at belly level, ready to move to either side. I drew up my sword one-handed, hilt high above my head, the blade hanging down across my body ready to parry any move he made. I leaned my weight on my back foot and smiled at him.

The chanting stopped in ragged confusion as I saw perplexity cloud Dagny's eyes. A sound like wind rushing through reeds hissed around the sand. 'Aldabreshin!' 'Aldabreshin!' I only hoped the ferocious reputation of

Archipelagan swordsmen had reached whatever marsh Dagny had crawled out of and that someone had mentioned my enslavement down in the islands last year. Now Fyle and the rest could see I'd learned something more cursed useful than a warlord's wife's bed tricks.

Tension crackled in the air so palpably I wouldn't have been surprised to see lightning strike. Dagny's mouth twisted and he launched a hacking stroke at me. I met it even before he'd got the full force behind the blow, stepping in and grabbing for his sword-hilt with my free hand. That sent him scuttling back in confusion, remembering the way I'd pinned him earlier.

He tried to spit on the ground again but now his mouth was dry. I waited patiently with a mocking smile and when he brought his sword level I took up the same Aldabreshin stance. Dagny thought he saw an opening and tried his favourite thrust down at my legs, but as soon as I saw his shoulders tense I angled my blade down to defeat the blow, hitting him hard enough to shake his balance. That gave me an instant of opportunity; I twisted my wrist over and sliced deep into his forearm, the blade falling instantly from his nerveless fingers. Scarlet blood saturated his sleeve in a moment but he just stood there, gaping.

I ripped the torn sleeve off my own shirt and shoved up Dagny's cuff to see the damage. It was a deep gash right along the meat of his forearm but I'd taken him so much by surprise he'd had no chance to turn his wrist. That should have saved the tendons but I'd hit a major blood vessel by the looks of it. I pressed the linen to the wound, my hands already sticky and slick. 'Hold this down hard.' I took his free hand and clamped it down.

'But they said I had to kill you,' he muttered unguardedly, shock at the unexpected wound doubling the garrulous impulse born of tahn.

'Who said?' I demanded, too soon, too curt, but people were crowding on to the sand.

He focused on me and realisation shuttered his eyes. 'I've

never fought against Archipelagan sword styles before. They said you weren't fit to be chosen anyway.'

'Who said?' I repeated, pressing down hard on his wound, more to hurt him now than to staunch the blood.

'Let me see!' Den Thasnet's man tried to pull my hands off Dagny.

'Back off,' I growled. 'Send for Mistress Fyle.'

'She's on her way,' someone said behind me.

'We've nurses of our own,' insisted Den Thasnet's man; I heard fear in his voice. 'Come on Dagny, we're leaving.' He wrenched at my bandaged hand.

I swore at him but hadn't the strength in the injured fingers to resist. A solid phalanx with trefoil amulets were pushing forward to surround Dagny, pushing everyone else away. I saw someone behind Stolley answer a brutal shove with a ready punch.

'Let him go!' I shouted. 'If the stupid bastard bleeds to death in some gutter, it's no loss to us.'

'Don't be a fool, man!' Fyle tried to hold Dagny back, but Den Thasnet's man smacked the provost's hand from the lad's shaking shoulder.

'You're stopping us?' A thick-set brawler with foul breath and pox scars pitting his face stepped up to Fyle.

'Provost!' My curt formality got Fyle's attention just before he shut the man's mouth with his fist. 'They came looking for a fight and they've had the only one they're going to get. Their man lost and that's all there is to it.'

I was relieved to hear a murmur of agreement behind me, led by Mistal and Temar.

'True enough.' Fyle looked at Den Thasnet's man without a hint of good will. 'Get your filth off my ground.'

The pockmarked man grabbed at Fyle's shoulders, ready to smash the provost's nose with his forehead. Fyle was too quick, making the self-same move an instant sooner and sending the big man stumbling back blindly.

'Ingel, leave it!' Den Thasnet's man was still trying to staunch Dagny's wound, the bandages already sodden with blood. The mob sworn to Den Thasnet gathered still closer as Dagny stumbled, face greenish white.

'Let them pass!' Fyle raised a commanding hand, his own fury vented in part by breaking the pockmarked man's nose.

'Wait.' Mistal stepped in front of Den Thasnet's spokesman. 'As an advocate sworn to the courts of law, I call all here to bear witness. You are removing this man from competent care of your own choice. Don't even think of making any claim that Fyle or D'Olbriot failed in their duty to succour the wounded.' His words rang with authority and I was pleased to see uncertainty flicker across Den Thasnet faces.

I watched them leave the rapidly emptying practice ground with frustration burning in my throat, that and the bitter chewing leaf. I spat it out. Who had told those men lies convincing enough to bring them here for a fight in blatant disregard of every custom?

'Dalmit?' I saw a sworn man I recognised from Tor Kanselin. 'You're not on duty tonight, are you?'

'Me? No.'

I spoke quickly in low tones. 'Someone wanted trouble here today. I want to know who, and so will the Sieur, but none of Den Thasnet's are going to give D'Olbriot's the steam off their piss now. How about you and a few lads swing round the inns and brothels where Den Thasnet's men slake their thirsts? See what you can kick or cajole out of some unwary drunk? I'll make your purse good for everything you spend.'

He looked at me thoughtfully. 'Do you think this ties in with whoever wanted your D'Alsennin dead?' A sworn man taking that kind of news to his Sieur would be remembered.

I shook my head. 'I've no idea.'

'It's got to be worth a look,' said Dalmit with a predatory grin. 'I'll let you know what I find out.'

'Shall we get you cleaned up?' Mistal tried for a smile. As he took his hands out of his breeches pockets and found some chewing leaf, I saw his hands were shaking. Temar by contrast looked like a hound who'd caught an interesting scent and then been chained up in the kennel yard.

'We agreed not to give them a fight, Temar,' I reminded him.

'Must that mean we *never* hit back?' he growled.

'We need to know who we're fighting,' I pointed out.

'Den Thasnet for one, that is clear enough,' he said scornfully.

I pulled off my bloodstained, sweaty shirt. 'We'll go back to the residence and start planning our campaign, shall we?' My injured hand throbbed and the strains of intense swordplay pulled at my muscles. I was going to miss Livak's skilful fingers working rubbing oils into my shoulders tonight.

'You need something to drink and something to eat!' Stolley reappeared, offering me an uncorked bottle. I drank deep, no way to treat a good wine, but I was too thirsty to care.

'Not until you've had that stitched.' Fyle elbowed him aside, bandages and salve at the ready.

I looked at the oozing slice on my arm and took another long drink of wine. 'Have you some tahn paste to numb it?'

'Rysh! Get yourself bandaged and we can start the serious drinking!' Jord raised a tankard to me as he shouted over the avid debates being joined all around us.

Mistal looked at me. 'This is probably our best chance of finding out if anyone put him up to answering the challenge, him and Lovis.' D'Istrac men all looked keen to join any celebration going.

Temar was bright-eyed with interest. 'It would hardly be courteous, to leave at once.'

I hesitated. 'We can stay for a little while.'

A Hireling Coach,
Summer Solstice Festival, Third Day, Evening

'And do you remember Inshowe, the tailor up by the portage way?'

Temar did his best to look interested at what would doubtless be yet another story about people he didn't know and places he was never likely to see.

'Had a wife with a limp?' Ryshad sat up straighter as the carriage carrying the three of them bounced over uneven cobbles. 'Three daughters, all with faces like a wet washday?'

'That's him.' Mistal could hardly speak for laughing. 'The wife, she was all for putting a wonderful new frontage on their house, squared-off stone, nice Rational lines, none of these old-fashioned bays and turrets.'

Ryshad frowned with the effort of recall. 'But all those houses are timber-framed. You'd be better to tear the whole thing down and start again.'

Mistal nodded with heavy emphasis. 'That's was Hansey said when they came asking. He totted up the men and materials for a job like that and her ladyship near fainted in the yard.'

Hansey and Ridner were the oldest Tathel brothers, Temar remembered belatedly, stonemasons down in Zyoutessela.

'Inshowe's never as rich as he likes to pretend.' Ryshad yawned. 'If he was, someone would have taken those whey-faced girls off his hands.'

Temar felt slightly let down by that unguarded remark.

'Hansey reckoned that'd be the last they'd hear of it,' continued Mistal. 'But next market day Ridner comes home saying the word round the well is Jeshet's going to do the work.'

'The brickmaker?' Ryshad asked, puzzled.

Mistal was nodding. 'He'd convinced Inshowe he could

reface the building in brick. It would look just like stone, he told him, built up to a nice flat roofline. Only someone reckoned to save time and coin by not taking the old roof off.'

Ryshad shook his head. 'I don't follow.'

He wasn't the only one, thought Temar sourly.

'They built up the frontage with brick and carried it up to the same height as the roof ridge.' Mistal illustrated his words with gestures. 'Then they filled in the gap, from the slope of the old roof to the frontage, with brick.'

Ryshad gaped. 'How did they secure it?'

'They didn't.' Mistal was still chuckling. 'Half a season later the whole top section slid clean off the old roof, bringing most of the facing down with it! The street was blocked for two days and Inshowe had to pay a fortune to get it cleared. Now he's arguing Jeshet's liable for all that coin as well as making everything good. Jeshet says he only did what Inshowe told him.'

'Was anyone hurt?' Temar was appalled.

Mistal looked perplexed. 'No, it all came down in the middle of the night.'

'A rude awakening,' Ryshad observed. 'Who are you arguing for?'

'Jeshet,' said Mistal promptly. 'He may only be a brickmaker but that's a more honest trade than tailoring.'

'That's good, coming from an advocate!' laughed Ryshad. Temar felt entitled to join in after what he had seen in the courts.

The carriage lurched to a halt and the driver hammered the butt of his whip on the roof. 'You wanted Narrow Shear?'

'Yes,' yelled Mistal. The door hung crookedly on stretched leather hinges as he got out. 'I'll need credentials from Burquest to get access to the Tor Alder archive, so I'll do that first thing. Oh, Temar, your clothes—'

'Return them tomorrow,' Temar said politely.

'First thing,' Mistal promised solemnly. 'When I've had a look at the records, I'll call round and tell you what kind of case we might make.'

Temar wondered how early Mistal might consider first

thing, given the bottles of wine he'd helped empty down at the sword school.

Ryshad waved his brother off and settled back against the greasy upholstery. 'Mist's always full of the latest news from home,' he apologised.

Temar managed a thin smile. 'I imagine Zyoutessela is much changed from the town I remember.'

'The colony expedition set sail from there, didn't it?' Ryshad looked pensive.

He was doubtless recalling those echoes of Temar's own memories left him by the enchantment; it was a shame he hadn't won some of Ryshad's knowledge in exchange, Temar thought crossly. Then he might not feel so utterly at sea this side of the ocean.

Ryshad yawned and fell silent, cradling his thickly bandaged hand across his chest. Temar watched the city go past the open window of the hireling coach. A puppet show was drawing a good crowd, rapt in the light of flickering lanterns in an alley mouth. Inns and taverns were doing a roaring trade on every side. Cheerful family groups bowled past in complacent coaches or walked along, arm in arm. Every so often some gathering blocked the flagway as people met with delighted greetings, exchanging news and embraces. The narrow houses of the tradesmen living below the old city were lit from cellar to garret, a season's worth of candles squandered over the five days of Festival as visitors were welcomed, parties given and the births, betrothals and weddings of the previous season all celebrated in the finest style that each family could afford. As the coach wound its way up to higher ground, wealthier merchants competed with their neighbours in more decorous but ever more lavish revels.

Temar looked at the proud dwellings, struggling between sadness and defiance. He had no family, no home, not on this side of the ocean anyway, and unless Burquest, Mistal and all their clerks could come up with some winning argument, he wasn't going to have a House or a Name to call his own either. He smiled thinly to himself at the weak joke.

What of it? He'd set his face eastwards when he'd first sailed to Kel Ar'Ayen, hadn't he? He'd promised his grandsire he'd raise the House of D'Alsennin to its former glories beyond the ocean, and by Saedrin he would do so still. He'd been mistaken to think all the cares of the colony were tedious and trivial, Temar realised. These so-called nobles, with their self-absorbed, trifling concerns, they were the petty ones.

Temar turned his thoughts determinedly to Kel Ar'Ayen. Rebuilding what remained of the original settlement had been their first priority, that and ensuring the remaining sleepers in the cavern were guarded in comfort and safety. Both those tasks had been pretty much complete when he'd set sail, hadn't they? What was left of the southern settlement, he wondered, where ocean ships had escaped Elietimm attack, salvation for those few who'd escaped under Vahil's leadership to carry the enchanted artefacts home? He'd find out, Temar decided, as soon as he got back. Making plans for an expedition occupied him as the carriage rumbled through the city and Ryshad dozed silently.

The horses slowed on the long incline leading to the D'Olbriot residence just as a new notion struck Temar. It was time the settlements of Kel Ar'Ayen had names, to honour those with the vision to found the colony, who'd shed their life's blood in its defence. Saedrin's stones, he wasn't about to let Den Fellaemion just be written out of history as subsumed into Tor Priminale!

He snorted with inadvertent contempt as the carriage pulled up in front of the D'Olbriot gatehouse and the driver banged on the roof once more.

'Did you say something?' Ryshad opened his eyes, swallowing a curse as he inadvertently leaned on his injured hand.

'No, but we are back,' Temar opened the door before turning to Ryshad with a faintly embarrassed smile. 'What is a fair recompense for the driver? I have coin, but—'

'A couple of silver Marks will give him something over for Festival.' Ryshad scrubbed his unbandaged palm over his face. 'Dast's teeth, I'm weary.'

'You have had a busy day,' Temar pointed out.

'I should have taken more water with my wine,' said Ryshad ruefully. 'At least you kept your wits about you.'

'Avila and Messire's surgeon were firmly agreed on that,' Temar shrugged. 'As little alcohol as possible after a blow to the head, they insisted.'

'Ryshad, Fair Festival!' The chosen man on duty in the gatehouse waved at them. 'One of Fyle's lads brought the news, and the Sieur said to broach a barrel for the barracks on the strength of it!'

'Fair Festival to you, Naer,' Ryshad grinned. 'What bet did you lose to be on duty tonight?'

'Is the Demoiselle Tor Arrial within?' Temar interrupted. 'You really must let her see that hand, Ryshad.'

Naer shook his head. He was as tall as Ryshad, Temar realised, with the same lean build but substantially more years thickening his waist and thinning his hair. 'The Relict Tor Bezaemar called for her late this afternoon, something about visiting a shrine fraternity? She's not back yet.'

'Are the Sieur and Esquire Camarl here?' Ryshad asked.

The swordsman shook his head again. 'They got back from the courts just after sunset but went out again as soon as they'd changed. I think they're dining with Den Murivance.' The swordsman looked at Temar with ready amusement. 'The Demoiselles of the Name are holding a musical evening, Esquire D'Alsennin. They were most insistent I remind you as soon as you returned.'

'Thanks.' Ryshad looked thoughtful as they walked away. 'I wonder how well Master Burquest argued today.'

'Tell me about Den Murivance,' Temar invited. 'What is their status compared to D'Olbriot? What is their interest in Kel Ar'Ayen?'

'I imagine the key there's the embarrassment of eligible and marriageable daughters blessing their House.' Ryshad took a deep breath of the cool evening air but it still turned into another yawn. 'Any one of whom would make a wife with rank to reinforce your claim to restoring your Name. That would certainly settle the rumours that the Sieur's planning to marry you off to one of his nieces. Another major House stepping into play over Kellarin would give Names like Den Thasnet pause for thought as well.'

They were heading for the residence, black shadows adding their own solid pattern to the complexity of the gardens. At every turn of these paths within hedges within walls Temar felt increasingly penned in.

'Den Murivance is extremely wealthy,' continued Ryshad. 'They've significant holdings from Lequesine to Moretayne. The only reason they don't have quite D'Olbriot's prestige is the last three Sieurs have been more interested in commerce than politics.' He looked at Temar with a wicked smile. 'So, did you find Gelaia easy on the eye this morning? A white-feathered fan means a girl's open to offers, did you know that?'

Temar struggled for an answer. Looking away from Ryshad's gently mocking gaze, he saw two figures coming down the path, their sudden hesitation catching Temar's eye. 'Who are they?'

'Visiting servants?' Ryshad peered into the gloom but the men had halted in the dimness where the flaming torches of the gatehouse fell short of the glow from the windows of the residence.

Temar shrugged and continued walking. The two men did the same, passing Ryshad with eyes firmly fixed on the ground. Their steps crunched with increasing haste.

Ryshad stopped and looked at Temar. 'I didn't recognise them, did you?'

Temar shook his head. 'And I have this old-fashioned habit of actually looking at servants.'

'And they look at you, more to the point, and bow.' Ryshad frowned. 'All the visiting servants have been told you're entitled to every courtesy, in no uncertain terms.'

They turned to see the two unknown men disappear abruptly behind a thick yew hedge.

'They're cutting round the residence to the stableyard.' Ryshad was scowling.

'Honest servants with permission to go out would surely leave through the main gate?' Temar's own suspicions were growing.

'Dast curse it,' Ryshad said crossly. 'It's probably nothing, but sometimes sneak thieves take advantage of Festival comings and goings. I'll go back and tell Naer to verify anyone trying to leave. You get over to the stables and tell whoever's on watch to get his thumb out of his arse. Tell them to shut the gates.'

Temar didn't need telling twice and ran down the shadowed path on light feet, settling his sword on his hip out of old habit.

The stableyard opened on to the lane running round behind the residence. The main block was a low, wide building and Temar passed doors warm with the scent of horses stalled within, more animals housed in wings reaching back into the darkness on either side. A steeply gabled coach-house flanked the stables on one hand while on the other a squat granary perched on stone-flanged pillars to foil greedy vermin. A newer dwelling for grooms and stable boys presented a squarely Rational face to these buildings, sharp stone corners and rigidly parallel windows in contrast to older, curving lines and ornate cornices. Beyond the beaten expanse of earth where coach wheels wore a rutted circle, wrought-iron gates stood open to the night. Carefully shuttered lanterns illuminated a couple of grooms playing an idle game of Raven on an upturned barrel.

Temar ran up to the liveried sentry on duty in a cubby hole by the gate. 'You – has anyone passed in the last few moments?'

The sentry stood smartly upright. 'No, Esquire, no one.'

Temar had never seen him before but the sworn man knew to recognise D'Alsennin with due courtesy. Ryshad was right. 'Chosen Tathel suspects thieves are in the grounds,' he said curtly. 'Close the gates and let no one pass without someone vouching for them.'

The sentry immediately blew three sharp notes on a whistle

hung round his neck. Four sworn men appeared from the new building.

'Ryshad says there's rats in the garden,' the sentry explained. 'You two, start looking. Iffa, rouse the barracks.' The remaining man helped him swing the heavy gates closed.

'What's to do?' A voice called down from the parapet high above their heads.

'Ryshad reckons he saw sneaks in the grounds,' yelled the sentry.

'There's no sign up here.' But the voice was already moving away in the darkness where the trees beyond hung black shadows over the walls.

'You'd best get yourself safe inside the residence, Esquire,' said the sentry with faint apology. 'The ladies are having a musical evening, aren't they?'

Temar nodded but didn't reply. No, he'd go and find Ryshad. He had a blade after all, and he knew how to use it, more than could be said for whatever fashionable nobles were hiding inside the house. Shrill whistles sounded, some high on the walls, some closer at hand, answering trills from the gatehouse.

Heavy boots thudded and a liveried guard skidded to a halt in front of Temar. 'Identify yourself! Ah, Esquire, beg pardon, but shouldn't you be inside?'

'Where is Ryshad?' Temar summoned all his grandsire's authority.

'Over yonder, sir, going to check the kitchen yard,' the man replied promptly.

'I will assist him.' Temar turned down what he hoped was the right path. These gardens were cursed confusing in the dark, he thought crossly. Light spilled across his way as an upper window in the house was unshuttered. Curious faces looked briefly out into the night and a spinet faltered to a halt before picking up its heedless merriment a moment later.

Temar tried to get his bearings, a hand on his sword hilt to balance it. If that was the new, west front, then the kitchens were on the other side of the house, beyond what would have been the great hall in his day, now given over to servants' quarters. He rounded the low wall skirting the kitchen yard and the two men with Ryshad levelled blades at him in a single movement.

'D'Alsennin!' Temar identified himself with a catch in his voice.

'Seen anything?' asked Ryshad.

Temar shook his head. 'But the stable gates are closed and the men on the walls alerted. And do not tell me I should be safer within doors,' he shot a warning look at Ryshad. 'I have two sound hands, which is more than you.'

Ryshad acknowledged that truth with a grin. 'Then watch my back.' He hefted a borrowed cudgel in his good hand. 'You two, turn the yard inside out. We'll take the physic garden.'

As the other two started a thorough search of every nook and cranny, Ryshad led Temar through a rose-garlanded arch into a small enclosure. At the older man's nod Temar moved to the far side, following a narrow path between low hedges of lavender framing tidy patterns of pungent herbs. A small plinth at the centre of the garden bore a dutifully garlanded statue of Larasion, the goddess proffering a stone branch bearing bud, blossom and fruit all at the same time. Temar tasted familiar scents waking beneath the rising dew as his steps stirred thyme growing in dense mats and sage lifting downy leaves silver in the light of the lesser moon. Mint waved scatters of black leaves as he brushed past.

'We'll check the store.' Ryshad pointed at a stone hut hidden in a thick holly hedge that screened the mundanities of the kitchen yard.

Temar peered into the recessed doorway, wondering if he saw movement or a trick of the darkness. He drew his sword.

Three urgent blasts sounded over towards the north wall. Ryshad and Temar turned as shouts rang out and in that instant a hooded figure darted out from the shelter of the holly, trampling sprays of fennel and comfrey. Temar sprang at the man but crushed slickness beneath his boot betrayed him. He fell to one knee and the thief kicked out, knocking

Temar's sword out of his hand. Temar scrambled up, catching the man round the waist and knocking him backwards. The thief fought hard, twisting, hammering at Temar with brutal fists. He punched the younger man hard on the side of the head and Temar's grip slipped.

'No you don't!' Ryshad was there, swinging his cudgel low, catching the intruder behind one knee. The man fell and Temar nearly had him pinned among the heady crush of herbs but the thief wriggled free with some inexplicable twist of his body. Ryshad couldn't reach the man with his club, could only chase him out into the darkness of the gardens. Temar raced to his side, breathing hard, salvaged sword bright in the night.

'Where did he go?' Ryshad turned slowly. Temar searched the patterned shadows of hedge and flowerbed, head pounding. Whistles rang out in the distance, beyond the wall as far as Temar could judge. Had one of them got away? Saedrin's stones, they'd best catch the other! The sound of a careless boot gouging into gravel rewarded his inarticulate prayer.

'Behind the stables,' Temar kept his voice as low as he could.

Ryshad nodded agreement and they walked warily through the dark, haste balanced by vigilance.

With the light of the lesser moon still all but full Temar noticed a black shape lying along the pentice roof of an outhouse built along the inside of the hollow square of the stables. He pointed it out to Ryshad in tense silence. The chosen man nodded him over into the angle of the buildings and moved towards the open end of the range. Temar walked carefully through stray straw, eyes fixed on the black shape. It lay motionless and Temar suddenly hoped it wasn't merely some trick of the shadows.

No, it was a man, abruptly kneeling upright as instinct or noise alerted him to their approach. Weight spread on hands and knees, he edged across the sloping tiles, away from Ryshad. Temar discarded his sword in sudden decision, climbing quickly on to a water butt. Startled, the thief froze and made to move back. Temar swung himself up, one boot on the edge of the roof. The intruder stood and ran up the slope of the pentice, only his speed saving him as tiles slid and broke beneath his feet, crashing down. Finding some handhold he swung himself up on the gutter, on to the roof of the stables, balancing as he ran along the roof ridge towards the outer walls.

'Shit!' Temar saw Ryshad hadn't the strength in his injured hand to pull himself on to the pentice roof. 'Temar? Can you get up there?'

'I think so.' Bracing himself in the angle of the walls he used every bone and muscle to press arms and legs against the unyielding stone, scraping skin, cloth and the leather of his boots as he forced himself up. Chest heaving he pulled himself awkwardly on to the stable roof, heart sinking as he saw the empty expanse of tiles.

Temar moved cautiously up to the roof ridge, fingers pressed flat. He wasn't about to give up. Ryshad was waiting below so the thief couldn't get off the roof unseen, could he? Moss squelched dangerously beneath Temar's hands and knees and he breathed a sigh of relief when he could swing a leg over the ridge, trying to ignore the bone-breaking drop on either side.

A noise pulled Temar's head round, nearly overbalancing him, but it was just a cat, hair fluffed to an indignant halo in the moonlight. Temar drew in a sharp breath of relief but a heavier sound beneath the light patter of paws made him hold it in. He let it go slowly, turning carefully, looking at the tall chimneystack foursquare at the angle of the stable buildings. The cats in his grandfather's yard had always favoured chimney corners, hadn't they? What had startled that mouser out of its cosy nook? Sliding down, Temar used the roof ridge to shield him and worked his way closer.

The thief was there, motionless in the shadow of the chimneystack, intent on the sentry pacing the parapet of the outer wall beyond, the only thing between him and escape. Temar watched, heart in his mouth as the sentry moved slowly away and the thief bent in a cautious crouch. Was he going to try and jump the gap? No, the man lowered himself over the edge of the roof, at full stretch to drop into the black shadows below.

Even if he called him, Ryshad couldn't get round in time. Temar scrambled as fast as he could across the roof, swinging himself over the edge as the intruder hit the ground with an involuntary grunt. The stone dug cruelly into Temar's hands. Curse it, he couldn't chance this, risk breaking a bone or worse. But it was too late, his own weight committed him, breaking his grip on the stone. Temar fell, landed, relaxed and rolled to break his fall, instinctive reactions learned from years in the saddle coming unexpectedly to his aid. He was on his feet with a speed that startled himself as much as the thief now crouching below the perimeter wall.

The man was on him before Temar could shout an alert, murderous purpose contorting his face. The thief threw a punch but Temar caught it in an open hand, gripping and twisting, grabbing the man's other shoulder as he did so. The thief kicked, nearly knocking Temar's foot out from under him. Temar stumbled and lost his hold, letting the man drive a brutal fist straight at his face. Temar knocked it aside with his forearm, the impact jarring him to the shoulder, then swung all his weight behind a punch of his own, catching the thief full under the chin and snapping his head back.

The thief hooked a fist to clout Temar's ear but Temar raised arm and shoulder in an instinctive block. The thief grabbed his sleeve, trying to pull him off balance. Temar smacked his fist backhanded into the man's nose and the thief let go, ducking backwards. Temar stepped in but the intruder met him with fists striking one after the other, spitting blood and fury. Temar took a blow on the ribs, another, a punishing blow to the stomach. The thief drew back his arm and Temar brought his knee up into the man's groin. The intruder went down like a sack from a broken hoist, retching and gasping.

Ryshad and a couple of sworn men came running up as Temar rolled the thief over, twisting unresisting arms behind his back. 'So we've got one at very least.'

'Got him in the stones,' Naer the gateward observed, seeing the man's agonised grimace and drawn-up knees.

'Always a good trick, if you can do it.' Ryshad grinned approval at Temar.

'Those mercenaries been teaching you their trade, Esquire?' Naer asked, harsh voice not unfriendly. 'Take a tip from a real warrior, eyes or knees is as good as stones and most men are slower to defend them.' He was searching the intruder as he spoke, rough hands brutally thorough. 'Nothing on him but that means naught. Lock him up.'

'A good kick on the side of a knee can send a man spewing,' added one of the sworn men as they dragged the unresisting thief along the path. 'We'll show you, Esquire, if our pal here doesn't give up his friend's den. What do you say?'

But the thief was too sunk in his present misery to worry about any new threat, from what Temar could see. 'What happens now?'

'He spends tonight in the gatehouse cell,' Ryshad replied. 'He'll face the Sieur's justice in the morning. In the meantime, let's find out what him and his mate were after. Naer! Me and D'Alsennin, we'll check the shutters.' He turned to Temar. 'Look for sprung hinges, loose slats, bent struts. Chances are it'll be an upper window.'

'Halcarion be thanked for at least one good moon,' Temar murmured as Ryshad began a slow circuit of the residence.

Ryshad spat as they rounded a corner. 'Shit!'

'What?'

'There.' Ryshad pointed to a louvred shutter where a strip of wood hung loose to cast an angled shadow over the rest.

Temar tried to work out what room might lie behind it. 'That must be where they tried to get in.'

'You think Messire's steward would let any shutter stay broken for Solstice, when half those bearing the Name come to stay and half the nobles in the city will be visiting?' asked Ryshad grimly. 'And those two were on their way out, Temar, so chances are they didn't just try, they got in. Come on.'

Temar followed Ryshad in through a side door, the chosen

man giving his frustrations free rein as they went up a servants' stair. 'We can't lock every door, every gate, not with so many people going in and out. It's always the same at Festival, guests arriving right round the chimes, coaches calling to take visitors hither and yon.' He stopped suddenly as they were halfway up a flight of servants' stairs. 'And half the best men will be down at the sword school this evening, three-fifths drunk. Do you suppose that's what the challenge was all about? Clearing the way for some theft here tonight? Curse it, I'm starting to sound like Casuel, seeing Eldritch-men conspiring in every corner. Here we are.'

Temar looked past Ryshad's shoulder into a small room cluttered with everything the ubiquitous maids needed to keep the residence in good order. Glass from the window shone like fragments of moonlight on the shadow-striped floor and the catch on the casement had been broken clean off.

Ryshad pushed the shutter open, setting moonlight free inside the room. 'We'd best set the valets and maids checking jewel cases. So, is this just theft or some new plot to discredit D'Olbriot? All these ifs and maybes could drive a man distracted!'

Mention of jewel cases turned Temar's thoughts instantly elsewhere. 'What lies beneath us here?'

He saw a reflection of his own fears spark in Ryshad's eyes. 'The library.'

Temar was out of the room, running down the stairs, Ryshad hard on his heels. They reached the library door together. Temar reached for the handle, praying it would be locked, his heart sinking as it gave way on silent hinges. 'Raise some light,' he snapped.

Ryshad turned to take a lamp from a table in the corridor. The subdued glow was too feeble to reach the book-lined walls but was enough to show them an expanse of crumpled linen empty on the table, a few remaining trinkets scattered beside the gaping emptiness of the ancient coffer.

'Poldrion's pustulent demons' arseholes!' Temar felt entitled to echo his grandfather's extravagant rages. 'Come on.'

Ryshad moved to stop Temar storming out of the room. 'Where to?'

'To see what that fellow in the gatehouse has to say!' Rage and dismay threatened to choke Temar. He'd had those artefacts, he'd held the means to restore so many people in his hands. How could this have happened?

'Justice within his own walls is a Sieur's prerogative, Temar.' There was regret as well as reproof in Ryshad's voice. 'You can't usurp it.'

Temar stared at him. 'So what do we do?'

'The one we caught will go before the Sieur in the morning.' Ryshad looked round the library and Temar realised the man's face was hollowed with exhaustion. 'But the other man must have got away with the loot. Do you think Demoiselle Avila has any Artifice that could help us find him?'

Temar was silenced by the appalling realisation that he'd be the one telling Avila about this disaster. He swallowed hard as two hesitant maids and a footman appeared in the doorway, eyes wide and wondering.

'Find out if anything's been stolen elsewhere,' Ryshad ordered them curtly. 'Come and tell me as soon as you've checked your mistresses' coffers, your master's jewels. Go on!'

Temar found his voice as the servants hurried off. 'Who would do this?'

'I don't know.' Ryshad spaced his words with barely controlled anger. 'Just like I don't know who broke into the warehouse in Bremilayne. Just like we don't know who stabbed you in the back, or who set me up for a sword in the guts today.'

'He was Den Thasnet's man, wasn't he?' Rage seared Temar's throat. 'Den Muret, Den Rannion, they were setting themselves up against us in the court. Can't we just call out the barracks and challenge them to prove their innocence?'

'If it were only that simple,' Ryshad growled. 'We need proof, Temar, something absolute, undeniable to tie a Name to all this. Something to lead us to the man who got away would be a start.'

'We have his fellow in the gatehouse,' cried Temar. 'He can answer to the Sieur in the morning all well and good, but can we not at least get him to talk tonight?'

Ryshad looked at him for a long moment. 'What do you suggest? Beating him? The Sieur will have Naer's hide if he presents a prisoner with the shit kicked out of him. We don't do that, not in this House.'

'Avila's not the only one who can work Artifice,' Temar said, exasperated. 'You know that. I could work the binding you were all treating so lightly before your courts for one thing. Then we will know if the man speaks the truth or lies to us.'

The unguarded distaste flickering across Ryshad's face set Temar's smouldering anger ablaze. 'You're going to have to come to terms with Artifice, Ryshad! Why not now? You cannot always just reject it out of hand because you were caught up in enchantment with me. Forget all this Toremal mistrust of mages – this is me, Ryshad, not Planir, not Casuel.' He burned with sudden determination to prove to Ryshad that some good could be wrought with Artifice. 'Even with the few incantations I know, I may just learn something from this scum, his name at very least. That could be enough to find some trail before the scent goes entirely cold. What would that be worth?'

He bit off his words abruptly but wouldn't drop his gaze. Ryshad looked away first. 'All right, let's see what you can do.'

Temar was taut with nervousness by the time they reached the gatehouse, neck stiff and tension pounding in his head. He realised he was rubbing his hands over and over each other and thrust them through the belt of his borrowed jerkin.

'Naer.' Ryshad nodded as they went into the watch room opening off the wide arch of the gate. 'The Esquire wants to see the prisoner.'

Naer rubbed a thoughtful hand over his heavily shaded chin. 'Don't leave any marks on his face.' He tossed Ryshad a heavy ring of keys.

'This way.' Ryshad opened a far door on to an age-darkened stone spiral. Temar followed him down steps chipped and worn at the edges. 'Watch your feet,' the chosen man advised him.

The stair opened on to a room divided with rough wooden partitions between the barrel vaults held up by thick pillars. A single lamp hung by the entrance, striking dull light from the chains holding the captured thief.

'Fair Festival to you,' said Ryshad pleasantly. 'This shouldn't hurt, not too much anyway.'

The man stiffened, chains chinking, defiance in his eyes. His lips narrowed, chin jutting forward as he braced himself.

Ryshad smiled again and folded his arms with slow deliberation. 'Esquire?'

Temar did his best to equal Ryshad's air of amiable threat. 'Aer tes saltir, sa forl agraine.'

The prisoner's confusion was plain to see. 'What's he say?'

'Never you mind,' said Ryshad with a satisfaction that only mystified the man further.

'His name is Drosel,' said Temar, trying to blend an offhand tone with an air of utter confidence.

'You don't know me,' the thief said before he could stop himself. 'You don't know that. Who told you? Who gave me up?'

'No one gave you up, pal. Esquire D'Alsennin here, he can pick things like that right out of your thoughts. You've heard about the Esquire, I suppose,' Ryshad enquired casually. 'He's from Kellarin, you've heard of that? Nemith the Last's lost colony, all the people sleeping away the generations under enchantment? Of course you have. Well, you're going to learn a bit more than most people about ancient enchantments, pal. The Esquire here's going to go looking for answers between your ears.'

Temar froze and hoped the shock didn't show on his face. He couldn't do that. Surely Ryshad wasn't expecting him to work Artifice that complicated? He cleared his throat.

Ryshad raised a hand. 'I know you want to, Esquire, but the

Sieur's a just man. We'll give this filth one last chance to save his sanity before you turn his head inside out. You see, the problem is he can pick your wits apart but he can't put all the pieces back together again.' He bent close to the rough bars and stared at the man, face grim with utter sincerity. 'Believe me, you want to cooperate. You don't want him inside your head, digging through every wretched memory you treasure. I saw this done to a girl once. She said she'd rather half a barracks had raped her and slit her ears and nose for good measure.'

Temar tasted blood inside his mouth as he bit his lip realising for the first time the depth of Ryshad's antipathy towards Artifice. The chosen man turned away from the prisoner, the lamplight harsh on his drawn face, mercilessly highlighting unfeigned fear and pain in his eyes. Then Ryshad winked, taking Temar utterly by surprise.

'So Drosel, we'll give you one last chance. The Esquire here will work a lesser enchantment, one that tells us if you're telling the truth. I'll ask a few questions, and if you tell us what we need to know we won't have to put a leash and muzzle on you when we take you before the Sieur tomorrow.'

Noise turned Temar's head and he saw Naer and a few of the sworn men on the stairs, peering round the stone curve with reluctant curiosity.

'Esquire?' Ryshad invited with a gesture towards the thief, who was edging back as far as his fetters allowed.

Temar cupped his face in his cold hands, eyes shut to concentrate all the better on the arcane words. He'd worked Artifice as complex as this once before and that was enough. He'd seen this done before his grandsire's seat. His own father had been accustomed to administer truth bindings for the House, after all. If Avila said she could do it, Temar most assuredly could. It had to work, or Ryshad would never trust him again.

'Raeponin prae petir tal aradare. Monaerel als rebrique na dis apprimen vaertennan als tal. Nai thrinadir, vertannnan prae rarad. Nai menadis, tal gerae askat. Tal adamasir Raeponin na Poldrion.'

He spoke the words with slow determination, every fibre of his being concentrating on the cowering thief. Ryshad took a bare instant to realise Temar had no more to say and slammed a hand into the wooden partition.

'Right, Drosel, who put you up to this? Don't lie to me, the Esquire will know if you do. Nothing to say? Sorry, if you play dumb, he'll just rip your mind apart and we'll get our answers that way.'

There was a strangled noise on the stairs and someone hurried away. Temar kept all his attention on the thief. The man opened his mouth, coughed and pawed at his throat with manacled hands.

'See?' Ryshad said coldly. 'You can't lie to us, can you?' He stared down at the man, face unyielding. 'And now you've tried, I'll tell you something else. Unless you tell us some truth, just a little one, you won't ever be able to speak again.'

The thief's jaw dropped and he looked at Ryshad with utter horror.

'Tell us,' Ryshad roared. 'Who sent you?'

'Master Knife, that's all he said,' the thief blurted out in panic. 'At the Valiant Flag, the tavern on the Habbitrot. He sent us just for that one box, just for whatever was in it.' He hid his head in his arms, hunched over his knees.

Ryshad turned and raised questioning brows.

'That will suffice for the present,' Temar managed an even disdain in his tone. 'We can always come back.'

The thief huddled into a tight ball of misery and terror. Ryshad jerked his head towards the stairs. Temar went ahead and found himself the focus of wary gazes from all sides of the watch room. Ryshad closed the door tight behind him and tossed the keys back to Naer. 'See, we didn't even have to unchain him.'

'What in the name of all that's holy did you do?' Naer asked.

'Have you really scrambled his wits?' whispered a white-faced sworn man.

'You didn't really believe all that, Verd?' Ryshad was

incredulous. 'I'd have thought Naer would have taught you better than that.'

'Watch your mouth, Rysh,' said Naer with a fair approximation of a laugh.

'Verd, that pile of shit had few enough brains to begin with,' Ryshad said reassuringly. 'Throw enough of a scare into his sort and any sense he's got left goes dribbling out of his arse.'

'Sounded cursed convincing to me,' the sworn muttered.

'Of course it did,' Ryshad agreed. 'I've got a brother who argues before the Imperial courts, and another who's a stonemason – you should hear him convincing some poor sailor to build a house three times bigger than the one he had planned.' That got a laugh all around the room.

'How did he know his name though?' a sworn man by the door hissed.

Temar spoke up at the same moment. 'Does anyone know this tavern, the Valiant Flag? What about this man who calls himself Knife?'

Someone laughed, abruptly silenced by a glare from Ryshad. 'Master Knife's a character in half the tales the puppetry men put on,' he explained. 'You'll find three down every alley at Festival.'

'But we can turn the Valiant Flag over and shake it till something falls out,' said Naer with relish. 'Verd, drum up the sworn and put the fear of the lash into the recognised. They'll be on watch for the rest of the night.'

'I'll need my sword,' Ryshad told him.

'When do we leave?' Temar felt growing excitement.

'You're not coming!' Naer told him. 'I'm not taking you down to the cloth yards, the Sieur would have my hide. Nor you, Rysh. All the proven are out being entertained, Stoll's down at the sword school even supposing he's still upright. You're senior man on the watch tonight, my friend, and that means you get the gate.'

'Naer!' Ryshad protested.

'He got in on my Watch, Rysh.' Naer's face turned ugly.

'I'll go and slap his pal in chains, not you. You lot, get yourself in hand!'

Temar watched Naer round up his troops, driving them through the gate with a mixture of harsh curses and warm encouragement.

'I'm too tired for this,' Ryshad said absently. He sighed. 'So we get the gate, well, I do. Go to bed, Temar; one of us might as well get some sleep.'

'I'll wait with you,' Temar insisted. 'I must tell Avila what's occurred as soon as she returns.'

'And I can tell Messire and Camarl,' said Ryshad without enthusiasm. He pulled up a stool by the watch room fire as a handful of eager young men in livery appeared. 'You, go and get the makings for some tisanes from the kitchens, will you? Plenty of white amella. And do any of you know your way around the North Bay well enough to take a letter?'

Temar watched as Ryshad rummaged in the sergeant's desk for paper and ink. 'I'll have that pen after you,' he said.

CHAPTER FIVE

Preface to the Chronicle of D'Olbriot, Under the Seal of Sieur Glythen, Winter Solstice in the 13th Year of Decabral the Virtuous

The Convocation of Princes was a fraught affair this year, and even allowing for the defences of wax and honour I wonder quite what I should record within these leaves. But I have my own duty to discharge, to leave an accurate record for those that take up the guardianship of our House after me. Raeponin be my witness and let the truth shame any hostile eyes that read this.

The proximate cause of the uproar among the Princes was an intemperate declaration sent to the Adjurist from the city of Col in the erstwhile province of Einar Sai Emmin. It has long been a treasured hope among the sons of Decabral that Col might be the first lost outpost reclaimed from the ashes of the Chaos and thus a foundation on which to build a new Empire among those ragged lordlings of the west. I would say any such expectation is now irretrievably dashed by the hostility provoked by Decabral's high-handed actions over this last year. This parchment over the seal of the Elected firstly confirms that the leading citizens of Col have revived their bygone forms of governance, and secondly vigorously refutes our Emperor's assertion that any such rule based on Old Imperial practice must acknowledge his suzerainty. The snub implicit in addressing this document to the Adjurist Den Perinal was unmistakable and served only to rouse Decabral's ire still further.

The Sieurs Tor Kanselin and Den Sauzet roundly rebuked the Emperor's behaviour in making such a declaration, particularly given all the Convocation's advice to the contrary last winter. Den Perinal agreed, saying hasty actions in times of uncertainty seldom prosper, making reference in the same breath to the confusion among the Princes after the unexpected death of the Emperor's late brother the Nervous. I dared hope such an attack might provoke Decabral into some folly but he restrained himself, choosing to argue in angry defence that securing Col is crucial to restraining the aspirations of the self-declared Dukes of Lescar and resurgent ambition in the Caladhrian Parliament. The Sieur Tor Arrial agreed that Tormalin strength in arms to east and west might well give both provinces pause for thought. This prompted widespread astonishment before Tor Arrial turned his speech to scathing condemnation of Decabral's fantasies. He speculated whether such nonsense was the result of overindulgence in strong liquors, aromatic smokes or apothecaries' nostrums, to wide amusement.

I had thought Tor Arrial might call for a formal censure but he sees as well as the rest of us that those Sieurs he has so hastily ennobled over the past ten years still slavishly support Decabral. Since these lapdogs know full well their place by the fireside depends solely on their master throwing them his half-gnawed bones, they will certainly defend him. We had thought Den Ferrand and D'Estabel were wavering over the summer but the Emperor bought their loyalty afresh with grants of monopoly rights to tax salt and lead production.

My sole consolation is that such typically shortsighted behaviour has only served to alienate the differing factions within Tor Decabral still further. The Empress's supposedly temporary departure for the Solland estates is now widely seen as a permanent move and her house there is taking on the air of a court in exile. Now that her eldest son is of age, he is of increasing interest to those scions of the Name who have been content to suffer Decabral the Virtuous's tactlessness for the sake of keeping the Imperial throne within the family. The Emperor's elder brother, Messire Manaire, has held himself aloof, and his own estates in Moretayne have long been a sanctuary for those hostile to the present regime. He was present in Toremal for Festival for the first time in some handful of years and made no secret of the extensive Solstice gifts he had sent his sister by marriage. Messire Manaire is past the age where he could reasonably expect elevation to Imperial honours, but his own sons would be well placed to succeed any son of the Empress who could succeed his father in short order. More significantly his trusted advisors have been hinting Manaire has finally forgiven his sister Maitresse Balene for her oppositon to his own ambitions on the death of their father, the Patient. Her marriage into Den Leoril could prove highly significant as her covey of daughers is now so widely married into so many influential families.

While many of us would prefer to see a complete change of dynasty, we might settle for a change of Imperial incumbent, since that would at least enable those newly ennobled Houses so dependent on Tor Decabral patronage to cover their treachery with a modest veil of continued loyalty to the Name. The year that opens with the dawn so rapidly approaching promises to be an interesting one.

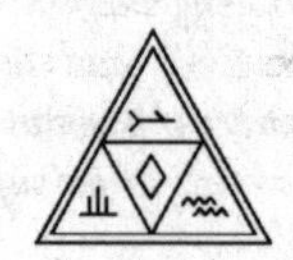

The D'Olbriot Residence Gatehouse, Summer Solstice Festival, Fourth Day, Morning

Shapeless horrors crushed me, faceless and formless, weaving a nightmare of inexorable, suffocating foulness out of my inarticulate terror.

'Chosen Tathel?' The soft but insistent knock at the door was repeated. 'Ryshad?'

I woke with a start, and for one choking moment it seemed the torment had come too, breaking out of my dreams to smother me. Then I realised someone had come in during the night and drawn the bed curtains closed around me, doubtless meaning to be kind. My heart slowed from its chest-bursting race.

'Yes?' I wished a silent pox on the uninvited curtain puller and for whoever was waking me up.

'There's a note.' The door muffled the voice.

Ripping back the curtains, I went to untie the latchstring. One of Stolley's newer lads held out a neatly sealed letter addressed in sloping Lescari script. He hovered hopefully, waiting for me to open the subtly fragrant folds.

'That'll be all, thanks.' I took the note with a grin and shut the door on his disappointed face. Leaning against it, I closed my eyes. Just at that moment, all I really wanted was one morning when I could sleep myself out, when I didn't have to get up for anything, not fire, flood or Poldrion's demons raising havoc round the residence.

Snapping the wax seal, I read the few terse lines from Charoleia. She'd be taking the air on the old ramparts between the second and third chimes of the day, would she? I'd better get up there. I threw the window open welcoming fresh air in to drive out the last remnants of nightmare and made myself presentable, hampered by a hand stiffened to near immobility. Unstrapping it showed me puffy knuckles dark with deep bruises. The cursed thing had kept me awake even after all my exertions, even after that highly uncomfortable interview with the Sieur well past midnight. I'd finally given in and taken a cup of tahn tea from Naer and I was paying for that now with a foul mouth and woolly wits, not to mention the horrors that had got through my sleeping guard.

This was no time for me to be less than fighting fit, I concluded reluctantly, rebandaging it as best I could one handed and resisting the temptation to scratch the stitches that were itching as the cursed things always do. I'd have to ask Demoiselle Avila for some healing. Temar was right, loath as I was to admit it. I couldn't turn down help I needed just because it came from Artifice. I only hoped the lady would be in a better mood this morning. She and the Sieur had arrived at nearly the same moment the night before, and the last I'd seen of Temar, Avila had been scolding him back to the residence, her consternation at the loss of the artefacts blistering his ears.

But the housemaids wouldn't even have unshuttered Avila's windows yet, so that would have to wait. I walked out of the gatehouse, sorely tempted to send round to the stables for a coach. No, the fewer people who knew what I was about the better. At least it was all downhill to the Spring Gate, and once I'd climbed the steps to the walls of the old city I had a cool salt-tinted breeze to clear my head.

As with most things, the old walls of Toremal hold up an example many lesser cities would have been wise to follow. Cities like Solland and Moretayne are both protected by a ring of masonry topped with a parapet three men wide, watch turrets set at every angle. But Solland fell to Lescari raids three times in the days of Aleonne the Resolute, and Aldabreshin pirates sailed forty leagues up river to raze Moretayne to the ground. It took Decabral the Pitiless to burn the isles of the eastern coast to barren ashes and finally drive the Archipelagans out.

The walls of Toremal have never been breached, not even in the worst excesses of the Chaos. On the outer face an immense wall of massive stones carries towers at regular intervals, each big enough to hold a fighting troop and close enough to reinforce its neighbours. They're backed with a colossal rampart of raised earth, levelled and reinforced in turn by an inner wall, the finest work any mason will see inside a season's travel. Three men can walk abreast round the walls of Solland or Moretayne; three coaches can drive abreast round Toremal's rampart.

But I was too early for the elegant gigs and smartly groomed horses that carry the wealthy and fashionable around the walls in these peaceable times. The nobility don't lead their cohorts in defence of the walls these days, they come to see and be seen, to flaunt their status and compete with their rivals far above the heads of the common folk. The serious business of socialising would start when the heat of the day had passed, so this early in the morning the rampart was deserted but for a few individuals taking a walk I followed the neatly swept earthen path, grass on either side clipped short around fragrant trees planted to shade benches for discreet conversation or safe flirtation. Passing the sharply pitched roofs of the old city on the one hand and the sprawling mass of newer building on the other, I looked briefly inside the Flemmane tower. Along with several others, it had been transformed into an elegant summerhouse where a lady might take a tisane or perhaps a little chilled wine carried up by dutiful servants.

There was no one inside. Where was Charoleia? I finally found her as the ramparts approached the Handsel Gate, where the Primeway leaves the city for the road to the north. Her elegance was unmistakable even draped in a sedate dun cloak. She was talking to some maidservant clutching a creamy shawl over a brown gown smudged with ash. I walked past, pausing some way beyond to examine a statue. It turned out to be Tyrial, Sieur D'Estabel, Adjurist to the Convocation of Princes under Bezaemar the Canny. I'd never heard of him.

'Good morning.' Charoleia appeared at my side. 'I'm sorry I wasn't at home when your message came.'

I smiled at her. 'This morning's soon enough.'

'Shall we walk?' She looked for me to offer a gentlemanly arm.

I did so with some reluctance. 'Please mind my hand.'

She tucked her hand lightly through my elbow. 'I heard about your exploits in the practice ground. Most impressive.'

I wondered if she were teasing me. 'Have you heard anything? Who put out the challenge in my name?'

'I've heard nothing beyond discreet satisfaction that you put Den Thasnet's man down. That's not a popular Name at present.' Charoleia shook dark hair dressed loose in glossy ringlets and I caught the same alluring, elusive scent that had perfumed her letter. She wore a light, rose-coloured gown beneath her cloak and a single ruby ring graced her delicate hand. 'So what did you want? Your boy told Arashil it was urgent.'

A Relshazri name; that must be the maid. 'Thieves broke into the residence last night. We snagged one, the other got away and, Dast drown it, he was the one with the loot.'

'Naturally.' Charoleia's fingers tightened. 'What do you want of me?' She was looking apparently idly from side to side, her shrewd violet eyes marking every individual taking the morning air up here.

'We had valuable artefacts stolen, Old Empire work.' I hesitated. 'They're bound to the colony and its enchantments. We have to find them if we're to restore those still sunk in sleep.'

'So when you say valuable, you actually mean priceless?' Charoleia turned guileless eyes to me, framed in the flawless beauty of her face.

'To us, yes,' I admitted. 'To whoever stole them, well, they may have no idea what they've got. The man we're holding doesn't seem to know much beyond Master Knife paying him enough gold to outweigh the risks.'

Charoleia laughed. 'Master Knife? Who might he be in his own coat? Come to that, who's pulling his strings? Do you think this was just theft for profit or another move to embarrass your Sieur?'

'All good questions and I want answers,' I said bluntly.

'Without Livak to turn over the stones where these people hide, you're my best hope.'

Charoleia frowned, a delicate cleft appearing between finely plucked brows. 'What's more important? Catching the thief or recovering the spoils?'

I chewed my lip. 'I'll trade the thief's neck for the artefacts if I have to. We must get them back. I'd certainly like to get a line on this Master Knife, but I don't suppose he'll have left any loose threads.'

'If I help, I want your word you'll keep my name out of this.' Charoleia sounded dubious. 'I mean it, Ryshad. I can't have your Sieurs or Esquires even knowing I exist, let alone anything more about me.'

'On my oath,' I promised.

'Are you prepared to pay?' Charoleia was all business now. 'To ransom the goods?'

'If we must,' I said reluctantly. 'I'll stand surety for anything you spend.' Gold won from my slavery would be well spent securing others' freedom.

'It all depends who's got the goods.' Charoleia pursed inviting cherry red lips. 'They may have already sold on the decent pieces, to be broken up or melted.'

'Saedrin save us.' Cold knives between my shoulder blades made me shiver with revulsion. What would happen if an artefact were destroyed? Would the hapless sleeper simply fall oblivious into the shades? Would they feel the furnace consuming their mind?

'Are you all right?' Charoleia was looking at me with concern. 'You've gone very pale.'

'It was a late night,' I offered lamely.

Charoleia pulled at her cloak falling away from one shoulder. 'What else do you know?'

'This Master Knife, he recruited our man Drosel and whoever his partner was, in a tavern called the Valiant Flag.' I grimaced. 'That's all. Naer took a troop down there last night and turned the place inside out but all he got was lice for his trouble.'

'Hardly surprising,' commented Charoleia with disdain.

'All right, I'll ask a few questions in the right quarters. I might hear something.'

'Send word to the gatehouse as soon as you do,' I urged her. 'Tell them to get a message to me at once.'

She was looking thoughtful. 'I've heard plenty of murmurs about D'Olbriot and D'Alsennin this Festival. What're they worth to you?'

I turned to face her. 'What have you heard?'

'In a moment.' Charoleia raised a perfectly manicured hand. 'I'll catch you up.'

She released my arm, giving me a gentle push, so I went to pretend an interest in a plaque on a crenellation. It celebrated the life of some D'Istrac long since ashes in an urn, who'd managed to kill himself falling off his horse.

Out of the corner of my eye I saw a thin-faced youth approach Charoleia. Glancing furtively around, he couldn't have been more obvious if he'd been carrying a scarlet pennant. Charoleia looked unconcerned, walking slowly with the boy, her elegant curls close to his cropped scalp. Charoleia reached beneath her cloak and passed the boy some coin. As he scurried off, still looking in all directions, she tucked a tightly folded bundle of letters securely within her cloak and came to join me looking out towards the sea.

'What was that?' I asked as she took my arm with easy familiarity.

'Information.' She smiled serenely.

'So you do have some game in play?' Had she been lying to me?

'Not as such.' Charoleia shook her head airily. 'I always walk here first thing in the morning, two full circuits of the walls. I wouldn't stay trim enough for close-cut gowns if I didn't.' She flashed a mischievous periwinkle glance at me and I tried not to think of the slender figure beneath her cloak. 'Servants with something to sell soon learn I'll be interested and this is the time and place to find me.'

'So what's worth your coin this morning?' I demanded. 'Anything to do with D'Olbriot?'

'No.' She took a step and I had to go with her or look churlish. 'At the moment it's nothing of any importance. But I'll keep this little bird in my coop, and when the time is right I'll send it flying out. One way or another, gold comes winging back.'

I decided that was best left unchallenged, like so many aspects of Livak's life. 'So what have you heard about D'Olbriot or D'Alsennin?'

'That the Name D'Alsennin will soon be as dead as ashes. That this colony over the ocean is a fool's smoke dream. But there's a hint of something more than gossip and spite.' Charoleia chose her words carefully. 'If I can find the right threads to pull, I might get a tug back from someone with word about that attack on your Esquire.'

'It'll be gold in your purse if you do,' I assured her.

She smiled. 'As for D'Olbriot, the chimney corner gossip says take his silver before you give him credit, because however high his flag flies at present, it'll be struck before long.'

'How?' I demanded.

Charoleia shook her head. 'That's where people get vague, which often means there's no substance to a rumour. Then again, there's this business with the courts fascinating everyone. There's gossip that the Sieur's fallen out of favour with Tadriol, that Lady Channis has returned to Den Veneta, that Tor Kanselin have broken Camarl's betrothal because D'Olbriot won't confirm him as Designate.' Charoleia's face was serious and all the more captivating for that. 'Which could all be the usual scum on a boiling pot, but someone's stoking the fire beneath it. I'll stake my stockings on that.'

'Can you find out who?' Dastennin save me, but she was beautiful.

She gazed at me with those entrancing eyes. 'If you make it worth my while. If you get me a card to the Emperor's dance tomorrow.'

I let slip a grunt of frustration. 'I told you before, I can't promise that.'

'Not even to save your Sieur's skin?' She held my hand tight.

I winced and shook her off. 'Dast's teeth!' I tried to flex my injured fingers and hissed with the pain.

'What have you done here?' Charoleia began undoing the bandage, ignoring my protests.

'I took a bad blow but I had to keep on using it,' I explained curtly. 'I've had worse.'

'I've no doubt, but this doesn't hurt any less, does it?' She sniffed in delicate reproof at the mottled bruising patterned by the pressure of the bandage. 'Halice and Livak are the ones used to patching up mercenaries; I prefer to stay within call of a decent dressmaker. But I've learned a few of their salves and tinctures. Come and have breakfast with me and I'll see what I can do to ease this.'

I was tempted, no question. 'I can't,' I said with real regret. 'The Sieur will pass judgement on that thief this morning and I have to be there.'

'Why don't you call on me this evening?' Charoleia's mouth curved in an engaging smile as she competently rebound my wrist. She stroked one finger across the hairs on my arm beside the tender line of the stitches. 'I can tell you if I've any news and you could stay for supper.'

'Some time around dusk?' I stood there awkwardly as she rebuttoned my shirt cuff.

'I look forward to it.' She tilted her head on one side, but just as it occurred to me to kiss her she turned swiftly, walking away, cloak floating lightly round her in the summer breeze.

I shoved my hands in my pockets as I headed for the nearest stair down by the Handsel Gate. Dastennin drown me but Charoleia was a piece of perfection. A man might do something really stupid in the face of such loveliness if he wasn't careful.

I reminded myself of all the reasons I had to be careful all the way back to the residence. Then I reminded myself of all my reasons for staying faithful to Livak, not least because she'd probably carve my tripes out with a dagger if I strayed – and I'd deserve it. I groaned with exasperation. Where was

Casuel when I needed him? I still hadn't found time to persuade the mage to bespeak Usara for me, to get some news of my absent beloved.

A coach with the D'Olbriot lynx on its door panels was slowing for the incline as I reached the conduit house so I jumped up on the running board beside the footmen, ignoring their frowns of disapproval. I swung myself down when we reached the gatehouse and watched as the coach turned down the lane to the stables.

'Ryshad!' Verd was the duty guard hailing me. 'We've just had word to send the thief over for the Sieur's judgement. You'd better get over there or you'll be neck deep in it!' His anxiety was mixed with justified reproof.

I hurried over to the residence, combing my hand through my hair and pulling shirt and jerkin straight, using my cuff to buff up my armring.

The sworn man guarding the audience chamber gave me a warning look. 'You're late.' He eased the door open just enough for me to slip inside the room.

The great audience chamber of any House is both a public space and a private one. It must welcome the supplicant while subtly reminding the importunate that rank should always be observed. The heart of D'Olbriot's residence reminds any and all coming before the Sieur that this Name has lasted more generations than most and still leads at the forefront of fashion and influence. It's an airy chamber, light pouring through tall windows with muslin drapes softening the sun. The room rises clear through two storeys and high above the white plaster ceiling is an orderly pattern of interlocking circles and squares, where borders of discreet foliage frame the D'Olbriot lynx and insignia of every House married into the Name. The walls are panelled with soft ash, the floorboards a welcoming gold, softened still further with a thick green carpet patterned with yellow flowers.

This sympathetic modernity has been carefully chosen because the fireplace harks back unashamed to antiquity. The massive hearth is framed by dark marble pillars and a great overmantel in grey stone reaches almost to the lofty ceiling. The central panel is inlaid with every colour of rock, crystal and semi-precious gem that those long-dead craftsmen could command. Marbles in every shade mimic the living blush of flowers, the vibrant green of leaves, marbled gold, smoky grey, lustrous blue, rich brown and smouldering orange. At the top, in the centre, Saedrin wears robes as bright as the morning sun, keys in hand with the door to the Otherworld closed behind him. Poldrion holds his ferry pole on one side, outstretched hand in inky black demanding his fee. Raeponin stands on the other side, gowned in blue, hooded in white, scales raised in mute warning. Below these three stern deities, Arrimelin is a girl dancing in a dream of delight, movement in every line of her white stone arms and scarlet skirts. Next to her, in a simple tunic the colour of rich brown earth, Ostrin holds out bread and wine, wheat and grapes springing around the feet of Drianon standing beside him. She smiles with motherly warmth, one hand resting lightly on the fecund belly beneath her harvest-gold gown. The whole is framed with black stone inlaid with every symbol of the gods, a riot of animals, leaves and tools in creamy marble relief.

The Sieur's face was as impassive as those of the stony-faced gods and he looked about as cheerful as Poldrion. He had the only chair, a heavy oak throne with a high-canopied back. Camarl sat beside him, upright on a cross-framed stool of reddish wood. The Sieur's brother Fresil stood to one side, glowering with Myred, who was carefully cultivating the stern indifference of his elders. Temar was straight-backed on a stool over by a window, face pale but determination in every line of him. Avila sat beside him, hands folded decorously in her lap, ankles crossed beneath her skirts, face emotionless. All the D'Olbriot men were in sober green, Avila wore a muted blue and Temar was an ominous figure in unrelieved grey, the great sapphire on his finger the only note of colour apart from his icy blue stare.

Stolley and Naer stood either side of the prisoner, polished and liveried, and I could see Stoll's collar cutting cruelly into his fat neck. A good number of other sworn and chosen were crowding the room along with most of the lesser Esquires of the Name. The air was tense with expectation and I could hear more feet scuffing above. A gallery rings the upper half of the room, and plenty of visitors had come to see the Sieur administer justice in their Name.

'You're late,' Casuel murmured, all but inaudible as he appeared at my side.

'What's happened?' I breathed.

'Naer and Temar explained how he was taken.' Casuel wavered on tiptoe, trying to see past a taller man. I took his elbow and we moved discreetly to get a better view.

'Was I called?' Not being on hand would be a mark against my name and no mistake.

Casuel shook his head but whatever he whispered was lost in the expectant shuffle of the crowd. The Sieur was speaking.

'You were taken within these walls uninvited. You have robbed us.' Messire's voice was calm. 'The only thing that could improve your situation is naming your accomplice and returning the goods you stole.'

Manacled behind his back, the prisoner's hands were shaking. 'Can't be done, my lord,' he said hoarsely, chin on his chest.

The Sieur raised sceptical eyebrows. 'Then you will be hanged and your head displayed on my gatehouse.'

A frisson ran through the room and the gallery above. The prisoner's chains rattled as he jerked upright.

'Can he do that?' gasped Casuel in a strangled whisper.

'He can if he wants to. He's the Sieur.' But I was as startled as the rest. I'd have to ask Mistal the last time any Head of a House used his ancient rights of life and death without deferring to the Convocation's privilege of ratifying such sentences.

'We will not pollute the sanctity of Festival. You will be hanged on the first day of For-Summer. This audience is concluded.' The Sieur nodded and Stolley and Naer seized the prisoner by the elbows. As they hustled the man to the door, all three with equally startled expressions, the onlookers parted to let them through. As the doors closed behind them, we heard chains rattling as the shock of condemnation wore off and the prisoner fought against his fate.

The sworn and chosen took themselves briskly off to their duties and the Esquires of the Name hurried away, avid to debate this unexpected turn of events. I stood, waiting, Esquire Camarl looking at me, displeasure mixed with disappointment in his eyes. He pointed silently at me and at Casuel before following the Sieur through a discreet door hidden in the panelling beyond the fireplace. Fresil ushered Avila through with stately courtesy and Myred did the same for Temar.

'Come on, mage,' I said grimly. 'We're wanted for a private reaming.'

The door led into the Sieur's sitting room where comfortably upholstered chairs were set out around a writing desk.

'Please sit, all of you. Where were you, Ryshad?' Messire asked without preamble. He didn't sound cross but then he seldom did.

'I know someone who might help us find the other thief,' I explained politely. 'I went to explain the little we know and to ask for help.'

The Sieur looked at me steadily. 'It really is time you reacquainted yourself with life in Toremal, Ryshad. By all means use your initiative to make suggestions, but when we're in a mire like this clear any such plan with myself or Camarl before acting upon it. A chosen man is far more visible than one from the nameless ranks of the sworn and his actions will be noted. Do you understand?'

'I apologise, Messire.' I dropped my gaze obediently.

'We need to keep a tight rein on who knows what, until this business before the courts is settled,' growled Esquire Fresil. 'We can't give anyone the means to make mischief.'

'Which is why the man will be hanged?' Esquire Myred

just failed to stop his words turning into hopeful question rather than firm statement.

'I see two possibilities here.' The Sieur caressed the patina on a bronze paperweight securing a sheaf of letters. It was shaped like a sleeping cat. 'The man was either put up to the theft by someone hostile to us and to Kellarin, or the criminally inclined think this House is somehow weakened by all these recent assaults. Either way, the thief's death will send a clear message.'

I saw Temar and Avila exchange an uncertain glance. 'What of the stolen artefacts?' the Demoiselle asked carefully.

The Sieur shrugged. 'He has, what, nearly two days and two nights. He may yet decide to tell us what he knows.'

'Will you release him, if he does?' Temar was looking concerned.

'Hardly,' scoffed Fresil. 'The man must die and that's an end to it.'

'Then what reason has he to cooperate?' demanded Temar. 'You think he will tell all in the hope of Saedrin's clemency?'

Myred opened his mouth to laugh, thinking Temar had made a joke. He hurriedly covered a feigned cough with one hand.

The Sieur spared his younger son a faintly reproving look before turning to Temar. 'We can't show any weakness, D'Alsennin. We must appear confident in the exercise of every right we hold. I don't think you quite realise the seriousness of our situation.' He invited his brother to speak with a courteous gesture.

Fresil scowled. 'Every third man coming up to me yesterday was a tenant working on our lands or a merchant contracted to our mines or shipping. All of them wanted to know if our patronage was still secure. I had to smile down men who've been buying from our estates for half a generation, who were worried about continued supply and quality. I had creditors politely hinting they'd appreciate early settlement of our accounts.'

'What did you say?' Esquire Camarl asked, voice tight with emotion.

'I told them they could have their money and be done with us,' rasped Fresil. 'If our word has no value, we'll take our business elsewhere. Most were only too happy to assure me they meant no insult, protesting every confidence in the House, but who knows who they met after me, Den Rannion, Den Thasnet or Den Muret? All doubtless undermining our House with Saedrin knows what lies!'

'Confidence is everything in Toremal.' The Sieur looked straight at Temar. 'If we show any lack of assurance, all those people who depend on us, whom we depend on in turn, they'll start to believe these lies. Our lands may be as fertile as ever, our ships as seaworthy, our mines as productive, but if the trust that shores up this House starts to crumble we'll be crippled like a penniless beggar.'

'But people will be outraged by this death,' Casuel interrupted with sudden consternation. 'What about the Rationalists? They always oppose the waste of a life and plenty of the Names approve of Rational philosophy. Oh, but maybe that's the point. Do you think the man meant to be taken? To test the Sieur like this?'

'I think we're hedged about with quite enough problems without seeing conspiracy under every bush, Master Devoir.' The Sieur smiled to soften his rebuke.

'What of the artefacts?' demanded Avila with rising colour. 'How do you propose to recover them?'

'Perhaps the thief could escape?' Casuel suggested with inspiration. 'He could be followed, back to his partner, back to wherever they've hidden the spoils!'

'Are you a complete fool, wizard?' Fresil's tone was scathing. 'What would that say for the House if we can't even keep one sneak thief securely locked away?'

'We've already had that lately come Den Turquand trying to get a hand in our strongboxes in return for whatever valuables he holds.' Messire D'Olbriot was still talking to Avila. 'While I don't think this conspiracy reaches as far as Master

Devoir might believe, I'd say it's a safe wager some other House put these men up to this theft. I think we wait for our unknown enemy's next move. With luck, they'll offer us the artefacts and we'll be able to agree a price. The worst that can happen is Den Whoever-It-Is locking the things away, to keep them from being used to help Kellarin rebuild. I'm sure they'll stay safe until we can tie someone's Name to this crime. Once we do that, the return of the artefacts will be the price of our silence.'

'So much for honour in this era,' said Avila with contempt.

'If we're dealing with dishonourable men, Demoiselle, the best we can hope for is pragmatism,' replied the Sieur steadily.

'So you will do nothing?' There was no mistaking Temar's anger.

Messire met his challenge head on. 'What would you have me do? Paste bills all over the city asking for the return of the artefacts? What measure of weakness would that show? Have you the means to pay five times their worth to whatever gutter thief manages to get his filthy hands on one?'

'Is it a question of coin?' Avila snapped. 'Like so much in this day of yours? What amount can weigh in the scales against the value of a life, a future?'

'What future will Kellarin have for anyone if the House of D'Olbriot falls?' retorted the Sieur. 'Without us to aid and defend it, your colony will be cast adrift across the ocean at the mercy of any looking to plunder it.'

Avila had no answer to that. She simply glared at the Sieur, lips tight, outrage hooding her eyes.

I stared fixedly at the carpet, hoping no one was going to ask me just what I'd said to Charoleia.

'But if we can't be seen to be searching for these artefacts, that doesn't mean others can't act for us.' Messire clasped his hands in front of him. 'Master Mage, Planir's been searching out these artefacts for years now. Surely he has some magical means of tracing them?'

Fresil snorted with contempt, Esquires Camarl and Myred exchanging sceptical glances as the wizard struggled for a reply. 'We have some techniques, some scholarship in Hadrumal—'

'Is there nothing you can do yourself, man?' demanded Fresil.

Casuel smiled weakly. 'I wasn't the mage who brought the things here. The girl Allin, she might have had some hope of finding the coffer, if the whole thing had been taken, but since it was emptied—'

'Is there any Artifice you can use?' Temar turned a beseeching face to Avila, who was studying her hands.

'Perhaps.' She looked up. 'I will send word to Guinalle and see what she advises. At least, I find no hint of Artifice being worked in the city, so I do not think we need fear Elietimm connivance in the theft.'

Myred looked as if he were about to speak but evidently remembered that Avila could use Artifice to send Guinalle her message rather than have to rely on a ship taking half a season to cross the ocean.

'If you're bespeaking the Archmage, ask if Livak's found any old lore that might help,' I suggested. Casuel looked as if he'd bitten into a quince.

'A good notion, Ryshad.' Messire looked thoughtful. He'd backed Livak's journey with coin and a measure of the House's prestige to secure a claim on anything she learned. That was primarily to give him the right to demand recompense for sharing the lore with Planir, be it coin or wizardly violence against any Elietimm landing on Tormalin shores. Now he might just get an earlier return on his investment. He smiled reassurance at Avila. 'Another resource we can call on.'

'Meantime, we simply do nothing?' Temar's frustration was building and I felt my own neck tense in sympathy. 'We allow all these enemies to ring us round? Can we never strike back?'

'It's clear enough Den Thasnet's deeply mired in all this.' Myred looked hopefully at his father.

The Sieur shared a look of silent understanding with Fresil. Both faces were hard with ominous determination. 'We'll see to Den Thasnet, never fear, and all the others snapping at our heels from the safety of the court. But we need time to get all our pieces in play, so your task is to show how confident we are by enjoying this Festival along with all the other youth of the House. You all have invitations for today, so I suggest you go and make merry, as if you haven't a care in the world.'

Camarl and Myred obediently rose to their feet but Temar's jaw set in a stubborn line. 'I will be needed to help Demoiselle Tor Arrial.'

'She can have the wizard,' said the Sieur with the first hint of irritation he'd shown. 'Think about those you have living and breathing in Kellarin, Temar, not merely the ones who still sleep. This Festival is the only opportunity you'll have this side of winter to meet the people you need to keep your colony afloat. So far you've attended one reception, got yourself stabbed and spent an illuminating evening drinking wine at a sword school. Making useful acquaintance must be your main concern today and tomorrow if you're to have any hope of raising your House again.'

'We're going to a garden lunch with Den Murivance,' said Camarl, looking first to placate his uncle and immediately after to suppress Temar.

'Perhaps I could—' The Sieur silenced me with a look.

'You're going nowhere beyond barracks and gatehouse, Ryshad. For one thing, whoever wanted to stick a sword in you yesterday might send someone for a second try. More importantly, the House opens to the commonalty tomorrow, had you forgotten? Imagine the opportunity for mischief that offers. After last night's disgraceful exhibition, I want you putting the fear of flogging into every man-at-arms who'll be on duty.'

'Stolley and Naer—'

'You've rank to equal theirs now, and in any case neither's shown himself to advantage over these last few days.' The Sieur smiled thinly. 'You're known but you're just unfamiliar enough to keep sworn and recognised on their toes. I want every man wearing my badge alert for the least thing out of the ordinary tomorrow. You're the man to make that happen.'

This was part compliment and part order. I bowed my head. 'Yes, Messire.'

'When does Ustian arrive?' Fresil turned from staring pensively out of the window to bark his question.

'Some time this afternoon,' said Myred hastily. 'And Uncle Leishal should be here later this morning.'

'Your brothers?' Avila looked to Messire for confirmation.

'Indeed, and we'd better have a plan to show them we're meeting this challenge to the House.' The Sieur looked at the rest of us with unmistakable dismissal as Fresil loosened the collar of his shirt, faded eyes distant with malice as he took a seat beside the Sieur.

Camarl led us out into a corridor. 'Are you coming to Den Murivance?' he asked Myred.

The younger man shook his head. 'I'm promised to a musical morning with Den Castevin – and I'm already late, so I'll see you this afternoon.'

Camarl nodded. 'Temar, I'll see you in my chamber.' He walked away without further ado.

Avila watched him go, thin lips pressed together. 'The library, now.'

She stalked off, skirts swishing angrily. Temar and I followed, Casuel catching up after hovering indecisive for a moment.

Dolsan Kuse, busy shelving books, was surprised to see Avila sweeping into his library as if she owned it. 'Leave us,' she commanded with scant courtesy. 'I need privacy to work Artifice.'

That sent the Archivist on his way with a hasty bow as Avila drummed impatient fingers on a jewelled purse chained at her waist. 'The Sieur can manage D'Olbriot's affairs as he sees fit but we need to discuss our own strategy. Guliel is right in part at least. Temar, you had best spend your day raising D'Alsennin's standard, for the sake of all in Kel Ar'Ayen. But you can keep your eyes and ears open all the same. Just avoid too many clumsy questions for Raeponin's sake.'

She turned to me with an irritated shake of her head. 'I was hoping to send you to watch Den Thasnet and follow that odious boy Firon for a start.'

'I can talk to the men as well as setting them weapons drills,' I offered. 'Someone may recall something from last night, someone might have heard a rumour worth following up.' Going beyond the Sieur's immediate commands wasn't the same as breaking them, was it?

'Master Mage.' Avila rounded on Casuel, who was examining the lamentably empty coffer. 'You will have to keep watch on Firon Den Thasnet. He is stupid enough to be indiscreet.'

The wizard's jaw dropped. 'Me?'

'Who else?' demanded Avila. 'You were put at my disposal and that is what I wish you to do. The Sieur's orders for everyone else were plain enough and you will have your elemental talents to assist you.'

'You're the best man for the job, Casuel,' I pointed out. 'No one knows your face, unlike me and Temar.'

'But how am I supposed to find him?' protested the mage. 'It's Festival, he could be anywhere in the city!'

'Scry for him,' said Avila briskly. 'That is the correct term, I believe. Or do you need me to use my arts?'

'No, no,' said Casuel with ill grace. 'I can manage that.'

'But what of the artefacts?' Temar began pacing in front of the fireplace. 'You cannot believe that fool of a Den Thasnet will simply lead Casuel straight to the thieves?'

'No,' agreed Avila, unperturbed. 'But I want to know to whom he speaks and, if possible, of what. I refuse to believe all this is just happenstance. If we can track some part of this malice back to its source, perhaps we can put a stop to the whole. Your magic enables you to listen from a distance, wizard, does it not?' That wasn't a question; Avila had clearly been keeping her eyes open around the mages Planir sent to Kellarin.

Casuel coloured slightly beneath her searching gaze. 'Technically, yes, but there are ethical considerations—'

'Take your scruples to Planir, when you ask if he has learned any lore that might help our search. Then apply yourself to Den Thasnet. I will contact Guinalle through Artifice,' she continued, oblivious to Casuel's outraged expression. 'Then, if I can get the Sieur's permission, I will ask that thief some questions myself. Artifice can loosen an unwilling tongue where threats prove ineffective.'

'No, my lady. That is, Temar—' Nausea thickened in my throat as I recalled the Elietimm enchanter searching my memory, breaking open cherished recollections, scattering hopes and fears to be crushed beneath brutal sorceries. Bluffing a man with fast talking and Temar's modest skills was one thing, truly setting Artifice on the man was quite another.

'I beg your pardon?' Avila looked at me in astonishment. Behind her I could see Temar looking aghast, frantically signalling me to silence.

'Only if there's no other way,' I amended my protest hastily. 'Word would be bound to get out and with the prejudice there is against magic, the notion that Artifice forced a man to talk – forgive me but most people would find that repellent. If Artifice is to rise above popular prejudice about magic—'

'Ryshad Tathel, let me tell you—'

A knock at the door saved me from the wrath building in Avila's face. Dolsan Kuse stuck his head into the room and looked at Temar. 'Excuse me, but Esquire Camarl's valet is looking for you and he's not in the best of tempers.'

'Camarl or the valet?' asked Temar sarcastically, but he was already on his way to the door. I followed him, bowing to Avila but avoiding her eye.

'Very well, go on, all of you,' she said ominously. 'Do not come back until you have something of use to report. No, Ryshad, on second thoughts, wait.'

I halted reluctantly. 'Demoiselle?'

'I want to see that hand.'

I walked over to her slowly, undoing the bandage as I went. 'It's not so bad.'

'Nonsense,' she said tartly. 'And there is neither virtue nor heroism in suffering unnecessary pain, my lad.' She held my hand between her palms, flat above and below, crossways in an oddly formal gesture. Her eyes softened and she seemed to be staring right through me as she whispered a soft incantation under her breath. A chill ran down my back as I heard echoes of ancient rhythms in the arcane syllables.

My arm and hand grew warm, not painfully but with the unmistakable, unnatural thrill of magic. A tingling throbbed briefly deep within my arm, as if I had slept crooked on it, waking to blood reawakening protesting flesh. I waited with growing dread for whatever shock of enchantment all this heralded.

But all that happened was the slow evaporation of the aching tenderness that had been catching me unawares with sharp jibes of pain all morning. The tingling sensation faded to nothing and the heat in my knuckles subsided to no more than a healthy glow, as if I'd been working the hand sparring. I looked down as Avila released me with a satisfied nod. The bruising had faded to no more than a faint discoloration and all the swelling was gone. I picked at the redundant stitches with a curious fingernail. Anyone would have sworn the cut was ten days healed.

'The Sieur's surgeon can take those out,' Avila instructed.

'Thank you,' I managed to say with a fair degree of composure.

'When we have leisure, we must discuss your own prejudices about aetheric magic, never mind those of the populace,' Avila said softly, her eyes searching mine.

'I had better go,' said Temar from the threshold. 'I'll come and find you when I get back.' Casuel hovered, unable to decide if he could go or stay.

'Is there something else?' Avila settled herself at the table. 'If not, I will contact Guinalle.'

'Come on, Casuel.' I ushered the wizard out of the room and shut the door firmly behind us.

'We have perfectly effective healing magics in Hadrumal you know,' he said with faint envy.

'I'm sure you do.' I realised I was rubbing the healed knuckles into my other palm and stopped. 'But do you have anything to find the stolen artefacts?'

'What exactly did she do? What did you feel?' Casuel was still looking at my hand so I shoved both in my breeches pockets.

'She stopped it hurting, which is good enough for me. Hadn't you better bespeak Planir? Find out what he suggests – and find out if Livak's discovered anything useful on her travels.' I spared a moment for a fleeting regret that I hadn't gone with her. A summer spent peaceably tramping through forests and mountains would surely have been preferable to all this confusion.

Casuel sniffed and stalked off down the corridor, back stiff with indignation. I watched him go then went off to make myself unpopular with the men I'd so recently been serving with. In some lights, this new rank was starting to look a rather tarnished prize.

The D'Olbriot Residence, Summer Solstice Festival, Fourth Day, Morning

Casuel walked slowly up to his bedchamber, so absorbed he quite neglected to bow to an elegant Demoiselle hurrying down the stairs. Shocked at the realisation he turned full of obsequious apology, but all he saw was a retreating head bright with a jewelled net encasing coiled braids. The girl had taken no more notice of him than of the maid on the landing below, a mere servant with arms full of linen and head empty of anything.

Goaded by complex dissatisfaction, Casuel locked his door behind him and picked up the bedside candle. He snapped his fingers at the wick, feeling little of the usual thrill at bending inert substance to his bidding. As he set the flame in front of his small mirror, he forced the burnished metal to submit, to reflect the image he wanted rather than the room around him. What Prince of Toremal could do as much, he thought. What Emperor? Constraints of distance were nothing to those who could manipulate the very elements of the physical world. Hearth-Master Kalion was right; such power deserved due recognition. He deserved recognition, him, Casuel D'Evoir.

An image snapped across the surface of the mirror as answering magic bolstered Casuel's own. 'Yes?' Planir looked up from tending a crucible on a charcoal stove. 'Oh, it's you. Good morning.'

'These people have no notion of courtesy to a mage,' Casuel spoke without thinking. 'How can they, when they don't meet a true wizard from one year's end to the next?'

'Is there some reason you're disturbing me to tell me this?' The Archmage stirred the contents of his pot with a metal rod.

Casuel missed the warning note in Planir's distant voice. 'No one in Toremal thinks a mage is any more than these tricksters Velindre's wasting her time with.'

Planir set down his rod with a rattle striking a faint echo from Casuel's mirror. 'You've something to say about Velindre?'

Casuel looked surprised. 'No, not as such. Just that she's doing herself no credit chasing round the city after every charlatan who claims the least sniff of an affinity.'

'Then perhaps you'll wait until you do have something to tell me before you bespeak me again.' Planir's displeasure came ringing through the shining metal.

'Oh, no, Archmage, I've plenty to tell you.' Casuel hesitated. 'Well, quite a lot. Messire D'Olbriot faced an array of accusations before the Imperial Court yesterday. That'll tie him up in argument until Equinox at least, the other senior Esquires of the House too, probably. Four other Names are claiming rights in Kellarin, there's been argument to declare D'Alsennin's House extinct, and someone or other has raised accusations of bad faith against D'Olbriot, using an advocate claiming to be a friend of the court.'

'Then find out who's behind it and let me know,' Planir said in exasperation. 'D'Olbriot defeated before the Imperial Court would have appalling consequences! It's been hard enough convincing Guliel and Camarl we're not all overbearing autocrats like Kalion, and they're the most open-minded nobles we could find. We have to have Tormalin cooperation over Kellarin, Cas, never forget that.'

'It's Kellarin I wanted to mention,' said Casuel reluctantly. 'You know those artefacts, the ones D'Alsennin somehow managed to find—'

Planir raised a hand. 'The ones Allin Mere helped him find? Which wouldn't have been recovered without her quick thinking?'

'Yes.' Casuel's lips narrowed. 'Well, they've managed to lose them, D'Alsennin and Ryshad. Thieves took the lot last night.'

The ochre light of the spell flared for a moment, heat palpable on Casuel's face. Planir's words were lost, but when the disturbance cleared Casuel could see the crucible beside him had cracked to spill molten metal over the slate-topped table.

'What are you doing to find them?' Planir demanded. 'We've pledged ourselves to support Kellarin. We may well need their Artifice against the Elietimm, don't ever forget that!'

'Allin didn't think to familiarise herself with the actual artefacts,' stammered Casuel. 'They didn't take the box, so she can't scry for that—'

'Did you make any study of the items?' asked Planir sharply.

'I wasn't able to,' said Casuel hurriedly. 'Demoiselle Tor Arrial sees such things as her business and no one else's.'

'Has she any aetheric means of finding the thieves?' Planir looked forbidding. 'Is there any hint that the Elietimm are involved?'

'Demoiselle Tor Arrial says no one's using Artifice in the city.' Casuel was relieved to have something definite to say. 'She's no way to trace the thieves herself but she's contacting Demoiselle Guinalle. I was wondering if Usara had found any lore among the Forest Folk that might help, or something from the Mountain Men? The book that girl of Ryshad's fussed over had ballads about following lost trails, didn't it?' he added hopefully.

'The book you gave so little credence?' Planir smiled for an instant before his face turned grim. 'No. There are some interesting leads for Mentor Tonin and his scholars to pursue, but nothing of any immediate use.'

'A shame,' said Casuel, trying to quell an inner satisfaction.

'Quite,' said Planir dryly. He looked at Casuel, and even as a small image reflected in magic his eyes were uncomfortably piercing.

'Doesn't Master Tonin have some means of identifying Kellarin artefacts?' Casuel asked hastily.

The Archmage shook his head. 'He can pick them out of an array of unenchanted objects, but only if they're to hand.'

A tense silence fell. 'Perhaps Guinalle will have some aetheric magic to find them,' Casuel repeated hopefully. If she did, he'd be the one giving the good news to Planir, wouldn't he? He would be suitably gracious to Usara when he had occasion to mention how much more use he had been to the Archmage.

'Perhaps and perhaps not. What are you doing in the meantime?' Planir demanded.

'I've an idea who might be behind this,' said Casuel rapidly. 'There's a scion of Den Thasnet I've my eye on. I was going to send Ryshad to follow him but I'd better do it myself. Obviously, as a rule I wouldn't dream of using magic to eavesdrop, but I think in these circumstances it's permissable?' He looked hopefully at the Archmage.

'Your high-mindedness does you credit,' Planir remarked with a flatness that made Casuel wonder if his spell was faltering. 'Be discreet.'

The mirror blinked to emptiness and Casuel looked blankly at it for a moment. He set his jaw, pleased to see the well-bred resolution in his reflection.

He poured water from the ewer into the basin on his washstand. This was an excellent opportunity to be of service both to D'Olbriot and to the Archmage, he realised with growing pleasure. D'Alsennin and Tor Arrial would be grateful as well when Casuel proved Den Thasnet was their enemy. Both Houses might have limited standing at present, but with the riches of Kellarin backing them the future was looking promising.

Casuel poured a little ink into the water and absently summoned emerald radiance to suffuse the bowl. A new notion warmed him. As and when D'Alsennin succeeded in reviving his long-extinct Name, Casuel would have an excellent precedent to argue before the Court of Prerogative when the time came for him to resurrect the House of D'Evoir.

But first he had more immediate matters in hand he

reminded himself hastily. He drew on his memory of Firon Den Thasnet, projecting his recollection of the uncouth stripling's sneering face into the ensorcelled water. An image coalesced in the green-shaded obscurity, clearing to show the youth reclining on a daybed in a conservatory.

Casuel looked down on Firon. There'd be none of this contempt for wizardry when even Names like Den Thasnet had to acknowledge D'Evoir, seeing a mage of indisputable noble rank was an ally of the Archmage, a confidant of men such as Hearth-Master Kalion.

Casuel looked up from the bowl. Perhaps it was time to consider how best to phrase a direct approach to Kalion? The Hearth-Master made no secret of his conviction that the mundane powers of the mainland must be made to recognise the resources wizardry offered an astute ruler. Kalion would certainly see the advantages of having one of their own to liaise with the Tormalin Names, and who would be better placed than Casuel? Once a few Princes acknowledged Hadrumal's influence, well-born girls would certainly consider joining him in renewing the Name of D'Evoir, wouldn't they?

Casuel glanced down and was startled to see his scrying dimming to a mossy dullness. Chagrined, he summoned the magic anew and the image sharpened. Breathing with exquisite care, Casuel drew the picture out, expanding the magic until he saw the Esquire was in a hothouse pavilion at the rear of the Den Thasnet residence. He frowned. The Den Thasnet residence was halfway to the northern heights above the city. There was no way Casuel could be expected to walk that far, not in the full heat of a summer noon. Arriving somewhere all sweaty and dishevelled would undermine the dignity both of wizardry and of D'Olbriot for one thing. But taking a gig from the stables would hardly serve the Sieur or Planir's insistence on discretion.

He lost his grip on the slippery scrying and the image floated into fragments on the water's surface. No matter. Casuel shook a remnant of green light from his hands and congratulated himself on visiting so many Houses when they'd last opened their gates at Equinox. He wondered in passing how best to mention this forethought to Planir as he built Den Thasnet's residence in his mind's eye, picturing the wide central block, new stone clean and white in the sun, the sloping roof bright with the finest tiles coin could buy, the wings on either side linked by corridors framing courtyards where sparkling fountains reflected in costly expanses of window glass.

Casuel reached for the substance of the breeze that drifted lazily through his open window. He made himself one with the air, feeling its paths and currents and travelling them with the ease of instinct honed with practice. In an instant of brilliant light he crossed the city and found himself standing in the midst of an elegant chequerboard of low-hedged flowerbeds.

'Hey, you!' A gardener shouted, outraged, letting his laden barrow fall to the path with a thud. 'Get off my summersilks!'

'I beg your pardon,' Casuel said hastily, trying to avoid doing any more damage as he struggled to the nearest path. He realised with dismay that his expensive boots were covered in some ominous-smelling mulch.

'Where did you spring from?' The gardener approached with growing perplexity. 'I thought the gates were closed to visitors today.'

'Don't concern yourself, my good man.' Casuel tried for a suitably noble tone as he walked off towards the residence. This was the kind of house he would build, Casuel thought, clean, Rational lines matching form and function in precise layout of grounds and building. No, his house would be even finer, given the way architects shared the same ridiculous prejudices against judicious wizardry as everyone else. After all, Casuel's sympathy with the earth made him the obvious person to judge the best stone to keep a house warm in winter and cool in summer. Even Velindre would find it simple enough to chart the flow of air through a house, and who better to consult about siting a hearth than a mage with a fire affinity? But no, all anyone ever wanted a mage for was shifting quantities of earth, for all the world like that nursery tale of Ostrin and the enchanted shovel. It simply wasn't fair that wizards were denied any genteel profession by Tormalin disdain for magic.

Conversation behind him interrupted Casuel's musing and he glanced over his shoulder to see the gardener walking slowly after him. Curse the fellow, he was talking to a man in livery, halberd in hand. Casuel looked from side to side for some discreet corner but Den Thasnet's desire to shape his gardens to the same height of fashion as his house meant there was precious little growing above knee height. A summerhouse offered the only sanctuary from the inconvenient underlings and Casuel hurried into it.

But what now? The little eight-sided shelter would barely hide an indiscreet kiss, and anyway the man had seen him come in here. Casuel looked out of the window to see the halberdier walking purposefully towards the gazebo. How was he to explain his presence if the House was closed to visitors?

Casuel drew a deep breath and summoned a shimmer of blue light between his hands. He hurriedly drew water from the earth beneath him and fire from the heat of the sun, wrapping himself inside a veil of magic to baffle prying eyes. He stood motionless, breathless as the puzzled man-at-arms looked into the summerhouse, the gardener behind him, brows raised in good-humoured curiosity. 'Where'd he go then?'

'Cursed if I know.' The gardener brushed earth off his hands. 'I'd have sworn he went in here.'

'Sure you've not been tending Esquire Firon's thassin too closely? Pruning it without opening the windows in the conservatory?' The sworn man laughed.

The gardener smiled thinly. 'But he went this way, some sour-faced chap all tricked out like a draper wanting to jump the counter and mix with his betters.'

'I'll pass the word,' the sworn man shrugged.

The two men walked away slowly, leaving Casuel all but throttled by indignation. What would some muddy day labourer know about fashion anyway? He was about to dissolve the blend of elements when a sudden thought stopped him.

The Archmage had told him to be discreet, so why not stay invisible? Casuel tightened his grip on the elements he was manipulating and added a complex lattice of air to baffle any sound he might make. Walking with agonised care, he went up stone steps to a broad paved terrace, searching for the pavilion where he'd seen Den Thasnet lounging.

There it was, an airy framework of white ironwork sheltering glossy citrus trees and a few unsightly pots of ragged ferns. Casuel peered through the windows to see Den Thasnet taking his ease, sipping from a glass in a silver holder. That was all the increasingly thirsty wizard had to see for what felt like half a season. Finally, as six chimes sounded from a distant timepiece, Firon slammed his drink down on a metal table, impatiently ringing a handbell. A lackey appeared, immediately sent away with brusque gestures and reappearing with a coat that Firon pulled on, tugging at his lacy cuffs with edgy hands. He shoved open a door to the terrace, slamming it back on hinges that squeaked in protest. Keeping firm hold on the sorcery sheltering him, Casuel followed as close as he dared as Firon ran lightly down the steps and through the gardens to the extensive stableyards. The mage's heart sank as he realised Den Thasnet wore riding boots and was carrying a whip.

'Get me the sorrel gelding.' The Esquire snapped his fingers at a lad carrying a basket of grain. 'At once, boy!'

The stable lad ducked away as if he feared a cuff round the ear. Casuel watched in an agony of indecision as the horse was brought out and saddled, Firon all the while tapping his switch impatiently on one boot.

'I'll need you to bring him back.' Firon swung himself into the saddle and reached a hand down to the boy. 'If you let him pick up a stone, I'll flay your back for you, understand?'

The lad tried and failed to take a pillion seat on the restive horse, getting a smack from Firon's whip across his shoulders for his pains.

Casuel moved forward slowly as the boy managed to mount. Invisible or not, he didn't like horses at the best of times and this beast was certainly not going to like what the wizard was about to do. He pulled a handful of wiry hairs from the horse's mane, sending the startled animal backwards in a clatter of hooves. The hapless stable boy slid off the sorrel rump and this time Den Thasnet's lash raised a scarlet weal on his raised hand.

'You're not worth your bed and board,' sneered Firon. 'Get up or I'll have you begging in the gutters.'

The lad clung on grimly to the saddle as Firon whipped the horse to a punishing trot. Casuel ran forward as two liveried men immediately began closing the tall gates behind the Esquire. Slipping through the narrowing gap just in time, he watched the retreating rump of the horse until it was lost in the busy traffic filling the route to the lower city.

But all was not lost, was it? Casuel looked with satisfaction at the ginger horsehair wrapped round his fingers. Ryshad would have been utterly at a loss, wouldn't he? D'Alsennin wouldn't have known what to do. Den Thasnet would have been lost to anyone without a mage's skills. Casuel walked round the corner of the residence wall, looking in the gully behind the shade trees. There had to be a puddle somewhere hereabouts? But no, not in high summer, not in Toremal. Casuel belatedly remembered years when no rain had fallen in either half of summer. How was he to scry for the cursed animal?

'If you want to take a piss, go and use the drain by the dung heap!' An old woman stood up from behind a low row of pease in the garden of a grace house, squinting belligerently at the wizard. 'I don't care what your Name is, we don't need you spraying round here like a filthy tom cat!'

Casuel realised his spells had come unravelled and coloured with embarrassment.

A younger woman appeared from behind an outhouse. 'Oh, do excuse Mother, your honour, she's not in her senses.' She bustled the old woman away, scolding her in a low, frightened voice.

Casuel walked hastily down the lane, smoothing his coat.

His gaze lit gratefully on a well, a horse trough beside it and a lower one for dogs. A few women were filling buckets with a desultory air, sparkling drops falling to be swallowed instantly by the thirsty dust. Casuel slowed his pace until they had slung their yokes across their shoulders and hooked on their pails.

He would have to work fast. Casuel hurried to the horse trough, hoping no one interrupted him. He dropped the horse hairs into the water, wrapping the coarse strands with verdant brilliance. A skein of emerald light coiled and twisted in the water, indistinct and blurred. Casuel wished helplessly for some ink to support the translucent image, laying his hands carefully on the surface of the water. The clear green took on a muddy hue. The image wavered but Casuel saw the sorrel horse making its way through a crowded street. Sweat beaded his forehead and he forced himself to draw unhurried, even breaths. Even the best scryers of Hadrumal couldn't be expected to hold a spell together long in these conditions, he thought with growing apprehension.

The horse slowed to a walk, and Firon Den Thasnet raised his whip to clear a few passers-by and pulled the animal up with a cruel jerk on the reins. The groom slid off the animal's rump, hurrying to hold the bridle as Firon dismounted. Casuel fought to still a growing tremor in his hands, watching breathless as the Esquire left horse and groom without a backward glance. He went into a tall building of brash orange brick, decorated with unashamed frivolity, an array of pipes fanned out over the double doors and stone swags beneath the windows heavy with fruit and flowers.

One might almost be tempted to credit the tales of Ostrin's warped sense of humour at times, thought Casuel, shaking the horse trough water from his hands with distaste. Of all places in the city, why did Den Thasnet have to go there?

The wizard began walking crossly in the direction of the lower city, heavy with fatigue. Firon Den Thasnet had better be staying a while in that theatre because Casuel needed some time to recover himself before working any more magic. No one had better try blaming him if the noble youth was gone before he got there.

A jangle of harness turned Casuel's head, and seeing a hireling gig coming up at the trot he waved it down authoritatively.

'Your honour?'

'The puppetry theatre on Lantan Straight,' Casuel curtly ordered the driver. He closed his eyes as the man whistled up the horse and tried to draw back some of the energies he'd used to manipulate the elements. It was all very well everyone expecting him to use wizardry to help them, but no one not mage-born knew what it cost, yet another injustice mages had to bear.

He opened his eyes as the gig stopped with a jolt and saw the driver turning expectantly. 'Is this the place?'

'Yes.' Casuel looked with displeasure at the tasteless façade as he climbed out of the gig.

'Fair Festival, but that'll be a silver Mark to you,' said the hireman indignantly.

Casuel tugged the D'Olbriot amulet out of his pocket. 'Apply to the gatehouse for your payment.' He dismissed the man with a gesture, ignoring disgruntled muttering as he walked slowly inside the lofty building.

The narrow lobby was empty but for some discarded flowers wilted in the dust and a chair with stuffing spilling out of a split seat. Casuel hurried past a detailed depiction of Ostrin embracing a maiden with his hands in most impertinent places. Had the artist deliberately chosen the most unsavoury legends he could find for these garish murals?

Beyond brightly painted double doors, laughter and chatter echoed round the vast windowless room that took up most of the hollow edifice. The stage at one end was busy with craftsmen hammering, sawing or painting. Their efforts fought with snatches of ragged music from somewhere beyond and a faint ache tightened across Casuel's temples.

'Come to see your brother?' A man clutching a bone-topped double pipe stopped on his way past.

'Yes, of course.' Casuel smiled weakly at the musician.

'Up there,' the man nodded at the stage. 'Go on up, no one'll mind.' The piper walked out, shirt tails loose over dirty breeches.

Casuel ignored the man, scanning the room for Den Thasnet, hissing with exasperation as he tried to find the Esquire in the constantly shifting crowd. Knots of people gathered and broke apart, dragging chairs out of ragged rows to make circles abandoned moments later. Cries of greeting cut through screeches of laughter as girls in dresses far too immodest for public display embraced in an excess of giddiness. The men were no better, coats and cuffs unbuttoned, lace collars untidily askew. Bottles of wine were being purchased from a side room and passed from hand to hand. Casuel sniffed with disapproval as he caught the sharp aromatic scent of stronger spirits. No wonder no one was wearing any insignia to identify the House they were disgracing with such behaviour.

The throng parted just long enough for him to see Firon Den Thasnet but in the next instant a giggling girl pulled her companion across the wizard's view. She turned her flushed face for a kiss that the youth was glad to supply before another lad folded the girl in a smothering embrace. Casuel gaped, horrified at such promiscuous indecency until a passing musician dug him in the ribs with a chuckle. 'She'll be letting more'n her hair down by sunset, won't she?'

Casuel turned abruptly to the narrow steps leading on to the stage. Watching warily as the busy craftsmen moved half-finished scenery around, he found a vantage point behind a curtain and looked for Den Thasnet again. There he was, sitting on a solitary chair, booted feet outstretched, scowling at people he tripped, his disgruntled expression deterring anyone thinking of including him in their conversation.

'Cas? Someone said you wanted me?' An impatient voice at his shoulder made the wizard jump.

'What? No, not particularly.' Casuel turned to see his brother looking askance.

'Then what are you doing here?' demanded Amalin.

'I'm about the Archmage's business,' said Casuel loftily, glancing back at Den Thasnet, who was still sitting alone. 'And Messire D'Olbriot's. Nothing to do with you.'

'It is if you're doing it in my theatre,' Amalin retorted robustly. 'Is this something to do with all those questions you had the other day? I told you, I've no idea which noble House is slandering another, and I've less interest. All that concerns me is which ones pay prompt.'

Casuel sniffed. 'Ever the merchant. You peddle your music like a wandering harpist.'

'At least it's a honest trade, Master Mage,' sneered Amalin. 'Mother's not ashamed to tell her sewing circle about my latest triumphs. Did I tell you I've written a new round dance for the Emperor's entertainment tomorrow?'

Casuel looked resolutely back at Firon, who was chewing a thumbnail and looking around sourly.

'So who are you spying on, Cas?' Appreciably taller, Amalin peered easily over the wizard's shoulder. 'The charming Esquire Den Thasnet?'

'Do you know him? Why? How?'

Amalin chuckled unpleasantly. 'Oh, you'll talk to me when you want to know something?'

'Don't play the fool, Amalin,' snapped Casuel. 'This is important.'

'So's rehearsing my musicians.' Amalin turned to leave.

'What would it do for your career if I told Messire D'Olbriot how uncooperative you're being?' threatened Casuel.

'Not much harm,' Amalin shrugged. 'They're saying the old Sieur's out of favour with the Emperor anyway.'

Casuel gaped. 'Who's saying?'

'Him, and his cronies.' Amalin nodded at Firon Den Thasnet. 'Not that I pay much heed. Den Thasnet owes more money to more entertainers than any other House in the city. Say what you like about D'Olbriot, the stiff old stick pays up by return messenger.'

'You'd go a good deal further in your chosen profession

with a little more respect for your betters,' said Casuel bitingly.

'Bowing and scraping to anyone entitled to call themselves Den Something?' scoffed Amalin. 'Why should I? Half of your so-called nobles live on credit and wishful thinking. It's honest traders like Father brought me the coin to build this place. They pay in full the moment the last note sounds at their banquets.'

'Paying for lewd masquerades danced by girls no better than common trollops, you mean,' retorted Casuel. 'I'm surprised to see you still bothering with proper puppetry.' He waved a hand at the marionettes hanging high above their heads, each as tall as a child, a masterpiece of woodwork dressed with a tailor's finest skill.

'I'll stage whatever pays, Cas.' Amalin's smile was mocking. 'Same as I'll let these wastrels use my place for their meetings and intrigues just as long as they pay with both hands for the privilege of drinking cheap wine while they do it.'

'It's all just counting coin with you, isn't it?' Casuel did his best to look down his nose at the taller man.

'At least I don't need Mother sending me money to put the clothes on my back.' Amalin winked at him. 'And my boots don't stink of horseshit either.'

'Then why do you look as if you fell out of some charity guild's ragbag?' countered Casuel.

Amalin brushed a negligent hand down his faded shirt, frayed at collar and cuffs. 'Work clothes, Cas, but you wouldn't know anything about that, would you?'

'Amalin? Where do you want this?' The summons from the far side of the stage saved Casuel from having to find a suitable retort. Amalin's arrogance really was intolerable, he raged silently. He had no respect for rank, wrapped up in his petty concerns and this tawdry sham of a world he'd built for himself. Casuel watched Amalin walk away with a faintly familiar-looking dark-haired man. No stomach for continuing the debate, little brother? Well, it wasn't the first time Casuel had set him right on a few things.

He looked back into the crowd to see Firon Den Thasnet

deep in conversation with someone. Who was it? What had he missed? Cursing Amalin for distracting him, Casuel struggled to calm himself sufficiently to float an invisible stream of magic drawn from air and light over the heads of the revellers. Concentrating hard, he waited impatiently for words to drift down the spell.

'—this, that, the other,' hissed Firon. 'I do it and what do I have to show? That fool of a boy got his arse well and truly kicked by D'Olbriot's man, so that dog won't hunt again. And your so-called advocate made a piss-poor showing over the Land Tax. What have you got to say about that?'

'I recommended the best advocate for the coin you were willing to pay,' shrugged the newcomer. 'I fail to see how you can blame me when D'Olbriot hires a more experienced man. Anyway, even if they're not being taxed on Kellarin for last year, there's been no judgement about next, has there? That game's still in play.'

Casuel moved as far as he dared beyond the shelter of the curtains, trying to work out who the man might be. Of an age with Firon's own father, and Casuel's come to that, he was a good height, iron grey hair soberly cut, face unremarkable in its placid pleasantness. He wore no identifiable colours, merely a plain brown coat and breeches well tailored from good cloth. Casuel frowned; the clothes were styled like livery and that was no merchants' fashion. Something about his manner was reminiscent of an upper servant as well.

'You said I'd find plenty of backing against D'Olbriot.' Firon's complaints were rising. 'Where is it? Any time I said yesterday they're just getting what they deserve, all I got was the cold shoulder.'

'Keep your nerve and people will come over to your way of thinking,' said the newcomer firmly. 'Bringing all the rewards we discussed. Look at the cases brought before the Emperor yesterday. At least one of them will trip Burquest, no matter how fast he dances round the truth. Your side of the scales will rise, just as soon as D'Olbriot's sinks.'

'Oh, will it?' Firon looked sceptical. 'High enough to match me to a girl of rank who can still bring a decent coffer of coin? My father's talking about selling me off to some fat-arsed merchant's ugly daughter, he's so desperate for some ready gold—'

The other man slapped a light backhand into Firon's mouth. 'Watch your tongue,' he said with genial warning. 'Show a little respect.'

Shock sent a shudder through Casuel's magic that nearly scattered the spell and he stepped back into the concealing curtains. Who was this man to dare such insult?

The blow hadn't been hard enough to leave a mark but Firon's face was scarlet all the same. 'Show respect, have more patience, set yourself up for a mighty fall if this all goes rancid! All our dealings go just one way, don't they?' he sneered. 'When will I see some return on this venture?'

The newcomer smiled thinly before reaching into the breast of his well-cut coat. He brought out a leather pouch and folded Firon's hand around it.

'Here's a little on account.' The man held Firon's fingers tight and Casuel saw pain chase perplexity across his spotty forehead. 'Spend it wisely for a change and don't let wine or thassin loosen your tongue. There are enough stupid whores, so don't bother with another one canny enough to pick some truth out of your boasting. Some girl you had down by the docks came knocking on my door a few days ago, looking for an open purse to shut her mouth.' The man's tone was amiable but the threat was unmistakable.

'What did you—' Firon looked sick.

'I paid her, what do you think?' As Firon smiled in hesitant relief, the man leaned close, voice cruel. 'Just enough to pay her way with Poldrion, then I made sure that's the last price the slut'll ever bargain.'

'I'm not frightened of you!' The sweaty pallor Casuel could see soaking the colour from Firon's face plainly contradicted his shaking words.

'Well said, your honour.' The other man released the Esquire's crushed fingers. 'Anyway, you needn't be afraid of me. I just follow my orders, after all. It's my principal you should worry about, who's not best pleased, truth be told.'

'I've done everything asked of me,' Firon protested.

'So you have,' smiled the newcomer. 'So go home and chew your thassin or find some warm little whore to cuddle. I'll let you know when we want something else. As long as you don't get greedy we'll all win out in the end, won't we?'

Firon fiddled with the purse in his hand, avoiding the other man's eye. 'When will I hear from you?'

The other man stood up. 'Soon enough.' He moved away as Firon was hailed by another young noble, whose expansive movements suggested he'd already drunk more than was wise so early in the day. Casuel tried to split his magic to follow both men but only succeeded in breaking the spell beyond repair, splinters of ensorcelled air darting invisibly in all directions.

The mage shifted from one foot to the other in an agony of indecision, trying to keep both men in view while staying within the protective shadow of the curtain. He drew back as Firon came closer to the stage, now intent on a girl with brassy blonde hair and a torn flounce to her gown. She was flirting with another young noble who Casuel couldn't quite put a Name to. Firon caught the girl by the shoulder and she turned with a well-rehearsed expression of delight that faded as soon as she recognised him. Firon raised the hand holding the purse and the girl smiled again.

'That's the only music sweet enough for her ears.' Amalin was a few paces away, studying a sheaf of music.

'Who is she?' Casuel asked.

'Too expensive for your purse, Cas.' Amalin looked up from his score. 'That's Demoiselle Yeditta Den Saerdel.'

Casuel's face reflected the question he hadn't dared ask.

'You thought she was a whore? No, she's far more choosy and far more expensive. You need an old Name and a fat purse before that one spreads her frills for you. Still, you'll get an education you'll never find in Hadrumal if you go sniffing after her.' Amalin went to stop a dispute between a carpenter and a painter.

Casuel watched an eager knot gathering round Firon and Yeditta, reckless youths in grimy linen and girls with cosmetics clashing brutally against the hectic colour rising on their cheeks. With brash boasts and extravagant gestures they all talked at once in an unintelligible muddle. At some signal from the brazen blonde the whole collection moved towards the door.

There was no way he could follow without being noticed, Casuel decided hastily. Nor was there anything to be gained watching whatever debauch they were planning to disgrace their Names. D'Olbriot already knew Den Thasnet was hostile. What Casuel needed to find out was who was pulling Firon's strings, as deftly as any puppeteer working Amalin's gaudy marionettes. He sighed with relief when he saw the man in brown talking to a dissatisfied maiden with heavily shadowed eyes trailing a wine-stained shawl from one hand.

A lutanist walked past and Casuel tried to match the musician's nonchalant saunter down the steps. Keeping that brown coat in sight was no easy task down on the crowded floor of the theatre, but this was neither the time nor place to work magic. Overlavish perfume and stale sweat caught at the back of Casuel's throat and he coughed. At least that made those closest step away with distasteful glances and Casuel caught a glimpse of the sombrely dressed man among the bolder colours all around.

This was no time for civility, Casuel realised, with these wastrels paying no one any heed, shoving and jostling without a by-your-leave. Biting his lip, Casuel used elbows and shoulders to worm his way between laughing embraces and belligerent disputes, ducking a retaliatory swing of some Esquire's arm, scarlet with embarrassment as he inadvertently set a covey of girls fluttering apart with shrill rebukes.

Finally gaining the fresh air outside with a gasp of relief, he couldn't delay to recover his composure. The man in brown was heading towards the old city, steady pace suggesting some specific destination. A gap opened up ahead of Casuel and he moved to outflank a goodwife laden with packages but a sturdy dray rattling past made him think again. Better to suffer the jostling on the flagway than risk being squashed flatter than a frog's foot. Casuel forced his way on through the crowd, apologising, tripping, heart pounding and hoping against hope the man in brown wouldn't hail a passing gig.

Den Murivance Residence,
Summer Solstice Festival, Fourth Day, Afternoon

'Are you enjoying the music?' Camarl offered Temar a crystal goblet of pale pink wine.

'Is this what they call the Rational style?' Temar asked cautiously.

Both men looked at the elegant quintet playing under a rose-garlanded bower in the middle of an immaculate lawn. Smartly dressed and richly jewelled nobles walked past, pausing here and there to admire the precisely patterned flowers. A riot of summer colour around the serene grass was confined within strictly clipped box hedges, an arc of orange here, a square of scarlet there, framed by sprigs of gold and green. Tall yew hedges rose dark behind the flowers, and beyond Temar could hear polite laughter. The musicians finished their piece with a decorous flourish, rewarded with appreciative applause.

'No, this is something new, reworking country tunes in the style of old shrine liturgies.' Camarl sounded a little vague. 'Adding counterpoint, harmonies, that kind of thing.'

'It is very pleasant.' Temar sipped the scented wine to hide his disdain. The gods couldn't even hold their music sacred any more.

Camarl was still talking. 'Amalin Devoir's one of the leading composers in the new style.'

Temar looked up. 'Casuel's brother?'

'Yes,' Camarl chuckled. 'Not that you'd ever know it from our mage. He's made quite a name for himself, Amalin that is. He started as a double-pipe player, I believe, but was soon hiring out his own troupe. He must have an eye for business because he built one of the biggest theatres in the city from the ground up a year or so ago.' He looked at the slowly circulating Esquires and Demoiselles. 'We should go down there one evening, once Festival's over. It's all very informal, just light-hearted nonsense.'

'That would make a pleasant change,' agreed Temar.

'Festival's all entertainment for the commonalty but that kind of leisure's a luxury our coin can't buy,' Camarl said frankly. 'There's so little time to see everyone. But you can take a little more time to enjoy yourself. The Sieur and I will secure Kellarin's interests.'

'For which you have my thanks,' said Temar politely. He looked round the myriad unknown faces and insignia. He'd still far rather be managing Kel Ar'Ayen's concerns himself, if only he had the faintest idea where to start.

'There's Irianne Tor Kanselin.' Camarl's tone brightened.

'Go and talk to her,' urged Temar. 'Unless you think I need a chaperone.'

Camarl's laugh surprised Temar. 'I'll see you later.' Camarl walked briskly towards his affianced and Temar watched as the girl's face lit up.

Temar sighed; Guinalle had never greeted him with that kind of delight, even during the brief dalliance that had meant so much more to him than to her. He began his own leisurely circuit of the Den Murivance gardens, exchanging polite nods and smiles. Whenever someone looked as if they might do more, Temar picked up his pace. He couldn't face trying to remember Names and families, more questions about his unexpected injury, his hopes for Kellarin, subtle enquiries as to his precise standing with D'Olbriot and what he thought of the arguments before the Emperor. A growing sense of inadequacy aggravated Temar. He hadn't spoken to a fifth the people Camarl had, arranging later discussions about ships for Kel Ar'Ayen, suggesting merchants who might link the distant colony's riches to a given House's resources. The knowledge he should be grateful to Camarl exasperated Temar still further, so he walked away through an arch of well-trained yew.

Shallow turf steps ran up to a broad terrace at the northern frontage of the house. Den Murivance's home had little of the harsh angularity of Tor Kanselin's, every brick and stone unmistakably ancient. But as Temar has been taken on a suspiciously extended tour, he'd noted all the furnishings looked brand new, quite the height of fashion.

Servants were still clearing away the remains of the recent elegant meal. Temar watched liveried footmen deftly piling plates and serving bowls, maidservants rolling table linen in neat bundles for the laundresses. Lackeys in workaday clothes waited to carry trestles and boards away while more outdoor servants dismantled the garlanded canopies that had shaded guests from the uncaring sun.

Temar castigated himself with painful honesty. You wouldn't know where to start organising an entertainment like this, never mind running the affairs of a House in this new Tormalin. So why was he here? This wasn't his place, and never would be. Why wasn't he out doing something to save those people still senseless in Kel Ar'Ayen, where he really belonged?

'D'Alsennin! You'll escort a lady into the maze, won't you?' A fresh-faced Esquire hailed Temar from the entrance to a circle of green hedge. He and a friend were gently teasing a group of Demoiselles somewhere between Temar's own age and Camarl's.

Temar identified the Esquire's marten mask badge as Den Ferrand. 'If she wishes.' He bowed politely to the girls. The closest giggled, hazel eyes huge behind her fan of black and azure feathers, but Temar couldn't identify the malachite insignia inlaid on the silver handle.

'I'm less concerned about escort in than escort out,' said a taller girl. Her chestnut hair was braided in a no-nonsense style and a tiny jewelled sword pinned her lace veil decorously to either shoulder. At least Temar could identify her as Den Hefeken.

'There's a summerhouse in the centre,' volunteered the youth, brushing unruly black curls with a hand beringed with a sizeable cameo of a rearing horse. 'There's always a steward there with directions out.'

'I'll go with Meriel,' Den Ferrand took the giggling girl's hand. 'Esquire Den Brennain, will you do me the honour of escorting my sisters?' He bowed extravagantly to the lad with the horse ring and then to two of the girls. One swatted her brother with her grey- and pink-feathered fan but the other blushed prettily as Den Brennain offered his arm.

'Demoiselle Den Hefeken?' Temar bowed.

'My pleasure, Esquire.' She smiled in friendly enough fashion.

'Which way do we go?' The girl Meriel looked around as they moved inside the ring of hedges.

'Do we split up or stay together?' Den Brennain paused as they reached a junction.

'Split up,' said Den Ferrand promptly. 'First ones to the middle win—'

'Head of the set at the Emperor's dance tomorrow?' suggested Demoiselle Den Hefeken.

The general approval suggested this was a prize worth winning. Temar didn't much care but he followed the Demoiselle obediently as twists and turns took the others down different pathways, conversation muffled by the tall hedges.

'Is this a popular form of entertainment?' he asked the Demoiselle, trying to get his bearings.

'More than listening to our elders and betters negotiating access and revenues and leaseholds,' the girl said cheerfully.

'Indeed,' said Temar with feeling. 'So, Demoiselle, do we turn or continue?'

'Call me Orilan.' She considered their options with a slight frown. 'Turn, I think.'

Temar followed, but after an abrupt corner the path delivered them into a dead end. Orilan Den Hefeken looked apologetically at Temar, but before she could speak a voice sounded from the far side of the hedge.

'Are you seriously thinking of marrying D'Alsennin, Gelaia?'

'My father's very keen to point out all the advantages.'

Orilan Den Hefeken smiled tightly at Temar before trying to step past him. He smiled back but didn't move out of her way.

There was more than one girl giggling beyond the wall of green. 'What advantages? He's handsome enough but he's four parts foolish! Ressy Tor Kanselin said he hasn't the first idea about anything.'

'I have, which is what matters to the Sieur D'Olbriot.' Gelaia sounded unconcerned. 'D'Alsennin can go back to digging ore and lumber out of his wilderness and I can turn it all into coin this side of the ocean.'

'So you wouldn't be going with him.' This new voice sounded relieved.

Gelaia was startled into laughter. 'Jenty! Have you had too much sun? No, he can keep all the delights of exploration and bad sanitation. I'll stay here with decent servants and some real influence to play with at last.'

'My Sieur says that D'Alsennin won't ever be more than a bastard line of D'Olbriot.' It was the first girl again, sounding dubious.

'That depends what I make of it,' countered Gelaia. 'And there are worse places to be in D'Olbriot's shadow. I'll still be Maitresse of a House, which is more than any of my other suitors can offer.'

The murmurs of agreement were coloured with envy.

'It'll be a mighty small House, just the two of you,' commented Jenty slyly.

'He'll need to come over for Winter and Summer Solstices for the first few years,' Gelaia said airily. 'It shouldn't take too long for him to get me breeding. In the meantime, I'll be entitled to a married woman's consolations.'

'Don't get caught wrong-footed,' Jenty warned. 'Everyone'll count the seasons when your belly swells.'

'I'm sure Lady Channis will advise me.' Scandalised laughter drowned the rest of Gelaia's words.

'But, Gella, taking him to your bed—' A young voice hovered between consternation and longing.

'Whatever else's changed since the Chaos, I imagine that's done the same way,' giggled Gelaia.

'My sister say a man generally wakes with a keen interest in his wife,' Jenty remarked with spurious innocence. 'What must a man be feeling after sleeping away twenty-some generations?'

Temar had heard enough. He offered Orilan Den Hefeken his arm and escorted her back down the path. She glanced at Temar over the orange feathers of her fan, colour high on her cheekbones. 'Gelaia wouldn't have spoken like that if she'd known you were there.'

'That is scant consolation,' said Temar tightly. 'I am old-fashioned, I know, but I look for mutual affection to prompt a wedding, not well-matched ledgers.'

'Affection grows, given time and good will on both sides, that's what my mother taught me. A good match with love to gild it is certainly a blessing, but marrying for passion is hardly rational.' Orilan stopped, forcing Temar to halt. She looked at him, grey eyes searching. 'Tell me it wasn't ever thus, even in your day?'

Temar recalled some his grandsire's forthright lectures. 'Certainly Raeponin always set restrictions in the balance against the privilege of rank.'

'Shall we try this way?' Orilan started walking. 'Forgive my frankness, Esquire, but surely you need someone to guide you through the complexities of Toremal, just as surely as we need some way through this maze.'

'Are you offering?' Temar tried for a flirtatious tone.

Orilan laughed. 'I was affianced at Winter Solstice. By the turn of the year I will be happily learning to love my husband under Den Risiper's roof.'

'My felicitations.' Temar concentrated on finding a path through the maze. In fewer turns than he expected, the hedges ushered them onto a small lawn around a little pool where Arimelin stood demure in greenish bronze beneath a tree-shaped fountain. A newly painted gazebo shaded a polite steward holding a jug.

Temar bowed to Orilan. 'Some wine?'

Orilan nodded as Den Ferrand appeared with a furiously blushing Meriel. Temar felt uncomfortably excluded by their laughter as he waited for the servant to fill a tray full of glasses. Worse still, Temar realised Gelaia and her friends were sitting behind the summerhouse.

'Esquire?' The lackey was waiting. Temar nodded and followed the man over to his new acquaintances.

'Well done, D'Alsennin.' Den Ferrand congratulated him with a friendly air.

'But you didn't have mazes in your day!' Meriel looked at Temar with eager inquisitiveness.

Orilan hid a smile behind her fan. 'We didn't have them in our grandsire's day, Meri.'

'You certainly have much we never knew, but equally it seems you lost much in the Chaos,' said Temar with studied carelessness. 'Customs, provinces, Artifice.'

'Is it true magic held the Old Empire together?' Meriel's eyes were wide and beseeching.

'A form of enchantment,' Temar replied carefully. 'Not this elemental magic of the Archmage and Hadrumal. We knew it as Artifice, and yes, it has many uses.'

'My Sieur says that magic is all tricks and fakery.' Den Brennain's words were half challenge, half curiosity.

Meriel exchanged an excited shiver with the Demoiselles Den Ferrand.

'You're in deep with wizards,' Den Brennain persisted. 'What have you seen?'

Temar sipped his wine. He'd hardly win any trust with tales of monsters spun from raging water, of lightning ripped from clouds to spear men where they stood. He didn't even want to remember magical fire crawling across empty ground to consume the enemy Elietimm without mercy. 'I have seen mages appear and disappear in empty air, crossing leagues in the blink of an eye. They can summon the image of someone far distant and speak with them. They can feel the passage of a river through unseen caves beneath the ground.'

'Or find gold within a mountain?' Den Ferrand looked speculatively at Temar. 'A House with such resources to call on would have significant advantages.'

Temar spread deprecating hands. 'Mages answer only to Hadrumal and Planir curbs any abuse of power.'

'You know the Archmage?' Meriel sounded disconsolate. 'I've never seen so much as a hedge wizard make candles dance.'

'No?' Temar ran a nervous hand over his close-cropped hair. 'When there are mages in Toremal?' He pulled a closely folded handbill from a pocket and cleared his throat. '*This is to give notice to all lovers of the magical arts and admirers of ingenuity that the famous Trebal Chabrin intends to fly from the Spring Gate to the Vintner's Exchange at the seventh chime of the fourth day of Festival. This feat will be followed by such diversions as the elements permit. All those attending are invited to make such payment as they are pleased to give.*'

'A wizard's going to fly?' Den Ferrand was incredulous.

'I have no idea,' Temar laughed. 'The words are rather too carefully vague, after all. I confess I'm curious though.'

Den Brennain looked up to check the sun. 'We could get there if we called for a carriage at once.' He sounded tempted. 'But it's hardly courteous to our hosts.'

'Yes, let's!' Meriel looked eagerly around. 'We've all been dutiful enough for one day, haven't we?'

'I've talked to everyone I was supposed to.' Den Brennain jabbed a finger at Den Ferrand. 'You wouldn't have suggested the maze if you still had people to meet.'

'Gelaia's just over there,' Orilan observed. 'We can make our farewells to her.'

She walked swiftly past the summerhouse. Temar heard a note of curiosity rising among the hidden girls. He forced a smile when Orilan returned with Gelaia and the other girls in tow.

'You're going to see a wizard?' A sallow girl with close-set eyes and a discontented mouth fiddled with expensive lace covering thin and lustreless hair.

'Esquire D'Alsennin, may I make known Demoiselle Jentylle Tor Sauzet,' Esquire Den Ferrand said perfunctorily. 'Either that or some charlatan. Either way, it'll be more interesting than staying here.'

'My thanks, Esquire.' Gelaia pretended outrage. 'I'll convey your compliments on his entertainments to my Sieur.'

Den Ferrand grinned. 'My gratitude, my lady.'

'Are we going or not?' demanded Meriel.

'Why not? I take it everyone's served their Name as they were instructed over breakfast?' Gelaia asked archly.

As everyone nodded, Gelaia led them confidently out of the maze. Outside, she summoned various lackeys with a wave of her fan, dispatching them with messages for her parents, her Sieur and concise instructions for the stableyard. Den Ferrand stepped aside to talk briefly to someone resemblance suggested was an older brother while Den Brennain made a bow to an elegant lady who soon sent him back with an unconcerned smile.

'I had better let Esquire Camarl know I am leaving,' Temar said suddenly.

'I've sent word we're going out together.' Gelaia took his arm with a proprietorial air. Temar managed to smile with apparent pleasure, even when he caught an avid glance from Jenty not meant for him.

Den Murivance was plainly a House with horses and grooms to spare, Temar decided, seeing two waiting carriages with polished portcullis badges on livery and harness as they reached the gatehouse. Gelaia organised everyone with casual adroitness and Temar found himself riding with her, Orilan, Meriel and Den Ferrand.

'Where are you committed this evening?' Orilan turned her back on the crowded streets.

'Tor Sauzet,' Den Ferrand replied promptly. 'And you?'

'Den Gannael. Tell me, is it true Den Rannion's designate spoke to Tor Sauzet about Jenty's prospects?' Orilan asked.

'Oh, I heard that!' Meriel sat forward eagerly. 'Which Esquire was proposed?'

Temar sat in silence as the others speculated good-humouredly. Let them chatter; they'd done what he needed after all. But his friend Vahil Den Rannion wouldn't have given Jenty a second glance, he thought. No wonder the plain-faced beanpole was envious of Gelaia; no one would ever make her Maitresse of a House. He watched Gelaia laughing and had to admit she was certainly pretty, golden skin warmed by a delicate blush, lips a tempting red. Her long black hair was woven round her head in a luxurious array of curls, a few delicate strands falling to her shoulders. Temar covertly studied the swell of her bosom above a narrow waist and speculated on what kind of legs her flurry of petticoats might hide. Was it time to serve Kel Ar'Ayen by taking his grandsire's advice, along with an attractive, well-connected bride who knew every turn around these latterday social circles? That would show Guinalle she wasn't the only berry on the bush.

'Are we there?' Gelaia broke off a convoluted anecdote as the carriage slowed and then stopped, a footman ready to open the door.

Den Brennain, Jenty and the others were spilling out of the coach behind them as Temar stepped down, offering a hand to Gelaia and Orilan.

'Let's see what there is to see.' Gelaia fanned herself, feathers today still white. 'Lemael, wait for us in Banault Yard.' The coaches rattled away obediently.

'Shall we stand over there?' Temar pointed to the steps of the desperately old-fashioned Vintner's Exchange, where a noticeable knot of nobility were laughing.

'We're not the only ones taking a break before the evening's duties,' remarked Den Ferrand with a grin.

'Only one more day of Festival to go,' said Orilan cheerfully. 'It's the Emperor's dance tomorrow. No one talks business, betrothal or anything serious there,' she added in an undertone to Temar.

He smiled absently at her as he scanned the crowd. With people of all ranks and none pressing close, it was impossible to see very far.

'It's just a rope trick.' Meriel sounded bitterly disappointed. Temar stopped searching the crowd to follow her pointing finger. They all saw a thin cable strung from a balcony on the front of the Vintners' Exchange up to the looming bulk of the old city walls.

'At that angle?' Den Ferrand sounded doubtful. 'I've never seen a rope walker go downhill.'

'I'm keeping my coin until I see something worthwhile.' Jenty clamped a bony hand on the silver mesh and emerald purse chained at her waist.

'When's something going to happen?' Den Brennain wondered.

'I will go and enquire,' Temar said obligingly. He went down the steps, heading for a doorway where several people were taking advantage of a mounting block to get a better view. 'Hello Allin. I got your note.'

'Temar! I'd almost given up on you.' The mage looked up at him with uncomplicated pleasure. 'Are you playing truant?'

Temar laughed. 'I persuaded a whole handful to come with me. I am relying on them to protect me from Camarl's wrath.'

'Good day to you, Esquire.' Velindre nodded a greeting.

'So, Allin—'

Velindre smiled as Temar broke off. 'She showed me your letter last night, and in any case Planir bespoke me, to let us know what had happened.'

'Can you help find these thieves?' demanded Temar.

Velindre grimaced. 'Not with any degree of certainty. Still, once we're done here I'll come back with you and we'll see what can be done.'

'Is this man truly a mage?' Temar looked up at the empty parapet on the far side of the broad street.

'I haven't been able to meet him to find out.' Velindre frowned. 'His handbills are nicely ambiguous, so he could just be some Festival faker willing to risk his neck. If he is a wizard, he's canny enough to conceal his abilities sufficiently to keep people guessing.'

'Then those who want to believe can, and those who feel threatened can just dismiss him as a trickster,' Allin explained, and Temar realised his confusion must have shown on his face.

Velindre nodded. 'And if he's shrewd enough to work that out, he could be a useful man to ask about Tormalin opinions of magic.'

A flurry of activity on the old city walls hushed the crowd to a murmur of anticipation. Temar looked round to see Gelaia staring impatiently at him. 'I had better get back.' He worked his way to the Exchange steps as every face gazed up at the lofty rampart.

'Look!' Meriel squeaked, clutching at Den Ferrand's arm. A man had climbed up on the parapet and was strapping something to his chest.

'What's he doing?' Den Ferrand squinted up at the man silhouetted against the bright sky.

'He's going to lie on it,' said Den Brennain slowly.

The man lowered himself slowly forwards, taking first one hand then the other off the rope. His feet still rested on the stonework of the wall but his body reached out over the emptiness supported only by the thin strand.

'That's some balancing act,' said Den Ferrand.

Gelaia took Temar's arm, face pale.

'Sliding down a rope is hardly flying,' objected Jenta, sounding pleasantly frightened.

The murmur of anticipation rose to a new pitch as blue-grey smoke appeared around the distant figure.

'Magelight!' exclaimed Meriel.

Hardly, thought Temar dubiously. He waited impatiently for the man to do his tricks, whatever they might be. Once Velindre was satisfied the man was no mage, she'd be free to help him search for the Kellarin artefacts.

The crowd exclaimed with fear and delight as the man launched himself off the walls, smoke still pouring from his outstretched hands, now more white than blue. The wide street was hushed as the would-be wizard gathered speed. A few nervous cries were hastily stifled but consternation swelled as everyone saw the man wobbling precariously.

The sliding figure slowed, tilted and the man slipped sideways. Gelaia screamed, shrill in Temar's ear along with every other woman in the rapt crowd as the man just managed to grab the rope, left hanging from both hands. Incoherent cries went up on all sides as the crowd beneath the hanging figure melted away.

'Someone should get a ladder.' Den Brennain looked around wildly.

'A blanket, a canvas, something to catch him,' Den Ferrand hugged Meriel, who was frozen in horrified fascination.

'Those cobbles will be the death of him if he falls,' Temar agreed in the same breath.

From the turmoil below other people were trying to put the same ideas forward but the press of bodies was hampering everyone. High above, the man was desperately trying to swing one leg over the rope. An anguished gasp burst from every throat as he failed, and worse, let go with one hand. Temar felt his heart stand still until the showman managed to regain his grip.

'Wait here.' He shook off Gelaia and pushed his way through the dithering crowd to the doorway. Allin was ashen, biting a thumbnail. Velindre in contrast looked as composed as ever, a little pity shading the contempt in her eyes.

'Can you get him down?' demanded Temar.

Velindre looked sardonically at him. 'The man claimed magical arts. Let him save himself.'

'You'll stand by and let him die?' Temar stared at Velindre in disbelief.

'He doubtless knew the risks.' Velindre sounded faintly regretful.

'You have the means to save him! In the name of all that is holy—'

'He's no reason to expect our help.' Velindre's stony eyes froze Temar's rebukes. 'If we weren't here, he'd have no hope beyond his own efforts, so what's the difference?'

'That fall will kill him!'

As Temar spoke screams erupted on all sides. Temar felt sick to his stomach, seeing the man falling, arms and legs flailing in futile terror. In the instant before anguish closed Temar's eyes, a flurry of iridescent azure light tangled round the plummeting figure, slowing his descent, toppling the hapless man over and over before he hit the cobbles with a crunch that made the entire crowd wince. A surge towards the man halted as soon as it began, people drawing away from the crumpled figure. As the circle widened, Temar saw the showman lying in a fading pool of radiance that rivalled the blue of the sky above.

'Who did that?' Velindre was keenly curious.

'How badly's that poor man hurt?' countered Allin robustly. 'Come on.'

She tried to force a path through the close-packed crowd but lacked both strength and height to make an impression.

'Clear the way!' Whether it was Temar's unexpected accents or just obedience to noble command, he couldn't tell, but at least the people moved. As he ushered Allin through to the wounded man, Temar saw another familiar figure being forced forward as the crowd retreated behind him.

'Casuel?'

'Curse the man for a fool!' The wizard's dark eyes were wide, almost black against his shocked pallor. 'I couldn't let him die.'

Allin knelt, heedless of the dust and litter. 'He's broken both his legs.' Her hands hovered over a sort of wooden breastplate the man wore, with a deep central groove that Temar realised must have guided the rope. 'We need a surgeon. I don't want to take this off until a surgeon has checked his ribs.' The showman's head lolled to one side, bruises already darkening beneath his tanned skin.

'Your control was a little lacking, Cas,' Velindre remarked, arms folded as she looked in, entirely composed.

'I did my best. It's not my element,' said Casuel defensively. 'You didn't lift a finger so you can hardly criticise!' His anger rang loudly through the tense silence.

'That's D'Olbriot's mage.' Temar heard a frightened voice behind him start a low current of speculation.

'You get away from him! You get away from him!' A frantic girl was shoving murmuring onlookers aside. An older woman followed with a narrow-faced man dragging a wicker basket behind him. All three wore cheerful motley that mocked their dismay.

'Trebal!' the girl shrieked hysterically. She would have swept the unconscious man into her arms but Allin grabbed her shoulders, forcing her back.

'Move him now and you could kill him.' The girl stared at her in blank incomprehension. 'We need a surgeon to splint his legs, to feel what other bones may be broken.'

'And who are you to say so?' the older woman demanded, twisting a gaily coloured kerchief in her work-knotted hands.

'We are mages of Hadrumal, my good lady,' said Casuel with a miserably inadequate attempt at authority. Repetition carried his words away like ripples through a pond.

'What have you done to him?' the girl screamed, trying to break free of Allin's unexpectedly firm grip.

'Saved him from certain death!' Casuel replied indignantly.

'Didn't do a very good job,' spat the older woman, kneeling and running gentle hands over the senseless body.

'You would rather he had died?' Temar asked angrily.

The woman looked up, face graven with the marks of a hard life. 'This is all your fault, you and this wizard.'

'What?' Temar and Casuel spoke in the same breath.

'You're D'Alsennin, aren't you?' The man stepped forward. 'You were raised from the dead by some old sorcery.'

A shudder of consternation ran through the crowd. Temar tried for a reassuring smile. 'No one was dead, we merely slept beneath enchantments.'

'You used your magics against Trebal, I reckon.' The man stepped close, hatchet face cunning. 'That's what made him fall.'

'He's only a hedge wizard, no threat to anyone.' The woman

gestured at the motionless Trebal, speaking to the crowd. 'But mages don't like to see rivals, do they? Not mages from Hadrumal.'

'No, that's not true—' Growing unease made the hairs on the back of Temar's neck prickle.

'That charlatan's no more mage than a stick of wood,' Casuel objected heatedly.

The man stared at Temar. 'Your sorceries ruined his show, that fall could have him crippled or dead. Who's going to keep his wife and family in bread?'

The girl looked up, face vacant in grief. The older woman silenced her with a hand on one shoulder, fleshless fingers digging in hard.

'Does the House of D'Alsennin make recompense?' The man raised his voice to carry clear to the Spring Gate and to the steps of the Vintner's Exchange.

The crowd rustled with expectation as the older woman fell to her knees, wailing and holding her head in her hands. 'How will we eat? We'll be turned out, all of us, the children, the baby, we'll be begging in the gutters.'

Temar wondered if anyone else noticed the pause before the girl joined the lamentations, albeit with slightly less expertise. 'This is ridiculous!'

By some quirk of ill fate, he spoke just as the weeping women paused to draw breath, his words loud in the silence. Affront stirred the crowd to new whispers.

'I think we should leave.' Velindre sounded calm enough but Temar could see her concern. 'Shall I clear a path?'

'No!' Temar didn't doubt the blonde mage could do it but he already had enough to explain to Camarl. He looked back at the Vintner's Exchange. 'Aedral mar nidralae, Gelaia,' he murmured under his breath. 'Gelaia, can you hear me?' He squinted over the heads of the crowd, seeing a sudden stir convulse the noble group. 'No, forgive me, you cannot reply. Please can you summon a coach to get us out of here?' He bowed curtly to the belligerent man. 'We will be on our way. You had best come with us, Master Casuel.'

'I can't,' protested the mage in confusion. 'You set me to watch Den Thasnet.'

'But the man's injured,' objected Allin.

'And he's their responsibility.' Velindre nodded at the wailing women.

'You don't get out of it so easy, you cold-eyed bitch. Not when you're the ones made him fall!' The man whirled round, hands outstretched, appealing to the crowd. 'Are you going to let them get away with this?'

'Come on, Allin.' Temar forced her gently to her feet with a hand under her elbow. 'If they will not take your help, you cannot force it on them.'

She shut her mouth in a mutinous line but drew close to Temar under the hostile gazes from all sides. Velindre continued surveying the mob with a regally icy gaze while Casuel knotted nervous hands together, looking all around. Temar wondered what he was looking for, but before he could ask the man in motley began ranting at them with fresh anger.

'Got nothing to say for yourself? Leave a man dying in the dirt and don't even open your purse for his widow and orphans?'

Temar ignored the taunts, looking over to the Vintner's Exchange, wondering how long it would take for Gelaia to summon a coach for them. She had better hurry, he thought nervously as he was jostled from behind. The restive crowd was drawing in, swayed by the charade being played out by the motley trio.

'Keep your eye on that man in brown, with grey hair, next to the woman in yellow.' Casuel moved to Temar's side, face intent.

'Why?' Temar found the man after a few moments.

'He seems to have some hold over our young friend,' the mage hissed urgently. 'They met earlier and that one was telling our friend what to do.'

Temar acknowledged Casuel with a nod and smiled reassurance he didn't quite feel at Allin.

'What are you whispering?' demanded the sharp-faced man. 'What are you planning?'

The older woman looked up from her repetitive lamentations, dry eyes suspicious. 'You don't leave here without paying us something.'

'Don't be ridiculous,' said Casuel coldly. 'You owe me that wretch's life!'

'Which will be lost, if you don't get a surgeon to him,' cried Allin.

'Shut your mouth, whore,' spat the thin-faced man.

'Shut your own before I break your teeth,' retorted Temar without thinking. Hooves clattered on the cobbles behind him and he sighed with relief. The crowd shifted, the mood growing uglier as the coachman's hoarse shouts urged them out of the way, the brassy note of the horn sounding above rising abuse. When the horses appeared between milling figures, the animals were tossing their heads, eyes rimmed white with panic.

'As quick as you like, Esquire,' the coachman puffed, reins wrapped painfully tight round reddened hands.

Temar found himself hampered by Allin clinging to him and Casuel managing to move precisely in his way every time he took a step. With people trying to leave as well as stubbornly holding their ground, getting to the coach was impossible.

'I've had quite enough of this.' Even Velindre's cool voice cracked a little. A wind appeared from nowhere, no passing summer gust but a sustained, strengthening breeze. People blinked as scraps of straw whirled up around their feet. Temar closed suddenly stinging eyes but opened them again as he heard a horse's indignant whinnying beside him. A space had cleared all around the coach, everyone retreating from something halfway between summer haze and a dust devil, dancing on a barely visible point of light.

'You see, Cas?' Velindre smiled 'That's control.'

The mage was too busy scrambling into the coach to answer. Temar ushered Velindre inside, then Allin, consternation on her face. 'They're not trying to move him, are they?'

'My dear girl, it is hardly our concern,' Temar said, exasperated. It was uncomfortably crowded inside the coach, since Gelaia had brought both Den Brennain and Den Ferrand.

'Please, do sit here.' Den Brennain tried to stand up to allow Allin his seat but fell back as the coach picked up speed.

Casuel forced his way through the window. 'I must see where that man in brown goes.'

'Who?' Den Ferrand looked out at the fast dissipating mob.

'There, next to Den Rannion's third son.' Casuel clenched his fists in frustration as the coach turned away up a road to the higher ground.

'That was Malafy Skern, wasn't it?' Den Ferrand looked to Den Brennain for confirmation.

The younger man twisted awkwardly to look before a building blocked his view. 'That's right.'

'Who is he and how do you know him?' Temar tried to make his question no more than idle chat.

'He was personal man to the last Sieur Tor Bezaemar,' Den Ferrand replied.

'The man who knew everything and everyone,' Den Brennain laughed. 'That's what they called him, but he was pensioned off a few seasons ago.'

'Then what—' Casuel subsided beneath a stern look from Temar.

'So who is the mage among you?' Gelaia's knuckles were pale as she gripped the spinel-set handle of her fan.

'Me.'

'I am.'

'I have that honour.' Casuel's stiff words fell into stunned silence as Gelaia, Den Ferrand and Den Brennain all tried to edge together, finding themselves unexpectedly surrounded by wizards.

'Three of you.' Gelaia fanned herself rapidly. 'What an unexpected pleasure.'

'May I make known Velindre Ychane, Allin Mere and Casuel D'Evoir.' Temar bowed to all in turn.

'My duty to you all.' Retreating behind formality seemed to reassure Gelaia a little.

'Our thanks to you, my lady.' Velindre's smile combined gratitude with considerable charm. 'You rescued us from an ugly situation.'

Temar could see both Den Ferrand and Den Brennain bursting with curiosity, but before either could frame a question Velindre stood to knock abruptly on the coach roof. 'We needn't trespass on your hospitality any further. Our lodgings aren't far and Casuel can escort us.'

He looked as if that was the last thing he wanted to do, but as the coach drew to a smooth halt Den Ferrand and Den Brennain both moved to let him out, smiles politely expectant. Casuel rose to his feet with ill grace, nearly falling over the footman hastily opening the door and letting down the step.

Gelaia looked out of her window. 'The other coach is behind us. You two had best see to your sisters, hadn't you?'

Den Ferrand and Den Brennain both looked as if they would have liked to stay but shared a rueful shrug and followed Velindre out of the coach.

'Call on me later.' Temar caught at Allin's arm. She nodded, blushing a little as both young noblemen offered her their assistance getting out of the vehicle.

The door closed smartly and the coach resumed its journey. 'Are we going back to your residence?' Temar asked.

Gelaia nodded. 'I think you'd prefer to tell Esquire Camarl your version of the truth before rumour drops some tattered gossip at his feet.'

'It was hardly my fault. It just all got somewhat out of hand.' Temar disliked the note of childish complaint he heard in his words.

Gelaia was fanning herself again, gripping the handle like a weapon. 'If the would-be flunkey with the filthy boots is D'Olbriot's pet mage, who's yours? One of the women? The dumpy one?'

Temar tried to identify the emotion threaded through her

words, but beyond deciding it wasn't jealousy he failed. 'Neither. I mean, you cannot consider a mage any kind of servant.'

'Which one used magic on me?' Gelaia pulled a loose feather from her fan with a sharp tug.

Temar bit his lip. 'I beg your pardon, but that was me.'

Gelaia looked startled. 'No one told me you were a mage!'

'I am no wizard.' Temar shook his head. 'I simply have a certain facility with minor aetheric enchantments.'

Gelaia looked down at her lap, her hands reducing the stray feather to shreds. She brushed at the fluff with a jerky hand but it clung obstinately to the silk.

Temar searched for something to say. 'Do you know this Malafy Skern?'

Gelaia visibly pulled herself together. 'Indeed. What of him?'

'You know these arguments persecuting D'Olbriot before the Emperor?' Temar said carefully. 'The man seems somehow involved, along with Firon Den Thasnet.'

'It's entirely possible. Skern always got all the gossip and he knows everyone's weak points. Firon has got plenty of those, after all.' The uncertainty in Gelaia's eyes was fading as she found herself on familiar ground.

'Whom does this Skern answer to?' Temar asked.

'The Relict Tor Bezaemar, who else,' shrugged Gelaia. 'Pensioned off or not.'

Temar frowned. 'But she wishes us nothing but good. She has been helping Avila, making introductions, free with her advice.'

'I'm sure she has.' Gelaia laughed without humour. 'You're the next best thing to a Sieur; she'll be sweetness from sunrise to sunset as far as you're concerned.'

'You think otherwise?' hazarded Temar.

'Oh she's not inclined to cultivate we lesser sprigs of the family trees. She clips us well back if she gets a chance.' Gelaia made a visible effort to seal her lips.

'Go on,' Temar prompted.

'Swear on all that's holy you'll not tell?' Gelaia leaned forward, eyes hard.

'May Poldrion loose his demons on me if I break faith.' Temar swore fervently.

'Last summer, Jenty and Kreve Tor Bezaemar got quite fond. He's the Sieur's second son and the one being groomed as Designate. That would have been an excellent match for Jenty, no question, but the Relict has other plans for her precious grandson. So she dropped a few hints but Jenty wouldn't take them, you know what she's like. Well, take my word for it. Anyway, after the Relict went to her mother, accused her of trying to get Kreve to bed her and get him married that way, Jenty told the old bitch to keep to her kennel.'

Temar winced at the anger in Gelaia's words. 'Which was not wise?'

Gelaia paled and fear tightened her voice. 'A few days later, Jenty's maid was snatched off the Graceway. She was raped in some cellar and dumped in front of the residence at dusk. Now the sworn men on the gate brought her inside before anyone saw, and everyone swore silence, for the girl's sake as much as anything. But next time Jenty met the Relict, the old dragon was full of sympathy. How could she know, when Jenty had done everything she could to make sure no word got out? Then the Relict just happened to mention, quite in passing, that such a dreadful thing might happen to any young woman if her luck ran out. Take my word for it, that dear old lady has more venom than a pit full of snakes if she's crossed.'

Temar sat back, not knowing what to say. Would Camarl believe any of this? What did it mean for Kel Ar'Ayen? Did this bring them any closer to recovering the stolen artefacts?

The D'Olbriot Residence Gatehouse,
Summer Solstice Festival, Fourth Day, Evening

'Ryshad!'

I turned to see Dalmit hailing me, Tor Kanselin's man.

'You look like a watchdog on a short chain!' he joked, squinting into the sinking sun.

I smiled without replying. It was fair comment though; I'd been pacing up and down in front of the residence since the bell tower had struck nine chimes and a running stationer who'd tried to interest me in his quills, inks and papers had certainly been mercilessly snapped at. The sworn men were studiously avoiding my eye, and given the way I'd drilled their duty into them through the heat of the day I couldn't blame them. Stoll was sitting inside the watch room, drawing up a roster with a fine display of attention to detail and disdain for my style of bucking up the recognised. I ignored him; it wasn't my fault the Sieur's orders had put his nose out of joint. I'd obeyed those orders, to the full, and now I was waiting for the ten chimes that would see me off watch. Then I'd have to decide whether or not to risk Charoleia's invitation.

'You've slipped your leash, have you?' I walked to meet Dalmit beneath a tall tree. 'Have you got time for a glass?'

'I'm on guard tonight.' He shook his head. 'Thanks all the same, but I'll be getting back.'

'What did you find out?' I got straight to the point. 'And what do I owe you?'

'A Crown or so should cover it,' he shrugged. 'Turns out Tor Bezaemar men passed on that bill of challenge to Jord and Lovis both. Different men, one of the sworn and a proven in from Bremilayne, but they were both spinning the same yarn about knowing for certain you weren't fit, saying you're carrying some injury from being taken for a slave last year.'

'And why were they passing this on?' I wondered sarcastically.

'No surprise there.' Dalmit grinned. 'Both of them were offering to make a wager if Jord or Lovis would put up half the stake.'

'Going shares in the winnings.' I nodded. We're not allowed to wager on ourselves in promotion challenges, but there are always ways round such rules.

'So, does that mean anything to you?' Dalmit asked guilelessly.

'Could be something, could be nothing,' I said casually. 'It's worth two Crowns at least, and if anything comes of it I'll let you know.' I wasn't going to quibble over coppers and if I could fit this piece into any larger pattern it would do no harm to let Dalmit know which way the wind was veering. 'Do you want the coin now?' I gestured up to my window.

Dalmit shook his head. 'Tomorrow's soon enough. I've nowhere to spend it tonight, have I?' He waved an informal farewell and began walking back towards Tor Kanselin.

As he did so a coach passed him, D'Olbriot's insignia on the door panel. I drew myself up smartly with all the other men on watch. The footman jumped down with alacrity but Esquire Camarl was already opening the door, getting down almost before the footman had the step unfolded. The Esquire barely turned his head to address me. 'Have my uncles all arrived by now?'

'Yes, Esquire,' I bowed. 'They're with the Sieur.'

Camarl nodded and walked rapidly towards the residence, round face uncharacteristically hard.

I looked at Temar, who was looking a little shame-faced, unbuttoning his formal coat by way of pretext to let Camarl get ahead of him.

'What did you do?' I asked. 'Step on some girl's hem and bring her skirts down round her ankles?'

Temar laughed. 'That would not have been so bad.' He

looked meaningfully at me. 'Shall we take a glass of wine?'

'Upstairs?' I led him through the watch room, ignoring the questioning look Stoll shot me behind Temar's back.

'Do you really want wine?' I ushered him into the narrow room that was a privilege of my new rank. 'I'll have to send one of the lads if you do.'

Temar shook his head as he sat on the bed. 'Not on my account.'

'So what's so urgent? Why's Esquire Camarl crosser than an ass with a wasp up his tail?' I took the stool by the window, scratching absently at the pinpricks left by the stitches in my arm.

'I talked Gelaia and some others into going to see some supposed mage doing tricks.' Temar looked unrepentant.

'The Sieur certainly wants you and Gelaia to be friends, if not more.' I frowned. 'I don't necessarily see the harm; plenty of nobles go to see such things.'

'My only interest was meeting Allin there,' Temar explained frankly. 'I had an answer from her this morning, saying she and Velindre would be watching this man's display. I had no chance to tell you before we went to Den Murivance.' Temar scratched his head. 'There was more than a little trouble. The man was no mage but some mountebank doing a spectacularly dangerous rope trick. He fell and Master Casuel had to save him.'

'Bad luck follows Cas like the reek on old fish.' I was puzzled. 'What was he doing there?'

'In a moment.' Temar sighed. 'Casuel plainly used magic to save the fellow from death, but the knaves with him immediately claimed it was Devoir's wizardry had caused their own man to fail. They began demanding money, nigh on turning the crowd on us.'

'Did they recognise you?' I snorted as Temar nodded. 'That kind never miss a trick?'

'Gelaia had to rescue us from the mob.' Temar sighed. 'Camarl has been telling me all the way back what a meal the broadsheets and gossips will make of it.'

'D'Alsennin and D'Olbriot publicly tied to arrogant wizards hurling careless magic round the city?' I winced. 'Perhaps, for a day or so, but today's broadsheets are tomorrow's privy paper, aren't they? It's the Emperor's dance tomorrow, and most of the Houses will be opening their gates to their tenants and the commonalty. Last day of Festival always turns up something to tempt the scandalmongers, so I don't suppose you'll be the tastiest tittle-tattle for long.' I tried to sound encouraging.

'I hope so.' Temar sounded glum.

'Was Gelaia cross?' Had that pretty face worked its charm on Temar's susceptibilities?

'More unnerved than cross.' Temar leaned back against the wall. 'I had to use Artifice to make Gelaia hear me and then Velindre used some magic of her own to clear a path through the crowd. I think Gelaia suspects any alliance with D'Alsennin will leave her hemmed in by sorcery on all sides.' He sounded more sarcastic than regretful so at least I didn't think he'd be breaking his heart over Gelaia.

A question prodded me. 'Did you get a chance to ask Allin or Velindre if they could help?'

'It seems not, sadly.' Temar sighed.

As he spoke ten chimes began sounding above us, the signal for the end of the day. I rose to my feet. 'Then if you'll excuse me I'll go and see this friend of Livak's, the one with a finger on the darker pulses of our fair city. I might just learn something useful.'

Temar pushed himself up. 'Let me get my sword.'

'Oh no,' I disagreed. 'You're committed to dine with Den Castevin.'

'To what purpose?' Temar's lip curled. 'Esquire Casuel will be talking, dealing, explaining. All I will do is to smile, look pleasant and make polite conversation.'

'Which reassures the nobility that they're being asked to deal with one of their own in Kellarin,' I pointed out. 'Proving you're not some grubby-handed mercenary or worse. Not turning up is an insult you don't want to give lightly.'

'I would not know any Den Castevin if I tripped over one in the street.' Emotion clipped Temar's words. 'The people whose lives depend on those artefacts are my friends, my tenants, my responsibility.'

'Which means they need you to look after their longer-term interests by not giving unnecessary offence.' I ushered him down the stairs again.

Temar glanced at the steps to the cellars as we walked through the watch room. 'Did Avila learn anything more from the thief?'

'She hasn't had a chance to try. As soon as she came out of the library Lady Channis whisked her away for a full day's engagements with Tor Arrial.' I tried to hide my relief; I still didn't think I could stand and watch a man undergoing such assault. 'Then they were going on to Tor Bezaemar, for tisanes with the Relict before coming back here to change for dinner.'

'Dirindal?' Temar's eyes were icily intent.

'You sound like you smell rats in the granary,' I commented quietly.

'What do you know of Tor Bezaemar?' Temar demanded, drawing a little way into the gardens, beyond the curious ears in the gate arch. 'Has that House any reason to bear a grudge against D'Olbriot?'

'You want Cas for this, not me.' I rubbed a hand round the back of my neck. 'It's no secret Tor Bezaemar took losing the Imperial throne hard, but that was nigh on a generation ago. Messire backed Tadriol the Prudent from the first, I remember that.' I thought back to my early days in D'Olbriot's service. 'There was some talk about Sarens Tor Bezaemar putting himself forward, but with so many Names following D'Olbriot's lead it never came to anything.'

'Sarens was the Relict's husband?'

'The Sieur as was,' I confirmed.

Temar scowled. 'The reason Casuel was on hand to save the rope trickster was he had followed Firon Den Thasnet only to see him meet a man whom Gelaia tells me still answers to Dirindal, for all he has been pensioned off. Casuel was following this man who was talking to some of the other nobles come for the spectacle.'

'Anyone in particular?' I asked, my own hackles rising in response to Temar's tension.

'Den Rannion's third son, for one.' Temar spat.

'You didn't arouse any suspicion?' I regretted the words as soon as they were out of my mouth.

'Hardly,' said Temar scornfully. 'I can ask all the stupid questions I want; everyone expects me to be ignorant of everything and everyone. But Saedrin be my witness, I swear this man is Dirindal's ears and eyes.'

'And he was seen with Firon Den Thasnet?' Perhaps there was a larger pattern to fit Dalmit's seemingly innocent news. 'It could still be nothing, Temar. We'd best wait until we can get a full tale from Casuel. Where is he?'

'Velindre wanted him.' Temar dismissed the mage with a gesture. 'What if Tor Bezaemar are part of this hostility? Gelaia was telling me the charming Relict can show a very different face if she is crossed, even vicious if it serves her turn.'

'How so?' I asked.

Temar shook his head. 'It is another's secret. I swore I would not tell.'

I opened my mouth and then shut it again. Trying to get Temar to break his word belittled us both. 'Did you tell Esquire Camarl about this? Is there any way we can send word to warn Demoiselle Avila?'

'We can let her know to be on her guard as soon as she returns.' Temar looked through the postern at the long shadows and the splendid sunset beyond. 'She cannot be much longer, she is due to dine with Den Castevin with me.'

'I wonder if she learned anything useful from Guinalle. You can tell me when I get back.' I was ready to go, Charoleia's letter tucked in the breast of my jerkin, my sword waiting in the gatehouse.

'Avila can make my excuses to Den Castevin—' Temar began.

'Messire will have my hide—'

'Ryshad!' Stolley was beckoning by the postern, a figure beyond him indistinct against the darkening rose and gold of the sky.

I hurried over. 'Yes?'

'Message for you.' Stolley moved aside to let the newcomer enter. It was Eadit, Charoleia's Lescari-bred lad.

I picked up my sword from its peg inside the watch room door. 'Outside.' We stepped out through the gate to lose ourselves in the shadows under the trees. Temar came too, but short of slamming the postern in his face I couldn't think of a way to stop him.

'I thought I was to call on your mistress?' I queried Eadit.

'Some news came that changed her plans.' His eyes sparkled. 'I'll take you to her.'

'Is this something to do with the matter I raised with her this morning?' I wasn't sure how much Charoleia was in the habit of confiding to this boy.

He grinned. 'She's run your quarry to ground for you and she's watching the earth as we speak.'

'Then I most assuredly will come with you,' Temar insisted.

'No,' I told him, exasperated.

'I come with you or I follow you,' he told me bluntly. 'Or will you tell Master Stolley to chain me alongside the thief? Nothing less will stop me!'

'It'd serve you right if I did,' I said grimly. But then I'd have to explain to Stoll where I was going and why Temar couldn't come too. Then I'd have Stoll rousing half the barracks to back me. He wouldn't miss a chance to succeed where Naer had failed and redeem himself in the Sieur's eyes.

'We should go,' Eadit said, looking uncertainly between us.

And bringing half a Cohort down on her wouldn't endear me to Charoleia either, not when she'd been so insistent on the need for discretion. Stoll would certainly want to know where I'd got my information, him and Messire.

'All right, you can come,' I told Temar. 'Go and get a sword from Stolley. Look haughty enough so he won't ask you why you want it. But you do exactly as I say, you hear? If that means hiding under a barrel until all the fighting stops, you do it, understand me?'

'Of course.' He was as eager as a child promised an evening at the puppet shows.

'The Sieur'll wipe that smile off your face,' I warned him. 'He'll be furious when we own up to this.'

'We had best make sure we have something to show for it,' Temar replied. 'Success can gild the most brazen act, after all.'

'I don't know about that,' I muttered as I watched him go back to the gatehouse. As soon as he reappeared we followed Eadit down the road.

He paused by the conduit house. 'Got your purse, chosen man?'

As I nodded, he flagged down a hireling gig and we all climbed in. 'Where to?'

'The shrine to Drianon down this end of the Habbitrot,' Eadit told the driver.

'Is that not—'

Eadit shot Temar an angry look and I silenced him with a sharp nudge. We all sat mute and expectant as the gig took us to that uncomfortable quarter between the southern docks and the lowest of the springs. A great swathe of the city is given over to making cloth hereabouts, dyeing it, printing it, cutting and sewing. Over to the east, where the land begins to rise again, pattern drawers and silk ribbon weavers live in comfort and prosperity. Down in the hollow where damp leaches up from hidden streams, women go blind knitting coarse stockings by firelight while their men search the refuse of the rich, knifing each other over bones to sell for bookbinders' glue or rag for the paper mills. The Habbitrot is the main road cutting through the squalor and I noted the Valiant Flag as we passed. Quite some distance past, Eadit turned to our driver. 'Anywhere here, thanks.'

I paid the man off and we watched him whip his horse into a brisk trot to get them both back to safer streets unmolested.

'Down here.' Eadit led us down a rutted lane, the summer-parched earth beaten hard underfoot, which was one blessing. Identical row houses faced each other, doors and windows cramped together beneath an unbroken roof ridge, all built many generations since by landowners eager to cram as many households as possible on to the smallest piece of land.

The lad moved confidently, gaze flickering constantly from side to side, lingering on any shadow that might conceal an unexpected threat.

'Parnilesse or Carluse?' I asked him suddenly. That was the most recent fighting that would have offered a lad like him the chance to serve with a mercenary corps.

'Parnilesse, up near the Draximal border. Where my people are from.' Disillusion clouded Eadit's eyes so I didn't pursue the matter. As long as I was sure he knew which end of a sword has a point, I was content. He turned into an irregular yard between two terraces, the gates open and ready.

'Good evening, Ryshad.' Charoleia was sitting in a shiny gig, an elegant bay horse idly chewing in its nosebag.

My blood ran cold at the thought of such a beauty waiting alone out here, with a horse worth more coin than the wretches round here would handle in a lifetime. Then I remembered how Livak had admired Charoleia's ability to take care of herself, and I'd met proven men more apt to need rescuing than my beloved. 'I thought I was to call on you.'

'I decided to save time.' She tilted her head. 'There's chatter running all along the gutters about this theft, given your Sieur's going to stretch the man's neck on the strength of it. The braver scum are egging each other on to try stealing a little magical power for themselves, the cowards just want to get their hands on the gold and melt everything down.'

Temar made a retching sound beside me.

'Fortunately, none of them know where to go sniffing for it, as yet.' Charoleia gestured casually with her whip. 'I, on the other hand, do. It's all a matter of knowing whom to ask for what.' Her voice turned serious. 'When this is done, you'll both owe me, and I don't mean just a card to the Emperor's dance, Ryshad.'

'This is my responsibility.' Temar was pale beneath the lesser moon still facing down her slowly waxing sister.

'I answer for my own debts.' I tried not to contradict him too flatly.

'Glad to hear it,' Charoleia said dryly. 'That's the house where your man's hiding.' She pointed some way down the narrow, foetid street.

'How do we know he's still in there?' I looked at the shuttered house, a candle glowing in a garret the only light. 'I wonder who owns this district, come to that.'

Temar whirled round as a door opened behind him, his sword rasping in its sheath. Charoleia's maid Arashil pressed back against the doorpost, hands clasped to her cheeks, and I swallowed an oath.

'Is our friend still at home?' Charoleia enquired.

Arashil nodded rapidly.

'Has he gone out at all today?'

'Has anyone left carrying anything?'

Temar's urgent question followed hard on the heels of my own. Arashil shook her head to both, evidently a woman of few words.

'We'd hardly have brought you here if the man had gone elsewhere.' Charoleia's rebuke was mild but unmistakable. 'A gang of luggage thieves live in the lower half of the house. They're gone for an evening's drinking, but I don't know how long you'll have before they come back.'

Temar moved towards the gate but Charoleia barred his way with her whip. 'Let Eadit unlock the door first.'

The Lescari-bred lad winked at Temar before sauntering idly out of the yard, head back and whistling. As he drew level with the house we were watching, he stopped, eased his breeches and stepped into the doorway. It was a quiet night hereabouts and we all heard the trickling sound.

I glanced at Charoleia as the noise stopped and Eadit remained in the entrance. 'How good is he?'

'Good enough.' She sounded confident. 'Livak taught him.'

I stared into the darkness. Charoleia presumably bought letters or any memoranda recovered by these thieves who cut chests and coffers from any carriage slowing long enough to be robbed. For all her beauty, Charoleia was deeply mired in this nether world of dishonesty, just as Livak had been for so long.

'There he goes.' Temar gripped my arm. We watched Eadit walk casually down the street until he turned into an alley.

'We cannot leave you ladies here unprotected,' Temar said with sudden concern.

'He'll be back soon enough. That ginnel comes around the back of here.' Charoleia pushed me. 'Go on. The game's all up if someone in there finds the door unlocked.'

I walked confidently out of the yard, hand on my sword hilt, Temar doing the same at my shoulder. As we walked openly up to the door I mimed a pull at the bell rope. After waiting a breath, I took a step back, hand raised as if greeting someone opening the door to us.

'What are you doing?' Temar whispered.

'Looking as if we've a right to be here. Get inside.'

The house seemed empty but had an expectant air, as if its rightful masters would be back at any moment. The door opened straight into a wide room, a simple curtain half pulled across an entrance to a filthy kitchen beyond. Pewter plates smeared with the scant remnants of a tripe and pease dinner were scattered across the greasy table, a few dry crusts of bread on the floor. The low fire was banked with small coal, ready to be stirred up to heat the battered kettle hanging above it.

'Up there?' Temar was already moving towards the rickety stair.

I nodded and touched my figure to my lips.

Temar walked carefully, weight on his toes, heavy boot heels making no noise on the bare wood. I followed, keeping a watchful eye first below and then on the upper rooms as we emerged on to a narrow landing. Two doors faced each other over a stained pallet heaped with filthy blankets. The place reeked of urine, sweat and decay, laths showing through the grey and crumbling plaster.

Temar looked a question at me. I chewed my lip, thinking. Ideally I'd want to know if anyone was in those rooms, but we might open the door on a man who'd fight or a woman who'd scream. Then our quarry in the garret would be instantly on his guard, whether or not this reeking place was in the habit of nightly fights. I took a slow breath and regretted it as the stink nearly made me cough. Shaking my head I gestured towards the sagging ceiling and drew my sword taking pains not to make a noise. Temar did the same, wielding a workaday blade not worth a hundredth of his heirloom sword.

Something halfway between a ladder and a stair ran up to the garret, turning back on itself to an open trapdoor. Temar climbed slowly up, ducking down as he reached the turn, hiding until the very last moment possible.

'What the—' As the man above swore in consternation, Temar sprang up the remaining stairs. I was after him, two and three steps at a time, into the garret and slamming down the door.

Temar had the thief up against the blind chimney breast rising up from the floors below, one hand gripping the man's throat, the other holding up his sword in silent warning.

'The house is empty,' I said in low tones. 'Start yelling and we'll gut you.'

Temar reinforced my threat with a tighter grip and the man raised futile hands to his purpling face. He was older than me, wild curls retreating fast from temples and crown, face thin from a hungry life.

'Enough,' I warned Temar. We'd taken the man by surprise, but that wouldn't last long and I didn't want him fighting back any sooner than necessary. 'Have you got him?'

'Like the rat he is.' Temar leaned all his weight into holding the man as I searched him rapidly for weapons. Knives at his belt and boots were easy enough to find, and thinking of Livak I also found them strapped to his forearms and one hanging from a thong round his neck. I slid all of them into a brimming chamber pot in the furthest corner of the room.

'Bring him here.' A broken-backed chair was piled high with unwashed clothes that this villain had never paid good coin for. I tossed them to the floor and Temar forced the man to sit. The shock was starting to wear off and he swung a kick at me, hands trying to break free of Temar. It was a valiant effort for a slightly built wretch, doubtless born and bred in these meagre streets. He'd probably have been scraping a living from hand to mouth until someone realised his stunted form was better suited than most for climbing in through narrow windows. That would have meant better eating, but nothing would restore his lost growth.

I slapped the thief hard across the face to stop his nonsense and found a belt among the litter of clothes. I bent back a little finger to distract him from his struggles, and, as he winced, had his hands tied behind his back. 'Temar, see if the goods are here.'

Dismay flickered in the thief's face as I was securing his legs to the chair but he didn't betray any hiding place with any instinctive look, trying to spit at me instead. I slapped him for that insolence, not with all my strength but an open hand was enough to split his chapped lip. I stepped back and laid my own sword across his shoulder, smiling with all the menace I could muster.

'Here!' Temar was on his knees, dragging a leather bag out from under a rope and plank frame supporting an infested straw mattress.

The thief couldn't hide his consternation. I snapped my fingers in his face. 'Is that everything? Have you passed anything on?'

'No.' The man was looking from me to Temar, eyes always returning to the bag.

'I think all is here.' Temar sat back on his heels, unable to hide his relief and surprise. 'That was easy.'

'It had better all be there.' I pressed the flat of my blade down hard and stared unblinking at the thief. I didn't fancy trying to track down anything already lost, not if it meant more evenings in cess pits like this, not to mention a deepening debt to Charoleia. 'And now we've got our goods back, we want to know who put you up to this.' We could spare just a little time to see if we could kill two birds with our stone.

The thief clamped obstinate lips tight shut. I set my sword down and drew gloves out of my pockets, putting them on with exaggerated care. 'You're going to tell me, you do realise that.' He was wearing a black velvet jerkin, the soiled pile rubbed bare across the shoulder. I ripped it down to pin his elbows to his sides. The man screwed his eyes shut, waiting, tense for the first blow. I obliged him with a smack around the ear, sending him rocking sideways. He grunted and recovered himself, opening his eyes to stare directly ahead, jaw set.

There was defiance in this studied blankness. I looked at Temar who was holding tight to the leather bag and then to the trapdoor. That had been open. The scoundrel had only cried out when he realised Temar wasn't whom he expected. So who was he expecting, and how soon?

I punched him at the base of the breastbone, a practised blow that stops the breath and causes agony out of all proportion to the damage it does. We may not beat up malefactors with the relish of some less honourable cohorts, but D'Olbriot's men are all taught how to use our fists. He gasped, tears starting from his eyes, falling on to his grey breeched knees as he hunched over. I grabbed a handful of matted hair and pulled him upright.

He tried to spit at me again so I shook him like a terrier with a rat, slapping him fore- and backhanded. 'Who put you up to this?'

He tried to twist his head out of my hand, determined defiance still nailing his mouth closed. This bastard had some hope to cling to, which meant beating the information out of him would take three times as long and we didn't have that time to spare. Perhaps we could wait to see who was coming to take the artefacts, but only from a safe vantage point.

I let go and patted the thief gently on the cheek, taking a pace backwards. 'So you've more backbone than Drosel.'

He opened scornful eyes. 'You can forget that bluff, bought man. Drosel wouldn't talk, and anyway, he doesn't even know this place.'

'He said enough,' I shrugged. 'How do you think we found you? Still, my congratulations; you're holding up well for a man hip deep in horseshit.'

'Save it for someone who cares, bought man,' he sneered. 'Turning friendly won't help you.'

I laced my fingers together and stretched them thoughtfully. 'How about ducking you in that a few times?' I nodded at the noisome chamber pot.

'I would not do so. He might pick out a knife with his teeth, he is so brave a man.' It wasn't Temar's mockery that made uncertainty fleet across the thief's eyes. What was it?

I looked at the thief. 'So, I can't be bothered to waste my time beating it out of you, and I don't fancy dabbling my fingers in your piss. All right, what's it worth?'

Surprise flared in the man's eyes. 'What are you offering?'

I pretended to consider the question. 'What about Drosel?'

'Don't make me laugh.' The thief recovered a little self-possession. 'Dro knew the risks. He wouldn't lift a finger to save me if the runes had rolled the other way.'

'And if we traded him to you, you'd only have to split the gold you're hoping to get for that little lot.' I sighed. 'If his life's of no value, what about your own? Do you want to share a ferry ride with him and argue over who pays Poldrion for the privilege?'

'My life won't be worth shoe buckles if I talk to you. They'll kill me, and where's my profit then?' He wasn't joking.

'You could flee the city,' suggested Temar, walking round to face the man, the bag secure on his hip. 'Perhaps with a fat purse for your trouble?'

The thief looked nervously down at the floor when I'd have

expected the offer of coin to give him pause for thought.

'The Esquire has coffers as handsome as his linen.' I gestured at Temar's elegant lace collar. 'He'd have paid a bounty for those treasures in any case.'

'Tell us who put you up to this, to whom they answer, if you may, and you can be well rewarded.' Temar offered with honest sincerity.

The thief's tongue poked at the oozing split in his lip but fear was still tarnishing the greed in his eyes. There was something about Temar that really unnerved him, I realised. I knew something else as well. This was taking too long. I had one ear cocked for any sound below and wouldn't have bet a Lescari Mark on the silence lasting much longer. I studied the thief's face; he wasn't just looking warily at Temar, his glance kept sliding to the leather bag and not because it held his spoils. 'You'll be glad to see the back of those things, whoever takes them, won't you?'

It was drawing a bow at a venture but the thief's sharp intake of breath and involuntary hunch of his shoulders told us both I'd hit between the joints of his harness.

'How well did you sleep, with all this under your bed?' Temar balanced a battered silver goblet on his outstretched palm, hand steady as a rock. 'Did you dream? Did you feel the imprisoned crying out for release? Did you feel their confusion, their pain?'

I was impressed. Temar was striking a resonant balance between sounding scarily archaic and speaking clearly enough to be understood by latterday ears. It was just a shame this bluff was so threadbare. But as I thought that I saw a new determination light in Temar's cold blue eyes. He reached into the leather bag, and what came next nearly made me cry out loud, never mind the thief.

'Milar far eladris, surar nen jidralis.' Temar slid into a rhythmical chant, eyes glazing. As he did so, a face coalesced above the black-streaked silver. Faint at first, like early streaks of mist lurking in hollows in the road, the image thickened like fog. It was pale as mist, a washed-out greyness to the skin, lips bloodless, unseeing eyes all but transparent. I couldn't tell if it were man or woman, old or young, indistinct, with hair no more than a wispy suggestion.

'Shall I send you to join these shades?' Temar stopped his incantation and the shape shivered in the air. 'Or shall I call them forth, to pursue you to the very borders of the Otherworld? If I do that, you can only be safe when you slit your own throat and Saedrin locks his door behind you.'

It was a good thing Temar was able to do all the talking because my throat had closed tighter than an oyster's arse. I moistened dry lips and saw the thief staring at Temar as if the young Esquire had revealed himself as one of Poldrion's own demons. A new stink added to the general stench in the room as the man soiled himself.

'His name's Queal, Fenn Queal.' He stumbled over the name. 'He works out of the Copper Casket, over near the limekilns on the bay.'

'What did he tell you?' demanded Temar. 'What did he promise?'

The door on the ground floor below rattled. Our luck had just run out. 'Hush, both of you.' I put my sword to the man's throat to ensure his silence.

'Jacot? Jacot, you putrid pig?' An indignant voice yelled up the stairs. 'You left the door unlocked, shit for brains!'

'Are you up there?' A second voice sounded faintly suspicious.

'Answer him.' I prodded the thief. 'Say sorry.'

Jacot managed a hoarse shout. 'Right, sorry about that.'

I cursed under my breath as I heard heavy boots on the stairs. 'You'll be more than sorry if anything's been lifted, dungface,' a halfway drunken voice threatened.

There was no time to untie Jacot, and anyway, if it came to a fight I didn't want him free. Whoever was wanting to pick an argument threw back the trapdoor and the indignation died on his lips as he realised Temar was standing there, naked blade ready to top his skull like an egg.

'We've no quarrel with you, pal,' I said with pleasant

menace. 'We're just about done with Jacot here and then we'll be leaving.'

The newcomer was a tall man with a weeping sore on his cheek that looked suspiciously like the scald to me. He was cleaner than Jacot, from what I could see of his shoulders, wearing a dun broadcloth jerkin over a plain shirt. All the better to go unnoticed about his thievery, doubtless. His dark eyes were red-rimmed and crusted but alert enough as they scanned the room; first the bed, the bound Jacot, myself and finally Temar, who smiled nastily at him.

'Whatever you say, you're the man with the sword.' He looked unconcerned at Jacot's reddened and bleeding face. 'Never was good for his rent, anyway.'

I'd been half wondering about taking the thief with us to give Messire a matched pair for the gallows, but bilked for his rent or not I couldn't see this bully letting us take Jacot with us. No matter. We had the Kellarin artefacts back and I'd wager gold against copper that Jacot would get his neck stretched soon enough.

I let my smile fade into hard-faced threat. The man gave the darkness under the bed one last look before sliding down the ladder, helpfully drawing the trap shut after him.

I raised a finger to shut Temar's opening mouth and, kneeling, lifted the trapdoor a fraction. There were too many voices asking puzzled questions for me to pick out the words clearly and then a door below shut them off.

I scowled. 'Do you reckon they'll let us just walk out of here with his loot on your belt?'

'I somehow doubt it.' Temar looked down through the crack of the trapdoor. 'We fight our way through?'

I sat back and looked round the garret. 'If we have to. I'd rather try and go round them and just run.'

'Almost certainly safer,' Temar said dryly. He bolted the trapdoor, which would give us a little more time to consider our options.

The tiny window was thick with soot, decaying round the frame, and it didn't look as if it had ever been opened.

Knocking it out would take time, make noise; I wasn't sure Temar could get his shoulders through it, let alone me, and in any case I didn't fancy trying to race thieves over the rooftops.

'Gag him.' Gesturing at Jacot, I went over to the chimney breast. A flimsy wooden wall on either side was all that separated this garret from the next house. I looked more closely. The aging stonework had shifted over the generations and pulled away, leaving the flimsy crosspieces none too deep in the walls. The cheap planks were rotting where last winter's rain had found a way through the coarse stone slates and most of the wood looked worm-ridden. I looked over at Temar, who was tying a thick knot in a stained rag to wedge into Jacot's mouth.

'Let's use him to weigh down the trapdoor.' I lifted one side of the chair. Temar took the other and we carried Jacot carefully over, fury choking him almost as effectively as Temar's gag. Temar took a deep breath, held it and then carefully moved the chamber pot to stand on the crack by the trap's rope handle. I nodded my amused approval as I stripped the pallet and greasy blankets off the bed and lifted up the frame.

'We smash through that wall and get clear as fast as we can.' Even if the thieves below thought we were just beating Jacot up, the noise would give them an excuse to interfere so we wouldn't have much time.

Temar swung the bed frame with me. 'On three?'

'On one.' I put all my strength behind the blow, Temar with me. The bed frame twisted and splintered but the wall buckled more, cross pieces ripped out of the chimney breast. We hit it again, and again, as hurrying boots came charging up the stairs. One last shove sent the ineffective partition crashing down and we forced our way through the gap. The garret next door was a mirror image of Jacot's and we raced to its trapdoor. Finding the bolt took a few unpleasantly tense moments in the half darkness, but then we were through and sliding down the ladder. Temar tried to pull it away but it was too securely fixed to the wall. I shoved him towards the stairs.

Shouts sounded in the room we'd just left, mainly of disgust as whoever tried to come bursting up through the trap was covered in Jacot's ordure.

I drew my sword and spared a breath to hope no innocents appeared and tried to stop us. Those runes rolled our way; this house was dark and we reached the ground floor unopposed. Temar cocked his head like a listening hound. The roar of pursuit from above didn't quite cover the shuffle of feet in the street outside the front.

'The back.' I was betting my hide and Temar's that there'd be an alley to match the one Eadit had used to get back to Charoleia.

This house had a door to its kitchen and we bolted it behind us as we ran. Once through the outer door, we found ourselves in a pitch black yard. Scrambling over the chest-high wall, we dropped into a narrow alley with an open sewer running down the middle. We ran on, swords in hand, eyes fixed on a spill of moonlight where the terrace gave way to a lane. Our footfalls echoed back from the walls on either side, rousing dogs from their kennels, hounds barking until doors opened on warning shouts. As we reached the open space we heard running feet to match our own and naked steel shone bright as three of the thieves came skidding round the corner.

The first one made a wild swing for my neck. This was no time for the niceties of a formal bout. I parried with a block hard enough to send him staggering. Grabbing his hilt with my free hand, I curved my sword down to rip it up the back of his calf. He dropped his blade to clutch at the wound as he fell crippled to the floor and I kicked it away into the darkness. The other two had both gone for Temar, each thrusting cuts that the younger man's ancient sword skills competently swept aside. One tried a vicious hack at his wrist but Temar saw it coming and pulled back. The thief leaned a hair's breadth too far forward and Temar had him, cutting down to the bone in the angle of his elbow. I was moving to take the last man but a shadow stepped up behind him, grabbing his head to draw a dagger across his throat in one practised movement. Temar and I recoiled but I still got spattered with hot sticky blood.

'Come on.' Eadit dropped the corpse and we followed him to the street. Charoleia was waiting, Arashil beside her, the gig barely pausing as we three grabbed the sides and back, scrambling to cram ourselves aboard. The whole neighbourhood was rousing by now, cries raising lights in curious windows. The thieves who'd pursued us down the alley came running after us and two men appeared from nowhere to grab at the horse's head. Charoleia ripped into their hands and faces with her metal-barbed whip and they fell away. The bay sprang forward but, hampered by the unevenly weighted gig, was hard put to outpace our pursuers. Charoleia wrenched the reins to turn it first round one corner, then another. We hit a wider road and she lashed the beast to a reckless canter, leaving the sounds of the chase fading behind us.

I stared backwards until I was satisfied we'd left anyone after our blood behind. 'What do you know of Fenn Queal, Charoleia?'

She kept her eyes on the road. 'If he paid that thief, someone is paying him ten times as much.'

'Would he have lied to us?' Temar asked. 'The thief, I mean.'

'Not and risk Queal finding out and skinning him for it.' Charoleia slowed the pace a little as we reached a street with ordinary people going about innocent Festival business. 'We'll discuss this indoors.'

'Where are we going?' I checked my bearings and it was clear we weren't heading either back to D'Olbriot's residence or north and west to Charoleia's house.

'Somewhere safe.' Charoleia glanced back at the three of us with a frown that still couldn't mar her beauty.

'D'Olbriot's is safe,' I protested.

Charoleia ignored me. I reached to touch her shoulder but Eadit held my arm back. 'You asked for her help, you take it.'

I gave him a hard look but he met my gaze squarely.

Charoleia turned down another back street and then another. She took a lane that ran right beneath the solid bulk of the old city walls and finally steered the weary horse into a tidily swept street where we drew up outside a respectable merchant's house. Eadit got out to take the horse's head while Arashil sorted the keys chained at her girdle. 'I'll need to wash that blood out at once,' she said, suddenly seeing the gore spattered all over me and Temar. 'Or you'll be going home in your drawers.'

'Sorry about that,' said Eadit perfunctorily, leading the horse away.

We went inside to find a small hall with a single lantern burning low on a table. Arashil lit a candle from it and opened a door on to a sparsely furnished parlour where she lit another lamp. 'Don't get blood on the furniture.'

Temar and I looked at each other and at Charoleia. 'I'll get some blankets,' she said with a faint smile as she turned to disappear up the stairs.

'I don't want to be at the laundry all night,' snapped Arashil. 'You've nothing I've not seen before.'

I stripped off my jerkin and shirt, folding them carefully to keep the bloodied sides innermost. Temar did the same with visible reluctance as I sat on a plain but well-polished chair to take my boots off. I didn't know just what I had trodden in this evening, but I didn't imagine Charoleia would take kindly to me tramping it through this house.

'And the breeches.' Arashil tapped an impatient foot. I considered refusing. I could feel the stickness against my skin, but once the blood had dried it would barely show on the dark cloth. Then I saw how the spray had caught Temar, leaving stains all across his pale breeches. He was blushing furiously and I couldn't leave him to be the only one standing there in his linen, not if it embarrassed him so badly. I stripped and bundled up the clothes, giving Temar an encouraging wink.

Charoleia came into the room as Arashil left and tossed us

each a warm blanket dyed an expensive blue. I tucked mine round my hips, not really wanting it in this heat. Temar wrapped himself tightly as he sat on a high-winged settle and some of the colour faded from his face.

'We all stay here tonight,' she said, businesslike with no hint of flirtation. 'If Queal was behind this, he won't take kindly to being robbed in turn. Will Jacot be able to tell him you were D'Olbriot's men?'

I nodded. 'We said his mate had given him up, so no one would go looking for who else might have passed on the word.'

'My thanks for that.' Charoleia dimpled. Perhaps I'd been wrong about the flirtation.

'You think Queal would try to get the artefacts back again?' I tried not to sound too sceptical.

'Do you want to risk it?' Charoleia turned melting blue eyes on me. 'Wouldn't you be staking out every road to D'Olbriot's residence if you were Queal? You won't get close enough to call out the guard before ten or twenty men rush you, believe me.'

'Can he rouse that many men so fast?' Temar frowned.

'He can,' Charoleia assured him. She looked back at me. 'Queal wouldn't only want a sackful of gold before he'd agree to organise robbing D'Olbriot. It would have to be someone important asking, important enough to make a marker with their name on it worth the risk.'

'Can you find out who that might be without putting yourself at risk?' I felt concern twisting my gut. 'Could he possibly suspect you were the one who gave him up? Is that why we came here, not to the other house?'

'I'm simply being careful.' There was a suspicion of laughter in Charoleia's voice. 'Queal won't trace anything back to me. I'll go home later tonight and then you two can leave here in the morning. No one hereabouts even knows Queal's name, let alone how to get word to him.'

I hoped Charoleia's confidence was justified but a yawn interrupted me as I tried to find a way of asking if she was sure without insulting her.

'Would there be anything to eat?' Temar asked hesitantly. 'And to drink?'

Charoleia smiled at him. 'Naturally.'

As the door closed behind her, I yawned again. 'I think we've managed a full day, haven't we? And just what were you thinking of back there? How much Artifice can you work now?'

'You have seen the sum total of my learning.' Temar looked somewhat embarrassed. 'Not much, I grant you but sufficient for bluff. I did no more than you last night.'

'You certainly picked that up quickly,' I complimented him. 'But that shade or whatever it was, that was no mere trick.' I managed to keep my distaste out of my voice.

'You are the one we have to thank for that particular incantation.' Temar laughed. 'Once Guinalle heard you had seen an Elietimm priest raise the image of its owner from an artefact for the Aldabreshin, she worried at the notion like a dog with a bone until she had perfected the incantations. She can still do it ten times better than any other adept, but Demoiselle Avila cannot do it at all. I have no idea why it came so easily to me.'

'Make sure you lock that bag somewhere secure and well away from the bedrooms for preference. We all need an undisturbed night's sleep.' Something must have shown on my face.

'I am sorry if raising that image reminded you of your enslavement.' Temar shifted a cushion behind his back to avoid meeting my eyes. 'Is that why you dislike Artifice so?'

'What made you suspect Jacot had been dreaming about the people still under the enchantment?' I countered.

'Thinking of the girl from the shrine,' Temar answered as if it should have been obvious. 'And of when Guinalle was devising that incantation to raise the images. I remembered Halice saying it looked like something out of old tales of necromancy, raising shades of the dead.'

'Halice is more Livak's friend than mine. How's she faring in Kellarin?' I asked, off hand, studying the purple line of the new scar on my arm.

'You keep turning the subject,' Temar said with blunt exasperation. 'Why does Artifice disturb you so?'

His irritation sparked my own anger. 'The first time I had aetheric magic used on me, Artifice, call it what you like, I was a prisoner of the Elietimm.' He'd asked and perhaps I owed him a fuller answer. 'That bastard who's been sending them over here, to rob and kill, he went ripping into my mind, looking for any information he wanted. I betrayed my oath, my Sieur, myself, and there wasn't a cursed thing I could do about it. That's what aetheric magic means to me. It happened to Livak as well, and I wasn't lying when I told that thief she'd rather have been raped.' I gave him a hard look. 'Have you ever met a woman who's been raped?'

Temar looked sick.

'Then I find I've been given your sword in hopes that whatever Artifice was within it might soak into my mind, my dreams, and give Planir the answers he was looking for. It worked, Dast save me, it worked, and Temar, I thought I was going mad! No, I don't blame you, I don't think anyone, not even the Archmage, knew quite what they were dealing with, but even then, I cannot forget that it was Artifice. Then there was the Elietimm enchanter trying to get his claws into the Archipelago, into Shek Kul's domain. He was using Artifice to dupe that stupid bitch Kaeska, and it got her killed. When he fought me, Artifice nearly left me dead a third time.' I lifted my arm to show Temar the new healed cut. 'This is precious little to weigh in the scales against all that!'

'And this is what you think of me, of Guinalle and the other Adepts, of Avila?' Temar was outraged and hurt at one and the same time.

'The Demoiselle wanted to get that thief to talk. How did she plan on doing that?' I demanded. 'With kind words and honeycake?'

Temar took a moment to consider his reply. 'Granted, there are ways to compel someone to speak the truth against their will, but those were only ever used when a death was involved or every other evidence indicated guilt. In any event, no one ever suffered as you did, my oath on it,' he insisted defiantly.

I shook my head. 'I'm sorry, but the idea still makes my skin crawl.'

'And your alternatives are so much more humane?' Temar challenged me. 'You trust a man to tell the truth when he has been beaten bloody? That hardly served you with Jacot, did it? Will a man not merely say whatever you want to hear, just to stop the torment?'

I had no answer to that. Temar sighed unhappily in the tense silence. 'I wish you could see all the ways Artifice can be a boon, rather than mistrusting it.'

'It's nothing personal.' I did my best to sound sincere. 'It's just – oh, as if I'd burned myself badly on a naked candle. Even a nice safe lantern would give me a qualm, wouldn't it?'

'I suppose so.' Temar grimaced. 'At least you accept wizardry, which precious few others seem to. Do you think your contemporaries will be as suspicious of Artifice? Do you think they will ever come to understand the differences between the arts?'

'It's hard to say. It depends how they see it used.' One reason I could keep my composure around mages is that I'd always had their spells used for me rather than against me, thus far at least. 'That worries you?'

Temar shook his head, eyes distant. 'I cannot see Kel Ar'Ayen surviving without Artifice.'

'The mercenaries are getting used to it.' I tried to sound encouraging.

'I think they have seen so many horrors, so many unexpected twists of fate, that nothing surprises them any more. And Halice would make a deal with Poldrion's own demons if they were going to be somehow useful to her.' Temar laughed, but there was still that lost look about him. 'But what if this mistrust of all magic deters those who might come from Tormalin to help us? We need them as well.'

Temar fell abruptly silent as the door opened and Charoleia came in with a tray of bread, meat and a bottle of wine.

She arched a teasing eyebrow. 'You two look very serious.'

'It was nothing of importance.' Temar shook his head. 'So, you want a card for the Emperor's dance tomorrow?' I wasn't the only one countering questions with questions.

'I think I've earned it.' Charoleia sat with composure that suggested she ate supper every evening in the company of partly dressed men.

'Have you been before?' Temar accepted a crystal goblet of pale golden wine.

'I've stood on the sidelines.' Charoleia talked about some previous Festival when she'd inveigled herself into the palace, being careful neither to name names nor specify the season. I helped myself to food, trying to recall if I could ever have been about my sworn man's duties when she would have been there. If I had been, I concluded, Charoleia had done nothing to bring her to my notice, which was presumably why she was quite so successful in her chosen line of work.

'Did you have such events in the Old Empire?' Charoleia refilled our glasses.

'Festival was very different in those days, first and foremost a time for due observance at a House's shrines. There was plenty of feasting and all the rest of the fun, but that was different as well, a way of bringing nobles closer to their tenantry.' For an instant Temar looked very young and very lost. 'Everyone knew they could rely on the protection of the Name they owed fealty to. It was not simply a tie of rent and duty paid, there was a real bond—'

'Things haven't changed so much,' I tried to reassure him, touched by the pain creasing his brow. 'The tenantry will be well fed and entertained tomorrow, and any of the commonalty who want to come besides. Messire will welcome them all, thank them, and anyone who needs his help can ask it.'

'How many times does that happen in a year?' Temar challenged. 'How many Sieurs do as much? How many begrudge the coin it costs them?'

I finished my wine, not wanting to argue with him, but Temar wasn't about to leave it.

'How long will D'Olbriot be available for his people? For

a chime or so in the morning, before everyone of noble blood escapes the commonalty by hiding themselves at the Emperor's dance?'

I stood up. 'I'm sorry, but this wine has gone straight to my head.' That was partly true, and I certainly had neither the energy nor the inclination for arguing the social and political intricacies of the present day with Temar. 'I really must get some rest.'

'Arashil will have made up the beds by now,' Charoleia said easily. 'Sleep well.'

'Temar?'

But Charoleia was kicking off her shoes and tucking her feet up under her maroon skirts.

'Tell me, just who among the D'Olbriot Name are visiting for the Festival?' Her tone was warm, maternal and inviting.

I smiled to myself and went upstairs. Charoleia was welcome to whatever information she could get out of Temar. It was her currency after all, and it might go some way to settling our debt with her.

CHAPTER SIX

The Chronicle of D'Olbriot Under the Seal of Andjael, Sieur by Saedrin's Grace, Winter Solstice Following the Accession of Kanselin the Confident

Let us give thanks to Raeponin that when Saedrin opened his inexorable door to our late Emperor Kanselin the Blunt, Poldrion forwent any claim to his youngest brother, now duly anointed and set above us. While it is but early days in this new reign, I find optimism warming my heart as I bid my screever set down my personal thoughts at this turn of the year.

Our late Emperor was a worthy leader and, in these uncertain times, a doughty guardian of Tormalin, but he was not called the Blunt out of idle fancy. His predilection for plain speaking had caused offence on more than one occasion and in some quarters provoked hostility slow to fade. Our new Emperor has now used the occasions of both Autumn Equinox and Winter Solstice to welcome such potential opponents of his rule to share his personal celebrations. Such open hospitality in plain devotion to Ostrin's name has done much to reunite the Princes of the Convocation and is the first of many hopeful signs I wish to relate.

As his brother was the Blunt, so his late cousin was the Rash. While few of us would condemn ambition to reclaim those provinces left fallow during the Chaos and its pernicious aftermath, we have all seen the consequences of those truly rash attempts to spread our meagre resources ever more thinly in hopes of restoring Tormalin authority in Lescar. This newly elevated Kanselin makes no secret of his belief that we must look to Tormalin interests first and foremost, resisting any pleas to involve ourselves in quarrels beyond our most ancient borders. He is deaf to those men of Lescar or Caladhria who beg never so pitifully for aid, seeking to trade on that fealty they so readily discard a mere handful of generations ago. I was myself present to hear the Emperor declare that, by Dastennin's very teeth, such men had chosen to plot their own course and must weather whatever storms might batter them. This is not to say Kanselin intends to return to the closed attitudes of the Modrical era. He has been vociferous in his encouragement of trade and generous in sharing the knowledge of markets and routes that has enabled Tor Kanselin to amass so substantial a fortune from all corners of the Old Empire.

In pious recognition of the binding oaths he swore, Kanselin has sanctified his role as Toremal's defender by taking up residence in the Old Palace and doing much to restore the dilapidation of the shrines within it. Rumour has it that he means to make a permanent court there, unwilling to spend his energies in crossing and recrossing the land when so much else requires his attention. This is of some considerable concern to those more remote Houses who know only too well that constant attendance on his brother was the only way to be certain of Imperial favour. I have ventured to differ with anyone I heard expressing such fears, trusting our Emperor's assertions that it is the duty of every Sieur and Esquire to care for their domains, no matter how distant, just as it is the Emperor's duty to secure the peace that enables them to do so. At Autumn Equinox Kanselin made no secret of his expectation that we would all depart for our various estates at the close of Festival, returning to celebrate Winter Solstice in unity undamaged for our sojourns apart. When we gathered for the rituals of Soulsease Night, even the most suspicious could not claim any greater good will apparent for those Houses proximate to Toremal. Nor could any claim disproportionate disadvantage accrued to far distant Names. I for one will gladly trade the expense and constraints of courtly life for the freedom to supervise D'Olbriot affairs more closely, if that can be done without risking a loss of status.

This Kanselin's whole rule is open to scrutiny, even to the lowest ranks of nobility. Any and all Esquires may petition him and

A House on Lavrent Cut, Toremal, Summer Solstice Festival, Fifth Day, Morning

The house was silent when I woke, an empty calm entirely unlike the rousing bustle of barracks or gatehouse. I rolled over, glanced at the window and sat bolt upright, swearing when I saw how high the sun was. Everyone would be wondering where in Saedrin's name we were. Messire would have Stoll and the sworn turning the city upside down by now.

'Temar?' I yelled out of the bedroom door as I wrenched on my underlinen.

'In the kitchen.' That halted me. Why did he sound so relaxed? I went, boots in hand. The door to the street was securely bolted, the front of the house dark, but the back was airy, with shutters open to the morning sun.

Temar was dressed and leaning against the table, eating soft white bread and drinking from a tankard. 'There is a note.' He nodded at a basket holding the other half of a flat, round loaf. The bag of artefacts lay beside it.

I read the note as I grabbed jerkin and breeches from a clotheshorse in front of the cooling range: *Leave everything just as it is, lock the yard door behind you and take the key. I'll send someone to collect it and my card at noon.*

'Did you read this?' I set the note down to pull on my clothes.

He offered me the flagon. 'So we have until midday to get the lady an invitation to the Emperor's dance.' He sounded amused.

'So how do we do that?' I couldn't see a joke. 'Is there any wine or water?'

'Only beer.' Temar poured me some. 'Better than the mercenaries make in Kel Ar'Ayen.'

I looked round the tidy kitchen; no sign anyone had spent

the night here, apart from the things on the table. 'Were the others here when you woke up?'

Temar shook his head. 'No, they had all gone. I did not even hear them leave.' A forlorn look fleeted across his face.

Charoleia could certainly take care of herself and her own, that much I was sure of. I took a swallow of weak, bitter beer to wash down the bread. 'We have to get back or the Sieur will be looking to nail my hide to the gatehouse door.'

'I used Artifice to tell Avila where we are.' Temar was unconcerned. 'Well, not where we are, because I do not know, but I explained to her what had happened.'

'Earlier this morning? Was she alone? What did she say?' I hadn't hidden behind a woman's skirts since I'd grown out of soft shoes, but if Avila had told Messire what had happened that might just save my skin.

'Yes, she was alone.' Temar couldn't restrain a childish grin. 'She was still abed and I hardly suppose anyone comes knocking at her door on the dark side of midnight.'

I was about to tell him to mind his manners when his bright smile made me suspicious. 'Someone came knocking at your door last night?'

Temar's attempt to look innocent would have done justice to a cat caught eating cheese. 'What has that to do with anything?'

I narrowed my eyes at him. 'Arashil?'

'No.' He couldn't hide the triumph in his eyes.

I took a deep breath but let it go. 'If you've eaten all you want, let's go and hire a ride.'

Temar followed me out of the kitchen door. I locked it, pocketing the key, and wondered how in Dast's name I was supposed to get an Imperial dance card for Charoleia by noon.

The alleys in this district were wide, well paved and clean, bringing us out on to a broad street where the morning's market was selling every fruit, vegetable or cut of meat a busy goodwife might need for the final banquets of Festival. Traders shouted loudly, as eager as anyone else to turn the day's coin and set about celebrating. I snagged a bunch of grapes from a high-piled basket, tossing coin over to a swarthy man. He caught and pocketed the coppers without taking a breath from his exhortations to passing women. 'Fresh as the dew still on it, good enough for any House in the city! Buy double and you can take a day of rest tomorrow, just like the noble ladies who never do half your work!'

That won him a laugh from a stout matron who reminded me of my own mother. She'd be at the markets by now, planning one last intricate meal before everyone returned to the usual routine of workaday life. Mother loved Festivals, especially if she could get us all together, eager for the day when we'd bring wives and best of all children home, to pack around the long table, swapping confidences and news, sharing triumphs and tragedies of the past season and planning ahead for the new. The only problem was that I couldn't ever see it happening. Mistal's passing loves usually went down like a pitcher of warm piss with our brothers, and on balance Livak would probably rather have her teeth pulled than spend another Solstice at home with me. Still, even Hansey and Ridner at their most irritating wouldn't have given me half the anxieties of this Mid-Summer.

'Here!' Raising voice and hand together, I caught the eye of a hireling driver. He pulled up a fresh grey horse.

'Fair Festival,' he said perfunctorily. 'Where to?'

'D'Olbriot's residence?' At his nod we climbed into the battered vehicle, narrow seats facing each other. It was an open carriage, so we both sat silent as the driver chirruped at his horse.

'A few more hires like this and I'll be stabled early today,' he said cheerfully over his shoulder.

'Good luck, friend.' I leaned back against the cracked leather and studied Temar, who was rapt in some happy recollection. I was sorely tempted to ask. If it hadn't been Arashil putting a spring in his step, it must have been Charoleia. But what was Charoleia hoping to get out of the lad? What had she learned from their pillow talk? How was I going to handle Temar lost in some romantic haze, given his tendency to fall headlong in love with unattainable women? Charoleia had to be the most unattainable yet.

All right, that was something of an exaggeration, if not downright untruth. It had only been Guinalle who had turned him down flat, bringing him hard up against the realisation that a woman who might agree to share your sheets might yet refuse to share your life. Something else we had in common, I thought wryly. No, before Guinalle had given him pause for thought Temar had been an accomplished flirt according to some of the memories that I wasn't about to let him know I shared. That was a startling notion. Had he charmed Charoleia into his bed? I didn't think so. Or didn't I want to think so? Was my pride injured because she'd travelled that road with him when she'd only taken a few steps along it with me? Was I jealous of Temar? I burst out laughing.

Temar was startled back to the here and now. 'What?'

'Nothing.' I could tell he didn't believe me but there wasn't much he could do about that in an open carriage.

The roads through the city were comparatively empty for a mid-morning, everyone busy at home preparing for the final day of Festival. The pace picked up as we approached the D'Olbriot residence. Wagons were delivering wine and ale, bread and pastries, all ordered up from the city to spare the House's cooks for more intricate confections. I could see a sizeable number of the commonalty already walking around the hamlet of grace houses where Stolley's wife was selling wine spiced with a little first-hand gossip about life in noble service.

Naer was on duty in the gatehouse, all spruced up in his livery. 'You're wanted, both of you, the Sieur's study.'

I'd have preferred to face Messire clean and shaven, but didn't dare risk delay. 'Come on, Temar.'

We hurried through the gardens. When I knocked on the door it was Camarl's voice not the Messire's that answered. 'Enter.'

I took a deep breath and opened the door. 'Good morning, Messire, Esquires.' I bowed low.

The Sieur was there together with all three of his brothers, sat in a close half-circle with Myred and Camarl to represent the coming generation. Painted, the faces would have looked like studies of the same man at different ages. Young

Myred, dutifully silent at the back, still had the bloom of early manhood, flesh softening chin and cheekbones but waist still trim beneath his close cut coat. Camarl showed the incipient family stoutness overcoming the fitness lent by youth but the years he had over his cousin sharpened his gaze with experience gained. Next in age was Ustian, Messire's younger brother, who still travelled seven seasons out of the eight, seeing how the House's vast holdings were managed at first hand. He was the plumpest of the four brothers, an inoffensive, round little man with a mind like a steel trap hidden beneath leaves. Long leagues on the road showed in lines around his eyes that Camarl as yet lacked. While the Sieur was still a man in his prime, Esquire Fresil, on Messire's left, was visibly further down the slope towards Saedrin's door. Leishal, master of the House's estates around Moretayne since the days of the old Sieur and seldom seen in Toremal, was not much older. But even those few years made a difference: his legs were thinned with old age, spindly beneath his paunch, his face sinking to show the bones of his skull. Where Myred's eyes were a vibrant stormy blue, Leishal's were faded nearly to colourless, deeply hooded beneath a wrinkled forehead. For all that, his wits were still honed sharp by three generations' unquestioning service of his Name.

'Good day to you, Ryshad.' Avila sat across the room beside the fireplace, expression bland, ankles crossed beneath a frivolously yellow-sprigged white gown.

'Where were you?' barked Esquire Leishal.

'Retrieving what was stolen from the House, Esquire,' I said politely.

Temar took a pace to stand beside me, one hand laid on the leather bag. 'We believe everything is here.'

Avila shifted in her seat with a rustle of silk but I'd have had to turn my head to look at her. I didn't feel that would be wise; displeasure hung in the air like the promise of summer thunder.

'You didn't have time to tell anyone where you were going?' asked Ustian.

'I chose not to, Esquire.' I faced him squarely. 'The person who gave me the information asked me to keep it in confidence.'

'There are no secrets between sworn man and master,' snapped Fresil. 'What do you mean by taking D'Alsennin into danger? The boy's barely out of bandages!'

'Your pardon, but I answer neither to Ryshad nor to any D'Olbriot.' Temar's face was stern. 'I crossed the ocean to seek these stolen treasures. Life and honour are both my own to risk in that quest.'

'Maitresse Den Castevin has no high opinion of your honour,' retorted Fresil.

In the corner of my eye I saw Avila sit forward, mouth thin with anger. The Sieur nodded to her and she stayed silent but from the surprise on Fresil's face I'd wager any coin she was giving him a very hard look.

'A great number of people tell you things in confidence, Ryshad,' Ustian said genially. 'Two are waiting to see you as we speak.'

Camarl rang a little hand bell and a blank-faced footman ushered two people through the far door, my brother Mistal and Charoleia's errand boy, Eadit, who was looking like a mouse in a room full of cats. I really did hope he wasn't here to ask for her dance card because I couldn't see Messire taking kindly to that.

'Fair Festival, advocate.' Camarl's smile was broad with all the confidence of rank. 'Anything you wish to say to Ryshad can be said before the Sieur and Esquires.'

Mistal bowed elegantly to the assembled nobility. 'I've been trying to determine who is paying Master Premeller to act as a friend of the court.'

'Why bring the news to your brother and not to Esquire Camarl or the Sieur?' asked Leishal sternly.

'I did not wish to presume on their honours' time.' Mistal bowed again.

'Just tell us what you've found out,' Ustian invited.

Mistal raised a hand to the front of the advocate's gown

he wasn't wearing. 'Master Premeller owes a sizeable sum to one Stelmar Hauxe, goldsmith.'

'Money-lender,' commented Leishal with disapproval.

'Quite so.' Mistal smiled without humour. 'According to the advocate who shares his rooms, Premeller's just defaulted on the interest for the second quarter running, but for some reason he hasn't suffered the bruising that kept him in bed for most of Equinox.'

'Why does Hauxe want Premeller snapping at our heels?' Fresil barked. 'We've never done business with the man.'

'Hauxe rents premises by the quarter from Aymer Saffan,' continued Mistal, 'who leases them by the five-year from Tor Bezaemar.'

'Which proves nothing,' Leishal grunted.

'Saffan has just granted Hauxe a season's exemption on his rent,' offered Mistal.

'You'll never trace that back to Tor Bezaemar,' Fresil scoffed.

'Indeed.' Ustian was considering this news. 'I could imagine a handful of explanations before implicating another noble House in deliberate malice.'

Training in the courts made Mistal equal to this. 'Would any of those alternatives explain Premeller's unexpected hostility to D'Olbriot? Has he ever shown any predilection for honourable disinterest?'

The Sieur raised his hand and everyone fell silent.

'Ryshad, introduce your other visitor,' Camarl prompted.

'This is Eadit.' I tried to put some reassurance in my voice. 'He works for the person who helped us secure the stolen artefacts.'

'Speak, boy!' barked Leishal.

Eadit cleared his throat nervously. 'I came to tell you Fenn Queal was visited yesterday morning by a valet recently dismissed by Tor Bezaemar. That valet's been seen drinking with one Malafy Skern, a pensioner from Tor Bezaemar's service. That's all I know.'

Camarl spoke up at once. 'I passed on Esquire D'Alsennin's

concerns to the Sieur yesterday.' His intent look forbade me to pursue the matter in Eadit's hearing. 'Advocate, Master Eadit, you have our thanks.'

Messire dismissed both with a gesture and Mistal hustled Eadit out of the room.

'More conjecture and gossip,' scowled Ustian.

'We can't set any of this before the court,' Fresil agreed.

'You cannot in all conscience ignore this,' said Avila with rising ire. 'In the Old Empire such weight of suspicion would have been enough to call out your Cohorts against Tor Bezaemar!'

'We have different fields of combat in this day and age,' Fresil said sharply. 'Never fear, Demoiselle, we'll set as much before Imperial justice as we can when the sessions resume after Festival. In the meantime we can take other steps against Tor Bezaemar, and who knows, sufficient provocation may prompt them to betray themselves.

'That would lend weight to our arguments,' agreed Leishal to general approval.

'If your Emperor declares against them in this court?' Temar folded his arms abruptly. 'Will that curb their malice?'

'We'll have won a significant battle,' said Ustian with a smile of amusement.

'Not the war?' persisted Temar.

'That will take a little longer.' But Leishal's dour words made it clear the outcome wasn't in question.

'That's our concern, not yours, D'Alsennin.' The Sieur spoke for the first time. 'You're to be congratulated on recovering your artefacts.'

'I could not have done so without Ryshad,' Temar said pointedly.

'Quite so.' The Sieur's bland face was unreadable. 'And now you can prepare to celebrate your good fortune at the Emperor's dance.' He smiled at Avila, who raised a sceptical eyebrow. 'My lady Channis will run through the etiquette.' Courteous as it was, Messire's dismissal was unmistakable.

'I must secure that bag first,' said Avila. 'If you are finally letting your tenantry inside your walls, Ostrin knows who might slip in unnoticed with theft on their minds.'

'As you see fit. Channis awaits your convenience.' Messire's face showed none of the indignation darkening Fresil's face beside him.

Camarl rang the bell to summon the doorkeeper. I moved to follow Temar.

'Where are you going, Ryshad?' barked Ustian.

I turned back, opting for silence as the safest response.

'Sit down, Ryshad,' Messire invited. I took a chair by the table as the door closed behind me.

'If you recovered D'Alsennin's spoils for him, you must know who stole them.' Camarl leaned forward. 'Why isn't he chained in the gatehouse?'

'His name is Jacot, and if I'd been able I'd have dragged him here by his heels,' I answered readily. 'But Temar and I would've had to fight through twice our number to do that. I'd have risked it with another sworn or chosen, but I wasn't about to chance D'Alsennin.'

'So he escapes to boast he robbed D'Olbriot and lived to tell the tale,' snapped Ustian.

'Why didn't you take enough men to capture this thief?' the Sieur asked mildly.

'I thought discretion more important than a show of strength,' I replied steadily.

'There's blood on your boots, Ryshad,' Messire pointed out. 'Someone spilled it. Granted I don't see you or Temar wounded, but you'd have been safer with sworn swords around you.'

'I didn't want to risk the safety of the person who betrayed the thief to me,' I said, shutting my mouth on further explanation.

'Who seems remarkably well informed as to the vermin crawling round this city's underbelly,' Messire observed. 'I take it we're talking about that Lescari lad's employer?

I nodded.

'Will you tell me who this is, if I ask?' the Sieur enquired casually.

'I will but I would ask you not to ask.' I looked straight at him. 'If we compromise that person's safety, we can't expect help from that quarter again. We recovered the Kellarin artefacts, Messire. I judged that more important than bringing the thief before your justice.'

'Did you?' Fresil plainly disagreed. 'Young Temar holds your oath now, does he?'

I kept my eyes on the Sieur. 'I serve D'Olbriot in serving D'Alsennin.'

The Sieur's smile came and went. 'I don't want to curb your initiative, Ryshad, but I said you were to inform myself or Camarl of such plans. I'm surprised I failed to make myself clear.'

I looked at the expensive carpet. 'I'm sorry, Messire.'

'I also thought I'd made it plain D'Alsennin was to fulfil the obligations of the rank he assumes.' Messire's voice got colder. 'You knew he was dining with Den Castevin.'

I stared at the Sieur's diamond-studded shoe buckles.

'Enough of this,' snorted Leishal crossly. 'What are we going to do about Tor Bezaemar?'

'We buy their timber for props and for charcoal for the Layne mines,' said Ustian promptly. 'Den Ferrand has land over that way that could supply us instead.'

'Tor Bezaemar hides keep our tanneries in Moretayne supplied,' Fresil mused. 'Could Den Cascadet pick up that trade without too much loss to ourselves?'

'We could split it between them and Den Gaerit,' suggested Ustian.

'What about closer to home?' Leishal demanded. 'Where are Tor Bezaemar holdings in Toremal in relation to our own?'

'Myred, the city plans.' The Sieur snapped his fingers at his son before glancing at me. 'What are you waiting for?'

'Your orders, Messire,' I said politely.

'Would you take them, if I gave them?' he asked lightly. 'I'm sorry, that was unworthy of us both.' He sighed. 'Finish this Festival as you started it, Ryshad, watching over D'Alsennin. You'd better attend him to the Emperor's dance.

Irianne will be there to distract Camarl, so we want someone watching Temar's back.'

Camarl looked up, startled, as he unrolled a detailed plan of the northern side of the bay.

'Never mind that.' Leishal was bending over the parchment. 'Look here, we own the road that gives access to all these Tor Bezaemar holdings.'

'So we do.' Fresil smiled with happy malevolence. 'I'm sure it's time we levied a toll thereabouts to pay for remaking the roadbed?'

'Those are mostly tapestry weavers in that district?' The Sieur stood and turned his back on me, taking a ledger from a shelf and leafing through it. 'Camarl, make sure none of our spinning mills deliver yarn to any Tor Bezaemar addresses from now on.'

I left, closing the door softly behind me.

'So they didn't skin you for a hearth rug, then?' The footman waiting in the corridor gave me a nod.

'Not this time.' I walked swiftly away. If the inner house servants knew I was in trouble, I'd really fouled my own nest. Where would Temar be, I wondered, dutifully learning etiquette from Lady Channis or intent on his own concerns? Heading for the library, I heard him in heated discussion with Avila from the turn of the corridor. At least I'd won that wager with myself. I knocked.

'Enter,' Avila snapped. She sat at the table, artefacts spread out before her, running a pointed fingernail down her list.

'What did the Sieur want with you?' asked Temar.

'To remind me where my oath rests.' I looked at Avila. 'Is everything there?'

'Thus far.' She looked up at me. 'What plot is Guliel hatching with those brothers of his?'

I rubbed a hand over my face and wished for a shave. 'As close to outright war with Tor Bezaemar as he can manage, without actually calling out the barracks.'

'On Temar's unsupported word?' Avila hushed his indignation with a curt word.

'The Sieur and Esquires must have their own reasons for suspecting Tor Bezaemar's ill faith,' I told her. 'I can't imagine they'd be doing this otherwise.' I wondered what the Sieur knew that the rest of us didn't.

'What are they doing?' Temar demanded.

'Wherever their businesses touch on each other, wherever Tor Bezaemar holdings or tenants rely on D'Olbriot services, the Sieur and Esquires will find ways to make Tor Bezaemar feel the shoe pinching. They'll break contracts if they can, refuse to buy or sell, deny Tor Bezaemar men passage over D'Olbriot lands, refuse carriage for Tor Bezaemar goods in D'Olbriot ships.'

'Will D'Olbriot interests not suffer? Will Tor Bezaemar not retaliate?' protested Avila.

'Fresil and Ustian will make sure Tor Bezaemar losses outweigh any D'Olbriot suffering.' I sighed. 'But it won't do the tenantry of either House any favours.'

'What does this mean for us?' Temar wanted to know.

'For Kellarin? You wanted less interference in your affairs, didn't you?' I queried. 'D'Olbriot's certainly going to be too busy with this to tell you how to run your colony.'

'We will be caught up in this regardless.' Temar looked at me. 'And if Tor Bezaemar or their allies believe hurting Kel Ar'Ayen will hurt D'Olbriot?'

'Any artefacts we still seek at once become pieces on this game board.' Avila was pale with anger.

I had no answer to that.

'These Sieurs, these Esquires, they can do this?' Temar began pacing round the room. 'Has your Emperor no power? Even Nemith the Whorestruck knew better than to let two Houses break each other's horns like this! His decree to end a quarrel was law.'

'A decision in the Imperial Courts should cut a lot of this short,' I offered.

'When?' Temar flung an impatient question at me. 'Aft-Summer? For-Autumn? This year? Next?'

'Who's to say your courts deliver justice, when Raeponin

is denied?' Avila was packing the artefacts back into their coffer with rapid, angry hands. 'When nothing holds a House's mouthpiece to the truth but their unsupported word?'

I was about to protest, at least on Mistal's behalf, when a footman followed a brisk tap on the door.

'My lady Channis sends her compliments,' he said as hastily as was polite. 'She invites you to attend her as soon as convenient.'

'My compliments to Lady Channis, and we will be there as soon as suits.' Avila barely managed not to vent her anger on the hapless servant. 'Find the mage Casuel Devoir and send him to D'Alsennin's chamber.'

The footman left with alacrity and I didn't blame him. Avila headed for the door. 'You two, bring that.'

Temar and I carried the coffer between us, following Avila up the backstairs, sharing a puzzled look. We'd barely reached Temar's opulent room when Casuel came hurrying along the corridor. 'Demoiselle, Esquire,' he puffed. 'How can I be of service?'

Avila stalked into Temar's chamber and looked around with disfavour. 'Where best to hide something? Under the bed?'

'The first place someone would look.' I was glad to let Temar give the obvious answer.

Avila smiled thinly. 'Then that is the place we want. Put it underneath.'

'But—'

'Master Mage.' Avila cut through Casuel's protest with a voice like steel. 'Can you make this box invisible?'

Casuel thought for a moment. 'Weaving an illusion of empty space might be more effective.'

'As you see fit, it is your magic.' Avila looked impatient as Casuel waited, smiling hopefully. 'At once, if you please.'

'Of course.' Casuel dropped to his knees and threw a dizzying burst of magic beneath the bed, azure shifting to jade and blending to startling sunset hues. I blinked as the afterglow faded slowly from my eyes.

'I should have done this before,' muttered Avila, pulling

up a stool. She sat down and drew a deep breath, laying her hands on the cream and crimson silk coverlet. 'Zal aebanne tris aeda lastrae.' She repeated the invocation, each time more softly until her words were a mere hint of a whisper in the rapt silence of the room.

'Suspecting Elietimm malice looking over our shoulders every time we use Artifice, we hesitate to do the most obvious things,' she said crossly. 'Master Devoir, has my enchantment affected your magic at all?'

Casuel bent down to peer under the bed and I couldn't resist doing the same. All I saw was empty carpet.

'Not at all, my lady.' Casuel stood up. 'What have you done?'

Avila smiled thinly. 'Laid an aversion over the bed and beneath it. Anyone not knowing the coffer is there will have no interest in looking. Anyone searching for it will dismiss such an obvious hiding place with contempt.'

'A fascinating combination of the two schools of magic,' Casuel looked intrigued. 'What—'

'Now let us see what Lady Channis thinks she can tell us about etiquette.' I hoped Lady Channis was equal to Avila's belligerence. Temar and I dutifully followed the Demoiselle and Casuel came scurrying after us.

'I suppose I'll have to bespeak Planir,' he was muttering. 'To tell him about your latest successes.'

'And your working magecraft to complement Avila's Artifice,' I pointed out.

Lady Channis's apartments are on the cool north side of the residence, furnished with all the elegance Den Veneta coin can buy. The lackey ushered us all in, assuming Casuel and I were both in attendance, and we couldn't retreat before two minor Demoiselles of the Name curtseyed themselves out, the door closing behind them.

'Demoiselle, Esquire, a tisane?' Lady Channis was wearing a simple cream chamber gown but her maid had already dressed her ebony hair high with amethyst-tipped pins. A naturally spare frame and the finest unguents lent her the appearance of youth. At second glance you would see the fine lines of age in her hands and neck but by then she'd have captured you with her charm.

I took a seat by the wall and Casuel did the same. Temar and Avila joined Lady Channis around a low table set with finest porcelain, crystal spice bowls and a small copper urn piping hot over a spirit lamp. The silver spoons and tisane balls marked with the Den Veneta sheaf of arrows gleamed with the soft lustre of antiquity. 'Ryshad? Master Devoir?'

Casuel jumped up with an obsequious bow as she turned deceptively soft brown eyes on us. 'My lady.'

'Your father is a pepper merchant, I believe?' Beauty had brought Lady Channis a long way from the minor House she'd been born in, and intelligence had carried her further still.

Casuel's smile became a little fixed as he selected spices for his tisane. 'He is, my lady, of Orelwood.'

'And your brother is the famous Amalin.' Lady Channis offered Temar a bowl of shredded citrus zest, ruby and enamel rings dark on her pale fingers. 'Your mother must be very proud of such talented sons.'

Casuel hesitated. 'Naturally, my lady.'

Channis filled Avila's cup with hot water and reached for Casuel's. 'So, Ryshad, what's your Sieur doing now?'

'He and the Esquires are planning to chastise Tor Bezaemar for their apparent hostility.' I filled my own tisane ball with a simple mixture of elder and sourcurrant.

'You can rely on the Sieur's judgement.' Lady Channis's dark eyes were shrewd in her flawless maquillage.

'I take it he acts on more than the suspicions Temar raised yesterday and the few things we learned this morning,' said Avila speculatively.

'Doubtless.' Lady Channis handed me my drink and waved Casuel and me back to our seats. 'Den Veneta will be sorely exposed in any clash with Tor Bezaemar, I'm sorry to say. That'll make things very awkward between Guliel and my cousins. But that's a problem for another day.' She shook her elegantly coiffed head. 'We're here to talk about the Imperial dance. In your day, I understand the last day of Festival was set aside for Imperial decrees? Well, Tadriol will certainly announce new betrothals, any major project a Name might be undertaking, but the emphasis is mostly on pleasure.'

I let her gentle voice fade into the background murmur of the busy residence. People all around were hurrying to ready everything before noon brought the commonalty into the residence and the nobility took their carriages to the Imperial Palace. I ran through the crowded events of the last few days in my mind. How might D'Olbriot's determination to attack Tor Bezaemar clash with D'Alsennin and Kellarin interests? Was there any way to head off such friction? Hadn't Temar said something about Artifice being a better means of achieving some aim than brute force?

I looked over to see him paying close attention to Lady Channis.

'It's been the custom, oh, since the days of Inshol the Curt that all rank is left outside the doors of an Imperial dance, along with hats and swords. No one's allowed to insist on deference and precedence, that kind of thing. Naturally any Esquire will treat any Sieur with due courtesy, that much distinction must be preserved but the erstwhile Imperial Houses aren't allowed to look down on lesser Names. You'll stand or sit as a lady pleases, of course, but there's none of this nonsense about Houses of lower degree having to wait until a senior Name decides to take the weight off his feet.' Lady Channis smiled as she ticked off points from a mental list on her beautifully manicured fingers.

'Keep your voice to a polite level otherwise the noise gets simply deafening. If you must debate some point or other, do it without anger or passion and naturally, if someone's boring you senseless, you'll oblige us all by not letting that show. You'll also do yourself more credit if you avoid boring anyone else. In general, I'd advise you to guard your own tongue and if you encounter anyone being indiscreet, do them the courtesy of not repeating what you hear, well, not outside the doors of the dance salon.' A fleeting smile softened her words.

'There'll be plenty to eat and drink but I can't imagine you need me telling you not to over-indulge.'

'I think I should be able to avoid disgracing myself,' said Temar politely but I could hear irritation beneath his words.

'These may be unwritten rules, Esquire, but there are penalties for infringing them,' Lady Channis told him firmly. 'If two or more people accuse you of indecorous behaviour, you'll be asked to pay a forfeit. It's quite a game in the normal run of things but with all that's going on, I'll wager my tisane spoons some scion of Den Thasnet or Tor Priminale will be only too eager to make you look a fool.'

'What would this forfeit be?' Demoiselle Avila demanded curtly.

'Since the days of Tadriol the Staunch's Maitresse, poetry has been the usual penalty.' Lady Channis waved a hand. 'Reciting the first few stanzas of *The Edicts of Perinal the Bold* is a favourite sentence. A serious offence can merit all three verses of *The Death of Decabral the Eager*. If you really tread on someone's hem, you could find yourself reciting *Drianon's Hymn to the Harvest* to the entire room.'

'I do not know any of those.' Temar shook his head cautiously.

'Which would make your humiliation complete, would it not?' Avila looked grim as Lady Channis continued.

Movement beside me prompted a glance for Casuel, who was listening avidly. His smugness suggested he knew all the relevant poems and epics. I remembered the mage's own ambitions to rank. What of other wizards with less narrow preoccupations? What would Planir do to protect his own concerns? How might his actions impact on D'Olbriot? How would Hadrumal seek to influence a quarrel between the Names that ruled the Empire? What could the Emperor do? Nemith the Last and his forebears might have ruled from the ocean to the Great Forest by unquestioned decree, but Emperors in this age have a different notion of justice. I pondered the bits and pieces of legal lore Mistal had bored me with when he'd first started his studies.

That led my thoughts to Hansey and Ridner. It wasn't only minor Names like Den Veneta who'd suffer once each Name dragged their allies into this struggle. My brothers are D'Olbriot tenants, but they buy their stone from Den Rannion quarries. Skirmishes over goods and services would break out from the Ast Marsh to the Cape of Winds, and people ill fitted to bear the losses would suffer first. I closed my eyes as I sought a way through this maze.

'That's all we need to know?' Avila's faint sarcasm roused me from trying to tease out all the potential consequences of a plan irresistibly forming in my mind.

'My thanks, my lady.' Temar shot Avila an unexpected look of reproof.

Avila smoothed her skirts as she rose. 'And now I have another chance to see how many different gowns one woman can wear in the same day.'

'May I take a moment of your time?' I stood, hands laced behind my back, formal stance stiffening my resolve.

Lady Channis smiled. 'Ryshad?'

I took a deep breath. Some ideas look perfectly convincing inside your own head and then sound like drooling idiocy once you try to explain them.

'We're sure, aren't we, that Tor Bezaemar's the House orchestrating hostility to D'Olbriot and D'Alsennin? But we can't prove it to the satisfaction of the courts.' I hesitated. 'The courts are the formal setting for the Emperor's justice but his authority as arbiter still applies anywhere, just as it did before the Chaos. Custom demands the Emperor hears every argument before he makes a decree, but there's nothing binding him to that. Tadriol could simply announce a verdict if he had sufficient weight of evidence to tip the scales.'

'The Emperor's word was law in our day.' Avila sat down again.

'What if we could prove Tor Bezaemar's enmity to the Emperor directly?' I looked at Lady Channis. 'Tadriol could act in support of D'Olbriot without waiting for the courts to grind every parchment into dust. The longer this quarrel drags on, the worse the consequences for everyone, from noble Names to commonalty. Tadriol is sworn to defend all ranks, isn't he?'

'He won't want open strife between D'Olbriot and Tor Bezaemar,' said Lady Channis slowly. 'Not if it can be avoided.'

'Would your Houses accept an Imperial decree cutting through all this convoluted argument before the court?' Temar asked Lady Channis hopefully.

'Given the consequences to the minor Houses if Tor Bezaemar and D'Olbriot go for each other's throats?' She looked pensive. 'Most would back an Imperial decree, if only to save their own Names.'

'We know Malafy Skern is still a favoured retainer of the Relict Tor Bezaemar,' I said slowly. 'She has to be involved.'

'No one drops a hairpin in that House without her knowing,' Lady Channis agreed.

'What if we could get her to betray what she knows?' I suggested.

'In front of witnesses?' She shook her head. 'She'd never do it, and in any case witnesses can always be discredited.'

'What if she didn't think there were witnesses? What if she were provoked into boasting or threatening?' I persisted. 'What if the Emperor heard her for himself?'

Lady Channis looked puzzled. 'You plan to provoke her to some indiscretion with the Emperor hiding behind a door like some maid in a bad masquerade?'

'Dirindal is too sharp for that, Rysh,' said Temar, disappointed.

'What if Artifice were prompting her to speak without her usual care?' I tried to ignore the qualms in my belly. 'What if she were alone with you, my lady, confident anything you claimed could be denied? There are enough rumours flying around the city; it wouldn't be unusual for you to discuss them with her?'

'Tor Bezaemar must still think themselves secure,' Temar said unexpectedly. 'They have no reason to believe we suspect their malice.'

'They'll know by the end of the day, if I know Guliel,' said Lady Channis rather sadly.

'Dirindal would be keen to know what the Sieur is thinking,' I suggested.

'If she were annoyed, Artifice would be all the more effective in urging her to speak her mind,' Avila observed.

Lady Channis waved her hands impatiently. 'How does it help to have Dirindal admit anything to me, however incriminating? It would be my word against hers, and I'm hardly an impartial witness.'

'The Emperor could see and hear it all if a mage worked the right magics,' I told her. 'Dirindal would never know.'

Lady Channis gaped at me.

'Scrying is mere sight without sound.' Casuel was frowning in thought. 'It could be done with bespeaking, but you'd need another mage with her ladyship as well as one with the Emperor.'

'We've Allin and Velindre to call on,' I pointed out. 'Either or both could help. Planir won't disagree, if it means we can head off this strife.'

'I would have to be close at hand, to work the Artifice on Dirindal,' said Avila slowly.

'Dirindal will never betray herself in front of three witnesses,' said Lady Channis flatly.

'Couldn't you be in the next room, Demoiselle?' I persisted. 'Out of sight?'

Avila thought for a moment. 'Yes, I believe so. Master Mage?'

Casuel nodded eagerly. 'A short distance would be no hindrance.'

Lady Channis shook her head in disbelief. 'It's a fascinating fancy, Ryshad, but it's completely irrational. How could we ever do it? Dirindal will suspect eyes and ears behind every curtain and closed door if she comes here, and I'm certainly not going to Tor Bezaemar's residence. I'd be seen, and when word gets out of hostility between the Houses that would prompt all manner of rumours weakening Guliel.'

'Can't you meet on neutral ground?' Temar asked impatiently.

'A dressmakers?' suggested Casuel hopefully. 'A jewellers?'

'Such people come to us, Master Devoir, we don't travel to them.' Lady Channis's words were kindly meant but Casuel still blushed to the roots of his hair.

I cast my mind back to my early sworn days attending the minor Demoiselles of the House. Where had they gone to gossip free from the discreet supervision of their elders? 'A feather merchant?'

'That's believable, at least.' Lady Channis smiled wryly. 'The cursed things come to grief so easily, we're always buying them at the last minute.'

'And even Maitresses of a Name have to go to the merchants, since none of them will risk hawking such fragile and precious wares from residence to residence,' I nodded.

'Is there a feather merchant where Dirindal would meet you?' Temar demanded of Channis.

'Masters Anhash and Norn,' Lady Channis replied with a mocking tone. 'Simply the only place for plumes this Festival, my child.' Faint optimism sounded in her voice for the first time. 'Where every noble customer is shown the choicest selection in a private room.'

'It has to be worth trying,' I urged. 'Outright enmity between D'Olbriot and Tor Bezaemar will serve no one.'

'True,' agreed Lady Channis. 'But if we're to try this madness, we've precious little time. Battle lines between the Houses will be drawn by nightfall.'

'Then send the Relict Tor Bezaemar some message enticing her to meet you at once, my lady.' I ticked off points on my fingers. 'We need you, Avila and Velindre at the feather merchant's before Dirindal arrives. Then we three need to convince the Emperor to listen to us.' I looked at Casuel, whose face was a potent mix of eagerness and apprehension. 'And we need some way of knowing when exactly Casuel needs to work his magic.'

'Allin could send word,' suggested Temar.

'I can't see you getting an audience with Tadriol, a scant half-morning before the biggest social event of Festival.' Lady Channis wasn't trying to make difficulties, but that was true.

I looked at Temar. 'You've not met the Emperor yet, have you? This isn't the ideal time, but I don't suppose anyone will gainsay you if you ask to introduce yourself. I'm sure you could claim a Sieur's right of immediate access to the Imperial presence.'

Lady Channis was crossing the room to an open writing case laid on a side table. 'You could cite that before the courts later on, if the Palace acknowledges you as such.'

'If that is what we need to do, to get before Tadriol, that he may see the magic.' Temar was looking nervous. 'But you will explain it all, Ryshad, when we see Tadriol. This is your idea after all.'

'He hasn't the rank to propose something like this to the Emperor!' Casuel was appalled.

'And he's sworn to D'Olbriot,' Lady Channis was writing rapidly. 'You owe no allegiance, Temar, for all your close ties with the House.' She sealed her note with perfumed wax.

'You're defending your own Name and your people in Kellarin,' I reminded Temar. 'The Emperor will respect that far more than any claim I might make to disinterest. We'll both be there to back you up, but you have to be the one doing the talking.'

'You do realise Dirindal may not come?' Lady Channis looked up. 'If she does, she may have nothing to say but platitudes and nonsense. You risk looking an utter fool, you do know that?'

'Compared to the risks we've run over the last few days, my lady, I think we can take this chance,' I assured her.

The Imperial Palace of Tadriol the Provident, Summer Solstice Festival, Fifth Day, Late Morning

'Cheer up, the worst they can do is refuse to let us in.'

Temar tried to smile at Ryshad's attempt at reassurance but saw the doubt shadowing the older man's eyes.

'With you so impressive in your livery and me in all this finery?' he retorted with considerably more bravado than he felt. 'Never fear, I do not intend returning to Avila with my tail between my legs.'

'All we need now is Cas,' Ryshad muttered. The carriage halted with a lurch that redoubled the nervousness plaguing Temar's stomach. What if the mage was delayed? What if he'd been unable to find Allin and Velindre?

'So this is the Imperial Palace,' Temar said softly as he stepped down from the carriage. It was a fair cry from the robust fortress Nemith and his forebears had held in trust as a last bulwark of noble power. Waist-high walls meant every passer-by could see the extensive gardens, though the narrow spaced railings were topped with vicious spikes curved in outward-facing claws. A small gatehouse of brilliant white stone gave a small detachment of liveried men-at-arms some shade from the sun hammering down from a cloudless sky. They were the only people in view.

'Where is everyone?' Temar asked, bemused. 'Do Tor Tadriol not gather as a family for Festival?'

'Not here they don't. This place is purely ceremonial. Their residence is over beyond the Saerlmar.' Ryshad fell into step a pace behind Temar. 'Remember, you're not asking the guard to let you pass. You're telling him you're going in.'

'Not without Casuel,' retorted Temar. About to wipe sweaty palms on the skirts of his coat, he realised that would mark the silk and reached for a kerchief. 'Where is he?'

'Over there.' Ryshad sounded relieved but Temar silently cursed the mage. If he had a little longer perhaps he could prepare himself a little more. 'What in the name of all that's holy is the fool wearing?'

Ryshad disconcerted did nothing to soothe Temar's qualms but the sight of Casuel in a long gold-brocaded brown robe raised a reluctant smile. 'That is the style the mages of Hadrumal wear, I believe, when they feel the need for ceremony.'

'It's the style everyone's great-grandsire wore on his deathbed hereabouts,' muttered Ryshad. 'Oh well, it'll distract the guard if nothing else.'

Casuel was walking rather too fast for the length of his garment, the cloth catching around his knees and ankles. 'Are we ready?'

'You tell me,' Temar demanded in sharper tones than he'd intended.

'Lady Channis and Demoiselle Tor Arrial are at the feather merchant's,' Casuel confirmed hastily. 'Velindre and Allin are on their way, and Allin will send word as soon as the Relict arrives. If she arrives.'

'Lady Channis seemed certain she would,' Ryshad reminded the wizard.

'I wonder what was in that note.' Realising the mage was even more nervous than he was put perverse heart into Temar. 'You look very formal.'

'Velindre suggested people will take us more seriously if I reminded them I've the power of Hadrumal behind me,' Casuel said with a sickly smile that soon faded. 'I'm sure she'll claim the credit for this with Planir, if it works. You'll put him right, won't you?'

Temar stifled a curt response. 'What now, Ryshad?'

'We have to be with the Emperor when we get Allin's message,' the chosen man frowned. 'It won't take the Relict long to get to the feather merchant, and we can't risk not hearing all the conversation.'

Temar saw the others were both looking expectantly at him. 'What do I say to the guards?'

'You're acting as Sieur of a House,' Casuel said acerbically. 'You need explain yourself to no one, least of all a gateward.'

Temar drew a deep breath and walked towards the iron gates. Ryshad's solid footfalls behind him were some reassurance, though Casuel's hesitant steps made him worry the mage was going to tread on his heels at any moment.

'Fair Festival.' Ryshad took a pace to the side to address the sentry. 'Make your obeisance to Temar D'Alsennin.'

'Fair Festival, Esquire, my duty to you.' The man bowed briefly, eyes never leaving Temar's face.

'Fair Festival.' Temar smiled graciously. 'I wish to see the Emperor.'

'Are you expected?' asked the guard politely.

'As senior surviving member of my House, I claim the rights of a Sieur,' Temar said just before Ryshad's prompting cough. 'That includes immediate access to the Imperial presence.'

The guard bowed again. 'Indeed.' Face impassive, he beckoned a sworn man waiting alert in the doorway of the gatehouse. 'Escort the D'Alsennin to the Steward.' He nodded at Ryshad and Casuel. 'Do you vouch for your companions?'

'Naturally.' Temar realised the guard was still looking at him expectantly. 'Chosen man Ryshad Tathel, of D'Olbriot, and Casuel Devoir, wizard of Hadrumal.'

The man's expression did not flicker. 'They may enter on your surety.'

Temar turned to see Ryshad unbuckling his sword-belt and moved a hand towards his own before Ryshad's minatory frown stopped him.

'Are you armed, Master Mage?' The guard looked warily at Casuel.

The wizard smiled with a superior air. 'Only with my skills.'

The guard looked dubious and glanced at Temar. 'Do I have your oath you'll keep him in check?'

'Poldrion be my witness.' Temar spoke loudly to cover some indignant noise from Casuel. He turned his head briefly to see the wizard rubbing a sore arm while Ryshad looked blandly ahead.

'This way, if you please.' The second guard walked ahead of them through the blazing colours of the gardens. Temar noticed inconsequentially that the paths were not carpeted with gravel but with crushed seashells and wondered why.

The shade cast by the north front of the palace offered welcome relief from the sun. It was a wide building rather than a tall one, only two stories above a cellar floor whose half-windows were shaded by deep arches at ground level. Steps down to the basement in the centre of the frontage were framed by a double stair curving up from the path to meet before double doors standing open. A spacious portico shaded steps and entrance, rising on faceted pillars to meet the roofline. Broad windows were set at regular intervals on either side, muslin blinds half drawn.

'When was this built?' Temar asked without thinking.

The man looked at him uncertainly. 'When Den Tadriol ascended to the throne.'

Once through the open door Temar found they were in a square room rising the full height of the building. Their escort was speaking to a man sitting behind a table set precisely in the centre of the grey and white chequer of the marble floor.

'D'Alsennin to see the Emperor, as of Sieur's right.' The guard leaned closer but the echoing room amplified his words. 'He's got a wizard with him.'

Temar couldn't resist a glance at Casuel, who was visibly preening himself. Ryshad was as stony-faced as the statues flanking the iron-balustered stair rising to the upper floor.

The Steward dismissed the man at arms and rose from his seat. 'Fair Festival to you, D'Alsennin.'

'Fair Festival.' Temar fixed the man with his best imitation of his grandsire's piercing gaze. 'I wish to see the Emperor.'

The Steward was a tall man, sparse grey hair clipped short and face mild above the Tadriol badge at his collar. He took a moment to answer. 'It's hardly convenient.'

Temar wondered if that was a refusal or merely a hint he'd be well advised to take. Either way, he ignored it. 'I appreciate the Emperor must be very busy, but I have to see him.'

'His highness will be at leisure this evening,' the Steward offered.

'I cannot wait,' Temar said firmly.

'He is preparing for the dance.' They could waste half the morning in these futile exchanges, Temar realised. He wondered how to shake the man out of his courteous obstruction. Then he realised the man was wearing a golden bull's head with enamelled horns and eyes set with chips of black opal.

'I must have approval for an insignia, before noon, that I may wear it at the dance.' Temar looked the Steward in the eye and hoped it wasn't too obvious he'd just thought of the excuse.

The Steward took a pace back and bowed. 'If you'll await the Emperor's convenience.' He walked briskly up the broad staircase without a backward glance.

'We wait here.' Ryshad indicated the maroon velvet chairs lining the walls.

Temar sat and looked at the portraits hung in regular lines framed by plaster moulding. 'So which one's your Tadriol?'

Ryshad nodded to a youthful figure holding a horse in front of the portico they'd just come through. 'Tadriol the Provident.'

'Fifth of his line, as you recall.' Casuel couldn't resist reminding Temar. 'Tadriol the Thrifty built this palace.'

'Does that happen every time there is a change of Name?' Temar looked at the mage. No wonder these Houses were all so obsessed with coin, if highest honour came at such a heavy price.

'It's only since Inshol the Curt that the Old Palace was turned over to the law courts,' Ryshad remarked. 'Tor Bezaemar built themselves a new palace but they weren't about to hand it over to Den Tadriol when they lost the throne.'

Casuel leaned forward in his chair. 'Tadriol the Vigilant wanted to build somewhere open to the populace, noble and common. One of the reasons Tor Bezaemar were deposed was their inclination to hold themselves aloof.' The wizard warmed to his theme. 'The Relict's late husband was caught up in quite a scandal in his youth. The House raised their rents at every Festival one year, not just at Winter Solstice, so when Solstice came round again a mob of their tenants turned up and pelted anyone bearing the Name with copper coin any time they showed their face. They claimed to be paying their dues, but—'

Temar turned to Ryshad. 'Is this place always so empty?' The silence was eerily disconcerting after the constant mass of people swirling through the D'Olbriot residence.

Ryshad shook his head. 'You wouldn't get a seat here after mid-morning outside Festival, and that Steward would have twenty men backing him up. But today everyone's getting ready for the dance.'

'The Emperor can hardly be polishing the silverware. Why isn't he free to see us?' demanded Casuel petulantly.

Temar turned his attention to statues set on plain white plinths between the paintings. Saedrin held his keys, Raeponin his balance, but a scaly snake curled round Poldrion's feet, head raised to the god's caressing hand. The beast's mouth was open to reveal disconcertingly sharp teeth. Temar wondered if that had any significance beyond idle decoration. He was ignorant of so much in this perplexing age.

He stared at the opposite wall, at the massed Sieurs of the House of Tadriol. All he could see in those varnished eyes was accusation. He was claiming to be their equal? Just what did he think he was Sieur of? Did he imagine he'd ever win respect, even if he did claw back some remnant of D'Alsennin lands? What difference would a few holm oak leaves make?

Temar gritted his teeth. They could judge him if they chose, but he would answer to his own conscience, his own values. D'Alsennin need not answer to any of these latterday Names. Even if this attempt to pull D'Olbriot's chestnuts out of the fire failed, he could return to Kel Ar'Ayen with his head held high. He'd recovered nigh on all the lost artefacts, hadn't he? He'd used Artifice in ways that would never have occurred to Guinalle, so she'd better not try putting him down as she was so apt to. A more beautiful, more intelligent woman than her hadn't scorned to take him to her bed and he'd acquitted himself creditably there as well.

'Are you ready?' Allin's distant voice startled Temar out of his reverie. He looked up to see a shimmering circle of air rippling in front of Casuel, Allin's homely face distorted as if through thick glass.

'We're still waiting for the Steward to take us to Tadriol,' said Casuel tartly.

'But the Relict's carriage has just pulled up.' Allin's anguish was clear if her image wasn't.

'We have to find the Emperor ourselves – now.' Temar was first to his feet, Ryshad a scant breath behind him.

'The backstairs are this way,' Ryshad pointed.

Casuel was winding the long sleeves of his robe round his hands in agonies. 'He'll call down the guard, we'll end up in chains—'

'You said I have the right to immediate audience.' Temar pulled Casuel to his feet. 'My grandsire says rights are like horses – useless unless you exercise them.'

'This way.' Ryshad opened a discreet door hidden beneath the grand stair. Temar dragged Casuel along by his stiff sleeve. They ran through empty marble corridors, down a long hall, up a flight of stairs.

A liveried servant on a stool beside a door looked at them in surprise.

'You're wanted below,' said Ryshad before the man could speak. 'The Sieur D'Alsennin has private business with the Emperor.'

Temar opened the door himself with as much authority as he could convey and strode into a small anteroom. Ryshad closed the door behind the lackey and wedged a chair back under the handle. 'In there.'

Temar clenched his fists before opening the plain single door. He found it a pleasant airy room hung with small paintings. A single band of floral moulding ran round the top of the walls but the room was otherwise plain white plaster, carpeted with thick bronze rugs. Walnut chairs softened with cushions in autumn hues were ranged to one side of a broad marquetry table, where a slightly built young man had been looking into a hand glass as he combed his hair into crisp waves, a jar of pomade to hand.

'What is this?' The habit of authority belied his simple shirt and plain brown broadcloth breeches.

'Esquire D'Alsennin, claiming Sieur's right to audience.' Temar bowed stiffly.

'Of course, I thought you looked familiar. But this is neither the time nor the place—'

The Emperor was already reaching for a silver hand bell resting on a stack of papers.

'Cas!' Temar snapped his fingers at the agonised wizard.

Casuel looked at him blankly but as the first note rang out he flung a handful of blue fire to knock the bell from Tadriol's hand. Documents fluttered in all directions as the bell toppled to the floor in uncanny silence.

The Emperor pushed his carved wooden chair backwards in visible consternation. 'I'll have your hide for that!'

'Forgive me,' stammered Casuel.

'Work your magic, wizard,' Temar ordered him urgently. 'Find Lady Channis.' He turned to the Emperor. 'We will explain ourselves presently, but I beg your indulgence.'

'It had better be a good explanation, D'Alsennin,' the Emperor retorted, wary eyes taking in every detail of his unexpected guests. 'You, D'Olbriot's man, does your Sieur know you're here?'

'Lady Channis does, highness,' Ryshad answered promptly. 'Messire is otherwise engaged.'

'Then what is so urgent—'

'I need something metal, something shiny.' Casuel looked vacantly around.

Ryshad grabbed a tray of glasses from a side table, dropping one in his haste. It shattered in a spray of crystal shards. 'Here.' He set the other goblets aside and threw the salver at Casuel who caught it as it hit him in the chest.

'I'll wait for my answers, shall I?' The Emperor's self-possession was returning. Nevertheless he unobtrusively retrieved his hand bell and set it on his desk in mute warning. 'But don't try my patience too long.'

'A candle?' Temar snatched a virgin taper from a small pot on the mantelshelf. He caught Casuel's arm and forced the wizard on to a chair facing the ornate table. Sweeping aside a clutter of letters, he thrust the taper at the wizard.

'Do you need a tinderbox?' asked the Emperor with faint courtesy. 'I take it you're one of the Archmage's underlings?'

'One of his associates, his liaison with D'Olbriot,' Casuel stopped to smile ingratiatingly. 'It has to be a conjured flame, your highness.'

'Then conjure it,' snapped Temar.

The mage snapped hesitant fingers, once, twice, but no scarlet magic flared to light the wick. Temar swallowed a curse and felt the blood pounding in his chest. A tentative knock sounded at the door and Ryshad moved to brace one booted foot firmly against the wood.

'You have done this often enough,' Temar encouraged the wizard in a tight voice. 'Even Allin can work thus.'

The taper spat a flicker of crimson fire, the spark strengthening to a modest flame. Temar handed Casuel the shiny tray. It rattled against the table as the mage's hand shook but a pinpoint of gold reflected steadily from the centre of the polished metal. It spread raggedly outwards like fire burning through paper, brilliant edges leaving a smoky void behind. Scars sparked across the emptiness like lightning splintering a stormy sky.

'It's Velindre,' Casuel said crossly. 'She's manipulating the spell from her end.'

'Then work with her, as best you can,' Temar urged him.

'She's not cooperating,' Casuel grumbled, but as he spoke

voices came out of the emptiness to echo round the silent room.

'My Lady Channis, I confess I was surprised to get your note.'

The Emperor looked at Temar, surprise and curiosity joining forces to win out over the last of his indignation. 'That sounds like Dirindal Tor Bezaemar.'

'Please look into the magic,' Temar begged. 'Then we will explain, I swear.'

The Emperor rose slowly from his chair to move behind Casuel. 'What's going on?'

Lady Channis was speaking. 'Granted gossip runs through this city like rabbits through corn but this particular rumour always seems to track back to your door.'

Temar looked into the magical reflection of distant reality. Lady Channis was sitting beside a round table covered with a plain white cloth where an array of gaudy feathers was carefully laid out for her inspection.

Dirindal Tor Bezaemar was standing by a fireplace filled with blue and purple flagflowers. 'I may have mentioned it, but only to try and find out who'd be saying such things.' Her genial face creased in a plump smile. 'Now I remember. That foolish Tor Sylarre girl was letting her tongue run away with her. I told her I didn't believe a word of it.'

Channis picked up a long grey plume banded with blue. 'That's curious, because Jinty Tor Sauzet is quite certain that you told her.'

'Talagrin himself couldn't tame Jinty's tongue.' The Relict's face turned a little weary. 'You know she was languishing after Kreve last year? Since he turned her down she's done all she can to make trouble for our House.'

'And what's Tor Bezaemar's excuse for brewing trouble for D'Olbriot?' Lady Channis laid down the grey feather and began examining a curling pink plume edged with black.

'My dear!' Dirindal sat down on a softly cushioned daybed.

Channis twisted in her chair to face the Relict. 'Jinty Tor Sauzet has no reason to tell all and sundry I'm about to leave Guliel and return to Den Veneta's protection. Den Muret on the other hand are plainly delighted to hear it.' Her tone was acid. 'I gather it has stiffened their resolve to pursue their case before the Imperial Court no end. Seladir Den Muret was telling Orilan Den Hefeken all about it, and Orilan told me. Seladir swears it must be true. After all, she had it from your own lips, and everyone knows you're as honest a woman as ever broke bread.'

Dirindal clasped beringed hands together. 'Orilan's a sweet child, but she's inclined to speak without thinking—'

'Don't,' said Channis bitingly. 'There's nothing you can say against Orilan, no threat you can use to silence her, no reason for her to lie. Our Houses have few dealings with Den Hefeken. How unlike Den Muret, whose roof would soon fall in without Tor Bezaemar bounty. Unlike Den Thasnet, whose wealth battens on your own like honeysuckle on a tree. Do you ask me to believe either House would attack D'Olbriot in the courts without Tor Bezaemar's approval?'

Dirindal's round face crumpled in distress. 'My dear, you must be mistaken. Let me talk to Haerel. He may have said something unwise, perhaps Den Muret mistook his meaning.'

'Do you seriously expect me to believe your nephew, Sieur Tor Bezaemar though he is, does anything without you knowing of it?' Channis flung the curled feathers down on the smooth linen. 'He barely wipes his arse without your permission.'

'My dear, I quite understand you're cross,' said Dirindal faintly. 'But I don't think I deserve these unwarranted accusations.' She fumbled in the silver net purse laced at her waist and dabbed her eyes with a lace trimmed kerchief.

The Emperor glared at Temar. 'I've no interest in hearing women scratching at each other's corn,' he whispered.

Casuel looked up. 'It's all right, they can't hear us.'

'Mind your magic, Cas,' snapped Temar, seeing the image waver and fade. 'This is no mere flurry in a hen coop, I swear.'

Lady Channis was making a careful selection of tiny iridescent emerald feathers. 'I took breakfast today with Avila Tor Arrial. She was telling me how you were encouraging young

D'Alsennin to secure his mother's portion from Tor Alder. She said how astonished he'd been to learn he even had such rights. But for Tor Alder to be ready to bring a case before the Emperor, they must have been convinced he knew, certain he'd be making a claim. If I go asking just who told them that, am I going to find your perfume hanging in the air?' Channis compared two feathers with a thoughtful eye. 'Then Avila told me about this business with the Kellarin artefacts. How she and Temar had looked to you for help before anyone else, explaining why they needed to trace such heirlooms. But you haven't helped, have you? First, you accept an invitation to dine with Den Turquand on the first day of Festival, such an honour for so minor a House. Then Camarl gets a note from that very Sieur telling him the heirlooms he wants will be sold to the highest bidder, and yesterday at the Den Murivance residence I learn Maitresse Tor Sylarre has been ransacking her daughter's jewel cases. She's accusing D'Olbriot of plans to use the courts to steal their wealth with some nonsensical tale of Kellarin's claims, I hear. You took lunch with her on the second day of Festival, I believe. Is that when she got this notion in her head?'

'Dast's teeth!' Involuntary anger escaped Temar.

'What's been going on?' The Emperor narrowed suspicious eyes at Temar.

'That is what we hope to learn.' He leaned closer to the image framed by the curlicues of the silver tray.

'You're full of accusations.' Dirindal was glaring at Channis, eyes dry and angry. 'Will Master Burquest be making such arguments before the court?'

Lady Channis laughed without humour. 'He could hardly build a case on such flimsy foundations. I suppose I should congratulate you on arranging everything so well.'

Dirindal opened her mouth but didn't speak, a puzzled frown deepening her wrinkles.

'It's just that I don't understand the depth of your anger,' Lady Channis continued smoothly. 'All our Houses are rivals, granted, but on the other side of the coin we're allies as well. We have to be, or lately come merchantry get ideas above their station; you told me as much when I was a girl.'

'They're doing that anyway, with the fool boy Tadriol encouraging their pretensions,' spat Dirindal.

Channis's hand shook with surprise and she dropped a feather to the floor. She bent to recover it. 'I know Guliel will be claiming the lion's share of Kellarin's bounty this year and probably next, but bear in mind all the costs the House has borne in recovering the colony. He'll soon see he needs to share the rewards to be had there.'

Temar gritted his teeth so loudly the Emperor looked at him.

'He'll allow us the crumbs that fall from his table, you mean?' said Dirindal sourly.

'That's hardly just,' Channis objected. 'Kellarin—'

'You think this is about Kellarin?' Dirindal interrupted in sudden, ugly fury. 'You think we have any interest in sorcery-addled paupers grubbing a living in muddy caves? I never thought to say it, Channis, but you're a fool!' She struggled to her feet and Temar's heart began to beat faster as the old woman crossed the room. She barely topped the sitting Channis by a head, and was easily a generation older, but rage lent speed to her feet and vigour to her gestures.

'Oh, it's about Kellarin, in so far as the wealth Guliel garners will extend his influence still further. He'll drop the sweetest plums into eager hands like some doting grandsire and the insignificant little Names will think D'Olbriot's so wonderful.' Dirindal's scorn was withering. 'Guliel will swan around, proud as a cob in springtime. All these dolts will be hanging on his coat tails whenever he goes before Tadriol – he'll give the lad a little advice here, some words of warning there. The boy won't dare ignore him; after all he speaks for so many. Guliel leads our so-called Emperor by the ring in his nose, just as he did his father, his uncles and grandsire.'

The Emperor gripped the back of Casuel's chair, the movement catching Temar's eye. An overlarge bull's head ring was Tadriol's only piece of jewellery, a battered golden antique secured by a fine black cord that looped up to tie round his wrist. Unlike the Steward's badge, this bull had no ring.

Lady Channis was protesting volubly. 'The House of D'Olbriot has only ever worked for the good of Tormalin. Guliel never uses his influence for selfish gain—'

'You expect me to believe that?' cried Dirindal. 'Oh, it's the quiet pigs that eat most fodder, my girl.'

'So this is about money,' said Channis with contempt.

'That's all Guliel's concerned with,' sneered Dirindal. 'Sending his nephews to dine with the merchantry, flattering their ambitions, telling Tadriol to listen to their whining. Saedrin save us, jumped-up draper's daughters are marrying into ancient Names with Tadriol's very blessing because their coffers of gold outweigh base blood! And all the while Houses with history back to Correl the Stout fall into rack and ruin because common parasites have leeched away their trade and prerogatives. Does Guliel do anything to restore the privilege of rank? Does D'Olbriot use any influence to stop the rot? No, he stands at Tadriol's shoulder and drips poisonous counsel in his ears and all the while his greedy little allies crowd round, drowning out wiser voices with their begging.'

'Would Haerel be offering better advice?' snapped Channis. 'Or Kreve? We all saw you encouraging him to invite Tadriol down to his fiefdom for last year's hunting season. I take it you're looking to sit your grandson on the steps of the throne in Guliel's place?'

'We should be sitting on that throne,' Dirindal hissed. 'I should be managing the marriage of an Emperor of my own blood, not worrying what slattern D'Olbriot's going to talk Tadriol into bedding. I should be an Emperor's Relict, with all the influence of a lifetime's rule. Don't think I don't know it was Guliel's uncle turned the Houses against my husband's claim, just as it's been Guliel and his brothers backing every Tadriol since. How else could those dolts hold the throne? How many more of them have to die before our House regains its rightful place? Well, it'll be different next time, when D'Olbriot's brought low and Tor Bezaemar can show the Names the true meaning of power.'

Temar saw Channis go as white as the linen covering the

table, even in the tiny image. Dirindal was leaning over her, rage twisting her hands in cruel claws. Channis gave a frantic push that sent the old woman stumbling backwards.

'Lay a hand on me and I'll scream!' Her frightened voice rang through the enchantment.

'Cas, tell Velindre to interrupt them.' Temar felt cold with apprehension.

'I can't, not without losing the spell,' said the mage tightly.

'Hold your magic, wizard,' ordered the Emperor, face grim. 'Channis can take her chances.'

But as Temar watched, nervousness making him nauseous, Dirindal walked slowly back to the far side of the room. She smoothed the skirts of her modest gown and ran a plump hand over her undisturbed coiffeur. When she turned her face was settled once more in amiable lines of serene old age. 'Dear me, Channis, I quite forgot myself. Oh, don't think I wouldn't slap you as you so richly deserve, but too many people know we're in here together. And as you so cleverly observed, I make a habit of not doing things that cannot be innocently explained away. You've done very well to discover so much but the people I've used will twist in the wind before they betray me, so you've nothing to show for it. All you've done is warn me to take better care in future, haven't you?'

'I'll tell Guliel.' Channis sounded like a petulant child, and from her expression she knew it.

Dirindal's laugh was kindly. 'And he will have no more proof than you, my dear and we have plenty of Names to call on, if he wishes to set his House against ours. I doubt he has the stomach for that when all he ever does is hide behind Tadriol's boy and whisper suggestions. If he had any true nobility he'd have taken the throne for himself by now.' She spoke over Lady Channis's indignant protests. 'Good day to you, my dear. I suppose I'll see you at the Emperor's dance this afternoon. You might want to purchase some white feathers while you're here. It won't be long before you'll be looking for another House to shelter you, if you can find some minor Esquire prepared to take on soiled goods.'

She turned her back on Channis and walked out, leaving the door ajar.

'I can't follow her, the Relict, I mean,' Casuel said hastily. 'Or rather, I can, if I scry for her, but I'll need ink and water—'

The Emperor smacked a furious hand into the silver tray, sending it skidding across the table and crashing to the floor.

Temar took a pace backwards as Casuel covered his head with frightened hands. Ryshad's hand moved instinctively to his swordless hip as he took a step to bring him to Temar's shoulder.

'Explain yourself, D'Alsennin,' demanded the Emperor. 'Tell me why I should believe any of that?'

'You saw it with your own eyes, you heard for yourself,' Temar retorted.

'What did I see?' The Emperor moved to put the table between himself and Casuel. 'Truth? Illusion? Some sorcerer's charade woven by Planir?'

'The Archmage would never stoop to such deceit!' Casuel looked up indignantly from beneath his hands.

'You expect me to believe Dirindal Tor Bezaemar, with all her years, would admit all that to her acknowledged enemy's paramour?' The Emperor scowled. 'What has D'Olbriot told Planir of the history of my House? What does your Archmage know of my father and my uncle's death?'

'No more than anyone else.' Casuel looked puzzled.

Urgent knocking on the door startled everyone in the room.

'Not now!' Tadriol yelled angrily.

Temar looked at the Emperor. 'She asked how many more of your Name had to die. Does that have some darker meaning for you?'

Ryshad was barring the inner door with his body. 'There've always been rumours, highness, among the sworn, but never leading back to Tor Bezaemar.'

The Emperor looked sharply at him before glowering at Temar again. 'And Dirindal conveniently half admits it!'

The knocking came again. 'Is everything all right?' a hesitant voice called.

'You, chosen man, get rid of them,' the Emperor ordered abruptly. Ryshad slipped out of the room. 'Wizard, do you spy like this for D'Olbriot, for the Archmage or both? How often?'

'I'm no spy,' Casuel protested weakly.

'I cannot believe Dirindal would forget herself away like that.' Tadriol looked grim.

'There are ways of loosening tongues.' Temar chose his words carefully, wishing Ryshad hadn't just disappeared. 'I know you have spoken with Planir, so you must be aware there is more than one kind of magic.'

'These so-called dark arts of the Elietimm?' The Emperor scowled suspiciously.

'Artifice is a tool, like any other. A knife can cut bread to feed a child or to stab a man to the heart.' Temar didn't dare let his indignation show. 'It was a cornerstone of justice in the Old Empire because no one could speak falsehood under the seal of their oath.'

'And how was that marvel achieved?' demanded the Emperor with obvious scepticism.

'With the oaths and invocations you still use in your courts,' Temar shot back. 'In my day they were backed with enchantment. And where Artifice can bind a false tongue, it can loosen another to speak the truth, all unwitting. Demoiselle Tor Arrial is a highly skilled Adept and she was in the next room laying an invocation on the Relict prompting her to speak.'

'Prompting her to speak her mind or merely making a puppet out of her?' countered the Emperor.

Temar struggled for an answer, hearing Ryshad arguing with someone in the outer room, seeing Casuel looking uncertainly from face to face. He closed his eyes to concentrate better.

'Aedral mar nidralae, Avila,' he said suddenly. 'Demoiselle, please get here as fast as possible. Bring Velindre and Allin.'

'I thought you were here to ask about an insignia!' The Steward's irate voice made Temar open his eyes. The man was standing in the doorway, Ryshad behind him ringed by menacing guards with swords.

Temar waved a frustrated arm. 'Give me just a little longer

and I can prove our good faith!' The evidence of his own eyes had convinced Ryshad, hadn't it?

'You don't raise your hand or your voice to the Emperor, boy!' The Steward snapped his fingers and the men-at-arms moved closer.

'Enough, Master Jainne.' Tadriol looked at Temar with a slight smile. 'Send D'Olbriot's man in here and wait outside. I believe some ladies will be joining us shortly.' He glanced at a small brass timepiece on the mantelshelf. The pointing arrow was very nearly halfway down the engraved scale. 'They'd better hurry or we'll all be late for the dance. So, D'Alsennin, you wanted to discuss an insignia? You think a badge will make you more secure? Have you chosen livery colours as well? I have to say, you'd be the youngest person I ever called Messire and D'Alsennin will still be a mighty small House. Do you really want to be Sieur in your own Name?'

The words weren't unkindly meant but still stung Temar like a slap across the face.

'I do not know if I want to be a Sieur on your terms; I do not know what the title means in this age,' he retorted. 'But I know what it meant in my day, and that was a duty of care to all who depended on you. By Saedrin's very keys, I will do my duty to the people of Kel Ar'Ayen. They crossed the ocean trusting in the Names of Den Rannion, Den Fellaemion and D'Alsennin. I am the last of those nobles and Poldrion drown me but I will defend their interests. I speak for people held under enchantment for nigh on thirty generations and many still lie insensible in the darkness. I want them back, and if I need some trumpery badge to make you people take me seriously then I will wear one, but it means precious little to me.'

'What he means is—' began Casuel in strangled tones.

'I can speak for myself, Master Mage!' Temar spat.

'Then speak,' the Emperor commanded.

'The only reason I came to you is my people will suffer still more in a quarrel not of our making. Kel Ar'Ayen is simply one more piece on the game board between Tor

Bezaemar and D'Olbriot, and I cannot let that go unchallenged. Tor Bezaemar has been orchestrating all the cases brought before you in the courts. By way of retaliation, the Sieur and his brothers are planning every assault possible on Tor Bezaemar property and allied Names. D'Olbriot's man there heard them.' Temar gestured at Ryshad who was standing motionless by the door, head raised, eyes level.

'You wear a chosen man's armring,' the Emperor observed, a distinct chill in his voice. 'Shouldn't you be keeping your Sieur's confidences?'

'I believe an open quarrel with Tor Bezaemar will harm the House.' Ryshad continued to stare straight ahead. 'My loyalties are to all who bear the Name, not merely to the person of the Sieur.'

'Guliel's not stupid, he must see this will only discredit his arguments in court,' said the Emperor, frustrated. 'Why's D'Olbriot taking justice into his own hands?'

'In my day we went to the Emperor for justice.' Temar stepped round the table to stand toe to toe with Tadriol. 'You must stop this quarrel before it gets out of hand. Before all your advocates have said their pieces, innocent men will have lost their livelihoods, and if Kel Ar'Ayen is cut adrift my people may well lose their lives.'

'When I see open antagonism between two powerful Houses I will act to limit the damage,' the Emperor protested.

'Can you not stop it before it starts?' demanded Temar. 'Do you wait until the roof catches before you tear down a burning house?'

'Then bring evidence untainted by magic before the courts,' repeated the Emperor with some heat. 'Where all can witness it and justice can be seen to be done.'

'If we had it, we would!' Temar cried, frustrated. 'We do not. Why else do you think we tried this?'

'I doubt shouting is going to achieve very much.' Avila strode into the room with Velindre and Allin at her heels. All three swept graceful curtseys to the Emperor, the swish of skirts the only sound to ruffle the abrupt silence.

'May I make known Avila, Demoiselle Tor Arrial,' said Temar, for want of anything better. 'And Velindre Ychane, Allin Mere, mages of Hadrumal.'

'You didn't get here by carriage.' Tadriol looked disconcerted for the first time.

'Velindre's magic served the purpose rather better.' Avila fixed the Emperor with an impatient glare. 'I take it you want us to prove ourselves?'

'How do you know that?' Tadriol looked instantly suspicious.

'Allin scryed for you when the Relict left.' Avila spared the girl an approving smile that set her blushing scarlet. 'It did not look a happy conversation and I have had a bellyful of Tormalin scepticism these last few days, so it seemed a likely guess.'

'You didn't translocate here when you only knew the place through scrying?' Casuel was looking scandalised at Velindre.

'Where's Lady Channis?' Ryshad asked suddenly.

'On her way home in her carriage,' Allin assured him.

'Can we stick to the point before us?' Avila asked, scathing. 'What kind of proof do you need, highness, to accept the evidence of your own eyes?'

Tadriol looked thoughtful, rolling the overlarge ring round his finger. 'You say this spell has to be worked between two mages?'

Velindre nodded.

'You, go with my Steward.' The Emperor pointed abruptly at Casuel. 'Master Jainne, take him to some room at the far end of the palace. No, don't ask me, I don't want anyone in this room knowing, not until this lady here finds him with her magic.' He inclined his head stiffly at Velindre.

The Steward relieved his feelings by slamming the door once he'd hurried Casuel through it. The wizard's anxious queries went unanswered and rapidly faded into the distance.

Silence swelled to fill the small room with tension. Temar found it impossible to sit or stand still. He walked around, ostensibly admiring the delicate paintings hung on the walls. Landscapes were picked out in subtle watercolour, a suggestion of trees framing a proudly Rational dwelling here, a tangle of ivy detailed over the ruins of some ancient house there. Tiny script engraved below identified it as the Savorgan residence of Den Jaepe. Temar sighed; those towers were clearly long since fallen from the heights he remembered. He moved on, a sideways glance showing him Allin perched on the edge of her chair, face unhappily flushed. Their eyes met, he gave her a momentary smile of encouragement, and the answering support in her gaze rewarded him. Ryshad was still by the door, stance straight as a lance. Avila was similarly stiff-backed, hands neatly folded in her lap, every year of her age plain on her weary face. The only people seemingly at ease were Velindre and the Emperor. The lady mage was looking around the room with unashamed curiosity while Tadriol relaxed in his chair, watching her.

'That should be long enough,' the Emperor said, suddenly sitting upright. 'Show us where he is.'

Velindre calmly retrieved the tray from beneath the window. 'I take it this is what Cas was using?' She glanced at Tadriol. 'Don't you think he'd have come a little better prepared if this was all some elaborate hoax?'

Temar fetched her a taper from the mantelshelf.

'Thank you.' Scarlet fire blossomed in her hand as she set the tray high on the mantel, holding the taper in front of it, face seemingly more angular than ever as she worked her magic.

A smooth golden glow in the centre of the shining metal deepened to a burning amber before splitting around a silver rift. Almost too bright to look at, the brilliant lines framed a widening picture of Casuel sitting indignantly in a small room with a single window high behind him, washstand and ewer just visible.

Velindre smiled. 'Your Steward seems to have put my esteemed colleague in a privy.'

'He's on his way to tell you that himself,' snapped Casuel crossly, glaring through the spell. 'Kindly send him back with the key.'

Temar had to turn away to hide his smile and saw the top

of Allin's head as she stared determinedly at the floor.

Velindre licked finger and thumb, snuffing the taper with a faint hiss. 'Sufficient proof? We could argue the rights and wrongs of it all day.'

'Your talents certainly seem to be all that your associates boasted,' Tadriol said slowly.

Velindre smiled. 'The cockerel can crow all he wants, highness, but it's the hen that yields the eggs.'

A smile tugged at the Emperor's mouth before he looked at Avila, face intent. 'You say you can compel the truth. Do so, to me, now.'

'If you wish.' Avila pressed bloodless lips together. 'Do you swear by all you hold sacred to speak truth not falsehood? This will only work if you are a man of your word.'

'I swear by the blood of my House and my father,' Tadriol said with forceful indignation.

'Raeponin an iskatel, fa nuran aestor. Fedal tris amria lekat.' Avila spoke with biting precision. 'Now, Emperor Tadriol the Provident, fifth of that Name, tell me you do not suspect Dirindal Tor Bezaemar of a hand in the deaths that have plagued your House!'

Tadriol opened his mouth, frowned and licked his lips. He swallowed hard, once and then a second time, tugging at the collar of his shirt. Fear creased his brow momentarily before he mastered a calculating frown. He coughed. 'True enough, my lady, I suspect her and with better reason than you know.' He pointed abruptly at Velindre. 'Do it to her!'

'I swear to speak truthfully, on the air that I breathe and the magic it grants me.' Velindre seemed unperturbed.

Avila repeated her incantation as Tadriol moved to stand in front of Velindre, searching her face with merciless eyes. 'Then was there any deception in what I saw? Is this some scheme concocted by Hadrumal?'

'No deception, no concoction,' she said calmly. 'You saw the plain, unhindered truth. Ask Channis, if you don't trust us.'

'I may just do that,' the Emperor retorted. Turning on his heel, he walked over to the window and stared out into the gardens. 'Get out, all of you. I have a great deal to think through and precious little time.'

Temar didn't move. 'You have to act before D'Olbriot and Tor Bezaemar bring chaos down on us all.'

Tadriol turned his head with a ferocious scowl. 'Chaos is no matter for foolish jests, D'Alsennin.' His anger faded in the face of Temar's evident confusion. 'I think this afternoon's dance should be soon enough, don't you? I'll see you all there, all of you, including you, chosen man. Ask Master Jainne for cards.' He looked back out through the window, arms folded across his chest.

Temar realised everyone was looking at him for guidance. 'Until this afternoon, then.' He led the way out through the anteroom. Out in the corridor the Steward came hurrying towards them with a faintly malicious air.

Temar spoke before the man could open his mouth. 'Yes, we know you thought it amusing to shut Cas in the privy. Go and let him out. We'll wait downstairs. Oh, and you can bring us five cards for this dance.'

Ryshad heaved a sigh of relief as the Steward left. 'The Sieur has already told me I'm attending you this afternoon. That means we've a card over to settle our account with Charoleia.'

Temar managed to set aside the distracting thought of dancing with the enticing beauty.

'Can you show us to the stairs?' Velindre was frowning as she spoke and not merely over the route out of the palace. Casuel was lost in ecstatic rapture but Allin was looking distraught.

'Is there some problem?' Temar asked her.

'What are we going to wear?' she said, aghast.

The Imperial Palace of Tadriol the Provident, Summer Solstice Festival, Fifth Day, Noon

The contrast with the morning's empty halls was startling when we returned to the Imperial Palace. Nobility in Festival finery thronged the grounds, bright sun striking fire from diamonds, sapphires and rubies, not that the well born spent much time beneath that merciless glare. Descending from their carriages in the great courtyard where the palace made three sides of a square, they paused just long enough for due admiration from the commonalty pressed ten deep beyond the black railings before hurrying into the cool of the interior. Den Janaquel liveries were well in evidence, keeping the endless procession of carriages moving smoothly in and out through the tall iron gates.

'I had not realised the palace was so big,' remarked Temar as our coach paused to cheers from the avid populace. He raised an absent hand to tug at the lace at his neck, something he'd been doing the entire drive here.

'You don't realise how far it goes back when you approach it from the other frontage.' The coach was getting uncomfortably stuffy and I was sweating in my close-cut livery. My stomach felt as hollow as a drum, what little food I'd managed to eat sitting leaden beneath my breastbone.

'Is the place used to any useful purpose, other than Festival frolics for the idle rich?' Avila fanned herself with a discreet spread of fluffy blue feathers that matched her summer blue gown. The shell inlay of the fan's lacquered handle reflected the pearly iridescence of her white lace overdress.

I turned to her. 'The Emperor is the main link between commonalty and nobility, Demoiselle. He hosts receptions for merchants here, meets with master craftsmen, with the shrine fraternities. If a Duke from Lescar or some Relshazri magistrate visits, this is where they stay and where anyone doing business with them has the Emperor as impartial witness. Most importantly for us, this is where the Emperor brings the Sieurs of the Houses together to discuss any concerns.'

That thought prompted me to look out of our coach window for Tor Bezaemar, Den Thasnet or Den Muret crests on passing door panels.

'Why do you suppose D'Olbriot sent us on in a separate coach?' Temar fussed with his shirt collar again, linen creamy against the dark blue of his coat and breeches.

'To remind people you've your own claim to rank?' I hazarded. I hadn't a clue what the Sieur was thinking. He'd accepted the startling news that the wizards were to come to the dance with bland equanimity and made no comment at all on our unexpected, unsanctioned absence for so much of the morning.

'You think cheap theatrics will convince anyone?' Avila sniffed. 'We've been dancing to D'Olbriot's tune this whole Festival, and everyone knows it.'

The carriage jounced as the gate opened for us and the horses trotted in. As we drew up before the shallow stairs, Tor Tadriol lackeys were already opening the white double doors. I jumped down to offer Avila my arm.

She descended with slow dignity and paused to arrange her skirts as Temar disdained the footman's offer of help. 'Where now, Ryshad?'

'Perhaps we should wait a moment.' I indicated the Sieur's carriage following us through the gates. As the driver pulled up his horses Messire was the first out of the door, splendid in peacock green brocade catching every eye in the sunlight. His brother Leishal, his son Myred and nephew Camarl were all dressed in the same cloth, cut in subtly different styles as befitted their ages and rank, an impressive statement of united D'Olbriot power and influence. Between them they wore an Emperor's ransom in emeralds.

Lady Channis's carriage drew up behind, the Den Veneta

crest of arrows proud on the door. Resplendent in crimson silk overlaid with pale rose lace, she escorted a posy of most eligible Demoiselles honouring the D'Olbriot name, the girls dressed in all the colours of a flower garden. Anyone doubting my lady's role in the House was plainly advised to think again. Ustian and Fresil followed in an open coach, preening themselves in the same peacock brocade.

As the carriages moved slowly round to the far gate, a smaller, uncrested coach was ushered in with scant ceremony. Casuel got out, stumbling awkwardly as he trod on the hem of his gold-brocaded robe. Velindre followed with easy grace, her undressed blonde hair striking among the intricate black and brunette coiffures. Her unadorned dove grey dress struck a muted note among the bolder colours all around but style and cloth were impeccable. I looked more closely.

'I see you have a good eye for a dress, Ryshad,' Avila remarked. 'Few men look at more than the seamstress's sums. Yes, it is the one I wore to Tor Kanselin. If Guliel's going to waste his gold buying me three changes of clothes for every day of Festival, someone might as well get the wear out of them.' She was plainly annoyed about something or someone but I couldn't be sure who or why.

The Sieur was greeting Lady Channis, embracing her with a fond kiss that won appreciative whistles from the watching crowd. As she took his arm the rest of the family paired off in practised fashion.

He nodded to Temar. 'If you and the Demoiselle Tor Arrial are ready?'

Temar offered Avila his arm with old-fashioned formality and she accepted with a glint in her eye. Seeing Casuel dithering over whether to escort Velindre or Allin, I bowed to Temar and to Messire and went down the steps.

'My lady mage, may I have the honour of escorting you?' Allin was holding herself with self-possession so rigid I wondered if she was breathing. I winked at her and she relaxed enough to give me a little smile. That was a relief; I didn't want her fainting on me.

'Come on, Cas.' Velindre slipped her arm through his and it was hard to say who escorted whom up the wide stone stair.

'That's a very elegant dress,' I remarked to Allin as we waited for the chamberlain at the door to admit each couple. The watered damson silk flattered her mousy colouring, and with luck wouldn't clash too badly with her inevitable blushes.

Innocent delight lent an unexpected appeal to her plain face. 'Demoiselle Avila had the maids turning out every wardrobe in the residence until they found something to fit me.'

I looked at the assembled ladies of the Name. The gown had probably come from Demoiselle Ticarie's closets, given the expert cut to disguise a short-coupled figure. Allin was lucky D'Olbriot ladies didn't run to height like Den Hefeken or willowy girls like Tor Kanselin.

'Your cards, my lady, my master.' We showed the chamberlain the folded pasteboard we each wore tied to our wrists and were duly ushered into a stylish salon.

'This is very impressive,' said Allin in faint tones.

'They say the floor's inlaid with wood traded from every corner of the Old Empire and the Archipelago,' I told her with a friendly smile.

The floor's pattern of circles and arcs was nicely balanced between rational restraint and exuberant display. Not that we could see much of it between the skirts and soft dancing shoes of the assembled nobles. The walls showed the same transition between older extravagance and later restraint, single fronds and blossoms moulded in the plaster rather than the intricate swags and garlands of an earlier age but still bright with gold leaf burnished to a delicate sheen. Vast double doors in the far wall would open in turn to the Imperial ballroom when Tadriol was ready to welcome his peers.

Temar had stopped to look up at the ceiling, heedless of people coming in after us. Plaster panels high above our heads were painted with the finest interpretations of ancient legends that the artists of the day had been able to offer the first Tadriol. In the corners, Dastennin with his crown of seaweed and shells was pouring out the seas between this realm and the Otherworld, while opposite Halcarion hung the moons in the sky before setting her diadem of stars to brighten the darkness. The animals of plain and forest knelt before Talagrin, garlanded with autumn leaves. Drianon, a sheaf of wheat in one arm, was bringing trees into blossom with a sweep of her other hand, while flowers bloomed in her footsteps.

Between each of these scenes other gods traversed the twin realms of existence in delicately painted ovals. Arimelin spun the dreams that might reach this world from the Other, Trimon raised his harp with music to echo through the Shades and beyond while Larasion summoned the wind and weather that knows no boundaries. On the one hand Ostrin healed the sick whose time to leave this realm was not yet come, and on the other he welcomed those about to be newly born, handing them the cup of wine that would wipe away any memory of their sojourn in the Otherworld.

'Impressive but none too subtle,' remarked Velindre, sardonic eyes on the centre panel, where the circle of Saedrin with his keys, Raeponin with his scales and Poldrion with his ferry pole stood equal in their authority. Lesser figures ringed the gods, echoing their stance and archaic dress.

'Are those actual portaits?' Avila studied the distant figures.

'Of the Sieurs of the day,' I confirmed.

'Do you suppose they remembered Saedrin's grant of rank brought them duty as well as privilege?' Temar speculated pointedly.

'Shall we move on?' I suggested. 'We're blocking the doorway.'

The large room was already crowded; Messire invariably timed his arrival to impress the greatest number of people while spending the least time possible in idle chatter before any festivities commenced.

'Are you committed to any dances?' Allin was nervously fingering her own card.

I shook my head. 'It's not really customary for chosen men.' But I wasn't the only one wearing livery. There were a few proven here and there, moving with easy familiarity among the nobles, well-dressed wives on their arms. I tried to imagine Livak making polite conversation about the latest Toremal gossip while I discussed some question of trade or dispute at the Sieur's bidding.

'Why does the Emperor want us here?' Allin wondered aloud.

'A very good question,' I agreed. This really wasn't my place, was it? I'd taken my turn outside the doors as part of a Duty Cohort when the honour and burden of keeping the Festival peace fell to D'Olbriot, but I'd never expected to be a guest inside.

'Temar's not going to lack for partners.' Allin sounded resigned. D'Alsennin was with Camarl by a side-table where ink and pens were laid out. Several D'Olbriot Demoiselles were noting their initials on his card and inviting him to return the compliment. A lackey hovered close by with an anxious eye.

Allin fiddled with her dance card. I saw faint regret on her round face. 'Do you like to dance?'

'Yes,' she admitted, round face colouring a little. 'That is, I used to, back home.'

'Don't wizards dance in Hadrumal?' I'd never really thought much about how mages might enjoy themselves.

'Sometimes,' Allin replied. 'But there are precious few musicians, and most wizards dance as if they'd their boots on the wrong feet.'

'It's one of the things that make a mage-born army an impossibility.' Velindre came up on my other side, her clear tones cutting through the well-bred murmur. 'Nine out of ten wizards seem incapable of holding a beat so they'd never be able to march in step.'

I smiled at her wry tone but dubious expressions around us suggested few others appreciated the joke.

'Planir, as you might expect, is remarkably light of foot and dances a very pretty measure,' Velindre continued, with unmistakable sarcasm. 'But then, he's so often the wizard that tests the rule.'

'You think rules should be observed?' I queried. 'Weren't you Otrick's pupil? He bends rules until they splinter.'

Velindre's face hardened into unflattering angles. 'At least those rules were the same for everyone, not one set for Planir and his cronies and another for the rest of us.'

'Have you any news of Otrick?' Allin peered round me with wide, anxious eyes.

'No.' Fleeting brilliance rose and vanished in Velindre's hazel eyes. 'And it's time Planir faced up to the truth. He cannot use this Kellarin business as the excuse for continually ignoring Hadrumal's concerns.'

'There's Casuel.' Allin seemed more concerned with matters in hand than quarrels in distant Hadrumal.

The mage was edging his way apologetically through the crowd, clutching his card in one sweaty hand. 'Has anyone asked either of you to dance?'

'Are you offering?' Velindre smiled innocently.

Casuel hesitated just a breath too long. 'Naturally, if you would do me the honour. Who else has asked you? Of what rank?'

Velindre showed him her unmarked card. 'You have your choice of dances, Cas.'

He frowned. 'Do you think Esquire Camarl would agree to me asking some of the ladies from the lesser families? From cadet blood lines?' The wizard looked around the crowded room. 'Where is he?'

I scanned the throng but couldn't see Esquire Camarl at all. What I could see were unmistakable knots of allied families. Firon Den Thasnet was standing with two Den Muret Demoiselles while his sister hung on the arm of the Sieur Den Rannion's youngest brother. Close by the Sieur Tor Sylarre was smiling as he chatted with an elder Esquire Den Muret. Even given the increasing press of people, they were keeping an emphatic space between themselves and Gelaia Den Murivance as she laughed with her brother Maren and Jenty Tor Sauzet. Further round the room Orilan Den Hefeken was talking to her affianced Esquire Den Risiper, other Esquires of both houses agreeing dances with a knot of minor Den Ferrand and Den Gennael girls. Beyond the stony-faced Sieur Tor Priminale stood with his extensive array of cousins in an unapproachable circle.

As I watched, a lackey in palace colours came up to whisper politely to the Sieur Tor Sylarre. A lifetime's training kept the Sieur's face impassive but he bid an immediate farewell to Den Muret and followed the lackey through a discreet door on the far side of the wide salon.

Temar came over, waving his dance card to dry the writing. 'Be careful not to brush against my leg, ladies,' he said breezily. 'Some clumsy girl has just spilt ink down me. I believe her badge was Tor Priminale.' Anger showed momentarily beneath his light words.

I looked at the barely visible dampness on his dark blue breeches. 'Fortunate that the Sieur suggested that colour.'

'Quite so,' smiled Temar thinly. 'Sadly, the Demoiselle's pretty orange feathers are now an unappealing brown. What might that signify in this complicated code these girls have concocted?'

I grinned at him. 'I hate to think.'

'Where does that lead?' Temar nodded towards the door Tor Sylarre had disappeared through.

'It goes round to the throne room,' I replied.

'Esquire Camarl and the Sieur were summoned as soon as they arrived.' Temar and I exchanged a speculative look.

'When's this dance going to begin?' Casuel demanded crossly. 'It's unbearably hot.' He fidgeted with the fronts of his heavy robe.

'Just be grateful this isn't an evening dance,' I told him. 'Add the heat of candles and we'd be melting faster than the beeswax.'

The salon ran the full width of the palace but even with upper windows open to breezes too high to disturb the ladies' elegant hair, the temperature was rising fast.

'We could work a little judicious magic, Cas,' Velindre remarked. 'I can start some air moving, and drawing the heat away would be a good exercise for Allin's fire affinity.'

'We can't use magic here.' Casuel was horrified. 'Not without the Emperor's permission.'

'We could ask him. Where is he?' At that moment, the brass-ornamented doors into the ballroom swung open and people spilled gratefully into the cooler space. Velindre looked into the ballroom as the crush in the anteroom cleared. 'Isn't your Emperor supposed to be receiving people?'

'The Sieur Tor Arrial's just been sent for.' Temar was still looking at the single doorway where a lackey now stood unobtrusive guard.

That prompted me to look for Avila and I soon saw her with the Maitresse Tor Arrial. The Maitresse's brother, Esquire Den Harkeil, was writing on Avila's dance card with a smile that was positively flirtatious.

'I am glad to see someone is enjoying the day,' remarked Temar rather tightly as he followed my gaze.

'I don't think Esquire Camarl is.' I nudged Temar as Camarl appeared through the side door, face impassive as he hurried to his uncles. The friendly smile on Ustian's face faded as we watched, and Leishal positively glowered. Fresil snapped his fingers abruptly to summon Myred, starting a buzz of speculation among more than the Tor Kanselin ladies so abruptly deserted.

Temar looked to me for answers but I hadn't any to give him. Then a stir in the ballroom turned every head but it was only footmen with trays crowded with glasses.

'I hope incautious drinking does not loosen too many inhibitions.' Temar beckoned with an authoritative hand.

I took a glass of deep golden wine. 'I've never heard of one of these dances turning into a free-for-all, but I suppose there's always a first time.'

'You don't seriously think there'll be violence?' Casuel asked nervously.

'He was joking, Cas,' Velindre told him scornfully.

Looking round the gathering, feeling the increasingly fervid undercurrents, I wasn't so sure.

A flurry of carriages outside caused another distraction. I welcomed it until I saw the late arrivals were a solid phalanx of Tor Bezaemar. The Sieur entered with his aunt the Relict on his arm, each son and nephew behind escorting dutiful daughters of the House. Every cadet line was represented, wearing the Tor Bezaemar martlet worked into pendants, rings and brooches, combined with the badge of every line subsumed into the Name over the generations. After pausing on the threshold until Dirindal was satisfied with the impact of their entrance, the family scattered like a flock of birds, alighting on every group and conversation, prompting smiles and welcomes, some less convincing than others. Dirindal relinquished her nephew to his wife and took her grandson Kreve's arm for a slow circuit of the wide salon. I saw a Tor Tadriol lackey heading immediately for the Sieur.

'This could be interesting.' Temar's discreet nod directed me to Dirindal, who'd drawn level with Lady Channis. Messire's lady was deep in laughing conversation with the Maitresse Tor Kanselin and neither drew so much as a breath as they turned dismissive shoulders on the Relict. Gathering the covey of assorted Demoiselles fluttering nervously around with brisk gestures with their fans, the two ladies walked away, never once making so much as eye contact with Dirindal. The Relict was left standing, a moment of unmistakable fury on her face before she raised a sweep of mossy feathers to conceal imperfectly an expression of wounded amiability. The Esquire managed no such masquerade, plainly outraged.

'Saedrin save us, Ryshad, you've certainly brought me to a fascinating occasion.' Charoleia's voice at my elbow nearly made me spill my wine. 'Good day to you, Temar.'

'My Lady Alaric.' He bowed to her, eyes sparkling and won a demure half-smile in return.

I did hope he wasn't going to make a fool of himself in public, but then again that might distract the assembled nobility. All those families with ties of blood and loyalty to D'Olbriot were taking their cue to ignore Tor Bezaemar, some with more grace than others. Indignation was swelling among

Den Muret, Den Rannion, Tor Priminale, leaving minor Houses exposed as the room divided into undeclared battle lines. Den Hefeken was looking to Den Ferrand for support while Den Gennael and Den Risiper drew into a defensive circle with Den Brennain.

'Aren't you going to introduce us?' Casuel's voice seesawed between rebuke for Temar and fawning in Charoleia's direction.

'My apologies. May I make known Lady Alaric of Thornlisse. This is Casuel Devoir, Velindre Ychane and Allin Mere. All mages of Hadrumal.' The laughter just beneath Temar's words set Casuel looking suspiciously for some hidden slight.

'You know Ryshad?' Velindre was measuring Charoleia with frank curiosity.

Charoleia returned the candid appraisal. 'We have acquaintance in common.' Her words were coloured with sufficient Lescari accents to lend a hint of foreign glamour, just as her pale lilac gown had a subtly northern cut. The gentian lace overlaying the silk brought out the colour of her eyes as well as emphasising the whiteness of her skin. A single silver chain carrying an amethyst and pearl pendant circled her elegant neck and more pearls studded a silver crescent lifting hair dressed high in an unmistakably Lescari style.

Velindre swung the fan chained at her waist. 'There'll be plenty here keen to make your acquaintance.' She sounded amused.

'That's what such functions are for,' Charoleia replied sweetly.

We were certainly attracting a fair degree of notice. An unknown beauty, three wizards and a chosen man who'd rather be outside holding the horses were certainly a welcome neutral topic for speculation in the tense atmosphere. I wondered how long we'd serve as a diversion, seeing Firon Den Thasnet draining yet another glass of wine, angry colour high on his cheekbones.

'Open hostilities here will suit no one's purpose,' Charoleia said softly. She was looking at two Tor Sylarre youths who were casting provocative sneers at a trio of Den Murivance Esquires, stiff-necked in their first appearance at such an exalted gathering.

'It's all this talking that's stoking up resentments,' I frowned. 'But it's the Emperor's privilege to open the dance, and he's nowhere to be seen.'

'But I am so ignorant of modern courtesies,' said Temar breezily. 'My lady?' He offered a hand to Charoleia.

She shook her head, smiling. 'I don't care to be quite so noticeable, Temar.'

He grinned and I realised whatever he felt for Charoleia was a fair cry from the prickly devotion he'd lavished on Guinalle. That puzzle had me tongue-tied just long enough to stop me calling Temar back when he sauntered off, idly swinging the card on its ribbon at his wrist.

I watched a touch nervously as he tapped Orilan Den Hefeken on one shoulder. The Demoiselle greeted him with a ready smile but that faltered as he spoke. She turned to appeal to her Sieur. Camarl strolled over as Temar spread beseeching hands to Orilan. Several other people drew near and a new murmur rippled outwards. We watched as the Sieur Den Hefeken sent a footman hurrying to the chamberlain, whose face was betraying considerable strain. Master Jainne was standing by a circle of musicians silent at the far end of the ballroom, pipers with single, double and double-reeded instruments of differing sizes and curves backed by lutanists and bowed lyres.

'Oh look, Cas,' said Velindre brightly. 'Your brother's leading the music. What an honour for your family.'

The mage's strangled reply was drowned beneath a lively chord. Temar led Orilan Den Hefeken into the centre of the floor and four other couples rapidly formed a set behind them. I hadn't seen Messire return, but he appeared on the far side, Lady Channis graceful on his arm. Assorted scions of Den Murivance, Tor Kanselin and Den Castevin followed suit. Kreve Tor Bezaemar promptly led one of Tor Sylarre's innumerable daughters out and Firon Den Thasnet followed with another.

'Competing over who dances the neatest figures should prove harmless enough,' said Charoleia with satisfaction. She took my hand and I found myself walking out to join the nearest set. She curtsied with consummate grace and I bowed, listening hard for the beat of the music, counting silently until I could move to one side with the other men. Charoleia swept past me with a sensuous whisper of perfumed silk and we both turned to join hands and follow the set in a series of rapid twists and turns, dropping and swapping hands as we went. I hadn't danced since Winter Solstice and that had been a servants' affair where errors were greeted with laughter rather than the contempt I could imagine here. Livak fitted into the lower halls well enough, but with the best will in the world I couldn't see her dancing these complex measures with a tenth the grace of Charoleia.

I managed the exchange of partners without error and when Charoleia came back to me could breathe a little easier.

'You look very serious,' she observed as the music changed to a partner dance.

I took her in my arms. 'Did you and Temar—' The words were out before I could bite my tongue.

Charoleia arched exquisite brows over limpid eyes. 'Is that any concern of yours?'

I felt ashamed. 'No, I suppose, forgive me.'

She laughed delicately. 'Since you ask, yes we did. But rather more importantly for that young man, we talked long into the night and again in the cool of the morning. I think you'll find him rather wiser to the differences between love and lust.'

I looked hastily from side to side in case anyone was overhearing this but we were safely isolated in the midst of the circling couples.

'I'd forgotten how tender an innocent can be,' Charoleia continued in an amused undertone. 'But I think I convinced him passion alone rarely sustains a love affair beyond first rapture, no matter how hot and strong that flame burns. I think he'll learn it's best to temper that charming ardour with friendship.'

Charoleia's indulgent satisfaction roused my indignation on Temar's behalf. Then I wondered if such newfound wisdom might help cut the tangle of emotions binding him to Guinalle. 'You had to take him into your bed to tell him that?'

'And to show him the delights of the flesh can be enjoyed simply for their own sake,' she replied easily. 'Don't tell me you've lived this long without learning that? I don't imagine Livak would have bedded you otherwise.'

I took up the challenge in those periwinkle eyes. 'What would you have done if I'd taken up your offer of such pleasures the other morning?'

'Compared notes with Livak.' Charoleia's smile was instantly ruthless. 'To let her know what manner of man you were, in case she thought different.'

I took a slow breath. 'Halice just promised to knock me senseless if I didn't do right by her.'

'That sounds like Halice,' Charoleia agreed lightly. 'We both look out for our friends in our own way. Wait until you meet Sorgrad and 'Gren.'

'That's something to look forward to,' I said with equal flippancy. 'If we get to the end of Festival unscathed.'

We finished the dance in silence and parted in mutual accord. I watched as Charoleia artlessly insinuated herself into a laughing group of Den Breval ladies escorted by various men from a cadet Den Haurient line. Then I went to escort Allin on to the dance floor.

The Imperial Palace of Tadriol the Provident, Summer Solstice Festival, Fifth Day, Afternoon

'Have you passed a pleasant Festival?' Temar could spare enough attention to attempt conversation with Gelaia Den Murivance now that the dance simply required them to advance hand in hand. At least he'd made his initial missteps with the amiable Orilan and various D'Olbriot Demoiselles.

'It's certainly been the most memorable of recent years.'

Temar thought Gelaia was about to say something else but they reached the end of the figure and had to turn away from each other. He smiled politely as he swept some unknown Demoiselle around, skirts swirling as he set careful hands on her slim waist. Gelaia raised her fan as they stood waiting their turn to pass down the middle of the set. 'Have you made any progress learning the language of feathers?' she asked archly.

Temar shook his head. 'It has been a busy five days.'

Gelaia's eyes kept sliding away from Temar's gaze. 'There are plenty of people here interested to see what colours I carry. But then no one knows what a D'Alsennin livery would be, do they?'

Temar studied her fan, a spread of glossy crimson layered over darker maroon plumes clasped in a golden handle studded with rubies and softened with a flurry of down. Vivid scarlet tendrils with tufted ends trembled on either side and Temar wondered what kind of bird those came from. He realised Gelaia was looking expectantly at him between glances at the rest of their set. 'You carry Den Murivance colours, do you not? Rather than the white plumes you used before?'

Gelaia raised a defiant chin. 'Which signifies I have no interest in any other House at present – and none has an interest in me.'

Temar took a moment to catch her meaning. 'Messire D'Olbriot will be disappointed.'

'Is he the only one?' Gelaia demanded with some indignation.

Temar took her hand to lead her down the middle of the other couples. 'I had barely realised I was being considered as a suitable candidate for your hand. Why am I now so quickly rejected?' Completing the last steps of the dance Temar turned with Gelaia to bow to the rest of the set.

Gelaia fanned herself, faint colour rising beneath her mask of cosmetics. 'There are too many complications.'

Temar looked at her in silent expectation.

'I know Toremal, I know how to dance the measures, how to play the games,' she said with sudden forthrightness, pulling her hand free. 'You don't, but you've already made dangerous enemies. I'll marry to suit my Sieur and I'll manage whatever affairs my new House requires of me, but I'm not ready to play for stakes as high as Tor Bezaemar. I don't know what else you're caught up in, and that worries me. You're laid low with a knife wound and yet sorcery has you healed by the following day. You associate with wizards who pluck a falling man out of the air.'

'I had little choice over any of that,' said Temar, stung.

Gelaia forced a smile. 'I do have a choice, Esquire. I choose not to get involved. I'm sorry.'

Temar bowed low and watched Gelaia hurry away to the security of her family. Looking round he smiled blandly at discreetly curious faces before sauntering over to Allin who was sipping a glass of wine, face flushed with pleasure. 'May I have the honour of this next dance?'

'Let me catch my breath.' Allin puffed out her cheeks inelegantly.

'Are you enjoying yourself?' Temar asked curiously.

'Oh, I'm determined to,' said Allin with a glint in her eye. 'Poldrion can loose his demons on these patronising women if I don't, especially that charming Den Rannion Demoiselle over there. She tells me how very old-fashioned my dancing is.'

'Your steps can scarcely be less up to the moment than mine.' Temar was about to continue but a flurry of activity turned every head towards the throne room door and the entire vast space fell as silent as an empty shrine.

Jainne the chamberlain's voice cracked slightly as he spoke into the expectant hush. 'Tadriol, called Provident by the grace of his peers and Emperor by the will of the Convocation of Princes.'

Temar realised he was badly placed to see anything going on but he wasn't about to draw attention to himself by moving. Movement spread in slow ripples from the far side of the room, the nobility clearing the floor to stand arrayed against the walls. Emperor Tadriol walked into the centre of the vast room. He wore plain breeches beneath a full-skirted coat of the same bronze silk brocaded with black. A wide collar of knotted gold links around his shoulders carried a central pendant of a mighty golden bull, head low and brandishing defiant horns. A narrow band of square-cut rubies set in gold confined the simple frill at his shirt collar. Matching stones shone on the brooches catching back the cuffs of his coat, revealing bracelets of thick gold chain adorning his wrists rather than lace. Each of his fingers bore a different ring in a mismatch of styles and gems that could only come from an extensive collection of heirlooms. The Emperor made a slow circuit of the floor, his pace never varying, his slight smile widening a touch as he made a brief half bow to each Sieur.

'I apologise for my tardiness and I hope you've been enjoying the music and wine.' Tadriol spoke with composed sincerity as he returned to the centre of the floor. 'I won't insult your intelligence by assuming that has been easy in the present climate – and I'm not talking about the weather.' His tone grew more formal. 'We are all aware of the unusual events of this last year and that matters have reached a crucial juncture. It is my duty to guide the Empire down the road most beneficial for all, so this lays a heavy responsibility on my shoulders. That's why I took this opportunity to consult with the Sieurs of those Houses directly concerned and also with those who have held themselves aloof. My thanks for your patience while I gained a fuller perspective.'

Tadriol paused to allow the whispers started by mention of Kellarin to run their course around the assembled nobles.

'Imperial verdicts are normally given in the Imperial Court, of course, but with the considerable ill feeling I see blighting the better judgement of some most influential Princes, I think it best to settle matters as swiftly as possible.' Tadriol's words were cutting in their measured delivery. 'I've heard representations in court and in private from the Houses concerned and I find the whole matter confused by malice, envy and misunderstandings both accidental and wilful. Outside interference has only worsened an already difficult situation. Accordingly, I have decided to issue a series of Imperial decrees.'

From the collective intake of breath, Temar judged this must be some considerable departure from normal practice. Allin gave his hand an encouraging squeeze. Temar squeezed back absently as he looked around for Ryshad. The chosen man was some distance away, Velindre and Casuel flanking him.

The Emperor raised a hand to brush back an errant wisp of hair. The chains around his wrist chinked, a slight sound heard in every corner of the room.

'The Imperial decree is not a power I use lightly,' Tadriol continued severely. 'I do so to prevent these disagreements getting any further out of hand, to the potential ruination of the Empire. This unseemly bickering has already done our Names no credit at all with the commonalty. It is my order that every House abandons these petty quarrels, on pain of my extreme displeasure.'

The Emperor smiled suddenly, speaking in more conciliatory tones.

'Look to the future rather than past grievances. But to the formalities. Firstly, I declare the House of D'Olbriot has no exclusive rights to deal with Kellarin or any persons living there. Any other Name or lesser trading concern is entirely at liberty to make whatever arrangements they see fit, free of D'Olbriot restraint.'

Temar glanced at Messire D'Olbriot but the Sieur's face was unreadable.

'Secondly, I declare the House of D'Alsennin has no claim on properties presently enjoyed by Tor Alder or any other Name. Grants and bequests made countless seasons ago cannot outweigh generations of care. I will not see ancient legalities used to upset the trades, households and livelihoods of so many innocent tenants. This decree also denies claims by scions of Tor Arrial, Den Domesin or any other noble House that ventured over the ocean in times past.'

The Emperor's tone of mild regret was no comfort to Temar, who felt sick misgiving hollowing out his belly. Was he being sent back to Kel Ar'Ayen deprived both of D'Olbriot aid and of any property that might have yielded coin to pay the mercenaries he'd surely need to defend his hapless colony now?

'But Raeponin's scales must be balanced, if justice is to be done.' The Emperor's stern words interrupted congratulatory smiles being passed between Tor Bezaemar and Den Thasnet. 'Just as D'Alsennin has no claims on this side of the ocean, no Name here may assert rights over or demand dues from the people of Kellarin. Haffrein Den Fellaemion was determined his new settlement would offer freedom from the shackles of greedy nobility . . .' Tadriol paused just long enough for affront to settle on various faces around the room. 'Hardly surprising, given they were fleeing the debauched excesses of Nemith the Last. I am minded to honour that great seafarer by respecting his wishes, so I repeat: no Name here has any rights over Kellarin.'

The Emperor took a slow sip from a glass of water.

'But the prestige of all our Names rests on the care we take of our tenantry. You have granted the House of Tadriol the additional responsibility of caring for the Empire as a whole and its peoples wherever they may be. I cannot simply abandon these colonists. Every Prince of the Convocation would rightly condemn me if these blameless people were left undefended, their wealth plundered and their liberties curtailed by unwanted settlers heedlessly shipped overseas.

'Fortunately, we have a ready solution to hand. If the House of D'Alsennin is a dead tree on this side of the ocean, it has a flourishing offshoot in the present holder of the Name. Accordingly, I decree that Temar D'Alsennin be raised to the dignity of Sieur of that House, with all the obligations and entitlements of that position. He will sit as the equal of any Sieur in the Convocation, where he may call any House abusing his tenants before the judgement of Emperor and Princes. All colonists of Kellarin are hereby designated tenants of the House of D'Alsennin and as such are under his protection. Anyone wishing to trade across the ocean must refer their proposals to the Sieur and submit to his scrutiny. I'm not about to leave Kellarin as a D'Olbriot monopoly but I'm not having some free-for-all where these people are bamboozled by any chancer who can hire a boat!'

The Emperor's sudden lapse into breezy informality won smiles from various Houses, some relieved, some reluctant. Tadriol raised a hand as subdued comment threatened to break into open conversation.

'But one man cannot build a House on his own. Since there are other sprigs of nobility planted in Kellarin's distant soil, I decree that these and their descendants be considered cadet lines of D'Alsennin and I ask the Sieur to ensure that they style themselves accordingly.'

The Emperor reached into a pocket and the entire room fell silent as he walked over to Temar. Temar swallowed hard. The hollowness he'd felt when he'd thought Kel Ar'Ayen was being abandoned was nothing compared to the crushing weight he felt resting on his shoulders now.

The Emperor halted in front of Temar and held out an open hand. A silver badge lay on his palm, three holm oak leaves, parallel and overlapping. 'Your insignia is granted, Messire.'

Temar studied the brooch for a moment, until he could be

sure his hands wouldn't tremble as he pinned it to the breast of his coat. The leaves shone bright and untarnished against the dark blue silk that echoed the great sapphire of his father's ring.

'My undying gratitude, my Emperor,' Temar said with archaic formality.

'From you, that's quite some promise,' murmured the Emperor in an undertone.

An isolated pair of hands began clapping somewhere in the crowd, soon joined by others. The Emperor turned to acknowledge the applause and the expectant faces.

'There are a few more trifles to settle before we can all enjoy the rest of the afternoon. One of the most noteworthy aspects to the Kellarin tale is the sudden reappearance of magic in our midst. I confess I'm still uncertain of much that's gone on, but some things I am sure of. Firstly, while the colonists of Kellarin owe a great debt to the wizards of Hadrumal, that changes nothing on this side of the ocean. All Houses may make whatever use they wish of magecraft, just as they have always done, and I will continue to listen to the advice of the Archmage Planir or any other wizard who wishes to offer counsel. But I will not grant such words any undue weight nor allow any wizard undue influence within Tormalin.'

Temar could see various people glancing smugly at the Sieur and his brothers, eager to see how they were taking this perceived rebuke.

'Indeed, what need do we have of Hadrumal's magic?' the Emperor asked abruptly. 'It was Tormalin Artifice saved the people of Kellarin in those far-off days, the same ancient skills that helped Correl the Stalwart carry Tormalin rule to the very edge of the Great Forest. I confess I'm curious to see what benefits Artifice bestows on Kellarin, and who knows, we may all benefit from judicious use of its proficiencies in years to come.' Tadriol paused and took a thick silver ring off one finger.

'But we cannot expect the people of Kellarin to share their Artifice with us if we deny them those still hidden in the enchantment that protected them through their lost generations. As many of you already know, Messire D'Alsennin came asking for our help. He needs to find the jewels and ornaments, the swords and badges of allegiance that safeguarded the very minds of his people as they slept.' Tadriol shrugged. 'I do not pretend to understand how this was accomplished, but I am shocked to learn some people have been tempted to extort coin or advantage in exchange for these items, all but demanding ransom for the very life of some helpless individual. This is my final decree, and I will summon a muster of the Cohorts to enforce it if need be. Every item that Messire D'Alsennin even suspects may be needed to restore his people is to be surrendered, without question, objection or recompense.' The Emperor's outrage shaded into scorn. 'We can all stand a little loss, even of heirloom pieces, and we gave up putting a price on a life in Tormalin when Inshol the Curt closed the slave markets.'

Tadriol handed the ring to Temar. The faceted band was flattened on the top into a hexagon carrying an inscription worn illegible by age. Temar's first thought was he'd never be able to manage the concentration needed to summon any image from the ring, his next that doing so would in any case be a very bad idea. He ransacked his memory, but before he could match the ring to any sleeper the Emperor had walked away to stand squarely before the Sieur D'Olbriot.

'Messire, as Adjurist of the Princes, do you need to summon a Convocation to ratify these decrees?'

D'Olbriot smiled calmly. 'Since we are returning to ancient forms today, shall we content ourselves with a simple show of hands? Forgive me,' he commented dryly. 'I didn't know I'd need the rod of office.' He turned to borrow Leishal's stick and thumped the floor three times. 'Stand forth, Sieurs, to uphold the dignity of your Name!'

The crowd shifted to allow the assorted heads of the Houses to stand forward.

'Do you commit yourselves and all who claim the shelter of your House to abide by these decrees? I charge you by the duty you swore to the Names that elected you and to the

Convocation that accepted you. Your oath remains to defend Tormalin from enemies without and tyranny within, with arms, with counsel and by enforcing the Emperor's writ.'

Temar watched as the Sieurs of minor Houses put their hands up at once, some hesitant, some with alacrity. Den Muret obstinately refused to look at Den Thasnet but Tor Priminale directed scathing contempt at Tor Bezaemar before slowly raising his hand. Den Murivance and Tor Kanselin both looked well content as they signalled ready agreement, a move spurring rapid compliance from Den Hefeken, Den Brennain and a score of others.

'Temar,' Allin hissed. 'Put your own hand up!'

Heat rising in his face, he did so, and was gratified to see that it prompted a further wave of agreement.

Messire D'Olbriot looked impassively at Temar before turning to Camarl, who was trying to hide his chagrin. 'As Adjurist, I must naturally call on my Designate to vote,' he remarked in an amiable aside to Tadriol that the entire room heard. 'Esquire Camarl? Does D'Olbriot stand with the Emperor for good governance?'

Camarl cleared his throat. 'Naturally, Messire.' He stuck an emphatic hand in the air.

Now all eyes were turned to the Sieur Tor Bezaemar. He raised a limp hand with a sickly smile in stark contrast to the white-faced fury of his aunt.

'Then we are all agreed,' said the Emperor happily. 'Thank you all for your patience. I suggest we enjoy ourselves.'

The musicians who'd been sitting studiously looking at their feet all this while began a lively tune but no one seemed inclined to dance. The crowd shifted and mingled, conversations breaking out on all sides.

'What are you going to say to Messire D'Olbriot?' breathed Allin at Temar's side.

'I really do not know,' he replied, still studying the Emperor's ring.

'He's coming over,' said Allin nervously. 'Do you want me to stay?'

Temar saw she was ashen with apprehension. 'Go and see what Velindre makes of it all,' he suggested.

All the same he felt uncomfortably bereft as he watched Allin sidle past Messire as the Sieur and his brothers advanced in matching step.

'Messire.' The Sieur D'Olbriot bowed politely and Temar returned the compliment.

'An unexpected turn of events,' was the best he could find to say.

'Indeed,' replied the Sieur. 'Quite unforeseen.'

'Can you manage all the affairs of Kellarin by yourself?' demanded Esquire Camarl, his voice hovering between belligerence and concern.

'Not without your help,' replied Temar forthrightly. 'I heard nothing forbidding me to ask anyone's counsel.'

'There'll be Houses queuing up to offer you advice,' said Camarl sourly.

'Then I will have to test it, to see if it's as sound as the guidance you have always given me.' Temar hoped Camarl wasn't going to sulk about this for long.

The Sieur smiled. 'We can discuss all this at our leisure. I just came to wish you luck, Temar. You're certainly going to need it.'

His brothers murmured their agreement, but Ustian surprised Temar with a friendly wink. 'Don't look at me like that, Fresil,' he rebuked his brother. 'Think it through and then argue if you must. While you do, I want a drink.' The Esquires and Sieur bowed and walked away, their conversation amiable.

'They'll be talking about this dance for years to come.'

'Ryshad!' Temar turned gratefully to find the chosen man at his elbow. 'Where were you?'

'With Casuel.' Ryshad nodded. 'He's choking on the ruination of his plans to be Imperial Sorcerer and Velindre's planning some come-uppance for Planir, if I'm any judge.' He broke off. 'It looks as if the Sieur Den Ilmiral wants to speak to you.'

Temar heaved a sigh. 'I would rather wait until I have some notion of what to say. Could we leave without causing undue offence?'

'Not really.' Ryshad frowned. 'But you can say you don't want to talk business on the last day of Festival. That's always been the custom, and if anyone doesn't like that it's their problem, not yours.'

'I hardly think that would be courteous, given the precedent the Emperor has just set,' muttered Temar glumly. 'How much longer does this entertainment last?'

'Not long, and I'll watch your back.' Ryshad managed a half-smile. 'The Emperor's Dole is distributed to the commonalty on the eighth chime of the day. That's when most of the nobility will leave.'

'If the populace is coming here to claim their bread and meat, can we risk going home without tripping over peasants and street urchins?' asked Temar sarcastically.

'The Emperor hands out coin these days, Temar.' Ryshad stepped aside to take a dutiful stance at his shoulder. 'Just smile politely and don't commit yourself to anything.'

Temar took a deep breath as the eager Sieur Den Ilmiral hurried over.

The Imperial Palace of Tadriol the Provident, Summer Solstice Festival, Fifth Day, Early Evening

'You must dine with us before you go overseas again.'

'As soon as I know what my plans are, I'll send word to your Steward.'

'Your Steward will contact his.' As the senior Esquire Den Haurient moved off, I leaned forward to murmur softly over Temar's shoulder. The lad was doing well with polite platitudes but there were still things he needed to learn.

We were circulating slowly around the anteroom while a few indefatigable dancers begged a few last tunes from the musicians. Temar paused to exchange some observation with the Maitresse D'Istrac before raising one eyebrow at me. 'What Steward?'

'You'll need one, now you're a Sieur,' I told him with a grin. 'And sworn men, and a residence, an archive, a Designate, a Maitresse, come to think of it.'

'I hardly think all that will be needed in Kel Ar'Ayen,' he began forcefully. He stopped and glared at me. 'You are joking?'

'Pretty much,' I allowed. 'But you do need a Steward of sorts.'

Temar looked thoughtful, but before he could speak the doors to the outer court opened and Tor Tadriol lackeys began discreetly alerting various nobles to the arrival of their carriages. 'Can we go now?' he asked instead.

'As soon as possible. We don't want to get caught up in the crowds coming for the Emperor's Dole.' I looked round for the Sieur and saw him coming towards us with Esquire Camarl at his side. 'Messire.' I bowed low.

'Ryshad.' He acknowledged me with a friendly nod. 'Temar, what are your plans for this evening?'

Temar looked nonplussed. 'Are we not going back to the residence?'

'I think we deserve a little time to ourselves, don't you?' Messire responded. 'Camarl and I are going to take a drive through the city, to find a quiet eating-house. Would you care to join us?'

'The residence will be full of girls giggling over the Esquires they danced with and comparing notes about dresses and fans,' Camarl added. He seemed in a better humour now.

'I've no wish to spoil my dinner with Fresil and Leishal arguing over today's surprises,' said Messire with unexpected frankness.

'Are they very displeased?' Temar enquired, equally blunt.

'Not so much displeased as wrong-footed,' said Messire judiciously.

'And yourself?' Temar asked.

'There's no sense in repining for what never was,' smiled Messire. 'Reason's a prop for a wise man or it's a cudgel for a fool.'

Temar looked at him somewhat uncertainly. 'So we all go forward as best we can?'

'Quite so.' Messire acknowledged a hovering footman with a nod. 'Are you joining us?'

'To show anyone wondering that we are still on good terms?' Temar hazarded.

'Festival is over, but the board will be set for a new game tomorrow,' Messire conceded. 'There's no harm in marking out our ground.'

'Getting ahead of those who've been so keen to trip us these last few days,' Camarl added.

Temar grinned. 'Then we will join you and gladly.'

'We're taking Ustian's expensive new equipage,' the Sieur explained as we walked out into the paved courtyard. 'He's going home with Fresil and Leishal.'

Temar wasn't listening and I saw he'd noticed Allin waiting, pleasantly pink and clutching her dance card like a talisman. 'Are you waiting for someone?' he asked her.

'Demoiselle Avila, if she can tear herself away from her conquests.' Something was amusing the young magewoman. 'Velindre was here a moment ago, but she's just been invited to supper with the Maitresse Den Janaquel.'

Voices behind us made me turn my head. Casuel was stalking along beside the leader of the musicians. Amalin Devoir had shed his coat and, with shirt collar loose and sleeves rolled up, he offered a sharp contrast to Casuel's precisely buttoned-up appearance.

'No, Cas, I insist. I've been well paid, and with a Festival gift from the Emperor himself I can buy you the finest meal in the city!' To my ear, Amalin's offer stemmed less from good will than from desire to lord over his brother.

'Ah, Master Devoir, my compliments,' the Sieur called. Casuel was about to reply but realised just in time Messire was talking to his brother. 'Your music was a perfect blend of the traditional and the innovative.'

The musician made a perfunctory bow. 'It was a day for novelty all round.'

Casuel bridled at this impertinence but Messire looked merely amused.

'Anyway, Amalin, thank you all the same but I'd better escort my apprentice back to her lodging.' Casuel nodded proprietorially at Allin but it was clear he'd just seized on the excuse she offered.

'She can come too,' countered Master Devoir promptly.

'Come where?' The excitements of the day seemed to have lifted years from Demoiselle Avila's shoulders.

Messire bowed. 'We're about to take a turn round the city and find a quiet place for supper.'

'I can recommend the Golden Plover,' Amalin interrupted to Casuel's obvious irritation. 'That's where we're going.'

Avila tapped her fan across her palm, a combative glint in her eye. 'Do you propose we all travel in that?' She pointed the bedraggled blue feathers at Ustian's open carriage, which had just drawn up, plainly only suitable for four passengers.

Amalin Devoir put finger and thumb in his mouth and split the genteel murmur of the courtyard with an ear-splitting whistle. 'My gig, as soon as you please!' A man in Den Janaquel livery turned to offer a gesture that would probably have been obscene if we hadn't had ladies standing with us. Seeing the Sieur D'Olbriot he sent a lad running out of the gates instead and a flashy gig soon came bowling into the courtyard. It was an expensive, tall-wheeled piece of work, driver's seat perched high in front of a highly polished body whose interior was luxuriously upholstered in purple. Ustian's carriage with its plain lines and dark green leather was a model of restrained good taste beside it.

'If you'll ride on the box with me, my lady,' Master Devoir favoured Allin with a blatantly flirtatious smile, 'there's room for two behind us. Cas and the Sieur D'Alsennin perhaps?'

Temar's expression instantly fixed as he tried to find some reason to avoid this. Fortunately Demoiselle Avila obliged. 'I'll ride with you, Master Mage.' Her tone suggested she was quite ready to squash the musician's pretensions.

'Let's make way for the other coaches.' Messire got into the open carriage with a discreet smile. 'This promises to be an entertaining evening,' he observed in an undertone as I sat in front of him, my back to the driver. Temar took the seat beside me as Camarl closed the half-door. As we pulled away I saw Firon Den Thasnet looking after us with naked hatred on his face.

Temar followed my gaze. 'I know Tadriol acted as he thought best, but it still galls me to think of Den Thasnet and Tor Bezaemar getting away with so much.'

'I agree.' Messire sighed. 'But we know what they did, as does the Emperor. I think we can rely on Tadriol to let judicious rumour circulate as appropriate. The main thing is that they failed.'

'But what manner of punishment is that? What about the Relict?' Temar wasn't going to let this go, and there wasn't room in the coach for me to shut him up with a discreet kick. 'She welcomed us in, all smiles and invitations, winning our trust, and all the while she was spinning snares like some fat old spider in the middle of a web. What of justice? She does us such injury and we have no revenge?'

'Revenge is overrated. We've half the egg each and all Tor Bezaemar's left with is an empty shell.' Messire's voice turned serious. 'Turn your thoughts to the future. You've a great deal of work ahead of you, young man, you and the Demoiselle Tor Arrial.'

'I am well aware of that,' Temar replied soberly.

'But not tonight.' Camarl acknowledged a merry salute from a group of revellers. 'Who did you dance with, Temar?'

The conversation turned to safely innocuous topics as the coach made slow progress through the raucous carousing of the lower city. As usual the commonalty were determined to squeeze the last drop of enjoyment out of their holiday. The morrow would see the first day of Aft-Summer calling them back to their workshops and duties, after all. I looked past Messire to see Allin giggling with the musician, who handled his mettlesome grey horse with considerable skill. Passers-by greeted us with cheers, some from dutiful loyalty, some too intoxicated to realise who was even in the coach but joining in regardless.

Once we were through the southern gate of the old town and on to the Primeway the crowds thinned considerably. An air of relaxation hung over aristocratic celebrations now that the demands of Festival had been met. The soft light of early evening gilded the city and a warm breeze caressed high- and low-born alike. Flambeaux were being readied and torches placed in brackets either side of doorways, ready to light the street when Halcarion wrapped up the sun in the soft swathes of dusk. Despite the heat a few traders were setting out braziers to cook delicacies to tempt passing revellers into spending their last few Festival pennies.

We turned into the Graceway and drew to an abrupt halt. 'What's the delay?' the Sieur called.

'Masqueraders, Messire.' The coachman twisted in his seat. 'Tumblers and jugglers.'

The footman sitting beside him looked back as well. 'Shall I move them on, Messire?'

'We're in no particular hurry,' D'Olbriot said carelessly.

'Cas was saying masqueraders are not fit entertainment for the well born,' Temar began.

I was about to give my opinion of the wizard's snobbery when movement caught my eye. We'd pulled up by the Den Bradile building where the frontage was being renewed and a wooden scaffold stood piled high with slates and heavy stone awaiting the morning's workmen.

A shadowy figure in an upper window jerked backwards. I'd barely time to realise he was bracing a pole against the aperture before the scaffold was levered outwards. Slates and marble came tumbling down, the heavy wood following.

'Move!' I lunged forward to grab the Sieur but Camarl was leaning sideways to see the acrobats, out of my reach. Temar was looking as well, his back to me. I sent him sprawling into the road, caught unawares by my brutal shove, as I hauled the Sieur out from beneath the deadly hail.

We fell heavily on to the cobbled road. The crash of the collapsing scaffold deafened me for a moment, muting horrified shouts and screams all around. With a cloud of dust stinging my eyes and choking my throat, I scrambled to my feet. Temar tripped and fell against me. We grabbed at each other, staggering sideways, and getting our footing we hauled the Sieur upright.

'Camarl?' Messire looked round wildly, blood oozing from a grazed cheek. The evening breeze scattered the dust and we saw the broken ruin that was the back end of Ustian's costly carriage. Worse, Camarl lay among the wreckage, gashed and bleeding, stunned beneath the slates and stones.

The horses were whinnying in panic as the coachman struggled to hold them. The carriage lurched, dropping hard on to its back axle as both rear wheels broke beyond hope. The shafts tilted upwards, harness gouging cruelly into the beasts, traces dangling dangerously near their frantically stamping hooves. Camarl gave an agonised yell as the shattered vehicle lurched forward, grating on the stones.

Messire hadn't suffered more than a few bruises and a coat of dust so I thrust him into Temar's hands. Ignoring the strain on my back and arms, I lifted the largest stone off Camarl's leg to uncover a nasty break, shards of bone visible in a ragged wound.

'I won't be dancing for a while,' the Esquire whispered shakily, face as white as the marble, blood oozing blackly down his leg.

'Hold on.' Guiding his arm round my neck, I struggled to raise him.

'Help, here, now!' Temar bellowed, looking up and down the Graceway.

A juggler came running, several masqueraders behind him. He raised a hand and in utter disbelief I saw him throw a heavy-weighted club with unerring aim. It hit the Sieur's coachman smack in the forehead, sending the man falling backwards like a poleaxed pig. The footman had very nearly got to the horses' bridles but this sudden disturbance sent them into a renewed frenzy, tossing their heads out of his reach.

'Ware behind!' Seeing a glint of steel in an oncoming masquerader's hand, I yelled a frantic warning. Dragging Camarl out of the wreckage, I could do nothing but watch appalled as the masquerader ran the helpless footman clean through. Heedless of his anguished cries, I dumped Esquire Camarl in a doorway.

'Temar! They're coming for us!' I caught up the juggler's treacherous club with one hand, grabbed Messire with the other, and shoved him behind me into the meagre shelter of the doorposts.

Temar had already got the measure of our situation, snatching up a broken scaffolding pole and bringing it round to sweep the feet out from beneath a masquerader rushing him with murderous intent. Another charged at me, live steel shining through the paint that covered his sword. I barely evaded the deceitful blade as I sidestepped his thrust, smashing the weighted club full into his face. The blow was hard enough to split his thin wooden mask clean in two. He fell back, clutching a smashed nose, blood gushing between his fingers. I snatched his sword away and drew a killing stroke backhanded across his guts, sending him on his way with a kick to one thigh.

Temar had scavenged a sword from somewhere too. He backed towards me, the blade held low and dangerous. As he did so, Halcarion threw us a little luck and the onward rush of the masqueraders was scattered by the horses charging headlong down the Graceway. The remains of the carriage swung wildly from side to side behind them. Startled Festival-goers fled in all directions, ducking to avoid splintered fragments of wood. One unfortunate chose the wrong direction, stepping directly into the frantic animals' path and disappearing beneath the horses' hooves. Screams of anguish from the woman with him added to the rising hubbub.

I whirled round as the door behind us opened. A startled face appeared in a handspan gap. 'Let us in, we've a wounded man! In D'Olbriot's Name!' I was shouting at wooden panels. The door slammed and we heard bolts being thrust home in panic.

'I can't stop the bleeding in this leg.' Messire had crimson stains spreading through the lace at his cuffs but his hands and voice were steady. He smiled reassurance at Camarl, who was shaking like a man in midwinter.

If one of the great blood vessels had been cut, Camarl would've died already. For the moment he was alive and I was more concerned with whoever might try to finish the job. The masqueraders were regrouping with malevolent intent but were now hampered by the uncomprehending crowd. People had spilled out of a tisane house across the road, wondering what was afoot. A tavern some way up the street was emptying, and confusion spread as indiscriminate attacks were launched, some on the acrobats, some on innocents mistaken for the scoundrels who'd started this.

A man in the buff breeches and plain shirt of a hireling servant hurried towards us. 'Send word to the Cohort,' I yelled.

He ignored me, breaking into a run and I saw a knife in his hand at the same time as the discarded mask in the gutter behind him. I swept a hasty cut at his wrist that Fyle would have mocked me for. All the same, he recoiled, so I tried to backhand him across the face with my sword. He ducked backwards again, harder to hit than a shade, but the knife hand curving round to my belly was no apparition. I blocked the thrust with my off hand, the force enough to numb his arm and send the blade clattering to the road. That didn't stop him stepping inside the reach of my sword, punching hard with his other hand, but at least my sideways step meant he only bruised my ribs rather than winding me. I brought my sword up to smash the hilt into the side of his head but the bastard threw himself bodily sideways. With an arm out before he landed, he rolled and was back on his feet with a tumbler's grace, eyes searching for his fallen knife. That instant of inattention was enough for Temar, who lunged to thrust his blade into the acrobat's side. The man staggered and fled, bloodied shirt flapping as he vanished into the crowd.

I looked to safeguard Temar's back and saw two men exchanging an uncertain look some paces beyond him. As I raised my sword with menace one broke, running headlong back down the Graceway. The other spread empty hands, gabbling in panic. 'Not me, your honour, not me.'

'Call out the Duty Cohort,' I bellowed at him. Looking up the road I saw other passers-by caught up in the spreading disorder, coaches and gigs held up in the distance and blocking the road. I cursed; Den Janaquel's men would almost certainly be on their way by now but they'd have some task breaking through to us. Men on all sides were struggling with masqueraders, either in self-defence, from a desire to help us or from simple drunken belligerence. Others were trying to leave, some frenzied enough to start new struggles around the initial skirmishes, hampering those intent on murdering us still further. But how to tell friend from foe? I sent a man who'd stumbled into me sprawling with a punch to the side of the head.

Could we escape down the road? Could we drag Camarl between us, and if so at what cost to him? As I looked I saw the hapless man I'd yelled at turn straight into the arms of two eager youths. They'd come running to see the commotion and immediately tried to wrestle him to the ground. 'No, let him go!' I yelled.

A whip split the air above their heads with a vicious crack. I saw Amalin Devoir's grey horse fighting to get its bit between its teeth, nostrils flared and eyes rolling wildly. The musician had the reins bunched in one hand as he laid about him indiscriminately with his lash, Allin clutching the seat with both hands. The lads and the man I'd sent for help all fled, ducking low with hands protecting their heads.

'Devoir! Casuel! Back off and get the Duty Cohort,' I yelled with a force that tore at my throat.

Devoir looked back over his shoulder but the confusion blocking the road made reversing impossible.

'Camarl is hurt!' Temar shouted with equal urgency. Allin caught sight of Messire kneeling beside the prostrate Esquire, her jaw dropping before she turned to relay information to Demoiselle Avila and Casuel, one hand gesturing.

'Temar!' I moved swiftly to intercept one man scrambling over the debris of scaffolding with evil in his eyes and a sword in each hand. Temar was about to follow but a hail of stones and juggling balls from two acrobats appearing in the mouth of an alleyway forced him to duck and dodge backwards. Temar snatched up a piece of broken panelling from the carriage to protect his head, moving to shield Messire and Camarl with his body.

The man facing me dropped to a wrestler's crouch. He had the brutish and battered face of a prizefighter but he had two blades and, for all I knew, was perfectly able to use them. He thrust at me, each hand in turn, clumsy strokes but fast and unhesitating. Moving back I felt splintered wood treacherous beneath the soft half-boots I was wearing. I took a two-handed grip on my sword and went in hard, circling the blade round and back on itself, half parrying, half attacking. Swordplay learned for the stage made a novice of the man, who instinctively fell into the trap of anticipating my strokes and moving to parry too early. Now I had the initiative I tempted him into an upward sweep and then ripped a sudden sideways cut underneath his arms. As I sliced his chest open his arms flung back in nerveless shock and I wrenched my blade up still further, tearing the notched steel into his bull neck. He collapsed, gurgling through a spray of blood.

I wiped drops off my face to see Temar smashing his improvised buckler into the head of some new attacker. The man turned and would have escaped down the nearby alley but the jugglers blocked his way and I realised they had their own problems. A swarm of what looked like ruddy, greyish hornets swirled around them, but there was no buzzing and whenever one of the dots darted in to land on cloth smoke rose briefly from black scorch marks. Angry red blisters appeared on the jugglers' exposed hands and faces, raised by scarlet sparks glowing and vanishing so swiftly they deceived the eye. I saw Allin still hanging on grimly to Devoir's frivolous gig, plump face intent with hatred as she glared at the acrobats. An empty brazier some way beyond the alley was smoking emptily but for a fading crimson light.

Devoir had beaten his horse into trembling submission, the poor beast too terrified to know whether it should flee forwards or back. Demoiselle Avila was struggling down from the back, Casuel wringing anguished hands as he followed her, cowering inside his ostentatious robe. Avila ignored the commotion all around as she headed straight for the doorway behind me. Temar ran forward to draw her into our frail circle of protection as fast as he could.

I'd have gone too but a vicious fistfight erupted in front of me, stones and broken wood hurled indiscriminately from the sidelines, and it was all I could do to stop the combatants falling over me, the Sieur, the Esquire. Temar and I were jostled from all sides, unable to tell hapless Festival-goers from murderous masqueraders, so forced to drive all comers off with harsh words and harder blows. Casuel yelped with outrage as I stood on his foot, but that served him right for trying to shelter between me and Temar. A stinging pain licked around the back of my neck.

'Shit, Devoir, watch that cursed whip!' But I forgave the musician when I saw he was laying about with it to keep the brawl from crushing Demoiselle Avila and the Sieur as they knelt in the doorway, busy with Esquire Camarl's wounds.

A brazen note pierced the tumult, Den Janaquel's horns finally giving notice of their imminent arrival. The strident signal came again, warning everyone to get clear or face the consequences. Efforts to struggle free of the fighting redoubled all around us and I saw several masqueraders ripping off their masks in hopes of disappearing into the anonymous crowd.

But three weren't abandoning their disguises and I wondered just who they might be, hacking a way through the turmoil with vicious swords, the bland wooden faces of folk tale heroes still tied on tight. They were heading for the alley opposite.

'Temar!' I yelled, pointing, as the crush around us lessened.

'Run them to earth, Ryshad!' The Sieur was at my elbow, a sword in his hand, Master Devoir with him, whip ready.

Temar and I used sword pommels, flat blades, fists and elbows to try to force a path to intercept the bastards. We were just too late and the three men hared down the alley, turning into a ginnel running between the backs of the close-packed buildings. I was after them like a loosed courser, Temar hard on my heels.

'Just run, man,' he was raging, and I realised we'd caught Casuel up in the pursuit. With the narrow alley giving him nowhere to step aside to let Temar pass, all he could do was run with us.

The masqueraders were holding their distance but only at

the cost of running at full tilt, not daring to try any doors or gates into yards or outhouses. Using every effort I could summon I was gaining, and I heard Temar behind me mercilessly driving Casuel on with ever fouler curses. The masqueraders turned a sharp corner into a wide alley. As I skidded after them, I realised the far end opened into a walled yard. A broad stone arch was carved with archaic flourishes, vines heavy with leaves and fruit on either side of open gates. I recognised it for the yard behind the Popinjay and frustration burned in my heaving chest. If they got out into the busy northern end of the Primeway, we'd lose the bastards for certain.

'Bring that down!' I turned to yell hoarsely at Casuel who was leaning in the corner of a wall, half doubled up, one hand clutching his throat. 'Block their way!'

'Noseless sons of pox-rotted whores!' spat Temar, racing past me.

That youth had been spending too much time with mercenaries. But I had no breath to say so and I ran after him.

Ahead of us the first masquerader was nearly into the yard, but just as I thought he'd escaped us the carved vines reached out from either side of the arch. They laced themselves together, coiling around each other, quicker than the eye could comprehend. A barrier of pale strands blocked the villain's way but he was running too fast to stop himself slamming into the crisscross of writhing stone. The tangle knotted and twined around him, each tendril swelling into a branch reaching up and outwards. Tugged this way and that the man struggled frantically, yelling in terror as he was lifted clear of the ground. His cries of fear turned to anguish as his body was twisted with audible wrenching, sinew and bone no match for the implacable pull of the rippling lattice. A final hideous snap silenced his howls, leaving his body hanging contorted in the coils of the warped vines.

The second man had stumbled to a halt a scant arm's length away but in the moment he took to recover his balance a yellow limb snaked out from the living archway. Leaves once wrought from solid rock waved softly as the sinuous vine coiled around his legs. The man screamed in horror and hacked at the curling stem but his blade simply struck sparks from the stone. A second tendril darted out to wrap itself round his sword arm, smothering it. As he tore at it with frantic, bleeding nails, new shoots sprouted to snarl around the hand he'd had free a breath before. New leaves budded and opened all over the intertwining stems now rooting his feet to the ground. But the vines binding his arms were still curling upwards in an insane parody of growth, racking the man ever more painfully. He shrieked some inarticulate curse with his last strangled gasps as the heedless branches forced him backwards in an agonising curve. His spine snapped like a dry stick.

All this happened in no more time than it took me and Temar to catch up to the third man. He was frozen in horror, but hearing our steps behind him he whirled round, eyes white rimmed with panic visible even through the holes in his mask. He was too appalled to raise his sword and I was too surprised. With a move nine parts instinct to one part training I punched him up beneath the rim of the mask, catching him full in the soft flesh beneath his jaw. He collapsed to his knees, choking and pawing at his throat.

'Let's see who you are, you shit.' As I yanked at the knotted ribbons holding on the concealing mask, I noticed for the first time that his clothes weren't the usual masquerader's shoddy pretence of noble dress. He was wearing the real thing, well-cut silk and expensive broadcloth. The hair I pulled out as it caught in the ribbons of the mask was perfumed with expensive pomade.

'Kreve Tor Bezaemar?' No wonder he had wanted to get away, identity hidden beneath this charade. Temar raised his sword in outrage and moved behind the kneeling man. 'Stand clear, Ryshad, and I will have this cur's head off!'

The last thing I wanted was the bastard going free to launch some new attack some other day, but I couldn't allow that. 'No!' I stepped between Temar and the still wheezing Esquire, eyes shut and tears pouring down his face.

'I have the right.' Temar glared at me.

'Yes, you do,' I agreed. 'But let the Emperor sanction his death. Wait until he's stood his trial in full view of every House in Toremal. That'll discredit Tor Bezaemar so thoroughly their Name won't aspire to the throne for fifty generations!'

'And if your advocates and their weasel words find him some excuse, some escape?' Temar challenged hotly.

'It won't happen,' I caught Temar's sword hand, speaking with absolute conviction. 'He raised open murder against two Sieurs in direct defiance of Imperial decrees given not half a day since. That's treason against the good order of the Empire and he'll die for it, trust me.' Ignoring Kreve's hoarse gasps I shoved the bastard on to his front and rested a heavy foot on his back.

Temar looked unconvinced but lowered his sword.

'If we're going to cut his head off, I'll do it,' I offered with savage humour as I released his hands. 'The Sieur D'Alsennin shouldn't soil his hands with such vermin's blood. And why don't you see who else Cas caught in his snare?'

'I suppose I may as well,' Temar agreed once a glance convinced him the incapacitated Kreve was going nowhere. Lifting the lolling head of the second man to die, he pulled off his mask with difficulty. 'Firon Den Thasnet,' he called back over his shoulder. 'I suppose we should have expected that.'

'I don't see Saedrin calling us to answer for him.' I glanced up as I secured Kreve Tor Bezaemar's hands behind his back with the ribbons cut from his mask. 'Who's the other one?'

Temar looked up uncertainly at the man hanging some way above him. 'My compliments to Master Devoir, but I am not about to try climbing this. Can you bring him down, Casuel?'

'I'm not sure I can.' The mage had come to stand next to me, white-faced at his own achievement.

'You must know how you did that?' I looked curiously at the wizard.

'Of course,' retorted Casuel with frosty dignity. 'In general terms, at least.' His poise melted as he stared up at his handiwork. 'I suppose we'll have to tell the Archmage about this, will we?'

The rear door to the Popinjay was opening slowly. After a long moment of hesitation on the threshold Banch advanced reluctantly into the yard, Ezinna urging him on with a savage hiss. He looked appalled at the enchanted forest sprouting from his ancient arch. At least it couldn't really be seen from the street, I realised with belated relief. Magic as dramatic as this would hardly suit the Emperor's declared prejudice against wizardry. We'd best get the evidence out of sight before it became a wonder for half the city to gawp at.

'We'll get it back to how it was,' I shouted to Banch, giving Casuel a dig in the ribs. The wizard was still gazing in some bemusement at the leaves and fruit, now all immobile unyielding stone again.

'You can stuff that where your mother never kissed you,' rejoined Banch shakily. 'Take a sledgehammer to it. I want it broken and carted away before the day's out, and I don't want so much as the dust from mortar left behind.'

'The magic is quite passed away,' protested Casuel indignantly.

'I want it gone, all of it!' Banch turned on his heel, pushing Ezinna back inside and slamming the door behind him.

I looked at Casuel. 'Can you break it down?'

'I suppose so,' he said a trifle sulkily. Scowling he rubbed his hands together, palms flat. Amber light sparked from his fingertips, incandescent shards of magic flying through the air to land on the coiled stone. Hairline cracks began spreading across the yellow stems, golden light darkening to a burning ochre as fractures gaped wider and wider, dust falling first, then small chips, finally pieces of stone as big as a man's fist. Temar backed away hurriedly and the body of the first man to die fell to the ground in a broken heap.

Temar moved forward with a cautious eye lest any masonry fall on his head. He shook his head when he'd ripped away the attacker's mask. 'I do not know the man.'

'No, nor me.' I stared down at the face now slack in death. 'Probably some minor Esquire, promised the sun, the moons and the stars in between by Kreve. Still, at least we've got him to face Imperial justice.'

Temar looked towards the prostrate villain. 'Not if he dies on us. How hard did you hit him?'

I was horrified to see Tor Bezaemar's face suffused with blood, his breath little more than a thready gurgle. 'Shit, I must have broken his windpipe.' Not checking on him had been a novice's mistake, for all I'd been distracted by Casuel's little display.

'Take him to Demoiselle Avila,' suggested Temar.

'At once,' I agreed. 'Cas, clear this all up and fast.'

'I hardly think—' he began indignantly.

'Do you want the Emperor asking Planir for an explanation?' I demanded. I held Kreve Tor Bezaemar under the arms while Temar caught up his legs. The bastard was an unwieldy burden and the distance back seemed thrice as far as we'd originally run, but fear for his worthless hide spurred us on.

We stepped out on to the Graceway to find a solid phalanx in Den Janaquel livery surrounding Messire and Camarl, sworn men with staffs levelled and sergeants-at-arms carrying unsheathed swords. More of the Cohort had the road blocked off for some distance in either direction and those caught inside the cordon were only being set free when two other people could vouch for their name and business. Several erstwhile masqueraders and acrobats were face down in the dust, trussed up like roasting fowl.

A number of sworn men moved towards us. I nodded with some difficulty at my armring, sweating freely. 'Where's the Demoiselle Tor Arrial? We need her at once.'

'She's busy with the injured.' Allin stopped as she went past with a steaming cup in each hand. 'Can I get you a tisane?'

'Get Demoiselle Avila,' I told her flatly. 'Otherwise this man dies and Tor Bezaemar escapes all punishment.'

Allin thrust the cups at a startled man-at-arms and raced off, hitching up her skirts. Temar and I laid the stricken Kreve down as gently as we could and looked guiltily at each other. Demoiselle Avila appeared and knelt beside the stricken youth without a word. Laying gentle hands on his throat, she began murmuring some rhythmical enchantment that soon had the dark colour fading from his face. As the Esquire's ribs laboured to draw air into his starved lungs my own breathing eased, along with the apprehension I could see mirrored in Temar's expression.

'I take it he turned out to be the worm in the apple?' Avila sat back on her heels, heedless of the filth on her gown, lace overdress torn in a handful of places. Her thin face was weary but the gleam in her eyes promised ill for Tor Bezaemar. 'I would rather be using my energies to tend the innocent injured.'

'Ryshad tells me it is for the Emperor to judge him,' Temar said, still rather mutinously.

'Quite so, though you seem to have done a fair job in the meanwhile.' Den Janaquel men parted to let Messire D'Olbriot through. He looked down at Kreve, who was still insensible, eyes closed. 'I'd say you have your revenge on Dirindal now, D'Alsennin. She's pinned all the hopes of the House on this lad since he first grew out of soft shoes.'

Temar looked suddenly disconcerted and sudden memories, not my own, assailed me. Temar had carried the burden of his grandsire's expectation throughout his turbulent youth and that in part is what had driven him to Kellarin.

'Is Esquire Camarl all right?' I asked abruptly.

'Thanks to my lady Tor Arrial.' Messire's poise was unmarred despite the lavish smears of blood darkening on his elegant clothes. 'As soon as Den Janaquel can get us a coach, shall we go back to the residence? We're hardly dressed for dining out now, and I think we've had enough excitement for one evening.' He brushed at a swathe of dust on one leg and I saw a faint tremor in his hand.

'What happens to him?' Temar demanded, prodding Kreve with a hostile toe.

'Den Janaquel's men will take care of him,' the Sieur

promised with steely authority. 'Their House is no friend to Tor Bezaemar, and they know well enough that the Emperor will have their necks stretched if anything goes awry.'

It galled me to leave Kreve in someone else's custody, but as a proven man in Den Janaquel's colours arrived with a carriage for the Sieur I had no choice. At least the grim expressions on the faces all around the unconscious Tor Bezaemar reassured me that these men would be as good as their sworn word.

CHAPTER SEVEN

The Sieur Endris D'Olbriot has caused this annal to be recorded and charges all who come after him to continue this work, in the sacred Name of Saedrin, Keeper of the Keys to the Otherworld, whose judgement every man must face

As Winter Solstice brings this year to a close, I do not know how to record a date, since all calendars are meaningless in the chaos that overwhelms us. The best I can offer is my recollection that this is the twenty-eighth year since the final solstice of Nemith the Last, also known as the Reckless. After the trials of this last generation I wonder if my father and uncles would have so rudely pulled even so wretched a ruler from his throne if they had suspected the calamities that would befall us. Should our once respected forebears be condemned as reckless in their turn? Do we suffer as a result of their impiety or does Raeponin weigh our own transgressions and finding us wanting, give Poldrion the nod to loose misfortune upon us?

The direst news I can attest to this Mid-Winter is that deaths of those bearing our Name have outnumbered births in this past year and who knows how many to those infants will succumb to the privations of hunger and disease in the seasons to come. Spurred by this, I have charged my scribes and Esquires to list each property remaining in the D'Olbriot Name, with a full list of every tenant, their claims upon us, the charges they have made on our coffers these five years past and the benefits we have gained from their loyalty. Raeponin be my judge, I have not seen the results as yet, but I predict a sorry tale of an ever shrinking fiefdom and who dares hope that there is not yet worse to come.

Let these words and the parchments appended thereto act as my defence down the generations, to whatever sons of D'Olbriot might survive to carry forward our Name, for the actions I am about to take.

We can no longer stand alone, on the dignity of our inveterate independence. The lone sheep is wolves' meat and we are beset with marauders on every side. I purpose therefore to join with those following the Den Modrical pennant, trading what force of arms we may muster for aid in defending our lands under direction of the Sieur Laenthal. I have watched over the seasons as this youth has risen to rule his House through proven skill as a warrior and by virtue of a character more forceful than any I have seen, even in men twice his age. Minor Names, cast adrift with the breaking of every tie to their earliest loyalties, have been flocking to his banner. Inside a year he has raised a formidable force, winning notable victories against the predations of brigands from the Dalasor grasslands.

Why must I seek to justify my course when Laenthal is so clearly an effective leader of action and resolve? Because I have reservations about both Den Modrical ambitions and practices and wish to make these known under the seal of our Name, lest I die before I can nominate a Designate in proper form and confide such vital matters in person.

I can forgive a young man the conceit that prompts him to invent spurious claims to a legendary lineage but I wonder why Laenthal encourages his fellows to swear so fervently that Den Modrical descends from so many ancient Houses. Whether this is truth or lie, the facts are lost in the mists of time. How do such fictions serve, when any man of my generation recalls full well the lowly status of the Name in the Nemith era? Are we supposed to be impressed with his array of pennants and badges of yore purloined from a miscellany of Houses? Still, such trifles are largely harmless compared to the daily perils we face.

Less harmless is the youth's assertion that anyone not with him will be deemed against him. Demanding allegiance at sword point can never be but folly. Nor can I approve Laenthal's subsequent tactics to ensure continued loyalty. True enough, service as a page to a companion noble House has always been part of an Esquire's education, but in these uncertain times the custom has been in abeyance for nigh on a generation. For my part, I see the gang of youths now travelling between the Modrical possessions under ostensible guard against bandits as little better than hostages for their families' good conduct. Yet I must nominate an Esquire from every branch of D'Olbriot, senior and cadet, and deliver them into Laenthal's custody before I can expect him to bring his lances and swords to drive the northern reivers and masterless men from our lands. That they will certainly learn their letters and reckoning at another's expense is scant consolation when I foresee they will also be inculcated with Laenthal's peculiarly ruthless philosophies.

But what other path is open to me? The gods have all but abandoned us, with every Artifice that priests were wont to use in our service found wanting. Shall I resort to these unsanctified sorceries that some can wield without blessing of god or man? Laenthal makes no secret of his loathing of such fell arts, putting any showing such skills to the sword without fear or favour. I might suspect some self-seeking in his ready condemnation but I cannot deny it gives any Sieur desperate enough to consider using a wizard pause for thought.

Den Modrical have been claiming their victories are proof of divine favour. Then let Raeponin weigh Laenthal's sincerity in the balance and Saedrin can judge him as he sees fit. I will not do so. All my efforts must be spent in service of my House, and as Poldrion is my witness I see no better choice to defend D'Olbriot than Den Modrical. Thereto I set my seal.

The D'Olbriot Residence, Toremal,
7th of Aft-Summer in the Third Year of Tadriol the Provident

'The Sieur's compliments and will you attend him in the library.' The footman delivered the message with a bland lack of emotion and I received it with a similar nod.

I was in the gatehouse watch room amending a duty roster, one of a whole collection of tasks allotted me as soon as the Festival had ended. With Naer and Stoll both senior to me, I was chosen for all the most tedious and recurrently exasperating responsibilities. That's always the way of it, I reminded myself sternly as I took my penknife to the recalcitrant quill. I had no right to complain. The lowliest sworn find themselves emptying privies and sweeping the floors until the sergeant-at-arms recruits someone new for them to look down on in turn. It's the longest sworn who man the gates, bowing and courteous to passing nobles and pocketing passing silver.

By that same custom Stoll was out visiting a swordsmith on the House's behalf, while by this chime Naer would be sharing a companionable flagon with Fyle, discussing just who they might recognise out of the eager would-be sworn who fetch up after every Festival. Which is why I was trying to make sense of hastily scribbled notes working out how to allow Verd leave to visit his sick father when Indar was out of the reckoning on account of coming back from Festival with a broken hand.

I took one last look down the roster; surely that would suffice? Then I cursed under my breath, seeing I'd placed three raw recruits all on the same watch. There was no way that could stand, with no one experienced to stiffen their backbone.

'Pense, you've got the duty.' I snapped the lid on the

inkwell and set down my pen. The senior sworn man came in with alacrity to take a stool in the watch room. 'Make the most of it,' I advised him lightly. 'We're on duty in the stableyard this afternoon.'

Pense groaned. 'Tell me we're seeing the back of the last guests today?'

I nodded. 'As far as I know.' I'd be as relieved as anyone else not to spend my days ferrying trunks, caskets and frivolous purchases to the carts and coaches that had cluttered up the yard and lanes for the last few days.

I walked through the empty grounds to the residence. The halls were strangely silent after the constant commotion of Festival. Everywhere was clean and polished, garlands all tidied away, the few servants round and about taking their time over minor tasks. There was a faintly tired air about the place.

Messire was alone in the library, where everything was once more in its customary place. The chests of documents and deeds brought out in anticipation of battles in the courts had been returned to the archive. Avila's casket, its hidden treasures and her lists were nowhere to be seen. Everything connected to Kellarin had been removed to a salon on the far side of the residence; everything D'Alsennin might need set apart. Temar had been receiving a steady flow of visitors while D'Olbriot held firmly aloof.

'Good day to you, Ryshad.' The Sieur sat in a chair on one side of the empty fire. He didn't motion me to sit.

'Messire.' I bowed.

'I understand you were summoned yesterday by the Justiciar gathering evidence for and against Kreve Tor Bezaemar?' Messire enquired.

'Indeed. I told him everything I knew.' And much that I suspected or merely guessed; it was the Justiciar's job to sort the wheat from the chaff. If he'd questioned everyone in the same exhaustive detail he'd demanded of me, it was going to be a long job.

'If you're on duty with the guard, D'Alsennin must be out this morning,' he observed. I'd been placed at Temar's disposal along with the empty reception chamber for whenever he was within D'Olbriot's walls. Beyond he was on his own, at least until he swore some men of his own.

'Where is D'Alsennin?' the Sieur enquired.

'He's visiting the Sieur Den Janaquel,' I replied promptly.

'In connection with what?' Messire raised an amiable eyebrow.

I hesitated half a breath before answering. 'To discuss that House's holdings around Kalaven.'

'To discuss how Den Janaquel grain might feed D'Alsennin's people,' said the Sieur with a faint hint of reproof. 'In exchange for what? Wood? Ore? Hides?'

'I can't say, Messire.' I said simply.

'Can't or won't?' Messire raised a hand. 'I'm sorry, but then that's not the first time I've said that to you, is it? I don't suppose you're finding this division of your time any more satisfactory than anyone else.'

He paused, clearly expecting an answer.

'I do my duty as it's presented to me,' I said stiffly. I'd found the constantly changing demands on me something of a trial, true enough, but at least it meant I'd been too busy to think about anything beyond that day or the next.

'D'Alsennin plans to sail for Kellarin around the turn of For-Autumn, I understand,' Messire remarked. 'When you're no longer so indispensable, we must arrange a grace house for you. You can send for that redhead of yours, if you're still so inclined. Then we'll assign you some permanent duties within the household. I know Leishal wants more assistance, and as a chosen man you should be helping manage the affairs of the House from a comfortable chair, not scurrying around wearing out boot leather.'

Something must have shown in my face because the Sieur burst out laughing.

'Forgive me, Ryshad, but you look like Myred bracing himself to dine with his aged aunts. It's my fault, I suppose. I kept you out on the roads for so long as an enquiry agent you're spoiled for this kind of duty, aren't you?'

I wasn't sure I liked that, but equally these past few days had shown me with brutal clarity that I really didn't like barracks life any more. 'I'll soon get used to it.' As soon as I spoke, I wondered how long the words would remain a lie.

'No doubt you would,' said the Sieur briskly, 'but it wouldn't alter the fact you'd be as well suited to it as a saddle horse pulling a coal cart. And there are other concerns.'

He paused again but I stayed silent.

'The time's come to speak frankly, Ryshad.' Messire leaned back in his chair, clasping his hands beneath his chin. 'You're a good man, always have been, but no man can serve two masters. D'Alsennin looks to you for advice – no, I'm not objecting. After Tadriol's decrees, there are few enough people he can turn to under this roof, and Saedrin knows the boy needs someone to guide him. But I cannot ignore the potential dangers. I'm sure you give of your best, you wouldn't do anything else, but sometime soon you're going to find what's best for D'Alsennin doesn't serve D'Olbriot, or conversely D'Olbriot interests will run counter to Kellarin's.'

This time his silence demanded a response and one sprang from the most basic precepts of my training. 'My first loyalty is to my oath.'

'Forgive me, Ryshad, but however much you might believe that I'm no longer convinced it's true.' Messire's conversational tone couldn't mask the severity of his words. 'Again, I bear much of the responsibility. I encouraged you to use your own initiative as an enquiry agent, your own judgement, but over this Festival I've seen too many occasions where your judgement has been to place D'Alsennin priorities over D'Olbriot's. You're acting as D'Alsennin's Steward in all but name as it is, and you cannot do that with a ring bearing my badge around your arm.'

I managed to keep my voice emotionless. 'Are you saying I should be wearing D'Alsennin insignia?'

'My business isn't with D'Alsennin, it's with you,' Messire shrugged. 'My concern must always be for this House and that means dealing with realities, however unexpected or unpleasant they might be. Some day, and one probably none too distant, you'll find yourself with a choice of either being true to yourself or true to your oath. I refuse to be responsible for putting you in such an invidious position, Ryshad, and that means I must hand you back your oath.'

Hollow confusion filled me. 'You're dismissing me from your service?' The Sieur's words and my own echoed inside my head.

'It's time for you to be your own man again,' the Sieur said with a sigh. 'You're a good man, Ryshad, and a loyal one. Since you'd see this choice as a betrayal, I have to be the one to make the decision for both of us. If I'm wrong, tell me so and I'll beg your pardon most humbly, but I gave you that armring to honour you and I won't see you wear it until it chafes you beyond bearing.'

All I could do was slide the gleaming copper down my arm and over my wrist. A selfish qualm assailed me; I could hand it back to the Sieur spotless but leaving his service like this would surely tarnish my reputation irrevocably.

Messire held out his hand and I took a step to place the gleaming circle on his palm.

'Thank you.' The Sieur turned the ring with careful fingers, frowning. 'I gave you this to honour you, Ryshad, and I won't see you dishonoured by such a turn of events. None of us could have foreseen the way this game would play out.'

He set the armring aside, reaching down into the shadow between his chair and the wall. Grunting slightly, he lifted up a pale wooden box, decorated in squares and rectangles cut with precise black inlay. 'This should convince you of the value I place on your service.' He fished in a pocket for the key to the neat brass lock. 'And anyone else looking to crow over you. You'll have to move out of the gatehouse, naturally, and it won't be fitting for you to eat with the servants any longer, but you can stay in a grace house until the turn of the season at least, longer if need be. Take your time to decide what you want from your future, Ryshad; don't make any hasty decisions. Don't let other people's needs sway you either, not D'Alsennin's nor anyone else. As I said, it's time for you to be your own man.'

I was still tongue-tied. I tucked the key in my belt-pouch and took the box. It was wide enough to need both hands and surprisingly heavy for its size. As I tucked it under my arm, the tight-packed contents made barely a chink.

'Come and see me if you've any questions,' the Sieur said briskly. 'Naturally, I'll vouch for you with any merchant or landlord or—' Inspiration failed him and I saw sadness hanging heavily over his head.

That wasn't something I could face so I bowed low. 'My thanks, Messire.'

Finishing the duty roster didn't seem important. I walked out of the residence and round behind the kitchens to sit on the stone rim of Larasion's fountain in the middle of the herb garden. I set the wooden box down beside me and looked at it. When a chosen or proven man is handed back his oath on retirement, all those sworn to the House assemble to see the Sieur hand over some valuable expression of his esteem. By long custom the man thus rewarded hands the coin back, declaring that the privilege of having served the Name has been honour enough. When that day came for Stoll or Fyle, they'd be well able to pay the Sieur such a compliment, secure in the knowledge that they had a grace house until their death and a pension to draw from D'Olbriot coffers at the start of every season. Now I had no such shelter from whatever storms might fall on my unprotected head.

I wondered what was in the box but made no move to unlock it. Whether it was copper or noble Crowns made no real difference. For the first time since I'd fetched up on D'Olbriot's doorstep, a lad desperate for some direction in his life, I was facing a future without certainties, without any right to a roof, to food, to support from my fellows.

So why did I feel so absurdly relieved? Emotions were tumbling through my mind in the peace of the herb garden and trying to make sense of them was as easy as trying to catch the sparkles of sunlight in the water of the fountain, but time and again what I felt was relief. It gave way to apprehension, then turned into perverse defiance, but each time I came back to relief.

I got myself in hand. What would I do now? Where would I go once my period of grace was over? The prospect of trying to convince my mother I'd not been turned out in dishonour was a daunting one, and the year would have turned and come full circle before Hansey and Ridner ran out of sly comments. That alone made the notion of going back to Zyoutessela unwelcome. Anyway I could no more go back to stonecutting than I could beg the Sieur to swear me to his service again.

Then there was telling Livak how dramatically our plans had gone awry. There'd be no future for the pair of us as proven man and his lady managing D'Olbriot affairs in some comfortably distant city. So some good had come out of all this, I smiled wryly to myself. The Sieur was right; I'd forgotten just how tedious close attendance on the Name could be. My smile faded. Perhaps he had done me a favour, but I still felt rebuffed. True enough, it was plain things couldn't have gone on as before, but I wasn't sure I liked having the decision taken out of my hands like this.

But that's what swearing your service away does for you, some rational corner of my mind scolded me. Sitting here in the sage-scented calm, I had to admit that submitting to other people's decisions had been galling me of late. Whatever else I might do, I decided, I wouldn't be swearing myself to Temar. Swearing service as a young man had been easy, putting my fate into another's hands a relief. Life had been clearer then, a puppetry tale of predictable characters in stock dilemmas making black and white decisions. As a grown man I'd learned life was far more complicated. My own desires were a mass of contradictions to begin with and I knew full well people around me wore more faces than a masquerader.

Which was all very well as far as philosophical musing went, but what next? My mother had never been one to tolerate indecision. 'You can't buy a bun and still save your penny,' she'd always told us as children. I unlocked the box to see how many buns I could buy with Messire's assessment of my worth.

'Dast's teeth!' I could buy my own bakery with the stacks of white gold packed tight with scraps of silk tucked in each hollow. I could buy the land to grow the wheat and a mill to turn the grain to flour and still have silver to squander.

My spirits rose. Messire always said there's no point repining over what's already done, didn't he? Livak and I had set ourselves to his service at the turn of the year in order to earn the coin that would give us choices for our future. Well, I had a whole casket full of choices here, and if Livak had won any aetheric lore from her travels whatever Planir or D'Olbriot owed her could only widen our options still further.

Before I made any decisions, whether to buy that flour mill or outfit a mercenary troop and go off to claim the throne of Lescar, I needed to talk to Livak. I locked my box and tucked it securely under my arm, trying to remember where Casuel had said he was going to be today. He could bespeak Usara, I decided. Usara would know where Livak was and what she was up to. Then I'd go back to the gatehouse and finish off that roster; I could at least take my leave of that duty on my own terms.

The Imperial Menagerie, Toremal
20th of Aft-Summer in the Third Year of Tadriol the Provident

'You have a remarkable collection of animals.' Temar hoped this was the right thing to say, and more, that he didn't sound as bored as he felt. Doubtless polite chitchat with the Emperor was a duty of his new rank but he'd rather be getting on with the five score and one things he had to organise before sailing back to Kel Ar'Ayen.

'Though it's not quite what one expects in such a nicely Rational garden, is it?' The Emperor tossed a nut at a tiny, white-faced, copper-haired ape sitting quietly in the corner of a cage. It watched the treat land without visible change in its expression. 'But it's become rather a contest between the Houses, to send me some beast never before seen in Toremal, some exotic rarity bought from an Aldabreshin warlord or some hairy curio snared in the Great Forest.'

Temar looked at the morose little ape and it glared balefully back at him. 'I will have to see what oddities Kel Ar'Ayen can offer.' Was that what was expected of him?

'That's one rivalry with the Names on this side of the ocean that I think you could enter into without too much danger.' The Emperor bowed politely at two distant Demoiselles who were looking with interest into an aviary where brightly coloured songbirds flitted above lavishly tailed fowl scratching around the floor. 'It's almost certainly what people will imagine we're discussing, which is why I asked you to meet me here.'

Temar looked around the gardens, seeing couples, young and old, sauntering between cages and enclosures, veils of lace drawn forward to shade sensitive skin from the sun and feathered fans busy in the heat.

'Some of those birds must be worth ten times their weight in gold, just for the plumes in their tails,' he commented.

The Emperor nodded. 'We have the occasional break-in but we give mastiffs the run of the place after dark. It's a shame we don't still have wolves to let loose. That would keep the chancers out for certain!'

'You have no such larger beasts then?' Temar wondered when Tadriol was going to come to whatever point he was aiming for.

The Emperor chuckled. 'It was a fashion in the days of Aleonne the Gallant for Houses to send the Emperor whatever beast they had on their badge. D'Olbriot sent a lynx, my forefathers a bull, that kind of thing.'

'At least a holm oak will not prove too difficult to catch,' Temar said with heavy humour.

'By all means send me one.' Tadriol waved a hand at a nearby tree laden with long, flame-coloured blossoms. 'That was planted by Den Bruern, before they were subsumed into D'Olbriot. No, the whole game fell into disfavour when superstition started running rife. The Sieur Den Haurient died two days after the wolf he'd sent to be reared from a pup dropped dead, and then half the Esquires of Den Somaer drowned when their ship went down not ten days after a flock of their pheasants all died of some cough.'

'So everyone watched the health of their beast as if it were their own?' guessed Temar. Was there some hint he should be picking up in all this inconsequentiality? He really had more important things to do.

'Quite so.' The Emperor walked on, pausing to throw a nut into an apparently empty enclosure. A small furry animal Temar couldn't identify darted out of a hole and vanished with its prize. 'Then some rumour started about the Tor Leoreil fox barking at any woman who wasn't a virgin and a handful of betrothals were broken off because of it. The final disaster was a wild boar D'Istrac sent down from Dalasor. Some Demoiselle or other tried to stroke it and it bit one of her fingers off.'

'How awful,' Temar said with feeling. He looked round the extensive garden. 'There was a menagerie in the Old Palace. Castan the Shrewd drained the moat, planted it with grass and fenced it off into sections. Houses would send him wolves and bears as a sign of Tormalin might taming the wilds of Dalasor, so my grandsire told me.'

'There's no record of that,' said the Emperor with some surprise.

'Lost in the Chaos, no doubt.' Temar smiled tightly. 'Anyway there were no beasts left by the end of Nemith the Last's fourth year on the throne. He wasn't prepared to pay for their keep so he had all the animals set against each other in baiting contests.'

'The more I learn about that man, the more I loathe him,' remarked the Emperor.

'It did him no credit, even with his sycophants,' Temar nodded. 'And he looked a fool more than once, like the time when nine lynxes refused to attack a bear.'

'That doesn't surprise me.' The Emperor ate one of his own hazelnuts. 'I've had Nemith the Last's example held up as a warning since before I was out of soft shoes.'

'What need have you to learn about such a sorry specimen?' Temar wondered aloud.

'Every boy who might one day lead his Name is taught about Nemith's reign. It's an object lesson on how to bring the Empire to its knees by favouring one faction over another, by disregarding the dignity of the Houses, by plundering the wealth of the rich and paying no heed to the trade and labours of the poor that support us all.' The Emperor spoke with evident sincerity, not merely reciting the rote of his youth.

Temar walked along the path, feeling the sun hot on his back. 'Kreve Tor Bezaemar cannot have paid much attention to the lesson.'

The Emperor sighed. 'It'd have been better for him if he had. But I've no idea what notions dear Dirindal addled his wits with. He's saying nothing to anyone, not to the Justiciar, not to his visitors, not to his jailers.'

'He will not escape justice, swear that much to me?' Temar caught the Emperor by the arm, courtesy be cursed.

Tadriol looked grim. 'He'll not escape. When the Justiciar has completed his enquiries, the Esquire Tor Bezaemar will face the fairest trial that Tormalin justice can display and thereafter the swiftest execution. Believe me, I've had my eye on Kreve, just as my father always suspected Dirindal of some collusion in his brother's death. Our enquiry agents turn up something to make us suspicious every couple of seasons, but we've never had anything that would stand the test of argument before the courts.'

'Thank you.' The words sounded inadequate to Temar but it was all he could find to say.

'No, thank you.' The Emperor started walking slowly. 'That's one of the reasons I asked you here today, to convey my gratitude. This whole sorry episode has offered me opportunities to do things it might have taken me ten years to achieve. Now I've the chance to be the kind of Emperor I want to be, the ruler my uncle would have been.'

'I do not understand,' Temar said cautiously. Now they'd finally reached the substance of this summons he was going to tread very carefully indeed.

'Think about it.' Tadriol stuck his hands in his breeches pockets as they walked. 'In putting a stop to those quarrels by making Imperial decrees, I've shown everyone I'm no D'Olbriot puppet dancing on the throne while the Sieur stands behind and pulls my strings. That suspicion's always been the price of his counsel.' He glanced at Temar. 'I was chosen as Emperor over my elder brothers because they were already married and deemed too closely committed to their wives' Names. That was a major concern to the Princes in the Convocation. On the other hand I was reckoned young enough to be easily manipulated, especially by those patrons used to giving the Emperor advice and seeing it taken without question. You'll come up against attitudes like this sooner or later.'

'I believe I already have,' Temar said drily. He'd learned to expect two visits from any Name he hoped to deal with, one from Designates hopeful he was some simpleton to be gently duped, and one from their Sieurs to talk serious terms.

The Emperor smiled knowingly. 'Later, in executing Kreve, I'll show the commonalty and the merchantry in the plainest way possible that I'm not going to defend noble privilege from the consequences of its actions. That's something you must take back to Kellarin with you, a sensibility to all your people, from highest to lowest.'

'I was raised in a tradition of far closer ties between noble and humble.' Temar thought he managed to swallow his indignation fairly well. Tadriol could learn a lot more from the Old Empire besides how not to make Nemith's mistakes.

'I'm only trying to offer advice,' said the Emperor mildly. 'My decrees have cut you off from D'Olbriot assistance and I'm concerned that'll hamstring you. Another reason I asked you here today was to offer my help. Let me know if you need an unbiased appraisal of any House for example, some discreet assessment of merchants you intend dealing with. I understand D'Olbriot's turned that chosen man of his loose but you'll need other servants soon enough, especially ones you can trust to manage your affairs on this side of the ocean without you here to keep an eye on them. I can have a Justiciar make enquiries about anyone you're thinking of swearing to your service.'

'My thanks again.' Temar's gratitude was unfeigned this time. 'I confess I do find the prospect before me daunting.'

'Almost as daunting as my acclamation to the throne, I don't doubt.' Tadriol took a seat on a bench shaded by a broad-leaved tree. 'In some ways, you and I have much in common.'

'Perhaps,' Temar said warily.

'So perhaps we can help each other as we go on,' suggested the Emperor with an innocent air. 'Have you managed to retrieve all the artefacts you were seeking?'

'All but a handful, and we believe we know where those are to be found.' Temar couldn't disguise his relief. 'When we have everyone awakened, families reunited, Kel Ar'Ayen will be far better able to look to the future.'

'Good.' The Emperor's warm approval was unfeigned. 'I've been meaning to ask, did my ring turn out to be one you needed?'

'No, as it proved.' Temar was a little embarrassed to have to admit this.

The Emperor laughed. 'It was a long-odds wager. That was the only heirloom I could find that was sufficiently old and obscure that people might believe it was from Kellarin.'

'I have it here,' Temar worked the heavy silver ring off his finger. 'And we cannot thank you enough for that decree.'

'Don't thank me too much.' The Emperor waved Temar's offer of the ring away. 'That whole business of enchantment, minds lost insensible among the Shades, it was giving me sleepless nights. More seriously, bickering over who held what gem or trinket had the potential to be highly divisive. There's a lot disturbing the settled order that I can't influence – new trade, new wealth, new ideas – but that was one wrangle I could settle. I'll be honest with you, one of the reasons I'll help you get Kellarin set fair for the future is to make sure your concerns disrupt life here as little as possible. We can afford to hand over jewels and trifles five times the value you've claimed; we cannot afford a tenth of this turmoil among the ruling Houses. Keep that ring to remind you.'

'And as a reminder of what we owe you?' ventured Temar.

'That too,' the Emperor agreed blithely. 'And as token of my pledge to always deal honestly with you, even when semblance and gesture might run counter to reality. But you've unique assistance when it comes to determining truth from sham, haven't you? I believe Demoiselle Tor Arrial can perform signal service in that regard.'

Here it came, Temar realised, the demand for payment. But wasn't that how the world had always worked? And settling a debt of coin or honour set a man free, didn't it? That wasn't so bad, as long as the price was one Temar was willing to meet. 'You'd appreciate some such service in return for all the help you've given us?'

'You've learned a great deal about the way Toremal works,'

the Emperor approved. 'Let's just say I'd appreciate some of the Demoiselle's time, so she can tell me just what Artifice might offer. I'd welcome a meeting with Demoiselle Guinalle if she ever visits these shores. Artifice held together a Tormalin Empire that reached from the ocean to the Great Forest, and while our boundaries are much reduced our affairs grow more complicated with every passing season. If an Emperor's duties in your day were largely military my concerns are almost all to do with commerce. It's my task to keep this great trading vessel on an even keel, balancing privilege and obligation, managing the conflicting interests of high and low alike. If you can offer me some means to help, I'll owe you more than I can say.'

Temar looked into Tadriol's eyes but saw nothing but sincerity. 'I will discuss it with Avila and Guinalle,' he promised. 'But I thought you did not like magic?'

'I don't like wizards,' the Emperor said firmly. 'But that's a different matter entirely. It's not their sorcery I mistrust, Saedrin be my witness, though the notion of people flinging handfuls of fire around certainly scares me. Any rational man would fear it. No, what I mistrust is wizards with political ambitions, that man Kalion for one, Hearth-Master or whatever he calls himself. He's someone else you'd be wise to be on your guard against.'

'Kel Ar'Ayen needs the mages of Hadrumal,' said Temar soberly. 'If the Elietimm attack, we will need their magic to defend us.'

'And if Ice Island ships turn up on our shores, I'll be the one calling loudest for Planir to blast them to splinters with whatever wizardry he likes,' the Emperor agreed. 'What I will not tolerate is any mage believing he can trade on that expectation for influence in Toremal's affairs. Wizards were a factor in the Chaos and I won't have them stirring the pot while I tend the fire hereabouts. I suggest you make the same thing clear in Kellarin.'

'I think Hadrumal will be looking to its own affairs for some while,' Temar said with some sadness. 'Cloud-Master

The Southern Docks, Toremal
35th of Aft-Summer in the Third Year of Tadriol the Provident

I'd been rehearsing what I might say to Livak for the best part of half a season but every word left me when I saw her standing on the gangplank of the ship. Dast save us, what had happened to her hair? When I'd last seen her, just after Winter Solstice, it had been long enough to her shoulders for my mother to hint at fond hopes of plaiting it for a summer wedding. Now it was cropped close to her head and the vivid red was tawny with mottled blonde.

She saw me and came running, the single satchel that was all she ever seemed to need slung over one shoulder. I caught her in my arms and held her tight, burying my face in her shoulder and wishing I need never let her go. Then her bag swung round and caught me under the ribs with a solid thump.

'What have you got in there – bricks?' I set her back on her feet. 'And what in Dastennin's name happened to your hair?'

She grinned up at me. 'Remind me to let Shiv know he owes me a gold Mark.'

I raised my eyebrows at her. 'Why?'

'He said the first thing you'd ask about was my hair. Anyway, hello to you.'

'Hello.' I stood there, grinning foolishly. 'And what did happen to your hair?'

'I had to lighten it, to pass for Mountain-born,' she said carelessly. She laughed. 'Do you recall, when we first met in Inglis we were talking about hair and disguises when we were both trying to track the Elietimm?'

'Are you trying to change the subject?' I teased her.

'What do you want to talk about?' she countered.

'How was the voyage?' I knew better than most just how much Livak hated ships.

'Not so bad,' she said shortly.

'It's just that I wanted you with me as soon as possible.' I felt a little guilty about not suggesting she make the shorter crossing to Caladhria and come the rest of the way overland. I'd have waited.

She smiled again. 'I wanted to be here. It was worth a little queasiness.'

I took her hand and we walked along the dockside. The rope walk was busy now, runners back and forth rigging yarn between the posts, ropemakers sweating as they wound handles to turn cogs and ratchets round and round, twisting the strands of hemp round each other and back against themselves so that one trying to unwind would tighten all the others and so hold it twisted in turn.

'After all those polite conversations relayed by wizards I'd have expected you to have more to say than this, now we're finally alone.' Livak tilted her head on one side and looked quizzically at me.

I laughed. 'I could hardly promise you endless delights behind the bed curtains with Casuel passing on every word.'

'He might have learned a few things,' she commented caustically.

'Or died of shock. So what did you learn over this summer?' If we were going to swap comparative successes, she might as well go first.

'Try this for weight.' She handed me her bag and I felt a solid weight in the bottom that could only be coin. 'That's what I finally managed to chisel out of that skinflint Planir.'

'So you brought back aetheric lore?' I reminded myself that it was a good thing one of us had managed to satisfy a patron. 'From the Forest or the Mountains? Was that song book all you hoped it might be?'

'We brought back a Mountain girl adept in their form of Artifice,' Livak said with that same evasion that was starting to make me suspicious.

'How did you manage that?'

She shrugged. 'It's a long story. I'll tell you later, over some wine.'

'So I've got something to take the edge off the shock?' I slung her bag over my shoulder.

'Something like that,' she admitted, slipping her arm round my waist. 'How was your summer? Have you made yourself indispensable to Messire? I've got lots to tell him about that song book and I'll expect him to pay up handsomely.' Livak halted, looking up with concern in her green eyes. 'Casuel told Shiv you'd performed signal service to the Emperor or some such?'

'I suppose that's one way of putting it. It's certainly been an eventful Festival.' I hugged her round the shoulders and we started walking again.

'What about the Sieur?' Livak persisted. 'How much further up that ladder have you climbed?'

I took an abrupt breath. 'I saved his life, him and Camarl, when ruffians hired by an enemy tried to kill them both.'

Livak's expression brightened. 'That must be worth a fair few Crowns.'

'He paid handsomely,' I assured her. 'And handed me my oath back along with the gold.'

Livak's arm dropped away and she turned to me, vivid eyes searching my face for any hint of my feelings. 'He dismissed you? After you saved his fat neck? How dare he?' Her indignation warmed me.

'It's a bit more complicated than that.' I heard a rueful note in my voice. 'I'd been helping Temar find those artefacts of his, looking out for D'Alsennin interests. The Sieur decided I'd find myself forced to choose between D'Alsennin and D'Olbriot and didn't want me backed into that corner.'

Livak snorted with contempt. 'That sounds like a flimsy excuse.'

'It'll hold long enough for me,' I assured her.

She looked at me for a long, considering moment. 'You're not angry? Hurt? Insulted?'

'I was, all of those things,' I sighed, 'but I'm mostly relieved. And the Sieur was right, in some ways. Accepting chosen status, when all I really wanted was a way of turning service to the House into some means of securing us a future together – that wasn't true to my oath. I was looking out for myself, not committing myself to the Name, and that's not entirely honest.'

'Not at all honest when the price of loyalty's no more than a bed and a full belly for nine men out of ten,' Livak mocked. Her voice turned serious. 'But you didn't foul the nest? You're still on fair terms with the Sieur? If we're thrown on our own resources we'll certainly need him to pay what he owes me and I'd rather he handed over the coin himself.'

'Or you'll go in through an upper window some dark night and find yourself a suitable settlement?'

'Something like that.'

I returned her mischievous smile but we both knew it wasn't a joke. 'I imagine the Sieur will see the logic of paying you your due,' I said drily.

Livak slid her arm through mine and we walked a little further along the quayside, pausing to let laden dockers pass, looking at the waiting ships with idle curiosity. The harbour was so close packed that we could barely see the water, the peaceful sea churned into a sandy green and dotted with flotsam.

'If we're not taking the Sieur's coin for the next few years, what are we going to do?' Livak gnawed her lower lip but she didn't seem overly distressed at the prospect of freedom. 'Is Charoleia still in town? She always knows how to double a Crown in no time.'

'We've had this conversation before,' I reminded Livak gently. 'Whatever we do, wherever we go, I'm staying on the sunshine side of the law, and Charoleia's just a little too fond of the shade for me.'

'Didn't you like her?' Livak asked with narrowed eyes.

'I liked her well enough,' I said placatingly. Dast knows, I knew just how important Livak's friends were to her. 'And she was a tremendous help, to me and to Temar. It's just that I don't intend taking up her trade.'

Livak smiled broadly. 'You're not pretty enough for one thing.'

'You forgot to mention that, didn't you? That she's such a beauty?' I prodded Livak with an accusing finger. 'Did you want to see if I'd fall down that bear-pit?'

'You gave that Aldabreshin woman what she wanted, didn't you?' she challenged.

I managed an injured expression. 'I was being a dutiful slave, doing as I was ordered.'

'You want to watch that tongue,' Livak commented. 'If it gets any longer someone'll hang you by it.' But she was smiling.

I drew her to me and kissed her soundly, ignoring a flurry of whistles and catcalls from appreciative dockers. I might have been tempted to a mistake with Charoleia, just for a few moments, but any man can mistake a thrush for a nightingale if he's got other things on his mind. But he'll never mistake a nightingale for a thrush, and now I had her in my arms I knew Livak was my nightingale. I might even tell her so, if I could find some words that wouldn't have her laughing at me for a sentimental fool.

'Ryshad! Well met!' A familiar voice called to me and then faltered as Temar saw I was otherwise engaged.

'And good day to you.' Livak turned in my arms and waved to him, unconcerned.

I held her close, my arms beneath her breasts, her hands on mine. I leaned closer to her ear. 'Temar on the other hand, fell right into Charoleia's honey pot.'

She glanced up at me and opened her mouth on a question but Temar arrived before she could frame it. Allin was with him, her usually open face closed and weary.

'Hello.' Livak's voice was warm with sympathy. 'I don't suppose it makes it any less hard to bear, but I'm so very sorry about Otrick.'

Allin's face reddened. 'He was always so nice to me.' She swallowed hard and didn't seem able to go on.

I looked at Temar as he put a comforting arm round the lass's shoulders. 'How's Velindre taking it?' The mage woman had been visiting every other day or so with a new chart or some alterations to an old one, offering advice on the winds and currents of the ocean deeps. I still hadn't fathomed her game.

'She tells me she cannot take passage with us to Kel Ar'Ayen in the circumstances.' Temar smiled without humour. 'She has to return to Hadrumal, since Planir no longer has any excuse to avoid appointing a new Cloud-Master – or Mistress.'

The notion that the Archmage might find himself too busy to interfere in our affairs wasn't unwelcome as far as I was concerned.

'Are you going back to Hadrumal?' Livak looked at Allin.

The girl sniffed defiantly. 'No. I'm going to Kellarin. I said I would and I'm going. I don't care what Casuel says, I can be useful there.'

'You are always useful,' Temar told her with warm approval. 'And I can settle Casuel's objections.'

'How?' I was curious.

Temar grinned. 'By telling him I've remembered that last D'Evoir he's so keen to tie himself to had both sons and brothers. The man married into Den Perinal and his brothers took wives from Den Vaedra and Den Coirrael.'

'So by the time Cas looks up from whatever archives he can trace for those Names, your ships will be the barest memory of foam on the horizon,' I concluded. 'Cas has ambitions to noble rank,' I explained to Livak, who was looking puzzled.

'Good luck to him,' she scoffed.

'Quite so.' Temar hesitated. 'But if we want to set sail this side of For-Autumn I have a great deal to get shipped down to Zyoutessela and then carried over the portage way to the ocean harbour. Please excuse us.'

Livak and I stepped aside to let them pass, Temar absently taking Allin's hand.

'I wonder how long it'll take for those two to realise they really should be more than friends?' she mused.

'It depends whether or not he's still got eyes for anyone else once he's back with Guinalle,' I commented. 'Allin's a very minor moon to outshine her glamour. Though Charoleia's little game certainly seems to have given him something to think about on that score.'

'Halice will make sure Temar notices Allin, if I ask her,' Livak said slyly. 'And it'll do that Guinalle no harm to have her nose put out of joint. If you sleep with a lad and then cast him off, you do it properly. Guinalle's not playing fair by encouraging him to keep hoping when she's no intention of taking him back. Usara'll be only too glad to console her, anyway.'

I looked down at Livak. 'Don't you like Guinalle?'

'I barely know her.' She was unconcerned. 'But she's too much like certain wizards for my taste. Why does magical talent of any ilk make people think they've the right to tell other folk how to live their lives?'

'Temar's not about to let Guinalle do that any more, not if the straight talking I heard him giving her the other day's any indication.' I laughed. 'Avila Tor Arrial was using Artifice to help him contact her and the enchantment nearly got away from her, she was so indignant.'

Livak frowned. 'That's the skinny old woman who always looks like she's biting a sour apple?'

'She's not so sour now,' I smiled. 'And she's not going back to Kellarin either, it seems. She's staying here to look after D'Alsennin interests and, if I'm any judge, to be wooed by a certain Esquire Den Harkeil.'

But Livak's thoughts were elsewhere. 'Halice said she always found the Tor Arrial woman's judgement pretty sound.' Which was high praise from Halice.

We walked on again and finally came to the end of the long stone-built quay. Below us the sea lapped on shelving sands where red-legged gulls picked over the line of weed and jetsam along the high-water mark.

For lack of anything more important to do, we stood there in close embrace while the busy life of the port went on all around us. Livak said something and I leaned back to lift her chin with one finger. 'I don't know how you ever expect me to hear anything, when you insist on talking into my shirt laces.'

She looked at me, new purpose in her emerald eyes. 'We could go to Kellarin. We could be useful there, like the mage lass said.'

'We could,' I said slowly. That notion had already occurred to me, but I'd wanted to see how the land lay with Livak before suggesting it.

'Halice is there and I miss her,' Livak continued frankly. 'I love Sorgrad and 'Gren like brothers, but it's not the same. And you're going to be wondering what D'Alsennin is up to wherever we are, aren't you?'

I was about to protest then thought better of it. 'True enough.' But I still wasn't going to swear service to him. The Sieur was right; it was time to be my own man, and where better than in an untested land where no one knew me. I'd certainly had enough of the whispers that were scuttling after me in Toremal.

I looked more closely at Livak's wide-eyed innocence. 'And there's something else?'

She smiled winningly. 'You know this Mountain girl I mentioned? She was one of what Sorgrad calls Sheltya, Mountain Adepts in Artifice. She didn't exactly come willingly, and it mightn't be a bad idea to get an ocean between me and the rest of them.'

I tried and failed to stop myself laughing. 'Let's go home. I think you'd better tell me all about it.'